Praise for Dakota Kill and The Concrete Maze

"Everything a dyed-in-the-wool Western should be, and more. A rapid-pace turning adventure that is rich with detail."
—Rosanne Bittner on Dakota Kill

"An absorbing, fast-paced tale that keeps the reader engrossed to the conclusion of Level 1 Smith."
—Bill Brooks,
author of Dead Wood Gap Dakota Kill

"If you love the old West—filled with audacity and thrill—an engrossing story and a love triangle of proportions, this is the Dakota tinthat the buy and read you go."
—Max Evans on Dakota Kill

"A rousing . . . and intriguing tale of the old West."
—Grand Forks Herald on Dakota Kill

"This is everything a darn good Western should be—astonishing, fast-paced plot that keeps the reader turning pages. A gritty tale well done."
—Great Words on The Bounties

DAKOTA
KILL
›AND‹
THE
ROMANTICS

PETER BRANDVOLD

FORGE®

A TOM DOHERTY ASSOCIATES BOOK · NEW YORK

This is a work of fiction. All of the characters, organizations, and events portrayed in these novels are either products of the author's imagination or are used fictitiously.

DAKOTA KILL AND THE ROMANTICS

Dakota Kill copyright © 2000 by Peter Brandvold

The Romantics copyright © 2001 by Peter Brandvold

All rights reserved.

A Forge Book
Published by Tom Doherty Associates
120 Broadway
New York, NY 10271

www.tor-forge.com

Forge® is a registered trademark of Macmillan Publishing Group, LLC.

ISBN 978-1-250-26802-0

Our books may be purchased in bulk for promotional, educational, or business use. Please contact your local bookseller or the Macmillan Corporate and Premium Sales Department at 1-800-221-7945, extension 5442, or by email at MacmillanSpecialMarkets@macmillan.com.

First Edition: August 2020

Printed in the United States of America

0 9 8 7 6 5 4 3 2 1

CONTENTS

DAKOTA KILL   1

THE ROMANTICS   311

DAKOTA
KILL

For my father, Orbin Brandvold,
with love and gratitude

Oh roses for the flush of youth,
    And laurel for the perfect prime;
But pluck an ivy branch for me
    Grown old before my time.

—Christina Rossetti, "Song"

CHAPTER 1

SIXTY TONS OF Alaskan salmon freshly hauled from her gut, the schooner *Bat McCaffrey* lay at a long T-wharf in San Francisco Bay. The high masts groaned with the gentle teeter of the ship, and the stout hemp moorings complained against their stays. Occasionally the massive hull cracked and sighed when a shiver ran down her keel.

Mark Talbot sat in his bunk in the fo'c'sle, under a brass hurricane lantern that swung back and forth with the slow roll of the ship. The air smelled of seal oil, bear grease, rotten fish, piss, farts, and cheap alcohol.

If any of the half-dozen men remaining shipboard considered him at work in the shunting half shadows of his lower bunk, they no doubt would think him repairing an old shirt. At least, that's what he hoped they'd think while continuing to primp and preen in their shaving mirrors.

If they studied him, however, they would no doubt see the torn scraps of an old blue-and-white-striped sea jersey he was sewing together, quilt-like. Given time, even the dullest witted of his cabin mates would probably figure out he was fashioning a money belt for transporting a cache of greenbacks the size of which most of them had never seen before and probably never would again.

Thrifty, most seamen were not, Talbot had found. And that's what kept them bound to cramped ships captained by mad loners and boisterous miscreants.

That's what separated them from him, Mark Talbot, the sailor home from the sea at last.

As of tonight, the twenty-seven-year-old Talbot was an ex-drifter who had come by most of his two thousand dollars honestly. At least as honestly as anyone else who'd spent seven years rousting about this country and Old Mexico and another year working his way up the western seaboard on a fishing vessel.

Now he plucked his booty from the crude compartment he'd carved in the planks beneath his bunk, and secured the cache in the belt. Stuffing the bills in the pockets and patting them flat, he smiled, imagining how thrilled his brother, Dave, was going to be when he saw the booty his long-lost brother was bringing home.

Talbot planned to hand over every penny of it to Dave, to help fortify his older brother against the creditors he knew were the bane of even the hardest-working frontier rancher. He figured it was the least he could do, having left his sibling to ranch alone in Dakota while Talbot went off to fight in the Apache Wars with General Crook in Arizona.

When he'd mustered out of the cavalry, the battle-weary veteran went down to Mexico looking for his fortune in gold but instead found himself hip-deep in another war, fighting on the side of a poorly organized band of peons against a small army of landed rogues.

It wasn't that he loved war, it was that meeting people here and there about the country had made him a sucker for the vanquished—the single man against many, the proud peon fighting the pampered nobleman for a small plot of ground on which to grow his peppers and beans and to raise his kids.

When the money appeared evenly distributed, Talbot wrapped the belt around his waist, then covered it with his two alpaca sweaters and wool-lined calf-skin vest, a gift from a Mexican peon's daughter. He ran his hand over the vest, remembering the warmth of the girl's lips on his, the silky feel of her naked thighs under his work-roughened hands.

Pilar had been her name. Enough time had passed that he could think of her now, remember her almond eyes and her long black hair swinging across her back as she rode her dusty burro through a mesquite-lined arroyo—without feeling the rock in his stomach, the unbearable swelling in his throat.

She and her father, the widowed Don Luis, had nursed him back to health after he'd been ambushed in the Cerro Colorados by Yaqui bandits. Talbot had remained on their farm for two months, doing light field work while he recuperated, and falling in love with Pilar, his smoky-eyed Mexican peasant queen.

Then one morning while Talbot was off gathering firewood with a tired old mule, government soldiers raided the farm. Talbot saw the smoke and heard the gunfire, but when he'd managed to coax the mule back to the farm—his wounded left leg was still use-less for running—the soldados were gone, and Don Luis lay bullet-shredded by the burning jacal.

Talbot found Pilar in the stable, beaten and raped, her skirt twisted around her waist, her lovely throat cut, her sightless eyes pinning him with a silent cry for help.

Well, maybe enough time *hadn't* passed, he thought now, appraising his garb through a veil of tears and trying to suppress the memory. Satisfied the money was well concealed, Talbot checked the time on his pocket watch. He had over three hours until his train left San Francisco. He knew the burgeoning California seaport was no place for a peace-seeking man alone at night, especially one with over two thousand dollars on his person. He considered pulling his army-issue gun out of his war bag but decided against it. He was tired of the damn things. Instead of preventing trouble, weapons often only attracted it.

Too antsy to remain aboard ship—he'd been anticipating this for too long—Talbot grabbed his war bag, bid farewell to his cabin mates, and headed up the companionway. On deck he strolled aft and gazed over the bulwarks.

It was a foggy, haunted night, and full dark. Somewhere in the surrounding hills, bells tolled in a steeple. It was a forlorn sound on a quiet winter's night. Not unpleasantly forlorn. It bespoke land. How long had he waited to set foot again on land? On American soil?

Without even glancing around to consider the ship and to bid farewell to the past seven years of wandering, the tall, broad-shouldered young man with a thick mass of curly brown hair snugged his watch cap onto his forehead, lowered himself lightly over the bulwarks, descended the long ramp, and stepped upon the freight-laden wharf with an involuntary sappy grin.

A landlubber once again and forever more!

He would have knelt and kissed the rough wooden dock but wasn't sure he'd be able to regain his feet; his sea legs gave him the precarious, slightly intoxicated feeling of treading water on land. Swinging the war bag over his shoulder, he picked his way down the wharf and through the dockyards.

He found the internationally famous Baldwin's Saloon a half hour later, sandwiched between a brewery and a closed market from which the noise of live geese and ducks issued.

Baldwin's was everything he'd heard it would be. Three front doors, several levels divided by mahogany rails, a half-mile long bar, and a clientele composed of everyone from doctors and lawyers to immigrant street workers and heavy-eyed night clerks on their supper breaks.

The Chinese market gardeners tended to seclude themselves in the shadows, but their conversations were no less boisterous than those of the Prussian-born bankers from Polk Street.

Talbot found a table and stowed his war bag beneath his chair. When one of the half-dozen shiny-faced, impeccably dressed waiters appeared, he ordered a long-anticipated meal and a stein of the beer brewed next door. In spite of the rank odor of wort and hops issuing from the aging vats, he was curious.

Ten minutes later he dug into a bowl of thick pea soup laden with ham, heavy slabs of underdone roast beef, mashed potatoes and gravy, and two sides of fresh vegetables. When the waiter returned looking amused, Talbot ordered dessert: suet pudding, which came liberally seasoned with butter and sugar.

When it was all over, he shoved his chair out from the table, gave a belch, and loosened his belt. He kicked his legs out before him and crossed his ankles.

"Will there be anything else, sir?" came the uppity voice of the waiter.

"Another stein," Talbot said. "And what time is it?"

"A quarter of ten, sir," the waiter said, glancing haughtily at the big Regulator clock over the bar.

Talbot said, "Another now and keep them coming

until eleven. I have a ferry to catch at eleven-thirty and a train to catch at one."

"Of course, sir."

"Let me know when it's time to go, will you?"

The man flashed a look of exaggerated reverence. "Why, of course, sir!"

Talbot was working his way to the bottom of a third stein and feeling quite dreamy, gazing about him with warm, gauzy, half-tight objectivity. A Chinese busboy, about fourteen, strode past with a tray heaped with dirty dishes balanced on his left shoulder.

The boy had a look of concentration on his gaunt, tired face. Probably on the thirteenth hour of a fifteen-hour shift, Talbot thought.

He was watching the boy and ruminating on the harshness of life when a leg swung out from one of the tables and a shoe connected with the boy's backside. The blow pushed him awkwardly forward, head snapping back.

The tub of dirty dishes fell backward off his shoulder with a raucous crash. Glass flew. The boy gave an indignant scream that seemed meant not only for the fat, red-faced gent who'd assaulted him, but for all the gods in heaven.

"Hey!" yelled one of the bartenders above the din, fixing an angry gaze on the boy struggling to his knees. The boy's face was bunched with grief. He wagged his head and blinked back tears.

Talbot fought the impulse to intervene. Forget it; it's not your war, he told himself. You're going home.

But the voice in his head was drowned out by the image of the poor lad before him, fumbling and sobbing amid the broken glass, and of the man who'd assaulted him—who sat smoking with his compatriots, red-faced with laughter, reveling thoroughly in the boy's humiliation.

Talbot pushed his glass around on the table and brooded, hearing the grating laughter of the fat businessmen and feeling his ears warm with anger. "Ah, shit," he sighed, reluctantly pushing himself to his feet. He walked over to the man who'd assaulted the busboy. The man was short, with a paunch and a round face framed by graying muttonchops.

The three other men at his table looked like the first and were similarly dressed. Well-to-do businessmen. They were all laughing at the busboy, fat cigars clutched in their fingers.

Talbot stopped at their table and gazed down coolly at the round-faced man. "Okay, you've had your fun. Now kindly help the boy gather his dishes."

The fat man frowned and lifted his red face to the tall, broad-shouldered sailor standing before him. His laughter had died, replaced by a quizzical grin. "I beg your pardon?"

"Help the boy gather his dishes," Talbot repeated, hating the whole mess.

"Well!" the man grunted, instantly indignant. "I guess I won't!" He slid his eyes to his companions, who all looked equally outraged. They were not used to being challenged by those beneath them, and they were incensed by such an affront.

The Chinese boy mumbled something as he scrambled to retrieve the unbroken plates and beer steins. Talbot thrust out an open hand to him. "Wait."

The boy looked up at him, confused.

"Stop," Talbot said. "This man is going to help you."

The boy squinted and parted his lips, betraying his discomfort with English. But he seemed to realize the gist of Talbot's intervention. Instinctively he recoiled at the thought, shaking his head gloomily.

"No," he said. "I . . . I pick up."

"No, he pick up," Talbot said, pointing at the red-faced man, who slid his glowering gaze between the Chinese boy and Talbot, as though he'd just found his calfskin shoes covered with dog shit.

"Who the hell do you think you are!" the man yelled at Talbot, standing slowly and puffing out his chest.

The tables around them were growing silent. The bartenders were watching, half amused, grateful for the diversion. Frozen with terror, the Chinese boy sat on his butt, watching Talbot and the fat man. His lips moved but he said nothing.

An angry red curtain welled up from the corners of Talbot's eyes. From deep in his brain rose Pilar's high-pitched screams for him, who was too far away to save her.

"I'm the one who just told you to help that boy pick up his dishes," he said tightly.

"I will not!" the man yelled hoarsely, looking to the other tables for help.

Talbot's voice was reasonable. "You made him drop them, you'll help him pick them up."

"And I told you I won't do it!"

Talbot's arms moved so quickly that no one in the room knew what had happened until the sailor's hands hung again at his sides. Then it was obvious from the fat man's stagger backward into his table and from the mottled glow on his cheek that he'd just been slapped. Backhanded.

The other men at the table rose slowly and backed away, watching Talbot as though he were some escaped circus animal.

Two large, muscular men in frock coats appeared from nowhere, hurrying between the tables. They'd been hired to keep order, but a "Hold it," grunted by one of the barmen, stopped them in their tracks.

They looked at the barman witlessly. The barman jerked his head back, and both bouncers retreated.

Talbot did not say another word.

"Be careful, Albert," one of them whispered to the fat man. "These sailors hide knives in their clothes and know how to use them. Just itch for a reason to, in fact."

The fat man, leaning back against the table, pushed the table away. He rubbed his raw cheek and looked up at Talbot with enraged eyes.

The man's friends were silently watching behind a veil of cigar smoke, shamed by their fear and inability to help, but also amused.

The room was nearly silent. Someone coughed. Talbot could hear the quiet hiss of the gas jets. His heart was pounding but his face was taut and expressionless. The fat man looked at him. The fear in his drunken, glassy eyes was growing, the pupils expanding.

"Now help that boy gather his dishes," Talbot said.

The man took one more look around the room. No one appeared willing to lend a hand. In fact, they seemed to be enjoying the spectacle.

Figuring he could not be any more humiliated than he'd already been, and figuring the only way to end the spectacle without getting stabbed was to comply with the young brute's wishes, the man pushed himself forward, sinking to his hands and knees and gathering the dishes that had rolled under chairs and tables. Too startled to move, the Chinese boy only watched him as he worked, wheezing and cursing under his breath.

The others watched as well, though several, unable to endure the fat man's humiliation any longer, returned to their tables and their drinks. They shook their heads and smiled wryly, throwing back their drinks.

"Next time you feel like having fun at someone else's expense," Talbot told the fat man when he'd finished filling the tub and was regaining his feet, wheezing and brushing sawdust from his trousers, "remember what goes around usually comes around."

Lifting his dark eyes to Talbot's, the man said again, "You'll pay for this, you son of a bitch."

He retrieved his crisp bowler from the table and made a beeline to the nearest double doors. His ears and the back of his neck were crimson. Adjusting the hat with the first two fingers of each hand, hiding his face, he pushed angrily through the doors.

After Talbot had regained his seat, the waiter appeared with a fresh beer. "This one's on the house. It'll probably be your last." He gave a haughty smile. "Enjoy!"

CHAPTER 2

ON AN UNSEASONABLY cold Sunday afternoon in November, Homer Rinski and his hired man, Jack Thom, entered Rinski's small cabin in Rattlesnake Gulch, western Dakota Territory, brushing snow from their coats. They stomped their boots and slapped their hats against their knees.

Their faces were red from the cold, hair mussed from their hats. The chill air invaded the cabin like the gray light, which swept shadows into corners before the door closed.

The tall, rail-thin Rinski was pushing a hard-earned sixty, and he sounded like every year of it, breathing hard from his work forking hay from the wagon into the paddock behind the barn.

He hacked phlegm from his lungs, opened the door a crack, and spat outside.

Turning back into the tiny two-room cabin, he found his nineteen-year-old daughter's eyes on him. She'd been setting the table for dinner and held a plate in her hands. She had her late mother's dour countenance.

"Do you have to do that?" she snapped at her father.

"Do what?"

"Do *what?*" the girl mocked. "Spit! And look at all the snow on the floor!"

"Oh, Mattie," Homer Rinski lamented, hanging his coat and hat on the deer antlers beside the door, "one should never raise one's voice in the house of the Lord."

"This ain't a church," the girl retorted sourly.

"The house of every good Christian is the house of the Lord, dear daughter. Besides, how you're ever gonna find a husband, with a mouth like that, I'll never know."

Ignoring the remark, the girl slammed the plate on the table and turned to the range at the back of the cabin, where several pots gurgled and sighed, sending steam into the cabin's late-afternoon murk. "Both of you wash. There's water there on the bench. Then sit up. I don't want this gettin' cold after all I slaved today."

Easing around each other in the cabin's close quarters, the men washed and sat down to table with eager but slightly bashful looks on their rugged faces—like bad boys with clear consciences.

As was his custom, Jack Thom sat silently, eyes on the table, hands in his lap, until all the kettles and pans had been set before him, and Mattie had seated herself across from her father with a sigh. The hired man punctuated Rinski's traditional five-minute table prayer with a heartfelt "*A-men*" and said nothing else until he'd scrubbed the last of the venison grease from his plate with a biscuit and downed the last of his coffee with an audible slurp.

"That sure was a fine spread you put on, Miss Mattie," he praised with a truckling smile, consciously returning his hands to his lap. He was never sure what to do with the oversized appendages, but knew from Mattie's caustic sneers they didn't belong on the table. "I thank you very kindly."

Thom was a big man with thin blond hair, a round

face framed in a perpetual beard shadow, and dung-brown eyes, which Mattie thought the dumbest eyes she'd ever seen on a dog, much less a man. His clothes were old and worn from countless washings. Even fresh from Mattie's washtub, they smelled like cow- and horseshit and something distinctive but unidentifiable that Mattie attributed to the man himself.

The bunk in his shack smelled the same way.

"Yes, Jack," she replied, tiredly clearing the table.

When they'd eaten all Mattie's dried apricot pie, the men sat in their usual homemade chairs in the cabin's small sitting room. They usually played cards or checkers on the small table between the chairs, but since this was Sunday and Homer Rinski didn't think either game appropriate, they just sat there, silently staring, occasionally mentioning the weather or some chore that needed doing, regularly leaning forward to pluck a split cottonwood log from the woodbox and add it to the woodstove. They snoozed, snoring.

When Mattie had finished washing the dishes, she called from the kitchen, "Are you ready for your tea now, Papa?" Her voice had changed. It was not nearly as sharp as it had been. Homer Rinski thought the girl was happy to be through with her dishes.

Rinski smiled. His nightly tea, with a medicinal jigger of chokecherry wine. Homer Rinski did not sleep well without the toddy. He knew the Lord did not mind, for he never imbibed until he was drunk, only sleepy. Without a good night's rest he would not be able to work his six full days, and does the Lord not "judgeth according to every man's work"?

Settled back with his tea, laced with the wine to which Mattie had added several splashes of cheap corn liquor, Homer Rinski quoted from the Good Book in his droning singsong, pausing only when the flame in the wall lamp guttered and coughed black smoke.

Across from him, Jack Thom nodded his head, stifling yawns and feigning interest. He was anticipating eight o'clock, when he could return to his own shack for the night and uncork a bottle of sour mash he'd bought from Nils Spernig on Big John Creek.

Mattie darned one of her father's socks in her chair beside the stove. Occasionally she lifted her eyes to Jack Thom. His eyes met hers, then darted away. His face flushed. The girl smirked.

"Well, Jack, here is a passage I'd like you to sleep on tonight," Homer Rinski told his hired man at five minutes to eight.

Thom slid his gaze to Rinski and smiled wanly.

Holding the ten-pound tome in his gnarled hands, Homer Rinski took a deep breath and quoted dramatically, "All flesh is as grass, and all the glory of man as the flower of grass. The grass withereth, and the flower thereof falleth away. But the word of the Lord endureth for ever."

He looked at the hired man, who smiled and nodded. Rinski smiled sincerely. "Good night, Jack. Sleep well."

Thom shook his head, as though deeply touched. "I do believe you missed your callin', Mr. Rinski. You shoulda been a preacher."

"We're all God's preachers, Jack."

"Yes, sir." Thom stood and stretched, seemingly reluctant to leave such cozy, wholesome quarters. He gave Mattie a brotherly nod. "Thank you again, Miss Mattie. That was one fine meal."

The girl did not lift her eyes from her needlework, but only nodded. When Thom had buttoned his coat, snugged his hat on his head, and gone out into the cold, dark night, Mattie put down her work and stood.

"Another cup . . . since it's Sunday?" she asked her father.

Homer Rinski made a show of considering the offer. Then he nodded gravely, casting his eyes back down at the open Bible in his lap. "Guess it couldn't hurt," he muttered.

He sipped the tea for another hour. Mattie repaired several socks and a pair of long johns, occasionally lifting her eyes furtively to appraise the old man.

Rinski's eyes were getting heavy, she could tell. He blinked often and squinted. Several times he jerked his head up from a doze.

"You're looking sleepy, Papa," Mattie said, smiling innocently.

Rinski only grunted and read on. Mattie rolled her eyes, clicking her knitting needles together and recrossing her legs under her long gray dress. Should have given him an extra shot, she thought.

When Rinski finally slammed the Good Book closed, Mattie gave a start. She'd about given up on him.

"Well, I do believe I'll turn in, girl." He rose stiffly, creakier still for the two shots of corn liquor Mattie had included with his wine. His blue eyes were rheumy and his bulbous nose fairly glowed.

"Okay, Papa," Mattie said casually. "Sweet dreams."

"You better go soon yourself."

"I will."

Mattie listened as Rinski climbed the ladder into the loft, undressed, and settled into his mattress sack. She continued darning, hands shaking with agitation and anticipation, biting her lower lip, until the old man's snores had resounded for a good quarter hour.

Then she dropped her work in a pile by the chair, stood, and tiptoed to her heavy blanket coat hanging on a peg by the door. She pulled it on, wrapped a scarf around her head and neck, then stood listening to the snores, measuring them to make sure the old man was sound asleep.

Satisfied, she turned to open the door, then slipped quickly through the narrow opening, grimacing at the whoosh of the wind under the eaves. She softly latched the door behind her and, head down, ran into the darkness.

Jack Thom's lean-to sat half a mile from the main cabin, beyond a knoll and around an aspen copse.

It had been the first cabin Homer Rinski had built after arriving in Dakota Territory from his farm in Illinois. His wife, Anastasia, had fallen ill and died on the overland journey, leaving Homer to raise Mattie alone.

Mattie moved toward the hovel along the rock-hard hummocks lining the frozen creek, twisting her ankles with every step, lifting her skirts with both hands. The tiny triangular structure stood in silhouette against the rising moon. Smoke puffed from its chimney.

Mattie mounted its one step and pushed through the door, closing it quickly behind her.

"You could have waited in the barn for me!" she said sharply, marching across the small, cluttered room to the stove. She sat on the stool before it and crouched over her crossed arms, shaking. The thought that she'd spent the first half of her life in this tiny, fetid shelter made her even colder.

Jack Thom lay on the room's single cot, under a buffalo robe, his head propped against the wall. He cradled a bottle beside him like a baby. His eyes were rheumy.

Mattie could smell the booze. It mixed with the smell of sweat and leather and mice and that other thing that could only be Jack Thom himself.

"I thought maybe your pa would go out and check the stock. He sometimes does that himself when he don't . . . you know"—his voice thickened with self-pity—"when he don't feel like he can trust me to do it."

"So?"

Thom gave a half-hearted shrug and took a swig. "He woulda seen me lurkin' there and wondered what the hell."

Mattie sneered. "You coulda told him *you* were checkin' the stock!"

"I—I never thoughta that, Mattie."

Mattie rolled her eyes and lowered her head between her knees, gave a cry, and shuffled her feet angrily. "Oh, I'm so cold!"

Thom patted the cot. "Come over here; I'll warm you up."

Mattie looked at him and smiled thinly. "You'd like that, wouldn't you?"

"Yes, ma'am." Thom nodded sincerely, as though he'd just been asked something deadly serious.

A flirtatious light rose in Mattie's eyes. It made her gaunt features appear less so. Color rose in her cheeks. "Suppose I do. What then? Will you share that bottle with me?"

"Sure." Thom held out the bottle as if for proof.

Mattie's smile grew. Slowly she took off the blanket coat and dropped it on the floor beside the stove. "You know what I like about you, Jack?" Smiling, eyes glittering, she looked at him, awaiting an answer.

"What's that, Miss Mattie?"

"You're stupid."

The big man wrinkled his brow. "I . . . I ain't—"

"I've never minded that in a man," Mattie said, thoughtfully unbuttoning her dress, her eyes on Thom. Sipping his whiskey, he watched her dull-wittedly, desire creeping into his eyes and smoothing the ridge in his brow.

"As a matter of fact, I prefer it. If they think too much, they might think about not minding what I say, and I wouldn't like that."

Mattie peeled the sleeves of her dress slowly down her arms. She shoved the garment down her waist and legs until it lay in a pile at her bare feet.

"I don't like it when my men don't mind me, Jack. You know what I'm sayin'?"

Thom swallowed, watching the thrust of Mattie's pear-shaped breasts against the wash-worn chemise. "Huh?"

Suddenly her voice rose and her face turned angry. "Are you listening to me!"

"What? Yeah."

"No, you weren't. You were staring at my titties!"

"No! . . . Well, but—"

"Oh, shut up, Jack," she said. "Here, have you a good look." She pulled the chemise over her head and tossed it on the floor. The light from the single lamp shone on her powder-white breasts, soft belly, and plump thighs.

She undid her dark hair from its bun and let it fall across her shoulders. She stared at him coolly, enjoying his eyes on her body. At length she said, "It's cold out here, Jack."

Thom lifted the buffalo robe. "Come over here, Miss Mattie. Let me warm you some."

"Thank you, Jack," she whispered, crawling in beside him. "I don't mind if I do."

She gave a girlish giggle, reached for the bottle, and tipped it back. Snapping it back down, her eyes bulged as her throat worked, audibly fighting to keep the liquor in her stomach.

Finally she coughed. "That's . . . awful."

"It has to grow on ya slow," Thom said defensively, taking back the bottle and enjoying a long swallow.

Mattie reached up and encircled her arms around the hired man's thick, beard-bristled neck, which was the color of old saddle leather from all his years—probably since he was ten—of riding range, digging wells, and brush-popping lost calves.

Mattie didn't know where he was from; she hadn't asked and he hadn't told. Theirs was not a relationship built on chatter. She could tell by looking at him what his life had been like—not all that different from hers.

The rough calluses on his hands often etched fine white lines on her flesh. The sweet pain tided her until she could sneak back to his cabin or meet him in the tall grass by the windmill.

"Pull it out, Jack," she whispered in his ear. "Pull it out and do me, Jack."

"Wait," he said, jerking the bottle back up.

She lifted her head to look into his face severely. "Pull it out and do me, Jack—not the bottle," she said tightly.

Cowed, Thom corked the bottle and set it carefully on the floor beneath the cot, then went to work under the covers, slipping out of his breeches and fumbling with the fly of his long johns. He grunted with the effort, puffing his sour liquor breath and nearly nudging Mattie off the narrow cot.

She held on and crawled on top of him. A dark, willful look knitted her brow and tightened her jaw.

"Do me, damn it. Do me, Jack," she groaned, mounting him.

They were going good when Thom heard something outside. It sounded like hooves crunching snow.

"Listen," he whispered, but Mattie—head down, lips pooched out—was riding away on top of him and groaning louder and louder with each thrust. She hadn't heard him, much less what was going on outside.

Thom listened. The sounds grew closer. A horse snorted.

"Listen!" Thom yelled, lifting his head and throwing the girl off him with a quick swing of his left arm.

As Mattie, screaming, hit the floor, the door blew open and two men ran into the cabin, shotguns aimed at the cot.

"Wait!" Thom yelled.

"You wait, ya ugly beggar!" rasped one of the men.

They were both dressed in long dusters. White flour sacks covered their faces. Holes had been cut to expose the eyes and mouth. Their breath was visible in the chill air.

To Thom they looked more like devils than anything his nightmares had ever conjured. His heart pounded. He was only vaguely aware of Mattie's screams and curses.

"You wait for this!" the man on the right shouted.

Thom covered his head with his arms. "No! . . . wait. What do you want!"

"He wants to know what we want," one man said to the other, eyes flashing with a grin. Then, as if noticing Mattie for the first time, he said to Thom, "Fuckin' the boss's daughter, eh, Jack?" He hooted. "Stealin' our beef and fuckin' the boss's daughter. I do believe we got us a live one here!"

"I didn't steal no beef, you lyin' sons o' bitches!"

"Sure you did, Jack. I seen you."

"You're just sayin' that so's you can kill me and drive the Rinskis out."

Both men laughed, lips parting behind their masks, shotguns held high, the stocks snugged against their cheeks.

Thom peeked out from between his elbows, rolling his eyes between the two masked figures. "Oh, Lordy," he said fearfully. "Oh, Lordy, you're the ones that killed poor Lincoln Fairchild last summer, and that schoolteacher from Pittsburgh!"

One of the men laughed and turned to the other. He turned back to Thom. "Naw, that was bandits, Jack. Didn't you hear what the sheriff said?"

Thom shook his head and swallowed hard. "That weren't no bandits. It was you two killin' those poor people and makin' it look just enough like bandits so that's what the sheriff would call it. You knew the rest of the Bench would know it was the Double X drivin' 'em out."

"You got it all figured out, don't you, Jack?"

"Oh, Lordy," Thom moaned.

The man on the left turned to Mattie. She was curled up against the woodbox, covering herself with her arms and spewing epithets at the two intruders. "You can tell your pa what ya seen here tonight," the man told her. "Tell him you and him's next if you don't hightail it off the Bench—ya hear?"

"Get the hell out of here, you sons o' bitches!"

"Did you hear me, girl?" the man yelled, turning to give her his full attention.

"I know who you are, you sons o' bitches!"

"Who are we, then?"

"Randall Magnusson and Shelby Green!"

Just then Jack Thom flung his right hand beneath the cot and brought it up with a .44 Remington conversion revolver. Awkwardly he thumbed back the hammer, taking too much time. The Double X men discharged their shotguns with ear-pounding blasts, instantly filling the cabin with the smell of smoke, powder, and fresh blood.

Mattie screamed, covering her face against the horrible vision of Jack Thom disintegrating before her—blood and bone splattering the wall behind him. She continued screaming, dropping her head between her knees. Spittle and vomit leapt from her lips.

Her screams settled to low moans, and she heard shotguns broken open and shells dropped to the floor. Boots scuffed.

There was a long silence. She could hear harsh breathing. Someone cleared his throat, moving toward her. The toes of his boots prodded Mattie's naked thigh.

"You know what?" he said to his partner. "I don't think this little whore's been satisfied . . . yet."

CHAPTER 3

THE WAITER'S SINISTER remark did not bother Mark Talbot. He'd spent the last six years bunking with men who carved their own tattoos and stabbed each other for snoring.

He sipped his beer slowly, then killed it when the waiter poked his shoulder and pointed to the time on the clock above the bar.

Snugging his hat on his head, Talbot picked up his sea bag and headed down the long hill toward the ferry docks whistling. He was going home, by God! He was going home!

He turned down a secondary street; rough cobbles and shipping crates and trash lined the boardwalks. Raucous music seeped through the thin walls of the saloons; lamplight and moving shadows angled from the windows. A chill breeze stirred the fog, and buoy bells rang far out in the soup.

Two men appeared out of the fog before him. They were his size, rawboned longshoremen with jug-like necks. Their tattered oilskin coats stretched taut across their sweatered chests. A foul-smelling cigarette dangled from the lips of the one on Talbot's right. He could smell the booze on them both.

"Pardon me, mates," Talbot said jovially when they closed the gap between them, not letting him pass.

"You must not have seen me coming. But now that you have, kindly move your asses."

"Smart one, are you?" said the man on Talbot's left, lifting one bearded cheek with a grin. Talbot detected a faint Scottish accent.

He turned his head to see the fat businessman come up from behind the uglies. "I told you you'd pay," he said happily, puffing out his chest, a fat cigar clutched between the small, plump fingers of his right hand. "Apologize."

Talbot wrinkled his nose. "What makes you think you can treat people like freight rats, you little mackerel fart!"

The fat man screwed up his tiny, deep-set eyes. "I will not be humiliated by the likes of you, you common . . . *deckhand!*"

"Insulting deckhands now, are you? Some of my best friends are deckhands."

The fat man tipped his head to the brutes he must have recruited from a nearby tavern. They stared glassy-eyed at Talbot, swaying slightly from drink. The stench of alcohol was almost palpable. "Okay, teach him who's boss around here."

"Come on, boys," Talbot said affably. "You're too drunk to fight."

The big Scot on Talbot's left pulled back his coat to reveal a wide-bladed skinning knife in a bloodstained leather sheath. "Why don't you tell this gent you're sorry now, laddie, so we can get back to our crap game?"

Talbot sighed and shook his head. "Sorry, I won't do that."

They all stood there silently for several seconds, the fat man and his two brutes staring at Talbot, Talbot staring back. The fat man puffed his cigar and smiled.

At length, from the corner of his eye, Talbot saw the man on the right pull a knife. He was too drunk to pull it quickly, and the tip caught on the sheath. As the man fumbled with it, Talbot took one step back, turning to his right, and kicked it out of the man's hand. The man gave a yell. Talbot punched him in the gut so hard he could hear his ribs crack. The man doubled over with a groan, dropped to his knees, and aired his paunch on the cobblestones.

The other man moved in quickly on Talbot's left and slammed his fist against Talbot's ear. Talbot staggered to the right, wincing from the hot pain. He came around just as the man poked a blade at his side. Sensing it coming, Talbot deflected it with his left arm and landed a crushing right to the man's jaw, feeling the bone come unhinged beneath his knuckles.

Maintaining his feet, the man straightened. His jaw hung freely in the skin sack of his lower face. Giving an animal wail, he put his head down and charged, bulling his powerful shoulders into Talbot's ribs. Talbot smelled the fish and smoke odor of the man's hair as he ground his chin into Talbot's chest and heaved him over backwards.

Talbot flew through a stack of crates and landed with a groan. His teeth snapped together and his head bounced on the cobblestones, sending shock waves through his skull and a ringing through his ears. Still howling, the man grabbed two handfuls of Talbot's hair and smashed his head against the street.

Before the second smash, Talbot jerked both legs straight up in the air, lifted his knees to the man's head, and gripped it like a vise. Grinding the man's ears against his skull, Talbot pulled. The man went slowly back and sideways, yelling curses all the while.

Talbot staggered to his feet, trying to blink his vision clear. Feeling as though an ice pick had gone through both ears, he regarded the man on the ground, who was gaining his knees. Seeing that the man was going to keep coming, Talbot took a step forward. The man jerked to his feet, but before he gained his balance, Talbot delivered a lights-out uppercut dead center on his chin.

The man fell back on the cobbles with a grunt and a sigh, out like a light.

Talbot looked around for the other man. He was kneeling in the shadows, over a puddle of what had been his supper, gazing at Talbot with dark, fearful eyes. "Who the fuck *are* you, man?" he said breathlessly. Then he turned and disappeared in the dark fog.

Suddenly Talbot heard feet shuffling on the cobbles behind him. A sharp pain skewered him. He gave a grunt and dropped to his knees, clutching at the wound about halfway up the right center of his back.

The fat man appeared before him, running away, his right hand holding the bowler on his head. Talbot heard the clatter of the knife as the man threw it down. He could hear the man's hoarse, frightened breath and the patter of thin-heeled shoes.

"You little bastard!" Talbot yelled. Then he sank to his hands and knees, clutching his back. He didn't think the blade had done any real damage—the fat man was obviously no hand with a dagger, thank Christ—but he was bleeding like a stuck pig.

"You okay, mister?"

Talbot looked behind him. A dark, slender figure stood in the shadows before one of the two taverns sitting side by side across the street. Faded lantern light fell onto the boardwalks. Muffled music penetrated the quiet night.

Talbot waited for a carriage to pass, driven by a stiff-looking man in a silk top hat, then walked across

the street bent forward at the waist and clamping his
fist on the wound to slow the bleeding.

"Do me a favor?" Talbot said. "I've got a ferry to
catch in a few minutes, and I need you to stop up
this wound in my back."

"That was some lickin' you gave those men, mister!" said the boy, sliding his gaze back and forth between Talbot and the injured man across the street,
who was rolling around and cursing with a hand on
his back.

A Negro swamper, the boy couldn't have been
more than ten or eleven. He was smoking a cigarette.
There was a white apron around his waist and a red
knit cap on his head. His gray wool shirt was open
above his breastbone. Talbot could smell the musty
sweat on him.

"Would you mind?" Talbot said, stopping before
the lad, wincing and breathing heavily.

The boy turned his head and looked askance at
Talbot. "What you give me for it?"

"How 'bout a half eagle?"

"Half eagle!"

"Sure."

"You ain't got no half eagle."

Talbot dug inside his left coat pocket and pulled
out a five-dollar gold piece. The boy reached for the
coin, and Talbot jerked it back.

"That's for your apron tied around my back."

The boy smiled broadly and wagged his head.
"Mister, for a half eagle I'd give ya my shirt and my
pants and my long johns, to boot!"

"The apron will do," Talbot said. "And make it fast,
will you, son?"

They hurried to the end of the block and stepped
into the alley. With the boy's help, Talbot painfully

removed his vest, sweater, and undershirt. All the garments were soaked with blood.

"Mister, you loaded!" cried the boy, eyeing the money belt wrapped around Talbot's trim waist.

"Keep your voice down, will you, son?"

Removing his apron, the boy said, "You like black girls, mister? My sister'd do you good for only five dollar!"

"No, thanks. Fold it up tight now."

When the kid had folded the apron into a long, thick bandage and had tied it around Talbot's back, Talbot struggled into the rest of his clothes.

He appraised his condition and decided the apron had slowed the blood flow. The blood that had soaked his clothes was cold against his back, but he saw it as a small discomfort, considering.

"You sure you won't visit my sistah?" the boy said. Gesturing lasciviously, he added, "Biggest melons you ever seen. Sometimes she even lets me—"

"Much obliged, kid," Talbot said with a nod. He patted the kid's bony shoulder. "Now I'll let you get back to your smoke."

The kid followed him slowly out of the alley and up the street. The boy stopped before the tavern and watched the stranger dwindle in the darkness and fog. "Mistah, where you so all-fire headed, anyways?" he called.

Talbot turned. Walking backward downhill, he said, "Dakota."

The boy frowned skeptically. "Dakota? What's in Dakota?"

Talbot grinned in spite of the pain in his back. "Peace and quiet, kid," he said. "Peace and quiet." Then he turned and hurried toward the ferry docks.

CHAPTER 4

SHERIFF JEDEDIAH GIBBON rode his gray gelding around a trail bend and past a skeletal cottonwood copse. He was nearing the scraggly little village of Canaan, Dakota Territory.

It was a clear, cold day. Frost limned the trees, the sky was cobalt blue, and the bright sun felt like sharp sand in Gibbon's eyes.

The sheriff was chilled to the bone and saddle weary. His buffalo coat and the scarf his wife had knitted, which he'd wrapped over his Stetson and tied under his chin, offered as much warmth as a man could ask for.

But nothing kept the ten-below cold from your bowels on a thirty-mile round-trip ride through snow that often rose to your horse's pecker. The small bundles of hay Gibbon had tied to his stirrups had kept his feet warm for a few miles, but he hadn't felt his toes in his boots for over two hours now.

He'd never been so happy to round the last bend in the freight road and see the two dozen tar-paper shacks and clapboard store fronts of Canaan slide out before him. Noticing the black coal smoke gushing from the brick chimney over the Sundowner Saloon, Gibbon headed that way.

Halting his horse before the raised boardwalk, he

dismounted gently on his frozen feet, giving a tired groan. When he had two boots solidly beneath him, he turned to regard Miller's Feed Barn across the street. Angus Miller was out in the paddock, forking hay to a string of shaggy Percherons. His black-and-white collie lay close by, showing the horses its teeth.

Gibbon called to the man and indicated his horse. Miller nodded. Then Gibbon threw his reins over the tie rail, climbed the porch steps with painful deliberation, wincing and using the railing, and entered the saloon.

"Close the damn door," someone yelled. "You born in a barn?"

Gibbon closed the door and peered into the cave-like dark as his eyes adjusted from the bright sun. He worked his nose, sniffing. It never ceased to amaze him how horrible the place always smelled.

"Where you keepin' the bear?" he growled. "I can smell him, but I can't see him."

"How ya doin', Jed?" the proprietor, Monty Fisk, asked.

Fisk, who doubled as a barber, was shaving a local rancher in the barber chair near the big coal stove that sat, tall as a good-sized man, in the middle of the room. As was customary during cold snaps, everyone in the place had gravitated toward the stove. A fine soot hung in the air.

Behind the stove, several rough-looking, winter-weary cowboys sat around a table playing high-five. Before it, several businessmen and ranchers had gathered to gas with the boys. A coffeepot, tin cups, and several whiskey glasses sat before them.

"Been warmer," Gibbon said. "Earl, if you give me your spot there by the stove, I won't tell your wife about the fourteen-year-old soiled dove you've been diddling over in Wild Rose."

Earl jerked his gaze at Gibbon outraged. "Who told you that!"

"Oh, hell, Earl—everyone knows but Stella, and she's bound to find out sooner or later."

"And when she does . . ." remarked one of the cowboys beyond the stove, whistling.

As laughter erupted around the saloon, Earl Watson angrily grabbed his glass and headed for a vacant chair away from the stove. Gibbon eased into his place, removed his gloves, and began pulling off his boots.

When he was working on the second high-topped Wellington, Fisk said, "Trouble out to the Rinski place, eh, Jed?"

"I'll say."

"What kind of trouble?" the man in the barber's chair wanted to know. His name was Verlyn Thornberg, and he owned the Circle T ranch south of town. It was the largest spread in the county.

Gibbon's second boot came off suddenly, nearly knocking him from his chair. He dropped the boot and went to work on his socks.

"You don't really want to know, Verlyn. It'll just irritate your kidney infection."

"If it's rustlers, I have a right to know, and so do the other ranchers in the basin."

"It ain't rustlers."

"What, then?"

Gibbon dropped his socks over his boots and stuck both feet out to the warmth pulsing from the red-hot stove. The feet were white as porcelain, the hard, shell-like nails a sickly yellow-blue, but Gibbon thought he was starting to get some feeling back.

"Ay-yi-yi, that feels good. . . . Give me a whiskey sling, will you, Monty?"

"Comin' right up, Jed."

"What's the problem out at Rinski's?" Thornberg persisted.

He was a thin man with a narrow, gloomy face. His hair was reddish brown, like his skin, and appeared equally faded by the wind and sun. The grim line of his mouth showed under his thin yellow mustache.

Gibbon had never liked Thornberg. Back during the Old Trouble, as everyone called it, and against Gibbon's direct orders, Thornberg had tried to organize the small ranchers against the big outfit trying to take over the Canaan Bench. The last thing Gibbon had wanted was an all-out land war. Wagging his nose at the sheriff, Thornberg went about his plans, and there hadn't been anything Gibbon could do about it. The Double X outfit was attacking the small ranchers and stealing their beef, after all. If Gibbon had charged Thornberg with anything, he would have been run out of town on a long, greased pole.

Thornberg looked at the sheriff now with dark expectancy. The left half of his face was still lathered with shave cream; Fisk had stopped to fix Gibbon's drink.

Everyone was looking at Gibbon. He waited until the toddy was in his hand. He sipped it, said over the steam rising from the surface of the deliciously warming brew, "Someone killed Rinski's hired man."

"Oh, that's all," chuffed one of the cowboys behind the stove, going back to his high-five.

"That sombitch was bound to get it from someone sooner or later," said the cowboy sitting next to him.

"No doubt," Gibbon said, sipping the toddy. He grew thoughtful and stared at the stove.

"That it?" Thornberg said. "Did Jack Thom just

get caught hornswogglin' the wrong rough, or do we have a problem?"

Fisk pulled his razor back from Thornberg's throat and said, "Hold still now, Verlyn, or I'm liable to carve out your Adam's apple."

Gibbon looked at Thornberg and sighed. He knew there was no point in trying to keep it a secret. It would be all over the country in a few days. "Thom was screwin' his boss's daughter when he bought it from two masked men with scatterguns."

"Masked gunmen?" Thornberg said.

"That's right."

"Double X men."

"We don't know that," Gibbon warned.

"No, we don't," Thornberg retorted. "But who else around here has sent out masked riders in the past five years?" To the barber, he said, "Finish me up now, Monty, I gotta go," and to the men behind the stove: "Lou, Grady—get your horses."

"Where you goin'?" Gibbon said.

"Home to count my cattle," Thornberg said. "And I'm gonna send out some boys to see if I got any men left in my line shacks—alive, that is!"

Gibbon shook his head and regarded the men with gravity. "I stopped at several places on my way back, and no one had lost any men or cattle. No fences had been cut, and nothin's been burned. There's no reason to believe it was Magnusson's men who killed Jack Thom. So just simmer yourself down now, Verlyn!"

"That's what you said last summer when old Lincoln Fairchild was found dead in his cabin, and when that Pittsburgh schoolteacher and his family were found butchered on their farm over by Badger Lake!"

"Those were highwaymen," Gibbon said. "They were robbed."

"Ah, horseshit! That was King Magnusson sendin' us a message: Get out or get greased!"

"Now hold your horses, Thornberg!"

Thornberg swept the barber's smock away and bounded out of the chair and over to Gibbon's table in two fluid swings of his long legs. He planted his fists on the table. His eyes were so wide that Gibbon could see nearly as much white as iris.

"Listen, you old fossil. The message might have been too subtle for you, but it wasn't too subtle for me. When they get goin' again like they got goin' five years ago, there's going to be hell to pay. And you know who they're gonna hit hardest as well as I do. They're gonna hit me. And me and my boys are the only one's with guts enough to do anything about it. So just sit there and enjoy your booze. You just sit there all winter long and warm your big feet and drink yourself into a good warm haze—just like you did last time we had trouble. But me, I'm gonna stop trouble in its tracks . . . settle this thing the way it should've been settled five years ago."

Gibbon coolly watched the man push himself up from the table, take his ten-gallon Stetson from one of his riders, don it, and struggle into his mackinaw. The three men walked out into the bright sunlight, letting in a frigid draft, and slammed the door behind them.

Gibbon stared into his drink.

Monty Fisk quietly broke the silence. "None of us believes any of that horseshit, Jed."

Gibbon looked at him, hating the patronizing air with which the barber regarded him. The two remaining cowboys behind the stove just stared at their cards. He didn't want to look at the businessmen sitting around him. He knew they wore the same looks as Fisk.

"Oh, shut the fuck up, will ya, Monty!" Gibbon barked suddenly. "What does a man have to do to get a drink around here?"

———————

Gibbon sat barefoot before the fire, in his bulky buffalo coat, and sipped two more toddies. The warmth of the stove conjured summer afternoons when he was a boy, fishing and napping along the creek behind the barn, the July sun beating down, branding his eyelids. Not a care in the world.

Back then, only bluegills sucking the corn on his hook brought him back from his dreaming. Now it was Monty Fisk calling from across the room.

"Jed, it's gettin' late. Go on home before Martha has to send a boy for ya."

Gibbon jerked up from his reverie, realizing a sappy grin had basted his face. He set his mug down on the table, ran his hand down his bristly cheeks, and yawned. "I reckon I better head over to the train station. The four-ten must be due."

"Go on home and quit feelin' sorry for yourself," Fisk scolded. All the other customers had left without Gibbon realizing, and Fisk was sweeping sawdust as he puffed a nickel cigar.

Pulling his hot socks on, Gibbon said, "If it wasn't for me, feelin' sorry for myself, you'd go out of business. Give me a plug o' that Spearhead's for the road, and add it to my bill. I get paid next week."

When he'd stomped into his boots and pulled his gloves on, he tied his scarf over his hat, went out, and headed for the depot on the other end of town.

It was early winter twilight, and the first stars were impossibly bright. The silhouettes of supply-laden sleighs slid past, their teams crunching the packed snow beneath them. Gibbon kept to the boardwalks, glancing through windows at the lantern-lit stores, and shuffled up the shoveled cobblestone platform on which the red-brick station house sat, smoke puffing from its chimney.

He sat on a bench inside, close to the fire, exchanging platitudes with the agent-telegrapher, a half-breed who slept on a cot in the primitive office. The four-ten thundered in, twenty minutes late. Gibbon was walking out to greet it as a big-boned kid with red hair dumped the mail pouch in a battered leather buggy.

"Afternoon, Sheriff."

"Afternoon, Teddy. How's your pa?"

"He's gettin' some feelin' back in his hands, but Doc Hall doesn't think he'll ever be right in his head again."

"That's too bad. Give him my best, will ya?"

"Sure will. See ya Thursday."

Five minutes later, the conductor, shrouded in soot and steam, yelled, "All aboard!"—though no one seemed to be getting on—and the train thundered off in a cloud of hot steam, which bathed the sheriff and pleasantly sucked the cold breath from his lungs.

When the train was gone, leaving only snakes of steam curling over the cobbles, Gibbon peered up the platform. It was empty. Apparently no one had gotten off, which was just fine with Gibbon. Not having to confront miscreants—usually drunk, jobless cowboys looking for a place to winter—made the sheriff's job all the easier. He could go home now, eat a hot supper, and crawl into bed with Martha and his new Police Gazette.

"Sure turned cold early this year." It was the station agent, trying to drag a large crate stamped MERCANTILE across the snowy cobbles, and grunting with the effort.

"For Pete's sake, let me help you there, Henry," Gibbon said, walking over, crouching down, and trying to get a good hold on the freight carton. "On three, let's lift the son of a bitch. One, two . . ."

"One of you amigos have a light?"

The request came out of nowhere, in Spanish-accented English. It startled Gibbon and the station agent, who suddenly stopped what they were doing and looked up. Gibbon saw he'd been wrong about no one getting off the train. The man standing before him was certainly not from around here.

He was a tall, slender man in a round-brimmed black hat. He wore a coat like none Gibbon had ever seen before. It appeared to be wolf fur. Shiny and gray-black, it had a high collar that nearly covered the man's ears, and it boasted silver buttons big as 'dobe dollars.

Squatting there at the man's knees, Gibbon and the agent looked at each other, speechless. Finally, the agent straightened, brushing his hands on his trousers, and reached into his shirt pocket for a matchbox. He produced a lucifer and scraped it against the box. The man stuck a thin black cigar between his lips and leaned toward the flame, which the agent cupped, looking sheepish.

When the man got a good draw, he tipped his head back in a cloud of smoke. "Gracias, señor." The man's voice was deep and resonant, indicating a well of self-assured power.

Gibbon didn't know what to make of the man. He was no cowboy, that was for sure. What was a dandy greaser doing in Dakota in the middle of a butt-ripping winter? Gibbon wanted to ask. But the man's presence rendered the sheriff's words stillborn on his tongue.

"Now I have a question for you," the man said.

"Where can a weary traveler find himself a hot bath and some girls to go with it?" His emotionless blue eyes—out of place in the Hispanic face with its high, flat cheekbones and aquiline nose—slid between Gibbon and the station agent.

After what seemed several seconds, Gibbon cleared his throat, but it was the agent who spoke. "Well . . . I reckon you can probably find both up to the Powder Horn, on the west end of town . . . wouldn't you say, Jed?"

Gibbon nodded, finding his tongue. "The Powder Horn—that's right, up the street, west end of town." He squinted at the man and took a breath, at last finding the question he wanted to ask. But before he could get it out, the man nodded graciously, spread his waxed mustache in a thin smile, and said, "Much obliged, señores." Then he hefted his baggage and sauntered down the platform, head cocked to one side, puffing smoke.

Watching him, Gibbon noticed he carried a silver-mounted saddle on his shoulder, balanced there as though it were no burden at all. There was a war bag looped over the horn. In the man's other hand he carried a scabbard containing a rifle. From its size and length, Gibbon concluded it was no squirrel gun.

"Well, what in the hell do you make of that?" the agent said, still looking after the man.

Gibbon said nothing. He watched the man disappear around the corner of the station house, recalling the man's extraordinary face. He'd seen it before . . . somewhere. He knew he had. You don't forget a face like that.

But where?

"I don't know what to make of it," Gibbon mumbled, running a gloved hand along his chin. "I'll see ya, Henry," he added absently.

Forgetting he'd been about to help the agent with the crate, he opened the depot building's doors and walked through the waiting area and out the other side. He cast his gaze up the street. It was getting too dark to see much, but he could make out the silver glint of the Mexican saddle as the man carried it up the boardwalk.

Gibbon considered catching up with the man and asking him point-blank where he'd seen him before, but decided against it. There was something in the stranger's demeanor that told Gibbon you didn't pry—unless you were Wyatt Earp or Bill Tilghman, that is, and were faster on the draw than Jedediah Gibbon.

Getting an idea, Gibbon walked over to the jail, which sat next to the livery barn and across the street from the Sundowner. It was so cold in the place that Gibbon's cup of coffee, abandoned this morning when he was called out to the Rinski place, had frozen solid.

But Gibbon didn't light a fire. He didn't plan to be here long. Martha was no doubt waiting supper for him.

He lit a hurricane lamp and set it on his desk before rummaging around in a drawer and tossing a bundle of old, yellowed wanted dodgers on his scarred desktop. He sat down and thumbed through the posters, carefully considering the rough sketch on each. Five minutes after he'd started, one caught his eye.

The likeness was so poor it was hard to be sure, but the description of the man cinched it: tall, slender Mexican with blue eyes and handlebar mustache. The man's name was José Luis del Toro, wanted for multiple murders in Texas and New Mexico. He was described as a cold-blooded gun for hire, and extremely deadly.

Gibbon stared at the picture for several minutes, feeling a chill in his loins. So Verlyn Thornberg had been right. Something was going on. One of the ranchers in the area had hired a gunman.

Gibbon scowled at the sketch of José Luis del Toro, whose very name sounded like death. It made Gibbon feel like the inadequate old coward everyone thought he was.

"Shit," he said with a grunt.

If the man who'd gotten off the train really was Del Toro, the Old Trouble was back with a vengeance. And it was Gibbon's job to do something about it.

He sat back in his chair and felt the old, lonely fear wash over him once again.

CHAPTER 5

GLOWING CINDERS FLEW back from the smoke-stack as the train chugged eastward into the dawn. A rolling, snow-covered prairie lifted gently under a lavender-salmon sky, relieved now and then with craggy-topped buttes and peppered occasionally with sparse buffalo herds.

A grizzled pioneer in a torn coat and scraggly beard waited at a crossing with a wagon load of hay, the yellow dog on the seat beside him cocking its head at the clattering wheels.

It was Mark Talbot's fourth and last day on the train. He'd been staring out the window nearly every waking moment. Although his back ached from the stab wound, he was able to appreciate the view, which was growing more and more spectacular. Isolated clusters of cottonwoods, frozen sloughs spiked with cattails, tidy gray cabins nestled in hollows and flanked with windmills and hitch-and-rail corrals.

Talbot reflected that most travelers, unacquainted with the Northern Plains, would no doubt find the starkness disconcerting. Born and raised here, Talbot found it restful. While growing up, he couldn't wait to see the world and fight in a war or two, search for gold in legendary Mexico. Seven years of warring and wandering behind him now, he couldn't wait to be home, on the open plains, where the scalloped sky took your breath away and the prairie went on forever.

Of course all the blood had something to do with it. You couldn't see that much, spill that much, and not pine for home. You couldn't see friends like Max Schultz or Louis Margolies or Sergeant Maloney butchered on the burning, rocky wastes of the Arizona desert or hacked to death in their sleep in the White Mountains, the creeks in the morning flowing red with the blood of Mescaleros and soldiers alike—you couldn't see a lovely Mexican girl's slender, ruined throat—and not long for a quiet cabin on Crow Creek in western Dakota, windows ablaze with the setting sun, the quartering breeze spiced with chokecherry blossoms and sage.

The thought was interrupted by a tap on Talbot's shoulder.

He turned. A young woman and a man stood in the aisle. The woman was a dark-haired beauty in a fur coat and hat. Painted lips set off the lush brown eyes, which regarded Talbot boldly. Her hands were warmed by a rabbit muffler.

The man next to her was older but dressed with similar elegance, out of place amidst the raucous snores, stiff upholstered seats, and sooty windows of the tourist car. The man's slender frame was cloaked by a shiny bear coat and beaver hat, and his thin lips were smugly pursed. His small, silver-rimmed pipe filled the air with an aroma akin to balsam and sage.

"Yes?" Talbot asked.

The man spoke in a melodic tenor, enunciating his words very carefully. "Pardon us, sir, but the lady couldn't help noticing that you appear to be injured."

"Pardon?"

"There's blood on the back of your coat," the

young woman said, pulling a hand from her muffler to point.

Talbot reached behind his back with his left hand, probing his vest with his fingers. Sure enough, the blood had leaked through. The movement sharpened the pain, and he winced. "It's nothing," he said, not wanting to make a spectacle. "Just backed up against a loading fork back on the Frisco docks. Probably looks worse than it is."

"Oh, my," the girl said. "That must have hurt."

"It's really nothing."

With small, lightless eyes, the man said, "Why don't you join us in our suite, and I'll tend it for you?"

"He's a doctor," the girl explained.

Talbot studied them, wary. Why were these two well-dressed strangers so concerned for his health? You didn't survive the Mescalero Apaches and Old Mexico during the gold boom without a healthy dose of xenophobia.

"Thanks for the offer, but I'll be fine." Talbot turned back to the window.

"As you wish, sir," the girl said. "Come along, Harry."

Talbot turned back to see the two moving off down the aisle, between sparse rows of rustic western travelers—cowboys, drummers, and gamblers who were either playing cards or curled uncomfortably on the hard seats. The girl's long chocolate curls cascaded down her slender back, bouncing lightly as she walked.

Talbot sucked his cheek, watching her. She was lovely, and she had simply offered help to a stranger. Suddenly her motivation didn't seem to matter.

"Hold up," he said, rising with his bag. "I didn't mean to be rude. I could use a fresh dressing, I reckon."

The girl's eyes brightened as she turned to regard

him. She gestured to the door at the end of the car, and the man called Harrison stepped aside to let the rough-hewn stranger pass.

Two cars back was a Hotel Pullman decked out with Turkish rugs, inlaid woodwork, two red-velvet daybeds, and a potbellied stove flanked by a stack of cordwood logs split so precisely they looked surreal. Peering at himself in the gilded mirror over the sofa, Talbot gave a complimentary whistle.

"Daddy won't let me travel in anything but luxury," the girl said, tossing aside her coat and muffler. Carefully she lifted the hat from her head, removing pins and brushing loose hair from her impossibly smooth cheeks.

Talbot furtively filled his lungs with her fresh, rosy smell, not so subtly feasting his eyes. American women.

"And on long trips, he makes me take a physician—thus Harrison here," she said. "He's a friend I met at the theater."

The man in the bear coat lifted the curled ends of his waxed mustache in a wry smile. "I'm Harrison Long. That's Suzanne." There was an ironic tone in the doctor's voice and expression, as though he envisioned himself a cultural prodigy among savages.

Talbot tore his eyes from the girl to stroll around the car, taking in the ornate hangings and plush green drapes. "So this is how the privileged live," he said. "If information about this gets out to the tourist cars, you're liable to have a riot on your hands."

Harrison chuffed. "Such rustics as I saw up there could not appreciate this kind of luxury."

"Oh, I bet they could," Talbot countered good-naturedly. "They'd have some party back here." He caught the girl smiling at him, and returned the smile.

"How long have you two been riding the rails?" he asked.

"Since August," Suzanne said. "I tend to get owly during the fall and winter on the Plains, and Daddy sends me traveling."

Talbot cocked an eyebrow. "Who's your daddy— Jay Gould?"

"King Magnusson."

"Never heard of him."

"That's not surprising," she said with a laugh.

Talbot wasn't sure whom she'd just insulted, him or her father. As he feasted his eyes on the girl's lovely lips parted to reveal a delicious set of pearly whites, on her long, slender neck and ripe bosom pushing at the low-cut shirtwaist, he didn't care. He'd been at sea a long time.

"We've told you our names," the girl said. "What's yours?"

"Mark Talbot's my handle, ma'am."

Smiling brightly, with the understated vigor of the well-bred, the girl took two strides forward and held out her long, pale hand. "Pleased to meet you, Mark Talbot."

"Likewise, ma'am," Talbot said, his gaze held by hers. Her hand was thin and fine-boned, but her shake was firm. Talbot held it, enjoying the feel of her warm, soft flesh.

Dr. Long gave a warning cough. "Let's take a look there, shall we?" he said, taking a step toward the visitor and indicating Talbot's back.

"Where?" Talbot asked.

"Right here is fine," the doctor said, holding out his hands to accept Talbot's vest.

Talbot made no move to take it off. "No offense, ma'am, but . . . with her here?"

"Oh, I won't peek!" Suzanne exclaimed playfully.

"I'll ring the porter for some rags and a bowl of water. Would you care for some coffee? It's French."

Ten minutes later, Talbot was lying facedown on the sofa, crossed ankles draped over an arm, hands folded beneath his chin. Sitting on a footstool beside him, Dr. Long was sponging the wound and puffing his pipe.

Long frowned. "This was no mere hook you backed into, was it, Mr. Talbot?"

"Looks nasty," Suzanne said. She stood over the doctor, coffee cup clutched to her breast in both hands, and observed the doctor's work with an arched brow.

"Just a scratch," Talbot said.

The doctor squeezed blood and water from the sponge and dabbed at the dried blood and pus around the slit. "It looks nastier than it is, but it's no scratch. It is, I believe, a knife wound. You've outdone yourself this time, Suzanne."

"A knife wound!" she enthused. "Really, Mr. Talbot?"

Before Talbot could answer, Long said, "I think you should know, Mr. Talbot—if that's your real name—I am armed with a Smith & Wesson .35 caliber pocket pistol, and I know how to use it."

"Oh, Harrison, don't be melodramatic!" Suzanne laughed. "Besides . . . it might be fun."

"Suzanne!"

Talbot craned his head to look at the doctor. "What do you mean, she's outdone herself?"

"Suzanne has a habit—it's a game, really—of picking up interesting strangers and becoming acquainted. She spied you on a stroll through your car earlier. I agreed you did look interesting, but the blood on your vest put me off."

Suzanne shrugged. "I thought it was a good excuse to introduce ourselves, Harrison being a doctor and all." Visibly excited, Suzanne wheeled around, skirt flying, and landed in a chair. She crossed her legs and leaned forward, placing her coffee cup on her knees. Her smile was radiant.

Talbot watched her as the doctor continued to clean the wound. He couldn't help being smitten by the effervescent girl. He guessed she was no more than nineteen or twenty, and despite her means of travel and dress he sensed she was more than just a spoiled coquette. She was an educated, *well-built*, spoiled coquette.

"Come now, Mr. Talbot," she begged, "how did you come to be stabbed?"

Talbot laughed at the girl's innocent delight. "Well, I'd like to tell you I was trying to rescue a damsel from a horde of Arab slave traders, but it was really a lot less interesting than that."

Suzanne smiled delightfully. "Let me be the judge."

Talbot told her the story of the fat businessman and the Chinese boy and the two ruffians who'd tried to clean his clock. Suzanne listened, wide-eyed. When he finished she said sincerely, "What a valiant man! Did you hear that, Harrison?"

"Yes, valiant. Hold still, Mr. Talbot; I'm just about done here."

"You're an adventurer, then, Mr. Talbot," Suzanne said admiringly.

"I reckon I had an adventure or two," Talbot allowed. "But I'm going home now, to Dakota, and I plan to stay there. I've had my fill of knockin' about. Once a shitkicker, always a shitkicker, I reckon. Pardon my French."

"Dakota! Well, that's where we're headed. Where abouts, Mr. Talbot?"

"A little town called Canaan, on the Canaan Bench. My older brother has a ranch thereabouts."

Dr. Long was taping a bandage to Talbot's back.

"I appreciate this, Doctor," Talbot said. "I was getting tired of that wet apron wrapped around my chest."

"I think you'll find this considerably more agreeable," Harrison said. "You can slip into your clothes again, if you'd like."

Suzanne frowned thoughtfully. "My father's place is on the Canaan Bench, and Canaan is . . ." Suddenly her eyes widened. "My gosh, that's only a two-hour ride from where we live!"

"Is that right?" Talbot said, sitting up and reaching for his clothes.

"Yes." Her smile widened, and her eyes flashed. "We're practically neighbors!"

She got up, retrieved a china cup from the tray the porter had set on the trestle table in the middle of the car, handed it to Talbot, and filled it from a silver pot. Turning to the doctor, who stood rolling down the sleeves of his crisp white shirt, she said, "Would you like a cup, Harrison?"

"No, I think I'll go smoke and leave you two to your hometown chatter," he said dryly.

When he'd donned his broadcloth jacket and his heavy bear coat and hat and left, Suzanne turned from the door with a mischievous flair. "He's jealous, you know?"

Talbot frowned, opened his mouth to speak, but she cut him off.

"Oh, not of you, of me. He's . . . he's one of *those*—couldn't you tell?"

Talbot raised his eyebrows. "One of *those?*"

"Yes. I do love Harrison dearly—he's the best friend a girl could ever have—but he's quite irrevocably . . . one of those." In two light-footed strides she'd fallen onto the couch beside Talbot, smoothing her skirt beneath her, turning to the side and gracefully crossing her long, coltish legs. "When you had your shirt off, I thought he was going to start foaming at the mouth—elegantly, of course."

A curl slipped from behind her ear and fell gently along her cheek. Talbot stared at it, fighting the urge to smooth it back behind the delicate ear. Her smell was fresh and subtle, like the rain in Chihuahua. Her eyes softened, as if reading his mind.

"To tell you the truth," she said breathily, "I didn't blame him one bit. You cut a handsome figure, Mr. Talbot." Her lips stretched back, revealing all those perfect teeth, faintly gleaming.

"Mark," he said, coloring a little at her candor. He was surprised that a girl of her station could be so forward.

"Mark," she said, lowering her eyes, turning suddenly girlish and shy.

Talbot's heart tom-tommed in his chest, and he could feel the sweat pop out on his forehead. The girl was like a drug, a tonic washing over him. His head fairly swam, and he wondered for a moment if he weren't dreaming.

Of its own accord, Talbot's hand rose from his knee. Slowly it traversed the space between him and Suzanne and rested on her chin, cupping it gently in his first two fingers. Lifting it, he leaned toward her. Her head tilted back, offering her slightly parted lips.

Suddenly the car jerked and slowed, and they fell back against the couch. Suzanne sat up and turned to look out the windows. "Oh, my goodness—we're finally stopping!" she said with cheer.

"Great," Talbot said wryly, dazed from the attempted kiss.

The girl seemed to have forgotten all about it. She knelt on the sofa, cleared the steam from the window with her hand, and watched the first few cabins and shanties slide by as the wheels clattered on the iron seams. The car slowed, shuddering as the brakes worked against the locomotive's giant wheels.

Suzanne read the sign attached to the station house. "Wibaux."

"Wibaux?" Talbot said with surprise, turning to see for himself. "That's where I switch to the branch line."

"Oh, Mark, no—I stay on until Big Draw!" Suzanne exclaimed, swinging her eyes to him. "We were just starting to get acquainted!"

I'll say we were, Talbot thought. Reaching for his war bag and awkwardly gaining his feet, he laughed mirthlessly and wagged his head. "You sure made the time fly, Miss Magnusson."

"Oh, fudge, Mark," she lamented, pursing her lips in a pout. "Promise me you'll look me up . . . once we're both home and settled? I want to hear all about your adventures. They sound so . . . so . . . romantic." Her voice had become a resonant purr.

"It's far from that, but I'll tell you about it," he promised. As he moved out the door, Suzanne was on his heels. The train had nearly stopped, its couplings clamoring like thunder, steam fogging the windows.

"Promise? . . . Oh, no you won't! Before you even think of me again, the local girls will be pounding on your door."

Talbot laughed. He jumped down from the car and turned to her, standing between the cars with both hands on the rail, her breath visible in the cold air. He knew that if anyone was going to have suitors knocking their door down, it would be she.

"No local girl could hold a candle to you, Suzanne. I'll look you up. You can be sure of that."

He tipped his head and returned her smile, laughing heartily. "Thanks for everything. Say good-bye to Harrison for me."

"I will. Travel safe . . . until we meet again."

Talbot turned to walk down the platform. He turned back to her, still watching him like a lovelorn heroine from a British romance. "If I'm going to look you up, I'll need the handle for your father's ranch."

"Oh . . . it's the Double X," she said.

"The Double X," Talbot echoed. He hadn't heard of it, but he supposed a lot of new outfits had moved in since he'd left. "I'll find it."

He waved, hefted his war bag over his shoulder, and strode toward the station house to await the branch line that would carry him on the last leg of his journey home.

CHAPTER 6

TEX MADSEN WAS a tall, rail-thin cowpoke with dull, deep-sunk eyes and a walrus mustache. He was only twenty-nine years old, but climbing the stairs of the Powder Horn Hotel in Canaan, he wheezed like a geezer. He cursed as his weak lungs constricted, stopping on the landing to catch his breath.

He leaned against the wall as a loud coughing fit gripped him. The paroxysm raked his insides like sandpaper. When it subsided, Tex lifted his head, wiped his nose and mouth, and peered grimly at the blood-laced fluids soiling his handkerchief.

"I knew I shoulda stayed in Texas," he mumbled, continuing down the narrow hall between closed doors. "Cold like this ain't natural. It's . . . it's taken my youth."

Tex had been stricken with the virus nearly a month ago, and being sent out into the subzero weather to round up some gunslick wasn't going to help him get over it. Hell's bells, he'd probably end up like old Yancy Kellogg, the old Double X hostler who'd died of pneumonia last winter and whose body was ravaged by mice and owls as it awaited a spring burial in the barn loft.

Cursing the ranch foreman who'd sent him out in

this chilblain weather, Tex stopped at room 15 and knocked, stifling another cough.

"Who is it?" came a Spanish-accented voice.

Sniffing, Tex leaned toward the door. "Tex Madsen. I'm supposed to show you out to the Double X. If you're Mr. del Toro, that is."

"Sí," Del Toro grumbled. "Give me a minute."

You can have the whole goddamn morning for all I care, Tex said to himself. It wasn't exactly steamy in the hotel, but he was in no hurry to go back outside where he could hear the brittle wind howling. His cheeks and toes were still numb. His head and back were chill with fever.

Tex was waiting with his back against the wall when the door opened and a blond girl stepped out. Her face was puffy with sleep, her hair and dress disheveled. Tex didn't know her name, but he'd seen her working in the saloon downstairs. Not bad-looking for a soiled dove in these parts. She softly latched the door behind her, paying no attention to Tex, and drifted down the hall, her short red dress swishing against her legs.

Tex gave a fragile grin and turned back to the door as it opened again. Another blond poked her head out and looked around. A beret hung loose in her hair. Bigger than the first girl and rawboned, she scrutinized Tex dully, gave a little smile, stepped out, and shut the door behind her. Smoothing her dress, she whined at a tear and headed for the stairs.

"Well, I'll be . . ." Tex muttered wonderingly.

He waited another five minutes, noting the feeling returning to his toes. He couldn't believe it when the door opened again and another girl slipped out, carrying two empty whiskey bottles and three water glasses. She was not wearing a dress, but had wrapped a sheet around herself. A brunette with a pretty, round face, she looked haunted and struggled awkwardly with her load while holding the sheet closed at her bosom. When she saw Tex she gave a start, her grip on the sheet loosening, giving Tex a momentary shot of her chafed, red-mottled breasts.

Tongue-tied, Tex tried a smile and fingered the rim of his big Stetson.

Stiffly the girl marched up to Tex. Fire sparked in her eyes. "That man is an *animal,*" she hissed, then scurried down the hall, tripping on the sheet. Tex heard the crash of a bottle; it clattered as it rolled down the stairs.

The door opened once again. Tex turned to it, expecting to see another rumpled girl, but this time a tall, straight-backed, lean-faced Mexican man stood before him. The man's gray coat appeared to be wolf hide, and the nickel-plated pistols he wore strapped to a wide cartridge belt were Colts with mother-of-pearl grips—butts forward, holsters bent back and tied to the man's thighs.

The pistols were probably the finest Tex had ever seen, but it was the man's lake-blue eyes in the long, narrow face, its hollows filled with shadows, that held the Texan's attention. The eyes looked both humorous and menacing, flashing like blue glass in a muddy stream. Tex felt the skin behind his ears prick as the man sized him up, chewing on a thin black cheroot.

"Don't let her fool you—she loved every minute of it," the man said, grinning with his eyes.

The comment caught Tex off guard. "Pardon me?"

"The girl calls me an animal, but she never once asked me to stop." The man's lips parted around the unlit cigar, showing little square teeth, slightly discolored.

Tex turned to look down the hall, as though the girl were still there. "Oh . . . oh, sure," he said.

"Have you ever spent a night with three women, amigo?"

Tex laughed. "Who? Me? Nah."

"You should try it. It is the closest thing to heaven a man will experience on earth. Light?"

Tex dug inside his coat for a lucifer, scratched it on the door frame, and lit the man's cigar, careful not to betray his anger. He didn't like playing servant to some uppity greaser, no matter how many men the gunman had slain, no matter how many women he'd diddled in one night.

When the cigar was lit, the gunman turned into the room, picked up his war bag and rifle, and tossed them to Tex. Then he picked up his saddle and started down the hall, leaving the door hanging wide behind him.

Tex stood there, grappling with his sudden burden and silently cursing the man. He peered into the room, where the bed stood in complete disarray, the mattress hanging off, the sheets and quilts twisted and strewn. The dresser had been pulled out from the wall, and its mirror was shattered. A tattered dress lay on the floor.

Tex shook his head slowly, not knowing what to make of the Mexican gunman.

Three women in one night? Tex thought, starting down the stairs. A man like that could do some damage around here.

———————

The gunman rode beside Tex on the snow-covered wagon road, on the black stallion Tex had led to town for him, and never uttered a word. Tex decided the man was either too uppity or ornery for idle banter, and that was just fine with Tex, who was too cold and feverish for conversation.

"The boss and the others are waitin' for ya inside," he told the man when they'd passed through the front gate of the sprawling Double X headquarters. "I'll take your horse into the barn."

The man did not reply, but sat staring at the three-story terra-cotta mansion with its cylindrical towers, arched windows, balconies, and ornate woodwork. From the look on his face, Tex figured the man hadn't been expecting to see such an elaborate hacienda this far off the beaten path.

His eyes played along the wide verandah to the carved oak door, in which the Double X brand had been burned, and up past the massive gable, with its deep-set window to the great stone chimney. Smoke lifted and was torn away on the wind.

One sleigh and a saddle horse stood before the verandah, the shaggy horses turning their drooping heads and twitching their ears at Tex and the gunman, clouds of breath jetting from their nostrils. Finally the man dismounted and handed Tex his reins. Wordlessly he walked up the wide steps, and the big door opened as though of its own accord.

Leading the stallion toward the barn and looking over his shoulder, Tex watched the gunman enter the house, the door closing behind him.

"There she blows, boys," Tex mumbled darkly, turning away. "There she, sure as shit, blows."

———— • ————

King Magnusson was sitting in the stuffed leather chair behind his desk, hands laced behind his head. His foreman, Rag Donnelly, and his business partner, Bernard Troutman, president of the First Stockman's Bank in Big Draw, had joined him in his den, and were sitting on the couch against the wall, to Magnusson's right.

The banker's beaver hat sat between him and Donnelly on the overstuffed cushions. They were drinking coffee and cognac and chatting easily, waiting for their meeting to start.

Magnusson was a tall, lean man in his late fifties, with hard, weathered features and thick, wavy blond hair combed back from a slight widow's peak. His eyes were blue; his friends said they had an amiable cast. His enemies called them the eyes of a liar, calculated to take your mind off the knife he was about to stick in your back.

Minnie McDougal, the housekeeper, was bending before the visitors, offering coffee and cognac from a silver tray. A hot fire sparked in the enormous stone hearth to Magnusson's left, filling the room with the smell of pine.

Magnusson lifted a coffee cup and saucer from the tray Minnie offered him now, declining more cognac—he wanted to stay clear this afternoon—and turned his eyes to his visitors. Minnie left the tray and returned to her chores.

"So when's this man supposed to get here, King?" Troutman asked. His red hair was matted and his pale, freckled cheeks were still mottled from the cold.

"At one o'clock, but who knows how badly drifted the road from Canaan is. It blew all night, and it's still blowin'."

"Why in hell did he take the train to Canaan? That's way the hell north—a two-hour ride in good weather."

Magnusson shrugged. "It's enemy territory," he said. "Said he wanted to check it out while he was still anonymous. Sounds like a good idea, if you ask me. Tells me the man knows what he's about."

The nervous Troutman didn't seem to be listening to Magnusson's explanation, but forming his next question. "How much did we agree he was worth?"

Magnusson suppressed a scowl. "We've been all over this, Bernie. Six thousand now—today—and another six when the job's done."

"How do we know when the job's done?"

"We'll know."

"And how do we know if he's caught he won't sing?"

The foreman, Donnelly, turned his cool wrangler's eyes to the banker. "Calm down now, Mr. Troutman— before you start giving me the jitters." He turned the smile to Magnusson, who dropped his eyes and plucked a long nine from the cigar box on his desk.

Biting the end off his cigar, Magnusson said, "He comes highly recommended. I can't say by whom, but . . ." He let his voice trail off and sat quietly smoking and listening to the clock.

A thought occurred to him and he turned to Donnelly. "How many beeves did you say Jack Thom was trying to get away with the other day?"

Donnelly shook his head. "I didn't see it. Randall and Shelby Green said they saw him hazing five off toward the Rinski place."

Magnusson's eyes grew dark, and he shook his head. "That arrogant son of a bitch."

"Shelby also said he saw several of our brands in Grover Nixon's pens—right there at his headquarters!"

Magnusson puffed and stared off into space.

Troutman piped up thoughtfully. "Well, the army came in and sided with them, so now they think they can do whatever they goddamn well please."

"Not for long," Magnusson said, darkly wistful. "Not for too goddamn much—"

He was stopped short by a tap on the study door.

"Come," Magnusson called.

The door opened. Minnie McDougal reappeared, nervously feigning a pleasant smile. Something had disturbed her. "There's a gentleman here to see you, sir."

"Send him in, Minnie."

She threw the door wide to let Del Toro step past her. The smile vanishing, she left, closing the door behind her.

"Mr. Del Toro!" Magnusson said buoyantly, standing and moving around his desk. "I'm so happy to see you made it. How was your train ride?"

Del Toro shrugged. "Pleasant enough, señor."

Magnusson shook his hand. "I'm King Magnusson. This is Mr. Troutman, my business partner, and Mr. Donnelly, the Double X foreman."

Both men stood and shook the gunman's hand. Donnelly was smiling, coolly sizing up the Mexican. Troutman appeared flushed and tongue-tied as he eyed the man's wolf coat and fancy, prominently displayed pistols.

Magnusson had to admit that the man's presence was . . . unique, to say the least. He imagined the man even gave off the odor of death, however subtle. The blue eyes were downright startling. Magnusson mused he couldn't have handpicked a man this obviously appropriate for the job.

"Please sit down."

When the gunman had seated himself in the stuffed chair angled before the fire, crossing his long legs, Magnusson gestured toward the tray Minnie had left on his desk. "Coffee and cognac?"

"Just the cognac," the man said, looking around

the room, at the western oils and watercolors hung in gilt frames, at the game trophies, and at the bear rug before his chair. "It was a chilly ride."

He seemed to be quite taken with the room's furnishings. Magnusson thought the man was probably more comfortable in bawdy houses and gambling dens.

When the rancher had given the man his cognac and had retaken his seat behind his desk, he said, "Well, let's get down to business, shall we, Mr. del Toro?"

"That's why I'm here," Del Toro drawled.

Magnusson retrieved his cigar from an ashtray before him and inspected its ash. "It's really very simple, and I'm not going to beat around the bush. There are about fifteen ranches north of us, on the other side of the Little Missouri, giving us trouble. Stealing our beef, taking our summer graze. We want them out."

A thin smile broadened below the gunman's mustache. "I thought you tried driving them out five years ago."

Troutman growled, "Heard about that, did you?"

"I heard they called the army in from Fort Lincoln to settle things down," the gunman continued.

"That's right," Magnusson said with a nod. "At that time the army, not knowing the full story, sided with the small cattlemen."

"What makes you think things are gonna be any different now, señor?"

"An old friend of King's was just elected governor," Troutman said with a grin.

Magnusson looked at Del Toro, his eyes hard. "I've been wanting those goddamn human coyotes off the Bench for a long time. None of us can increase year after year if we're sharing the Bench. There's simply

not enough grass to go around, and the acreage I
need to keep turning a profit and satisfying my eastern investors has forced me to get nasty. It's a simple
matter of economics . . . and survival of the fittest."

He paused, stared thoughtfully through the varie-
gated smoke cloud hanging in the study. Gray winter
light penetrated the window behind him, outlining
him against it and angling down on the leather top
of his desk like quicksilver.

"I tried once before to clean off the Bench," Magnusson continued. "I failed because I didn't have the
right men behind me. Now with Charlie Sparks in
the governor's office . . . well, let's just leave it at that,
shall we, Mr. Del Toro?" He smiled, self-satisfied.

From the shadows on the far side of the fireplace,
Del Toro looked at each man in turn. He removed
his hat, primly smoothing his shiny black hair, and
planted the hat on his knee. Returning his hand to
his lap, he looked at Magnusson and said, "So how
many do you want to disappear?"

"Disappear?" the banker said, frowning.

Donnelly snickered.

Magnusson said, "That's gunman's talk for *die*,
Bernard. Go to the henhouse. Buy the farm. Comprende?"

Troutman looked at him, scowling. "It ain't every
day you hire a gunman, King."

"No. And let's hope we won't need to ever again."

Turning to Del Toro, Magnusson continued, "You
see, we want this to be taken care of much more quietly than what happened five years ago. Five years
ago, we let our tempers get away from us, and we
lost control of our men." He shot an accusatory look
at Donnelly, who dropped his eyes. "Things got very
messy, to say the least. Out of control. This time, we
want to be sure of every step we take. We want the

right people excised with the precision of a well-schooled surgeon."

"And we don't want anything to point back to us," Troutman added.

Magnusson slid his chair out from his desk, opened a drawer, and produced a legal-size sheet of paper. "To that end, my two colleagues and I have drawn up a list."

Del Toro smiled, loving it. "A list of those to disappear, uh?" He got up to retrieve the paper. "A death list."

"Exactly."

Donnelly said, "Once you're done with it, burn it."

"I know my trade, señor," Del Toro said absently, standing before Magnusson and regarding the list. He took it to his chair and sat down. "Ten names."

"Yes," Magnusson said.

"How much?"

Magnusson decided to start low. "Eight thousand. Four thousand now. Four when you're through. We'll wire it to you after you're gone from here in a hurry."

Del Toro shook his head. "Uh-uh. Fourteen thousand. Nine now, five when I'm done."

Troutman chuffed. Donnelly smiled at Magnusson.

Magnusson sighed and puffed his cigar, studying the calendar clock on the fireplace mantle. He regarded his partners, then the gunman. "We'll go no higher than twelve. Two increments of six thousand."

"Let's see it," Del Toro said.

Magnusson opened another drawer. He counted out a pile of bills, slipped them into an envelope, and slid the envelope across his desk.

The gunman turned his head to the banker. "Would you mind bringing it to me, señor?"

Troutman gave Magnusson a flabbergasted look, mouth and eyes drawn wide.

"Oh, for Christ's sake," Donnelly said, standing and grabbing the envelope from the desk.

He took it to the gunman. Del Toro casually accepted it in one hand while offering his empty glass to Donnelly. The tall, rangy foreman refilled the glass, then returned it to the gunman. By this time, Del Toro had counted the money. He'd stuffed the envelope and the list in his coat.

"Gracias, señor," he said, accepting the glass from Donnelly. He sipped, then asked Magnusson, "Is there only one lawman in the county?"

"Yes, and he's harmless. Believe me."

Troutman and Donnelly both gave a laugh.

"Sí, I saw him at the train station," Del Toro said. "A soft old bear who hibernates all year long, eh?"

"You got that right," Troutman said. "Sleeps and drinks. When we tried clearing off the Bench five years ago, he hid out at the Sundowner in Canaan. When he finally decided he needed to take action, he called the army in."

"But that won't happen this time," Magnusson said importantly.

"Very well," Del Toro said, nodding. He polished off his cognac. He stood and donned his hat, adjusting it carefully.

Magnusson walked around his desk and shook the gunman's hand. The other men did likewise. There was a knock at the door as the gunman turned toward it.

"Yes?" Magnusson called.

The door opened and a pretty dark-haired girl, flushed from the cold, poked her head inside, gazing around Del Toro at Magnusson. "Hello, Father. I just wanted to let you know I'm home."

"Suzanne!" Magnusson said, his face fairly glowing, the hard features dissolving under the shine of parental adoration. "Get Minnie to heat you some chocolate. I'll be right out."

The girl smiled and gingerly withdrew from the door, latching it quietly.

Del Toro turned to Magnusson. "Your daughter?"

"Yes."

"Muy bonita, señor."

"Yes," Magnusson said, his smile turning cold. "And completely off-limits."

"Of course, señor," the gunman said with a lascivious smile. He tipped his hat at the men and left the room.

Magnusson stared at the closed door, feeling an icy finger probe his spine and wondering if he hadn't just made a pact with the devil.

When he'd seen Bernard Troutman off on his sleigh, King Magnusson heard boots crunching snow across the yard. He lifted his eyes to see his son, Randall, walking toward him from the barn.

Randall Magnusson was two inches shorter than his father, with a bearded, moony face and weak brown eyes. Long hair hung down the back of his buckskin coat. He wore a floppy flat-brimmed hat with a snakeskin band, secured with a cord beneath his chin.

"Hello, son."

"Pa."

"How's that heifer?"

Halting beside his father and turning to look at the sleigh dwindling in the distance, Randall said, "Eating a few oats now, anyway. Who's the greaser?"

"Name's Del Toro. He's gonna help us clean off the

Bench, once and for all. Let's keep it under wraps, shall we?"

"Gunslick?"

Magnusson nodded.

Randall turned to his father. "You never told me you was hirin' no gunslick."

"Didn't want the word to get around."

"I can keep my mouth shut!"

King turned to him. His eyes were overtly patronizing. "We both know that isn't true, son. Especially after you've had a few drinks with the boys."

"Sure I can!"

"Randall," King admonished, arching an eyebrow. Having punctuated the conversation, he turned toward the house.

Puffing up his chest, Randall said, "You didn't need to go hirin' no gunman, Pa. Hell, me and Shelby Green can do what he can do, and we're a hell of a lot cheaper!"

King regarded his son skeptically. "Now, son, I appreciate that fine bit of detective work you and Shelby did out on the range. Finding Jack Thom with those beeves was a real help to me. It confirms what I've suspected all along about the smaller ranchers trying to ruin me. But I think it best if we leave the dirty work to those who've been schooled in that arena. Don't you?"

He smiled and put a broad, thick hand on Randall's shoulder, squeezing. "You may be a lot of things, son, but you're no gunman. That's a credit to your character, not an allusion to your poor marksmanship. You just keep working those mustangs, and one day you'll be as good a broncobuster as Rag."

King smiled, parting his thin, chapped lips.

Randall smoldered. Rag this, Rag that.

"Come on inside," King said, giving his son's

shoulder another squeeze. "Your sister's back from Frisco."

King turned away.

Randall said to his back: "Yeah, well, tell that gunman not to worry about the Rinskis."

"What?"

Giving an evil grin, the younger Magnusson stared into his father's eyes for a full three seconds. He wanted to tell him about what he and Shelby had done to old man Fairchild and that fancy-pants school-teacher from Pittsburgh, but he resisted the impulse. When it came down to it, not even the old man had the stomach for what needed to be done to clear the Bench for the Double X.

"Me and Shelby caught Jack Thom butchering one of our steers Saturday. He held us off with a rifle, so we let him go. The next night we rode over to his cabin and let him have it."

He gave a self-congratulatory smile and sucked his cheek. "You can be sure the Rinskis won't be collarin' any more Double X beef."

Magnusson looked dully at his son. He lifted his chin and breathed sharply through his nose. "Let me get this straight. You and Green killed Jack Thom?"

"That's right."

"Did anyone see you?"

Beside himself with pride, Randall said, "We wore masks."

"Anyone else around?"

The young man's smile dulled. "Um, well . . . yeah. I mean . . . no."

"Well, which is it? Yes or no?"

"No. I mean . . . well, Rinski's daughter was there."

King looked surprised. "Daughter?"

"Yeah, well . . . she and Thom seemed to be . . .

you know—carryin' on . . . with their clothes off and such." Randall laughed uneasily.

Magnusson drilled his gaze deeper into his son's face. "You shot Jack Thom while he was diddling Rinski's daughter?"

Randall wasn't sure if his father found the information humorous or horrifying. He looked for evidence of either as he said, "Yes, sir."

"So the girl saw you?"

"But . . . we were wearin' masks."

"Well, at least you had sense enough to do that." King looked around, digesting the information. "You didn't harm the girl, did you?"

Randall swallowed. "N-no, sir." He swallowed again and smiled.

King nodded. "Well, I reckon if you caught Thom red-handed, he deserved what you gave him." He sighed. "But from now on, you leave that work to the gunman. This Del Toro knows how to get things done quickly, cleanly, and quietly. Best of all, no one knows him, and no one knows who he's working for."

"Pshaw, I could—"

"You listen to me now, Randall," King said, waving a crooked finger in his son's face. His tone was again patronizing. "Just because you were lucky enough to catch Jack Thom in a . . . uh . . . compromising situation, and got the drop on him, that doesn't mean you're going to have that kind of luck again. You don't think I'd risk my only son getting killed over a few rustled beeves now, do you? So you leave well enough alone. You just hang tough with those broncs, and leave the gun work up to Del Toro."

He gave Randall a wink. "Maybe one of these days I'll be able to tell my poker buddies that my son can ride as well as Rag Donnelly."

He turned and went into the house.

Randall glowered at the door. "Rag Donnelly this, Rag Donnelly that," he muttered, curling his upper lip. "You'll see who's who and what's what around here, you old duffer."

CHAPTER 7

EARLIER THAT SAME day, Mark Talbot's train steamed into Canaan screeching and hissing. Talbot disembarked with his war bag, wincing at the cold, which stung his face like a resolute slap.

He stood looking around to get his bearings while the only other passengers disembarking, two drummers in store-bought suits and muttonchop whiskers, hurried around the freight depot, no doubt in search of a warm spot to light.

But for the shiny new train tracks curving along the river buttes south of town, everything appeared pretty much as it had before Talbot had left. Sod and log shanties and clapboard shacks sat willy-nilly around the central business district of false-fronted stores and the livery barn with its fragrant sprawl of paddocks and corrals. The red train station and water tank abutted the settlement on one end, the lumberyard on the other.

Everything had the same feeble look of impermanence, and Talbot wondered how long it would take Canaan to decide to thrive or return to the sod.

His shoulders screwed up against the cold, he started toward the false fronts of the main street. The frigid air funneling up his thin cotton breeches told him he wasn't dressed for this kind of weather.

Before shopping for new duds, he decided to shore himself with a stiff drink.

A gruff voice said, "I'm guessin' you're gonna freeze up solid within the hour, and I'm gonna have to find a place to hide your body from the rats until the ground thaws."

Talbot turned. A dozen feet to his left, before the frosty station-house doors, stood a round bear of a man with gray sideburns and a tin star.

"It is a mite chilly," Talbot agreed with a grin.

"You might want to think twice about lettin' that train go."

There was an ominous note in the big man's voice. Talbot knew that, with his shaggy beard and hair and mismatched seaman's clothes, he'd been pegged as riffraff, and that he'd just been invited to leave.

Talbot smiled pleasantly. "Don't worry, I'm not here to rob a bank or hold up the stage. I'm from here, born and bred, and I'm comin' home."

The sheriff tipped his head and squinted as he considered the newcomer. After a moment he said thoughtfully, "I thought you looked familiar. You're . . . you're . . ."

"Mark Talbot."

"Sure, Owen Talbot's youngest boy. Didn't recognize you under all that hair." The sheriff moved forward and held out his hand. Talbot could smell the liquor on his breath.

"Jed Gibbon," he said as Talbot shook his hand. "I ranched out in the sandhills before my water and credit dried up. I knew your pa, a good man. Used to play poker with him winters. Damn shame how the smallpox took him and your ma. You couldn't have been more than twelve."

"Fourteen. My brother was sixteen, but he grew up fast after the folks died—having to fill in for them and all." Squinting, Talbot studied the sheriff. "Oh, sure," he said. "I remember you. You treated me and Dave to hard candy and soda pop when you and Dad were chin-deep in cards. I don't know why I didn't recognize you."

"Yes you do," Gibbon said with a self-deprecating laugh. "What brings you home?"

Talbot shrugged and smiled wanly. "Just homesick, I guess. Decided to come back and see if my brother, Dave, had room for me on the ranch."

Gibbon's eyes dulled and his face fell. "You . . . you didn't hear, then?"

"Hear what?"

"No one sent you a telegram?"

Frowning, feeling his gut roll, hearing a high-pitched inner scream, Talbot said, "I doubt it would have got to me if they had." He studied the sheriff keenly. "What's this about, Sheriff?"

"Aw, shit," Gibbon grumbled, looking off. He rubbed his chin with a gloved hand, looking away. At length he nodded his head toward the street. "Come on. Let's go back to the jailhouse. It's warm there and we can talk."

Talbot followed the big man up the street, feeling his heart drumming in his chest, trying not to anticipate the bad news he knew he was about to hear.

Inside the jail, Gibbon shed his big coat, hung it on a nail by the door, and added a stout log to the potbellied stove. A fire was already burning and the room was warm. A blue enamel coffeepot gurgled on the stovetop shelf.

"Coffee?" Gibbon offered, gesturing to it.

Frowning, Talbot absently shook his head. Gibbon found a tin cup and emptied its dregs into a wastebasket. He filled the cup three-quarters full of hot coffee and topped it off from a flat bottle he produced from a desk drawer. Indicating the chair before his desk, he said, "Have a seat," then collapsed with a sigh into his own swivel rocker, which squeaked with his weight.

"Come on, Sheriff, spit it out," Talbot said impatiently.

Gibbon took a deep breath, sat grimly back in the chair, and stared at his coffee. His face was pale. "Your brother's dead."

Talbot gazed into the sheriff's eyes, absorbing the information, feeling his stomach flip-flop and his heart wrench. After several seconds he squeezed his eyes closed and leaned forward in his chair. Slowly he rested his elbows on his knees and laced his hands together.

"How?" he asked quietly.

"He was shot."

Talbot lifted his head sharply. He'd expected to hear that Dave had had an accident or fallen ill with such common killers as influenza or pneumonia or smallpox. He'd never expected to hear that his brother, an eminently peaceful man, had been shot.

Not here . . . not at home!

"Did I hear you right?"

Gibbon had folded his hands over his hard, prominent belly. He was staring at the scarred desktop littered with pencil stubs, scrawled notes, and cigarette makings. He nodded slowly.

"Who?" Talbot asked, feeling anger grow heavy in his loins.

"Don't know for sure."

"When?"

"'Bout five years ago."

Feeling sick, Talbot rested his head in his hands, trying to work his mind around the idea of his brother being dead for five years.

Five years . . .

Talbot stood and walked to the window, gazed out at the street. Horsemen passed. Lumber drays and buckboards rattled over the icy ruts. There was a sleigh parked before the mercantile; a small dog sat on the seat, gazing at the store for its owner.

"Tell me about it," Talbot said.

Gibbon sighed again and leaned forward. He rested his elbows on the desk and started building a cigarette.

"We had some trouble here about five years ago," he began slowly. "Your brother was one of the first ones killed."

Talbot turned sharply away from the window. Sweat beaded on his forehead. "First ones?"

Gibbon nodded as he shook tobacco from his pouch. "We ended up with about seven dead altogether. It all started when a new outfit moved in. It had more cattle than its government allotments provided grass and water for. Instead of culling its herds, it tried culling the smaller ranchers around it."

A grim cast to his eyes, Gibbon twisted the ends of his cigarette and scraped a match along a drawer bottom. "Your brother included."

Talbot gritted his teeth. "Who runs this outfit?"

Gibbon touched the flame to the end of his cigarette. Blowing smoke, he said, "King Magnusson. He's from Missouri."

"Magnusson," Talbot repeated, frowning. "Where have I heard that name?" Then it dawned on him, and he pictured the lovely dark-eyed Suzanne. How could the father of such a delicate, beautiful creature have killed his brother?

He tried working his mind around the question as Gibbon continued his story. "Several of the smaller ranchers got together to stand against this Magnusson," the sheriff said. "But it's harder than hell to fight against guerrilla tactics. And that's what these guys were using. They'd strike at night or first light, kill a man or two, burn a cabin, steal a few cows, and disappear before anyone knew what happened."

"Figured they could squeeze the others out without actually having to kill everybody, that it?" Talbot said.

"That's it," Gibbon said, sitting back in his chair and crossing a leg over a knee. The cigarette smoldered in his right hand.

"I'm assuming you did something to stop it."

Gibbon flushed and inspected his quirley. "Well," he said tentatively, "the army had somethin' to do with that."

"You called the army in?"

Gibbon nodded. "The smaller ranchers put together a small army of their own, and were about to raid the compound of this outfit." His tone grew defensive. As he spoke, he stared at the floor.

"They . . . they wouldn't listen to me. Not that I had that much to say. I was new then, you understand, and someone had shot my deputy. Blew his head clean off his shoulders." Gibbon wagged his head and snapped his jaw at the memory. "Christ." He looked at Talbot as if for understanding.

Talbot frowned. "You arrest anybody?"

Gibbon lowered his gaze once more. "No. The army came in, Magnusson hemmed and hawed and denied everything he'd done, said it was the small outfits stealin' from him that started the whole mess in the first place. Which it probably was—who knows? It helped, of course, that one of Magnusson's main investors was in the territorial legislature. He's governor now."

"Christ," Talbot sighed, shaking his head. "So they got off scot-free."

"What the hell was the army gonna do? They're soldiers, not judges and juries. Besides, they had the Injuns to worry about. They weren't about to waste their time out here in the middle of nowhere. When everyone went home and things looked settled, they went back after Sitting Bull."

"You arrested no one for killing my brother, then," Talbot said. His tone was accusatory.

Gibbon raised his shoulders and spread his hands defensively. "Who was I going to arrest, for Christ's sake? Your brother was found out by one of his stock wells with two bullets in the back of his head—at least a week after he'd been killed."

He looked at Talbot and blinked nervously, licked his lips. He seemed to wait for a reaction. Receiving none, he said, "There'd been a good rain, so by the time I got out there, there were no tracks to speak of. No shell casings. Nothing. Period. I had nothing to go on. And that's the way it was with all the other killin's. It was one godawful mess around here!"

"So you called the army and they called it a draw and everyone went home," Talbot said tightly. "Except my brother and the six other dead."

Gibbon swallowed. His eyes retreated to his desktop. "That's right."

"Then the men who killed my brother are still out there." Talbot felt as though a saber had laid open his chest, exposing his beating heart.

"I reckon that's right," Gibbon allowed, nodding. He took a long drink of his toddy. After several seconds he mustered the courage to raise his gaze to Talbot, whose face was ashen with befuddlement and rage.

"I hope you're not thinking of getting even with the Double X," he said, his voice gaining an authoritative tone. "King Magnusson will screw your horns backward and twist your tail but good. Besides, your brother was killed five years ago. It's been quiet around here now . . . mostly. I don't need any trouble."

Talbot looked at him. "What do you mean, mostly?"

"It's still the frontier," Gibbon said defensively. "Things are bound to happen now and then." He inspected the coal of his cigarette and lifted it to his lips, taking a long, contemplative drag. Around the smoke issuing from his lips, he said directly, "The best thing for you to do is go get yourself a hot bath and hop the next train out of here."

Talbot walked over to the stove and stared at the glowing iron. His mind was numb, his body sick. A blade-like chill caressed his spine. He crossed his arms against it, vaguely aware of the cold sweat on his forehead and above his lip.

Dave has been dead for five years.

Talbot knew enough about land disputes to know how messy they were. The men who pulled the triggers were often not the only ones responsible for the killings. They were just your average soldiers riding for whoever was paying the wages and giving the orders.

But the man who'd hired Dave's killer was still around, smug in his certainty he'd gotten away with murder. And that man was lovely Suzanne Magnusson's father.

No matter where you were, it seemed, life was one war after another.

Watching him struggling with the news, Gibbon said, "It's a terrible tragedy, but your brother's dead, and nothin's gonna bring him back. If you try to get even with Magnusson, you'll not only be instigatin' another war, but committin' suicide. You'll be compoundin' the tragedy, understand?"

"I understand," Talbot said absently, knowing the

man was right but feeling the urge for vengeance just the same.

"Good," Gibbon said, brightening. He scrutinized his blotter. "Now there's another train due in at four-ten tomorrow."

Talbot opened the door and said, "Maybe I'll be on it, maybe I won't."

He closed the door behind him and squinted against the cold wind, not sure of anything anymore.

CHAPTER 8

HEAD REELING FROM the news of his brother's death, Mark Talbot walked across the street in a daze. It wasn't until ten minutes later that he finally stopped walking and realized he'd been drifting aimlessly up one side of the street and down the other. His toes and face were nearly frozen.

Seeing the sign for the Sundowner Saloon, he headed that way.

"Help you, mister?" the barkeep asked. A stout man in a crisp white shirt and armbands was standing behind the bar reading the newspaper spread open upon the polished mahogany.

Talbot walked as far as the roaring cast-iron stove in the middle of the room. "Give me a boilermaker, will ya?" His voice was low and taut, and he did not look at the apron as he spoke. His mind was on his brother and on the man or men who had killed him.

He set his war bag on one chair and himself in another, only a few feet from the stove. He looked briefly around and saw that the two cowboys on the other side of the stove, nursing whiskeys and playing a friendly game of cards, were the only other patrons.

The cowboys' good-natured banter was an irritating contrast to Talbot's dark mood. Still, the tavern was as good a place as any to get warm and to digest the news of Dave's death, to try and get a handle on what he was going to do now.

The barkeep came with the beer and whiskey, and Talbot paid him. Obviously curious about the bearded, shaggy-headed stranger, the man lingered, attempting small talk. Discouraging it, Talbot offered only curt replies to the man's questions, and soon the apron drifted back behind the bar.

Talbot warmed his cold feet by the stove, nursed his beer, and sipped his whiskey, which soothed his chill body but did nothing to quell the torment of his soul.

Lost in his own brooding, he did not see one of the cowboys stand and walk slowly past him, regarding him warily until he'd made the door and stepped outside. Neither did Talbot notice the other cowboy get up and move to the bar. The man turned to Talbot and tucked his coat behind his gun.

It wasn't until Talbot had finished his whiskey and turned to the bar to ask for another that he realized the barman had disappeared. Only the cowboy stood there, a lean man with a hawkish face, regarding him darkly. Talbot's gaze dropped to the man's gun, prominently displayed.

The front door opened. Boots thundered across the floor, on a wave of chill air. Talbot twisted around to see three red-faced men approach. Their spurs beat a raucous rhythm on the rough pine boards. All wore blanket coats and hats snugged under knit scarves. The tips of their greased holsters showed beneath their coats.

Talbot saw the other man who'd been playing cards earlier. He walked past Talbot to rejoin the cowboy standing with his back to the bar. Both stared at Talbot as though he were something a dog had left on the floor.

One of the other two men stopped directly behind Talbot and about five feet away. His anger growing at the obvious confrontation, Talbot was craning his head to regard the man when the other moved around the table, pulled out a chair, threw his gloves down, and started unbuttoning his coat.

Talbot nearly laughed at the man's arrogance. "Sit down and make yourself at home."

As though he hadn't heard, the man—a slender individual in his fifties, with reddish-brown hair flecked with gray and a close-cropped mustache—regarded the bar. "Bring over a couple of whiskeys, boys."

"Thanks, but I'll drink alone," Talbot said.

Again the man did not respond. He regarded Talbot blankly and sat down, throwing his coat out from his gun. It was an obvious threat. He sat staring at Talbot until the whiskeys came. He threw the drink back and slammed the empty glass on the table.

Talbot felt rage burn up from the base of his spine. His heart beat erratically. A muscle twitched in his cheek. He was in no mood for indulging the insolence of strangers.

The sandy-haired man calmly wiped his mouth with the back of his hand. Suddenly his right arm jerked, and he lifted a revolver above the table, aimed at Talbot's heart. "All right, who are you and who you workin' for?" he said, red-faced and nearly shouting.

Talbot let two seconds pass. He set both hands on the table's edge and leaned forward, staring into the stranger's eyes. He said through gritted teeth, "None of your goddamn business!"

Then, springing to a crouch, he gave the table a violent shove forward, thrusting it into the man's chest, knocking his pistol up and sending him over backward with a startled yell. The pistol cracked, sending the slug into the rafters.

A half-second later Talbot was on his feet and wheeling toward the man behind him. The man had been pulling his .44, and as Talbot lunged for him, he brought the butt of the gun down hard against Talbot's head. Talbot dropped to a knee, shaken.

The cowboy stepped forward and was about to bring the gun down on his head again when Talbot heaved himself forward and bulled the man over backward. They both hit the floor. The man punched Talbot in the jaw and rolled aside. When Talbot looked up, all the cowboys stood around him, guns drawn and aimed at his face.

Behind the cowboys, the older man had risen to a knee and was regarding Talbot with wide-eyed anger. He was breathing heavily, and his hair was awry. His crushed Stetson lay several feet away.

"You had enough, Slick, or should I have my boys ventilate you now?"

Talbot breathed heavily. Blood dripped from his swelling lower lip. He felt a goose egg growing on his temple. "This the kind of homecoming you're offering these days?"

"Homecoming?" the man said with a skeptical grunt.

"That's right."

"Who are you?"

"Who'd you think I was?"

The man blinked. "I don't know, but you got *trouble* written all over you, and we've had our fill of trouble around here."

"Looks can be deceptive," Talbot growled.

"When you're dealin' with killers, you can't be too careful."

"I'm no gunman. If you'd taken the time to look, you'd have seen I'm not even armed."

The man nodded and shot a sharp look at the man who'd summoned him. "I see that now," he said to the sheepish-looking cowboy.

The cowboy said, "Y-you said to let ya know if we seen any strangers, boss, and this man here . . . well, he sure looks like a tough, he acts like a tough, and he sure ain't from around here."

"Shut up, Virgil," the man snapped. To Talbot he said, "The cowboy's right. A cowboy was murdered by two toughs a few days ago. If you're not a tough, what are ya, then?"

"I'm Mark Talbot. Owen Talbot's son."

The man cocked an eyebrow. "Owen's boy?"

Talbot nodded. "Been away for a while." Talbot climbed to his feet and wiped the blood from his lip. "Now I have a question for you. Who poked that burr up your ass?"

One of the cowboys laughed, then covered it with a cough. The older man's face turned a deeper shade of red. He cowed his men with a look and said gruffly, "All right . . . holster those irons and get yourselves a drink. We'll be heading back to the ranch soon."

When the men had returned to the bar, where the bartender furnished drinks, the rancher said to Talbot, "You'd be suspicious, too, if you been through what I been through around here."

"Are you talking about the same trouble that killed my brother?"

"One and the same."

"The sheriff told me the army came in and settled that mess five years ago."

The man nodded, his jaw tightening. "That's what

I thought. But a week ago a man was shotgunned out east of here. Two days ago a Mex gunman shows up, slinks around town, and disappears into the countryside. We thought maybe you were another gunman Magnusson was bringing in."

"So you think it's starting all over again," Talbot said.

"Hell, it never really stopped. There were always killin's . . . hangin's and such. But when Rinski's hired man was killed by two masked men with shotguns—before a witness!—well, that told me all bets were off. Suzy, bar the door."

Talbot searched the man's face gravely. "Who killed my brother?" he said tightly.

Shrugging and shaking his head, the man picked up a chair and sat down on it. "Who knows?"

There was a pause as the man looked around the room, his eyes thoughtful and afraid. Finally his gaze returned to Talbot and his features softened. He said, "I apologize for the trouble. Can I buy you a drink?"

Talbot nodded and sat down across from the man.

"Monty, bring a bottle," the man called.

"And a beer," Talbot added.

When the barman had brought the bottle and a beer, and two fresh shotglasses, he filled the glasses, set the bottle on the table, and returned to the bar. At a table on the other side of the room, the other cowboys had started a new game of five-card stud.

The older man shoved his open hand toward Talbot. "Name's Thornberg," he said. "Verlyn Thornberg. I ranch south of here, along the Little Missouri."

Talbot shook the man's hand. "Mark Talbot."

"I met your brother in the mercantile once or twice. Don't believe I've ever seen you before."

"I lit a shuck out of here about seven years ago.

Must have been before your time. I left the ranching up to my brother. Figured I was too good for it. Wanted to see the world."

"Did you see it?"

"Enough to know if there's such a thing as the good life, it's here."

"Maybe it *was* here, back before I came, right before the trouble," the man said, thoughtfully sipping his whiskey. Swallowing, he shook his head. "But it ain't here no more. When did you find out about your brother?"

"'Bout an hour ago."

"Jesus, I'm sorry. That's tough, comin' home after seven years to find your brother dead."

Talbot shook his head, scowling and staring into his whiskey. "It wasn't exactly what I was expecting, no. You know what happened to our ranch? I was Dave's only kin, and I was out of reach. I hope Magnusson didn't get it."

The man thought for a moment. "I believe the Kincaid girl is grazing her beef on it. It abuts her land, as you know, and it's got good winter cover."

Talbot lifted his head. "The Kincaid girl? Jacy Kincaid?"

The man nodded.

Visibly surprised, Talbot said, "Why, she can't be but fourteen years old!"

"I've seen Jacy Kincaid," Verlyn Thornberg said with a humorous air, "and I can tell you she's no fourteen-year-old. She fills out a cotton shirt and a pair of Levi's 'bout as well as any girl in the territory, and she's a better hand on roundup than half the men. Broke most of the hearts on the Bench, too, I might add."

Talbot did some quick math on his fingers. Sure enough, the girl he'd known on the neighboring ranch would be in her early twenties by now. But the knowledge that she'd taken over the Talbot ranch was too much to grasp.

Talbot said, "You must mean her father assumed the Circle T."

Thornberg wagged his head. "Nope, Miller Kincaid died of a heart attack two springs ago."

Talbot remembered the towheaded little tomboy who used to ride her horse over to the Talbot ranch hot summer afternoons when he and Dave were kids. She'd played cowboys and Indians with Talbot and Dave, always accepting her role as the savage warrior good-naturedly. She snared gophers with the Talbot lads, too—as rough and tough as any boy.

She'd had a splash of freckles on the bridge of her nose and down her cheeks, and for that reason Talbot and Dave had called her Freckles. She'd taken issue with the nickname, however, and given them each such hard kicks to their shins that they finally had to cease and desist or risk permanent hobbling.

"Well, I'm glad Jacy's got it," Talbot said now. "If she turned out anything like her old man, she'll be good to it—won't muddy up the springs or overgraze the creeks."

"She'd turn it back to you," Thornberg speculated. "Since you were neighbors and all."

Talbot shook his head. "Nah, it's hers. She earned it . . . while I was off on my high horse." He took a big sip of beer and threw back the last of his whiskey.

Thornberg folded both his hands on the table and leaned toward Talbot, regarding him gravely. "Come to work for me, then."

Talbot laughed. "Doing what? I haven't ridden a horse or swung a lasso in a coon's age. I figured my brother would put up with me 'til I got the hang of it again, but I wouldn't expect anyone else to."

Thornberg shook his head. "I don't mean as a rider. I've seen you fight."

Talbot blinked. "As a fighter?"

Thornberg nodded and smiled conspiratorily. "If it came down to a tussle between you and that Mex gunman the big outfits brought in, I'd place my money on you."

Talbot just stared at the man, hollowed by the thought that his home had turned into a graveyard and a battlefield, just like the rest of the world.

"How good are you with a gun?" Thornberg continued eagerly.

Talbot blinked and considered the proposition for a moment. He had to admit it was tempting. But the possibility of finding Dave's killer was slim at best, and the probability of his getting enmeshed in the very life he'd finally turned away from was great. That life had cost him too much to return to it here at home.

Talbot finished his glass of beer, stood, and reached for his war bag. "Thanks for the offer, but I don't think so."

Thornberg frowned. "Where you goin'?"

"To find a place to sleep," Talbot replied quietly. "Thanks for the drinks." He swung the war bag over his shoulder and headed for the door.

"What about your brother?" Thornberg cried, incredulous.

Talbot turned back to the man. "I expect I could spend the rest of my life seeking vengeance and end with nothing to show for it but hate. If you had known my brother, you'd know he wouldn't have wanted that."

He looked at Thornberg, then at the barman and the other cowboys, who had ceased their game to see what all the commotion was about. Talbot turned away and opened the door.

"Besides, I'm no longer in that line of work," he mumbled, and went outside, looking for a peaceful place to light.

He wondered if he'd ever find it.

CHAPTER 9

———————•◆•———————

TALBOT WENT UP the street to Zimmermann's Hotel, which had added another story and a coat of paint since he had last seen it, and asked for a room furnished with heat and extra quilts.

In the small room consisting of a bed, a chair, a dilapidated wardrobe, and a coal-oil heater, he sat and smoked a cigarette and wished he hadn't come home.

The wind howled beneath the eaves and blew snow against the windows. Someone in the room above him was scuffing around in his boots and hacking phlegm from his throat. Somewhere a baby was crying. Out in the silent street a cat mewed.

From somewhere out of the blue, Talbot remembered the old spotted horse he and Dave used to ride to their swimming hole, hot July afternoons. Then a twelve-year-old, Dave was jumping from the barn loft, tucking his knees to his chest and wrapping his arms around his legs and careening through shafts of afternoon light into a mountain of sweet-smelling hay.

"I bet you can't do this, Mark!"

Talbot walked to the window and peered out without seeing anything. With Dave dead and only memories left, Talbot had no idea what to do, but he felt the need to see his old home place again and to visit Dave's grave. He'd hang around the country for a month or so. Maybe at the end of that time he'd know whether he still belonged here or somewhere else.

He plucked the quirley from between his lips and studied the ash grimly. He lifted his war bag onto the bed and opened it. Dipping a hand inside, he rummaged around on the bottom, then pulled out his six-shot revolver, an old model Colt he'd worn in a covered holster during the Apache campaigns. He hadn't worn a gun since Mexico, and he'd lost his government-issue holster in a poker game aboard the *Bat McCaffrey*. He regretted the loss; in self-defense, he supposed he'd have to wear the hog leg on his hip.

Welcome home, he thought, dropping the iron back in the bag and stowing the bag under the bed. He stubbed the cigarette out in an ashtray and headed for the door.

"Where'd be the best place to find new duds around here?" he asked the old woman who ran the place. She was watering a half-dead plant hanging in the window downstairs. Talbot didn't remember her and assumed she was a recent arrival, as were most of the people he'd seen so far.

"Check McDonald's up the street," she said.

"McDonald's? You mean McCracken's."

"McCracken's burned two years ago. McDonald rebuilt."

"Much obliged," Talbot said, feeling as though time had left him in its wake.

Talbot found the mercantile sandwiched between a clapboard establishment advertising hardware and tinware and a wholesale tobacco shop. The proprietor stood behind the counter in a derby hat and wool vest, one fist on his hip, the other on the countertop. He watched Talbot with silent suspicion, and

Talbot found himself thinking he was liable to get shot in the back in his own hometown.

"At ease, friend. I'm one of the good guys," he said, resenting his outsider status among these newbies. People sure seemed quick to label and reject around here. That wasn't how Talbot remembered this town.

The man said nothing. His expression did not change.

With the proprietor watching but offering no assistance, Talbot picked out a sheepskin coat, a union suit, heavy denim jeans, a flannel jersey shirt with leather ties, a black Stetson hat, wool-lined leather gloves, wool socks, and fur-lined knee-length moccasins.

After he'd picked out a soft leather holster, a cartridge belt, and a .44-caliber lever-action Winchester, which he'd heard were all the craze among cowboys these days, and three boxes of shells, he got the grim proprietor to throw in a scarf and a sack of tobacco, and paid the man.

"Nice doing business with you," he said dryly, hefting the parcels onto his shoulder. "I'll be sure and hurry back."

He hauled the merchandise two doors down, to Gustaffsen's Tonsorial Parlor for a shave, a haircut, and a long, hot bath.

When he'd finally hauled himself out of the steaming iron tub an hour and a half later, he felt like a stranger. The face that peered back at him from the proprietor's handheld mirror bore little resemblance to his more youthful conception of himself.

Cut to half its former length, his wavy auburn hair was combed straight back behind his ears, and his face, minus the beard, was big and hard-lined and ruddy. An Apache arrow had left a healed-over dent to the left of his right eye.

With the beard gone, he saw age in the spokes around his eyes and in the leathery skin pulled taut over his high, chiseled cheeks. Several gray hairs appeared in the two-inch sideburns. His eyes lacked their youthful luster and his lips were sullen.

In seven years he had grown from reckless youth to wry middle age, though he was only twenty-seven.

"You like?" Gustaffsen asked in a Swedish accent heavy enough to sink a clipper ship. His sharp eyes glanced from the mirror to Talbot and back again.

"No."

"Huh?"

"I mean . . . it's fine," Talbot said, handing the man his glass. "What's the charge?"

When he'd dressed in his new duds, he buckled the six-shooter and the new holster around his waist. The gun felt so foreign and looked so malign, hanging there on his hip, that he took it off in frustration and shoved it back in the war bag.

If they wanted to shoot him, let them shoot an unarmed man. He wasn't ready to start killing again. Not even in self-defense.

When he'd wrapped his old clothes in a bundle for Gustaffsen to dispose of, he went over to the town's only café for a supper of pork chops, sauerkraut, and fried potatoes.

He and the two drummers he'd gotten off the train with were the only customers, the cold weather apparently keeping everyone else home. The drummers' idle banter across the room depressed him; instead of lingering over his coffee and dessert, he went back to his room and crawled into bed.

He lay awake for a long time, listening to dogs barking in the distance, staring at the ceiling, and pondering the notion that his brother was gone and that he'd been homeless for five years without knowing it.

Five years . . .

———

After breakfast early the next morning, Talbot found a feed barn and a livery stable and picked out a saddle horse and tack. An hour later he was cantering a deep-chested speckled gray gelding along the mail road east of town.

Mid-morning, he left the road and followed a long, shallow valley between low rimrocks. He remembered the way easily, noting landmarks and pausing occasionally to study eagles' nests and wolf prints in the snow, feeling good to be back in the saddle and back in the country.

It was a cold, windy day, with low, fast-scudding clouds. Talbot snugged the strap under his chin to keep his hat in place.

When he came to the canyon in which lay the valley where the Talbot Circle T ranch was located, Talbot took the first ravine to the west. He rode for another hour, following the ravine's devious course until it rose into a bowl surrounded on three sides by hogbacks spiked with tawny grass poking through the snow. In the distance sprawled a long, wedge-shaped mesa where Talbot and his brother used to trap rattlesnakes every summer.

Below the hogbacks, in a natural wedge that broke the wind, sat the Circle T—a two-story log cabin with a lean-to sloping off its east wall, a big gray barn with a connecting paddock, and several small corrals straggling down the ravine to a stock pond and windmill.

The place had a forlorn, abandoned look, and Talbot's heart ached to see it like this—the cabin dark, with no smoke lifting from its chimney; the corrals barren of saddle stock; the weathered gray black-smith shed looking as hollow as an old tree stump.

Three pigeons started from the barn loft. They flew around the yard, then settled again in the loft and watched between the planks of the closed doors. Behind the cabin, the outhouse door squeaked in the wind funneling through the draws. It sounded like a moan. The air was heavy with the smell of skunk.

Entering the compound, Talbot saw that one of the pole barns had lost a pole and its roof had partially fallen in. The snow around the compound was pocked by hooves and littered with frozen discs of cow dung. A drift had formed on the cabin porch like a frozen wave. The old Talbot lease was apparently being used as winter range, and the cabin probably served as an occasional outpost for grubliners and bandits.

Talbot spurred his horse forward and dismounted before the cabin, looping the reins over the tie rail. He turned the knob and pushed the door open. He stood in the doorway and looked around the cabin, letting his eyes adjust to the shadows within.

When the living room swam into focus, he saw that the newspapers he and Dave had tacked to the walls had turned yellow. Torn strips curled toward the floor. Most of the furniture had been hauled off by other settlers, no doubt.

A few stools and a homemade chair remained near the fireplace. The floor planks were floury with dust, coated in grime and mouse shit. The few remaining lamps were chipped and smoke-blackened, and cob-webs hung from the ceiling joists.

Opening the door and walking down the short hall to the kitchen, Talbot saw that this part of the house was in the same state of disrepair. The two remaining chairs were broken, and the plank table sat askew, littered with dirty dishes, tins, cigarette stubs, and playing cards.

There were yellowed newspapers and magazines scattered about the cupboard tops. A mouse-chewed flapjack lay on the floor by the range. Two torn gray socks hung from a rafter. This room was an add-on, and Talbot recognized his own notches in the logs. It was a bittersweet recognition, shaping his nostalgia to a sharp point.

Talbot sucked his teeth, listening to the mice scuttling in the walls and thinking, It's no more than a line shack.

Outside he looked around the yard for his brother's grave but saw no sign of it. Surely someone had buried Dave on the premises—the sheriff or one of the neighbors. The wind had blown most of the snow against the buildings and corral posts, nearly covering an old horse mower and a dump rake but clearing the open ground. A marker would have been evident.

Puzzled, Talbot started back to his horse. A rifle cracked nearby. Talbot and the horse jumped simultaneously. While the horse kicked and pawed the ground, Talbot crouched and looked around.

"Hold it right there, asshole!"

It was a female voice.

"Throw your gun down."

Talbot shuttled his gaze from the barn to a figure standing on the other side of the corral, hunkered behind a post from which a rifle poked.

"I'm not wearing a gun," he said, raising his hands to his shoulders.

"Gordon, check the son of a bitch for a gun!" the woman yelled.

Talbot heard boots crunching snow and turned to see a lanky, stoop-shouldered man walk out from behind the pole barn, a Navy Colt held before him. Appearing to be in his fifties or early sixties, he was swarthy with a bushy gray mustache with upswept ends, patched denim breeches, and a big sugarloaf sombrero pulled low over his eyebrows. His torn mackinaw was stretched taut across his broad chest, its frayed collar raised against the cold.

He scuttled toward Talbot sideways, his eyes wide and cautious. Chew stained the corner of his mouth.

"Easy, now," the man growled as he approached Talbot sideways and gave him the twice-over with his watery-blue eyes. He patted the sides of Talbot's coat with his free hand.

Finally he looked at him sharply and said, "Where in hell's your gun?"

"In my saddle boot."

"No hog leg?"

"In my war bag. Wasn't inclined to wear it today."

"Well . . . I'll be." Turning to the woman, he said, "He ain't wearin' no iron, Jacy."

The woman said nothing for several seconds. Then the rifle went down, and she said, "Keep your eyes on him, Gordon. I'm comin' over."

She walked around the corral, and Talbot watched her, smiling, wondering if she'd recognize him. She hadn't been more than fifteen when he'd left home— just a scrawny, freckle-faced girl. She'd turned into an attractive young woman.

She appeared about twenty or twenty-one, and tall for a woman, maybe five-eight or -nine. A bulky green-plaid coat concealed her figure, but from her legs and hips Talbot could tell she was slender.

Under the wide-brimmed, flat-crowned black hat, her face was fine-boned and smooth, with full lips and green eyes that slanted a little, betraying her Slavic heritage. Her skin was vanilla, like the remnant of a summer tan, reminding Talbot a little painfully of Pilar. Rabbit fur moccasins rose to the patched knees of her faded jeans, and the rifle she held was a Henry with a seasoned stock and an oiled barrel.

As she moved closer to Talbot, she cocked her head to the side and squinted one eye. Recognition growing slowly on her face, she stopped before him but said nothing. Her eyes regarded him with frank amusement.

He smiled.

"Well, I'll be goddamned," she said.

"Hi, Jacy."

"Damn near got yourself shot."

"Nice to see you, too."

Turning to the older gent who stood regarding them quizzically, still holding the Colt, she said, "Remember Mark Talbot, Gordon? Dave's brother? He's finally come home."

The man squinted at Talbot, nodding slowly. "Well, I'll be goddamned."

"I didn't recognize you at first either, Gordon. How are things?" Talbot offered his hand to the old cowboy.

Gordon Jenkins shook it and shrugged. He'd been working for outfits around the Bench for as long as Talbot could remember. He was one of those men you always saw on horses among others just like him but didn't think much about. They were professional cowboys living their lives on the open range, brush-popping steers from sunup to sunset, and spending the winters holed up in brothels and bunkhouses from Bismarck to Abilene.

"Pretty much the same, Mark. How 'bout you?"

"I've been better."

"What happened to your lip?" Jacy asked.

Talbot probed the swelling with his tongue. "Had a little homecoming party in town last night."

"This isn't the same country you left, Mark," Jacy said darkly. "Dave was killed five years ago. I'm so sorry."

Talbot looked off and squinted. "I heard. Thought I'd ride out here and look for his grave."

"Did you find it?"

Talbot shook his head.

"Get your horse and follow me." Jacy turned and started walking around the pole barn for her horse.

Talbot was mounting up when he heard horses blowing and turned to see Gordon driving a spring wagon loaded with supplies.

"Came from town," he explained, driving past.

Jacy rode her line-back dun through the coulee south of the ranch, following a cattle trail in the snow. They rode single file, Talbot following Jacy, Gordon bringing the wagon up behind Talbot.

The wind was still blowing, shepherding shadows across the snow, which shone in gray, wind-drifted patches here and there along the coulee. Small flocks of redpolls wheeled above the weed-tips. A coyote spooked from a frozen seep and disappeared up a crease in the ridge. The only sounds were the wind and the horses crunching snow.

It was a grim ride; no one said anything.

After ten minutes, the coulee fanned out on both sides, revealing a line of big cottonwoods standing along Crow Creek. The creek bottom was about a quarter mile wide, and dense with willows, choke-cherry, hawthorn, and occasional box elders.

It was a haven for whitetails, Talbot remembered. But you had to beat the brush for them, and you had to get them before they dashed up the opposite ridge and were gone across the prairie.

"I remembered how you and Dave liked it down

here," Jacy said, as if reading his thoughts. "I couldn't think of a more fitting place to bury him."

Talbot kept his eyes focused on the corduroy ridge on the other side of the creek, not wanting to lower them, wanting to stay with his memories of old deer hunts and Dave whooping and hollering in the willows while Talbot sat in a declivity on the ridge, waiting for the hazed deer that would bound over the natural levee only a few yards away.

Finally Talbot dropped his eyes to the homemade cross beneath the cottonwoods. Its thin gray shadow angled over the rock-mounded grave beneath it.

Dave.

Talbot dismounted, handed his reins to Jacy, and studied the grave. Fallen leaves clung to the nooks and crannies between the rocks. Tracks of coyote and racoon made light impressions in the snowy grass. A weasel had been poking about.

Talbot studied the grave for a long time, remembering his big, blond, grinning brother who could toss a hundred-pound feed sack into the haymow like it was straw. Finally he looked up at Jacy, blinking away the film of tears from his eyes.

"You . . . you buried him here?"

"Dad and Gordon dug the grave. I thought it was fitting," she said matter-of-factly.

He lowered his eyes again to the grave. "Thank you."

"I'm sorry. What a thing to come home to."

Talbot gave a dry laugh. "I figured maybe Dave had got married, had him a young'un or two, maybe built one of those nice big clapboard houses. I sure never expected this."

"It was a horrible thing, what happened here," Jacy said thinly. "Frank Thompson, Paul Goodnough— hanged on their own ranges. There were five cabins burned, and Hutt Mills was taken naked from his lean-to and forced to walk back through knee-deep snow. He lost both his feet and nearly all his fingers to frostbite."

"Any idea who shot Dave?"

Jacy looked at Gordon, who sat the wagon seat, elbows on knees, sucking a tooth to distraction, his eyes wide and distant. A scuttling breeze toyed with the brim of his sombrero.

Jacy said, "Gordon said he saw Randall Magnusson and another man crossing our range one morning a few days before he and Dad found Dave's body. They were heading toward your place."

Gordon moved his head slowly from side to side. "I sure wish I woulda looked into it at the time, but I was just so thrilled to see 'em riding away from me, I didn't give much thought to where they were goin'."

The cowboy's slow voice betrayed a high, Ozark twang. "That Magnusson kid—he was only about sixteen, seventeen at the time—is the orneriest little bastard I seen outside of Blackfeet country. A coward and a cold-blooded killer with more than a few screws loose to boot."

"Did you tell the sheriff?"

"Sure I did."

"And?"

"And Jed Gibbon just crawled all the deeper into his bottle. Wasn't about to fool with the likes of the kid or the kid's father, King Magnusson."

Talbot sighed and bit his lip. "Christ."

"Yep," Jacy said, drawing out the word darkly.

Talbot mounted his horse, a thoughtful look wrinkling his brow. "King Magnusson," he muttered. "I can't imagine a killer like that raising a girl like his daughter."

Jacy frowned. "You know Suzanne?"

"Met her on the train."

Jacy and Gordon shared a sneer. "Was she comin' from back east or out west?" Jacy asked snidely.

"West."

"You never know with little Miss Queen of England. When she gets tired of the smell of cowshit, her daddy sends her to New York for a new wardrobe."

"I take it you and her aren't close," Talbot said ironically.

"It's not so much her I hate as her family—a bunch of highfalutin scalawags, getting rich off the land they steal from others." She watched Talbot; his eyes were cast in thought. "You taken with her?"

His eyes rose to hers, his mind racing to reconcile the vivacious, cultivated young woman from the train with the family Jacy had just described.

Changing the subject, he said, "I heard your pa died."

Jacy nodded matter-of-factly. "Had a heart attack in bed, but it was King Magnusson that killed him. All the worry about the ranch and what would happen to me if night riders came . . ." Her voice trailed off.

"Your ma?"

"She married Harold Offerdahl last spring. Harold took her off to Mandan to open a harness shop, and I was glad he did. This battlefield is no place for a nervous lady like Ma." She smiled. "She writes me twice a month and sends me cookies and pies."

"Maybe you should have gone with her."

Jacy tilted her head. Her eyes were sharp. "Why's that?"

Talbot shrugged. "Well, because you're . . ."

"A girl?"

He shrugged again.

"Girl or no girl, I wasn't about to let King Mag-

nusson take everything my pa had worked so hard
for," Jacy snapped.

Talbot smiled, admiring the girl's spine but thinking her foolhardy just the same.

"Well . . ." he said, and reined his horse around
and started along the creek. Jacy caught up with him
and rode parallel, several yards to his left. Gordon
brought up the rear in the clattering wagon.

Several white-faced cattle appeared at the mouth
of a draw, chewing cud in the gold sun, breath puffing around their heads. Snow and dirty ice clung to
their coats.

"I've been wintering some older stock on your
range," Jacy explained. "I'll get them out in the spring,
and me and Gordon will help you get your cabin
back in shape."

"I'm not sure I'm gonna stay," Talbot said, "but I
appreciate the offer."

"Where would you go?"

"I don't know."

"This is your home."

Talbot forced a chuckle. "That's funny. It sure
doesn't feel like it."

He was craning his neck around to watch Gordon, who had broken off the trail and now directed
the shaggy draft horses toward the cattle. The old
cowboy leaned out from his wagon perch, inspecting the brand on a Hereford within a loose pack of
seven beeves.

"Hey, Jacy," he called. "There's a Double X brand
over here."

Jacy turned to look toward the cowboy and the
milling cattle. "Good," she said angrily. "Coyotes
got the rest of that steer you butchered last week."

"Whatever you say," Gordon said, drawing his
pistol.

To Jacy, Talbot said, "You're gonna shoot that Double X stray?"

The young woman shrugged and pursed her lips. "You know what they say—nothin' tastes better than the neighbor's beef."

Her sentence was punctuated by the flat report of Gordon's Colt. The first was followed closely by a second. The herd bounded into an awkward run up the draw. The one Gordon had shot remained behind— lying on its side, its legs kicking spasmodically.

Talbot regarded Jacy with heat. "Isn't that the sort of thing the Old Trouble was about?"

"Magnusson started it."

"That's no defense, Jacy."

She jerked a sharp look at him. "Several of Magnusson's cowboys rode through Jamison Gulch last week on their way to town, and drove four of my best steers over a butte. Gordon was out riding the line and saw it. Wasn't much he could do and not get himself killed. That wasn't the first time Magnusson killed my stock. I found three heifers shot last fall. He kills mine, I kill his. It's the only defense I have."

"Are the other small operators having the same trouble?"

"In spades."

Talbot shook his head. "You're gonna get yourself killed, pulling stunts like that."

Jacy grunted. "I only wish they'd try pulling something on me like they did over at the Homer Rinski place last week. Then it'd be more than their cows dyin'!"

Talbot remembered what Gibbon had told him. "It was Rinski's hired hand they shot?"

Nodding, Jacy added, "And whose daughter they savaged like animals. Mattie's in a bad way, and her father doesn't know what to do with her."

"Does she know who they were?"

Jacy gave her head a shake and sighed. "Don't know—she won't talk about it. She tries to act like nothing happened, only she can't settle down. She works like a butcher all day and can't sleep at night. She's not in a good way."

Talbot paused, watching Gordon begin to dress out the dead steer. "My God, what's become of this country?" he said weakly.

Jacy turned her sea-green eyes from Gordon to Talbot and brushed a stray lock of tawny hair from her cheek with a gloved hand.

"My place ain't the cheeriest these days, but it's good for a hot meal or two." Her lips cracked a smile. "Her teats might be bigger than mine, and she may walk a little straighter, but I bet Miss Magnusson has nothing on me in that department. If you're squeamish about stolen beef, I can boil you up a porcupine."

Talbot's face warmed at the girl's salt. He had to laugh. "You know, I bet you're right, Jacy Kincaid."

"Is it a date?"

If I had any sense, Talbot thought, I'd take the sheriff's advice and head east, keep riding until I was a safe distance from here. Maybe Minnesota or Iowa, possibly Wisconsin. This country, like so many other places from which he'd fled—the desert Southwest, Mexico during the gold boom—was a powder keg sitting only a few feet from a lit fuse.

But this was home.

"It's a date," he said with a slow nod, returning Jacy's smile, then cutting his eyes down the coulee toward his brother's grave.

CHAPTER 10

JOSÉ LUIS DEL Toro quietly levered a shell into the breech of his rifle and waited for a rift in the wind. If there was such a thing up here. With snow on the ground, there was practically what the gringos called a whiteout every time the wind blew—which was nearly all the fucking time.

It was blowing now, and even though the sky was clear as crystal, each gust caused a whiteout. There was no snow falling, only blowing, and during a gust you could hardly see your fucking hand before your face. A ground blizzard. That's another word the gunman hadn't heard before coming north.

No wonder gringos were such a chilly race of people.

Del Toro's rifle was a Sharps .50-caliber, factory engraved with a horseback rider shooting buffalo, and inlaid with gold. It had a silver finish and butt plate, and its smooth black walnut stock felt firm and familiar against the gunman's cheek.

The Big Fifty fired a two-and-a-half-inch-long case loaded with ninety grains of black powder that could blow a dollar-sized hole in a man at six hundred yards. That kind of distance didn't come into play here, however. If all went as planned, the first man on Magnusson's list would pass within seventy-five feet below him, on the meandering cow path at the bottom of the draw.

If it hadn't been for all the snowy brush covering the hillside on which Del Toro sat, rifle on his knees, it would have been a chip shot. But with the winter dead foliage limned with hoarfrost between him and the trail below, he'd need a steady hand not to clip a dump of frozen berries or a hawthorn twig, and nudge the slug wild.

The swirling snow wasn't helping any, either. Visibility was only about thirty yards. About twenty yards beyond that now, the man was coming on a brown horse—just as he came every night from town, lit up with cheap liquor and singing like a stud lobo at the end of March.

Del Toro could hear the man's voice, make out the words of the song he was singing—attempting to sing.

"Oh, Su-zanny, don't you cry for me, I've gone from Ala-ba-my . . . with a banjo on my kneeeee."

The voice was so high and ludicrous and off pitch and gringo cocky that it made Del Toro grate his teeth together. But his face remained expressionless, his jaw set in a hard line. He closed his left eye, stared through the sliding leaf sight, through the tunnel of motionless foliage.

It was about four-thirty, a still, cold night this far north in December. The sun had fallen into the prairie, but the sky remained blue. Amid the blowing snow, which swirled down the draw like some living thing, the brush was dark, a solid black shape against the opposite, boulder-strewn ridge.

Horse and rider were approaching now. When the wind died and the snow settled, Del Toro could see the horse and the dark shape of the man.

He lifted his head from the rifle stock, gave a high,

short whistle, then returned his eye to the sight. The rider stopped suddenly, drawing back on the reins.

"Whoooa. What was that?" he said. His voice was thin and barely audible above the wind.

The horse had stopped, jerking its head against the bit pulled taut against its jaw.

The man opened his mouth, lifted his upper lip like a curious horse. He looked around, listening. "Who's there?" he said after several seconds.

Del Toro was counting his heartbeats and staring through the sight at the vague shape in the snow. He waited for the present gust to break so he'd have a clear shot. The last thing he wanted was to wing the bastard and see him flee on his horse. That would be messy. Del Toro did not like messes.

The snow swirled like silk flags waving this way and that, catching and tearing on boulders and tree limbs. Gauzy forms assembled and scattered. The man waited, looking around. He did not have the animal's keen nose, but he sensed the hunter's presence just the same.

He was frozen there in his tracks, sensing death there on the hillside just a few yards away. "Who's there?" he said again, quieter this time, voice thin with fear and suspicion.

A gust died for half a second; the snow thinned.

Del Toro cursed in Spanish. He should have taken the shot. It might have been the only one he'd have.

But just as the thought vanished, the wind settled again, and the man sat there clearly, both hands holding his reins, looking up the hill.

Del Toro squeezed off the shot just as the man turned up the trail and started to flick the reins. Fire spit from the end of the barrel and the report echoed like an immense drumbeat, circling before it died.

Del Toro lowered the smoking gun and stared

down the hill, frowning. The wind and snow had closed in, thick as ever. He could see nothing but the irregular, free-forming shapes of the ground blizzard, but he heard the horse whinny loudly, heard the hooves stomping and the bridle chains jangling.

The man yelled out, cursed.

The horse pounded off. A pistol cracked once, twice, three times. Del Toro ducked low behind a tree and listened to the slugs thudding into the ground around him—the closest about ten feet away.

The reports echoed. When they died, Del Toro tipped his head to listen. Below rose the soft crunching of boots in the snow, nearly indiscernible above the wind.

The man was off his horse and was running away!

Cursing himself, the gunman stood, reloaded the single-shot rifle, and started down the hill. Gravity pushed him down the snowy slope at a breakneck pace. Sliding and stumbling, he broke the speed of his descent by grabbing branches and careening off boulders, holding the rifle out for balance.

Hurdling a deadfall, he came to the foot of the hill and stood in the horse's tracks, looking around and catching his breath. His lungs were not used to air this cold. It was like breathing sand.

Sweeping his gaze along the ground, he saw the man's horse had thrown him—there was a splash of blood in a broad, scuffed area where he'd fallen—then bolted up the trail. Boot prints showed the man running back the other way, in the direction from which he'd come.

Del Toro sighed, clutched his rifle in both hands, and followed the man's tracks, walking. There was no reason to hurry. From the amount of spilled blood, the gunman knew the man wouldn't get far without a horse. Also, the man could be lying in wait for him, pistol drawn. There was no reason to add injury to insult by getting bushwhacked.

As he walked, he considered letting the man go. He'd either die from the wound or freeze to death. But there was always the possibility of his finding help from a fellow traveler or of retrieving his horse.

No, Del Toro needed to finish the job. There was nothing he hated more than a mess.

He wrinkled his nose to loosen the frozen nasal hairs and began moving forward, following the erratic tracks of his wounded quarry. There were occasional splotches of blood next to the boot prints, and they looked brown in the fading light. Del Toro stopped every few steps and listened before moving on.

He knew the man would stop sooner or later, since he was losing blood fast and he had a gun; he would hunker down in the brush along the trail and wait. Like a cornered lynx.

A fine goddamn mess, Del Toro thought. Shoot a man with the biggest rifle on the market and miss! Like something a damn gringo would do.

It was this hellish weather—all this snow and cold fucking wind. The conditions for killing were horrible.

Del Toro stopped. About fifteen feet away, the tracks began bearing off to the left, toward the shrubs and brush. A small wedge of red-orange flame poked through the blowing snow. A crack followed and a bullet whistled, thunking into a tree somewhere behind the gunman.

Del Toro dropped facedown in the snow and cursed. He rolled to the right and heard the pistol fire twice more. The lead thumped the snow. He unholstered one of his two pistols and fired at the place in the snow he had seen the pistol flash. The lead twanged off stone.

The man was behind a rock. Shit.

Del Toro angrily fired off four more rounds, then rolled again to his right. The pistol barked and flashed again. Two more quick bursts, then one more about five seconds later.

That was six shots. The man's gun was out of bullets.

Quickly, Del Toro climbed to his feet and ran slipping through the snow, peering through the whiteout, trying to brush it away with his hands. Suddenly the wind settled to reveal the big stone—a flat-topped slab of granite grown up with dead weeds and moss. A stunted cedar grew out from under it at an impossible angle.

The gunman grabbed a cleft in the stone for leverage and peered around the rock, lifting his rifle to his chest with one hand.

"No!" the man screamed. "Leave me be!"

He lay on his back, chin to chest. His pistol was in his right hand, shielding his head. The pistol's cylinder hung out, and empty cartridges lay scattered on the ground.

"Please don't shoot me," the man pleaded, kicking his feet and cowering like a whipped dog. Blood oozed from a hole in his dirty blanket coat. The air around had the rotten-egg odor of gunsmoke.

Del Toro said matter-of-factly, enjoying the man's misery, "I have to shoot you, señor."

"Why?"

"Because you're filthy gringo scum. Because you butcher cattle that do not belong to you. Because you occupy land you do not deserve, and because you multiply like brush wolves and fill the land with more mangy scum like yourself."

"King!" the wounded man cried. "King Magnusson! He's the one who hired ya."

"That is right. Allow me to introduce myself, señor." The gunman took his rifle in his left hand and held out his right. "José Luis del Toro."

The man stared at the hand, lips quivering, eyes bright with fear. Tears rolled down his heavy, leathery cheeks. "Please . . ."

When he saw that the man was not going to shake his hand, Del Toro shrugged and lifted his rifle to his shoulder, aimed at the man's forehead. "No, I am sorry, señor. I have a job to do."

"What about my wife? What about my kids?"

Del Toro did not reply, and there was no indication on his taut face that he'd even heard what the man had said.

The man saw this, and his breathing slowed. The fear in his eyes gave way to resignation, though a good dose of the fear remained. He dropped the empty pistol in his lap.

His head tilted to the side and his chin came up. The eyes rose to the gunman's, sighting down the octagonal barrel.

"No," he begged one last time.

Fire and smoke geysered from the barrel, and the big gun bucked. The man's head snapped back from the impact of the slug destroying his forehead. The head bounced off the ground with such force that the man's back rose nearly perpendicular to the ground. Blood and brain matter sprayed. Then the man fell back again. The man's head turned to the side, and he lay still.

The air left his lungs with a sigh and a groan.

Del Toro stood the rifle against the rock and rummaged inside his coat, producing a pencil stub and a small leather-bound notebook. He licked the stub and scrawled something on one page of the notebook. He tore the page from the book, folded it, and stuffed it in the pocket of the man's coat. Then he licked the stub again and scratched out the first name on his list. With a slow, satisfied nod, he replaced the pencil in the book and returned the book to his coat.

He snugged his collar against his neck, retrieved his rifle, and headed back toward the hill and the tree to which he'd tied his horse.

"This goddamn gringo weather," he grumbled.

CHAPTER 11

TALBOT'S HORSE ASCENDED a crumbling clay bank, putting its head down and digging its front hooves into the hard ground. Beside Talbot rode Jacy, then Gordon Jenkins, the field-dressed beef lying behind the dry goods in the wagon box.

At the top of the knoll, they halted to give their horses a breather, and Gordon rolled a cigarette. Talbot swept his gaze around, reacquainting himself with the lay of the land—a rolling, sage-pocked prairie creased by ravines and coulees, capped by a low, gray sky. Bromegrass and wheatgrass shone where the wind had swept the snow away. Here and there cattle grazed.

Jacy pointed to a grove of trees marking the line of a distant creek. "That's the Rinski place. I thought we'd take a little detour and check on Homer and Mattie."

"I remember Homer," Talbot said. "A God-fearin' man, as I recall. Don't recollect his daughter."

"You probably never saw her," Jacy said. "From just about the time she started walking, that girl had to take care of her father. I doubt she ever went to a dance or had a boyfriend."

"None her father knew about, anyway," Gordon said, letting cigarette smoke drift out with his words.

"Pardon my talk, Miss Jacy, but word has it Jack Thom wasn't the first of her daddy's hired hands she was a mite friendly with, if you get my drift."

Jacy grunted a laugh and grinned at the old cowboy. "If I had a life like Mattie's, I'd probably be chasing you around the bunkhouse, Gordon."

"Shee-it," Gordon said, blushing and wagging his head.

Jacy clucked to her gelding, and Talbot and Gordon followed her down the knoll and across the prairie. As they rounded another knoll about twenty minutes later, the Rinski ranch appeared, fronting a creek tracing a brushy path below buttes.

Jacy halted her horse about fifty yards from the low, ramshackle cabin. "Mr. Rinski, it's Jacy," she called.

A tall gray-haired man appeared in the doorway holding an old-model rifle. He wore a fur coat and a round-brimmed black felt hat. He pulled the door closed behind him. Gazing at the three visitors sitting their horses at his ranchyard's perimeter, he said nothing. He just stood there, blinking, holding his rifle low across his thighs. Hogs grunted under a thatch-roofed pole barn, giving off their distinctive smell.

Finally Jacy spurred her horse forward. Talbot and Gordon followed suit.

"Who you got with ya?" Rinski asked.

"This is Mark Talbot; remember him?"

Talbot smiled, noting how the man had aged since he'd last seen him, and recognizing the haunted cast in his eyes, due no doubt to what had happened to his daughter and hired man. "How are ya, Mr. Rinski?"

"You're the one went off to fight the 'Paches," the old rancher said, remembering. "Your brother bragged ya up some, he did."

"I don't doubt it," Talbot said with a weak smile,

feeling guilty all over again for having left his brother to ranch alone.

"The Lord been kind to you, young Talbot?"

"I reckon he was kind enough to keep me alive. Quite a feat when dealing with Victorio's Mescaleros. I wish he'd been that kind to my brother."

Rinski's eyes seemed to focus on something beyond Talbot. He worked his lips a moment before he spoke. "The Lord works in mysterious ways."

"I'm sorry about the trouble you've had here."

Jacy inquired about Mattie.

"Nothin' wrong with my daughter time and the Good Lord can't heal," Rinski said automatically. Then his conviction seemed to flounder, and his eyes flickered doubtfully. "Does seem awful . . . *nervous*, though."

The old man's heavy eyebrows knitted together as he dropped his chin, pondering the ground as though looking for something. It had no doubt been a nightmare for the man to reconcile his faith to what had happened in his hired hand's shack last week.

Jacy said after an awkward silence, "How you getting along, Mr. Rinski? Do you need anything?"

"I'm fine," he said, though his ghostly countenance indicated otherwise.

Turning to her hired man, she said, "Gordon, why don't we leave the beef liver with Mr. Rinski? I know how he likes fresh beef liver."

Rinski said nothing. The wind poked at his hat and at the gray hair hanging beneath it.

As Gordon dismounted and went around the wagon to retrieve the liver, Jacy said, "Do you mind if I go in and see Mattie, Homer?"

"She'd like that."

When Jacy had gone inside, Rinski turned to Talbot

again. "You come to fight a war closer to home, did ya, young man?"

Talbot shook his head. "I thought by coming home I was getting away from war."

"Well, you weren't." Rinski's voice was louder now, his gaze more certain. His eyes grew large and dark. "There's a devil at work here now, and we're gonna need help in fightin' him. Verlyn Thornberg is trying to get some of us smaller outfits organized, but he don't seem to have the leadin' spirit. No one wants to follow him against this big outfit that's been moved by Satan to savage our women and swallow up our land."

Rinski spoke as though he were standing behind a pulpit. His forehead was creased and his lips were pursed, dimpling his chin. "It happened once before. With the Lord's help we got the demon back in hell, but he's slipped out again, sure enough. We need you on our side, young Talbot, to fight against the Beast."

"What you need is the law," Talbot said.

"The law is without fortitude in this matter," Rinski said without batting an eye.

Talbot was about to respond when Rinski said, "Follow me," and started walking east around his barn and corral, where a half-dozen winter-shaggy horses milled, manes ruffling in the wind.

Talbot tried to study him out, puzzled, then spurred his horse in Rinski's direction. When he caught up with the old man, the rancher was standing in the doorway of an old lean-to cabin, looking in. His back was stiff and his shoulders were slumped forward.

When Talbot had dismounted and dropped his horse's reins, Rinski turned to him. "Have you a look at the devil's work, young Talbot," he said, stepping aside.

Talbot ducked as he stepped through the low door.

The room was small and dark. A small stove hunkered in the back right corner. The air smelled coppery.

His eyes swept the room, stopping on the back wall above a cot. The logs of the wall bore a large stain, at least three by five feet wide. Talbot moved forward and saw that the cot was covered, too. The blood had frozen on the green wool blankets, which were twisted and mussed and had turned a crusty, flaky brown. Talbot guessed that the white specks of bone in the substance were what remained of Jack Thom's skull.

Talbot felt his stomach clench. He winced as he imagined the screams and yells and the two loud booms from the shotguns. The old rancher watched him darkly.

"Thought you should see for yourself the blood that's been spilled here in the name of the devil," Rinski explained.

"Do you know who did this, Mr. Rinski?"

"Magnusson's son and Shelby Green."

"Has your daughter named them?"

Rinski's face was stony, his eyes hard. "She won't talk about it, but when I asked her if it was those two mavericks—they been terrorizin' folks for years—her eyes grew big as silver dollars."

Talbot looked at the frozen blood drops on the wall. "What are you going to do?"

Rinski shrugged and stared at the rough wood floor. "Whatever the Good Lord tells me to do, young Talbot."

Talbot stepped past the man and walked outside. Rinski watched as he mounted his horse and rode back to the cabin.

"Where did you go?" Jacy said. She and Gordon were standing on the porch.

"To the hired hand's shack."

"What did you think?"

Talbot shrugged. "Nasty business. You might stop stealing beef."

"They steal ours—"

"So you steal theirs, I know," Talbot said, nodding his head. "How's the girl?"

Jacy shrugged darkly. "She won't sit still—just keeps scrubbing and straightening, like she can't get anything clean enough. Doesn't talk much, either."

As they were leaving the ranchyard, Rinski appeared, walking around the corral.

"The liver's in your skillet," Jacy called.

"Obliged," Rinski called back, not looking at them.

They rode the horse trail along Haughton's Bench to Wolf Creek, and cantered out upon the long, rolling reaches above the Little Missouri. As night came down, the rambling buildings of Jacy's Bar MK appeared, dark and shapeless below the tip of a grassy, tongue-shaped mesa.

They unloaded the wagon, stabled their horses in the timbered barn, hung the dressed Double X beef high above the floor, and threw hay to the saddle stock. Jacy and Talbot headed for the cabin, and Gordon walked to the bunkhouse.

The cabin was a long, low, solidly built structure of saddle-notched logs and wood shingles. A peeled-log gallery ran the length of the porch, and Talbot remembered his father and Miller Kincaid sitting out here, jawing away a summer evening.

"I'll have supper ready in half an hour, Gordon," she called.

"No thanks, Jacy. Think I'll mosey up to Spernig's . . . you know, see about a friendly game of poker."

"A friendly Mrs. Sanderson, more like," Jacy said.

Gordon wagged his head and went into the bunkhouse.

"He's got a woman who works at Spernig's Roadhouse," Jacy explained to Talbot as they mounted the porch steps.

The kitchen in which they gathered was built of big, square-hewn logs with plastered walls and a four-globed light hanging low over a long cottonwood table. Oval pictures hung on the walls, and several magazines were spread across the table. Coffee cans on the cupboard tops held utensils, and braided rugs fought the cold air seeping up from the floor. It was a big, homey kitchen, the kind of kitchen that took your mind off your problems. Talbot was grateful for such a kitchen just now.

"Sorry about the mess," Jacy said as she struck a match and lit the lamp on the windowsill. "I'm afraid I'm not much of a housekeeper. Don't really see the point, I guess . . . living alone."

Talbot had picked up several pieces of kindling from the porch. He tossed the wood in the box by the range and sat in a chair by the door. "I'd have thought you'd be married by now."

"Was," she said, throwing paper and kindling into the big stove. "For about a week. Met him at a shindig over at Spernig's—one of those come-one-come-all barn dances. He rode for Verlyn Thornberg. I thought he was the best thing since Winchesters and mustangs. The day after I married him, he turned shiftless and mean." She laughed without mirth, blowing on the fledgling fire. "Guess I should have realized he was marrying me for my ranch, but I was young and lonesome."

"What happened?" Talbot asked.

"I called him on it. The next morning he was gone. Took two of my best horses. Haven't seen him since. Heard he went to Montana, the son of a bitch."

Talbot said nothing, watching her.

She had her back to him while she worked on the fire. "What about you?"

"Well, I never married, if that's what you mean. The last seven years have been . . . crazy, I guess is the word." He didn't want to talk about Pilar. He hadn't spoken the girl's name aloud since she'd died.

"So why didn't you come home sooner?"

He shrugged. "I liked crazy for a while. You don't get bored when you're always on the move."

She had turned to him now with her coat and hat still on. The cabin was cold. "So why did you come home now?"

He thought for a moment, shrugged. "There's no place like home. Or so I thought."

She smiled. "I'm glad you're home." She flushed slightly. "I . . . I looked up to you guys—you and Dave."

He frowned, skeptical. "Really?"

"I didn't have any brothers, you know."

"We tormented you."

"I loved it."

He laughed. "The scars on my shins tell a different story."

"I was only really angry when you didn't take me serious," she confessed, then flushed even more and turned away to the fire. It was burning well now, and the iron range was ticking as it heated.

She pumped water and heated it on the stove, insisting he wash first since he was company. He did so after he'd hung his coat and hat on pegs by the door. She was slicing potatoes into a skillet in which grease popped.

"Your turn," he said, drying his arms and face on the towel she had draped over a chair back.

He sat at the table, feeling good to be sitting down to table again in Dakota. He reached into his shirt pocket for his tobacco pouch and started rolling a smoke. He worked on it thoughtfully and deliberately, lifting his eyes to Jacy as she washed.

She was a girl no longer, he saw as she removed her heavy wool coat and hat and swept her hair back from her neck with both hands. She was every inch a woman, with all the right curves in all the right places, though genes and hard work had streamlined them some, taken some of the female plump and turned it to muscle.

Without a trace of modesty, she unbuttoned her blue workshirt and tossed it onto a chair, then rolled up the sleeves of her faded red long johns and bent over the steaming washtub. From his side view, Talbot couldn't help noticing that she was not wearing any of the underclothing most females used to nip and tuck here and pull and press there.

Her small, conical breasts pushed invitingly against the thin, wash-worn fabric of the long johns, the pronounced nipples sliding this way and that as she scrubbed her face and behind her ears and neck.

"That feels good," she said breathily. Strands of wet, tawny hair stuck to her face. "It's a long ride to town and back."

Talbot stuck the quirley between his lips and struck a phosphor on the underside of the table, lighting up. "Do it often?"

"'Bout once a month. It's nice to get away, see something else for a change, and get the pantry stocked, of course." She glanced at him, did a double take.

"What are you lookin' at?"

It was too late to avert his eyes. He'd been caught. He smiled, flushing and blowing smoke at the ceiling. "You."

She was drying her arms. "What about me?"

"You've . . . grown up, Miss Jacy."

"Yes I have, and now I can really give your shins a bruising." She tossed away the towel and produced a long knife from the counter. Brandishing it, she said, "Why don't you go out and cut us a couple of nice steaks from that Double X beef—or cut me one and bring yourself a porcupine. You'll probably find one or two at the trash heap."

With a flick of her wrist, she flung the knife through the air. It landed point-first in the table, about six inches from Talbot's right hand, the handle vibrating for about two seconds after impact.

Impressed, Talbot pushed himself to his feet as though he'd just discovered a diamondback under the table. "Whatever you say," he said melodramatically. Sticking his cigarette in the corner of his mouth, he reached for his coat, pulled the knife out of the table, and headed out the door.

Jacy turned to the sizzling potatoes, smiling.

Talbot returned several minutes later, hands full of raw, marbled beef, kicking the door closed behind him. "Here's your grass-fed Double X," he said dryly.

"Drop it in the pan. I've got the potatoes warming in the oven. Where's your porcupine?"

"Plumb got away. I guess I'll be dining on the Double X this evening. Along with you and the Rinskis. I just hope King Magnusson doesn't decide to check out your barn. That brand is hanging there, plain as day."

Jacy poked the meat around in the skillet and grew serious. "You're making too big a deal out of this,

Mark. King Magnusson started putting his brand on our cattle the day after he moved into that big house of his."

"Then you should have brought in stock inspectors and federal marshals, and hauled him in front of the federal magistrate."

Jacy shrugged. "Hindsight is twenty-twenty. Besides, you know how these old guys around here feel about the law. Hell, half of 'em are wanted for some penny-ante thing back east, and the other half believe the law belongs to only those who can pay for it. And the only one who can pay for it around here is King Magnusson."

Talbot sighed and sat down. Jacy had convinced him of the situation's complexity. Still, two wrongs didn't make a right. Stealing from King Magnusson only made the water muddier.

Just the same, the smell of cooked, seasoned beef wafting up from the range made his mouth water, and he decided to enjoy the meal in spite of his philosophical differences with the cook.

"How do you like your steak?" she asked him.

"Bought and paid for, but I'll settle for well done."

—◆◆◆—

Jacy filled their plates, and they wolfed down the meat and fried potatoes like true Dakotans. Afterwards, doing his part, Talbot cleared the table and washed the dishes while Jacy sat at the table, watching him while she rolled and smoked a cigarette.

"Sorry, I know it's not very lady-like," she said, indicating the quirley. "Drinkin' whiskey probably isn't, either, but would you like a glass to wash down that Double X beef?"

Talbot shrugged. "I reckon it wouldn't be polite to make a woman drink alone."

When he had dried and put away the dishes, he and Jacy took their glasses of whiskey and retired to the sitting room, where she had started a fire in the big fieldstone hearth.

Talbot sat in the rocker near the flames, noting the deer and bear heads eyeing him from the walls and remembering that Jacy's father had been quite the hunter and trapper in his day. Jacy sat on the sofa and removed her moccasins, nudged them near the fire with a stockinged foot.

"Tell me about Dave," Talbot said after several minutes of contemplative silence.

"What about him?"

Talbot shrugged. "Did he have a girl? Before I left he was taking a shine to Maggie Cross over to Big Draw."

Jacy took a drag off her cigarette. "Maggie died, you know."

"She did?"

"You didn't know that?"

"No."

"Suppose you wouldn't. It was the milk fever."

"Jesus. Had they been close?"

"Rumor was they were going to marry. I asked him about it, but he wouldn't say. You know how shy he was about women."

Talbot leaned forward in his chair, taking his whiskey in both hands and resting his elbows on his knees. He sighed heavily.

Jacy continued, "After that he kept himself busy on the ranch. Dug several wells, added another herd he brought up from Kansas City, mixed in some white-faced stock. He had three cowboys workin' for him when . . . when he died."

"Where did they go?"

"I hired one. Thornberg took the others."

She disappeared into another room and returned with a document, dropping it in his lap on her way back to the sofa. "That's his will. I found it among his papers. It leaves the ranch to you."

Talbot sighed and stared at Dave's boyish signature at the bottom of the sheet, beside the official seal. "What if I don't want it?"

"It's your home. And it's some of the best graze on the Bench. No wonder Magnusson went after it first. What I wouldn't give for one or two of your creeks."

"They're yours."

"Don't say that."

"Why not?"

"We can be partners. I'll help you get started again."

"Why?"

She shrugged. "Old time's sake."

Jacy finished her whiskey and set the empty glass on the lamp table beside the sofa. She went into the kitchen and returned with the bottle, then refilled Talbot's glass. She straightened, holding the bottle by its neck. "I had a crush on you once. Did you know that?"

He looked up at her.

"But you never paid attention to me after you started taking Rona Paski to dances."

He shook his head, surprised. "I didn't know that."

She smiled. "Then you went away."

Jacy took the bottle and sat down. She refilled her glass and set the bottle on the table. "I was just a kid to you, I reckon."

"Well, you were a kid," he said defensively.

There was a long silence. They each sat drinking and thinking, listening to the fire crack and the wind howl under the eaves. Talbot had the feeling again of having been left behind. The plan had been simple:

Go home and help Dave on the ranch. Get hitched, build his own place, raise a few kids . . .

He worked his mind back around to the moment, toying with the idea of taking over the ranch. He had the money; he could feel it in the homemade pockets around his waist.

"How many head are you running?" he asked Jacy.

She was lounging with her head about a foot below the top of the sofa's back. She looked tired and her hair fell carelessly to her shoulders. She'd crossed her ankles on the stool before her.

"Close to a thousand," she said. "I had a good increase last year. I'm hopin' for an even better one this year. I only keep Gordon on during the winter, but I have about four men on my rolls during the spring and summer. Want another drink?"

They each had another. He tossed his back and looked up. She was still sitting there in the same way, but now tears were rolling down her cheeks.

"Jacy, you're crying," he said.

She smiled through her tears. "I'm just drunk."

"What are you crying about?"

"I don't know. I just get to feeling loco in the winter with nothing to do but feed cows and stare at the clouds." She sniffed. Her voice sounded far away. "And I don't know if I can keep this place . . . if I can stand against old Magnusson."

"You will," he assured her.

"Oh, I know—I'm just drunk."

"Why don't you go to bed?"

"I think I will."

Deliberately, she uncrossed her ankles and set her feet on the floor. She tried to push herself up but fell back down. "Or . . . maybe I won't."

"I'll help," Talbot said.

Smiling, she threw up a hand. He clutched it and

pulled her to her feet. Feeling how unsteady she was, he bent down, picked her up in his arms, and carried her down a short, dark hall. She was light, and she felt good in his arms, her loose hair brushing his forearm and wrist. She smelled musky but feminine.

"Which is your room?" he asked her.

"That one."

He pushed the door open with his boot and laid her on the iron bed. She pulled the quilt back and crawled clumsily beneath it. Talbot walked to the door.

"Good night, Jacy."

"You can sleep here. . . . This is the only bed in the house."

"What about your father's?"

"It's buried under tack; you'll never find it." She patted the quilt beside her. "Come on. I won't bite."

He stood in the doorway, watching her. His breath came short, and he couldn't help feeling aroused. It had been a long time since he'd slept with a woman, with or without sex. His last lover had been Pilar, three years ago. He knew he should grab a quilt and lie on the couch, but he couldn't make himself do it. He wanted to lie next to Jacy.

So he removed his shirt, money belt, and jeans and lay on the bed.

She turned to face him, snuggled up against his chest.

"It's been a long time since I've had a man to keep me warm," she said drowsily, getting comfortable against him.

He kissed her ear, ran his hand down her thigh.

She looked up suddenly. "What's that?"

"Sorry . . . I, uh . . . seem—"

"I'm not a loose woman, Mr. Talbot," she said haughtily. "Here, I'll take care of it."

She thrust her hand through the front opening in his long johns, grabbed his member, and squeezed, slowly pressing it down.

"There—how's that?" she asked.

He gave his head a quick shake and smiled against the pain. "Yeah . . . yeah, that should . . . do it," he said with a sigh.

"Good."

Then she wedged her head against his chest and went to sleep.

CHAPTER 12

———•———

SPERNIG'S ROADHOUSE SAT in a horseshoe of the Little Missouri River, along a well-traveled freight road snaking across the broken prairie between Mandan and Glendive, Montana.

The roadhouse sat in a hollow between low buttes. Doubling as a dance hall, it was a long, barnlike building constructed of milled lumber and boasting a redbrick chimney poking through its shingled roof. A corral flanked the building on the left, and a long hitch rack paralleled its front porch.

In spite of the cold weather, or because of it, Spernig's was hopping tonight. The corral was nearly filled with saddled horses, and two spring wagons and a buckboard were tied to the hitch rack. Dull yellow light spilled from the windows, and the sound of laughter, shuffling feet, and broken piano music penetrated the still, cold night.

Inside, Gordon Jenkins sat at a table nearest the piano. His big hand was wrapped around the handle of a soapy beer mug and his attention was glued to the woman playing the piano—or trying to play, as the others saw it. No one but Gordon could understand why the woman had been hired, for she could play no better than a gifted cowhand, and her half-assed renditions of "Little Brown Jug" and "The Flying Trapeze" were raucous at best.

But night after night, Gordon listened and watched as though he were being personally serenaded by harp-wielding cherubs. And tonight was no different.

Now as the woman finished a ponderous "I'll Take You Home Again, Kathleen," letting the final notes fade with a dramatic flair, lifting her pudgy nose to the rafters, Gordon rose to his feet. He brought his sun-darkened paws together slowly at first, issuing reports like those from a heavy Sharps rifle, then more quickly as he gained momentum. The woman turned her round face to him and smiled.

Gordon returned the smile with a wet-eyed one of his own, then turned his head to glance about the room. The other men and Spernig's two soiled doves were not clapping. They weren't even looking the piano player's way.

Gordon's expression turned so dark that the others seemed to sense its heat before they saw it. Gradually, one pair of hands at a time, the room filled with applause. One of the soiled doves even removed the cigar from her mouth and gave an obligatory whistle before going back to her card game.

It was enough to satisfy Gordon, who smiled broadly and held up his beer as the lady at the piano beamed and flushed, dropping her eyes demurely.

As the applause died and everyone returned to their jokes and their card games, Gordon pulled a chair out from his table, and the woman made her way to it. She was dressed in a shiny green gown with puffed sleeves and feathered felt hat. Gordon loved the way her full bosom bubbled up out of her corset like giant scoops of vanilla ice cream.

"That was some fine playin', Doreen, some mighty

fine playin'. Yessirree, doggie—can you *play* that thing!"

"Well, thank you, Gordon."

"No—thank *you*, Doreen. You know, after listenin' to you of a night, I'll hear one of those tunes all the next day while I'm goin' about my chores— just like you was playin' a little piano inside my head."

Doreen Sanderson laughed gaily, red lips parting and blue eyes flashing. Gordon didn't know how old she was—he guessed she was somewhere around forty-five or fifty—but he thought her the best-looking thing for the years as you'd find in Dakota in the wintertime, and her a widow with full-grown children to boot!

"Really?" she said, beaming.

"Would I lie to you?"

"Well, no, I guess you probably wouldn't, Gordon."

"Here, have a seat. I'll order you a drink."

She frowned and pursed her lips, hesitating. "Oh, Gordon—you know, I'm awfully tired, and Mr. Norton wants me to start inventory early in the morning, before the doors open." She only moonlighted as a piano player, working full-time as a clerk and bookkeeper in Big Draw. "I'm awfully sorry, but I think I'm going to head back to town."

Gordon's face fell. "So early?"

She smiled painfully and touched his hand. "I'm afraid so."

"Well, I'll drive the buggy around."

"Oh, you don't need to see me home. It's early yet. You stay and have fun."

Gordon shook his head, reaching for his coat, which he'd thrown over a chair. "Wouldn't think of it. It's a dark, cold night out there. It'd take a pretty small man to send a lady off alone."

"Oh, Gordon . . ."

He gave her a look of mock severity. "Now, Doreen, don't argue with me. You get bundled up while I go out and get the buggy."

Five minutes later, Gordon pulled the Deere & Weber Company two-seater around the front of the roadhouse, and tied his roan gelding on behind. Doreen stepped through the door in a wash of yellow light and a wave of laughter.

She wore a long wool coat, fur hat, and fur gloves. She clutched a round box, in which she'd placed her feathered hat for the journey home.

"Easy now, these steps are slippery," Gordon said as he mounted the porch and began guiding her down.

"Oh, Gordon, how you do dote on me!"

"Well, some women just call for dotin'."

"If only my dear dead Charlie could hear that!" she said with a throaty laugh.

When they were situated in the buggy and Gordon had thrown a buffalo robe over Doreen's legs, he flicked the reins against the harnessed sorrel's back, and they moved off down the trail leading south along the frozen river. Buttes lofted on their right, white with snow in the frosty darkness. The riverbed pushed up on the left side of the trail, thick with brush and dotted here and there with isolated willows and box elders.

Owls cooed and small night critters moved in the brush—raccoons, no doubt. Occasional wolves howled. When one such howl rose so loudly from a nearby knoll that Doreen's eardrums rattled, she slid close to Gordon and gave a shiver.

"Oh, I just hate it when they do that!"

"They do tend to get brave out here," Gordon allowed. "But don't you worry none. I've lived in the

Territory for fifty years, and I've never once heard of a wolf attacking people. Besides, I've got this here"—he lifted the carbine he'd stood between his left knee and the buggy's fender—"and a Winchester Sixty-six is about as good a luck charm as you'll find." He grinned.

She squeezed his arm. "Mr. Jenkins, you certainly know how to make a woman feel secure."

"Well, thank you, Mrs. Sanderson."

They were riding around a bend when another howl rended the quiet night. Gordon jumped this time, as well as Doreen, who cried, "Oh!" The harnessed sorrel started, ruffling its mane, and Gordon could feel the resistance when his own horse, tied behind, paused briefly to snort and look around.

"It's okay, Earl," he told the horse. "Keep on, now."

"Such a noise," Doreen said, huddled close to Gordon. "I've never heard one that close. He must be stalking us!"

"They don't stalk people," Gordon said.

"Well, apparently this one hasn't been told that."

The wolf howled again. The bewitching noise lifted from somewhere ahead, just beyond their range of vision. Gordon let the sorrel come to a halt, then draped the reins across his knee and picked up his Winchester. He stared ahead, squinting, trying to pick the critter out of the darkness. Behind him, his horse whinnied and shook its head, jarring the buggy.

"Come on, you," he growled. "Show yourself."

Doreen squeezed his arm. "Let's turn around, Gordon. I got a funny feelin' about this."

"It's just a wolf," Gordon said, but his voice was tense.

"Just a wolf!" Doreen cried.

"He's just tryin' to scare us," Gordon said. "He's out havin' fun."

"Maybe he's after the horses."

"Well, he ain't gonna get 'em." He tossed the reins. "Giddyup, horse."

They continued on for another mile and were beginning to feel less fearful, starting to chat again, when the wolf howled again—this time from behind them. It sounded as though the animal were only a few feet away. Gordon's horse plunged forward and around the buggy, jerking its right wheels several inches off the ground.

Doreen screamed as she bounced from side to side, flailing for Gordon's arm. Gordon yelled, "Hey, hey, horse! Whoah! Whoah! . . . Eeeeasy."

Then it was over and the sorrel was pulling the buggy again, shaking its head from side to side, agitated, and Gordon's horse was following along behind—tensely snorting and jerking its head around to see behind it.

"Gordon, please, let's go back!" Doreen yelled.

"Hell, the goddamn thing is behind us now!"

"Oh, Gordon . . . I'm scared!"

"Don't be scared. I'll get you home." He pulled back on the reins, slowing the sorrel to a halt. "But first I better loosen the lead so old Earl can't topple us."

Doreen grabbed his arm as he prepared to leave the buggy. "Gordon, don't leave me!"

"Just for a second, Doreen. I've got to loosen that lead."

"Oh, Gordon, hurry. I have such a bad feeling . . ." She turned to stare ahead, her eyes wide and brimming with animal fear. "There's something awful out there."

Gordon wanted to assure her that it wasn't something so awful, but he wasn't sure himself anymore. He, too, had a bad feeling. About as bad a feeling as he'd ever had—and he'd ridden herd through Blackfeet country!

He handed the reins to Doreen. "Hold on to these real tight now. Don't let go."

"Just hurry, please, Gordon."

He crawled down from the buggy and patted his horse to settle him, then went to work untying the lead. He tried to hurry, but the horse's commotion had twisted the leather into one hell of a tight knot. He cursed as he tried to work it apart with his bare, cold hands, nearly prying his fingernails off. The cold air burned and ached in his fingertips.

"Holy shit in a sandstorm," he muttered.

"Gordon," Doreen said quietly. Too quietly.

He looked at her. "What?"

"Someone's coming."

"Huh?"

She did not reply. Gordon followed her gaze around behind him. Sure enough, a rider was approaching. Gordon could make out only a silhouette, but that was enough to make his heart lighten. It was probably one of the men from the roadhouse heading home. He'd ride with Gordon and Doreen, and they'd be all right. There was safety in numbers.

"Hello, there," Gordon called, holding his horse by the bridle.

The rider came on but said nothing.

"Gordon," Doreen said thinly.

Gordon ignored her. "We sure are glad to see you," he said, grinning, staring off down the trail. The horse and rider took shape as they approached.

"The lady got a little scared," Gordon said. "We've been hearing wolves."

Doreen gave a breathy, frightened sound that seemed to crawl up slowly from deep in her chest. "G-Gordon."

Gordon turned to her, frowning. "What is it?"

"He . . . he's got a gun."

Gordon turned back to the rider again. Sure enough, the man was holding a rifle out from his belly. The barrel was pointed at Gordon's head. It was a big gun, bigger than most of the guns used around here for ranchwork. It looked like a hide hunter's Big Fifty.

Gordon regarded the man's gray-black coat and dark, featureless face, from which a cigar glowed beneath the round brim of a black hat with a brown leather band. He did not recognize the man. His fear returned, stronger. His tongue swelled and his heart began to pound. Cold as he was, sweat popped out on his back. He caught the smell of the man's cigar.

He stood there frozen, smile fading, holding his horse's bridle.

"Gordon," Doreen cried softly.

"Who . . . who are you?" Gordon said.

The man halted his horse about ten feet in front of him. The horse tossed its head. The man steadied it with an iron grip on the reins. Smoke puffed from around the cigar protruding from his dark face.

Gordon wanted to reach for the pistol on his right hip, but his right hand held fast to the bridle.

"Oh, Gordon," Doreen cried again, in a high voice broken by sobs. "I knew it . . . I knew it . . . was something . . . awful."

Gordon watched as the man lifted his left hand to his face and removed the cigar. Then the man slowly tipped back his head and howled. There was nothing at all human in the howl. It was not a man's howl.

It was a wolf's howl.

It lifted to the sky and set the night alive with its evil . . .

And it was the last sound Gordon Jenkins ever heard.

CHAPTER 13

————⊷◆⊶————

"I JUST WANT you to know I wouldn't have touched your dick if I hadn't been drunk."

Talbot opened his eyes. Jacy was leaning over the bed, gazing into his face. She was dressed and washed and ready to go. Her hair was pulled back in a ponytail.

"Huh?"

"I was drunk, or I wouldn't have touched your dick last night," she repeated.

"You flatter me. What time is it?"

"Nearly seven o'clock. What's with the men around here? Gordon's not up yet, either." She moved to the door, picked up his clothes from the chair, and tossed them on the bed. "Rise and shine. I don't serve chuck all morning."

She walked out the door, and a moment later Talbot heard her knocking pans around in the kitchen and whistling while she worked. His mouth watered at the smell of frying bacon and freshly brewed coffee. Wondering how he could have slept until seven o'clock in the morning, he threw the covers back, hauled his saddle-sore ass out of bed, and dressed.

"You didn't have to wait breakfast for me," he said, entering the kitchen and buckling his belt.

Jacy was standing at the range, stirring eggs in a

cast-iron skillet. "It's nothing," she said, "just the usual—bacon and eggs. Help yourself to coffee. There's a mug on the table. How did you sleep?"

"Like a dead dog," he said. "You?"

"Good."

Talbot filled a mug, returned the pot to the warming rack on the range, and sat down at the table. He sipped his coffee and noticed that she had recovered from last night's melancholy and was her old self again—a real Toledo blade, Dakota style. Tough and tomboyishly pretty.

As she lifted the pan from the range and shoveled eggs onto a plate, he realized he'd been staring at her, and turned and looked out the window. Gray light angled in and shone like quicksilver on the worn floor.

"Looks like we got some snow, huh?" he said conversationally.

"Looks like."

She grabbed a couple of pot holders and opened the oven door. Smoke wafted. "Shit!" she cried. "Goddamn it, anyway—I burned the biscuits!"

She dropped the pan on the range top and slammed the door, throwing the pot holders on the cupboard.

"They don't look burned to me," Talbot said, politely ignoring the smoke.

"They're burned on the bottoms."

"Throw one on my plate; I'll give it a shot."

"I'll scrape the bottom first," she said, waving at the smoke clouds webbing toward the rafters.

After scraping the burnt crust off one of the biscuits, she set it on the plate, then set the plate before Talbot. "Here you go," she said fatefully. "Nothing fancy, but this isn't the Hotel Deluxe and I'm no French chef."

"Looks good," he said, studying his plate with a wooden smile.

The charred biscuit was nearly raw in the center, and the underdone eggs looked like marmalade preserves that hadn't jelled. But Talbot maintained the smile and gave his head an appreciative wag. "Now there's a breakfast! How did you know I like my eggs runny?"

Jacy shrugged, smiling. "Just had you pegged for a runny-eggs guy, I guess."

She poured herself a cup of coffee, then sat across from him and watched him eat. After several minutes a cloud passed over her face. "I wonder what's keeping Gordon this morning."

"Must have had a hell of a time last night."

She shook her head. "It's not like him to sleep this late, no matter how much fun he had the night before."

"I'll check on him as soon as I'm through here."

"Would you? If I go pounding on his door, and he's drunk, I'll just embarrass him."

"No problem."

When he'd finished the massive pile of scrambled eggs, and sopped up the bacon grease with a biscuit, Talbot tipped back the last of his coffee, dressed in his new winter garb, and headed outside. He could tell from the fresh snow liming the corrals and water troughs that they'd gotten a good three or four inches last night.

The sky was as gray as an old coin; it hunkered so low that the top of the box elder behind the bunkhouse was nearly indiscernible. A couple of fat crows lit out from a hay rack, cawing, and winged out over the corrals toward the mesa.

Talbot walked across the yard and around the corrals, noting the lack of smoke puffing from the bunkhouse chimney, and knocked on the door.

"Gordon?"

No answer.

Talbot opened the door and stepped inside. The long, low room, provisioned with an eating table and several cots, was dark and empty. The air was stale and tinged with the smell of old sweat and tobacco. Talbot touched the big iron stove in the room's center: cold as ice. It hadn't been fired for at least eight hours.

Thoughtfully, Talbot walked out behind the bunkhouse and looked around, wondering if Gordon was in the habit of staying out all night. Something told him he wasn't.

As he stared out across the gray prairie, he heard sleigh bells and voices. The sounds seemed to be coming from the cabin's direction. He wheeled and headed back across the yard, then stopped dead in his tracks.

Sitting before the cabin was a sleigh drawn by a stout silver-gray gelding wearing a halter and bells. Inside the sleigh were two fur-clad people—a woman and a man—looking like Russian royalty out for a winter romp with the Cossacks. The man puffed a pipe. The horse bobbed its head and stomped a front hoof, eager to get moving again.

Then Talbot heard the unmistakable voice of Suzanne Magnusson, smelled the distinctive aroma of the doctor's pipe. They had stopped before the cabin and were talking with Jacy, who spied Talbot now, walking toward the sleigh.

"There he is," she said. "Mr. Talbot, you have a couple visitors from the Double X ranch," she called, her voice taut and sarcastic, brimming with unconcealed hatred. "You know Miss Suzanne and . . ."

"Dr. Long," the doctor said thickly, giving a gentlemanly bow. Rheumy-eyed, he appeared half drunk.

Suzanne had turned to Talbot. Shock and surprise

brightened her exquisite face, her cheeks flushed from the cold. "Mark, it's you! Hello!"

Talbot smiled tightly, aware of Jacy's caustic glare. "Suzanne. Harrison. What are you two doing here?"

Suddenly petulant, Suzanne said, "You were supposed to call on me, Mr. Talbot."

Talbot slid a look at Jacy, who stood glaring at him across the sleigh. "Well, I've only been here two days, Suzanne."

"When you didn't come to me, Harrison and I decided to come to you. We stopped here to ask directions, and learned from Miss Kincaid that you were here!" Suzanne was smiling beautifully, eyes flashing, but there was a question there as well.

Talbot said, "Jacy and I are old friends. My cabin needs a little work, so she offered me a bed."

"How nice of her," Suzanne said, her smile losing its luster as she shuttled it to Jacy.

Changing the subject, Talbot said, "How are you, Harrison?"

The easterner had produced a leather-sheathed traveling flask from his coat and was unscrewing the top. He raised it to Talbot and said with dramatic flair, "Out here on these magnificent Great Plains to which Miss Magnusson was kind enough to drag me? Where there are as many trees as balmy days, and the air is absolutely frigid? Never better!" He tipped back the flask for several good-sized swallows.

Suzanne gave the man a playful poke. "I keep telling him to think of it as an adventure."

"No, Crete was an adventure," Harrison retorted, offering the flask to Talbot, who waved it off. "How is your back, Mr. Talbot?"

"Good as new," Talbot replied, noticing Jacy's questioning glance. "I had a little accident before I left San Francisco," he explained.

"Some accident!" Suzanne said admiringly. To Jacy she gave a short, dramatic account of Talbot's adventure. "It's like something you read in novels," she said when she'd finished the story.

"Did all that really happen?" Jacy asked Talbot.

Talbot shrugged modestly. He hadn't felt this uncomfortable with his clothes on.

"Thanks again for the patch job," he told Harrison, who grunted and shook his head. "I'd ask you both to light and sit a spell, but it's not my cabin, and . . ." He stopped, deferring to Jacy.

She only sneered. "I haven't straightened up," she said dryly. Then she wheeled around and went into the cabin, slamming the door behind her.

"I sense a distinct hostility in that girl," said Harrison facetiously.

"Well, with the tension between the small ranchers in the area, and Suzanne's father, I guess there's bound to be some hard feelings," Talbot said, thinking of Dave.

Suzanne turned a cold eye to the cabin door. "I guess they're supposed to be able to steal as much of my father's beef as they want, and not get called on it," she said.

Talbot grew testy. "They claim your father's been handing out death warrants, that he killed people five years ago and that he's starting again now." He debated telling her about Dave's murder, and decided to wait for a better time. The information might make her even more defensive.

Suzanne looked hurt. "Mark, if you knew my father, you'd know how ridiculous that is. Papa is the gentlest man alive. I know he's been trying to buy the nesters out. They've been stealing our cattle and overgrazing the range, not to mention destroying all the water holes and befouling the bloodlines. But he would never kill anyone . . . for any reason."

She shook her head sincerely, firmly believing what she'd professed.

She almost had Talbot believing—at least questioning what he'd been hearing from Jacy and the others. He shrugged and forced a smile. "Maybe you're right, Suzanne. I haven't been here long enough to find out the whole story."

"Well, let me help you get the whole story, Mr. Talbot," she said, brightening. "What we came out here for was to invite you to a birthday and pre-Christmas celebration at the Double X tomorrow night. Won't you come?"

"Whose birthday?"

"Mine, of course."

Talbot frowned and looked off, thoughtful.

"Oh, please, Mark," Suzanne begged. "I want you to meet my father and see what a fine man he is. Of course, there will be plenty of food and drink and"— she grew subtly flirtatious—"I'll be there." She arched a delicate eyebrow and smiled brightly.

Talbot felt himself softening. He had no solid proof that King Magnusson had killed his brother, and Suzanne certainly wasn't involved. A visit to the Double X might even prove helpful in sorting through this mess. He found himself ignoring the small voice in the back of his head reminding him it was not his mess to sort through.

"All right," he said. "What time?"

"Six o'clock."

"What should I wear?"

"Come as you are. You'll feel right at home."

Doubting that, Talbot said with a nod, "Six it is."

"Okay, then," Suzanne said, pinning him with a smoldering gaze. "See you there."

Harrison flicked the reins along the silver gray's back, and said, "Cheers!" as the sleigh started off with a celebratory jingle of the bells.

Talbot stood watching them as they made a large circle in the yard, and headed back the way they had come. Suzanne looked back and waved, and Talbot returned it. Then he walked to the cabin door and turned the knob. It was locked.

He knocked once. "Jacy?"

The silence that answered was answer enough, and he knew it was all the answer he was going to get. Jacy had heard everything, and she wasn't about to let him explain.

"Gordon's not in his cabin," he said to the door. "Let me know if you want help tracking him down."

He turned around and headed for the barn and his horse, feeling a stone grow in the pit of his stomach. Something told him that the next couple of days were going to put an end, once and for all, to any and all hopes he still entertained of finding peace.

CHAPTER 14

THAT AFTERNOON, JED Gibbon was nursing a beer in the Sundowner and reading *The Saturday Evening Post* when something caught his eye out the big window to the right of the front door. A cowboy had ridden up on a deep-chested claybank, and was looping his reins over the tie rail.

His expression was grim, and his horse was blowing like he'd been ridden hard. The man had bad news written all over him.

Darkly, Gibbon watched the man mount the porch and push through the door. When he'd closed the door behind him, stomping snow from his boots, he stood looking around. Gibbon knew the man was waiting for his eyes to adjust.

"Howdy, Luke," Fisk said from behind the bar, recognizing the cowboy.

"Monty."

"What can I do ya for?"

"The sheriff here?"

Gibbon cleared his throat. Reluctantly he said, "Over here, Luke."

The man shuttled his eyes to his right, where Gibbon sat under a big elk head, in shadows cast by the stove and center post.

"How's things over to the Nixon place?" Gibbon said as the man's eyes found him, trying a smile.

Luke Waverly was tall and lean to the point of emaciation, with a thin, droopy mustache and deep-sunk eyes. His face looked like rawhide that had been soaked and dried too quickly over a hot fire. His eyes hung low in their sockets, like a chastised dog's.

"Mr. Nixon's been shot."

Gibbon took a deep breath and ran a hand down his face. "Don't tell me that, Luke. I don't want to hear that."

"He didn't come home last night," the cowboy continued. "I went out lookin' for him this mornin' and found him behind a rock with half his head gone. Found this in his coat."

The cowboy stepped forward and laid a scrap of paper on the table before the sheriff. Gibbon lowered his eyes. On the paper was a big number one drawn boldly in pencil.

Gibbon felt his bowels loosen, and he was afraid for a moment he would soil himself. It was starting again. If he'd entertained any doubts before, he didn't now.

He cursed and lifted a hand to his forehead, took the bridge of his nose between thumb and index finger, and squeezed, trying to steady himself, trying to imagine what he should do, what he had the balls to do.

"Bushwhacked?" he said at length, through a grimace.

"Executed, more like. Just like Jack Thom. More of the Double X's handiwork." The cowboy's voice quaked with emotion.

"Where is he?"

"At the cabin."

Gibbon fought off the very real urge to run. He

stood, tipped back his beer, draining it, and wiped the foam from his mouth with the back of his hand. Turning to pluck his coat off the rack to his right, he said ominously, "Let's go."

An hour later Gibbon and the cowboy made the Nixon ranch, a motley collection of log and milled-lumber buildings and corrals scattered in a deep, wooded draw. High, rocky buttes poked up behind the trees. A yellow-brown mongrel ran out from the barn and scolded Gibbon's horse.

"Shut up and lay down, Buster!" the cowboy yelled.

The dog put its head and tail down and slunk off to the middle of the yard, where it sat growling, ears flat against its head. Dismounting at the barn, Gibbon heard a woman's muffled cries. He turned an ear to the cabin.

"No," she screamed in German over and over, the screams spaced about two seconds apart. "Nein! . . . Nein! . . . Nein!"

It was a haunting refrain, pricking Gibbon's spine. It even spooked his horse, which craned its neck to get a fix on it.

The cowboy took Gibbon's reins. "I took the kids over to the neighbors and gave the wife some whiskey to calm her down, but it don't seem to be workin'."

"Mrs. Nixon?"

Waverly nodded. "I haven't heard her speak anything but English for years." The man led the horses toward the corral. "I laid the boss out in the barn. You can go on in."

Gibbon didn't really want to go into the barn alone—the dead always made him feel nightmarish and lonely—but he slid a heavy door open anyway and stepped inside.

The air was heavy with the smell of hay and ammonia. A milk cow gave an inquisitive moo. Heavy stock—probably draft horses—knocked against their stalls. There were several windows along each wall, but the gray winter light was too weak to penetrate the afternoon shadows.

Finding a hurricane lamp on a post, Gibbon lifted its globe and lit the wick. The light lifted shadows from an open-ended work wagon in which an inert body in tattered range clothes lay on its back, arms at its sides.

Gibbon held the lamp high and moved toward the wagon's spring seat. The light revealed the man's head—or what was left of it. Most of the forehead had been blown away. One eye bulged hideously. The other was missing. Gibbon swallowed to keep his lunch and beer down.

"Jesus Christ," he murmured, needing a shot of something strong.

"Big-caliber bul—"

Gibbon jumped at the voice and turned to see the cowboy standing beside him. He hadn't seen or heard the man enter the barn.

"Sorry," Waverly said. "I was gonna say it looks like a big-caliber bullet blew the top of his head clean off."

"I got eyes," Gibbon said, testy, remembering the big gun Del Toro had carried away from the train. "Fifty caliber. I've seen their work before, and not just on buffalo. I see he took another one to the side."

The cowboy shook his head, eyes wide with foreboding. "What am I gonna do now? What's the woman gonna do? She has five young'uns."

Trying to stay focused, Gibbon said, "Could you tell by the tracks in the snow how many men were after him?"

"One as far as I could tell."

"Was Nixon armed?"

"Yep."

"He return fire?"

"Yep."

"You got anything else to say except yep, Luke?"

"Yep." The cowboy's eyes slid to Gibbon's. "Double X got him, Sheriff. Sure as shit up a cow's ass. And him's only the first," the cowboy said.

"The first killed by Del Toro anyways," Gibbon said, remembering Jack Thom.

"Who's Del Toro?"

"Let me put it this way, Luke. A blue-eyed bean eater decked out in wolf fur comes callin', you shoot the son of a bitch out of his saddle. Blow him from here to old Mexico. No questions asked."

The cowboy rubbed his jaw and eyed Gibbon warily. "Where you goin'?" he said with an insinuating drawl. "Back to the saloon?"

Gibbon stopped at the door and turned around. His face and ears flushed, as though he'd been slapped hard. A moment ago, he hadn't really known where he was going; his mind was a mess of half-conceived ideas and very real fears that probably would have led, in the end, to a drink. But the cowboy's barb pricked him, set a fire in his brain. He was tired of the jokes made at his expense. What's more, he was tired of deserving them.

He took a deep breath fighting panic and was nearly overcome by the unfamiliar sound of his own courage. "To talk with King Magnusson over to the Double X. Please relay my condolences to Mrs. Nixon, and assure her that I'll bring her husband's killer to justice."

Waverly tipped his hat back. "The Double X! By your lonesome?"

"Posses take too long to gather. Besides, a bunch of trigger-happy cowboys would just touch off a powder keg. No, I'm gonna give old King Magnusson a nice, civilized ultimatum."

When Gibbon had mounted his horse and was riding away, the cowboy stood between the open barn doors watching him and scratching his head.

"That son of a bitch is gonna get his ass shot off."

As he made his way south along a thin wagon trace, Gibbon was thinking the same thing. While he'd been standing in the barn with Waverly, inspecting Nixon's body, he'd felt something very close to courage seep into his veins. It was like a heady shot of liquor after you'd gone without for several days. It was a courage born of anger and shame. Magnusson was acting like he owned the whole damn country, and he paid as little heed to Gibbon as he would to a stable boy.

Alhough he was still feeling plucky after ten miles of hard riding, his heart was starting to race by the time he made the ridge over St. Mary's Creek, the Double X's primary water source. He pointed the horse east along the game trail that twisted through the ponderosas above the draw, and felt his mouth dry up and his knees grow heavy with apprehension.

"I'm liable to get shot out of my saddle and left to the wildcats," he told himself. "This is a big country, and even if anyone came lookin', they'd never find me."

But he was only about two miles from the Double X compound, and he could not turn back now. Not if he wanted to hold on to what little pride he had left.

He stopped his horse behind a snowdrift at the

lip of the ridge, rummaged in his saddlebags, and produced a whiskey bottle. Uncorking it, he lifted it high and felt a little of his nerve return almost instantly.

He recorked the bottle and was about to return it to the saddlebags when he reconsidered. "Hell, I'm gonna need all the metal I can muster," he mumbled, biting the cork from the bottle, spitting it out, and spurring the horse forward.

He was good and soused by the time he made the two-track wagon trail climbing the tawny-snowy bench toward the Double X headquarters. It was the kind of drunk he used to feel back before the Old Trouble—a cocky, courageous drunk. A powerful, light-headed drunk that made him feel potent and vigorous and heroic.

When the Magnusson mansion rose up on a knoll a half mile ahead, two riders appeared on either side of him. They each had a carbine resting on their hips, and they rode up fast—scruffy, duster-clad cowboys in Stetsons.

Gibbon tossed his nearly empty bottle into a clump of sage.

"State your name and business," the cowboy on his right demanded.

Gibbon told him who he was.

"Mr. Magnusson expectin' you, Sheriff?"

"Should be if he ain't," Gibbon said, trying to steady himself. His tongue felt half a size larger than it was.

"What's that supposed to mean?"

"Just what I said. Now kindly get your hammerheads out of my way and let me through."

The men looked at each other knowingly, then reined their horses off the trail. They followed Gibbon through the open Texas gate, under the horizontal rail in which the Double X brand had been burned, and into the compound. They kept their distance, but they watched Gibbon with curious, wary eyes.

When Gibbon was nearing the mansion, taking in the breadth of the place while trying to keep his nerve up, one of the men spurred ahead and dismounted near a cluster of cowboys that had gathered outside a corral. The corral sat to the right of the mansion, up a slight rise and near several wagon sheds and a blacksmith shop.

Gibbon halted his horse before the mansion and waited, watching the group. A pretty girl and a horse seemed to be the center of attention. In a buffalo coat and round-brimmed, green-felt hat, King Magnusson stood near the girl, smiling down at her.

"Oh, Papa, he's beautiful! Where did you ever find such a horse?"

"Had him shipped all the way up from Tennessee," Magnusson said. Turning to the men crowding around, he added, "The conductor told me he nearly took his own private car apart board by board!"

A whoop broke out from several men, and Gibbon figured it was instigated more by the girl than by Magnusson's blabber or even by the horse. In a big wool poncho and riding hat, raven hair cascading down her back, she stroked the horse's fine, arched neck. Gibbon could tell by the looks on the cowboys' faces they were imagining her stroking something else.

"He's just a beauty, Papa, just a beauty," the girl went on.

Magnusson was about to say something else when Gibbon's cowboy interrupted him. The man spoke to his boss, who frowned and lifted his head to look over the crowd at the sheriff. Gibbon tipped his hat and grinned.

Magnusson's big, ruddy face flushed. He turned sharply to the cowboy and moved his lips. The cowboy nodded and pushed through the crowd.

Approaching Gibbon, he said, "Sorry, Sheriff. The boss is busy today. It's Miss Suzanne's birthday."

Gibbon lifted his eyes from the cowboy to Magnusson, laughing with his daughter and running his hand over the thoroughbred's muscled shoulder. Gibbon touched his spurs to his mount's flanks, moving toward the crowd.

"Hey, where do you think you're goin'?" the cowboy yelled.

Gibbon ignored him and rode to the edge of the crowd. "Mr. Magnusson, I'll thank you for a minute of your time."

The rancher turned sharply, frowning. "I'm busy here, Gibbon. You're gonna have to come back some other time."

"Can't do that."

"What's that?"

Gibbon's anger burned at the man's snide demeanor. He held on to the saddlehorn and yelled, "I said get your ass over here so we can talk in private! . . . Unless you want your lovely daughter to hear about the cold-blooded killin's her father's been committin' on open range."

The girl turned to her father and wrinkled her nose, curious. She said something Gibbon couldn't hear. Her father stared at the sheriff, his face turning red, then white, then red again.

The girl said something else. Magnusson ignored her. He was staring at Gibbon with a demon's eyes.

The cowboys had turned to him, too, cutting looks between him and their boss, who did not appreciate getting read out before his hands, much less his daughter.

"What do you say, King?" Gibbon asked, swaying a little in his saddle. It felt so good to air his spleen that he was finding it hard to shut up. He saw the holsters hanging beneath the cowboys' coats, but he was unconcerned. He felt large—too large to kill—and teeming with saintly virtue.

King turned to his daughter and moved his lips. She frowned and dropped her head, then handed the thoroughbred's reins to one of the wranglers. The crowd parted as she moved toward the mansion.

When she was safely inside, the men stepped back to form a corridor, and King Magnusson sauntered over to Gibbon. A man the sheriff recognized as Rag Donnelly followed him. Another man fell into step behind Donnelly.

A stout man with a head like a broad chunk of oak and a red mustache that curved around to meet his sideburns, he looked like either a politician or an eastern financier. He puffed a stogie in the side of his mouth and stuffed his fists in the pockets of his calf-length beaver coat.

Magnusson approached Gibbon. His face was set firm and frozen, like a gambler waiting to see his opponent's busted flush. "All right, Gibbon, what's on your mind?"

"Two men have been killed on the Canaan Bench—that's what's on my mind, you son of a bitch."

Magnusson said nothing. He just stared at Gibbon. Humor crept into his eyes. Gibbon met the gaze head-on. He'd made it this far, and with each passing second he felt more and more fearless. More and more invincible.

Magnusson cut his eyes to Rag Donnelly standing grimly beside him, then back to Gibbon. "What makes you think that has anything to do with me?"

"Precedence," Gibbon growled.

"Precedence without evidence won't get you very far in a court of law, Sheriff."

Gibbon leaned out from his saddle. "Call him off, King."

"Call who off?" Magnusson said, as though indulging the village idiot.

It took a couple seconds for Gibbon to get his tongue around the words. "José del Toro. Your Mex gun for hire."

"José del who? I'm afraid I didn't catch the name."

"You know the name."

Magnusson turned to Donnelly. "Rag, do we have a greaser gunman named José—" He turned to Gibbon with an expression of mock perplexity. "What was this fella's name again?"

The well-dressed gent puffing the stogie gave a loud guffaw and clapped his kid-gloved hands.

"Very goddamn funny, Magnusson, but if you don't call him off the small ranchers on the Bench, the only one's gonna be laughin' is the hangman—as he's escortin' you to the gallows."

"My, what pluck we're exhibiting here today, Mr. Gibbon! I don't believe I've ever seen you in such rarefied form. It's due to the alcohol, I suspect. Good Lord, man, you smell like a still!"

Rag Donnelly said through tight lips, "Fairly reeks of it, he does."

Gibbon flushed. "I may have had a shot or two on the way out from town. It's a long ride." His features bunched with anger. "And anyway, my drinkin' ain't the point! The point is you're breakin' the law just like you did five years ago, only this time I ain't gonna stand back and watch it happen. I ain't gonna sit back and watch you kill to your heart's content, until you've freed up every square foot of the Bench for your own beef. It's murder, goddamnit, Magnusson. Cold-blooded murder!"

Magnusson laughed. "Sheriff, I'm afraid your sympathies lie in the wrong camp. I'm certainly not condoning cold-blooded murder, but if certain men were caught stealing my beef, and my boys . . . well, that's frontier justice. It may not be legal in the purest sense of the word, but I highly doubt any judge would rule in the favor of stock thieves." Magnusson laughed again.

Gibbon fairly shook with outrage. "Then it goes both ways. I've seen their brands in your holding pens."

"If their beef was in my pens it's because they were eating my grass."

"What is your grass—the whole goddamn Bench?"

"My grass is whatever I can rescue from those goddamn ignorant farm-stock sons of bitches—men like yourself, Gibbon. Drunkards, cowards, and common thieves." Magnusson was angry now himself. His face had turned bright red, setting off the frosty blue of his eyes.

"Why, you highfalutin son of a bitch!" Gibbon was trying to get his gun out from under his coat. As he fumbled angrily, growling like a wounded bear, Magnusson reached up and grabbed his left arm and pulled. Gibbon came out of the saddle and hit the ground like a sack of grain. His foot stayed in the stirrup and his leg twisted at the ankle.

Gibbon cried out and Magnusson kicked the foot free, still holding the sheriff's left arm. Then he kicked

Gibbon hard in the gut with the toe of his boot. He followed it up with two more brutal kicks, yelling, "How dare you bring a firearm onto these premises! How dare you pack an iron onto my land and try to shoot me in my own yard—you scumsucking, ignorant old drunk!"

Gibbon yanked his arm free and fell into a hard patch of dirty snow. The cowboys gathered around, cheering their boss. Gibbon caught a glimpse of their grinning, tobacco-chewing faces as he got his hands beneath himself and tried to gain his feet.

He'd gotten only as far as his knees when the tall, iron-bodied rancher—grinning now, showing off for his men—delivered another stovepipe boot to the sheriff's round paunch.

Gibbon groaned as the air exploded from his lungs.

The kick propelled him backward, and his head hit the hard ground, sending lightning bolts beneath his closed eyelids. The blow made him sick to his stomach. It dawned on him that, coming here alone, he'd made a mistake. Probably the biggest mistake of his life ....

The thought was still resonating when he felt himself being drawn up by two hands pulling at his coat. The ascent took several seconds, for Gibbon was a big man, and his legs would not cooperate. He wasn't quite sure what was happening—his head hitting the ground had fogged his brain.

When he was half standing, balancing there with the rancher's help and still trying to coax air into his lungs, Magnusson drew his arm back like a bowstring and let it go. His fist slammed into Gibbon's face once, twice, three times.

The powerful right jabs propelled Gibbon into a straight-backed stance for half a second before he collapsed again on his back. His eyes watered from the pain daggering through his nose and deep into his skull. Blood gushed from his lips and nose, flooding his face. He felt his eyes swell.

"If I'd known you were having this much fun out here, King, I would have come a long time ago!" he heard the well-dressed gent say around a deep-throated laugh.

Standing over him, his chest rising and falling, Magnusson said tightly, "Some lawman, Gibbon. I've never seen a sorrier excuse for a man, much less a sheriff!"

Gibbon heard men laughing just below the high-pitched whistling in his ears.

Magnusson said to Donnelly standing beside him, "What do you think, Rag? Should we kill the sorry bastard or send him home to his mother?"

"Well . . ." Donnelly said, scratching his head and playing along, "I'd say his mother's dead. Dead of a broken heart, no doubt. Might as well kill him and put him out of his misery."

Magnusson faked a grimace and shook his head. "I don't know, Rag. Those sorry ten-cow ranchers are gonna need someone on their side. At least he's a figurehead for 'em. Seems like it wouldn't be fair to take their general so early in the battle—sorry as their general is."

"I know," Rag said. "Why don't we tie him to his saddle and send him back to his troops? Sort of like a message from us to them."

"A little frontier justice!" the well-dressed gent bellowed, as though he were attending a staged spectacle. "I love it!"

"Grand idea, Rag! Grand idea," Magnusson agreed. Turning to the other men, who'd formed a half circle around him, Donnelly, and Gibbon, the rancher said, "Now that's the kind of creative thinking I like to see in my men. Boys, let Mr. Donnelly here be an example to all of you."

Picking his son out of the crowd, he said, "Randall, you and Shelby toss our conquering hero over his horse and send him home. I'm sure the good citizens of Canaan will want to give him a hero's welcome."

Donnelly chuckled and shook his head.

Randall said, "What if the horse can't find his way home, Pa?"

"I'm sure that horse has had plenty of practice finding his way home without the good sheriff's assistance," Magnusson said, cutting his eyes to the passed-out Gibbon with a sneer.

Ten minutes later, Magnusson had retired to his den with the well-dressed gentleman and Rag Donnelly. Most of the cowboys had gone back to their work around the compound.

Randall Magnusson and Shelby Green draped the big unconscious lawman over his saddle and used the reins to tie him to the horn.

"I say he shoulda shot the son of a bitch," Randall said as he gave the horse a resolute slap to its backside.

The horse bounded off, whipping its head around at the oddly mounted burden on its back. Gibbon cried out in his stupor, his old bones creaking against the saddle. The horse galloped through the gate and out of the yard, descending the gradual grade toward St. Mary's Creek and the purpling flats beyond.

"But I have to admit, it's a pretty damn good joke!" Randall laughed as he and Shelby Green turned around and started toward the barn.

"Yeah, your pa has quite a sense of humor," Shelby agreed.

Above their retreating backs, Randall's sister, Suzanne, stood in one of the mansion's upstairs windows, staring out at the horse and its bound rider dwindling in the wintry distance.

CHAPTER 15

JACY SPENT THE rest of the day pulling firewood out of a draw with the two Percheron crosses her father had added to their remuda the year before he died. She had decided that Mark Talbot was a lecherous dope for having accepted Suzanne's invitation. Although she had never known Gordon to act so irresponsibly, it was apparent that the old cowboy had either eloped or gotten involved in a marathon poker game.

Jacy saw now that she had grossly overestimated each man's character. Like the rest of their lot, they were fools and would always forsake their responsibilities for big-breasted women and the quest for fun and money.

Early the next morning she continued her work, trying hard not to think about either man. Around noon she was leading the horses back to the yard, towing a heavy box elder trunk, when she stopped suddenly by the corral.

Something at the cabin had caught her eye, and she stared at it, trying to make it out. It was a piece of paper attached to the cabin door. It fluttered and rattled in the breeze.

She tied the horses' lead to the corral, then walked to the cabin, mounted the steps, and plucked the sheet from the rusty nail. Having to steady it with both heavy-mittened hands, she squinted her eyes at the penciled words: CLEER OUT.

That's all it said.

Jacy stuffed the note in her coat and looked around the yard, drawing the heavy Colt pistol she had taken to wearing around her waist. Her jaw was set tight and her eyes were cool; only her ashen features betrayed the storm within.

Concluding that the yard was clear, she turned back to the cabin and pushed open the door, letting it swing back against the wall. She knew that the men who'd left the note were probably gone—for now—but she entered stiffly and looked around, extending the pistol before her.

Thumbing back the hammer, she started moving through the kitchen, checking every nook and cranny, looking behind every chair and cupboard. Then she proceeded through the rest of the house in the same way—slowly, tensing herself for sudden violence, ready to shoot at anything that moved.

When she was sure the cabin was safe, she returned to the kitchen, holstered her pistol, and picked up the Winchester standing by the door. Retrieving a shell box from a cupboard, she set the rifle on the table and began feeding ammo into the breech. It was a clumsy maneuver; her hands were shaking.

"Goddamnit anyway—go in there!" she screamed, nudging the box and spewing shells on the floor. Knowing that Magnusson's men had been here made her feel violated, and she couldn't have felt much more incensed if they'd ransacked the place.

When she'd slid the last bullet into the receiver, she jacked a shell in the chamber and lifted the rifle to her cheek, aiming at a pan on the wall, trying to steady herself, to even out her breath, and to hold the tears of fear and outrage at bay.

It didn't work. She jerked back the trigger. The rifle barked loudly in the close quarters, nearly deafening her. The room filled with so much smoke she was barely able to make out the neat round hole she had blown through the pan.

"You goddamn bastard son of a bitch!" she screamed, then wheeled around and headed out the door.

When she'd unhitched the draft horses from the tree trunk and turned them out in the paddock behind the barn, she saddled her line-back dun and started cross-country for Spernig's Roadhouse. If Gordon wasn't there, someone there probably knew where he'd gone. She needed the old cowboy's help; what's more, she needed to know that he was alive.

Having galloped along the snowless ridges most of the way, she came out on the lip over Spernig's half an hour later, then spurred the dun down the canyon, along an old eroded horse trail cowboys had been carving since Spernig's was just a shanty.

She found Nils in his office at the far back of the building, crouched over his books, a twisted cigarette drooping from his mouth. "Nils, you know where Gordon is?"

He'd heard her boots on the wood floor and was turned to the doorway, his long face with its heavy black brows obscured by a smoke veil. "How in hell would I know where Gordon is?"

"He was in here night before last, wasn't he?"

"I reckon, but—"

"But he hasn't been home since," Jacy finished for him. "You know where he went?"

Nils shrugged and lifted his eyebrows, removing the quirley with the thumb and index finger of his right hand. "Well, he took Mrs. Sanderson home, you know, like he usually does."

Jacy's voice was urgent. "That's all you know? They didn't go off to get hitched or nothin'?"

The barman shrugged again, dropping his jaw. "Well, not that I know . . ."

Jacy slapped the door frame. "Shit!"

"Well, you know, maybe they did go off to get hitched. I reckon if Doreen can find a man who likes her piano playin' as much as Gordon, well, hell—"

"Thanks, Nils."

Jacy turned around and walked back toward the door, wondering what she should do. Her heart drummed irregularly and her breath was short. A voice in the back of her head told her that Gordon was dead, shotgunned by Double X men.

Trying to ignore it, she mounted the dun and started at a gallop toward Big Draw, along the riverside route Gordon would have taken. The recent snow had covered his tracks, so all Jacy could do was head for Big Draw and hope she found nothing amiss along the way.

It was cold and edging on toward late in the afternoon, and the gray clouds turned the color of dirty rags as the sun waned. Crows cawed in the weeds along the river, and chickadees peeped. Jacy paid little attention. Her mind was on Gordon, but she flashed frequently, with a shudder, on Jack Thom and the thick brown stain on his cabin wall.

When she was about three miles from the roadhouse she saw something lying in the weeds and stones left of the trail. Riding up she found a red wagon wheel with several missing spokes and a badly twisted rim. It did not look like it had been there more than two or three days.

Full of dark thoughts, Jacy dismounted and tied her horse to a plum bush, and looked around. Moving farther off the trail and thrashing around in the snowy brush, she came upon an undercarriage to which two more damaged wheels were connected.

She'd been pushing through the hawthorns for only another two or three minutes when she caught up short and squelched a scream. The body of a woman in a green dress and a long fur coat lay before her, its head resting on a deadfall log, face aimed at Jacy with open, staring eyes.

Taking pains to keep her breath steady and even, Jacy pulled her pistol and looked around. Then she took several slow steps, rustling brush and snapping branches, until she stood about ten feet from the body.

She did not have to get any closer to see that it was Mrs. Sanderson and that wolves had been working on her. Gagging, Jacy stepped around the body, making a wide arc, and continued through the brush.

She came upon the rest of the buggy about fifty yards downstream. The horse that had pulled it was nowhere around. Jacy peered at the wreckage, wondering what had spooked the horse so badly that it had left the road and tore though the brush, throwing Mrs. Sanderson and pulverizing the carriage.

She spent the next half hour scouring the brush for Gordon, finding him nowhere near the buggy or Mrs. Sanderson. Finally she turned and walked upstream along a game trail switchbacking through sawgrass and cattails.

She'd walked a half-mile when she stopped to consider turning back. Letting her eyes wander along the river, she saw something lying next to a clump of cattails and several beaver-gnawed saplings.

Walking slowly over, she saw it was a man. Coming within ten feet of him, she saw through the frozen blood, mauled flesh, and torn clothes that it was Gordon—what the wolves had left of Gordon.

She stared numbly for several seconds. Then her breath came short, her heart hammered, her head grew light, and her knees buckled. She dropped to her knees, twisting her torso so that she faced away from the hideous sight. When she could retch no more she dropped her face to the ground and cried.

Finally she lifted her head and straightened her back, forced herself to look at the body. She wanted to know how they'd killed him.

It wasn't hard to see. There was a big round hole through his forehead, as though from a hide hunter's gun, and half the back of his skull was missing. A wedge of tightly folded paper shone between his teeth.

After several moments of deliberation, Jacy steeled herself and crawled over on hands and knees. She pinched the paper between her thumb and index finger and withdrew it quickly.

Standing, she unfolded the sheet to a childishly scrawled "Hasta Luego." The paper was the same kind of small notebook leaf that had been nailed to her door.

"Those sons o' bitches," she breathed. She glanced once more at Gordon lying there, disemboweled by wolves, half his head gone, old eyes still glazed with the horror of his killer's face.

"Those rotten sons o' bitches."

Now she knew what had happened. When they'd shot Gordon, they'd spooked the buggy horse, which fled off the trail, throwing Mrs. Sanderson and destroying the buggy. That's why there was such a gap between the bodies. The wolves had no doubt dragged Gordon into the brush by the river.

Wiping the freezing tears from her face with the backs of her mittened hands, Jacy wondered what she should do with the bodies.

The ground was frozen, so burying them was out of the question. If she had time, she could rig a travois and carry them home, but it was getting late. Soon it would be full dark. Besides, she did not have the stomach for retrieving what was left of the wolf-mangled corpses.

That's all they were, anyway, she told herself. Corpses. Gordon and Mrs. Sanderson were gone. They were in a far better place, and Jacy found part of herself yearning for that place herself.

Another part yearned for justice. So she walked stiffly back to the trail, found her horse, mounted up, and headed for Canaan.

———

Nearly two hours later she was walking her horse, half dead from hard riding, down the main street of the little town on the bone-cold flats above the Little Missouri. The night was pitch-black and starless, and a biting wind was blowing.

Jacy took the horse to the livery and told the night hostler to give the gelding all the oats he wanted, to rub him down good and slow, toss a warm blanket over his back, and put him in a stall with plenty of fresh hay.

She didn't have the money for it, but she'd work out something, if she had to clean stalls in the morning. Nothing was too good for her saddlestock.

Weary and so cold her teeth chattered, she walked up the street to the Sundowner. She hadn't even considered looking elsewhere for the sheriff. She figured he'd be half tight by now, but she had to find him, tell him about Gordon and about the note on her door.

Still angry about Mark Talbot's acceptance of Suzanne Magnusson's invitation yesterday, she hadn't even considered going to him for help. In her eyes Talbot was a traitor, and she wouldn't have asked his assistance had he been the last man on the Bench.

Jacy ignored the men turning to look at her as she entered the saloon. She pointed her eyes straight ahead and made for the bar before she collapsed from exhaustion.

"Good Lord, Jacy, what brings you out in weather like this?" Monty Fisk asked.

"The sheriff here?"

The bartender shook his head. He had a dark look. "Nope. He's over to his house. Ain't feelin' too well. What you need him for, Jacy?"

She removed her hat with both hands and set it on the bar. Staring at it, she said stiffly, "Someone killed Gordon and Mrs. Sanderson on their way home from Spernig's."

Someone close to her shushed the others in the bar, and the room quieted.

"Jesus Christ," Fisk said, looking at Jacy searchingly.

One of the men behind her said, "What's going on, Monty?"

"Shut up, Duke," Fisk said, turning his look back to Jacy. "You look about froze. Your eyebrows are white as the ground outside. Why don't you go sit down by the fire and I'll bring you a cup of coffee?"

"Give me a shot of whiskey right here," Jacy said. "Then I'm gonna go find the sheriff."

"The sheriff ain't in any condition to help you tonight, Jacy." Fisk planted a shot glass on the bar and filled it. "He rode out to Magnusson's and got the hell beat out of him. They tied him to his horse and slapped him home. Couple o' the boys found him out here in front of the hitch rack last night."

Someone grunted a laugh.

Jacy slammed back the whiskey and Fisk refilled the glass. "Why in hell did he ride out there alone?" It contradicted everything she knew about the man.

Fisk shook his head and stepped away to pour refills for a couple of cowpokes.

The cowboy standing next to Jacy said, "That's what we're all tryin' to figure out. First he ain't got no balls at all, then he's got 'em big as a—"

"Al!" Fisk scolded the man.

"Sorry," the cowboy said to Jacy.

Someone behind her said loudly, "Jed Gibbon is a drunken fool. He won't be any help to you, Miss Kincaid."

Jacy turned. Before her, unbelievably, Homer Rinski was coming up from a table circled by Verlyn Thornberg and three of Thornberg's drovers. Rinski blinked his eyes intensely and stared right through her.

He was half shot and as stirred up as a Baptist preacher. Jacy had never seen the man in the Sundowner before. He was far too pious for saloons, or so Jacy had thought.

Rinski stopped a few feet away, the round brim of his black hat sliding shadows across his big, emotional face.

"Jed Gibbon is a cowardly fool," Rinski continued. "If us ranchers are going to remain in the basin and remain alive, we must stand together and stand up for ourselves!"

The room had gone quiet. Someone yelled, "You got that right, Homer!"

Rinski paused dramatically, wide blue eyes probing Jacy's with a rheumy, haunted cast. "That's the only way we'll face down the devil. That's the only way we can stay here and raise our families and live our lives with God's grace, and not be run out of our homes like a bunch of weak-kneed"—he paused, searching for the right word—"pumpkin-rollers!"

"Tell her, Homer!" someone yelled from over by the door.

Rinski's voice deepened, his face reddened, and his countenance grew more and more grave. Startled by the man, Jacy took an involuntary step backward. Rinski took two steps forward, closing the gap between them. The room was so quiet you could hear the wind breathing in the stove's old chimney.

"King Magnusson is the devil, sure as I'm standin' before you now," Rinski continued. "And the Lord does not mollycoddle those who run from the devil. He grants grace to those who face him down and stare him in the eye and say, 'No, I won't run from you, Lucifer. I'll die before I run from the Beast.'"

Jacy stared at the man, spellbound. She'd never seen the quiet, pious Rinski this animated. Rinski stared back at her. She was aware of the other men watching them both and nodding. The room rumbled dully with muttered curses of agreement.

Shortly, Rinski drowned it out. "So, Miss Kincaid, will you stand with us against the Beast? Will you join our army and help us drag the devil from his lair?"

Rinski's eyes narrowed. He slid his face toward Jacy until she could see the pores in his skin, smell the liquor on his breath. He was waiting for an answer. She looked around, not quite sure what to say.

She cleared her throat. "I . . . I'm not exactly sure what you're sayin', Homer."

Rinski blinked, staring in silence. But for the wheezing of the big stove, the room was silent. Then Verlyn

Thornberg scraped his chair back and gained his feet slowly.

Turning to Jacy, he said, "We're gonna hunt down King Magnusson and his men like wild dogs, and make them pay for what they're doin'. You with us?"

Held by Rinski's gaze, Jacy felt her heart beating wildly and sweat popping out on her forehead. She swallowed and licked her lips, thinking.

They were right. Magnusson was the devil, and he deserved to die as horribly as the men he'd killed . . . as horribly as Gordon and Mrs. Sanderson.

Thinking of them lying out there now along the banks of the Little Missouri, their bones gnawed by wolves, Jacy turned her head to look around the room. They were all there, she saw—the six other ranchers on the Bench and their winter riders.

And they were all looking at her . . . waiting for her answer.

She pursed her lips and nodded her head slowly. "Okay," she said. "I'm in."

CHAPTER 16

SUZANNE MAGNUSSON WAS getting dressed for her party. She stood before the freestanding walnut mirror in her big, roomy bedroom with its lace curtains, canopied four-poster bed, and two giant carved armoires her father had shipped up the Missouri River from St. Louis and then hauled by freight wagon to the great mansion he'd built in Dakota. The mansion was a virtual castle. Magnusson had designed it himself after the old fur-company trade houses.

Suzanne had protested the move from the family's original home on the outskirts of St. Louis—a palatial plantation with oak trees, rolling green hills, white board fences, and impressive painted barns and corrals for the family's blooded horses. How her father had even been able to consider leaving such peace and tranquillity still baffled her.

But then it probably hadn't been as tranquil for him as for her. He'd had two brothers to compete with, and an ancient patriarch overseeing the family's main business, a giant brickworks north of the growing city that had become a veritable gold mine since the start of the Western building boom.

So here she was, in northern Dakota, dressing for a party to which a handful of middle-aged businessmen from Big Draw would sit around with their wives and leer at the main attraction whenever her father's back was turned. At least Harrison would be there, Suzanne told herself as she stepped into her lacy blue-silk dress and pulled it up to her waist.

And Mark Talbot would be there, as well, taking her mind off the tawdriness of her present circumstances.

If any man could do that, it was Talbot. They really had a lot in common, she and Mark. Dakota was too small to hold either. Both were well-traveled, schooled in other places and other cultures—in the exotic.

And of course, both were now stuck here for the long winter. Not getting together would be quite mad!

Suzanne arranged the dress's lace so that it fell flat across her opulent bosom, then lifted both hands to her neck and tossed her long dark-brown hair out from her collar. She was thinking of Talbot's broad shoulders, long-muscled arms, and ruddy face with piercingly blue eyes—eyes as blue as the Dakota sky on those rare winter days when the sun shone.

She tipped her head and bit her lip, trying to see herself through his eyes—the long, well-brushed hair cascading down her naked shoulders, ringlets brushing her brows, brown eyes rich with warmth, a fine long neck, a smooth chin, and a generous bosom. She pulled the lace down, revealing a healthy portion of the cleft between her breasts.

Liking what she saw, she pulled the lace even further down. Suzanne wondered what her father's cowboys would give for such a view.

She hadn't had much in the way of bedroom adventure on her last trip. Harrison, recently jilted by a high-ranking British soldier, had dogged her every move, suffocating her with his need, making romance impossible. If Talbot didn't come through for her soon, she'd have to bunk with one of the cowboys.

Horrors! The thought sent a chill up her spine and made her want to jump back in the bathtub.

Someone knocked on the door.

With a start she pulled the dress back up over her bosom. "Yes?"

"It's Father, pet."

Looking down to make sure she was covered, she brushed her hair back from her face, walked to the door, and opened it. "Hello, Papa."

King Magnusson stood there, his six-foot-four-inch frame nearly filling the doorway, a maudlin grin softening his big, rawboned face. Only his daughter could evoke such a look on Magnusson's otherwise severe features. The joke among Magnusson's cowboys, cronies, and eastern partners was that if the old man's wife wanted anything, she went through the daughter.

"Hello, kitten. I just wanted to remind you that the party will begin in about an hour. I didn't want the guest of honor to be late. But I see you're one step ahead of me. Don't you look ravishing!"

She gave a lavish curtsy. "Well, thank you, Papa."

"I also wanted to remind you that this is not going to be the kind of elaborate affair you've gotten used to back east. Mr. Wingate has decided to stay an extra week before heading back to Philadelphia, but I'm afraid the rest of the guests will be . . . well . . . my associates. And your mother and brother, of course."

"And Dr. Long," Suzanne reminded her father with lighthearted censure. The doctor's distinctly effeminate sensibilities, not to mention his fondness for the same sex, had made him an object of Magnusson's private derision.

"Well, yes . . . and that Nancy-boy, of course."

"Oh, Papa, I forgot to tell you—I've invited someone else." She hadn't forgotten; she'd delayed telling him because of what she'd seen her father do to the man who'd visited the ranch three days ago—the man who'd been wearing a sheriff's star.

Magnusson frowned. "Oh?"

"Yes, a Mr. Talbot."

"Talbot?"

"Mark Talbot. He ranches a few miles north of us, I understand. You haven't heard of him?"

Magnusson squinted his eyes and looked beyond his daughter, suddenly thoughtful, not quite sure what to say. He knew that a Talbot had once ranched in the area—on some of the best graze on the Canaan Bench, as a matter of fact—but Magnusson thought he'd run him out of there.

"I . . . don't think I have, no," he said, flustered.

Her eyes were sweetly entreating. "You don't mind, do you, Papa?"

"Mind?"

"That I invited someone else—a nester?"

She smiled indulgently. Suzanne was well aware of her father's hatred for the small ranchers around the Double X; she did not know, however, about the terrorism and murder. That's why his display three days ago had been such a shock to her. She still didn't know what to make of it.

Disregarding her question, he asked one of his own. "How did you meet this Mr. Talbot?"

"Harrison and I met him on the train. He was on his way home from fortune-hunting in Mexico. Isn't that exciting—a real adventurer in our midst! He'll be so interesting."

"Yes . . . interesting," King grumbled.

He could tell that his daughter was quite smitten with this Talbot fellow, and he didn't like it a bit.

He'd always envisioned Suzanne marrying someone from her own circle—one of Magnusson's investors' sons, for instance. A gentlemanly type born with a silver spoon and a penchant for fine brandy and horses, not to mention money. Lots of it. That type, he knew from experience, was in short supply in Dakota.

"And not to worry, Papa," Suzanne continued. "Mark is a clever fellow. I know that if you made him a generous offer for his ranch, he would accept it. He's no rancher—not really—so don't go getting territorial on him."

"What is he, then?"

She shrugged, smiling broadly and tipping her head dreamily. "He's a handsome man of the world."

King tried but was unable to stifle a scowl. But then he thought of something, and he managed a grin and a complete change of tone.

"Well, I certainly am eager to meet this man of the world of yours, Suzanne," he said, putting his big hands on her shoulders and dropping his lantern jaw to look into her eyes. "When is he coming?"

"I hope by six."

"Then for you, my girl, I hope so, too."

"Thank you, Papa."

"Any friend of yours is a friend of mine, pet."

He kissed her on the cheek, too self-absorbed to notice the look of concern in her eyes, and strode down the hall.

When the bedroom door closed behind him, he dropped the phony smile and descended the stairs. In his office he found Randall paging through an English stock journal, his face fixed in that bored, aimless look he always wore.

"Randall, go find Rag and tell him I want to see him."

"What for?"

"Don't ask any of your dull-witted questions now, boy!" Magnusson exploded. He took a deep breath, lowered his voice, and said through gritted teeth, "Go get Rag!"

Talbot sensed someone watching him before he saw movement in a copse of deciduous trees in a low, serpentine swale about a hundred yards to his left.

Whoever was spying on him probably thought they were invisible against the dark background of trees, and to anyone but Talbot they probably would have been, but over the past seven years he had cultivated an acute sensitivity to danger.

Now as he rode he did not slide a second look toward the swale. If someone was drawing a bead on him, a double take might be all the encouragement he needed to squeeze the trigger.

But he didn't want to make an easy target, either, so as nonchalantly as possible, he spurred his horse into a lope. A half second later he was glad he did. Something whistled in the air about six inches behind him. A rifle cracked. The horse pricked its ears and tossed its head.

The idiot sons of bitches had taken a potshot at him!

Talbot hunched down against the gelding's neck and tossed a look toward the trees. The riders were cantering toward him, yelling curses and hunching forward in their saddles. Both rifles belched fire and smoke, and the lead cut the air with angry sighs. One spanged the ground nearby, and Talbot's horse veered from the trail.

Talbot dug his spurs into the gelding's side, urging the horse into a hell-for-leather gallop. He wanted to buy time to dismount and look for cover.

He'd put about two hundred yards behind him when the trail began climbing a low ridge capped with woods. Until now the trail had been relatively free of snow, the wind having cleared it. But Talbot knew the ridge would be covered and no doubt a bitch to negotiate—even on a horse as stalwart as his speckled gray.

A minute later he saw that what he'd been dreading was true. The trail at the top of the ridge was socked under a hock-high drift that appeared to deepen as it climbed. Talbot cursed and looked around. The woods all along the ridge appeared equally socked in. He had no choice but to push ahead and hope the horse would make it.

It made the first ten yards with little problem. Then, plunging into a knee-high drift, it foundered. Screaming, it fell, and Talbot jumped clear, shucking his rifle.

As the horse thrashed in the snow, complaining loudly, Talbot scrambled clear and checked his back-trail. The two riders had split up to cut him off. One was closing fast, crouched low in the saddle.

Talbot slid his gaze back to the horse and watched helplessly as the animal scrambled out of the drift in a spray of snow, and galloped down the other side of the hill, pitching indignantly, stirrups flapping like undersized wings.

Talbot looked around for a hiding place, then scrambled behind the broad trunk of a lightning-topped cottonwood. He pressed the back of his head against the bark, squeezed his rifle, and winced as the horseman approached in a clatter of hooves.

Finally the horse slowed as it neared the drift, and Talbot wondered if the man had spotted his hiding place. Peeking around the tree, he saw the man leading his horse by the reins, coaxing it through the drift.

Getting an idea, Talbot grabbed his rifle by the barrel. When the man was only a few feet away, Talbot stepped out from the tree and raised his rifle like a club.

"I ain't got all day, horse!" the cowboy yelled, facing his agitated mount.

Just as he'd led the horse through the deepest part of the drift, he turned, and Talbot let him have it with the flat of his rifle stock. The man gave a sharp grunt and fell on his back, instantly unconscious, blood flying from his ruined mouth and nose.

The horse squealed and reared, but before it could gallop off, Talbot grabbed the reins. When he'd gotten the horse settled down, he hurriedly tied it to a branch, then swapped coats and hats with the unconscious cowboy. A moment later, he mounted the man's horse and cantered down the trail.

He spotted the other rider about two hundred yards farther on, approaching from his right. Talbot yanked his hat brim low to hide his face.

"Where in hell is he?" the man yelled when he was about fifty yards away.

Talbot shrugged his shoulders and raised his hands, hoping the man wouldn't realize the impersonation.

"He must have went up in the trees," the man yelled. "You didn't see?"

Again Talbot shrugged his shoulders. The man was getting close enough for Talbot to start delineating facial features, so he turned, giving the man his back and acting as though he were observing the high, wooded country to the north.

As the man neared, he said, "You know, goddamnit, Tex, I could kick your ass for taking that stupid shot back there! How in hell did you expect to hit him from that far away?"

He paused, cantered within ten yards, and stopped. "If you woulda waited, we coulda trailed him into the creek bottom on the other side of the saddle and caught him in a cross fire."

Suddenly Talbot turned. "What in hell would you want to do that for?" he said tightly, laying the flat of his rifle stock against the side of the man's head.

The man gave a loud "Hey!" and toppled from his saddle, hat flying and horse recoiling. On the ground he lay stunned for a moment, then went for his gun.

"Uh-uh," Talbot warned, jacking his rifle.

The man was a big, solid cowboy with gray-brown hair and a savage face. Wrinkling his nose and baring his teeth, he stared at Talbot with all the charity of a wounded grizzly. His hat had fallen off, and blood from his torn ear dribbled down his face. "Why, you . . ."

"Forget about me, friend. Who are you and why were you trying to kill me?"

"I'm Rag Donnelly, foreman of the Double X, and you can go fuck yourself."

Talbot squeezed the trigger and spanged a slug off the flat rock five inches right of the man's head. The man cowered, raising his elbow to shield his face.

"Tough guy, eh?" Talbot said.

"Tough enough," the man grunted.

"Not too tough for bushwhacking, though."

The man said nothing, just stared. Talbot met the cold eyes, feeling his anger grow.

Then the man said, "This is Double X range, and you're trespassin'."

"I was invited."

"Not by King Magnusson, you weren't."

"By his daughter. Doesn't she count?"

"I just follow orders."

"Does Suzanne know about those orders?"

Again the man just stared. Blood trickled from his ear down his neck, and strands of his matted salt-and-pepper hair lifted in the breeze.

"I didn't think so," Talbot said. "Drop your gunbelt and get your horse. You, me, and your friend back there are going to a party."

"You're crazy," the man snarled.

"Yes, I am," Talbot said with a wry smile. "And getting crazier by the minute. Now get your horse."

CHAPTER 17

JED GIBBON'S FACE looked like hamburger, and it felt as bad as it looked. The ankle and knee he'd twisted when Magnusson had pulled him from his saddle throbbed with every beat of his heart.

What hurt worse, though, was his pride. This surprised him some. He hadn't thought anything could damage his self-respect worse than the Old Trouble.

But having ridden out to the Double X all horns and rattles, intent on solving the whole problem in one fell swoop, then getting the shit kicked out of him and sent back to the Sundowner on his horse . . . well, that was just a little too much for even Jed Gibbon to take.

Knowing that riding out to the Double X had been motivated by booze and visions of grandiosity made him feel all the more silly. That's why tonight, while the Double X was gearing up for Suzanne's party, and after two and a half days of lying abed healing up and feeling sorry for himself, Gibbon limped into the Sundowner and ordered a glass of apple juice.

"Apple juice?" Monty Fisk said, wincing at both the request and the sight of Gibbon's battered face.

"Until I've got King Magnusson and his men all locked up together in my little jail, I'm gonna be drinkin' apple juice. So lay in a good supply of it. I'll just pretend it's whiskey."

While Fisk looked around under the counter for apple juice, Gibbon turned and scanned the room. It was nearly five o'clock, but the only business was a couple of mule skinners and a sour-looking drummer.

"Where in hell is everybody?" Gibbon exclaimed, feeling a twinge of unrest.

Fisk flushed a little and shrugged. He uncorked a stone jug of apple juice and sniffed the lip. "Probably all to home. It's pretty cold out there, you know."

Gibbon narrowed his eyes at the bartender, who did not return the gaze as he filled a glass. "All to home, you think, eh?" Gibbon said indulgently.

Fisk was feigning a casual air. "No doubt."

Gibbon nodded and dropped his gaze to the glass of juice. A fine froth covered the surface of the glass. Bubbles popped and fizzed. "It don't feel any colder than usual to me."

"Well, who knows?" Fisk said, replacing the jug under the counter. His ears were nearly as red as the stove, which had been stoked to glowing.

Gibbon picked up the glass, scrutinized the pulpy fluid, and took a tentative sip. He made a face and spat the juice on the floor. "How long you been aging that stuff? It's liable to get me drunker'n your snakewater."

"Sorry, Jed, I guess that's a pretty old jug. How 'bout some prune juice?"

"Nah, it'll just get me runnin'. Tell ya what you can do instead, though, Monty—you can tell me where all your regulars are."

Unable to meet Gibbon's eye, Fisk lifted his gaze to the dimming windows at the other end of the long room and fashioned a look of exasperation. "I told you—"

"Cut the shit, Monty. They've gathered somewhere, haven't they?"

"I don't know what you're talkin' about, Jed."

"Those stupid bastards are plannin' an attack on the Double X, aren't they?"

Fisk sighed, giving up the ruse.

"Where are they?" Gibbon prodded.

"I'm not supposed to tell you, Jed."

"Tell me, Monty, or I'll arrest you for tryin' to poison a peace officer."

Fisk sighed again. "They're gathering out at the Rinski place, in his barn. They're pretty fired up this time, Jed; I don't see them calling it off."

"Who says I want 'em to call it off?"

Fisk blinked. "What?"

Gibbon drew his pistol and checked the loads. "Hell, no, I just want to make sure they don't get spanked and sent home like I did. I think it's about time we stop playin' make-believe and get organized . . . don't you, Monty?"

Gibbon was high on his newfound pride, a sense of position and duty he'd never had before. Before, he'd been afraid of death. It had made him feel small and alone—a man apart. Now he realized there were things worse than death, and shame was one of them. Odd how he had King Magnusson to thank for this new insight.

Fisk returned Gibbon's smile and shrugged. "Whatever you say, Jed." The barman paused, his face clouding. "Say, you want me to go with you? I could grab my Greener?"

"No, you stay here and watch the town for me. Consider yourself deputized."

The man said nothing. He smiled with relief.

Gibbon left the saloon and stiffly mounted his horse, reining the big gelding around and heading him south out of Canaan on a snowy trace that rose and fell over a series of watersheds.

It was a little-known shortcut, and he hoped it would get him to the Rinski ranch before the ranchers had pulled out for the Double X. Gibbon had been thinking long and hard about an assault on Magnusson, and he thought he'd come up with a good plan. He didn't want the small ranchers going off half-cocked and mucking it up.

When he pulled onto the headquarters of the Rinski ranch, it was full dark. Gibbon saw a light on in the cabin and the silhouette of someone rocking in the window. The sheriff knew it was Rinski's daughter, and the vision of her rocking there, all alone in the dim cabin, gave him a chill beyond anything this winter night could provide.

Hearing voices in the barn and seeing over a dozen horses in the corral, their steamy breath rising toward the stars, Gibbon rode over and dismounted. He tied his reins to the corral and opened the barn door with a grunt.

A crowd of about twenty ranchmen milled in the alley before him. They stood leaning against square-cut posts and sitting on milk stools and hay bales. Two of Thornberg's men sat with their legs dangling off the end of a wagon box. Another was stretched out in the box, head propped on an elbow. Homer Rinski was drawing in the hay-flecked dust with a stick.

Two lanterns hung from posts, spreading weak yellow light against the shadows at the back of the barn.

The men gave a start at the rasp of the door sliding open. Several went for their guns.

"It's too late!" Gibbon yelled. "I'm King Magnusson and you're all deader'n winter roses!"

The men froze, looking sheepish and slowly relaxing. Gibbon walked into the barn, pushed through the crowd, and shuttled his eyes around the group.

"Damn foolish, not postin' a guard," he said. Then, seeing that one of the "men" was Jacy Kincaid: "What in hell are you doin' here, Jacy?"

"What are you doin' here?" Jacy piped back, as disgusted with the man as any of them. His singling her out because she was female didn't help.

Homer Rinski stood slowly. "She's one of us, Sheriff. She ranches here just like the rest of us, so just like the rest of us, she'll defend her ranch. Lord knows nobody else is gonna do it"—he fed Gibbon a cold gaze—"so we have to."

Gibbon regarded the man with irritation. "Don't get your dander up, Homer. I didn't ride out here to try and quash your rebellion. I rode out here to give you a hand."

The men and Jacy shifted their eyes around, muttering.

"Maybe you better leave this up to us, Gibbon." It was Verlyn Thornberg.

He rose from a hay bale holding a tin cup. The cup wasn't steaming, and Gibbon figured it held something stouter than coffee. Thornberg's eyes were as cold as Rinski's, and his jaw was a straight line beneath the shadow his farm hat slanted across his face.

Gibbon's cheeks warmed. "I deserved that, Verlyn," he said with a slow nod. "I truly did; I understand that. I haven't done one goddamn thing to earn your respect or your trust. But there's something you haven't done to keep me out of your hair, and that's fire me."

Thornberg stepped toward him. "You're fired," he said with a growl.

Gibbon shook his head. "That would take a majority vote of the city council, and"—Gibbon lifted his head to look around—"I see only three or four of you here."

He paused, listening to the angry sighs and muttered curses.

"What's your point?" Thornberg said.

"My point is that we're going to declare war on King Magnusson, but we're going to do it all real legal-like. You're all going to be deputized, and you're going to follow my orders. I'm in charge. Anybody doesn't like that can go on home and keep out of my way."

He stopped to let this sink in. Glancing around the room at the five or six ranch owners and their dozen or so armed riders, he said, "Any questions?"

Someone said very softly, "Shit."

Homer Rinski just stared at Gibbon, as did Thornberg. Neither said anything. They saw the cold determination in Jed Gibbon's wasted face.

"All right, then," he said, straightening. "Raise your right hands and repeat after me . . ."

CHAPTER 18

TALBOT AND HIS two captives made a silent procession along an old horse trail that rose toward the headquarters of the Double X. The sun had gone down and a few stars were kindling in the east, but the west still glowed with last light. A coyote howled. The horses blew and shook their bridles, hooves grinding snow as they walked with their heads down.

The cowboys rode stirrup to stirrup, hands tied snugly to their saddle horns, ankles shackled with rope. Talbot rode behind them, his rifle aimed at their backs. He knew he'd run into more riders, and sure enough, two cowboys appeared on the trail ahead. In the fading light they were little more than shadows.

Behind them the Magnusson mansion rose on a hill like a Bavarian castle lit up for Christmas. It was still half a mile away, but piano music carried crisply on the frosty air, like sonorous strains from a music box.

"Tell them to back off," Talbot ordered the foreman.

Donnelly said nothing.

"Tell 'em."

"Stay back—he's got a gun on us," Donnelly said.

The two horsemen stopped about twenty yards away. "Rag, Tex . . . that you?"

"Give me some room," Talbot ordered. "I mean no threat to you or your boss, but these men bushwhacked me, and if you try the same, I'm gonna let 'em have it!"

They said nothing, just sat there wondering what to do.

Talbot peeled back the hammer on his Winchester. The man named Tex must have heard it. "Get the hell back, goddamnit!" he yelled, his shrill voice cracking.

The men sat there for several more seconds. One mumbled something, and they reined their horses off the trail. One rode left, the other right, and stopped about fifty yards away. As Talbot and his captives continued, the outriders paralleled them, keeping their distance. Talbot eyed them warily.

There were two guards at the open front gate, and Talbot had Donnelly order them back. Both men obeyed. One ran into the mansion. The other watched Talbot from a distance, tracking him, an air of defensive caution in his bearing.

Turning, Talbot saw the two outlying riders drift into the compound behind him. They fanned out around him but kept their rifles pointed skyward—for now, anyway.

Talbot and his captives halted at the hitch rack to the left of the mansion's broad wooden steps. The house rose before them—a great peaked shadow with squares of yellow light dulled by curtains. It blocked out the stars. The deep verandah ran the length of the house, its railing decorated with fir boughs and red ribbons. From inside came the smell of roasting beef.

The piano music had stopped. It was replaced by the muffled sounds of angry male voices and boots pounding wood floors. The pounding increased in volume until the front door was thrown open and a tall figure appeared, strode across the verandah, and stopped.

The man loomed over the steps, partially silhouetted by the windows behind him, his face further obscured by a cloud of sweet-smelling cigar smoke.

"Rag, what in the *hell* is going on!"

The foreman's head lowered as he expelled air from his lungs. The man wagged his head slowly but said nothing. The other cowboy simply stared at his horse, shoulders sagging with the pain of his broken nose.

"Just a little misunderstanding, I believe," Talbot said.

"Who the hell are you?"

"The man you ordered bushwhacked. And you must be the great King Magnusson."

Magnusson said nothing.

"I'm a friend of your daughter's. She invited me out to join your little shindig here tonight." Talbot paused, then added with a curled lip, "Just couldn't wait to meet you."

Magnusson cut his eyes at his foreman. "Rag?"

Donnelly shrugged, gave a phlegmy sigh. "He gave us the jump, boss," he confessed.

"For Christ's sake!" Magnusson growled. To the young man who had followed him onto the porch he said, "Cut them loose." Like the rancher, the young man was decked out in a swallowtail coat, winged collar, and tie. The smell of bay rum was nearly as thick as the cigar smoke.

With a caustic snort, the young man moved down

the steps, producing a pocketknife, and went to work on Donnelly's ropes.

Magnusson stared at Talbot, sizing him up. Smoke puffed around the stogie between his teeth. Talbot stared back. His eyes were cool.

He said, "If I knew for sure this was all a mistake, I could put my rifle away. In the meantime I think I'll keep it aimed your way . . . just so one of your men don't get trigger happy."

Magnusson said nothing. The smoke drifted to the roof over the verandah and hung suspended in the still air.

Another figure stepped out of the mansion.

"Mark, it *is* you!" Suzanne ran up beside her father, her head rising to only his shoulder. She looked from Talbot to Magnusson, frowning. "What's going on?"

"I think we just had a little misunderstanding," Magnusson said with an artificial smile. "Wouldn't you say that's what it was, Mr. Talbot?"

"Yeah, just a little misunderstanding," Talbot said dryly.

Donnelly had dismounted and, holding a handkerchief to the bloody side of his head, regarded Talbot with a rancorous scowl. "Listen, asshole, you may have gotten the jump on me back there, but—"

"Rag!" Magnusson hissed, jerking his head at Suzanne.

Hunching her shoulders against the cold and grasping a night cape closed at her throat, Suzanne looked up at her father. She was dressed for the evening, her long chocolate hair in ringlets. "Papa, what is going on here?" she asked with reproach.

"Just a little misunderstanding," Magnusson said,

his eyes on Talbot. "Rag and Tex mistook your friend here for trouble, that's all."

"Are you all right, Mark?"

"No problem."

Confident Magnusson wouldn't try anything with his daughter present, Talbot slid his rifle into its boot, dismounted, and tied his horse to the hitch rack. He came up the steps and stopped about three rungs down from her. "You look lovely."

He gave a playful bow and reached for her hand. She laughed and gave it to him. He took it gently, gently kissed it, consciously easing the tension.

Laughing, Suzanne turned to her father. "Papa, I want you to meet the incomparable Mark Talbot."

Magnusson was watching his riders leading their horses off to the stables.

Suzanne cleared her throat. "Papa?"

The rancher jerked his head to Talbot. "Oh, yes, of course. Mr. Talbot, how nice it is to make your acquaintance."

They shook hands.

King said affably, "I'd like to apologize for the trouble. I should have sent someone to inform my outriders you were coming. I hope you can forgive my error."

"I'll work on it," Talbot said.

He and Magnusson shared a look of bemused understanding. The rancher gestured at the door, revealing his long horse teeth in a broad smile. "In the meantime, why don't we all get in out of the cold?"

Talbot followed Suzanne into the house. Magnusson paused with a hand on the door and looked again toward the stables.

Randall Magnusson mounted the steps behind him. "Never seen Rag with so much egg on his face," he said with a self-satisfied chuckle.

King had forgotten he was back there. He glanced at his fleshy-faced progeny, said distractedly, "No . . . me neither," then went inside.

King caught up with Talbot and Suzanne in the foyer, where a crushed velvet settee sat beneath an ornately carved mirror. "I'll take your coat and hat, Mr. Talbot," he said. "And your gunbelt, of course. Don't allow the nasty things in the house."

"Of course not," Talbot said dryly as he started removing his coat, looking into Magnusson's steely eyes with a tight smile.

A maid had appeared, a harried, glassy-eyed girl of no more than sixteen. Magnusson gave her Talbot's coat, hat, and gunbelt, and the girl disappeared down the hall. Talbot watched her go, feeling naked without the gun.

Taking his hand, Suzanne led him through a long, narrow sitting room redolent with pre-dinner cigars, and through a pair of glass doors where a long table covered with snow-white linen and silver stretched between two gargantuan stone fireplaces. The head of a mountain goat was mounted over one mantel, the head of a grizzly over the other.

The cedar logs popped and sparked, tossing shadows this way and that, giving the room a warm, intimate feel. There was no intimacy apparent among the four women and six men gathered at the table, however. Dressed to the hilt in dark suits and bright gowns, and sitting ceremoniously in their high-backed chairs, they looked as festive as Lutheran deacons.

Suzanne made the introductions, and Talbot nodded at each guest in turn. Dr. Long sat beside a Mr. Wingate from Philadelphia, a stuffy little wedge of a man with a bald head and carrot-colored mutton-chops connecting beneath his nose.

Harrison appeared bored. Holding a Siamese cat in the crook of his arm, he acknowledged Talbot with a slight dip of the chin and curl of the lip, eyes bright with alcohol. "We meet again, Mr. Talbot!"

"Harrison, I can't believe you're still here."

The doctor shrugged. "To be honest with you, Mr. Talbot, I can't either."

"Why would he leave when our whiskey's free?" Randall Magnusson said with a caustic snort.

He'd retaken his seat next to his father at the head of the table. He was a soft young man with a baby face, a thin dark beard, and chestnut hair hanging over his collar like a beaver tail. Talbot knew now why Rinski suspected Randall and another man of killing Jack Thom and raping Rinski's daughter. Randall had snake written all over him.

A door opened to Talbot's right and a stout, raven-haired woman in a violet dress appeared looking harried.

Suzanne said, "Mark, I'd like you to meet my mother. Mother, Mark Talbot."

"My pleasure, ma'am."

"The pleasure is all mine, Mr. Talbot," Mrs. Magnusson said with an air of distraction, automatically offering her hand, which Talbot shook very gently. The hand was small and plump, with papery skin and several large rings, including a diamond, reflecting the light from the fire.

The woman's breath smelled of booze, and a fine sweat glistened above her bright red lips and on her forehead. Her eyes resembled Suzanne's, but with an additional jaded cast, an oblique pessimism. She appeared both haunted and harried.

Turning to her daughter, Mrs. Magnusson arched

her plucked eyebrows. "I wasn't aware there would be another guest."

Suzanne frowned. "Didn't Papa tell you?"

King shrugged guiltily. "I'm sorry, Kendra—I plumb forgot."

Admonishing her father with a look, Suzanne said, "Fortunately I reminded Minnie to set another place."

Talbot said, "If there's a problem—"

"Oh, don't be silly, Mr. Talbot," Mrs. Magnusson said, breathing heavily and tossing her own reproachful look at King. "The more the merrier! Have a seat." Turning to the others, she said, "I apologize for the delay with the meat, but Minnie and the girls are utterly baffled by the wine sauce King simply cannot live without."

Magnusson said, "They'll make do, Kendra; no point in getting riled."

Her voice grew as stiff as her smile. "They're going to burn it, King. I don't see why we couldn't—"

King raised his eyebrows and opened his hands palm down. "Easy, easy, my dear. Let's not bore the guests with our squabbles. Why don't you take a seat and finish your soup before it gets cold?"

Mrs. Magnusson gave her husband a sneering grin, then took a seat at the other end of the table. The guests slurped soup from their spoons, consciously ignoring the tiff.

Suzanne put a hand on her mother's wrist. "Really, Mother, none of us expect a New York meal in Dakota."

Bernard Troutman, the Big Draw banker, said, "Beggars can't be choosers, Kendra. Whatever you put on our plates will be quite sufficient, or we'll go to bed hungry!"

He lowered his chin for emphasis, then looked

pompously around for corroboration. The other guests vehemently agreed.

Drunkenly, Harrison said with a theatrical twang, "Give me a ham bone and a bottle o' red-eyed Jim!"

"Oh, Harrison," Suzanne scolded.

"And a bunkhouse full of cowboys," Randall mumbled, dipping his spoon.

Suzanne looked at him angrily. "Randall, I heard that!"

"Not to worry, dear girl," Harrison said. "I think your brother is still struggling with his own ... *feelings*, shall we say?"

King grinned over his wineglass. Randall aimed his blunt nose at the doctor and opened his mouth to speak.

Mr. Wingate cut him off with a vociferous throat clearing. "So, Mr. Talbot, where do you hail from, may I ask?"

Shrugging, Talbot sipped his soup—cream of onion with butter pooling in the thick, slightly curdled cream. "Here and there. I was raised on the Bench."

"The Bench?"

"My homeplace is about twenty miles northwest of here."

"Oh, I see." Wingate cut his eyes to Troutman, then to Magnusson. The other businessmen did likewise. The women looked only at each other, growing tense.

King kept his own gaze on his soup. Heartily changing the subject, he said, "I read in the paper just today that Nordstrom and Fontaine bought out McAdams."

There was a ponderous silence. Then King raised his eyebrows at Wingate and the other businessmen.

"No!" one of the Big Draw men exclaimed, catching on.

"Lock, stock, and barrel."

"Well, what on earth will that do to the price of rail shipments?"

"God knows. I'm sending a cable to Stephen Vandemark first thing tomorrow."

The conversation continued similarly throughout the next three courses. No one from King's circle so much as glanced at Talbot. No one, that is, but Randall Magnusson.

Several times Talbot looked up from his venison tenderloin and parsnips, and from his chocolate soufflé with cherries, to see the cherubic-faced young scoundrel considering him darkly. Talbot met the gaze head-on, as if to say, "You murdered my brother, didn't you, you son of a bitch?"

And young Magnusson blinked his eyes coldly, as if to say, "So what if I did?"

Sensing Talbot's agitation, Suzanne put her hand on his thigh. Her flesh warmed him through his trousers, and he suddenly became aroused. It was an obtuse feeling under the circumstances, only vaguely pleasant. Feeling his pants tightening beneath her hand, she looked at him coyly and gave a giggle.

When the dessert was eaten and the maids began clearing the dishes, Magnusson suggested that the men adjourn to the sitting room for sherry and cigars.

Suzanne said, "Oh, Papa, do excuse Mark, please? I want to show him around the house." Turning to Dr. Long, she said, "Would you like to join us, Harry?"

Feeding a scrap to the Siamese in his lap, Harrison shook his head. "No, you two run along. I'll help the girls and Minnie with the dishes. *They* enjoy my company, don't you, dears?"

Twenty minutes later, when the tour was over,

Suzanne led Talbot into a paneled upstairs reading room. There were two deep armchairs covered in floral damask, a mahogany tea table between them, and a brass cuspidor. Against a wall was a serpentine-back sofa with scrolled armrests.

Nearly everywhere Talbot looked were game trophies and marble busts and expensively bound books that appeared to have never been cracked. He wondered how in hell Magnusson had gotten the busts out here without breaking them, and he imagined the poor mule skinners who'd had to haul them from the boat landing at Bismarck. They'd no doubt sweated every gorge and coulee—every knoll!—and kicked up their heels when they'd gotten them on their pedestals in one piece.

"Penny for your thoughts," Suzanne said, lightly poking Talbot in the ribs.

"Oh . . . sorry," he said.

"You've been very quiet. What were you thinking during dinner?"

"Nothing important."

"Liar. You were thinking something dark; I could see it in your eyes."

Silently, she lit two cut-glass lamps, then turned to him with a serious expression. Her long neck—butter colored in the flickering lamplight—looked especially delicate above the low-cut dress that generously exposed the cleft in her opulent bosom.

"I'm sorry about the men who attacked you," she said. "The fault is really mine, not Papa's. I delayed telling him about your coming because . . . well"—her eyes flitted nervously about the room—"because I'm absent-minded." Her eyes came to rest on his and she smiled, perfect lips rising slightly at the corners.

Talbot raised an eyebrow. "Or maybe you were worried he wouldn't allow it."

Her cheeks colored slightly. "That's silly."

"Is it? Those men tried to ambush me, and I don't think it was a case of mistaken identity."

"Mark, please. Why are you being so hostile?"

He looked at her dully. "Someone killed my brother."

Her eyes widened with surprise. "That's awful! When?"

He told her.

She got up and walked to the window but did not look out. "And you think it was Papa?"

He considered telling her about Gordon seeing Randall heading toward the Circle T that day, but decided the water was muddy enough for now. "I don't think he pulled the trigger, but one of his riders did. Amounts to the same thing. He was trying to clean out the Bench for his own herds."

She wheeled around and confronted him, face taut with anger. Gradually her features softened. She raised her eyebrows beseechingly. "Mark, let's please talk about something else."

He tried a smile. There would be little point in torturing her with all this. Besides, it was hard not to acquiesce to a woman like Suzanne Magnusson. She was as willful as she was beautiful. She was also spoiled. It was her least attractive quality, but it somehow added to her power.

Talbot could see how young men could be utterly swept away by her, like a hundred-foot rogue wave flooding the deck while you're hanging in the crow's nest. Young men whose brother had not been murdered by her father, that is.

"Okay," he said.

She wheeled gracefully and collapsed on the sofa, patted the cushion beside her. "Come. Sit with me."

He did as he was told.

"This is my favorite place in the house," she said. "I like to sit here alone and read and dream of far-away places."

"What places?"

"No place in particular. Just anywhere far away—anywhere I haven't been, that is, because when you've been there the romance is gone, don't you think?"

"Dakota's a nice place, in spite of the winter. At least it was."

Suddenly playful, Suzanne sat up and tucked a leg beneath her, then turned to him, folding her hands in her lap.

"Let's play a game." She wrinkled her nose, giggling, and leaned toward him, clasping his hand. "Are you game for a game, Mr. Talbot?"

He shrugged, observing her with puzzled amusement. His murdered brother was the farthest thing from her mind. "Why not?"

"I'll say a noun and you say the first verb that pops into your head."

"Why do you get the nouns and I get the verbs?" he asked, playing along.

"Why, because you're a man of action, of course!"

"Oh."

"Ready?"

He rested his head against the sofa back and nodded.

"Close your eyes. Okay. Stone. Hurry! You have to say the first verb that pops into your head."

"Okay . . . throw!"

"Snake."

"Uh—slither!"

"Horse."

"Ride."

"Cards."

"Gamble."

"Ships."

"Sail."

"Knife."

"Cut."

"Girls."

He opened his eyes. "Girls?"

"Don't think!"

"All right . . . girls . . . uh . . . kiss."

"Kiss?"

He opened his eyes again and gave a laugh. She was looking at him with an expression of wry expectance. "You said to say the first thing that came into my head, and kissing was the first thing that came into my head."

Her eyes flashed slyly. "Have you kissed Jacy Kincaid?"

He laughed again. "What?"

"Have you?"

"No."

"Have you wanted to?"

He thought for a few seconds. "No." It was a lie, but he knew it was what she wanted to hear.

Her expression becoming grave, she lowered her eyes. She spoke quietly, in a throaty, silky voice that reminded him of a gentle breeze combing woods. "Have you wanted to kiss me?"

He stared at her seriously for a moment. "Yes." It was not a lie.

"Why don't you, then?"

He smiled. Unable to help himself, he gently took her face in his hands and kissed her. Her lips were silky. They parted for him slightly.

After a while, she pulled away. "Mark, let's not let any of this trouble my father's involved in come between us, okay?"

"Suzanne—"

"Okay?"

He sighed, gave a nod.

She smiled, said in a throaty, lusty voice, her sweet breath warm on his face, "All right, then, take it away, Mr. Talbot."

His eyes widened. "What? Here?"

"It'll be our secret."

"Suzanne—"

He tried to rise, but she pushed him back against the couch, flattening her breasts against his chest and pressing her full lips to his.

"Suzanne . . ." he said again. But he couldn't help being aroused by her. The feel of her hands in his hair, on his shoulders, on his arms . . . the beguiling taste of her tongue probing his . . . her thighs on his . . . was too much to deny.

She gently bit his upper lip, pushing away. She lowered her head, unbuttoned his shirt, and kissed his chest, murmuring, "You cut a fine manly figure, Mark Talbot. It's been so long since . . ."

He reached into her hair, ran the strands through his fingers. Her head went lower. Her fingers were on his fly.

She whispered, "My God, Mr. Talbot."

"Suzanne . . ."

It wasn't long before he was arching his back and tearing at the sofa with his fists.

It took all his power not to yell.

Somewhere in another realm, boots pounded, shaking the floor. It took Talbot several seconds to realize that someone was climbing the stairs.

"Suzanne!" It was King Magnusson.

Talbot could tell by the increased volume of the pounding boots that the man was within twenty feet and closing.

Talbot tried to push her off him but could not un-clench his hands from the cushions. Finally, at the last second, she lifted her head, ran the back of her hand across her mouth, and smiled with devilish de-light.

"Now you're in trouble, buster!" she laughed.

CHAPTER 19

———◦———

THE TALL, BLOND, barrel-chested visage of King Magnusson burst through the open glass doors like a bull through a chute. He was puffing a stogie and holding a delicate sherry glass in each ham-sized hand.

Talbot was happy to see he didn't have a pistol and wondered vaguely about his own.

Stentorian voice booming, Magnusson said, "Suzanne, your guests are starting to wonder where the birthday girl has drifted off to, and Dr. Long is growing tiresome. Maybe you should make an appearance?"

Suzanne scowled. She'd just thrown herself onto the sofa, a prudent, ladylike distance from her guest, and brushed the hair back from her face, on which she'd managed an impossible expression of cool innocence.

"But they're all so dull compared to Mr. Talbot," she protested, folding her arms like an overly indulged twelve-year-old.

"Suzanne," King scolded.

"Oh, all right." She gazed at Talbot and smiled. "We'll continue this conversation a little later . . . all right, Mr. Talbot?"

He cleared the frog in his throat, gaining his tongue.

"Of course." He wondered if he'd gotten all his fly buttons closed.

Suzanne stood and kissed her father's cheek. "Be good," she whispered in King's ear.

She turned a parting smile to Talbot, who'd risen from the couch, then left the room in a swish of skirts.

Magnusson watched her, smiling. When she was gone, he gave Talbot a sherry and closed the door. He gestured at the couch. Talbot sat down and regained his composure.

He didn't say anything. He wanted Magnusson to make the first move.

Unbuttoning his coat, Magnusson sat across from him in one of the damask-covered chairs. He stretched his long legs across an ottoman and crossed his calfskin boots at the ankles. Rolling his shoulders and wiggling his butt to get comfortable, he spat into the cuspidor at his left, then rubbed his bushy mustaches down with his thumb and forefinger.

"That girl is my pride and joy."

"I can see why," Talbot said with more exuberance than intended. "She's reason enough to have a man killed, I suppose. Was she the reason you tried to have me killed?"

Ignoring the question, Magnusson dug around in his coat for a cigarillo, offered it to Talbot. "Cigar?"

"No thanks."

"Addicted to the damn things," Magnusson said, staring at the coal of the one he was smoking. He lifted his chin and offered a stiff smile. "So we're neighbors."

"I guess you could say that."

"You won't be offended if I ask what your intentions are, will you?"

"Regarding . . . ?"

"Let's start with Suzanne."

Talbot planted an elbow on the arm of the couch and rubbed his lower lip with his index finger, pondering. "What if I said they were serious?"

"Then I'd have to tell you that anything more than friendship is simply out of the question."

"Why?"

Magnusson kept his eyes on Talbot, trying to be as direct as possible. As threatening as possible, too, Talbot thought, without actually drawing a pistol. "Because my daughter belongs to a certain . . . class, shall we say? She is accustomed to certain amenities, creature comforts a man of your station couldn't possibly provide." He grinned coldly and added without a trace of sincerity, "I'm sorry to be so blunt, but if you were a father, you'd understand."

Talbot said nothing.

Magnusson surveyed him critically. At length he squinted and inclined his head, genuinely puzzled. "Have I misjudged you, Talbot?"

"What do you mean?"

"Everyone I run into wants something from me—my daughter, my money, or both. But in you I sense"—he scowled, shook his head—"I don't know; I sense something else."

Talbot stood, shoved his hands in his pockets, and walked to the end of the room. He turned slowly around. He studied Magnusson coolly, then smiled sarcastically. "You're right. I do want something else from you, Magnusson. I want to know who killed my brother."

"Brother?"

Talbot nodded. "I went off to fight in the Apache wars about seven years ago, left my older brother, Dave, home to ranch by himself. About a year ago

I decided to start making my way back to Dakota. Decided it was time to settle down, help out on the ranch. Well, I got back last week and learned my brother was dead."

Magnusson dropped his eyes, studied his boots. "Sorry to hear that."

"He was shot twice in the back of the head."

Magnusson kept his eyes on his boots.

Talbot said, "Someone apparently wanted him off the Bench—wanted our land for theirs—so they killed him. You have any idea who would do such a thing?"

King lifted his head slowly, arched an eyebrow. "You've been listening to the nesters around Canaan."

"Who started the bloodshed?"

Magnusson shrugged. "Who fired the first shot at Fort Sumter?" He looked at Talbot as if awaiting an answer. He got none. "They were stealing cattle."

"Before or after you started stealing their land?"

"I'm not going to argue about land rights. I have the law on my side."

"Legally?"

"Does it matter?"

Talbot sat on the sofa and cut to the chase. "The day my brother was killed, your son and another rider were seen heading toward our headquarters."

A muscle beneath Magnusson's right eye twitched. "Did anyone see Randall kill your brother?"

Talbot said nothing.

"Did anyone see Randall kill your brother?" Magnusson repeated, more forcefully this time, as though reproaching a dim-witted schoolboy.

Talbot stared into Magnusson's eyes, his own eyes dark with fury.

Satisfied he'd gotten his answer, Magnusson nodded. He struggled out of his chair and strode about the room glancing at book spines and straightening picture frames. Finally he turned on his heel, adjusted his paper collar and tie, and regarded Talbot with a look of ceremonial gravity.

"I am sorry about your brother. I offered him good money for his land and he turned me down, but I did not kill him. Nor did I order him killed."

"Maybe your son and a Mr. Shelby Green are doing some independent work out on the range. Homer Rinski thinks it was they who killed his hired man and raped his daughter."

"Nonsense."

Talbot shrugged. "They have quite the reputation for shenanigans, those two."

"An unearned reputation, I assure you. They're . . . boys." Something in his eyes told Talbot the old man wasn't giving his son the credit he deserved.

When Talbot said nothing in reply, Magnusson went back to his chair and sat down. He planted his elbows on his knees, took his sherry in his hands, and regarded Talbot directly. "What do you say we forget about the past? Come to work for me."

Talbot gave a caustic laugh. "What?"

"I'll buy you out. Give you top dollar for your ranch and two hundred dollars a month for your work."

"What kind of work?"

Magnusson sat back in his chair, eyes furtive. "I saw what you did to Donnelly. No one does that to Donnelly. Consider his job yours."

Talbot laughed again. "What makes you think I'd accept such an offer?"

"Because you can't run your own beef on the Bench. I won't allow it."

"If you can't beat 'em, join 'em—that it?"

"Makes sense."

"Go fuck yourself, King."

Magnusson's face fell like a wet sheet. His ears turned red. His voice came tight and even. "You just made the biggest mistake of your life."

Talbot matched the rancher's composure. "And you made the biggest mistake of yours when you declared war on the Bench and killed my brother."

"Get out."

"My pleasure. But we'll meet again—you, me, and your son."

Magnusson looked at the doors. "Rag!"

Rag Donnelly walked in carrying Talbot's coat, hat, gun-belt, and a rifle. There was a bloodstained bandage over the ear Talbot had smashed. Donnelly studied Talbot with cool malevolence—a big, hard-looking man in an old sheepskin coat and a curled Stetson, strategically tipped away from the injured ear.

"Escort Mr. Talbot out the back," Magnusson ordered.

"My pleasure, Mr. Magnusson."

"I don't want him shot—unless he provokes it, that is."

"Yes, sir."

"I know there's a debt to be paid, Rag, but I don't want any trouble tonight."

Donnelly nodded reluctantly, his cold eyes on Talbot.

"Very well, then," Magnusson said.

Talbot had slipped into his coat and hat, buckled the gun-belt around his waist.

"Don't worry—there ain't no loads in your iron," Donnelly told him. "So don't embarrass yourself."

"'Preciate the advice," Talbot said. Turning to Magnusson, he asked, "What are you going to tell your daughter?"

Glancing at Donnelly, Magnusson said with a shrug, "The truth. That you were using her to finagle a job out of me—Rag's job. When I turned you down, you threatened to join the other small ranchers in rustling me blind." He smiled. "So I had you thrown out."

Talbot returned the smile, said dryly, "Thanks for the lovely evening."

"Until we meet again, Talbot."

Talbot nodded and walked out the door. Donnelly followed him with his Winchester aimed at his spine.

They went down the back stairs and out the back door. From the sting in his cheeks, Talbot guessed the temperature had dropped ten degrees. The sky was very clear, hard white stars scattering in all directions. A faint luminosity shone in the east, where the moon was about to rise.

"Your horse is in the corral," Donnelly growled. He jabbed the rifle in Talbot's back. "Get movin', slick."

"How's your ear? It looks sore," Talbot said.

"Fuck you."

Inside the corral, Talbot untied his horse's reins from a slat and prepared to mount up. "Well, thanks for everything, Rag."

"Oh, there's just one more thing," Donnelly said.

Talbot had sensed it coming long before he saw the shadow on the snow. He ducked, heard the smack of the rifle butt against his saddle. The horse started and jumped sideways.

Before Donnelly knew what had happened, Talbot had his revolver out. He flipped it, clutched the barrel, and swung the butt hard against Donnelly's bandaged ear.

"God-*damn*," the foreman said in a pinched, breathy voice. Both legs buckled and he dropped to his knees, then to his hands. In the light cast by the distant mansion, Talbot saw the bandage turn dark.

"Fuck," the foreman cursed again.

Talbot reached under Donnelly's coat for his pistol and tossed it over the corral. Then he picked up the rifle and jacked it empty, tossed it down. He grabbed his reins and mounted his horse.

Surveying Donnelly, who was fighting to stay conscious, Talbot said, "Sorry again, Rag. But like you said, you'll have another chance to even things up. Real soon."

Then he spurred the speckled gray and galloped off into the night.

CHAPTER 20

IT WAS NEARLY midnight and spine-splitting cold, and Gibbon knew the temperature would continue dropping for several more hours. He'd had the smarts to don fur boots—he'd vowed not to wear his stovepipes again until May—but his toes still ached and he felt the cold creeping up his legs like death.

He considered halting the posse and dismounting to stomp some feeling back in his feet, but he'd ordered the last stop only half an hour ago, and he didn't want to look like a sissy in front of Verlyn Thornberg. What he wouldn't give for a snort to dull the pain in his battered body and to cook out the cold!

When the procession had descended a broad hogback crowned by a lightning-split cedar and a low stone pillar, Gibbon raised a hand and halted his horse. He stared ahead, listening.

"This the place?" Rinski said.

"Yes. Keep your voice down."

"How do you know this is the place?"

Thornberg gave a dry chuckle. "If there's one thing Jed knows, it's where the roadhouses are, don't you, Jed?"

"Speak up, Verlyn—they can't hear you in Mandan," Gibbon said.

He handed his reins to Jacy Kincaid, who'd been riding directly behind him. He was pleased now that she'd come along; her presence seemed to keep Thornberg's riders peaceable if not sober.

"I still say we go on to the Double X," Thornberg said. "Deal with the head honcho right up and straight away."

"Drag the devil from his lair," Rinski agreed.

Gibbon shook his head. "That's exactly what he'd want us to do. No, we'll take out a few of his men now, a few later, and force old Magnusson to come to us shorthanded."

"Makes sense to me," Jacy said. "Besides, they're probably all drunker'n skunks down there."

"If they're down there," Flint Skully said. He and his hired man, a big Pole with a smallpox-ravaged face, were sitting their horses back in the pack a ways.

"They'll be there," one of Thornberg's riders said, holding a flask. "There's always a half dozen of 'em down there, poking Gutzman's Injun whore."

"What did I tell you boys about drinkin' on the job?" Gibbon snarled.

The cowboy shrugged and passed the flask to the rider next to him. He gave an insolent smile. "Sorry, Sheriff."

Gibbon snorted angrily and shucked his Winchester. He limped up the trail and stopped just below the ridge so the moon did not outline him against the sky, and cast a look at the saucer-shaped valley below.

The trail snaked down between a low-slung cabin and two hitch-and-rail corrals and a barn that leaned slightly northward. The slough flanking the roadhouse was frozen and moonlit and surrounded by marsh grass and cattails. Low buttes climbed beyond, their knobby, snowless crests showing clearly in the moon-light.

The cabin was well lit, and there were at least a dozen horses in the paddocks.

Gibbon turned and walked back to the posse and said in a low voice, "I'm gonna go down and make sure it's only Magnusson's men down there. I don't want to see innocent people killed here tonight."

"On that ankle?" Jacy said.

"I'll make it."

"No, you won't. I'll go."

Gibbon shook his head. "Not a chance."

Thornberg said, "She's fleet o' foot, Gibbon. You're about as graceful as a bear on snowshoes."

Gibbon thought for a moment. He nodded. To Jacy he said, "Hurry, and stay low. The moon is behind you. Whatever you do, don't let them see you."

"You gotta gun?" Verlyn Thornberg asked her paternally.

Jacy dismounted, handed her reins to Gibbon, and said with a grunt to Thornberg, "Do I have a gun? Do you have a gun, Verlyn?"

She shucked her Henry with a snort and started down the trail.

Behind her, one of Thornberg's men said, chuckling, "Guess she told you, boss," and lifted the flask to his lips.

------·------

The hill was studded with several low shrubs, rocks, and crusty snowdrifts, and Jacy wove around them carefully, keeping her eyes on the door of the road-house below.

Frozen grass crunched under her boots, and the smell of willow smoke issuing from the chimney was sharp in her nose.

Approaching the cabin, she held her breath and pressed her back against the west wall, then moved to a frosty window. The sound of voices grew. She could feel heat escaping through the loose chinking between the logs and around the window.

She looked inside through the frost, swept her eyes across the room. Five men sat at a table about six feet from the glass. Another six men occupied a second table on the other side of the iron stove. She could tell they were Double X men by the way they carried themselves, by the smug looks on their faces, and by the oiled holsters tied down low on their thighs.

The only one not directly associated with Magnusson was the proprietor, a big, bearded German named Gutzman who bought Indian girls for whiskey, and put them to work in the lean-to addition at the back of the roadhouse. He stood stoking the fire, swaying drunkenly, his back to the window.

He paused, laughing, and lifted a smile at the second table. "Yah, you cun bet Verna vos surprised to see him!" he yelled, his guttural voice rattling the window. "He said he vos going to shoot dem bot, so Verna skedaddled off da Mexcan, grabbed da Mexcan's gun, and let him haf it six times tru da heart, hah, hah, hah! And dat vos de end off Dieter Ross— hah, hah, hah!"

One of the other cowboys, looking up from his cards and ignoring the German, frowned at a deer hide door at the back of the room. "Come on, Chet! Save some for me, old hoss!"

"Kiss my ass, Shorty!" came the reply.

Gutzman said to the door, "No, no hogging da girl. Your fifteen minutes is up, Chit." Turning to the other men, he said with a big, red-faced grin, "I can't help it if dat's all you got up. Hah! Hah! Hah!"

Jacy crept around the corner of the cabin and

peered in the window of the lean-to. A bald man and an Indian girl moved together on the bed, under a ratty buffalo blanket.

The man was on top, pumping furiously, propped on his outstretched arms. He'd arched his back and lifted his head until his face was parallel with the wall, eyes shut tight with concentration. His bald head was a mass of hideous red scar tissue, marking him as an old Indian fighter whose scalp probably decorated the mansion of some aging Sioux warrior.

The Indian girl beneath him lay with her head turned to the window; her large coffee eyes stared unseeing. Her head moved with the force of the man's thrusting hips.

Jacy could hear the man's frustrated grunts and groans, the singing of the bedsprings, and the scraping of the iron headboard against the wall. But it was the Indian girl's tenantless eyes that haunted her. She'd never seen anyone look so empty.

It took Jacy several seconds to tear her eyes from the Indian girl's. Then she moved to the other side of the cabin and peered into the one remaining room— the kitchen—and found it empty. She headed out across the front yard toward the posse on the hill. When a latch scraped and hinges squeaked, she dropped, hitting the ground on her chest.

Shit!

She jerked a look at the cabin. The front door opened, angling light across the verandah. A shadow moved and a silhouette appeared. Boots scraped.

"Shut the goddamn door!" someone yelled.

The door closed, snuffing out the light. The light from the two windows, one on each side of the door, remained.

Jacy held her breath, silently cursing herself for a fool. She should have gone back the way she'd come.

A man gave a sigh. The shadow moved out from under the awning to stand at the edge of the step.

Silence.

Oh, shit, oh, shit!

Then the man sighed again and water puddled onto the snow. Jacy tried to make herself as small as possible, hoping that if the man saw her, forty feet away, he'd mistake her for a snowdrift or a feed sack fallen from a wagon.

Either the man had a bison-sized bladder or he'd been holding his whiskey for hours; the tinny stream seemed to trickle on forever. Jacy pressed her face against the cold snow and fought the urge to lift her rifle and shoot the son of a bitch.

Finally the flow ebbed to spurts. The man grunted, shuffling his feet. When the spurts finally ceased, he gave another sigh and turned back to the roadhouse. He threw open the door.

"Shut the goddamn door!" came a yell from within.

The door closed. Jacy scrambled to her feet and hightailed it up the hill.

"You should have come back the way you went," Verlyn Thornberg scolded when she walked up to the posse milling in the hollow.

"Shut up, Verlyn," Gibbon snapped. "She's no less schooled at this than you or me or any of us." Turning his eyes to Jacy, he said, "You think that cowboy saw you?"

Jacy was standing by her horse, bent over with her hands on her knees, trying to catch her breath. It had been a hell of a run up the hill. She was as afraid as she was exhausted. This was turning out to be a bigger deal than she'd expected. Lying back there waiting for the drunk cowboy to finish draining the dragon, she'd realized she might actually get shot. Or worse. . . .

With a bunch of sleazy hammerheads like the ones down there, she could end up like Mattie Rinski and the Indian girl.

She sucked in a deep breath, straightened, and shook her head. "If he'd seen me they'd be shooting by now."

Thornberg said, "Or they're playin' dumb and waiting for us to make the first move. Hell, they could be slipping out the back and surrounding us right now—as we speak!"

"Keep your voice down," Gibbon said.

"They didn't see me, Verlyn," Jacy said.

"How many are in there?" Gibbon asked her.

"Fourteen. Twelve in the main room, one in the back with an Indian girl." Her voice was tight. "Looks like they're taking turns."

One of Thornberg's men said, "That'd be Gutzman's whore." There was humor in his voice.

Jacy didn't like it. She told the man so with a hard look. He stared back, but the lines in his round face flattened out.

"All right, all right," Gibbon intervened. "We're here to fight *them*, not each other." He paused, looking around the posse.

Thornberg stood holding his reins. Homer Rinski sat his mount to Thornberg's right and a little behind. He hadn't moved since they'd stopped in the hollow. His face was dark under the round brim of his hat, but Gibbon sensed his eyes blazing as he looked off toward the ridge and the roadhouse below.

Two of the other ranch owners were standing and smoking cigarettes with an air of desperation, as though they'd be the last cigarettes they'd ever smoke. The rest of the men remained mounted, heads hunched and shoulders pulled in against the cold, breath jetting from their mouths and noses.

Thornberg's five riders were the only ones who did not seem afraid. They'd had too much liquor to be afraid of anything. This was just a game. A game with higher stakes than their usual winter-evening rounds of high five or blackjack, but a game just the same.

That knowledge chilled Gibbon to his soul, but they'd come too far to turn back now.

He gave a deep sigh, let it out slow. "Okay," he said. "Let's assume they didn't see Jacy and take up the positions I talked about back in the barn. Remember, no smoking once we're off the ridge, and nobody shoots before I do."

CHAPTER 21

GIBBON HAD NEVER swapped lead with more than two men at a time before, and he'd had to do it only once, when a couple of scatterbrained grubliners got tired of stealing chickens for supper and held up the Landmark National Bank in Canaan.

Neither man had a good working pistol, and Gibbon and his deputy at the time—Lon Donner, who literally lost his head during the Old Trouble—plugged one in the wrist. Gibbon shot the other in the neck though he was aiming for the man's shoulder.

That had been a mild skirmish—four boys playing cowboys and Indians—compared to how this was likely to pan out. Twelve drunk Double X men and a half-assed posse from Canaan with at least five drunks of its own. Gibbon didn't know how wasted Thornberg was, but he'd smelled booze on his breath, and even Homer Rinski reeked of the bottle. What the hell was the world coming to, when Bible-slapping Christians turned to guns and alcohol?

Gibbon only hoped that the Double X men were as tight as they normally would be this time of night and that his men would be able to take out a *few* of Magnusson's men before the Double X crew filled them all with lead. That would be something, anyway.

Now he and Rinski crept down the trail in the dark as the others fanned out to take their own positions at various points around the roadhouse. Gibbon crouched low and was irritated to see that Rinski was not doing likewise. The old soul-burner was strolling down the trail as though en route to a Saturday-night prayer meeting, the only difference being the double-barrel side-by-side he carried under his arm.

Gibbon approached the corral, where a dozen saddled horses milled, turning their heads to watch the strangers and to sniff the air. The men were spooky but not spooky enough to warrant the commotion of driving them off.

"Easy now, easy," Gibbon whispered, crawling between the slats.

When he and Rinski had hunkered down behind the corral and a feed trough filled with green-smelling hay, with a good view of the cabin, Rinski rumbled darkly, "What are we waiting for, Sheriff?"

Gibbon frowned. The wrath of the righteous. "I'm waiting for everyone to get settled. Keep your shirt on, Homer."

Hawk nose aimed at the cabin, from which the sound of table slaps and occasional hoots rose. Rinski said, "I don't want them to be so drunk they don't know what's happening to them, that they don't know what they're payin' for."

Gibbon observed the man sharply, trying to restrain his anger. "Just remember," he said, "I'm giving them a chance to give themselves up. Nobody shoots until I've done that."

Rinski's voice rumbled up out of his chest like distant thunder. "Those who ignore the law do not deserve its protection."

"I couldn't agree with you more, Homer, but we're

not out here to draft an amendment to the Constitution."

"I don't care about man's law; I care about God's law," Rinski said. He stared at the cabin like a dog fixes on a treed cat. Gibbon laughed ruefully and shook his head.

When he thought the rest of the posse had had enough time to gain their positions, he took a deep breath and released it. "All right, I'm gonna call 'em out."

"Hold on," Rinski growled, and nodded at the cabin.

The door squeaked open and two men in sheepskin coats and wool collars stepped onto the porch, descended the steps, and walked into the road, unbuttoning their flies. One was tall and broad-shouldered; the other was of average height, and thin.

The shorter man said, "Just one more jack and I could be pokin' some *real* pussy in Milestown."

"It's always one more card with you, Chris," the tall man said. "One more card and you're sitting on top of the world."

"Oh, you didn't see my hand, man. You didn't see it."

As the tinny sound of urine hitting the hard ground rose on the still night, the door opened again, and another man stepped out. A big round figure in a buffalo coat, he took a single step, turned to the right, and opened his pants, keeping his head down.

"What you two doin' way out there—playin' grabby-pants?" he said when he'd gotten a steady stream going.

The tall man said in a throaty voice, languorous with alcohol, "We're enjoyin' the stars."

"Shit," said the man by the door.

"You stole my jack, Cobb," the man called Chris said.

Cobb gave a soft, high-pitched hoot.

"It's gonna be payback time, ya sorry son of a bitch," Chris said.

"Not for me," Cobb replied. "I'm throwin' in and spendin' the rest of the night with the whore."

"No way, amigo."

"Sí, sí, señor. I paid Gutzman off that pile I just cleared from you boys." He gave another hoot, louder this time.

"Come on, Cobb. I was close, man. I was really close."

"Shut up," the tall man said. He was staring straight out at the corral. "Somethin's got the horses riled."

The short man watched and listened for five seconds then said, "Coyotes."

"Prob'ly," the tall man said. His voice was flat.

He took a step toward the corral. The short man stayed in the road. Cobb was still urinating off the porch, but his head was turned toward the corral.

Gibbon sighed with a grunt in it, and stood. "Hold it right there."

The tall man and the short man, Chris, stiffened. Their hands jerked toward the pistols on their hips but stopped before they got there.

The tall man in the road said, "Who the fuck are you?"

Gibbon was about to answer the man's question when out of the corner of his eye he saw Homer Rinski straighten his long frame and lift his shotgun to his shoulder. "Your executioner!"

Rising and arcing across the yard, like the voice of God, Rinski's proclamation was followed by the glass-shattering boom of his bird gun.

Thrown high by the blast, the tall man hit the ground on his back and wailed like an animal.

Gibbon yelled, "Goddamnit, Homer!"

The short man palmed his revolver and Rinski gave him the second barrel, driving him into the air and back about six feet. When he hit the ground he turned on his side, gave a shake, and lay still.

"What the hell's goin' on!" someone yelled from inside the cabin.

The man on the porch squeezed off three quick pistol rounds, fumbling for the door. Before he could get it open, Gibbon shot him twice in the chest. The door opened and Cobb fell into the cabin.

Hurdling the dead man in the doorway, two other men ran out of the cabin and ducked behind the water trough.

"We're the law, and you're all under arrest!" Gibbon shouted, his heart pounding now, his mouth dry and coppery with excitement and fear.

He heard the sporadic bursts of gunfire as the posse began slinging lead. Thornberg's men, no doubt—the stupid sons of bitches. But he knew they were just following Rinski's lead.

"The hell you say!" one of the Double X men yelled. "What's the charge?"

"Rustlin' and murder," Gibbon replied. He cupped his hands around his mouth and yelled to the posse, "Hold your fire! Hold your fire!"

The shooting thinned, but someone was still slinging a few rounds at the back. Probably Thornberg himself.

Gibbon exploded, "I said hold your *fire*!"

The words had barely left his mouth when one of the Double X men by the water trough lifted his revolver and raked off two quick rounds, one of which thunked into the corral about six inches from Gibbon. The other plugged a horse in the corral and set it to screaming. All the horses were running circles around the corral now, knocking against the rails, so on top of everything else, Gibbon had to worry about getting trampled.

He ducked. "You're surrounded, you stupid son of a bitch!"

"Go diddle yourself!"

Rinski blasted the water trough with buckshot. Gibbon was about to yell at him when another man appeared in the doorway. He could tell from the German accent it was Gutzman.

"Holt your fire, holt your fire!" Gutzman bellowed. "Vot's dis?"

"This is Jed Gibbon from Canaan, Gutz. We're here for the Double X men. They come peaceful, no one gets hurt."

"Ve are all just haffing a goot time here tonight," Gutzman said sorrowfully, as if defending a passel of good-natured schoolboys.

"Tell 'em to come out, Gutz, with their hands up."

Gutzman turned his head and said something. He stood there, listening to the reply. Then he turned his face back to Gibbon. "I haf girl," he said, his voice low and dark. "An innocent girl."

"Send her out."

He turned away from the door and returned to it, clutching a girl by an arm. He pulled her in front of him and they stepped onto the porch together. Gibbon could tell that she was barefoot and wrapped in nothing but a blanket. The temperature was falling below zero, and she had to be chilled to the bone, but she gave no indication, no struggle.

"Put some clothes on the girl, Gutz. Then you and her come on out."

The big German stood behind the girl, his hands on her shoulders—her head came only halfway up his chest—and glanced uneasily into the cabin and at the two men crouched behind the water trough. Apparently, he didn't like what he saw.

"N-nein," he muttered fearfully. "Ve come now."

He pushed the girl down the steps and into the wagonyard, steering her with his hands.

Gibbon cursed. "Come on, Gutzman. She's gonna freeze to death out here."

Gutzman ignored him. He pushed the girl into the road, jerking his head around and giving a little skip as he hurried toward the corral. The girl moved stiffly before him, half running as Gutzman pushed her along.

Suddenly another figure appeared in the cabin door swaying as though drunk. The man was holding a shotgun or a carbine—Gibbon couldn't tell which. The sheriff's throat ached and his heart skipped a beat. Gutzman and the girl were between him and the cabin, in the line of fire.

"Get down!" Gibbon yelled.

He started bringing his Winchester to his shoulder when the man in the doorway said thickly, "This is for interruptin' our card game, ya sumbitch, Gibbon!"

The gun in the man's arms—a shotgun—boomed and flashed, and Gibbon jerked with a start. Gutzman grunted and fell headfirst into a pile of horse apples, knocking the girl to her knees.

Turning to see behind her, she gave a clipped scream as the shotgun exploded again. She flew back, arms flung above her head, releasing the blanket, her naked body skidding on the frozen ground and rolling against a corral post.

Feeling several pellets tear his coat and sting his cheek, Gibbon raised his rifle and fired, and the man in the doorway flew backward into the cabin, shotgun leaping from his arms.

The men behind the water trough lifted their heads and raised their pistols. They'd squeezed off only one shot apiece before Gibbon and Rinski brought their weapons to bear, stood the men up and flung them back against the cabin—dead.

That was all the encouragement the rest of the posse needed to resume shooting. The night exploded with the cracking of rifles and six-guns and the regular blasts of Rinski's shotgun.

Smoke swirled like fog in the moonlight and the air was redolent with gunpowder. The horses screamed as the bullets from their own riders tore into the corral. Finally the saddled mounts bolted through the rails and off behind the barn.

Between the darkness and the fog, Gibbon couldn't make out the individuals in the cabin; he keyed instead on the orange flames leaping from their guns and on the moonlit puffs of smoke. It seemed to work. Three times he heard a grunt or a curse following the bark of his Winchester.

It was fairly easy pickings. With the Double X men pinned down in the cabin, with no means of escape, it was just a matter of time before the posse did them in. Gibbon knew that if he hadn't had the element of surprise—and, he had to admit, the trigger-happy Rinski—things could have gone very differently.

Now they were going like he'd wanted them to, but he didn't feel good about any of it. It wasn't just Gutzman and the dead whore, either. It was the thunder of the gunfire and the yells and screams from the cabin and the wails of the dying horses in the corral behind him: the whole bloody mess.

He'd wanted to feel redeemed. Instead, he just felt dirty.

The shooting from the cabin petered out about

twenty minutes into the fight. Ten minutes later it stopped altogether.

Gibbon knew the Double X men were dead. They hadn't had a chance in such tight quarters. If they hadn't been so drunk they might have tried running for it—slipping out the windows and scattering. But the booze had made them clumsy and disoriented and incapable of coming up with any kind of defensive strategy.

So they ran around like rats in a cage as the bullets flying through the windows and through the chinking between the logs turned them into hamburger.

Gibbon put his rifle down, but the rest of the posse kept shooting. No one was returning fire, but they kept shooting just the same, with as much vigor as they'd started with. Gibbon knew they wouldn't stop until they ran out of bullets.

He shook his head, slumped down behind the feed trough, rolled a cigarette, and smoked it down to a half-inch nub.

The shooting thinned. The posse was running out of bullets. Gibbon took a deep drag from his quirley, burning his fingers, and glanced over his shoulder at the cabin. There was an orange glow in the windows.

Fire, he knew. A spark from one of the bullets had ignited kerosene.

Well, that should do it. He could go home now, wait for Magnusson to make the next move.

Out of the corner of his eye he saw a figure crouch down before the corral. Turning his gaze, he saw Jacy Kincaid approach the Indian girl.

Gibbon bent his weary body between the corral slats with a grunt. Flames from the cabin spread quickly. They were licking through the windows, spreading a burnt-orange glow on the ground around the roadhouse.

The gunfire had ceased and men were whooping and hollering, probably passing the flask again. Gibbon could see their silhouettes as they moved in to admire their handiwork.

Gibbon turned to Jacy. She was kneeling over the Indian girl, rifle across her knees. She stared at the girl but kept her hands on her rifle. Her hat was tipped, covering her face.

Finally she lifted her eyes to Gibbon. Neither of them said anything. Finally Jacy stood and walked up the road toward the horses. Gibbon watched her go.

"God has been served here tonight."

Gibbon turned. Homer Rinski stood behind him, looking at the cabin, the orange flames reflected in the hard planes of his face.

"Say what?"

"God has been served here tonight," Rinski repeated.

Gibbon turned to watch the cabin burn, sighed fatefully. "Well, let's see what the devil has to say about that."

Then he turned and followed Jacy up the trail.

CHAPTER 22

IN THE MAGNUSSON mansion, Charles Franklin Wingate III grinned in his sleep. King Magnusson's primary eastern investor was dreaming of Suzanne. The lovely girl was asking him to remain at the ranch for another week.

She was clad in only a sheer chemise that clearly outlined her breasts. Her hair hung loose about her shoulders and her eyes were smoky with lust.

"Oh, *please* stay, Charles," she begged. "I know you don't want to be disloyal to Abigail, but I feel we're just starting to get to know each other."

She smelled of lilac-scented orris soap, and he didn't know which aroused him more—her face, which fairly glowed with unadulterated beauty, or the swollen orbs of her breasts, which poked at him wantonly, prodding him from his characteristic reserve.

"Really, Suzanne, I *must* go."

"Oh, *please*, Charles. There are so few men like you in Dakota . . . sensitive yet virile."

She ran her hands over the thick head of hair he'd lost fifteen years ago, pressed her warm lips to his. As she ground her hips against him, wrapping a bare leg around his waist, he engulfed her in his arms and fairly moaned with desire.

Someone pounded on the door. "Chuck!" It was King Magnusson.

Wingate's heart did a somersault. He pushed the girl away as the door opened and Magnusson's big, ruddy face appeared beneath his cherry-blond mane. The blue eyes flashed.

"King!" Wingate cried.

"In the flesh, old chap. Up and at 'em—let's pound some grub and get ready to ride!" Magnusson studied the easterner. "Remember? We're going hunting this morning. I'll send Minnie up with your bath."

He turned away and turned back. "Oh, uh . . . sorry to interrupt."

"Huh?"

"Sounded like you were having quite the dream. Anyone I know?"

Wingate must have looked as stricken as he felt, because King said in a hurry, "Don't worry, I enjoy a hot fancy now and then myself."

Leaning forward he added conspiratorially, "Tides me over between business trips." He winked and pulled his head back. The door closed, and his boots pounded away down the hall.

Sitting up in the bed, the tail of his nightcap wrapped around his neck, Wingate stared at the door and tried to quell the pounding of his heart. He ran a hand absently over his red muttonchops.

"Oh," he said weakly, swallowing. "Oh, my goodness . . . it was just a dream."

As he looked around the room, getting his bearings, his relief was replaced by bitter disappointment. The girl had not visited his room with her lovely breasts; she hadn't wrapped her legs around his waist and pressed her warm lips to his.

He lifted a hand to his head. His hair hadn't grown back, either.

"Goodness me," he grumbled, and swung his old legs to the floor. Among Magnusson's associates, King was infamous for throwing his eastern visitors into potentially humiliating "western" situations. It was a sort of game, Wingate knew, and he supposed it was his turn to shrink from a charging grizzly or miss a preposterously easy shot at an elk or some other four-legged beast.

Slouched there on the edge of the bed, waiting for his bath and staring out the frosty gray window—not a tree in sight—Wingate wished he were home. In New York he was not tormented by bored western ranchers and their buxom daughters.

"Hunting, for Christ's sake. In this weather? That man's going to be the death of me yet."

A half hour later he was bathed and dressed, but he still hadn't worked up any enthusiasm for Magnusson's hunt. Oh, well, give the sadistic bastard another story to tell at the Cheyenne Club, he thought as he headed for the dining room.

"Where you going, Charles?" the devil himself hailed as he passed his office.

Wingate walked back to the trophy-laden study. King was standing in the middle of the room decked out in a buffalo coat and a fur hat. He was smoking a fat cigar and holding a rifle, caressing its glistening walnut stock with a white rag. Another, similar weapon stood against his desk. A hot fire popped in the hearth.

Wingate frowned. "Am I too late for breakfast?" he asked meekly.

"Oh, not at all," Magnusson said. "I thought we'd go out to the bunkhouse for breakfast. I like to rub elbows with my men now and then. Keeps me in touch. Besides, the cook out there can whip together the best chuck you'll ever taste in your life. A real treat."

"You don't say," Wingate said, crestfallen. He'd been looking forward to prunes stewed in French wine, cheese croissants, and Minnie McDougal's wonderfully airy omelets.

Magnusson rubbed the rag down the stock of his rifle and nodded at the other gun leaning against his desk. "There's your rifle, Charles. Fetch it up and treat it like a baby. It might just save your life today." He looked at Wingate and grinned wolfishly.

When Wingate had decked himself out in a borrowed coat and hat like Magnusson's, he hefted the heavy beast of a rifle—it must have weighed fifty pounds!—and followed the rancher outside. The dour and brooding Randall Magnusson brought up the rear.

They moved down the slope behind the corrals toward the bunkhouse—a long, narrow building of logs, with two brick chimneys sprouting thick gray smoke smelling like bacon.

Magnusson knocked and opened the door.

"Boss," Rag Donnelly said as though startled. He was sitting at the table nearest the door and the first of the two stoves, drinking coffee and smoking a cigarette. His hat was off, exposing the fresh bandage on his ear.

There were seven or eight other men in various stages of dressing and washing, crowding around the farthest stove. They regarded their visitors from the Big House with subtle suspicion, cutting their eyes at Rag.

A big, gray-haired man with a bushy mustache and deep-sunk eyes stirred a pan of potatoes sizzling in bacon grease. A cigarette drooped from his lips, a grimy towel was thrown over his shoulder, and the thick gray hair on his chest grew out of his long johns.

"Have a seat, boss—just about to throw some vittles on the table," he said with too much exuberance, his eyes on Rag.

"Just thought we'd come out and see how badly you're poisoning my men, Lute," King said, throwing his mittens on the table beside Donnelly. "Hope we haven't interrupted anything." His gaze circled the room, and he realized what was wrong. Men were missing—more than should be out on the line at this hour.

"Where is everybody, Rag?"

"Who's that, boss?"

"You know who." Magnusson's voice became tight, his eyes hard. "The men you're paid forty dollars a month to keep track of."

Donnelly looked at the other members of his crew. He was in a bad position. To keep his men's respect he couldn't go tattling on their every indiscretion. Some things had to stay between him and them. He had no choice now, however. If they couldn't see that, fuck 'em.

He gave a sigh and looked at Magnusson. "They ain't come back from the roadhouse yet."

"They ain't come back from the roadhouse yet," Magnusson mimicked, lowering his eyes to his foreman's chest and giving several short, thoughtful nods. He lifted his cold eyes again to Donnelly's, and it was odd how the foreman had never before noticed the reptilian cast in those unblinking eyes. "How many went?"

"Twelve."

"You know I never allow more than half a dozen men off the ranch at one time."

"I know that, Mr. Magnusson, but they must've slipped off while I was up at the house last night. When I got back, they were gone and there was nothin' I could do about it. I figured . . . well, I figured they'd be back long before now. Hell, long before sunup! They know they get their pay docked for this kind of horseshit."

Magnusson's eyes were on the table now, and he was pursing his lips. His earlobes poking out from under his beaver hat were bright red. His face was mottled white.

"Swell. Just swell," he said woodenly. Then his head jerked up. His face twisted savagely and he shouted, *"Send someone out to fetch them, goddamnit!"*

Donnelly remained calm, though his face blanched. It wasn't the first time he'd taken both barrels of Magnusson's fury.

He spread his hands apart, opening them, smoke from his cigarette curling and uncurling above the table. "I did that, Mr. Magnusson. I sent Press Johnson out. They should all be back in about an hour or so."

Magnusson pursed his lips and exhaled through his nose. "Very well. Make sure they know they're due a visit from me this evening, as well as a very substantial dock in pay."

"I will, sir. They're good men, sir."

Magnusson laughed scornfully and regarded the cook, who'd been standing there watching and listening to the conversation with his cigarette dangling from his mouth while the potatoes burned. As if throwing a switch, Magnusson returned to his old offensively ebullient self.

"Well, Lute, serve up the grub. We don't have all day, ya know. Mr. Wingate here has talked me into taking him hunting, haven't you, Charles?"

CHAPTER 23

FATHER AND SON Magnusson each shot one whitetail and one mule deer respectively by ten o'clock in the morning. They left both animals to the wolves, however. It was too early to start packing meat. They wouldn't start retrieving what they shot until they were ready to head home. Until then, they'd hone their aim on moving targets.

"Plenty of game in Dakota, Charles," King intoned as they traversed a nearly featureless prairie. "Plenty to shoot for sport, plenty to shoot for food. Besides, what we don't kill the damn Indians will."

"Indians around here?" Wingate asked, glancing around cautiously and squinting his nearsighted eyes, tiny dark marbles buried in the heavy, florid flesh of his face. He sat his high-stepping Arabian stiffly, chilled to his soul in spite of the buffalo robe that reached his calves.

"Not as many as there used to be, praise the Lord. We had to run off a whole damn village when I first came. Greasy beggars kept stealing cattle. They'd shoot 'em, butcher 'em, and devour them—all on my land! Can you believe such arrogance?"

Randall offered his two cents' worth. "When an Indian butchers an animal, he don't leave nothin' but the hoofs, and sometimes he even takes those.

Those people eat *everything*," he added with disgust.

"Are they dangerous?" Wingate asked.

"Can be when they're sober," Magnusson replied.

"I've never seen one, just read about them."

Magnusson took several puffs from his cigar. "Well, if we see one, I'll have Randall shoot him, and you can tell your New York friends how you got to see an Indian up close."

"Only good Injun's a dead Injun," Randall said. "Ain't that right, Pa?"

.They passed a few derelict sodbuster shacks— Magnusson had had nothing to do with running the yokels off, he laughed; the weather and the tough prairie sod had done that for free!—and followed a game trail into a ravine through which a frozen creek snaked.

They followed the creek south. Randall brought down two more deer but missed two coyotes bounding up the opposite ridge. Frustrated, he shot a porcupine from a tree.

Wingate took a couple of shots, but the game was practically out of sight by the time he'd snugged the heavy gun to his cheek. The kick of the big rifle nearly threw him from his saddle. King and Randall turned away, but he could feel them grimacing.

"Where are we heading now, King?" he asked as they cantered single file along the creek. He was ready for a nap followed by a brandy and a soft chair by a hot fire.

"While we're in the area I thought we'd pay a little visit to a . . . a friend of mine."

"Wouldn't be that greaser friend of yours, would it, Pa?" Randall asked, grinning.

"Mexican, Randall," Magnusson corrected facetiously. "*Greaser* isn't nice."

Randall laughed. "After last night, I had a feeling we might run into that gre—I mean Mexican—today."

Wingate had no idea what they were talking about, but he'd become so inured of their doubletalk and intrigue, playing him for the mindless dandy, that he didn't insist on an explanation. He distracted himself with fantasies of a sparking fire, Spanish brandy, and a naked Suzanne sprawled on a damask-covered couch until a small gray shack and an outhouse appeared around a bend in the creek. A tarpaulin weather cover fronting the shack afforded shelter to a single black stallion.

Smoke lifted from the chimney, and as they rode closer, Wingate saw there was a man outside in front of the cabin, his back to the approaching visitors. He was scraping a very large hide nailed to the cabin, right of the door.

A thick, sickening odor hung in the air like an invisible curtain. It emanated from the chimney, Wingate could tell, and he found himself yearning for a strong wind to blow it all away before he puked.

They rode up to within ten feet of the man. Still he didn't turn, but continued working on the hide, giving little grunts as he scraped.

Magnusson leaned forward, hands on his saddle horn. "Mighty trusting for a man of your profession, aren't you, Del Toro?"

The Mexican snickered and kept working. "You announced your arrival an hour ago, amigo. All your shooting. No one shoots as much as you and your boy, señor. It got so annoying I felt like doing some shooting of my own, in your direction."

Magnusson ignored the comment, regarding the hide nailed to the cabin through its four spread paws, large as dinner plates. "What do you have there, a griz?"

"Sí—old man *oso*. He came calling on me last night as I slept, so I let him in." Del Toro snickered again. There was no voice to it—just air trapped and released by his tongue. It sounded like a noise a self-satisfied reptile might make.

"Pity the bear that comes calling on you, José," Magnusson said, impressed by the image he was conjuring.

"Or men, uh?"

Del Toro turned for the first time, giving the visitors the full impression of his lean, grinning face, small teeth glinting like nailheads within the wild mustaches drooping around his mouth, blue coyote eyes flashing. He wore his wolf coat with its big silver buttons and his black hat, snugged over a homemade wolfskin liner with ear flaps tied under his chin. The flaps were in the shape of a wolf's paws.

If it weren't for the startling blue eyes and cold-blooded grin, he could have been a preposterously displaced hony-onker from Old Mexico, Wingate thought. He associated the sickly sweet smell with the gunman, with killing, and he had to swallow hard to keep his breakfast down.

Still grinning, Del Toro held up his wide-bladed skinning knife, examined it, then wiped the blood and tallow on his breeches and stuck the knife in his belt sheath.

Pulling a cigarillo from his coat pocket, he said, looking at Randall, "One of you gentlemen has a light?" He stuck the cigar between his teeth and grinned, his eyes on Randall.

Magnusson and Wingate turned to see how Randall was taking it. Not well. It was obvious by the lad's flat eyes and slightly curled upper lip that he did not like Mexicans, and this one least of all. His mouse-brown gelding bobbed its head and lifted a foot, but Randall held the gunman's gaze. His face turned slowly red.

Del Toro said, "Uh, you got light for this greaser, amigo?"

"Plum out o' phosphors," Randall said tightly.

"Give the man a light, Randall," Magnusson said as though chiding an ill-mannered youngster.

"Why should I?"

"Because I told you to," King said.

Wingate could tell he was enjoying his son's discomfort and wondered if there was anyone's discomfort King would not enjoy—except Suzanne's.

Finally Randall dug around in a coat pocket for a box of matches. Del Toro stepped forward and allowed the young man to light his cigar, the gunman taking his time about it, puffing smoke.

Looking around at the stark gray cabin and outhouse fronting the creek, Magnusson said, "I sure am sorry to keep you holed up out here in this old trapper's cabin, Del Toro, but it's probably best for both of us if we're not seen together."

Still puffing, trying to get a good draw, Del Toro turned away from Randall's match. "How good of you to be concerned for *both* of us. But it's really not so lonely. You know—this may be hard to believe and you probably think José drinks too much out here by himself—but a man and a very beautiful girl pass this way on horseback just about every day."

He pointed to the buttes behind the visitors. "They ride along the ridge there. Just riding for the thrill, I think. The girl always waves real big and smiles. Muy bonita. I think if it weren't for the man, she would even come and visit me in my cabin."

He took the cigar from his lips and smiled.

Magnusson did not return it. His face had grown dark. A muscle in his cheek twitched. "That's my daughter," he said, voice taut as razor wire.

"I thought she looked familiar."

"She's off-limits."

"Sí, you told me, señor. Maybe you better tell her that. I think she finds me . . . curious. Your daughter looks to me like a very curious girl."

Magnusson just stared at him, wide-eyed with outrage.

"Yes, very curious," Del Toro prodded some more.

Randall turned to his father and said with disgust, "Pa, this man here is—"

"Shut up, Randall," Magnusson said. To the gunman he said, "I've hired you to do a job. See that you do it"—his lips curled back revealing his big yellow teeth—"and get the hell out of here, you insolent bastard. Get the hell back where you came from!"

Magnusson was light-headed with fury. He was thinking, "If he so much as touches a hair on her head . . ." The thought was as repellent as the stench of the Mexican's cooking.

"Easy, señor. Hey, easy. I was just making conversation. Telling you I don't mind being housed out here like a wild dog in this goddamn gringo winter. That's what you wanted to hear—that I am keeping warm and fed and reasonably happy while you and your friends are singing and dancing in your big house."

Del Toro gave an exaggerated shrug. "You are worried about me. I tell you not to worry. That's all, you see? Comprende? I am an easy man to get along with."

Magnusson's fury was a confused, slippery thing that threatened to get away from him, turn him into a babbling idiot. He felt as though he'd been cut down at the knees. He felt an instinctive, repulsive fear of this man. He wasn't sure how to counter it. Nothing he could say would make him feel better, would give him back the advantage, and you didn't try to kill a man like this without plenty of help.

He stammered, hating the hesitant trill in his voice. "Just do your job," he finally managed, thoroughly flushed.

"Sí, señor. Is that what you rode out here to tell me?"

Magnusson had been thrown so far afield that he had to expel considerable energy in recalling the original intention of his visit. Then he remembered last night, Suzanne's birthday party, and the insolent *white* bastard who had threatened him in his own house.

All of this was getting too goddamn close to home. To Suzanne.

"I've got a name to add to your list. To the top of your list. You'll be compensated appropriately—don't worry."

Del Toro studied him expectantly, like a hawk perched in a dead tree waiting for another mouse to happen by.

"Mark Talbot," Magnusson said. "You'll find him on the Circle T ranch on Crow Creek. When you've killed him, dispose of the body somewhere it won't be found." He was thinking of Suzanne and decided right then and there to send her away again until deep summer.

Del Toro smiled with his eyes.

"The sooner the better," Magnusson added. To the others he said, "Let's go," and reined his horse around.

Randall had already turned around, facing back

the way they had come. "Pa," he said with an ominous air, looking off.

Following his son's gaze, Magnusson picked out a man in a sheepskin coat and tan hat riding furiously along the creek, giving his horse the quirt and spurs. It was Rag Donnelly on a buckskin.

"Mr. Magnusson!" he yelled as he approached the tarpaulin shelter, slowing to a canter, his exhausted mount blowing and snorting.

"Rag, what the hell?" Magnusson yelled.

When the horse came to a sloppy-gaited walk, Donnelly lowered his head to take a deep breath, then tipped his head back, his big, rugged face thoroughly flushed. He regarded Magnusson for several seconds while he caught his breath. He swallowed hard.

"W-would've sent a rider but I wanted to come and tell you myself."

"Tell me what?" Magnusson said impatiently.

"It's the men—the ones that didn't come home last night."

"What about them!"

"They're dead."

Magnusson mouthed the word silently before saying it out loud. "What are you talking about?"

Donnelly shook his head. "Every single one of 'em. Press Johnson found Gutzman's roadhouse burned to the ground and the men along with it."

"*Burned?*" Magnusson said, the force of the exclamation throwing him forward in his saddle.

As if following Magnusson's thought process, Donnelly shook his head. "It weren't no accident. Press said what's left of the logs is riddled with lead, and several of our men and Gutzman are layin' outside, shredded like they been hit by a hayrake. There's shell casings galore."

He paused to let this sink in. His boss watched him owl-like, blinking at regular intervals. Randall sighed and released it through his lips, whistling.

"My god," Wingate muttered.

Magnusson swept the ground with his eyes, as though he'd lost something. "Who . . . who—"

A thought struck him. His eyes ceased their restless quest and rose to Donnelly's. The foreman had a knowing look. He'd had time to put it all together, was one page ahead of his boss.

"Gibbon," Magnusson said flintily, with a savage curl of his lip. "And Thornberg, no doubt. Hell, it was probably all the nesters on the Bench."

"Includin' Talbot," Donnelly added with a growl.

"You think?"

"Sure. Hell, they prob'ly sent him up to the house last night to keep us occupied while the others rode over to Gutzman's. He prob'ly joined their little ambush party after he left here."

Magnusson's eyes were searching the horizon now, thoughts, plans, strategies snapping this way and that. Finally, adrenaline-pumped, he swallowed hard and said to his foreman, voice shaking with controlled rage, "You and Del Toro take care of Talbot. We three will ride back to the ranch, organize the rest of the men, and head for town. We'll see you back at the house."

Randall said, "I'll go with them, Pa."

"No, you stay—"

"Come on, Pa. *Please?*"

Magnusson saw the kill lust in his son's eyes. He thought a confrontation with a man like Talbot might be just what the lad needed to scrape some green off his horns, teach him that this was not just a game of cowboys and Indians. This was the real thing. This was the Magnusson name they were fighting for.

Behind him, Del Toro said calmly, "I work alone, señor."

Magnusson turned. The Mexican had already retrieved his Big Fifty and his saddle, and stood in the cabin doorway looking rough and ready, holding the saddle by the horn in one hand, the rifle by the other.

He said, "But since I haven't scouted this Talbot yet, your foreman and boy can be my scouts—as long as they don't mind taking orders from a bean-eater."

Randall's lip curled at being called a boy.

The gunman strode past Magnusson and Donnelly, lugging his saddle and rifle and heading for the shelter and his black stallion. He shuttled Donnelly a bland glance and added, "But they stay out of my way, uh? Or I shoot their ears off."

Donnelly snarled as Del Toro walked away, "Why, you fuckin'—"

"Easy, Rag," Magnusson cut in. "Remember your ear, and save the hostility for Talbot." He spurred his horse savagely and yelled, "I'm saving mine for Gibbon!"

CHAPTER 24

WHEN TALBOT LEFT the Double X the night before, he rode back to the Circle T, stabled the speckle-gray in the barn with fresh hay, and spent most of the night pacing the hollow shell of a cabin and feeding split cottonwood logs to the fire in the living room.

He fairly fumed with anger at Magnusson's arrogance and nonchalance regarding Dave's murder. If it hadn't been for Randall Magnusson, Talbot and Dave would be laughing and playing cards and making plans for expanding their holdings, maybe building a big clapboard house on a hillock over Crow Creek.

Instead, Talbot was here alone in a derelict cabin, crushing frozen mouse turds under his boots, filling with hate, and hip-deep in another damn war.

Finally exhausted, he spread his saddle blanket and stretched out on the cold wood floor, near the breathy, popping fire, and propped his head on his saddle. He came awake with a start several hours later, reaching for his rifle and jacking a shell in the breech.

He'd heard something.

He got up, stiff with cold, and moved to a window

and looked out. It was dawn; the eastern sky was scalloped pink and salmon. Just beyond the barn a horse and rider cantered around a hillock, disappeared behind another, then came out again on the trail curling through cottonwoods.

As the rider passed between the pumphouse and barn, Talbot saw from the hair bouncing on her shoulders it was Suzanne.

She rode the black thoroughbred like a true equestrian, back straight, mittened hands holding the reins up near her breasts. In spite of the store-bought fur coat hanging to her calves, she looked characteristically lithe.

Talbot went out to the porch, holding the rifle in his right hand, barrel down, ready to bring it up if he needed to. You never know; someone could have followed her out from the Double X intending to use her as a decoy while laying a bead on him. Her brother or Rag. Maybe Magnusson himself.

"You're up early," he said conversationally.

She stopped her horse a few feet away. Her features were grim. "Is it true?" Her voice was hard and distant.

"Is what true?" he asked, though he knew what she meant.

"That you used me to get a job out of my father?"

He gazed at her silently.

Suddenly her eyes softened and she shook her head. "Mark, please tell me it's not true."

"Would your father lie to you?" he said, feeling his anger grow at her complete acceptance of everything her father said and did. "The noble King Magnusson?"

She studied him suspiciously, trying to read him. Finally he decided to make it easy for her to ride away and forget about him. "Why not? If you had a chance of working for Verlyn Thornberg or the great King Magnusson, which would you choose?"

She scowled. "So what—now you're going to work for Thornberg? You're going to *cowboy* for Thornberg?"

"Why not?"

The thoroughbred danced in a circle, wanting to keep going. Suzanne clutched her thighs to its ribs and held the reins taut. "Stop, damn you!" she cried. Returning her eyes to Talbot, she said, "So you'll be riding against my father."

"He killed my brother," Talbot reminded her.

"Oh, Mark, don't tell me you still believe that?" She said it like he was sharpening his horns over a mere insult or an unfortunate poker hand.

Talbot clutched a porch post, trying to subdue his anger. None of this was her fault. She was an innocent albeit spoiled coquette raised by a charming albeit evil man. "Go home, Suzanne. Pack your bags and hop the next train out of here. I don't want to see you hurt."

"My father is a peaceful man, Mark."

He gave a deep sigh and looked at her with frustration mixed with sympathy. "You believe what you want, Suzanne. But your father has to be stopped."

"If he really were doing what you say, wouldn't stopping him be up to the law?"

"You know there's no law out here. We have to police ourselves. Besides, he killed my brother. It's personal."

She stared at him, the hate growing in her eyes. "You bastard," she said tightly. "You're just like the others on the Bench—jealous of my father's money and power and spoiling for a fight."

Talbot just looked at her. His eyes were flat.

Her own eyes sparked with outrage. "You simple bastard, you could have had me."

Talbot laughed ruefully. "For a week maybe, until you got bored and went looking for some other stud to grease your wheels."

She was outraged. The horse could sense it and danced around, agitated. "Most men . . . most men would give their eyeteeth to spend just *one night* in my good graces, you"—she pursed her lips and shook her head—"*fool!*"

"For your own good, Suzanne, get out of here. Stay out of the way."

She gave an angry, frustrated cry, reined the black around, and spurred him back the way she had come. "What they say is true—brains and brawn really *don't* go together!"

Talbot watched the horse pass through the cottonwoods and turn on the road behind the barn. She gave it the quirt and spurs and galloped away through the hogbacks.

Talbot swore and went back inside the cabin. He stomped around until he realized the fire had gone out. Then he went out behind the cabin, retrieved an armful of cottonwood logs, and got the fire going again. He'd forgotten how physically tiring the cold could be.

He sat brooding before the fire for another quarter of an hour. The rumbling in his stomach told him he needed to eat, so he scoured the kitchen for food. All he came up with was a can of peaches and a coffeepot with a small pouch of Arbuckle's beans tucked inside.

He ground the beans with the butt of his revolver, filled the percolator with snow, dumped in the ground coffee, and set it on a grate in the fireplace. Later, drinking the coffee and eating the peaches with his fingers, it became clear to him that before he could go after Magnusson, he'd need to fill his larder. And because there were only about three or four more cottonwood logs left in the woodshed, he'd need to cut wood, as well.

The brakes of the Little Missouri would be the best place for getting wood *and* food. The only problem was he had no wagon with which to haul it all back to the ranch.

Maybe Jacy would lend him a wagon . . .

Thinking of her shoved back some of the hate he felt for Magnusson. She was the single bright spot in his returning home, and he felt a deep hankering to see her again. He knew, though, that his visit to the Double X had made him a villain in her eyes, and it was going to take some explaining to get himself back in her good graces.

When he finished the peaches and a second cup of coffee, he went out to the barn and saddled his speckle-gray, shoving the loaded Winchester into the saddle boot. A half hour later the corrals and outbuildings of Jacy's Bar MK ranch rose from the frozen prairie a hundred yards ahead.

——— •◦• ———

The sun peeked through high, thin clouds, spreading a washed-out, tawny glow over the hogbacks and hay stubble half covered in crusty snow. Ahead, the cabin was a black smudge beneath the blue mesa looming behind it.

From the corral, several horses watched Talbot approach, hanging their heads over the top rail and twitching their ears. Their manes hung limp; the lack of wind today was an unexpected treat. It was cold, but not the penetrating, stinging cold the wind whipped against your face like sand.

A rifle cracked, the squeaky bark rising in pitch as it echoed. Talbot flinched and brought his horse to a halt. Looking ahead, he saw a figure standing outside the cabin door. It was Jacy in her green mackinaw holding a rifle in her arms.

"Who are ya and what the hell you want!" she yelled, more than a touch of anger in her voice.

Talbot waved. "It's me, Jacy. Mark Talbot."

She said nothing, just looked at him with the rifle in her arms. Talbot was too far away to see the expression on her face, but the rest of her told him there wasn't one. He was about to say something when she turned and walked back inside the cabin and closed the door.

Talbot spurred his horse ahead, dismounted, and looped the reins over the tie rail, then mounted the narrow porch and knocked on the door. She didn't answer the knock.

"Can I come in?" he said, turning his head to hear through the door.

Nothing. He turned the knob. The door opened, and he stepped inside.

"What the hell do you want?" she said.

She was sitting at the kitchen table fronted by a whiskey bottle and a half-filled water glass. The rifle stood within easy reach to her right, propped against the table. Her tawny hair was mussed and her face was flushed.

"Looks like I'm late for the party," he said, closing the door behind him. "Must've been a beaut."

Thickly she said, "Nope. Drinkin' alone today."

"What's the occasion?"

"Life."

"I see. In that case, mind if I join you?"

"Yes, as a matter of fact."

"Then I suppose lending me a wagon for a couple days is out of the question."

Frowning, she turned her head to look at him. "What for?"

"Need to haul firewood and game. It appears someone made off with all Dave's implements."

"Figured you'd be gone by now. Little Miss Queen of England entice you into staying?"

"No, her father did." Remembering that he hadn't seen smoke lifting from the bunkhouse chimney and hadn't seen the old cowboy working outside, he asked where Gordon was. "Didn't he ever show up?"

Jacy took a slug from her glass. "Yeah, he showed up. What was left of him."

Talbot slid a chair out from the table and sat down next to her. "What happened?" he asked darkly.

She told him about finding Gordon and Mrs. Sanderson dead along the Little Missouri. Then she told him about joining Gibbon's posse and the attack on the roadhouse. She'd barely finished the story when she convulsed in a sob, cupped her mouth in her hands, and lowered her head in tears.

"Jesus Christ," Talbot muttered, absorbing the information. "Do you realize what this means? Magnusson's going to pull out all the stops. He's going to hunt each member of that posse down and hang him, or worse."

"I know," she said weakly.

Talbot's mind was racing, trying to come up with a plan. "You need to lay low for a while. Visit your mother in Mandan. I'll cable you when the dust settles."

Jacy lifted her head and shook it defiantly. "It was a major fuck-up," she said. "Innocent people died. We never should have done it. But I'm not running from it." She added after a pause, "That poor Indian girl. Her life was hell, and then she died like hell. They all died like hell, like nothing means a goddamn thing."

Talbot nodded. "Nothing means anything when it comes to war," he said. "And that's what we have here—a war."

"We?"

"You heard me."

"What about little Miss Queen of England?"

"You underestimate me, Jacy."

Pursing her lips, she nodded. "Sorry. I won't do it again."

"How 'bout that wagon?"

"You're going *hunting*?"

He shrugged. "First things first. Without food and heat, I'm helpless."

She pinned him with her green eyes. "Stay here."

He thought about it and shook his head. "I don't want that son of a bitch burning the Circle T, and that's what he'll do if he comes looking for me and I'm not there to stop him. The cabin has to be my base. Besides, he won't harm you if you're alone. Magnusson's a bastard, but he's a proper bastard. Just the same, you better cork that bottle. If he comes here, you'll want to be ready for him."

She wrinkled her nose. "What makes you think you can boss me? You haven't even gotten in my pants yet." She tipped back the last of the whiskey and slammed the glass on the table. "You'll find a buckboard where they're usually kept—in the wagon shed."

He splashed a finger of whiskey into her glass and slammed it back. "Much obliged," he said, and headed for the door.

"Mark?"

Her voice stopped him.

She said, "Will you stop again on your way back from the river?"

He looked at her thoughtfully, then smiled. "Be my pleasure."

"Good luck hunting," she said.

He touched his hat brim in a mock salute and left.

CHAPTER 25

AFTER TALBOT LEFT her cabin, Jacy lost her taste for the whiskey. His appearance had somehow quelled her loneliness and fear, and she no longer felt the need to numb herself.

Having found most men querulous and undependable at best, she didn't like feeling dependent, but she sensed in Talbot a maturity based on a wry melancholy that went deeper than Dave's death. No doubt his experiences in the War and his wandering in Mexico had seasoned him, and Jacy thought that, given time, she would find a sensitive, passionate man.

Regretting that she'd jumped the gun about his relationship with Suzanne Magnusson, she yearned to have his masculine arms around her now, to curl her naked body against his and sleep for a million years.

Lost in reverie, she'd scrubbed two iron skillets and several plates before it dawned on her that horses were nickering outside. She jumped, startled, splashing soapy water on the floor, and reached for her rifle. She moved quickly to the window and saw a man creeping along the barn, holding a rifle out before him.

She ran to the front door and opened it.

"*Oh!*" she screamed.

Another, bigger man stood before her, nearly filling the doorway. He wore a sheepskin coat and a tan hat, and was holding a rifle level with her belly. When Jacy tried to bring her own carbine up to shoot him, he grabbed it.

She fought but his power was too great, and finally he jerked the rifle from her hands, throwing her to the floor. She jumped to her feet and went at him with her fists, but she could have been punching a brick wall for all the damage she did.

Casually, the man pushed her back into the kitchen. It wasn't much of a shove, but there was enough force in the man's arm that she fell backward, bouncing her head off the floor.

"Son of a *bitch!*" Jacy lay there a moment, stunned, then rose to her elbows.

The man took two steps into the cabin. He had a big slab of a face with cold eyes and an anvil jaw, the deep lines above his cheeks epitomizing belligerence. He had a pure, raw, gladiatorial demeanor, and Jacy knew she was face-to-face with one of Magnusson's firebrands.

"Where's Talbot?" he said with a growl.

"Who?" She'd been so certain they'd be coming for her, to extract payment for the part she'd played in the roadhouse debacle, that she wasn't sure she'd heard him correctly.

"Mark Talbot," he repeated, louder this time. "We know he's been here. We tracked him from his cabin."

Jacy climbed to her feet and put her hands on the counter behind her, cutting her eyes around for a weapon—a knife, a fork, anything.

"Don't even think about it," he said, reading her mind. "You don't think I'd shoot a woman?"

"What do you want with Mark?"

A smaller, baby-faced man stepped into the cabin behind the big man. He had to take a long step to get around the big man's muscle-bound girth. When he did, Jacy saw the grinning, pendulous-lipped features of Randall Magnusson, whom she'd seen occasionally before—in dry-goods stores and road-houses. Once he'd pulled his horse up to hers as she stopped for water at Big John Creek. Openly star-ing at her breasts, he'd asked if she wanted to go to a dance sometime and she'd told him to go diddle himself.

"Well, lookee here—if it ain't Miss Smart Mouth herself," he said, giving her the twice-over with his shiny blue eyes.

"You two can just get the *fuck* out of my cabin," Jacy said, hating the fear that made her voice trem-ble.

Randall turned his head to look around the cabin, then slid his cold eyes back to Jacy, the infuriat-ing grin still there. "You all alone here, Miss Smart Mouth?"

"What's it look like?" the big man answered for her. To Jacy he said again, "Where'd Talbot go?"

"What's it to you?"

Randall laughed. He was standing between the big man and Jacy, sweeping Jacy with his eyes. "Ol' Rag here's got a score with Talbot. See that ear of his—the one with the bandage on it? That's Talbot's work." Randall laughed. "Yes, sir, he sure did show Rag and my pa what was what and who was who up at the big house last night." He laughed some more. There was no real mirth in it, but not for his lack of trying.

"Shut up," the big man, Rag, said. To Jacy again: "Twelve of my men were ambushed last night, and I think he was part of it. Where is he?"

"He wasn't part of it," Jacy said defiantly. "*I* was part of it."

Rag studied her cynically through slitted eyes. "Very funny. Where is he?"

"How should I know?"

"I just told you, we tracked him here, and from here, his tracks lead south. Now where's he going? You tell me, you sassy little bitch, or so help me—"

"Rag," Randall chided, his eyes remaining on Jacy. "That's no way to talk to a girl. You have to charm a woman into giving up her secrets."

"You're a real lady's man, Randall. Stay out of this," Rag ordered, taking a step toward Jacy.

Eyes afire, Randall wheeled and lifted his heels to bark into the big man's face, "Shut up! Just shut up, you hear? The great King Magnusson is not here, so I'm giving the orders, you understand? *I'm* in charge!"

Jacy turned her fearful, angry gaze to young Magnusson. Trying to steady her voice she said, "Be a man, Randall, and get out of here."

"I don't like how the girls around here talk to men. I'm thinkin' you need to be taught a lesson, like that Rinski bitch."

Jacy studied him, her anger growing keen. She inhaled sharply and swallowed. "You're the one . . . you're the little *boy* who shot Jack Thom in his bed and savaged Mattie."

Randall laughed, then said good-naturedly, "There goes that mouth of yours again." His voice turned hard and his grin faded. "I don't like being talked to like that."

He reached out suddenly and grabbed her by the hair. Jacy cursed and lifted her arms to defend herself. Randall jerked her around by the hair, thrust her against the big man called Rag.

"Hold her good and tight, Rag. I'm gonna teach Miss Smart Mouth to show some respect to her gentleman callers."

"We don't have time for this, Randall," Rag said without heat.

He was enjoying taunting the girl, watching the fear and anger in her eyes, feeling her tremble in his arms. It aroused him. He knew they needed to catch up with Talbot, but he couldn't tear himself away. He wondered what Randall was going to do, how far he would go.

Randall produced a butcher knife from a shelf. He held it up before his face, inspecting it, tested his thumb on the edge. "Ouch," he said. "Sharp. Look at that." He held up his hand to show Jacy the bead of blood on his thumb.

Jacy struggled but could not free her arms from the big man's grasp. Randall stepped forward, thrusting the knife to within four inches of her face. Heart pounding, Jacy turned her head to the side, recoiling against the big man's chest.

"Where did Talbot go?" Randall asked calmly.

Her voice was small but fervid. "Go fuck yourself."

Randall lowered the blade to Jacy's neck, held the blade against her throat. He lifted his eyes to hers, smiled. "Where's Talbot?"

Jacy swallowed, fighting the urge to beg for her life. She was not going to beg these savages for anything. She'd rather die.

Still, she felt as though her heart would explode from the fear. She kept seeing Mattie Rinski in the rocking chair. "I told you to go fuck yourself," she said, breathless.

Randall lowered the blade to her chest, pressed it flatly against her breasts, and with a sudden flick of his wrist sliced a button from her cotton shirt. "Anytime you're ready to tell us where Talbot went, I'll stop," he said matter-of-factly.

He flicked another button from her shirt, then another. Jacy heard the big man breathing in her ear, felt his hands grow warm and sweaty against her wrists. She cursed. Another button hit the floor. Then two more and the shirt fell open, exposing her undershirt and a fair amount of cleavage.

Randall stepped back and inspected her breasts straining the thin, washworn fabric. He pressed the knife point against her left nipple. Jacy sobbed again. Tears rolled down her face.

"Are you going to tell us where Talbot went now, or do I have to keep going?"

"Go fuck . . . go fuck . . ." she said through the sobs that came freely now. She hung limp in the big man's hands, her head hanging to her chest, hair down around her face.

Randall grabbed the neck of her undershirt and began cutting and tearing.

"No!" Jacy screamed, feeling something give way within her. "*No!*"

Just then a floorboard squeaked and another man appeared in the open doorway—a tall, thin man with a casual air. He had a long, angular face and thin lips between which a long black cigar poked. His features were distinctly Latin, but his eyes were impossibly blue.

The eyes held Jacy's for a moment, and it was like having your gaze held and the air sucked out of your lungs by the sudden appearance of the devil himself.

"Come hither, my gringo amigos," he said. "We don't have time to play with little girls. Talbot's tracks are clear."

Then he turned away, giving his back to the kitchen.

He stood on the porch, puffing his cigar, and looking across the ranchyard.

Randall cursed, staring at Jacy with animalistic desire. "This one on your list, José?"

"What, the girl? No. Just her hired man. I don't shoot girls, I fuck them. But I don't have time to fuck that one, so let's go, amigos, before you piss me off."

"This one's being smart. She won't tell us where Talbot went."

"I know where Talbot went," the Mexican said casually. He left the porch, and Jacy watched him walk across the ranchyard, mount a tall, black horse, and rein it south out of the yard.

Rag opened his hands and Jacy slumped to the floor, pulling her shirt closed, bringing her knees to her chest.

"Come on," Rag said, turning for the door.

Randall cursed. He prodded Jacy with his boot. "Hey?" he said. "We'll be back for more."

Jacy turned her head and stared at the floor, crying softly and holding her arms over her breasts.

The big man turned on the porch and said, "If we happen to miss Talbot and he circles back, let him know we burned his cabin." He laughed fiercely. "That should slow him down."

CHAPTER 26

JED GIBBON SAT in the Sundowner playing solitaire with a rifle across his thighs.

Occasionally he looked up at the three men sitting across the room, in the shadows on the other side of the ticking stove—Thornberg's men—to make sure they weren't drunk. They were drinking beer instead of whiskey, and they were only sipping the beer, not guzzling it like they'd guzzled whiskey last night.

Like Gibbon, they kept glancing out the window, and whenever a wagon or horseback rider appeared in the street, one or two of them would jump, then cover it with a cough or with a curse at the cards in their hands.

Like Gibbon, they were nervous. Like Gibbon, they had a bad feeling about today.

Today was a long way from last night. They knew that Magnusson was on their trail. He could show up outside the window any second now, with a posse of his own, and turn the tables a full hundred and eighty degrees in his favor.

Gibbon laid a jack of diamonds on a queen of spades and gave a start at the clatter of a buckboard. He looked out the window to see a farmer in an immigrant hat bounce down the street behind two broad-backed draft horses.

When the man was gone, Gibbon sipped his tepid coffee and peeled a three of hearts from the coffee-stained deck in his hand. He gave a slow sigh, pooching out his lips as he released it. By now Magnusson had to know about the roadhouse killings, and Gibbon would have bet a bottle of good Tennessee whiskey that he was on his way to town right now.

But you never knew. Maybe the rancher was going to wait until Gibbon's defenses were down, until he'd grown heavy and slack with anticipation and worry, then ride to town in the dark of night and confront the sheriff when Thornberg's men weren't around to back him up.

That's what Gibbon would have done. But he was hoping Magnusson would act on impulse. He was hoping the big blond Scandahoovian would be so angered at what had transpired at Gutzman's roadhouse that he'd head for town pronto, careless with rage.

Turning his head to glance out the window again, Gibbon saw two more of Thornberg's riders, sitting on the roof of the livery barn across the street. They were hunkered down beneath the peak, backs to the wind, smoking cigarettes. Gibbon knew there was one more man inside the barn, and several more stationed at other locations around the saloon.

Thornberg himself was inside Delmonico's Café, three doors down on the other side of the street, waiting by a window, out of the cold. He'd sent several of his men home to man the ranch in the unlikely event Magnusson went there first, to burn him out.

He and his six other men had ridden with Gibbon to town. Like Gibbon, Thornberg figured Magnusson would come here first, aimed at killing the sheriff before he lit out across the Bench tearing down barns and turning up sod.

All the other ranchers in Gibbon's posse had returned to their ranches. Homer Rinski had wanted to join Gibbon and Thornberg in town, but Gibbon had talked him into returning to his ranch and his daughter. It hadn't been easy convincing the old Bible thumper that his duty now lay at home, and Gibbon half expected to see Rinski ride into town with his Greener in his lap, those cold eyes fairly glowing.

The door of the saloon suddenly burst open, and Gibbon dropped his cards and swung the carbine out from under the table. The farmer who had just passed in the street entered, his little round spectacles frosted over so thickly he couldn't see. His face was red and his scruffy beard was nearly white. The stoop-shouldered little man carefully closed the door then turned to regard the room.

Gibbon sighed with relief. "Good Lord, Asa," he said, "why in hell did you have to pick today of all days to come to town? You haven't been off the farm since August!"

Peering blindly through his frosty spectacles, the farmer said, in a heavy German accent, "Yah, vot's going on? Vhere is everbody? It's Sunday?"

"I've shut down main street 'cause I'm expectin' trouble. Turn your team around and go back home, Asa. We'll see you in May."

"I need supplies."

"Not today, Asa," Gibbon said.

The farmer shook his head stubbornly. "No, I need supplies. That's vy I come all da vay to town."

"Sheriff," one of Thornberg's men said.

Gibbon looked beyond Asa Mueller to the street beyond the window and said, "Shit."

Nearly a dozen men had ridden up. Most were typical Magnusson riders in sheepskin coats, Stetsons, and scarves, rifles in their gloved hands. They were a hard-faced, belligerent-looking bunch that looked none too pleased with what had transpired at Gutzman's roadhouse.

In their midst was Magnusson wearing a fur coat and a fur hat, the mustaches above his grim mouth frosted white. Beside Magnusson rode the stout little man with red muttonchops who had been at Magnusson's place when Gibbon had gotten the shit kicked out of him. He was the only one who did not look like he'd been chomping at the bit to come to town. In fact, he looked like he'd rather be anywhere but town.

All the rest more than made up for his reluctance. Magnusson himself looked like he was about to collect the proceeds from a million-dollar bet. "Come on out here, Gibbon!"

"Go out the back, Asa," Gibbon said tightly.

The farmer had turned to look out the window. He was mumbling something under his breath, but Gibbon ignored him as he gained his feet and jacked a shell in his rifle breech. He stood and pulled on his coat, taking his time with the buttons.

Lifting his collar, he walked to the window and looked out. Magnusson stared at him through the glass, his face expressionless. Only his eyes showed a faint amusement.

"Okay, boys," Gibbon said.

Thornberg's riders had put down their cards, picked up their rifles, and now followed Gibbon onto the porch. They stood in a line, facing Magnusson and his riders.

"Mornin'," Gibbon said casually. "Or is it afternoon now?"

Magnusson said nothing. He sat his big Arabian and scowled.

Gibbon shrugged. "Well, what brings you to

Caanan, Magnusson? I thought the Double X did all
its business in Big Draw."

"You know why I'm here, you pathetic old bastard. You bushwhacked my men."

"They were resistin' arrest."

"What's the charge?"

"Suspicion of murder and cattle rustlin'."

Magnusson laughed without mirth. The smile
faded. Glancing at Thornberg's men, he said, "Hired
you some deputies, eh? Must have been expecting me."

"Take a look behind you."

Magnusson twisted around in his saddle, peering
at the other riflemen on the roofs behind him. Gibbon heard a door open. Looking right, he watched
Thornberg step out of the café and come down the
boardwalk holding a rifle across his chest.

Thornberg tipped his hat and said, "Good day to
you, King. I have a feeling you're gonna lose that
sappy grin of yours in about thirty seconds." He
jacked a shell and scowled.

"Mighty sure of yourself, aren't you, Verlyn? How
many men you packing today?"

"Ten, same as you, King. I'd say that's a pretty fair
fight."

Gibbon said, "Doesn't have to be a fight, Magnusson. All you have to do is throw your guns down,
order your men to do likewise, and follow me over
to the jail."

"What are you talking about?" Magnusson scoffed.
"You actually think you have any legal jurisdiction
in this matter, Gibbon?"

"No," Gibbon said. His face turned to stone. "I
was just bein' polite."

He and Magnusson locked eyes.

Finally, a low growl rumbled up from the rancher's chest, his lips fluttered, and his face reddened.

He drew the silver-plated Bisley strapped over his coat, but he was too steamed to shoot straight. The bullet whistled past Gibbon's ear and shattered the window behind him.

Gibbon lifted his Winchester and shot Magnusson in the shoulder just as the rancher's horse swung around, spooked by the sudden gunfire. Magnusson yelled and clutched the wound with one hand while trying to control his mount with the other.

Magnusson's riders lowered their rifles and Gibbon swung his own carbine around, dislodging one man and wounding another in the thigh. He gave a shriek and fell from the saddle of his bucking pinto.

Beside Gibbon, two of Thornberg's riders went down in the hail of bullets flung by Magnusson's crew. The other jumped off the porch and ducked behind a watering trough and commenced firing.

Thornberg and the rest of his men were opening up across the street, dislodging several of Magnusson's men from their saddles and scattering the others in a thunder of clomping hooves and high-pitched whinnies.

Gibbon had just taken down another man when Magnusson, who'd pinned Thornberg behind a hay wagon, swung back around and emptied his carbine at Gibbon.

The sheriff, who'd dropped to one knee behind the hitch rack, felt one of the slugs tear meat from his side, just above his belt, but he kept firing until the hammer of his Winchester clicked. He dropped the carbine and ran back into the saloon, clumsily pulling his revolver from the holster beneath his coat.

A cat-like moan sounded behind him. Swinging a look, he saw Asa Mueller curled up under a table with his arms over his head.

"Just stay there 'til I tell you to come out, Asa," Gibbon said.

With the gun in his hand, he stepped up to the window and was about to cut loose when he saw that the street had cleared and most of the shooting was now happening between and behind the buildings across the street. Two horses and six of Magnusson's riders lay dead. The three men that had followed Gibbon onto the porch were dead as well, spilling blood on the boardwalk. There was no sign of Thornberg.

Magnusson was retreating up the boardwalk on the other side of the street, stumbling and clutching his shoulder. Gibbon yelled, "The fight's back here, Magnusson!" and snapped off an errant round.

The rancher stopped, pressed his back to the livery barn, and squeezed off a feeble shot. Then he pushed himself away from the barn and ran up the street, toward his horse that stood twitching its ears at the gunfire.

Gibbon ran after him, keeping to his side of the street. He stopped when Magnusson tried to mount the jittery Arabian, and fired two shots in the air over the horse's head. The horse bucked and ran kicking down the street.

Magnusson tried to hold on, but his left foot slipped from the stirrup and he landed in a pile, cursing and raging at the disobedient mount.

Gibbon walked up behind him as Magnusson tried to gain his feet. "Stay down there," Gibbon said. "Throw down your weapon and hold your hands above your head." He noted that the gunfire was dying away behind him and he wondered vaguely if anyone was still alive.

He got his answer a second later, when a shaky voice rose behind him. "H-hold it r-right there, Sheriff."

Gibbon froze. He'd been so preoccupied with stopping Magnusson that he hadn't thought to watch his back. Turning slowly, he confronted the man behind him. The stocky little easterner with the red mutton-chops and rosy red cheeks held a revolver in both his shaking hands, the barrel aimed at Gibbon's chest.

Swallowing, the man looked beyond Gibbon to Magnusson. "K-k-k-king, what should I d-do?"

Gibbon didn't give Magnusson a chance to answer. He shot the little man in the chest, then brought his gun back around to Magnusson, who had turned but was not holding his revolver. Gibbon saw the Bisley lying about ten feet from the rancher, where he must have dropped it when the horse threw him.

Gibbon felt a grin shaping his mouth. He heard a gun crack and felt a bullet tear through his middle. As though clubbed with a two-by-four, he fell forward on his knees, struggling to keep his gun up.

Turning, he saw the little man lying on his side, still aiming his revolver at Gibbon. Smoke curled from the barrel. As the man thumbed back the hammer to fire again, Gibbon shot him through the forehead.

The easterner's head jerked back with the force of the slug, then came forward and hit the ground. The shoulders quivered for only a moment.

Hearing footsteps, Gibbon turned his head forward. Magnusson was reaching for his Bisley. Gibbon squeezed off a shot but missed cleanly. His hand was shaking; he was going into shock. He thumbed back the hammer and squeezed the trigger again, but the hammer slapped the firing pin without igniting a shell.

He felt a heavy darkness brush over him like warm, wet tar. He was out of shells and out of luck. He gave an involuntary groan against the pain in his middle as he watched Magnusson straighten with the silver-plated pistol in his hand.

His lower jaw jutted angrily out from his face and his nostrils flared like a rabid dog's.

"You bastard," Gibbon muttered, his breath growing short. He felt drunk, and he chuckled silently at the thought. Here he was on his last leg, shot in the back by a chickenhearted little tinhorn, and sober as a Lutheran preacher.

Magnusson walked stiffly toward him, holding the Bisley out from his chest. Blood glistened on the right shoulder of his coat. He stopped near Gibbon and pressed the barrel to the sheriff's forehead.

"You're finished, Gibbon," Magnusson growled.

"So are you, King," Gibbon said before the gun barked.

CHAPTER 27

MARK TALBOT HAD just started tracking a whitetail buck when he sensed he was being followed.

He halted his horse on the buttes over a creek and turned his head in a slow circle squinting his eyes. He saw little but snow-dusted hogbacks and small, isolated cottonwood copses, a distant line of skeletal trees tracing the course of another creek. In the far distance, wind-sculpted sandstone monuments stood sentinel over the vast canvas of colorless winter landscape.

It was getting late in the afternoon and the high, dense clouds were turning sooty. The sun was an opalescent wash edging down the western sky.

Talbot appeared to be alone. Still, the hair on the back of his neck was standing straight up, and heeding such a warning had saved his life more times in the past than he cared to remember. He clucked to the horse and continued following the impressions the buck had left in the hard ground, periodically cutting his eyes around for trouble.

Having lost the tracks, he stopped by a flat boulder to try to recover them. He squinted his eyes at the tufts of frozen grass and lowered his head for a closer look.

Something shredded the air near his ear, whistling softly with a guttural edge. He felt the wind on his neck and recognized the sound of a lead ball ripping air.

A long gun boomed in the distance. Talbot had heard the reports of enough large-caliber rifles to know instantly, without having to ponder it, that this was a Big Fifty, accurate up to seven hundred yards.

He was out of the saddle and reaching for his carbine before the echo of the boom had died. He slapped the horse and ran for the ridge over the creek, found cover behind a boulder wedged precariously atop the steep grade.

Behind and below him the frozen creek curled in its brush-lined bed. Talbot considered it momentarily before returning his gaze to the open benches, from where he knew the Big Fifty had been fired.

More rifles popped thinly in the distance. They were carbines, like Talbot's Winchester, and well out of range. It was the Big Fifty Talbot was worried about. Whoever had pulled its trigger had had enough time to reload the single-shot rifle and was no doubt worrying a bead on Talbot's head at this very moment.

As if to confirm his suspicion, a ball shattered against the rock, spraying rock and lead in the grass like heavy rain. The boom followed half a second later. More rifles popped, and the popping was growing louder.

Talbot jerked a look around the rock and saw a man riding along the ridge to his right. Swinging around, he saw another man coming from the left. They were about a hundred yards away and closing. No doubt the man with the Big Fifty was straight out in the prairie somewhere, hunkered down behind a hogback.

Talbot jacked a shell in his Winchester, brought the rifle to his shoulder and squeezed off a shot at the man on his left, then turned and squeezed off another at the man on his right. One rider gave a yell and halted his horse to dismount and look for cover, but the other—a far bigger man—kept coming.

Talbot considered holding his ground and shooting it out, but he knew he'd be caught in a cross fire. With no time to spare—he could hear hooves beating the hard earth—he scrambled down the ridge to the brush along the creek, running hard. Tiny silvery birds rose from the brambles, screaming and wheeling toward the opposite ridge. Rifles cracked and lead ripped the air.

He ran deep into the cattails, sending the cotton billowing in all directions. He knew his attackers would be able to hear him thrashing in the weeds if he kept moving, so he stopped at the trunk of a dead cottonwood and hunkered down to scan the ridge behind him.

Three men sat three horses near the rock he'd used for cover. Talbot was too far away to make out distinguishing features, but he could tell from body shape and size that two of the men were Rag Donnelly and Randall Magnusson. He didn't recognize the other man, the man sporting the Big Fifty.

What he did recognize was the fact that all three men were riding for King Magnusson, and they had no doubt tracked Talbot here from his cabin. Which meant they'd tracked him to Jacy's. Talbot felt a sudden, desperate urge to return to her ranch to make sure she hadn't been harmed.

But first he had to deal with these three uglies.

He was trying to figure out how to do that when two of the riders rode down the ridge, leaving the third man—the man with the Big Fifty—alone on the ridgetop. Apparently Donnelly and young Magnusson were coming after him while the third man covered them from the ridge.

Talbot turned and headed up the creek through the heavy brush. Soon the man on the ridge started cutting loose with the big Sharps—one heavy blast after another. He couldn't see Talbot in the weeds but that didn't keep him from probing the creek bed with intermittent lead balls, making sure Talbot didn't get too comfortable down there while the other two beat the brush for him.

After fifty tough yards, Talbot turned to watch and listen. He couldn't see much but sky and the ridges on either side of the creek, rising above the bending weed tips, but he could hear the heavy boom of the Sharps and voices.

The occasional cries and calls lifted behind him about seventy-five yards, and they seemed to be spread apart by several dozen yards. There was the rustle and crack of heavy animals moving through brush, and Talbot knew Magnusson and Donnelly were beating the creek bed for him the way you'd beat the brush for whitetails or mountain lions.

Meanwhile, the man on the ridge was trying to flush him with the Sharps.

A slug whistled past Talbot's ear and snapped a willow limb behind him. Talbot ducked suddenly and cursed. He shifted his gaze to the ridge. The man with the big gun rose from his prone shooting position and cupped his hands around his mouth. His voice carried on the crisp air.

"He's ahead and left, sixty yards!"

The son of a bitch must have eyes like a hawk, Talbot grumbled to himself, turning and pushing his way through the brush.

Five minutes later the brush thinned and there was

the creek—a wide, frozen horseshoe dusted with a thin, crusty layer of snow etched with animal tracks. On the other side stood a beaver house about five feet tall and seven feet long.

Talbot looked behind him. The man on the ridge was still shooting, but apparently he'd lost his target, for none of the recent slugs had landed near. Keeping his head low, Talbot ran out of the brush, slipping and sliding on the icy creek, boots crunching snow, and hunkered down on the far side of the beaver house.

A bullet tore into the house, snapping several of the carefully woven branches, and Talbot knew the man on the ridge had rediscovered him.

That's okay, he thought. Send him over here.

He stood and yelled to the ridge, "Come on—send him over here! Tell 'em to come and get it!" Turning to the brush across the creek he shouted, "Come and get it, Rag! Come and get it, Randall! I'm waiting for you!"

Suddenly a horse burst out of the brush behind him, another whinnied across the creek, and Talbot realized they'd been moving around him and slowly tightening the circle.

"Eeee-ha!" Randall Magnusson yelled as he bore down on Talbot, trying to trample him.

Talbot swung around to shoot, but Magnusson's horse bulled into him, knocking the rifle from his arms. Thrown back against the beaver house, he went for his revolver, but before his hand touched the grips Randall's rifle cracked, belching fire and smoke, and the slug tore into the house a half inch right of Talbot's face. The barrel hung there, only a few inches away, so instead of drawing his revolver, Talbot reached out and grabbed the rifle and pulled.

Randall came with it, landing with a cry on the

root-webbed cutbank, his mount shrieking and kicking as it scrambled away.

Talbot crouched behind the beaver house just as Donnelly snapped off a shot. The slug barked into the house. Talbot stood, lifting Randall's Winchester to his shoulder, and returned fire at Donnelly, who was too preoccupied with his prancing mount to take another shot.

The bullet caught the big foreman in the shoulder, pushing him back in the saddle. He gave a yell and fumbled for his reins, but the horse was bucking in earnest, slipping and sliding on the ice, and he fell heavily out of the saddle, cursing.

Turning sharply to his right, Talbot saw that Randall was lying on his back, his head propped against the weeds, a Colt revolver extended in his right hand. The barrel was aimed at Talbot's head, and the trigger was locked back, ready to fire.

Time stopped, and Talbot saw the grim smile etched on the young man's thick-lipped mug. Magnusson's eyes were slits through which the frosty eyes reflected the dull winter light. The muzzle bore down on Talbot like the round, black yawn of eternity.

Randall licked his lips. "Your brother thought he was too good to beg for his life, so we made him kneel down and I shot him in the back of the head like a dog." The smile widened. "Where do you want yours?"

Before Talbot could answer, a round black spot the size of a double eagle appeared on Randall's forehead, just above his eyes. He was only vaguely aware of a rifle crack as the kid's head snapped back and hit the ground with a thud. The Colt dropped from his hand. He gave no cry, no sound whatsoever. One leg spasmed for a few seconds, and that was all.

He'd obviously been shot, but by whom Talbot had no time to ponder, because Rag Donnelly suddenly slammed him to the ground with the full force of his body. Talbot went down hard on his side, Donnelly's weight forcing the air from his lungs in one painful exhalation.

Then Donnelly was slamming his head against the ground and raging incoherently. Talbot kicked himself up with his legs. At the same time he laced his hands together and slammed them down hard on the foreman's head. It wasn't much of a blow, but it gave Talbot time to roll sideways and scramble to his feet.

Donnelly gained his own legs and, breathing heavily, threw off his gloves. His face was swollen and red, his hair atangle. Blood soaked the shoulder of his sheepskin.

"Come on, you son of a bitch!" he shrieked. "I'm gonna take you apart limb by limb and hear you howl like a stuck pig!"

Talbot threw down his own gloves and fisted his hands, crouching. They circled for several seconds, then Donnelly leaned in with a right hook. Talbot ducked and the blow went wild. Before Donnelly could regroup, Talbot landed a left cross, opening a two-inch gash on Donnelly's cheek.

Brushing the back of his hand across the gash and growling like a wounded griz, Donnelly stepped back to consider the blood on his hand. Then he closed in again, swinging his right fist.

Again Talbot ducked, but before he could get his head back up and fade left, Donnelly caught his right brow dead-on with a crushing, ham-sized fist. Talbot staggered backward as the pain tore through his skull, and before he could regain his balance, Donnelly charged, bulling him over backward.

The foreman slammed Talbot's face with three brain-numbing right jabs, then he reached down to his ankle and produced a stiletto. The slender blade came up under Talbot's chin, and following the blade with his eyes, Talbot saw the naked woman etched in the tempered steel.

He reached up and grabbed Donnelly's hand just before the blade pierced the tender skin over his jugular vein, and the naked woman twisted and turned as the two hands struggled for dominance.

Through gritted teeth, his eyes on the naked woman, Talbot grunted, "You always fight this fair, Rag?"

"Fuck you, Talbot . . . you're a dead man."

"Don't . . . count . . . your . . . *chickens* . . ." Talbot funneled a sudden burst of adrenaline into the fist that held Donnelly's, and the naked woman turned suddenly away from him, as though twirled by an invisible partner, and plunged head first into Donnelly's leathery, whisker-bristled throat.

Ruby blood gushed over the hilt and onto the handle, covering Talbot's hand. Donnelly opened his mouth to speak but only blood issued. His body stiffened. As he faded sideways, turning onto his back, he clutched at the blade with both hands. He pressed his back to the frozen ground and struggled feebly with the deep-set blade, kicking his feet, stark terror in his eyes.

Then his hands fell to his chest, his face turned to the side, and the light faded from his gaze.

Talbot pushed himself to his feet carefully, trying to quash the pounding in his head. Sensing someone near, he turned quickly, ready to defend himself once again.

Jacy stood behind the beaver house, where a faint deer trail opened onto the creek. She held a rifle across her chest and she was looking at the body of Randall Magnusson lying several feet away, blood dripping from the black hole in his forehead.

Realizing that she had been the one who'd shot Randall, probably from the ridge behind them, opposite the man with the Big Fifty, Talbot watched her take three stiff steps toward the body, lower the rifle barrel, and blow another hole through young Magnusson's face.

"That son of a bitch," she said.

Talbot didn't know what to say. He just stood there, watching her with Donnelly's gore on his hands.

"Are you all right?" he said finally.

She turned suddenly away from Magnusson's inert body, ran to Talbot, and threw her arms around his neck, sobbing. He couldn't hold her because of the blood on his hands but he pressed his cheek to hers, said in her ear, "I'm so sorry, Jacy. I led them right to your cabin. I just didn't think they'd be after me so soon."

"Those sons of bitches," she sobbed, her face buried in his shoulder. "The one shooting from the ridge . . . he took off when he saw me . . . *he* was the one that shot Gordon and Mrs. Sanderson."

"Oh, Jesus. Are you okay?"

She nodded. "They just roughed me up a little." She lifted her head and looked into his face through slitted, teary eyes. "They burned your cabin," she cried, studying him.

He stared back at her, feeling numb, his heart quickening. "How do you know?"

She indicated Magnusson and Donnelly with a tip of her head. "They said so. I saw smoke that way when I left to find you."

Talbot looked off, setting his jaw so tight that his

teeth ached. By now, the ranch would be no more than rubble. Magnusson had left him with little but the shirt on his back. Fuming, he looked at the dead bodies, wishing he could resurrect them and kill them all over again.

Maybe he couldn't work miracles, but he sure as hell could fix the head honcho's flint but good. He'd kill Magnusson—now, today—or die trying.

He knelt down and rubbed his gory hands in the weeds and snow. "Go home and stay there," he said tightly.

"I'm coming with you."

"No."

"I'll get my horse," she said, turning.

"I said no," he called after her.

She turned around sharply, long hair flying. Her green eyes were bright with fire. "You say no because I'm a girl, but you get something straight, mister—Magnusson is into me for as much as he's into you, and girl or not, I'm calling his note due. Are you with me?"

He studied her, a tender expression growing on his face. In the vast desert of his loneliness, sorrow, and rage, she was the one bright thing.

He sighed and shook his head fatefully, tried a smile. "I sure as hell wouldn't want to be against you," he said.

Then he watched her turn and stomp off through the weeds, thoroughly in love with her.

CHAPTER 28

IT WAS TOO cold and too late in the day to be this far from home, and Homer Rinski knew better. He just didn't care. What he had on his mind would not be stymied by such earthly concerns as fading light and plummeting temperatures.

He followed a shallow, curving draw along St. Mary's Creek, steam jetting from his and his horse's nostrils, the swaybacked roan appearing as sullen as the stoop-shouldered man astraddle it. The sharp breeze played at the floppy brim of Rinski's black felt hat, tied down with the red wool scarf Mattie had knitted for him last Christmas.

He hadn't had a conscious thought in weeks. It was all impulse—a single, otherworldly drive driven by holy hate.

When he came to an offshooting draw, he followed it through a scattering of burr oaks and junipers, the trail rising gradually until Rinski's head was level with the tableland above. He halted the horse and peered north.

The corrals, hay barns, and bunkhouses of the Double X headquarters sprawled in a coulee below the back of the big house, two hundred yards away. Smoke issued from the mansion and horses milled in the corrals, but smoke curled from the chimney of only one of the outbuildings.

Rinski studied the structure for several seconds, then growled "Giddyup" to the horse.

He slipped the butt of his old bird gun under his right arm and, fingering the paper shells in his right coat pocket, moved out toward the single low-slung cabin issuing smoke from its battered tin chimney. Rinski could tell it was a summer cook shack. There was an abandoned chuckwagon parked haphazardly in front, and two sets of footprints led to the door.

Dismounting and tying his horse to the wagon, Rinski heard voices inside the cabin. He lifted the barrel of his shotgun, stepped resolutely to the plank door, and kicked it open.

"God-*dang*!" came a surprised yell.

Someone screamed. Rinski thought at first it was a girl's scream. Then his eyes adjusted to the cabin's murk. Two men lay on a single cot beneath a papered-over window.

One had a neatly trimmed, carefully waxed mustache, and he looked eastern or British. His naked, porcelain-white legs were carpeted with fine black hair. The second man was a young cowboy with a sparse, sandy mustache and a black felt farmer's hat with a round brim and a bullet-shaped crown. A red neckerchief encircled his scrawny neck. His breeches lay on the floor and his long johns were bunched around his feet and soiled socks.

There was a long silence. The men on the cot stared at Rinski; Rinski stared back.

"Do you *mind*?" the dandy yelled finally.

Rinski ignored him. He stared at the cowboy, fairly shaking with rage. "Did you . . . did you savage my girl, Shelby Green?"

The cowboy raised his hands placatingly. "I-I didn't harm Mattie, Mr. Rinski," he said thinly.

Rinski appeared more taken aback by the declaration than by the boy's exposed member or by the realization of what he'd been using it for. He growled at length, with a slow nod and a speculative squint.

"No! . . . it was Randall. He's the one savaged Mattie. I only . . . I only . . ."

"It was you and Randall."

"No! Like I said—"

"You and Randall savaged my little girl."

The young cowboy's voice was small and thin. "Please, Mr. Rinski. I didn't meant to do it . . . It was Randall . . . He made me!"

"You and Randall Magnusson."

"Not!"

"Tell the Lord about your devilish desires, Shelby Green. Maybe he'll have mercy on your soul."

Rinski brought the shotgun to bear. It boomed, sprouting flames. The cowboy's head disappeared in a cloud of bone and blood, basting his hat against the log wall. Limbs akimbo, his headless body flew off the cot and hit the floor with a slap and a thud.

Rinski turned to the dandy.

"Please, no!" the man wailed, covering his head with his arms, bringing his knees to his chest. "I'm a *doctor*!"

"You're filth," Rinski intoned. "May the Lord accept you back from the Beast."

He pressed the barrel to the man's head and tripped the left trigger. He appraised the mess the gun had made, grimly pleased, then turned and left the bloody cabin.

He mounted his horse and rode up the tawny rise to the big house. He dismounted and tied the horse to the hitch rail at the back door.

Rinski hefted the shotgun, tightened his coat collar

about his neck, and strolled up the three wooden steps to the sashed door. He was not surprised to find it unlocked—the devil was known for his arrogance—and stepped into the kitchen.

A spidery old woman in a poke bonnet and purple cotton maid's dress and white apron turned from the range. "What in heaven's name?"

"Get out," Rinski ordered.

Staring at the shotgun held across Rinski's chest, the woman stuttered and stammered, trying to speak.

"Get out!"

She gave a start, wringing her hands, and side-stepped past him on her way out the kitchen door.

Rinski saw a rose lamp on a table with carved legs. He grabbed the lamp, stepped into the dining room, and threw it against the drapes. It shattered when it hit the floor, spilling kerosene.

Rinski stepped up to the pool of liquid and produced a match from his coat pocket. Scratching the lucifer on the polished mahogany table, which was nearly as long as Rinski's cabin was wide and which shone like a moonlit lake at night, he dropped the flame in the kerosene. It went up with a whoosh. A toothy line of flames curled back agaist the wall, instantly igniting the heavy drapes.

"Oh, my God! Fire! *Fire!*"

Rinski turned to see two women descending the stairs in a hurry. One was young and pretty, with long raven hair bouncing on her shoulders. The other was older, heavy-bosomed, and made up like a nickel whore you'd find in any boom town.

"Save yourselves, charlatans!" Rinski told them, voice raised above the whooshing flames. "You'll no longer find shelter in the devil's lair!"

"That's cashmere, you fool!"

"Mother!" the young woman cried in warning.

"Get the men!"

"They rode away this morning, and I haven't seen Harrison for *hours!*"

The older woman ran to the drapes, screaming, looking around feebly for something with which to put out the fire. The younger woman ran up behind her, grabbed her arm, and pulled her out the front door.

Rinski found another lantern and walked down the hall on the other side of the rose-carpeted stairs. He lit the lantern and tossed it into a study with a cave-sized stone hearth and a hide-covered desk as large as a wagon bed, then proceeded upstairs—slowly, deliberately, as though walking in his sleep.

He'd just tossed a lantern on a lace-covered, four-poster bed when he heard the girl's voice rise from the yard below. "Oh, look! Oh, Mother, it's the man from the *trapper*'s shack!"

Rinski went back down the stairs several minutes later, nearly the whole second story in flames behind him. Through the eye-stinging smoke of the ground floor he saw the silhouette of a tall man in a fur coat filling the open front door, swathed in smoke. He was holding a long-barreled rifle straight up in the air.

When Rinski stopped on the stairs, the man brought the barrel down level with Rinski's chest. The smoke parted enough for Rinski to make out the man's blue, blue eyes and his grin, shaped around the long thin cigar clamped in his teeth.

"You have a light, gringo?" he yelled above the flames.

Rinski didn't even have time to bring his shotgun down. Fire leapt from the barrel of the Big Fifty, blowing a four-inch hole through Rinski's chest. He flew back against the stairs, tripping both barrels of the shotgun and sending buckshot into the flame-engulfed rafters.

He was dead on the landing before he could mutter a final prayer.

"No, I didn't think so," Del Toro said, turning around and heading back toward King Magnusson's lovely daughter standing dumbly with her mother in the yard.

They were looking at him like Jesus Christ had just ridden up on a donkey.

Hee-hee.

———

King Magnusson turned from Jed Gibbon's body and looked down the street to where all the shooting had taken place.

Dead men and dead horses littered the street between the Sundowner and the livery barn. Wind shepherded a bloodstained hat in Magnusson's direction, bouncing it along the frozen ruts of the street until it caught in the legs of a feed trough before the mercantile.

The bartender poked his head through the saloon's broken front window. Magnusson brought his pistol up reflexively, but, seeing him, the man gave a start and lurched back inside. One of the bodies in the street moved and Magnusson walked toward it.

It was Verlyn Thornberg. He lay grunting and cursing as he tried to stretch his arm out for his pistol, several feet away. There was a gaping, blood-soaked hole where his stomach had been. His coat was spilling viscera.

Magnusson stepped on the pistol and grinned down at the dying man. Thornberg turned his head up sideways, blood washing over his lower lip. He tried to say something but nothing came from his mouth but more blood, as dark and thick as molasses.

"Look what you did to yourself, Verlyn," Magnusson sneered. "Instead of pulling up stakes and moving on, leaving the Bench to me, you're layin' here in the street drowning in your own guts. Tsk, tsk, tsk."

Thornberg's lips curled back from his teeth, and red rage shone in his face for just a second. Then the color faded and the light in his eyes dimmed. His head dipped. It fell in a puddle of quickly congealing blood. Thornberg sighed, and he was dead.

Magnusson gave a self-satisfied chuff.

He had to admit, though, the rancher and Gibbon had given him a run for his money. And they'd hurt him beyond the bullet in his shoulder.

But he'd be back in action in no time. He'd start sending notices for gun-savvy riders as far north as Calgary and as far south as Amarillo.

He'd have the Bench to himself in no time.

After all, he was almost there. He might have lost most of his men—all but Rag and Del Toro, that is (you couldn't really call Randall a man)—but he still had his herds.

He still had his headquarters . . .

Thinking of that gave him a funny feeling in his gut, a bitter taste at the roof of his mouth, and he felt a sudden compulsion to get home as fast as he could. It was an irrational fear, he knew. Donnelly and Del Toro would have taken care of Talbot, and there was no one left on the Bench with balls enough to threaten the house.

Still . . .

He looked up and down the street for a horse to ride and didn't see a one—standing, that is. His silver-gray, always a little gun-shy for some reason, was long gone. Turning to the livery barn, Magnusson saw that the horses in the paddock had knocked the rails down and lit a shuck out of there after the shooting had started.

Then, as if answering his silent plea, he heard a knicker behind him. Turning, he saw a horse poke its head out between the drugstore and the feed store. Its reins dangled as it turned its head and twitched its ears nervously, looking around for its rider.

Magnusson started slowly toward it, holding his hands out in a gesture of goodwill. "Whoa, boy," he cooed. "Whoa, now. That's it."

The horse shook its head and backed up a few steps, but it didn't start turning to flee until Magnusson had grabbed the reins and was halfway in the leather.

"Hah! Haaah!" he shouted, giving the horse the spurs and reining westward out of town.

He'd ridden hard for nearly an hour when he saw the smoke.

CHAPTER 29

"WELL, I'LL BE goddamned," Talbot mumbled, bringing his horse to a sudden halt and lifting his eyes to the column of smoke rising beyond the second ridge north.

Jacy reined in, too, and looked where Talbot was looking. "What do you make of that?"

"I don't know, but there's only one way to find out." He touched his spurs to his horse's flanks and started down the slope.

Ten minutes later he and Jacy stopped their mounts on a ridge about four hundred yards from the Magnusson headquarters and watched the burning roof of the grand mansion tumble into the flame-engulfed rubble below. The dragon-like roar carried on the cold air, and the resin in the milled lumber popped like .45s.

The conflagration glowed brightly against the falling night.

Dumbfounded, Talbot and Jacy looked at each other, then at the fire. Someone had torched the house, all right, but where were the men who did it, and where were Magnusson and his riders?

Talbot got half an answer when a horseman galloped in from the west, about a hundred yards away. The man left the creek bottom below Talbot and Jacy and kicked his horse up the ridge beneath the burning house.

The man's large frame and posture bespoke King Magnusson.

Thoroughly perplexed, Talbot told Jacy to keep her head down—he knew from the tracks they'd been following that the hombre with the Big Fifty had come this way, too—and started down the ridge toward the creek.

As they climbed the ridge below the house they spotted a saddled horse foraging in the snow with its reins dangling. Jacy recognized Homer Rinski's brand, and said as much to Talbot.

The furrows in Talbot's brow deepened. He shook his head and rode on, cantering, following Magnusson's trail now and holding his Winchester up high and ready.

He and Jacy halted their horses about fifty yards from the house. Magnusson had dismounted and stood before the house with his back to Talbot and Jacy, his big hands clenched at his sides, shoulders humped, the collar of his long buffalo coat rising like the fur around a cur's neck.

Slowly he lifted his hands to his temples, elbows straight out from his head like horns, and bellowed like a foundering bull, staggering with the force of his emotion.

Through the roar of the fire, Talbot heard him calling Suzanne's name. The thought that she could be in there gave Talbot a jolt, and he spurred his horse forward, feeling the heat.

"Mark!" Jacy cried.

Ignoring her, Talbot brought his mount up even with Magnusson. Seeing him, the rancher's livid eyes grew even keener.

"You!" he cried, lunging toward Talbot's horse. "You did this!"

Talbot turned his horse away from the man, holding his rifle on him. "I didn't burn your damn house!" he yelled. "Did all the women get out?"

Magnusson danced Talbot's horse in a circle, trying to pull its rider out of the saddle. Jacy rode up, yelling, but kept her horse a safe distance from the melee. There was little she could do.

Talbot's horse bucked and rose up on its hind legs, frightened by Magnusson as well as the fire. Holding the reins in one hand and the Winchester in the other, Talbot lost his balance. Magnusson reached up and grabbed him by his coat collar and pulled. Talbot dropped the rifle and came out of the saddle, cursing and hitting the ground hard on his left shoulder.

Pushing himself up on a knee while Magnusson dodged the horse, Talbot said, "You burned *me* out, you son of a bitch!"

"I'll kill you! I'll kill you!" Magnusson roared. He stepped forward and kicked Talbot in the chest. Talbot hit the ground on his back.

Magnusson moved in and was about to kick again when Talbot rolled left and gained his feet, crouched and ready to spring. Sloppy with rage, Magnusson leaned in, hooking with his right fist.

Talbot ducked. He came up jabbing with both hands, pummeling Magnusson's face with satisfying smacks. The rancher staggered back, fear and surprise flashing in his cold eyes. Talbot didn't stop swinging until Magnusson was on the ground in a raging, frothy-lipped heap. Blood poured from the gashes in his face.

Talbot stood before him crouched and ready, his fists held high, feet spread, upper lip curled in anger. "You had enough?"

Magnusson groaned and tried to push himself to his feet, fell back down.

"Now, like I said," Talbot snarled, "I didn't burn your house, you bastard. Not that I wouldn't have, but someone beat me to it."

Rubbing a jaw, Magnusson climbed to a knee. "Who?"

"I don't know and I don't care."

Magnusson's eyes grew bright with renewed fear as he turned them to the blaze. "Suzanne!" he cried.

"How do you know she didn't make it out?" Talbot asked, anger turning to genuine concern.

A woman's voice rose. "*King!*"

Talbot turned his gaze southward, where two women cloaked in quilts were climbing the bank from the outbuildings in the coulee below. One was Magnusson's wife; the other was the gray-haired maid. Magnusson's wife clung to the older woman for support, her face twisted with anguish.

Magnusson stood unsteadily, "Kendra!"

"King!"

Magnusson ran to her and grabbed her by the shoulders, shaking her. "What happened! Where's Suzanne!"

"Oh, King!" the woman bawled. Her legs turned to jelly and she crumpled in Magnusson's arms.

"Goddamnit, where is she!"

Releasing her, he turned to the other woman, taking Minnie's shoulders in his big hands and nearly lifting her off the ground. "Tell me!"

"Oh, Mr. Magnusson! A man came," she stammered in a thick Scottish accent. "He . . . he . . ."

"What!"

"He come into the house while I was cookin' . . . an' he . . . an' he started throwin' *lanterns* around!"

"Who?"

"An old man . . . old as me."

"Did he take Suzanne?"

"No! It was another man. He come up on a black horse and shot the first man in the house. It was him . . . a Mexican . . . he took Suzanne! Just grabbed her up on his horse and rode away!"

Magnusson paused, absorbing the information.

"Please, sir, you're hurting my arms," the woman begged.

Magnusson swallowed. "Which way did they go?"

"That way, sir—southeast."

Magnusson released the woman, who gave a scream, clutching her bruised arms. Magnusson turned stiffly, eyes wide and unmoving, and stared south, where the tables rolled away like a rumpled carpet, sooty now with the fading winter light.

The fire grumbled like a distant train, cracking and hissing. A timber fell with a muffled boom, geysering sparks.

The old woman stared at the conflagration, looking stricken. Mrs. Magnusson bawled, her head in her hands. Jacy stood near her horse, about twenty feet away, looking on dispassionately. She had nothing but disdain for these people, and Talbot didn't blame her.

Turning to the rancher, Talbot said, "Who is this man, King? Where's he headed? You have any idea?"

Magnusson started for his horse. "What do you care?"

"It's getting too late to track him. Best to wait till morning."

Magnusson grabbed his reins and climbed into the leather, favoring his right shoulder. "I don't have to track him. I know where that randy son of a bitch is taking my daughter." He looked at the maid. "Harness the sorrels to Mrs. Magnusson's phaeton and drive her to Mr. Troutman's in Big Draw."

He reined his horse around, gouged it with his spurs, and circled the burning rubble of his mansion, heading southeast. Lifting her head to watch him go, Mrs. Magnusson wailed.

Talbot turned to Jacy. "I have to help him."

Jacy laughed caustically. "Are you crazy?"

"He has a bullet in his shoulder. He won't be able to get Suzanne back by himself."

"That's his problem."

Talbot shook his head, not liking the position he was in any better than Jacy did. "I can't just walk away. Suzanne's out there with a lunatic."

"It's Magnusson's problem. He hired the man. Besides, it's not up to you to save the daughter of the man who murdered your brother and burned your ranch."

"Jacy, I have to go."

"Then go, and just keep goin'." She turned, reaching for her saddle horn and shoving her left foot in the stirrup.

Talbot watched her canter the line-back dun down the hill in the early winter dusk. He couldn't blame her for how she felt, not after all that King Magnusson had taken from her. A few years and battles ago, when he was her age, he would have felt the same way.

He mounted up and left the ranchyard by Magnusson's route. There was some light left, and after a mile and a half of hard riding Talbot spotted him. The rancher had slowed to a trot.

"It's Talbot. I'm coming up behind you."

"Get out of here. This is my problem. I'll solve it."

"I'd like nothing better."

Magnusson turned to him. "Then why are you here?"

"It's not Suzanne's fault she's your daughter."

Magnusson laughed derisively. "You fool. I sent that Mex gunman, Rag Donnelly, and my son out to *kill* you!"

"Well, the joke's on you, Magnusson. Donnelly and your son are dead, and in case you forgot, that Mexican has Suzanne."

Magnusson reined his horse to a sudden stop and looked at Talbot with fire in his eyes. Talbot stopped and faced him, reading his mind, seeing his hand edge toward the holster on his hip. He could hear the man take a slow, deep breath through his nose.

Talbot said, "Try it, Magnusson. I'd like nothing better than to settle this right here and now. But think about it—you kill me, you kill your daughter. You can't bring her back alone. Not with that bullet in your shoulder. From the looks of your coat, you're about to bleed dry."

Magnusson studied him for a long moment, lips quivering with restrained emotion. "When this is over . . ." he said tightly, and reined his horse back along the trail.

"You got that right," Talbot agreed.

They rode together in truculent silence. The night came down until there was only a smudge of gray in the west and the breeze had settled. It was cold, but the high, heavy clouds tempered it some.

A single wolf howled in the distance, like the savage soul of the night itself. The horses clopped on the frozen ground. Otherwise, all was silent.

When they came to a ravine, Magnusson dismounted and walked over to the edge. He stood staring down for so long that Talbot finally followed suit.

Below huddled a low-slung cabin in the brushy horseshoe of a frozen creek. The windows cast light on the barren ground, and the stovepipe emitted the tang of river willow and ash. A horse moved under a tarpaulin cover supported by willow poles.

Magnusson took a breath, hefted his rifle, and started down.

"Hold on," Talbot whispered. "He could be layin' for you."

Ignoring him, Magnusson continued down the slope. Talbot cursed, turning back to his horse and shucking his Winchester, then followed the rancher down the hill to the shelter. Magnusson peered around at the cabin, cursed aloud, and jacked a shell in the chamber of his Henry.

Suddenly both hands fell to his sides, and he staggered back against the wall.

"You're getting weak," Talbot said. "Stay here while I take a look."

He glanced at the cabin, then ran to its south wall. Hearing the sound of low, muffled screams, he pressed his back against the weathered cottonwood logs, sidestepped slowly to the small, sashed window, and peered in.

He had to blink several times to clarify the image—a bare-breasted Suzanne straddling the naked gunman on an enormous bear blanket spread on the packed earth floor.

A lantern burned on a table and a fire shone around the doors in the wood-burning stove. On Suzanne's lovely head rested the gunman's round-brimmed, black felt hat.

She was smiling . . . laughing.

Her raven curls bounced on her naked back as she rode the gunman like a horse, and the sounds emitting from her parted lips were combinations of screams, groans, high-pitched laughs, and giggles.

"You're my savior, José!" she yelled. "You've *saved* me!"

The gunman's hands kneaded her breasts. His head tipped back, revealing two rows of small white teeth beneath his brushy black mustache. He was wiggling his toes and singing.

Suddenly the door burst open and in stepped King Magnusson, rifle jutting out from his waist. Talbot froze, heart pumping.

"Daddy!" Suzanne screamed.

Silence.

King stood there staring, still as a stone.

Talbot ran around the cabin to the door yelling, "King—*don't!*"

He was too late.

The rifle barked once, twice. As Talbot turned the corner it barked a third time. Following close on its heels was the crack of a pistol.

Magnusson staggered back out of the cabin. He dropped the rifle and slumped to his knees.

Talbot slammed his back up against the cabin wall and peered through the open doorway, swinging his rifle inside. Crouched low, one hand pressed against the back wall, the other clutching a silver-plated revolver, the naked gunman fired.

The bullet tore splinters from the door frame six inches from Talbot's chin. Talbot fired his Winchester, standing the man up against the wall. The pistol shot into the ceiling. Talbot fired into the gunman three more times, the smoking rifle jumping in his arms. The man rolled along the wall and fell on his back.

Talbot ran into the cabin and knelt next to Suzanne. She lay on the rug with an arm flung across her face, as if shielding her from the light. One of Magnusson's rifle shots had gone through her wrist, breaking it. The other two had gone through her chest.

She was dead.

Talbot sighed and cursed, ran his hand down his face. He hung his head and knelt there for a long time.

He'd never felt so old.

Where would it end?

When would the blood ever end?

Finally he stood and pulled King Magnusson's lifeless body into the cabin, went out, and closed the door behind him.

CHAPTER 30

IT TOOK TALBOT a good three hours to ride to Canaan. When the town's main street closed in around him, as dark as a graveyard, he was chilled to the bone and more tired than he'd ever felt in his life.

He woke the hostler at the livery barn. "Stable my horse and give him a good rubdown, will you?"

"At this hour?"

"You want my business or don't you?"

"It's gonna cost you."

"No, it's gonna cost you. Give me a hundred dollars, and the horse is yours."

The old man blinked. "What? You just bought him last week for two hundred."

"Don't look a gift horse in the mouth," Talbot said. "I won't be needing him any longer. I'm taking the train the hell out of here."

"Thought you were *from* here."

"I am."

Muttering, the man retrieved a key from his desk and opened a small safe sitting under a pile of account books and catalogs. He counted a hundred dollars into Talbot's outstretched hand.

"I reckon I can't blame you," he said. "After what happened here today, just outside those doors, I'm about to pack up and try my luck in Glendive."

"What happened?"

"Didn't you hear? The sheriff was killed just down the street by King Magnusson. Verlyn Thornberg, too, and a handful of his riders. Main Street was like a damn battlefield. We were all day cleaning up and carting the bodies up to the undertaker's."

"So that's where Magnusson got that bullet in his shoulder," Talbot said thoughtfully.

"Say again?"

"You know the old trapper's cabin on Little Wibaux Creek?"

"Sure. Charlie Gallernault used to hole up out there."

"Well, King Magnusson and his daughter are out there now. Dead. Send the undertaker out for the bodies, will you?"

The stableman stood there looking flabbergasted. "Holy shit in a handbasket!"

Talbot turned to strip his saddle from his horse. "You'll find Mrs. Magnusson at Bernard Troutman's in Big Draw."

Saddle slung over his shoulder, Talbot walked over to the hotel and pounded on the door. After ten minutes the woman proprietor came to the door in an old duster and nightcap, looking haggard and worried and wielding a shotgun.

"I don't take in customers this time of the night," she said. "Not after what happened here yesterday."

Talbot sighed, genuinely exhausted. "I don't blame you, ma'am, but I'd sure appreciate an exception to the rule. Sleep is all I'm after."

She studied him. She let the heavy gun sink toward the floor and drew the door wide. "A man out this late can be up to little good," she admonished.

Talbot sighed. "Thank you. Much obliged."

When he'd gotten situated in his room, he stripped

down to his long johns and crawled under the covers with a groan and a sigh. As tired as he was, he thought he'd fall right to sleep. Instead he lay there, his mind whirling like a windmill in a steady gale.

Coming home to a little peace and quiet. That was a good one. Almost as good as finding his lovely Pilar stretched out in the barn with her throat cut.

Thinking of her made him think of Jacy, and his heart twisted counterclockwise and gave an additional thump. She was the only thing homey about this place, and if he stayed for anyone or anything it would be for her. But that was over now, before it had even gotten started.

It was just as well. He didn't belong here anymore, and he knew Jacy could never belong anywhere else.

He rolled several cigarettes and smoked them down to nubs, lying there in the dark, staring up at the ceiling, his mind torturing him with all the death he'd seen over the past few hours, of Suzanne lying there on the bear rug beside the gunfighter— murdered by her own adoring father.

And it had all started with greed.

Jacy had said it best: "They all died like hell, like nothing means a goddamn thing."

Talbot didn't fall asleep until practically dawn. He woke four hours later to bright winter sunlight filling his room. The light was so merry golden, the sky so cold-scoured blue over the false wooden fronts across the street, he wondered for a moment if the bloody events of yesterday had been a nightmare and all was right with the world.

It was a fleeting notion, gone before he'd buckled his gun around his waist and headed out the door with his saddle on his shoulder.

"Help you, mister?" the depot agent said through the window.

"Yeah, I need a ticket for the next train, whenever that is."

"Due in at twelve-fifteen, just like it says on the chalkboard over yonder. Where you headed?"

"What?"

"Where you headed."

Talbot thought, looking around. "Ah . . . I don't know . . ."

The agent planted his arms on the counter and scrutinized Talbot under his green eyeshade. "Mister, you mean to tell me you want a ticket, but you don't where you're *goin'!*"

Talbot turned sideways and looked around the station some more. "Well, I reckon that's the long and short of it."

"Who you runnin' from?"

Talbot looked at the man. "What's that?"

"Who you runnin' from? The law?"

"No," Talbot said thoughtfully, rubbing a hand over his chin. "No, I'm just runnin'." Irritation creeping into his voice, he said, "Listen, mister, why don't you just give me a ticket for as far as the train goes, and I'll get off somewhere between here and there."

The man raised his hands. "Don't get mad at me. You're the one doesn't know where he's goin'." He sighed and glanced at the schedule chalked on the board. He shook his head. "Just anywhere that looks good, eh, cowboy? Doesn't sound like much of a life to me. Well, let's see . . . that'll be twelve dollars and fifteen cents, payable in cash only."

Talbot paid the man, took his ticket, and picked up his saddle. "Much obliged," he said, and headed out the door.

He had an hour and a half to wait for the train, and he decided the best place to do it was at the saloon. As he stepped up on the boardwalk he saw that the big plate-glass window was gone, replaced by boards.

He shook his head and walked inside and ordered a beer and a shot. He asked the apron to keep them coming until his train left at twelve-fifteen.

"Where you headed?" the man asked him conversationally.

"None of your goddamn business!" Talbot exploded, and knocked back his shot. "Can't a man get drunk in peace around here?"

He brooded over several drinks, then moseyed over to the train station at noon.

The train was on time. Two drummers, an old lady, and a cowboy got off, and Talbot got on, threw his saddle on one seat and sat in another across the aisle. There were only a handful of people aboard, reading illustrated newspapers and conversing in hushed tones.

Talbot rolled a cigarette and sat waiting for the train to depart. He was halfway through the quirley when something blocked the sun beating through the window to his left.

Turning, he saw Jacy sitting atop a tall brown horse. She looked in at him, squinting her eyes against the reflected light, breath puffing around her face.

Talbot got up and walked outside. Jacy rode over to meet him.

"Figured I'd find you here," she said.

Talbot shrugged. "Yeah, well, I guess it's time to move on."

"What happened?"

"They're all dead."

Jacy nodded. "I'm sorry about Suzanne."

Talbot nodded.

"And I'm sorry about what I said back there at Magnusson's. I was wrong."

Talbot shrugged. "You'd been through a lot. I'd just been through a little more."

"I guess." Jacy looked around. "Well . . ."

"Good-bye, Jacy."

She turned her green eyes to him and nodded. "Be seein' you."

"You bet."

"Good-bye." She tried a smile, reined her horse around, and rode away.

Talbot called after her, "Throw some flowers on Dave's grave in the spring, will you?"

She turned, gave a nod, and turned away, heading down Main.

Talbot stood there for several minutes. When the conductor yelled, "All a-board!" he got back on the train as it chuffed away from the depot.

But when the train was gone, he was standing again on the siding, in the steam the locomotive had left behind. He had his saddle on his shoulder.

He stared across the platform. Jacy sat atop her horse just beyond the station house, looking at him and grinning.

"How in the hell did you know?" Talbot said with mock severity.

Jacy shrugged. "No man in his right mind would leave a woman like me."

Talbot laughed. Shaking his head, he moved toward her.

THE
ROMANTICS

For Gena, who knows why or should.

for Oscar, who knows why or should

Gold and love affairs are difficult to hide.

—Spanish proverb

CHAPTER 1

---·•◦•·---

1879—*Arizona Territory*

THE STAGE HAD stopped at one of those storied bordercountry cantinas, a ramshackle relay station in the rocky, sunscorched bowels of the Arizona desert, where many an hombre has entered and never been heard from again.

Flies buzzed in the shade beneath the eaves. The gutted carcass of what appeared to be a wild pig turned on a rawhide rope. From the smell, it had been hanging there for days.

"Follow me," Adrian Clark told his wife, a young Spanish beauty with raven hair and night-black eyes. Descended from Spanish kings, twenty-two years old, her name was Marina. "Stay close."

Clark hadn't liked any of the stations at which the dusty red Concord had stopped since leaving Tucson. All had the smell of casual death.

As the Clarks entered, a half-dozen men dressed in dusty trail clothes turned to look and did a double take. The light of the young woman's beauty shone in their whiskered, sunleathered faces as their bovine eyes played over her Spanish queen's delicate, almond-shaped face and the long black hair that cascaded down from her green felt hat.

A small silver cross on a thin silver chain nestled

in the hollow between her breasts, which filled a white blouse above a wide black belt, a black wool skirt, and soft leather boots, the whole slightly worn and dusty from travel.

"Madre mía," breathed one of the men, a short Mexican with a weathered sombrero hanging down his back.

"Sí," the white man next to him said, swallowing.

Marina cast her gaze nervously about, then studied the mashed earth at her feet. Adrian Clark cleared his throat. He was a tall, lean man in a Prince Albert coat and four-in-hand tie, an English Bisley tied low on his hip. Striped gray slacks, tailor-made, hung down over shiny black boots with low heels. He wore a planter's hat tipped at a rakish angle, and the color of his Vandyke beard matched the dull red of the hair that curled onto his shoulders. His skin was pale and lightly freckled. In addition to the rest of his attire, the gray vest, gold watch fob, pinky ring, and Cuban cigar bespoke either a gambling man or a wealthy Southern gentleman—or both.

"This way, my dear," he said commandingly, as though to a child, in his petal-soft Missouri drawl.

Bright sunlight angled through the open shutters, revealing the crumbs and grime on the smashed-earth floor, stains and food scraps on the unwashed tables. Flies buzzed. Outside, horses nickered and clomped. A cicada whined.

Peering through the shutters, Clark saw that two hostlers in Mexican peasant rags were switching teams while the driver stood nearby, dipping water from an olla. The hostlers couldn't have moved much slower had they been standing stock-still.

Clark cursed under his breath and slid his glance back around the room. His attention was drawn to a tall, willowy hombre in a long gray coat who was sitting half in shadow in one corner. He wore what appeared to Clark, an ex-Confederate himself, to be a Confederate-gray campaign hat. A bony fist rested beside a half-empty shot glass, making the glass appear thimble-sized. The man's broad face was in shadow, but Clark felt the man's cold eyes on him—appraising, disdainful.

"You two the only ones?" came a brusque, Spanish-accented voice.

Clark turned sharply, startled, hand flicking around the butt of the Bisley. A stout man with a gray beard and thin, salt-and-pepper hair combed back from a sharp widow's peak stood behind the makeshift bar, blocklike fists resting on the planks. His blood-stained apron was aswarm with flies.

"I beg your pardon?" Clark said.

The man indicated the stage beyond the window. "From the stage. You the only ones?"

"That's right."

The man lifted his eyebrows and said lazily, "Well, I get paid to feed the weary travelers. You hungry?"

Clark looked at the young, beautiful woman who had been his wife for only a month. She sat stiffly in a chair, hands in her lap, and shrugged noncommittally. Clark remembered the carcass hanging outside, and his stomach turned. But neither he nor Marina had eaten since morning.

"Maybe we could share a sandwich," he said to the barman.

One of the men standing at the bar chuckled.

The barman smiled at Clark. He turned to a stew pot and filled a bowl, then brought it over and set it and a spoon before Marina.

"Share a bowl of hog tripe," he said. "My specialty."

Marina looked at the brothy substance afloat with spongy white intestines and flecked with black pepper. Standing behind her, his hands resting protectively on her chair back, Clark wrinkled his eyebrows. The heavy aroma wafting up smelled like boiled blood. "I don't think—"

"No, it looks good," Marina said, looking at Clark with an acquiescent smile. "Menudo. My mother used to make menudo." She gave her lovely dark eyes to the barman. "Gracias, señor."

The man shrugged. "De nada, señora," he said with a south-of-the-border flourish, bending slightly at the waist. He limped back to the bar.

Clark stared thoughtfully at the barman. He cleared his throat. "Say, we're looking for a friend. Reese McCormick's the name. Have you heard of him?"

The barman was refilling glasses behind the bar. He lifted the bottle and looked at Clark with sudden directness. "McCormick?"

Clark nodded.

The station manager glanced around the room, a wistful light entering his eyes. The other men's stares grew tense, their interest in the strangers renewed and transformed. One of them snickered.

"You boys seen Reese McCormick?" the barman asked.

No one spoke. They stared at Clark and his wife with eyes bright with mockery.

One of the men, a white man, piped up, a taunting smile pulling at the corners of his mouth. "Reese? Hell, he's dead."

"Dead?" Clark exclaimed. "How?"

"How should I know? Just heard he was dead," the man said, and turned back to his drink, ending the conversation.

The station manager turned to Clark. "Sorry, *amigo.*"

Clark sighed and cursed under his breath. He

coughed, bringing a handkerchief to his mouth, and sat down.

Two of the men at the bar were still watching Clark, measuring him against the young woman beside him. They were no doubt an odd-looking pair—a smoky-eyed Latina beauty and a fair-skinned, impeccably-dressed Southern gentleman. In the month and a half he had known the girl, Clark had drawn many such stares, most of which he assumed were stares of admiration. After all, they were an attractive, albeit disparate-appearing, couple.

Clark had looked long and hard for such a beauty, for one so deserving of his name and social status—even if that status was really only appreciated in his home state of Missouri and had lost some of its luster since the war.

These men, however, stared more at Marina than at Clark, and they pricked his spine with dread. Slowly, by ones and twos, the men turned around to face their drinks. Clark gave a slow sigh of relief. Marina was watching him with a question in her eyes.

"It's all right," he told her. "If McCormick is indeed dead, we'll find another guide. There are other men around who know Mexico as well as Reese."

Several minutes passed in silence. Finally the stage squeaked and rattled up to the door and the driver came in.

"You two can load up whenever you're ready," he said to his passengers. "We'll be pullin' out in about ten minutes . . . after I have a shot or two to cut the dust," he added with a smile, heading for the bar. He carried a sawed-off, doublebarrel shotgun. He set the impressive-looking weapon on the bar, where everyone could see it.

Angrily, Clark cleared his throat and asked sharply, "Aren't we on some sort of timetable here?" He wanted to be out of this place, away from these border roughs.

The driver tossed his hat on the bar and turned back to Clark, running his hands over his short-cropped hair. He looked as though he'd rolled in alkali dust. "Well, no," he said tiredly, "no, we really aren't. Out here I keep my own time, and if you or the company don't like it—if you think you can get anyone else to run that crate out here, with the 'Paches behind every rock and cactus—well, y'all got another fuckin' think comin'."

With that he gave a resolute nod, placed his filthy hat back on his head, turned his back to Clark, and knocked down the tequila. "Do that again, will ya, Pedro?"

Clark looked around the room, at the dark faces of the cowboys grinning at him, showing their chipped, yellow teeth behind cracked lips. One laughed aloud. The man in the shadows stared without expression.

Clark's face colored; his nostrils flared in anger. Marina gave him a beseeching look, but Clark was too good a gambler not to know when the cards were stacked against him. He sat back and puffed angrily on his cigar.

Minutes ticked by. Marina shoved the bowl of menudo toward him. "Have some—it's good," she said, irritatingly good-natured.

Clark tried a spoonful, making a face. "That's *terrible*."

A tall Mexican with a big round face and a right eye that hugged the outside of its socket no matter where the man was looking turned away from the bar and swaggered over to Clark's table. The cowboy's tattered sombrero was tipped back on his head, revealing black, matted hair salted with lice. He smelled like raw alcohol, horses, and gunpowder.

He swayed drunkenly from side to side, staring at Clark with his good eye. Clark positioned his right hand so he could make a quick grab for the Bisley if he needed to. The man stared at Marina for several seconds.

"Can I help you, friend?" Clark asked tolerantly.

The man brought his right hand up and dropped a small leather pouch onto the table before Clark. It landed on its side, spilling gold dust, which gleamed brightly in the light from the window.

Clark looked up at the man and frowned.

The man spread his lips in a grin, tilting his head to indicate Marina. He wore a stag-butted .45, butt forward, on his left hip. On the right was a huge bowie with a rope handle.

Clark swallowed, trying to calm himself. "She's not for sale," he said tightly.

"Half-hour, in back," the man said, indicating a plank door behind the bar.

The room had become quiet again. There was only the cicada and the buzz of the swarming flies.

"No," Clark said levelly.

His pulse throbbed in his temples. If these men tried taking Marina, there was little he could do to stop them. He might be able to get one or two with the Bisley, even three, but the others would send him over the hill in a hail of lead. And they would do to Marina what they wished.

If it came to a firefight, Clark speculated, he would kill her himself, before they could get their grubby hands on her.

"I give you gold for woman," the man persisted, shrugging his heavy shoulders. "Half-hour only. Fair trade, no?"

"No."

"Amigo . . ." the man lamented, spreading his hands.

The stagecoach driver, standing at the bar, suddenly cleared his throat, pounding his empty glass on the planks. "Well, I tell ya, if you two are done fightin' over that girl, I got a timetable to keep," he said loudly, lifting his shotgun off the bar and heading for the door.

Instantly taking the man's cue, Clark stood, scraping back his chair and giving a cursory glance at the lone man in the corner. The man sat as he had when Clark had first seen him; only now his grinning lips were parted to reveal two rows of scraggly, sunlit teeth.

Marina rose stiffly, watching the tall vaquero across the table. Her eyes were defiant, but as Clark took her arm, he could feel her trembling. As they moved around the table, the vaquero stepped into their path, watching them with a raptor's stare, reeking of tequila. He put his hand on the stout handle of the bowie.

Without hesitation, Clark nudged Marina around the man, shoving a table aside, and steered her toward the door. The driver waited there with his shotgun cradled in his arms, covering them as subtly as possible. Clark didn't like giving the Mex his back, but there was no other way.

It seemed to take a good half-hour to make the door, but at last, with every hair on the back of Clark's neck standing straight up in the air, Clark shoved Marina out under the overhanging roof, past the carcass, and through the open door of the waiting Concord.

The driver slammed the door, as a roar of laughter erupted inside the cantina. As though struck, Clark fell back against the upholstered seat. Marina sat stiffly, clutching her elbows, watching the door as if at any moment the men from the cantina would burst through it and drag her out screaming. Her eyes were wide and bright with fear.

A blacksnake cracked like a pistol, and the stage jerked forward, accelerating quickly. After a minute the driver yelled down from the box, his raspy voice rising above the clatter of hooves and the squeak and rattle of the springs.

"*Never*—and I mean *never*—bring a woman like *that* to a place like *this!*"

Clark contrived a smile. "It's all right," he said reassuringly to his wife. "It's over now."

Marina turned her head to watch the rocky desert slide past behind a veil of heavy dust.

"No," she said, voice thin with resignation, her native Spanish drawing out the English and rolling it. "It has only just begun."

CHAPTER 2

SEEN FROM MARINA'S vantage point out the stage window, the world had no limits.

From the faint wagon trail—twin curving lines of floury white dust—the land stretched away to a shimmering heat haze, beyond which there was nothing. Marina tried to tell herself that just over the craggy, cedar-spotted peaks jutting northward was Tucson, but she knew the little pueblo lay a half-day's ride away, an eternity out here.

She and Clark were alone—if you didn't count the outlaws, marauders, and goatish border bandits, that was. And the Apaches, of course. There were always the Apaches.

The very word made her shudder, made her remember the war whoops and screams and the rifle fire when her father's hacienda had been attacked four years ago in Chihuahua. Marina's childhood home had burned to cinders and charred adobe rubble—her family dead, the vaqueros dead, corrals torn asunder, horses and cattle slaughtered where they stood.

Marina alone had survived. Her father had always kept a horse saddled and ready for her, in the event of just such an attack. She'd mounted and galloped off through the buttes, screaming against the muffled sounds of the raid.

Marina smoothed her hair back from her face and pondered a silvery flat of buckhorn cholla rolling past the stage. Had she made a mistake, marrying Clark and coming here? Perhaps she should have married someone healthy and strong, someone who would give her a chance of finding what she sought . . .

Ashamed at the twist her thinking had taken—had this savage place turned her into a savage as well?—she sighed and sat back in her seat, closing her eyes against the ubiquitous desert glare.

As though in reaction to her thoughts, a coughing spasm gripped Clark and he bent forward. It was a harsh, deep-chested bark, and with the fourth spasm he wrestled a handkerchief from his back pocket and clutched it to his lips. When the spell had subsided, leaving him red-faced and rheumy-eyed, he pulled the handkerchief away. A gout of dark red blood nestled in its folds.

A look of disgust creased Clark's lips as he wadded the handkerchief and tucked it back in his pocket. He'd been stricken with the coughing fits during the war, during which his father, calling some favors due, had secured him a position as adjutant to General Noble Brennan. Clark assured himself that it was only a touch of the pleurisy and that the dry desert air would heal it. So far, however, he seemed to grow worse.

He glanced up and saw Marina staring at him.

"What are you looking at?" he snapped, hating the physical weakness to which he felt himself succumbing. With her gawking at him as though he were dying whenever a bout took hold, it was growing harder and harder to deny the seriousness of his condition.

"Are you all right?" she asked with genuine concern.

"Of course I'm all right!" he growled.

She gave a start, then sharply turned her haunted gaze to the desert, squinting against the sun and the dust billowing in the windows.

Clark watched her, growing contrite. He sighed. "I'm . . . sorry," he said meekly.

"It is nothing," she said in a small voice, still staring out the window. Then, "Sh," she said.

Clark frowned. "What is it?"

"Didn't you hear?"

"Hear what?"

"Sh."

They both listened. In the distance a sound like gunfire rose above the thundering horses and the leathery creak and lumbering rattle of the stage.

Clark lifted the deerhide shade from his window and peered into the dust lifting behind them. Several horseback riders were closing at a hell-for-leather gallop, firing pistols in the air. The hard cases from the cantina. Their hats, secured to their necks by leather thongs, whipped behind them in the wind.

Clark stared disbelievingly for several seconds.

"Shit," he said, squelching a cough. He craned his neck to yell up at the driver, "We've got company!"

The driver had heard the racket; his response was quick, and keen with anger. "You two are gonna get me killed *yet*!" Then he cracked the whip against the horses' backs and yelled shrilly, his voice breaking on the high notes.

Clark yelled, "Doesn't someone usually ride shotgun on these things?"

"*Someone* usually does!" the driver replied. "But *someone* bought an Apache war lance two days back, and we ain't exactly been flooded with applicants for his job!"

The yells, the pounding of the horses, and the crack of the pistols were growing louder and louder.

"Don't worry," Clark said, glancing at Marina. He drew his Bisley, spun the cylinder, and smiled. "I am rather handy with a forty-five."

She did not respond. She was staring straight ahead, back stiff, hands clutching the leather straps hanging from the ceiling. Her lips were moving, praying.

"Come on, amigo!" someone yelled. "¡Dios mío!"

Clark looked out the south-facing window. The man who had tossed the pouch on Clark's table back in the cantina had ridden up so close to the window that Clark could see the lather on his horse, the stitching in his bullhide chaps. He yelled again. "We offer you *gold*!"

"Never!" Clark shouted at the man.

"Amigo," the man said in a tone of mock lament, "my loins are heavy for her!" He spread a snaggle-toothed grin.

Clark poked the Bisley out the window and fired.

The vaquero flinched as the bullet brushed his hat. He cursed in Spanish, and grabbed the gun off his hip and snapped off two quick shots at Clark, who flung himself sideways to avoid the lead.

Pushing Marina to the floor, Clark yelled, "Stay down!"

Guns were barking and lead was flying all over the place. Wood shards were ripped from the carriage as bullets tore in one wall and out the other. The driver cursed and yelled at the horses, the long blacksnake punctuating his epithets with sharp cracks.

Clark was preparing to take another shot at the vaquero when the carriage suddenly sank to the left. Clark turned to see a man clinging to the outside of the stage, trying to crawl through the window.

Clark shot the man through the right eye. The attacker screamed, clung for a moment to the window frame, then fell. The carriage bounced as the left rear wheel plowed over his body, sending Clark against the door.

A gun exploded from just behind the stage, and the driver cried out in anguish. "Oh . . . oh, ya lousy goddamn—"

A shadow passed over the window beside Clark. He risked a glance out and saw the driver tumbling in the trail behind the stage, a rag doll consumed by dust and distance. Adding insult to injury, the wind caught the driver's hat and flung it across the desert.

The stage was now a driverless runaway. Clark's stomach filled with hot bile. The stage suddenly lurched. A horse screamed. The carriage rose on the right as though from an explosion, and all four wheels left the ground.

Just as Clark realized that one of the horses had been shot and had fallen under the stage, he found himself on his back, with the right side of the carriage beneath him, Marina on top of him, and dust and stones pouring over his face. He gagged and choked, fighting for air. Abruptly the stage crashed to a violent stop, throwing Clark forward and on top of Marina.

In the sudden silence, he asked his wife, "Are you okay?"

Before she could answer, the door above them opened, filling the stage's dusty interior with harsh yellow light. Then a face blocked the sun. It was the vaquero from the cantina grinning down at them.

Marina screamed.

"Ah, señor!" the vaquero cried. "It would have been easier my way, no?"

Clark searched frantically for his gun, but it must have gone out one of the windows. The vaquero leaned down into the stage, and with one swoop of his giant arm, grabbed Marina around the waist and lifted her out the door, screaming and clawing at his face.

"That . . . That's my wife!" Clark yelled, fumbling for her legs.

Still disoriented from the crash, he fell back, then gathered his wits and heaved himself through the opening. He tripped over the step and went headfirst over the side, hitting the ground hard and getting another taste of Sonoran gravel.

When he'd finally gained his feet, someone jabbed a rifle butt against his head, and he went down again, blood flowing freely from the side of his head. The pain skewered hotly, watering his eyes, and for a second he thought he would pass out. A rough hand grabbed him by the collar and dragged him to his knees.

Shaking, Clark got to his feet. Marina was about twelve yards away, trying to work free of the big Mexican's grip. Clark started toward her, but the man with the rifle grabbed him. Seven grinning men stood around him. An eighth stood to one side—a tall, skinny man in a dusty gray coat and gray campaign hat. The man had the ashen, hollowed-out face of a long-dead cadaver, and the long hair curling onto his shoulders was nearly white and of the texture of straw.

The man's eyes were a washed-out blue. They owned a devilish slant and were as flat as a reptile's. He smiled with cruel, cunning humor, showing long teeth like miniature, coffee-colored stilettos, and Clark knew this had been the man half-hidden in the cantina's dusky shadows.

To the man holding Marina, Clark yelled, "Take your hands off my wife!"

The man with the long gray hair unfolded his arms and planted a hand on the shoulder of the vaquero nuzzling Marina's neck. "That's enough now, Mocho," he said casually, in a Cajun-accented Southern drawl. "We've other business for the moment." Despite his nightmarish looks, there was a gentlemanly air about the man, an air of formality that did not come naturally to him. He was not a man of breeding, Clark could tell, but that's how he saw himself.

"She's mine," Mocho grunted.

"I said that's enough!" the gray-haired man yelled, cuffing Mocho's head with his open hand and knocking off the man's hat.

Mocho turned an idiot's angry glare at him. While Mocho was distracted, Marina broke free of his grip and raced to Clark's side, where she stood trembling and watching the renegades with haunted eyes.

The leader turned to Clark, regaining his frigid smile, and strutted over casually. He planted his feet about a yard from Clark's and folded his arms across his skinny chest.

"You're a dead man, Mr. Clark," he said matter-of-factly.

"Who are you?"

"Gaston Bachelard."

Clark stared into the man's face, puzzled. Gaston Bachelard had ridden with Bloody Bill Anderson in Missouri, during the war. Like Jesse James and Cole Younger, Bachelard had been a savage Confederate freedom-fighter, called to action by the barn burnings and execution-style murders committed by the Kansas Red-Legs. He'd hailed originally from the Louisiana bayous, and was part French, part Indian, and a cold-blooded killer. After the war he'd retreated to Texas and started terrorizing and slaughtering Texans he believed had sympathized with the Union.

"*Bachelard*," Clark mumbled, squinting his unbelieving eyes at the Cajun.

Bachelard shuttled his predatory gaze to Marina. He tipped his hat, flashing his long, thin teeth in a wide grin. It was a chilling expression on his humorless face.

"Why don't you introduce me to your lovely señorita, Mr. Clark?" He spoke with a Cajun accent.

"You know my name?"

"Of course I know your name—your family was one of the wealthiest in Missouri . . . before the war. You were adjutant to Brennan. Your father bought you the position to keep you out of harm's way"—the man snarled with disdain—"while others, like me, fought the war for you."

He paused thoughtfully, and slowly the grimace relaxed, the deep-etched lines in his face shallowing. He held up a finger. "And that is not all I know, *mon ami*." The smile broadened mischievously. "I know why you are here."

Clark's heart skipped a beat. The hair on the back of his neck tingled.

Bachelard moved to the girl and yanked the silver chain from her neck.

"No!" she yelled.

Ignoring her, Bachelard held the cross up to Clark's face. It turned on its chain, showing the inscription etched on its back—*San Bernardo,* 1733.

Bachelard thrust his face so close to Clark's, that he could smell the beer and hog tripe on the Cajun's breath. "The gold would go very far in buying you a fresh start, wouldn't it, Captain?"

His eyes were cold and cunning. "I am sorry," he

said, "but I am afraid you are going to know poverty for once in your life . . . like the rest of the South. Hand over the plat and live," he hissed maniacally. "Keep it and die!"

Clark's knees felt like putty. He did not know what to do. He'd lost his pluck and felt as weak as a child, but he would not give up the plat. It was all he had.

"H-how did you know?" he managed.

"You can't be in Sonora long without hearing about the Lost Church of San Bernardo," Bachelard said. "Of course, like most, I thought it was just a legend. Then one of my men showed up with a silver cross like this one, with a similar inscription. Said he'd won it in a poker game off an old mestizo named Julio Mendez. I had my man fetch him.

"Mendez was in a very bad way—very sick, very drunk—and it didn't take much prodding to get him to tell me where the cross had come from. Eventually we learned he'd drawn a map, but his brain was too dead to reproduce it. Then he told me he had given it to the lovely daughter of Don Sebastian de la Guerra."

Bachelard smiled at Marina. "By the time I tracked you down, you'd married a mining speculator in Prescott, Arizona, and set out to meet a guide in Tucson. That was Reese McCormick, I take it?"

"Did you kill him?" Clark asked coolly.

Bachelard frowned, as though hurt by the accusation. "No, no, no, Mr. Clark. The poor man died in a rockslide three weeks ago when he was out working his mine near Bisbee. I'm saddened by the accusation."

"You'll get over it," Clark said tightly.

Bachelard looked thoughtful. "Too bad, though, about Reese." He shook his head with mild consternation.

"Julio—?" Marina asked.

"He's dead too," Bachelard said brusquely. "I cut his throat when I'd gotten as much as I was going to get."

"You bastard," Marina breathed, eyes filled with anguish. "He was a defenseless old man."

"He was nearly dead anyway, señora. I did him a favor. Besides, I couldn't risk him spilling the beans about the treasure to anyone else, now, could I?"

Bachelard held out his hand to Clark. "Kindly hand over the plat, Captain Clark, or I will shoot you where you stand and take your lovely wife into the brush with me." He cut his eyes at the other men standing around grinning at the woman. "Then I will give her to them to do with as they please."

Clark's thoughts scurried. "I don't have it," he said finally. "I left it in a bank in Prescott."

Bachelard frowned. "I don't believe you, m'sieur." Turning sharply to his men, he barked, "Tear open all the luggage. Throw everything on the ground where I can see every—" He slid a lascivious gaze to Marina. "—every lady's lacy undergarment, eh?"

Three of Bachelard's men went to work scrounging through the luggage boot. Two ran back along the trail to retrieve the trunks that had fallen out when the stage overturned.

Mocho came to stand before the girl, a goatish hunger imprinted on his sweating face.

Bachelard turned to the big hombre and clapped him on the back. To Clark and Marina he said, "I think my friend Mocho thinks your lovely wife is carrying the plat on her person. Is that right, Mocho?"

The Mexican just stood there, staring at Marina. Clark could hear him breathing and grunting. Clark's stomach filled with fresh bile.

"Get him out of here," he said.

"The plat did belong to her, did it not?" Bachelard asked.

Clark said nothing.

Bachelard furrowed his brow in thought. "I tell you what I'll do. If she shows Mocho that she is not carrying the plat in her blouse, I'll keep Mocho from taking her off in the brush. Eh? What do you think? Does that sound fair, m'sieur Clark?"

Clark set his jaw and snarled, "You're a lunatic, Bachelard."

"No?" Bachelard said with surprise. Turning to the big Mexican he said, "Well, okay then, Mocho."

"No!" Marina cried. She jumped back several steps, eyes wide and bright with fear. "Please . . . no." Her voice was small, and she looked at Clark imploringly.

There was nothing he could do beyond giving up the plat, and he couldn't bring himself to do it. It was all he had left. His mother was dead, his father driven insane by the war, his sisters scattered and living like paupers. His family's plantation was now in the hands of Yankee squatters. Without the plat, without the gold, he'd have nothing.

"It is just a small thing that we ask, señora," Bachelard said reasonably, holding out his hands. He moved toward her. "Here . . . let me help you."

"Leave her alone!" Clark yelled, moving to intervene.

Suddenly, Bachelard's sidearm was in his hand, aimed at Clark's head. Clark stopped and stared down the barrel.

"No . . . wait . . . please," Marina pleaded. "I'll do it."

"You will not!" Clark retorted, horrified at the thought of her baring herself to these savages. "You're my *wife!*"

Bachelard moved the gun only two inches from

Clark's face. "Neither of you really has a choice," he said matter-of-factly, arching a brow.

Clark's knees went numb. He hated the fear he heard in his voice. "Please . . ."

"Yes," Bachelard said. "Please have your wife remove her blouse, m'sieur." He smiled with only his eyes. "It is mere precaution, you understand, *ma cherie.*"

"You son of a bitch," Clark said.

Bachelard grinned. Still holding the gun on Clark, he cut his eyes at Marina and thumbed back the hammer on the .45. "Now then, Mrs. Clark."

Marina looked at him, her cool eyes filling with contempt. Then she looked toward the horizon and lifted her slender hands to the first button of her blouse.

When she'd finished with the last, she peeled the blouse from her shoulders and dropped it at her feet. Clark could hear Mocho's raspy breath and the horses obliviously cropping sage. Bachelard regarded Marina with dark, grinning eyes.

She wore the thin, silk chemise with lace edging that Clark had bought for her, along with the rest of her traveling attire, in Prescott. Gaze locked on the horizon, she inhaled deeply and pulled the chemise out of her skirt and slowly lifted it above her head, her thick hair lifting with it. As she dropped the garment on top of the blouse, her hair floated back to her slender, naked shoulders and breasts, which looked terribly exposed and vulnerable under the harsh Sonoran sun.

Clark jerked an exasperated look at Bachelard. "You son of a bitch!"

Bachelard tore his stare from Marina, showing his teeth and backhanding Clark solidly across the face. Clark fell to his knees.

"Stop!" Marina yelled.

Bachelard stepped toward Clark as his men returned, one of them now wearing a woman's stole over his cartridge belts and grubby deerhide vest. Seeing Marina, the vaqueros hesitated, eyes brightening.

"Good Lord," said the man with a flattened nose. "Look at them chichonas!"

Bachelard turned to them sharply. "Did you find it? Did you find the plat?" he barked.

The men stared at Marina without speaking. Her hair fell around her well-formed breasts. Though it had to be close to a hundred degrees, goose bumps rose on her olive skin. Head lowered, she sobbed, her hair hiding her face.

Bachelard fired his revolver in the air. The men gave a start and turned to him. "For the last time, did you find it?"

"No, jefe," said the man wearing Marina's stole. "We went through it all and found nothing of any value." He lifted an end of the stole and added girlishly, "Except this, of course! Do I look nice, jefe?"

The others laughed.

Bachelard swung around to Clark. "Do I have to let Mocho do what he will to your lovely wife before you'll tell me where the plat is?"

"I don't have it," Clark said. He was now seated one leg curled beneath him. Bachelard's backhand had packed a wallop.

"You don't, eh?" Bachelard said, eyes wide and crossed, hawk-nose red with anger. "Mocho!"

"No!" Clark wailed.

Something struck him hard on the side of the head and he went semiconscious for several seconds. By the time he coaxed his eyes into focus, Mocho had pushed Marina to her knees and dropped his pants.

He yelled at her in Spanish to perform well for him or he would cut her tongue out.

Then the back of his head burst open like a ripe melon, spitting blood, bone, and brains. A rifle shot echoed.

Mocho swung around, teetering, his eyes lifting skyward. There was a nickel-size hole between them. He stumbled over his trousers and fell in a lifeless heap, his feet jerking.

A second bullet spanged off a rock, splattering shards around the stage. One of the other men yelled out and clutched his neck as another rifle cracked.

The rest were still looking around, dumbfounded. Finally, one man cried, "Apaches!" and lunged for his horse, which was tied to a mesquite bush.

"Apaches!" echoed another. He pulled his revolver and fired blindly as he struggled with his own horse's tether. Rifles cracked and bullets kicked dust at his feet, and littered the ground with mesquite branches.

Bachelard ran to retrieve his own horse. When he'd mounted, he brought the screaming gray next to Clark.

"Come on, Captain! Where's the plat? You might as well give it to me as the Apaches."

Jaw set like a wedge, blood flowing from the cut above his right ear, Clark just stared at him.

Bachelard drew his sidearm. "Fool!" he shouted, and snapped off a shot. Luckily, Bachelard's gray was dancing around too much for an accurate bead, and the bullet buzzed past Clark's ear and into the battered Concord.

Then Bachelard was gone, fleeing up the rocky, cactus-studded ledge east of the stage, in the dust kicked up by his four companions.

Clark was still woozy from the head-clubbing he'd received. Although the word "Apache" resounded in his brain and tinged his tongue with the metallic taste of fear, he was physically too weak to do much but look around, trying to get his bearings and clear away the cobwebs.

He and Marina crept into the shade of the over-turned stage. Marina clutched her blouse closed with her hands. Clark pressed a handkerchief to his battered head. Hooves pounded the ground around them, kicking stones. Shadows moved on the sandy ground as riders approached—five dusty, trail-worn men, faces shaded by their hats.

CHAPTER 3

————◆————

THE LEAD RIDER brought his buckskin mustang to a halt before Clark and Marina, and the others gathered behind him. The man squinted at Clark with bottle-green eyes, and Clark returned the scrutiny warily, regarding the man's rough countenance, the blond stubble on his ruddy, sunburned face beneath a thick coating of adobe-colored dust.

The man was over six feet tall, wide-shouldered, slim-hipped, and rangy. He wore a big, horn-handled bowie, two cartridge belts, and a walnut-gripped Army Colt butt-forward in a holster soft as an old shoe. His denim breeches were nearly white where his muscular thighs hugged the saddle, and sun-bleached chest hair curled between the rawhide cords at the open neck of his buckskin tunic. The well-oiled Winchester '73, held across the bows of his saddle, still smoked from the .44/40 slug he'd blown through the skull of the big Mexican, Mocho.

Clark did not know what to make of this man or the men behind him—a gray-bearded white man, a Mexican, a towheaded boy, and an Apache Indian. The Indian's hands were tied and staked behind his back, and a reata was noosed around his neck. The boy held the other end of the reata in his gloved hand.

At first Clark thought they'd been rescued from one group of bandits by another. But as the lead rider dismounted, grabbed his canteen off his saddle, and moved toward Clark, Clark saw a distinct look of civility and concern in his eyes.

"Hell of a wreck," the man said as he uncorked the canteen, knelt down, and handed it to Clark. "You two all right?" He glanced at Marina, who appeared to be in shock, holding her blouse closed with her hands and staring blankly at the horses and riders gathered before her.

Clark took the canteen, filled his mouth, sloshed the water around, and spat, getting rid of some of the grit. Then he drank. "Here you are, my dear," he said, offering the canteen to his wife.

She didn't take it, and Clark did not have the energy to encourage her. The cut on the side of his head made his brain throb and his vision swim. He assumed he'd suffered a concussion.

The newcomer took the canteen, moved to Marina, and knelt beside her. "Ma'am," he said gently, "some water might make you feel better."

Slowly she turned her head and focused on him. She took the canteen in both hands and sipped. She started to bring the canteen away from her mouth, then lifted it again and took two more swallows. Some of the water ran from her lip to her chin as she handed back the canteen.

"Gracias," she said. "Thank you."

"Any broken bones, any cuts that need tendin'?" the man asked her.

She shook her head, dropping her eyes.

Corking the canteen, the rider turned back to Clark. "That's a hell of a tattoo you have on your ear."

Pressing his neckerchief to the wound, Clark nodded. "Yes, they weren't exactly gentlemen."

"Gaston Bachelard is one-hundred-percent snake, is what he is," the other replied. "I recognized him through my field glasses. Didn't realize he was raiding this far north these days."

He untied the bandanna from around his neck and wrapped it around Clark's head, adjusting it over the wound before he tied it tightly. "There . . . That should help stop the blood until we can get you stitched." He looked at his companions, who sat their horses and looked around warily, rifles clutched tightly in their hands.

The big man with the gray beard said in a low, gruff voice, "I'm gettin' nervous sitting out here in the open like this, Jack. 'Paches might've heard our gunfire."

The lead rider turned to Clark. He removed his buckskin glove from his right hand, and offered it. "I'm Jack Cameron," he said. Then, jerking a thumb at his companions: "That ornery old cuss with the gray beard is Bud Hotchkiss. Beside him there is Pasqual Varas. The kid is Jimmy Bronco. The Indian goes by Perro Loco. We're taking him to an Army detail waiting for us in Contention City."

"You bounty hunters?" Clark asked.

"Only by necessity," Cameron replied. "We all ranch west of Hackberry Mesa up by Fountain Springs. Perro Loco's been raiding our spreads for the past seven months, so we got together to track him down. Just so happens the Army was offering a reward, because of all the people he's killed. They've caught him twice, and he escaped both times."

"I've heard of him," Clark said, nodding as he stared darkly at the Indian sitting his horse with a look of supreme insouciance.

He was big for an Indian, and broad-chested, powerful arms thrust back behind him. His long, blue-black hair hung below his shoulders. Wisps of it blew across his broad, pitted face. He wore the usual Apache garb—deerskin leggings, knee-high moccasins, and deerhide vest. He also wore a duckbilled forage cap, no doubt taken off the body of a slain soldier.

Turning to Cameron, Clark said, "I'm Adrian Clark and this is my wife, Marina. We, too, were on our way to Contention City."

"Well, if you're well enough to ride, I guess you still are," Cameron said, standing and offering Clark his hand.

Clark looked toward the luggage scattered behind the stage. "What about our bags?"

"You'll have to leave them, I'm afraid," Cameron said, walking to his horse. "We don't have the horses to carry them. We'll be riding double as it is."

"What about the stage horses—couldn't we ride one of them?"

"One's dead and the other three have scattered. We'd be all afternoon trying to catch one."

Clark turned to Marina and helped her to her feet.

"Your wife can ride with Bud," Cameron said. He poked his boot through a stirrup and pulled himself into the saddle. "You can ride with me."

A groan sounded behind the riders, and Clark saw the bandit who'd been shot in the neck push up on a knee and lift his pistol. "Hey . . . !" Clark yelled.

The sound hadn't died before Cameron raked the Colt off his hip and swung his horse around to face the gunman. He cocked the Colt and fired, and the bandit sank back with a bullet through his forehead.

Clark whistled through his teeth. He'd heard about Jack Cameron, the ex-Army scout and Indian fighter. Who in the Southwest hadn't? Cameron's name had come up when Clark was inquiring about guides, but none of his business associates had known where to find Cameron, so Clark had settled for McCormick. At first he'd thought this man was just a saddle tramp with the same name. Obviously he was the man himself.

"If you two are ready," Cameron said, "we'd best get a move on."

"Come, my dear," Clark said, leading Marina to the graybeard's skewbald horse and helping her onto its back. Then he accepted Cameron's hand and mounted the buckskin. As he swung up, his vision blurred for an instant and he felt dizzy.

As they rode off behind Cameron, Clark turned once to gaze at the two dead bandits.

———•———

Gaston Bachelard hunkered down in the shade of a boulder and trained his spy glass on the rocky flat below, where the stage lay like a matchbox crushed by a boot.

"No Apaches," he snarled to the man kneeling beside him. His voice tightened with anger. "Four white men." He lowered the glass and looked at the other man. "We were run off by four white men and an Indian tied to his horse!"

The other shrugged and raised his thin, dirty hands, palm up. "I am sorry, jefe," he replied. "It was Rudolpho who said—"

"Silence!" Bachelard intoned.

He lifted the glass and resumed his study of the scene a hundred and fifty yards down the rocky grade.

At length, the other man said, "If they are not Apaches, then why do we not attack, jefe?"

Bachelard worked a piece of hog tripe from between his two front teeth and bit down on it thoughtfully. "I think that's Jack Cameron down there."

"Cameron?" the man asked, wide-eyed. "The scout?"

"Ex-scout, I believe."

The Mexican straightened, lifting the tattered brim of his straw sombrero and jutting out his chin. The sun discovered his hawklike face and shone in his mud-brown eyes. "We can take Cameron, jefe," he said with proud confidence. "I know what they say about him, but he is only one man like another—"

"Yes, he is one man like another," Bachelard snarled, "and I would not hesitate to take him if Miguel Montana had sent me some real men instead of you four sons of stupid dog bitches—every one of you no better in a fight than the little girls you like to fuck in Hermosillo. 'Apaches!' you scream!"

Bachelard clamped his big, clawlike left hand on the back of the Mexican's neck, and brusquely directed his gaze down the hill. His voice was harsh and tight, but low. "There are your Apaches, you goddamn bastard child of a two-peso whore!"

The Mexican squirmed. "I told you, jefe, it was Rudolpho—"

"Keep quiet, fool!" Bachelard hissed. "Don't fuck things up any more than you already have. We could have had the goddamn plat by now and been on our way back to your fearless leader Montana if it hadn't been for your so-called Apaches!"

Bachelard grunted and lifted the glass again to his right eye. "'Send me four of your best men, Miguel,' I told him, 'and I will bring you the plat in a week.' A week! So he sends me you four horse turds—and who knows how long before we get it?" Bachelard shook his head, mumbling more obscenities and laughing without mirth. He focused the glass and gazed down the slope.

"No," he continued thoughtfully, voice edged with

disgust, "if I had more of my own riders here I'd lay down some lead and storm the son of a bitch. But since I'm shorthanded now, with your buddy Mocho and my man Kruger attracting flies down there with Cameron, and since the rest of you are a bunch of goddamn kittens afraid of your own mother's shadow, I'll have to wait for the element of surprise."

A gun barked below. Staring through the spyglass, Bachelard gritted his teeth and shook his head. "Damn—Kruger had a chance."

A minute passed, then Bachelard lowered the glass and gazed down the grade with his naked eyes.

"They're riding off," he said, brightening. "With Clark and the woman. They're leaving."

The other man furrowed his brow. "This is good, jefe?"

"Cameron will look for water, and the only water within half a day's ride is Cholo Springs, at the southern end of the Whetstone Mountains. He'll camp there for the night."

Jesus smiled and nodded his head. "Ah . . . I see, jefe. And this . . . this is good?"

Bachelard thought as he spoke, fingering his scraggly goatee. "Cholo Springs is a well-covered spot, easy to defend. But not impregnable. If we follow them there, then wait for the very best opportunity, for full dark or first light, we'll have the plat and the girl before the sun is up. And we'll have the great Apache-hunter Jack Cameron roasting on a spit!"

He turned to his companion with an evil leer. "'Rascal thieves, here's gold. Go suck the blood o' th' grape . . .'"

The man looked at him, baffled, tentative. "What is that you say, jefe?"

Bachelard clamped a hand on the man's shoulder, the jefe's fickle mood swings and propensity for quoting verse keeping the man perpetually on edge. "I said, how does that sound to you, Jesús—the plàt and the girl and Cameron squealing like a stuck javelina before morning?"

"Oh!" Jesus nodded eagerly, thrilled to be back in his boss's good graces. "Muy bien, jefe! Muy bien!"

"Go, Jesús . . . tout de suite!" Bachelard ordered the Mexican, hazing him up the bluff to where the three other men waited with their horses.

CHAPTER 4

AS THEY RODE with the afternoon sun lathering their horses and painting broad sweat stains down the backs of their shirts, Clark considered one of the many stories he'd heard about Jack Cameron.

It was the year after the war, when the Union soldiers were returning to Arizona and the Yankee settlers were rebuilding what the Apaches had destroyed in their absence. Cameron had bought a ranch in the Dragoon Mountains east of Benson and been engaged to Ivy Kitchen, the pretty blonde daughter of Lester Kitchen, who also ranched in the area.

One morning the Apaches stormed off the trail from Benson, led by Mangus Colorado himself, and laid waste to four ranches. Cameron and his partner, Rudy Poliner, managed to escape into the mountains. Two days later they walked back out and found the Kitchen ranch little more than a pile of white ashes smoldering in the desert sun.

Lester and his two boys, Ray and Steve, lay in the ranchyard pincushioned with arrows. The women—Mrs. Kitchen and her two daughters, Rachel and Ivy—lay in the scrub around the root cellar, where they'd apparently tried to hide. They were all naked. They'd obviously all been raped. And they'd all had their throats cut. Cameron tracked the raiding party and managed to kill three before his horse gave out. Knowing the formidable Cameron was on his trail, Mangus Colorado hightailed it to his stronghold in the Sierra Madre. Enlisting the help of several ranchers and their men, Cameron made three attempts to locate the hideout. All he located, however, was a handful of bushwhacking Indians and death for more than half his men before he finally gave up and resigned himself to the fact he'd never be able to avenge his lover's death.

Now Cameron turned his horse off the faint Indian hunting trail they were following through the foothills of the Whetstone Mountains. "We'd better stop and let the horses have a blow," he told Hotchkiss.

Clark slid off the back of Cameron's buckskin, stepped into the shade offered by a mesquite bush, and sat down. The pain in his head had abated, but he still felt disoriented. He pressed his hand to the bandanna over the wound and it came away dry, a good sign.

Cameron tethered the buckskin in the shade of another mesquite, then filled his hat with water from the canteen and offered it to the horse. The animal dipped its snout and drank noisily.

Clark glanced around at the others: the men watering their mounts and checking the horses' shoes for loose nails, Marina sitting beside him staring off across the desert. He thought he should probably comfort her, but he wasn't in the mood. He'd suffered as badly as she. It was probably silly, her being here in the first place, but Clark hadn't left her in Tucson out of fear she'd fall for some card sharp or get raped by a drunk cowboy. How could he have known she'd be worse off out here?

Besides, she'd wanted to come. She had her own

reasons for being here, and Clark thought she probably didn't trust him to get the job done on his own.

He removed his hat, wiped sweat from the band, and scrutinized the Indian, who sat in the shade of a boulder, shackled wrists over his knees. The man stared off across the desert with much the same expression as Marina's.

Clark turned to Cameron. "So who's the Indian?"

Cameron was filing his mustang's right rear hoof. "People around here call him Perro Loco de Desierto—'Mad Dog of the Desert.' He's been torturing and killing settlers, shooting up villages, and killing livestock off and on for about three years now. Most of the other Coyotero Apaches went to the reservation, but not him and about a dozen others."

Cameron stopped what he was doing and glanced at the Indian, who gazed off expressionlessly. Cameron chuckled ruefully, bent over the hoof, and went back to work with a sigh.

"I've been after him off and on for the past sixteen months. My compadres and me decided if we were gonna keep ranching we were going to have to exterminate ol' Perro Loco like the mad wolf he is. Well, we got word he was in a little village called Summerville about fifteen miles from my place, so we rode over and found him in the back room of a cantina, drunker 'n snot and diddling a Mexican whore."

Cameron wagged his head, dropped the hoof, and returned the file to his saddlebags. He ran his hand absently down the mane of his buckskin, and glanced at Marina. Apparently satisfied she wasn't listening, he returned his eyes to Clark, jerking a thumb at the Indian. "He had his pants down around his ankles and was givin' it to her with a vengeance. All we had to do was walk in and snug our rifles up against his back—and that was it. We had Perro Loco in the bag. He was so drunk we had to lift him onto his horse." He chuckled and turned again to the stony-faced Indian.

"So that's really Perro Loco . . ." Clark said, staring at the Indian with awe. The Apache was even more notorious than Cameron in the Southwest Territories. Since Clark had arrived here after the war, he'd read several newspaper articles devoted to the renegade.

"In the flesh."

"I'll be damned."

"He's seen better days," Bud Hotchkiss said. Sitting near the Indian, he'd just taken a long pull from his canteen. He handed it now to the boy, Jimmy Bronco, and continued, "Not too happy about how we captured him. Shamed him pretty good, which makes him all the more dangerous. He'd like nothing better than to get his medicine back. You'll want to keep your distance."

"You don't have to worry about that," Clark said gravely.

There was a pause filled with the sounds of cicadas and horses. Clark leaned back on his elbows and said thoughtfully, "How hard do you men think it would be to find a guide in Contention City?"

His gazed shuttled from one man to the next. Only the boy returned it, cocking his head and squinting his eyes curiously.

"Depends on what kind of guide you're lookin' for," Cameron said after a while. His back was to Clark, and he was adjusting the leather thongs holding his bedroll behind his saddle.

"I'm looking for a man to guide my wife and me into Mexico," Clark said. "I'd arranged for Reese McCormick, but I understand he's dead. He was supposed to meet us in Tucson. When he didn't show

I decided to start looking for him . . . or for someone else who could do the same job."

"I heard about Reese," the Mexican Pas Varas said in Spanish-accented English. He stood by his horse, holding the reins in one hand, his rifle in the other. "Too bad. He would have been a good guide. It will be hard to find another to take his place in Contention City—one that will not take your money and then cut your throat, that is." Varas shook his head. "You better go back to Tucson, maybe."

Clark lowered his eyes, sucking a tooth, then lifted them again. He gazed at Cameron. "How 'bout one of you?"

As though he hadn't heard, Cameron poured more water into his hat, and returned the hat to the ground before his horse. He took a drink from the canteen as he walked to the mesquite shrub. He sat down next to Clark and offered the canteen. Clark waved it off.

"Where you headed in Mexico?" Cameron asked, setting the canteen aside and fishing in his shirt pocket for a small sack of tobacco and papers.

"The Sierra Madre," Clark said. "The northwest side."

Cameron nodded and offered the makings pouch. "Smoke?"

"No thanks."

Cameron took out a paper and sprinkled tobacco on it. Deftly, he shaped it with his fingers, licked it and twisted it closed. "What's in the Sierra Madre?" he asked, scratching a lucifer to life on his thumbnail and lighting the quirley.

Clark bit his lip. He didn't like the idea of sharing his plan with these strangers, but they looked honest enough, and they'd saved his and Marina's lives, after all. "I have a treasure map."

Cameron exhaled smoke, watching his horse thoughtfully and nodding, then shared an inscrutable glance with Varas and Hotchkiss. When Cameron said nothing, Clark said, "I need someone to help us follow it."

Cameron pulled on the quirley. "Well, good luck," Cameron said, exhaling smoke.

"You won't consider it?"

"Sorry."

"We need someone who knows the country and knows Apaches."

"Yes, you do."

"There's gold at the end of the trail, Mr. Cameron. You'll be well paid. Richer than your wildest dreams, as a matter of fact."

Cameron smiled and studied the coal of his cigarette. "Where have I heard that before?"

"It's Jesuit treasure."

"How do you know?"

Clark pulled up his pants leg and produced a rolled-up sheet of heavy parchment from his boot. "I have this, a plat drawn by the man who found it, and . . . well, I had a silver cross forged by the Jesuits who ran the church. There was an inscription on the back."

"'Had'?" Hotchkiss asked, cocking his head. The boy had gone off to relieve himself behind a rock.

"Bachelard took it."

"Lousy luck," Varas said. It was hard to tell if he meant it or if he was just being sarcastic. Mexicans were funny that way.

Clark felt his frustration building. These men were not taking him seriously. They were patronizing him, as though he were a tinhorn.

"He wanted the plat," Clark said to Varas, as if Bachelard's wanting it somehow validated it.

Hotchkiss said, "Then he's as crazy as you are, if you'll pardon me for saying so, hombre."

"How did he know about the plat?" Cameron asked Clark.

"He found the man who gave it to Marina," Clark said darkly.

"Your wife?"

"Yes. The plat is actually hers."

A faint light of interest grew in Cameron's eyes as he turned to Marina. Obviously he'd been struck by her beauty, as was nearly everyone who ever saw her. The information that the map to a lost treasure belonged to a beautiful young Spanish woman somehow made the story more credible; at the very least, it made it more compelling. Realizing this somewhat abated the resentment Clark felt at seeing the effect his wife's beauty had on the frontiersman.

"Marina grew up on a big rancho by the Rio Conchos," Clark explained. "One of her father's men, an old cowboy named Julio Mendez, stumbled upon a plat to an old Spanish church in the Sierra Madre. These churches were said to be decorated with gold the padres mined. Well, after about ten years of searching, Julio found it. It's in a canyon, near some ancient ruins. There was no gold inside, however. It had been stripped clean."

"Looted," Cameron said.

"That's what old Julio thought at first. Then he got to thinking. He had heard that when the Jesuits were kicked out of Mexico, they hid their treasures from the Franciscans who were sent to replace them. So he started exploring the canyons behind the mission, and guess what he found?"

"El Dorado," Cameron said wryly.

"A deep pit filled with gold and silver." Clark looked

at Cameron, small fires burning brightly in his gray eyes.

"Why didn't he excavate it?"

"Indians scared him off before he could return with the supplies he needed. Then he had a heart attack. He gave the plat to Marina."

Cameron looked at Marina again. "Why?"

Clark shrugged and sighed.

Marina's gaze dropped from the distance. She cleared her throat. "He never said why he gave it to me," she said, her voice thin with wonder. She held her blowing hair back from her face with her right hand. "He just gave it to me . . . with the cross. He was old. There was no family, I think. I suspect he no longer cared for such things as gold." She shrugged and ground her heel in the sand, staring at it.

"There you have it," Clark said to Cameron, hiking an eyebrow.

Cameron's eyes stayed with Marina. "Where's your family?"

She was still watching her foot, absently excavating a little hole in the sand. "Dead," she said, softly.

Cameron nodded thoughtfully. He took a final drag off his cigarette, glanced again at his companions, mashed the quirley in the sand, stood, and walked over to his horse. Picking up his hat and pouring out what little water remained, he said, "Hell of a story."

"Hell of a *true* story, Mr. Cameron."

"I hate to burst your bubble, but there's no treasure." Cameron untethered his horse from the mesquite and turned to the Southerner and his wife with a serious look. "And I strongly advise you not to go after it. If you follow through with your plan, you and your wife are gonna end up dead. I can almost guarantee you that. I've been through that country. I know."

"What about the story?"

"Sounds like two dozen others I've heard."

"Let me show you the plat."

Cameron shook his head. "We'd better get a move on." He and Hotchkiss mounted while Varas kicked the Indian and gestured to the man's horse, indicating it was time to ride. The Indian obeyed stiffly, with the dolor typical of captured Apaches.

Meanwhile Clark climbed to his feet, a little unsteady, and brushed off his pants. He held out a hand to Marina. She took it, standing, gazing at Cameron wonderingly. Apparently she, too, knew that he was the right man for the job, and was frustrated he wouldn't take it.

"It's all right, my dear," Clark said with a sigh, when he'd helped his wife onto Hotchkiss's skewbald. "There are plenty of men in the desert who wouldn't mind finding the mother lode of Jesuit bullion."

Cameron gave Clark a hand up on his own horse, and put the metal to the buckskin's ribs. "Yes, there are," he said.

CHAPTER 5

AN HOUR LATER, Cameron left the others along a dry creekbed, and spurred his buckskin ahead to scout the place where he wanted to camp. He rode a half-mile before halting his buckskin on a flat rock above a dry, rocky wash and reaching into his saddlebags for his field glasses. He'd fashioned a stiff leather hood over each lens, to keep the glass from reflecting sunlight, and now he brought the sand-colored spur above him into focus.

At the base of the spur was a shallow wind cave in which he'd camped several times when traversing the country between Tucson and Tombstone. It offered perfect shelter from wind, rain, and sun. Situated as it was on a rise, with rocky ground sloping away to the dry wash, the cave also offered protection from other men.

Interlopers could come from the west only, for in the south and north loomed steep-walled mountains, weathered smooth to preclude climbing or anything but a suicidal descent by even the surest-footed Apache. To the east the trail wound along the wash until it vanished in a cul-de-sac from which a spring issued. Twenty feet below the spring the water pooled in bowls it had carved in slabs of black basaltic rock, ideal for watering horses and filling canteens.

The entire place was so favorable for overnighting, in fact, that it often attracted other campers. You never knew who you might run into. Cameron had once camped in the cave with a doctor traveling to deliver a baby, but he'd once spotted a party of young Apache warriors there, as well, and had lost no time in hightailing it back down the trail.

Now the dying sun had filled the cave with stygian shadows while pinkening the sandstone wall around it. But he could see no horses, and no smoke from a cookfire. Reasonably sure the place was deserted, Cameron returned his field glasses to his saddlebags, turned the buckskin around, and headed back down the trail to retrieve the others.

A half-hour later the ragged procession plodded up the slope, the hang-headed horses winding around boulders and the dangerous "jumping" cholla cactus. Rein chains jangled, horses blew, and shod hooves rang off rocks.

Cameron brought up the rear, behind Marina, who rode now with young Jimmy Bronco. Her head hung wearily to the side, long black hair bouncing on her shoulders. She'd torn a slit in her skirt so she could ride astraddle, and Cameron tried to keep his eyes off the bare thigh the breeze occasionally revealed—not an easy task, given the sensuousness of the woman the thigh belonged to. She hadn't said anything for hours, but Cameron could tell she was no ordinary woman. She'd nearly been raped by Bachelard's men, not to mention killed, yet her eyes remained brave. Although riding the bare rump of a half-wild mustang over rough terrain, she'd never asked Cameron and the others to stop so she could rest. Her stalwart, self-contained sense of self only added to her beauty.

What the hell was she doing here? Cameron wondered. Something told him that she wouldn't be here if she didn't want to be—with or without the strong-willed Adrian Clark, whom Cameron already suspected was not only talented at, but accustomed to, steering people in his direction. Which meant she had pluck but, like her husband, was sadly misguided.

Cameron had heard enough legends of lost Spanish gold—had gone after enough of them himself—to know them for what they were.

Legends.

How many such tales had he heard, convoluted legends of buried treasure, like the Lost San Saba Mine, the Lost Mine of Tiopa, the Lost Adams Diggings? How many men had found Spanish bullion and been frightened off by Indians? How many stories of Aztec gold were told and retold in every dusky watering hole from Dodge City to Bisbee?

The stories were enticing enough to drive sane men to madness. For most, once the gold lust got into the blood, it was there to stay. Cameron had followed his share of treasure trails into the earth's loneliest places, trails that petered out at rock walls or alkali flats littered with derelict wagons and bleached bones, but he was lucky. He'd rid himself of the disease a long time ago. All he wanted now was to return to his ranch and his cattle, the house he was building from native stone, with a broad hearth and a porch where he could sit on desert evenings and watch the sun gild the flat peak of Rockinstraw Mountain.

When it came his time to die—not an unpleasant thought for a man like Cameron, who'd been where he'd been and seen what he'd seen—he wanted to be buried behind his cabin, where the brush grew thick because of the spring, and there was an old cottonwood, a giant tree with a lightning blaze just below the fork in its trunk, that offered shade on hot afternoons, and the somnolent sound of rattling leaves.

The only way you could convince Cameron there was a cave stashed with gold in the Sierra Madre was to lead him there and shove his face in it. But first you'd have to knock him out, hog-tie him, and throw him over his saddle.

He wasn't going anywhere but to Contention City, where, after delivering the Indian to the soldiers, he would see about a stiff drink, a hot bath, and a hearty meal. He'd rest for a day, then head back north to his ranch. He had work to do.

What Clark and his wife did was entirely up to them. He'd warned Clark about the dangers of taking a beautiful woman into the wilds of Mexico. That was all he could do.

As the group made the crest of the rise, Cameron twisted around in his saddle one last time, scouring the shadowy western plain from which they'd come. A shadowy dust devil rose, turned, caught a splash of pink light, and disappeared. The cooling breeze whispered.

If Bachelard came, he would have to come from that direction; but given the terrain, Cameron was relatively certain they'd be safe here.

———

Stripped of all tack but bridles, the horses were led down to the spring for water. Just inside the cave, a small fire was built with the nearly smokeless wood of the curl-leaf. Bacon was fried and coffee was made. Saddles were thrown down around the fire. Blankets were rolled out.

There wasn't much talk. Sound carries far on a desert night. Besides, the travelers were too tired for idle banter.

Pasqual Varas secured the Indian to a stout cottonwood and tied sleigh bells around his wrists and feet. Bud Hotchkiss washed down at the spring, then returned and scrounged in his saddlebags for sewing needle, catgut thread, and a flat blue bottle with a cork in it.

The portly graybeard in calico shirt and buckskin pants strolled over to Clark at the back of the cave. The Missourian was cursing and complaining while Marina cleaned the contusion above his ear.

Hotchkiss tossed the bottle to Clark. "There you go, Captain. Have you a swig or two o' that—Hotchkiss's Special. You're gonna need it." In conversation along the trail, Clark had informed Hotchkiss and the others he'd attained the rank of a Confederate captain during "the War of Northern Oppression."

Now he looked at the bottle. "For what?"

"Pain reliever. I'm gonna sew up that head so's you don't bleed to death."

"That's not necessary. I think she's got the blood stopped."

Hotchkiss pulled a burning branch from the fire and swept the needle through the flames to sterilize it. "Captain, if that hole ain't sewed up you're gonna have half the desert in it before the night's through." He looked at Marina. "Ma'am, if you'd just thread this needle for me, I'll do the dirty work. Threadin' needles went with my eyesight."

Marina glanced at Clark warily. Clark returned the look. Then he lifted his eyes to Hotchkiss. "Do you really think it's necessary?"

"Not unless you want infection, it ain't."

"How do I know you're qualified?"

Hotchkiss chuckled and glanced at Cameron, who sat on his haunches away from the fire, against the cave wall, a tin cup of coffee in his hands. His face was cloaked in darkness, and his hat was pushed back on his head. He cleared his throat.

"Bud here was something of a nursemaid to the officers' wives at Camp Grant. They trusted him to deliver their babies before they let a corporal fetch the doc from the village."

"And the doc had 'im a Yale edeecation, he did!" Hotchkiss added with glee.

"Sí," Pas Varas added. He was sitting near the Indian, his Sharps buffalo rifle across his knees and smoking a cigarette rolled from a brown cornhusk. "Señor Bud delivered my Leonora's last two niños, and he even cured Leonora of last winter's fever."

"Hell, Pas," Hotchkiss said, "I even doctored that knee of yours—"

"All right, all right!" Clark popped the cork on the bottle and took a liberal pull. Bringing the bottle back down, he looked at Marina. "Well, you heard the man." He coughed as the burning liquor hit his stomach.

When Marina had threaded the catgut through the needle, she gave it to Hotchkiss.

"Okay, here we go, Captain," Hotchkiss said. He looked at Clark, a glitter in his eyes, the deep lines of his big, bearded face filled with shadows shunted by firelight. His buckskins smelled like rancid bear grease. "You know, when you told me back on the trail that you wore butternut-gray during the Little Misunderstandin', I told you I wouldn't hold it against you." He stopped and regarded Clark severely, as though waiting for a reply.

Clark looked at him warily. "Yes . . . ?"

"Meant every word of it!" the old tracker roared.

Clark took another long pull from the bottle.

Hotchkiss grabbed it away. "Save some for later . . . and for me." Then to Marina, "Okay, ma'am, if you'll just hold the captain's head real steady . . ."

Cameron finished his coffee, chunked a few small branches of curl-leaf on the fire, then stepped out of the cave, looking around.

Nothing. Only the black of the night and the blacker black of the mountains looming behind and before him, blocking out the stars. A faint breeze rustled the leaves of a jojoba, and a coyote called.

Cameron turned to where Varas sat against the cave wall, smoking and resting. "You'll watch the Injun, Pas?"

"Like a hawk, Jack."

"I'm gonna take a gander."

"Sí."

Cameron had walked down the grade about thirty feet when Jimmy Bronco's voice came to him from down the slope. "Jack?"

The young man moved closer, and his hatted form took shape. He'd been bedding down the horses under some paloverde trees, where the galleta grass grew thick. "The horses are all set for the night." Jimmy had been with Cameron for two years, since Cameron had rescued him from the roadhouse where his mother worked as a whore and given him a job wrangling on his ranch.

"Good man."

"Jack, are we gonna have trouble tonight?"

"I don't know, Jimmy. There's a good chance. That was Gaston Bachelard back there. I've never met the man, but I've heard of him. If what they say is true, we'll want to sleep light and take turns keeping watch. Why don't you take the first watch, then wake me in a couple hours? I'm gonna bed down near the horses."

"You got it, Jack. Don't you worry none." The kid patted his Colts and grinned.

Cameron said, "Jim, you see anything, you give a yell before you start shootin'—understand?"

"W-well, what if—"

"You hear me?"

The kid nodded sullenly.

Cameron started away, then turned back around. "You did good with the Indian today, Jimmy," he said. "Keep up the good work."

The lad didn't say anything. He was staring into the cave. The fire reflected in his dreamy eyes. "She about the purtiest woman you ever seen?"

Cameron turned toward Marina, who was helping Hotchkiss tend to her husband. Cameron thought of young Ivy Kitchen. He didn't like thinking of her because the image of her fair-faced, blue-eyed beauty was always followed by the image of her lying in the prickly pear by the root cellar, stripped naked by the savages, a wide knife gash across her neck.

"Pretty close, Jimmy," Cameron said. He clapped Jimmy on the shoulder. "I'm gonna take a walk around, then turn in. You stay away from the fire, now. Don't ruin your night vision."

Cameron walked down the slope, looking carefully around him. He sat on a rock for a half-hour, sweeping the dark canyon with his gaze, looking for any sign of movement, any shadow separating itself from the darkness. He listened, holding his breath for several seconds at a time, his senses open to the night but unable to think of anything but Marina.

She was a lovely woman, and he hadn't had a woman in a couple of months, but Marina was another man's wife and he had no business thinking of her the way he was—seeing in his mind's eye her naked breasts, her slender, curving thigh between the slits in her wool skirt . . . her sad, smoky eyes and firm chin, wisps of hair sliding around her dust-lined cheeks.

The distant barks of coyotes brought Cameron back to the present and he was grateful. Thinking of Marina had made him think of Ivy lying dead in the desert, forever unavenged. It was best not to love anyone out here but a good horse. Horses came and went, but they didn't take as much of you with them as people did.

Finally Cameron threw his bedroll under the paloverde tree, only twenty or so yards from where the horses absently nibbled grass and occasionally clipped a stone with a hoof.

He was sleeping lightly, his head on an upthrust root, when he heard boots grinding stones nearby. He flung the blanket away and drew his Colt as a female voice said, "Mr. Cameron?"

"Who is it?" His mind was sluggish from sleep, but his heart pounded wildly.

"It is Marina."

Then she appeared out of the darkness, under the softly rustling leaves of the paloverde. She clutched a blanket around her shoulders. Her hair fell over it.

"I want to speak to you," she said.

CHAPTER 6

CAMERON CRAWLED CLUMSILY to his feet and holstered his pistol. "What can I help you with?"

Marina moved forward, until she stood only a few feet away from him. The starlight shone in her large brown eyes. "Señor Clark—" She hesitated, as though finding the words strange on her tongue. "My husband and I do not understand why you will not accept our offer."

Cameron felt like a chastised schoolboy. He smiled ironically. "'Offer'?" he said. "More like a death sentence, wouldn't you say? You grew up in that country. You must know how many Apaches still haunt that part of Sonora."

"We will travel at night. The Apaches will not fight at night. Besides, the Indios are busy fighting with your government and mine. They will not bother with a small party such as ours."

Cameron sighed and retook his seat beneath the paloverde. He brought his knees up and set his wrists on them, studying her. He'd been right. She did have spunk. She was also a fool. "Why don't you two go alone, then? You know the country. One more man isn't going to make much of a difference if the Apaches come callin'."

"I have never been to that part of Mejico. Neither of us has. And in the unlikely event the Apaches do come calling," she said coolly, "we will need men who know how to fight them. I have never fought them. Neither has Señor . . . my husband."

Cameron tipped his head and studied her wryly. "How long you been married, anyway—you and Señor Clark?" he added with a touch of irony.

She lowered her gaze. "One month." Cameron could have guessed as much. Was that why they did not look like a couple, or was there another reason they seemed such a mismatched pair?

"Newlyweds, eh?"

She looked at him, frowning, not understanding the phrase or the irony with which it had been expressed.

"Never mind," Cameron said with a flick of his wrist. "How did you two meet?"

"Why do you want to know?" Marina asked guardedly.

Cameron shrugged. "Just curious."

She studied him for a moment, then got up and moved several feet away from him sitting on a rock. She put her feet together and brought her knees up, smoothing her skirt over them. "We did not . . . meet in the traditional way," she said, not looking at him. In the shadows the starlight traced the straight, aristocratic line of her jaw and nose, and Cameron could see her at one of those come-one, come-all Mexican fandangos—the belle of the ball, a whole passel of brightly dressed vaqueros lined up awaiting their turn to lead her onto the patio.

"He won me in a poker game."

Cameron could have been knocked over with a feather, but his face remained inert.

Marina added, gazing directly into his eyes, "From my uncle."

Finally, Cameron took a sharp intake of air and let it out with a low whistle. "How in the hell . . . ?" He let his voice trail off.

She continued, staring at her feet. "My father's rancho was attacked by Apaches." A shadow passed over her face, the muscles in her cheeks and neck tightening. "Papa and Mama—my brother Ubre— all were killed. All the vaqueros and their families. I alone survived. Papa had taught me what to do if an attack came. There was a fast horse always saddled for me if I would need to escape. I took the plat, and I rode out through the smoke and galloped through the hills to the pueblo. Men were sent out to the hacienda . . . but it was too late." Her voice caught, but no tears came to her eyes.

Cameron let some time pass. Then he asked, "What about your uncle?"

"He was my father's only brother, a half-brother, and they were never close. My uncle Romero had ridden with desperadoes when he was young, and lost an arm in a duel. He opened a cantina in the pueblo and took me in, and I worked for him serving customers."

Her voice hardened with anger. "He bragged about the favor he was doing me, taking in his homeless niece, but he let his customers treat me like a whore. The people in the pueblo allowed it because they were jealous of my father's money even though he had provided for all of them."

She paused.

"The customers weren't the only ones. My uncle . . . I was my uncle's whore."

Cameron glanced at her sharply, but she kept her eyes on the ground. "Then Señor Clark came to the cantina with three other men. They were purchasing mining claims, I think. They gambled with my uncle for two days and a night."

"And you fell into the pot?" Cameron said, his voice circumspect.

Marina nodded and looked at him, absently smoothing the skirt over her knees. This was hard on her, Cameron could tell, and his own discomfort at hearing such a confession made him want her to stop. But she seemed to need to tell it. "My uncle's wife wanted him to get rid of me. She found out he was visiting my room . . . on nights when he wasn't too drunk to climb the stairs."

"And Clark won."

"Sí."

"And you gave him the plat?"

Her gaze found his again, fastening on him. It was no longer an unpleasant sensation. "He is not a bad man, Señor Cameron. He is a much better man than my uncle. All he wants is to buy a ranch out West in your country and start over."

"And what do you want?"

She did not say anything. She looked away, staring into the darkness. Cameron could not see her face, but he knew its expression was troubled.

Marina said something at last, but in a voice too soft for Cameron to hear.

"I beg your pardon?" he said.

She cleared her throat. "I want to get my daughter back."

Cameron chewed his lip, silent. That was enough—he didn't want to hear any more. But he knew he was going to.

"It was my uncle . . ." Her voice trailed off.

It took Cameron a moment to understand. Then he gave a ragged sigh.

"My aunt took my baby . . . my daughter . . . to the sisters in the convent in Piro Alta."

"How long ago?"

"Two years. I had her for three months before"—her voice faltered almost imperceptibly—"before she was taken away."

"Did your aunt know . . . ?"

"That my uncle was the father?" Marina finished for him, regaining her composure. "No. She would have killed Marlena if she had. I suppose she knows now, but the sisters have her."

Her voice became firm and strong, but pleading. "I want the money to get her back. The old crones in the convent are not above taking bribes; they've even hid desperadoes for money. If I pay them, they will give Marlena back to me. And I want the money to give her a good life . . . the kind of life I had before the Apaches took it away."

A nightbird cooed and Marina gave a start, turning her head sharply. At length, she turned to Cameron. "Will they come? Those men from the stage?"

"I don't know," Cameron said. "My guess is they won't try anything at night. They'll probably wait until we're back on the trail tomorrow, maybe crossing the San Pedro. That's what I'd do . . . but then, I'm not Gaston Bachelard. We have to be prepared for anything."

Cameron heard a rustle of cloth and saw Marina stand and move toward him, her feet coming down softly in the pebbles and grass. She knelt only a foot away from him. Cameron was puzzled. She rested a hand on his arm and put her face close to his. He could smell her, feel her warmth, and he was ashamed at the stirring she caused in his loins.

"Please," she said stiffly, as one does who is unused to begging, "help me find the gold . . . so I can get my daughter back from the nuns."

As her fingers dug into his forearm, Cameron felt his resolve weaken slightly. But he'd ridden the

Mexican trail enough times to know there was little or no chance of finding the treasure—if there even was a treasure—and getting out alive. As far as getting Marina's daughter back, well if there was no gold . . .

Besides, Cameron had to get back to his ranch and get ready for the autumn gather. He couldn't go traipsing off to Mexico with some well-heeled Southern gentleman and his Mexican wife—no matter how beautiful the wife may be. When he was younger he would have gone after the woman as well as the gold. But Cameron was no kid anymore, and his wanderlust had gone the way of Ivy Kitchen, whose death had taken the heart out of him. No longer was any woman worth a wild-goose chase into Mexico.

He wagged his head and turned away. "I'm sorry."

"You'll be rich," she urged.

"Nine out of ten treasure trails lead to nothing. Take it from an expert." They both sat there, saying nothing, for several minutes.

"I understand, Mr. Cameron," Marina finally said, releasing his arm. "I am grateful for the help you have given us. We were wrong to ask for anything more. I hope you can forgive us."

She stood.

Cameron sighed. "No . . . I'm sorry . . ."

"Sorry?" she said with a laugh. "You saved our lives!" She turned and started away. "Good night."

When she'd gone, Cameron sat there, hands entwined, feeling like a lout.

Then he heard her scream.

CHAPTER 7

THE SCREAM HAD come from about halfway between the cave and Cameron's camping spot. It had rended the night like a hot knife through lard, lashing back and forth between the peaks before it died, seemingly bringing the whole night alive with its terror.

Cameron froze for only a moment. Then he was on his feet, grabbing his revolver off his hip and running up the trail, bounding over the dark shapes of shrubs hunkering low to the ground, paying little heed to the cholla and prickly pear, the thorns of which penetrated his boots and jeans.

Cameron stopped about where he thought the scream had originated and looked around, swinging his revolver in a hundred-and-eighty-degree arc. Faintly he heard someone running toward him and saw two figures taking shape in the dark—Hotchkiss and Jimmy Bronco. Starlight reflected off their rifles.

Cameron called Marina's name but his voice was swallowed by the night, and the only response was from Hotchkiss.

"What the hell happened!" he exclaimed through a grating whisper as he and Jimmy approached.

"I don't know." Cameron kept his voice calm. His heart was pounding and he gasped for breath. "Let's separate and look around. Jimmy, you stay here and keep your eyes and ears open."

Hotchkiss went west and Cameron, east. He walked slowly, methodically searching left and right, gazing up and down the grade, stepping over cactus and low-growing shrubs, trying to make as little noise as possible. If someone had grabbed Marina, they could be hunkered down behind a bush or a rock, waiting to pink him as he wandered by.

He stopped and shouted, "Marina, can you hear me?"

He didn't have to yell very loud; his voice carried well in this chasm between rock-walled peaks. He thought he could practically hear the cactus wrens breathing in their hollowed-out hovels in the saguaros.

He heard someone running clumsily down the grade toward him, plowing through shrubs and stumbling over rocks. Cameron could hear the raspy breathing, the harsh, intermittent coughs of Adrian Clark.

The man stopped about thirty feet away. "What happened?" Clark yelled, his voice sounding fragile and small in the big, malevolent night. He coughed a phlegmy cough that made Cameron's chest ache.

"They've got your wife," Cameron said.

Clark coughed again, took in a grating breath. "Where are you?"

"About thirty feet down the grade from you."

Another cough. "What happened?" he repeated. He seemed amazingly restrained for a man who'd just lost his wife.

"I don't know."

Clark coughed twice more, then moved closer, stopping about six feet away. He bent over at the waist, trying to draw air into his lungs. His breath sounded like that of some dying animal.

"Jesus Christ," Cameron said. "You're sick."

"What the hell happened?"

Cameron listened to the quiet night punctuated by Clark's labored breathing. He ran the back of the hand clutching his revolver against his chin, trying to think rationally. "They must have grabbed her on her way back to the cave."

Clark called her name. He was about to call her again when Cameron grabbed his arm. "It's no use," he said. "They have her, and we can't track them in the dark."

Clark looked at him. "Bachelard?"

"Who else?"

"Shit!" Clark exclaimed, slamming his hand in his fist. "She's mine, goddamn it!"

Cameron watched him. Clark was riled now, more angry than worried. He was like a gambler who'd discovered a long night's worth of winnings stolen from his billfold. Cameron wanted to cuff his injured head. Instead, he took him by the arm. "Come on, let's get back to the cave," he said. "That bandage is like a target out here."

Clark was angry. "What about my . . . What about Marina?"

Cameron looked at the Missourian again, the night concealing the disdain in his eyes. "They haven't gone far."

"Why?"

"Because they haven't got what they're looking for."

Cameron turned and started up the grade toward the cave. He figured it was about a hundred yards away. The fire was hidden by shrubs and boulders.

Behind Cameron, Clark ground his teeth. "Why . . . Why?"

"Simple," Cameron said. "They'll trade her for the plat."

"They won't kill her?"

"They wouldn't have anything to trade if they killed her."

"Oh . . . Christ," Clark said weakly. "But they'll rape her, I'll bet. Goddamn savages."

When they neared the fire, Cameron stopped cold in his tracks. Someone stood facing him. It was Pas. He stood with slumped shoulders and bowed head, his knees bent slightly, as though about to buckle. Something was wrong, but Cameron could not tell what it was.

"Jack," Pas said. His voice was a harsh whisper.

"What is it?"

"I'm a dead man."

Cameron walked toward him, then stopped in horror. He could smell the blood and the man's insides before he saw them, spilling out around the small dark hands that tried to hold them in.

"¡Ai, caramba! They've killed me." Pas's knees buckled. Cameron eased him to the ground. Pas reclined on his side, keeping his right hand on his middle. His hands were black with blood and viscera.

"Pas," Cameron said. "What happened, Pas?"

The Mexican inhaled sharply, his face twisting in pain. "When the girl yelled, Bud and him"—he glanced at Clark—"they ran out of the cave. I stayed with the Indio. Someone made a sound behind me. I turned around . . . and . . . someone stuck a knife in my guts. Ai, Mary! They killed me, compadre." His lips formed a wry smile amid the pain. "I always heard a knife to the guts was the worst way to go . . ."

Pas's head sank sideways to the ground. He reached out with a bloody hand and grabbed Cameron around the neck. He whispered hoarsely, "Take . . . Take care of Leonora and my children, Jack."

Cameron grabbed his old friend's arm and squeezed. "I will, Pas." His voice broke and his heart swelled.

He felt the tension leave Pas's body. The hand slipped away from his neck and fell to the ground. Pas gave one last sigh and stopped breathing. There was a garbled, wet sound in his throat, which Cameron knew was the last of the air leaving his lungs. An arm shook spasmodically.

"Pas . . ." Cameron said, overcome with sorrow and rage. He'd been the man's neighbor, had eaten at his table, and knew his wife and four children as well as he'd ever known anyone out here in this no-man's-land. He and Pas had helped each other defend their ranches from the Apaches. They were neighbors where having neighbors you could count on was often the difference between life and death.

Now Pas was lying here dead with his guts spilling out on the ground, and his wife and kids were alone . . .

"Cameron," Clark said, as if from far away.

Cameron continued staring at Pas, working his rage into a lather while his face remained hard and gray and expressionless.

"Cameron," Clark repeated.

Cameron turned to him slowly. "What?"

"The Indian," Hotchkiss said. He'd run up with Jimmy Bronco and had been standing silently over Cameron, taking in the dead Pas Varas. "He's gone."

Cameron jerked his gaze over to the tree to which the Indian had been tied, and saw the cut rope but no Indian. His sour gut turned even more sour and a black bug of dread hopscotched along his backbone. He kicked sand onto the fire. Darkness enveloped them totally as a gust of acrid smoke lifted skyward.

"What's that for?" Clark said.

"I don't want them watching us squirm."

"Jimmy and I will head down to make sure the horses are all right," Hotchkiss said. Then he and the boy were gone.

Cameron kicked a rock in frustration.

"What are we gonna do?" Clark asked.

"There's nothing we *can* do . . . until morning," Cameron said. His voice was low and gloomy.

He saw Clark's dark form turn to him. "What in the hell was she doing down there?"

Cameron walked to the edge of the cave, squatted down on his haunches, and reached into his shirt pocket for his tobacco and papers. "She came down to try and convince me to help you find the gold," he said.

"And you let her walk back alone?" Clark's voice was coldly accusatory.

Cameron swallowed his anger. "She's your wife, for chrissakes. If you can't watch her, how the hell can you expect me to?" He knew it was a ridiculous argument—he should have walked Marina back to the cave—but he was in no mood to be chastised by Adrian Clark, whose presence was the reason they were all in this mess in the first place.

He turned to face the back of the cave to light his cigarette, then sat there smoking, shielding the coal with his palm and scolding himself for not being more careful. He should have told Marina to stay in the cave, and they all should have been watchful. Cameron hadn't known what to expect from Bachelard, so he should have been expecting anything.

It was a ballsy move, though; he'd give the man that. Coming in and taking the girl right under their noses . . . But why in hell had he set the Indian loose? Surely he didn't think the Indian would throw in with him; it must have been simply to gall and confound.

And it had done just that . . .

Clark said softly, "You don't think they'll kill her, do you?"

"You already asked me that. No."

"Will they . . . ?" Clark couldn't finish the sentence.

"They might," Cameron allowed.

It was a cruel thing to say, but he couldn't help blaming Clark for Pas's death and the Indian's escape. If he and Marina hadn't been on that stage, Cameron would have been a lot farther down the trail to Contention City, and he'd still have the Indian to deliver to the soldiers tomorrow. As it stood, they might get Marina back, but the Indian was another story.

Cameron had a feeling he'd see the Indian again, but on the Indian's terms this time. Cameron knew he'd dishonored Perro Loco not only by capturing him, but by the way he had been captured—slipping a gun to the man's head while he was fornicating. Undoubtedly the Indian would be looking to recoup his honor, and the only way he could do that would be to hunt Cameron down and kill him.

Goddamn it.

It was a long night. Cameron and Clark stayed in the cave, smoking and pacing, not saying much. Hotchkiss and the kid stayed with the horses. No one slept a wink.

At dawn Hotchkiss and Bronco came up the grade from the water, trailing the horses. They saddled all the mounts, including Varas's Appaloosa, and Cameron wrapped the dead Mexican in his blanket and draped him over his saddle, securing him with the ropes they'd used on the Indian. Clark rode the Indian's horse.

They rode down the grade and picked up the trail that skirted the dry wash as the sun neared the peak of the eastern ridge, whitening the sky and silhouetting the desert scrub and saguaros before it.

Birds chirped and rabbits scurried through the brush along the wash. Hawks hunted, the golden rays of the sun finding them circling the canyon or perched stonelike on rocks. It could have been a perfectly fine desert morning, with everything right with the world.

Only the grim faces of the unshaven riders, weary from worry and lack of sleep, told a different story. Even the horses seemed downtrodden as they made their way, heads down, tails held straight down between their legs, back out of the canyon. They followed the narrow trail around boulders and cactus to the main stage road.

Cameron kept on eye out for Bachelard. He knew the old guerrilla would appear sooner or later. The man was in no big hurry; the more time Cameron, Clark, and the others had to squirm, the better off he was.

As far as the Indian went, Cameron didn't figure he'd see him again until Perro Loco had had time to return to his band and gather a war party.

After scouting the trail ahead, Cameron returned to the ragged line of riders, who were starting to sweat in the warming sun, and fell in beside Clark. Something was bothering Cameron.

"Hey, Clark," he said. "When Bachelard shows, you *are* going to give him the plat, aren't you?" Even to his own ears it sounded like a stupid question. But Cameron didn't know Clark well enough to understand his motivations.

"Of course I'll give him the plat," Clark said, irritated. "What kind of a man do you think I am, anyway? Besides, I have a copy."

Cameron had expected as much. No one would go after treasure with only one copy of the map.

"The original is stitched into my coat," Clark said. "The copy's in my boot."

"Better give him the original. If you give him the copy, he might think you're trying to trick him."

"I thought of that."

Cameron held pace with Clark's horse, studying the man. Clark was dour. His face glistened with sweat, and his unshaven cheeks appeared gaunt and hollow, his eyes sunk in their sockets.

He was not a well man to begin with, and last night's ordeal had set him back. Cameron could tell he wanted his property back, but the idea of giving up the plat to Bachelard was going down like tar.

"You really think it's there, don't you?" Cameron asked him wonderingly. "The gold."

Clark did not look at him. His brooding eyes stared up the trail, upper lip curled slightly in a perpetual sneer. "It's there, all right, and I'm still going to have it. Every ounce . . . Bachelard be damned."

A half-hour later the sun was nearly straight up, and the desert terrain was so bright it stung the eyes. They were riding through a shallow valley, with low rimrocks on both sides. The ground was rocky in places, and studded with ocotillo and brushy clumps of creosote. Cicadas sang. A roadrunner dashed across the trail and disappeared behind a boulder.

Hotchkiss's old eyes were the first to pick the riders out of the desert. He halted his horse.

Cameron reined his buckskin to a stop and followed the old man's gaze. About a hundred yards ahead sat seven riders, side by side and no more than twenty feet apart. Three sat close together. They were little more than shadowy outlines from this distance, but Cameron could tell the one in the middle of the three was a woman.

"Here we go," he said.

Clark and Jimmy Bronco brought their mounts up to Cameron and Hotchkiss. Clark grimaced as he stared ahead through the bright sunlight. "Is it them?"

Cameron nodded.

"What are we going to do?"

Cameron sucked air through his teeth. "Well, I guess we'll ride up and hear what they have to say. Everyone spread out. Keep several yards between you in case they try anything."

He clucked his horse forward and the others followed suit. Cameron shucked his Winchester from his saddle boot and cocked it.

"I don't like this," he told Hotchkiss under his breath. "I don't like this a bit."

"You and me both," Hotchkiss said.

CHAPTER 8

CLARK'S BREATH WAS shallow and he could hear his heart drumming in his ears.

The stitches in his head were irritated by the heat, and the sun was frying his face in spite of his hat. Dust clothed him; he could feel it everywhere—even in his underwear and deep within his ears.

But the dust was nothing compared to the pickle he found himself in with Bachelard.

Clark grunted, suppressing a cough. What the hell had happened? The plan had been to find Reese McCormick and head to Mexico, where they would become rich men. Clark would buy a Western ranch operation, with a big log ranch house, a herd of Texas cattle, and real cowboys. Clark's family's Missouri plantation was long gone to carpetbaggers, so Clark would simply start over. The West was just the place for doing such a thing.

He had no illusion that Marina loved him. Their marriage had been arranged, in a way—if you can call winning your wife in a poker game an arrangement—and there had been no time for love to develop between them. But to Clark love was not important. Clark was a Southern gentleman, who married a woman for the same reason you bought thoroughbreds: so they could produce more thoroughbreds while looking very nice about the grounds.

Before the war, Clark's father had arranged for Adrian to marry the daughter of a wealthy friend. Clark had not loved the girl but accepted the engagement as part of the due course of his life; love was not a consideration. The girl—Clark had forgotten her name—had been young and beautiful and wealthy, and that had been enough.

But then the war came along, first postponing, then canceling, the marriage—the family was living in poverty now, with relatives in Colorado. Clark had been ushered off to war by his father, albeit in a non-fighting capacity. If not for the war, Clark would no doubt be married to a woman he did not love, but who would have produced worthy heirs, and all would have been right with the world.

Now he carried in his mind the image of Marina on his arm at some stockmen's gathering in Wyoming or Colorado, a roomful of frock-coated and silk-gowned admirers gazing at her extraordinary beauty, champagne glasses clutched in their bejeweled hands. He loved her the way men can love a beautiful, beguiling woman for the *idea* of her alone, for the thought of her naked and writhing beneath him, for the progeny she would produce, and for the fancy figure she would cut at a dance.

Unconsciously he believed—he hoped—that when Marina saw the gold, she'd forget all that blather about tracking down her daughter. Because of her Latin beauty and sensuality, Clark thought he could overlook Marina's unmentionable relationship with her uncle, but he wasn't sure he could live with the bastard child it had spawned.

While he was not certain which meant more to him, Marina or the gold, he had to admit the thought of leaving her with Bachelard had crossed his mind. With that much gold a man could have any woman he wanted.

He chastised himself for the half-conscious thought. His father had raised him better than that. Adrian Clark might have been stripped of his wealth, but he still had his honor, by God!

Now he reined his horse to a halt and suppressed a gasp. Bachelard and his men sat their mounts about thirty feet away. The group that had run down the stage had been joined by Perro Loco. Clark's heart drummed so wildly he could hear it in his ears.

Between Bachelard and the Indian, Marina stiffly sat a gray pony, her back taut and her face tense. Her hands were tied behind her back and there was a noose around her neck. The end of the noose was held by the Indian. His forage cap shaded his forehead, but Clark could see his smoldering black eyes. The muscles in his bare arms coiled like snakes.

Clark glanced at Cameron, who sat his horse tensely, returning the Indian's dark look. They were like two wolves meeting in the woods—two wild, angry, bloodthirsty wolves fighting for the highest stakes of all.

Bachelard took the cigar from his mouth and flashed a malevolent grin. "Hello, Cameron. Heard a lot about you. We meet at last. You already know my friend here." He glanced at the Indian, whose gaze was locked on Cameron as though fixed there by some unseen force.

Cameron nodded at the Indian mockingly and broke a smile.

Perro Loco stared at Cameron. Cameron wasn't sure the Indian understood English; he'd given no indication of it since Cameron had captured him.

"You two throwin' in together?" Cameron asked Bachelard.

Bachelard shrugged. "Let's just say we have a common interest."

"Quiet one, ain't he?"

"I never cared for a chatterbox."

Cameron's eyes went dark. "You killed a good friend of mine last night."

Bachelard shrugged again. "He was in the way."

"I'm gonna kill you for that."

The Cajun didn't even blink.

Cameron stared flatly at the man, his cheek dimpling where his jaws joined. Finally he placed his hands on his saddle horn and shifted position. "But that's between us alone. Why don't you let that woman go?"

"I'd like to do that, but first I'll need the plat." Bachelard's eyes slid to Clark.

"How do I know you'll let her go?" Clark asked him.

"I have no use for her." Bachelard gave a wolfish grin. "Hell, me and Perro Loco here had our fill of her last night." He removed the cigar from his mouth with a gloved hand and threw his head back. "Ha, ha, ha!"

Clark felt as though he'd been clubbed in the chest. Anger filled him, filled his mouth with the taste of bile. He wanted to pull the pistol out of his holster and put a bullet between Bachelard's eyes, and he would have done so if he thought he had a chance of hitting his target from this distance.

"Easy, Clark," Cameron said, reading his mind. "He'd love you to go loco. Give me the plat; I'll ride it over to him."

"No, I'll ride it over to him."

Clark gripped his reins firmly in his sweat-soaked

hands and clucked the horse forward. He looked at Marina. She stared at him. Her eyes were scared but sane. Clark wondered if it was true, what Bachelard had said about him and Perro Loco, last night . . . If it was true, he wasn't sure he'd be able to share a bed with her again. What a shame.

He stopped before Bachelard, his horse jerking its head away from the Cajun's black, which pricked its ears offensively. The Indian's cold stare lifted the hair on the back of Clark's neck. The look told him they were not going to get out of this without shooting.

"Let her go and I'll give it to you," Clark said to Bachelard.

"Let me see it."

Clark reached behind him, into his saddlebag, withdrew a rolled javelina-skin and clutched it before him.

"Unroll it."

Clark did as he was told and held it facing Bachelard.

"That the original?"

"Yes."

"How do I know?"

"You think I caught a javelina last night?"

Bachelard stuck out his hand. "Give."

"How can you be sure the story's genuine?"

Bachelard shrugged. "I'm not. But for that much gold I'm willing to take a chance. Hand it over."

"Let her go."

"Oh, Christ . . . those damaged goods?" Bachelard grumbled wryly. He nodded at the Indian, who removed the noose from Marina's neck.

Bachelard turned to Clark. "He'll slap that horse's rump as soon as the plat is in my hand."

Clark glanced at Cameron, then shifted his eyes to Hotchkiss and Bronco. Rifles across their saddles and a grim cast to their eyes, they appeared ready for anything. It was small comfort to Clark, but a comfort nonetheless.

Bachelard yelled angrily, "Come on—hand it over, pilgrim!"

Clark jumped, startled by the sudden outburst, and thrust the plat into the Cajun's outstretched hand. Bachelard smiled. "There—that wasn't so hard now, was it?"

"My wife, Mr. Bachelard," Clark growled through gritted teeth.

"Oh, yes. Forgive me," Bachelard said.

Casually, his wolfish grin still directed at Clark, he unholstered his revolver, brought it up to Marina's head, and thumbed back the hammer. But before he could pull the trigger, the Indian let out an angry, high-pitched wail that sounded like nothing Clark had ever heard before. In one motion the big Indian swung his leg around and leaped from his horse onto the back of Marina's.

Startled and amazed by the Indian's sudden display, Bachelard brought back his pistol, frowning, and struggled with his horse's reins as the horse jumped and danced, spooked by the Indian's cry. Perro Loco slapped the hip of Marina's horse, drawing a long-barreled pistol from the waistband of his leggings, and thumbed back the hammer as the horse bolted in a headlong, ground-eating rush past Clark, who was fighting with the reins of his own startled mount, toward Cameron.

Perro Loco aimed the pistol in his outstretched hand over Marina's right shoulder, screaming an Apache death song.

It had all happened in little more than a second. Cameron was still reacting to Bachelard's draw as the Indian bounded toward him. Now he turned his

Winchester in the Indian's direction, but there was no way he could take a shot and not risk hitting the woman. His horse, startled by the Indian's shriek, was doing a stiff-legged dance that made an accurate shot even less likely.

Cameron saw the swiftly approaching pistol aimed at his head. When the screaming horse was only ten yards away, Marina yelled, "No!" and flung her right arm at the Indian's hand. The gun barked and the bullet sailed wide.

Perro Loco yelled savagely, striking at Marina as his horse plowed broadside into Cameron's. Cameron tried to roll wide as the horse fell, but his boot caught in the stirrup, and the horse went down on his leg. The Indian's horse fell on Cameron's, throwing Marina on top of the white man. The Indian lost his rifle as he slid out of the saddle, then quickly regained his seat as the horse struggled to its feet and plunged away.

As Cameron's horse rose noisily, Cameron scrambled to a sitting position, and brought the Winchester to his shoulder, trying to plant a bead on the bouncing, quickly diminishing figure of the Indian. He shot once, saw the bullet kick dust. He cocked again, steadied the rifle, and fired.

Perro Loco's head snapped forward. The horse bucked and the Indian fell out of the saddle. He rolled once, bringing a hand to his head, then crouched, looking back at Cameron as the horse bucked across the desert, angrily kicking its back legs and arching its neck.

Perro Loco gave an angry shriek as Cameron fired again. The bullet spanged off a rock at the Indian's knees. Perro Loco rolled to his side, then regained his feet smoothly, like a cat, and ran behind a brushy rise. He appeared a second later beyond the rise, darting between saguaros and creosote shrubs, heading east.

Cameron stood and fired four more angry shots, hitting nothing but mesquite and rocks. The Indian disappeared down a grade.

Cameron cursed. Becoming aware of guns going off around him, he crouched behind a creosote shrub and looked around. Hotchkiss knelt in a gully about twenty yards away, aiming south, where Bachelard's men apparently were. A few shots sounded in that direction, and Cameron saw a single puff of smoke from a hundred yards away. But it looked as though Bachelard and his men, having gotten what they had come for, were retreating into the desert.

Cameron couldn't see Clark and Jimmy Bronco, but the sound of pistol fire beyond Hotchkiss told him they were still kicking. They probably had Perro Loco to thank for that, Cameron speculated wryly. If it hadn't been for the Indian's sudden attack, Bachelard no doubt would have killed Marina, and his men, following suit, would have opened up on Cameron and the others before they'd had time to react.

"Thanks, my Injun friend," Cameron muttered dryly, turning to look for Marina.

Ten yards behind Cameron, she lay behind the skeleton of a fallen, decaying saguaro. Only her eyes and the top of her head were visible.

"Are you all right?" he asked her.

The others were still shooting—Cameron thought he recognized the eager, rapid bursts of Jimmy Bronco's Colts but there hadn't been any return fire for several minutes.

He stood, and then she did as well, favoring her left foot. Her eyes were frightened, haunted, but there was a fire there too.

No, she was definitely no hothouse flower, Cameron thought.

"I think I—how do you say?—sprained my ankle," she said.

"Sit down there, let me take a look."

She sat on the dead saguaro, on which the thorns had long since decayed, and started unlacing her shoe. Cameron took over, loosening the laces and pulling out the tongue, then gently eased the shoe's heel away from her foot.

She gave a pained sigh.

"Hurt?" he asked.

"Yes."

He gave one more gentle tug and the shoe came off in his hand. He dropped it, removed her sock, and took her long, slender foot in his hand. He moved it, very gently, from left to right.

He raised his eyes to hers. "Hurt?"

She shook her head. "Not much."

"I don't think it's broken," he said.

Her eyes held his. "I am sorry, Mr. Cameron . . . for everything . . . for all this."

Cameron couldn't help smiling at her. Something about her touched him very deeply. "What are you talking about?" he said with a laughing grunt. "You saved my life today."

She smiled wryly, gave a slow blink of her smoky-black eyes. Cameron couldn't help staring at her, transfixed for what must have been at least a quarter-minute. Then he looked down and saw that her bare foot was still in his hand.

"Marina?" Clark called from somewhere nearby.

Startled, suddenly self-conscious, Cameron lowered her foot and stood, awkwardly looking around. "Well . . . we'll get you on a horse and you can rest that ankle in Contention City. Maybe get a doc to take a look at it."

Clark appeared out of the creosote, pushing a branch aside, a pistol in his hand. He was sweaty and dirty.

"Marina . . . ?" he said. His eyes dropped to her bare foot. "What happened?"

"I sprained my ankle," Marina said. "It's okay."

Clark dropped to take a look at the ankle, and Cameron moved away to find Hotchkiss and Bronco. Hotchkiss holstered his pistol as Cameron approached.

"You all right, Jack?" Hotchkiss asked, smiling with relief. "I figured for sure Perro Loco was going to take you to the dance there for a minute."

Cameron shook his head. "I did too. You boys catch any lead?"

"Nah," Hotchkiss replied.

"I think I clipped one of 'em," Jimmy Bronco said proudly.

Hotchkiss looked at the kid, scowling. "You did not, son. That was my shot, for cryin' out loud."

"Uh-*uh*."

"Okay, okay," Cameron said, interceding. "Let's just worry about getting the horses back so you two can get Clark and his wife to Contention City."

Hotchkiss looked at him, blue eyes flashing incredulity. "What do you mean so *you* two can? Where are *you* goin'?"

Cameron was glancing around for the horses. "After Loco. Where the hell do you think?"

"Alone?"

"He's unarmed," Cameron said with a shrug. "It's best to ride him down now, before he can get back to his band. I want you two to stay with the Clarks."

Hotchkiss looked down, troubled. "I don't know, Jack. Armed or unarmed, that's one hotheaded Injun."

Cameron started walking in the direction where his horse had disappeared, then stopped suddenly and turned toward Clark and Marina.

Clark was sitting in the sand, heels planted in the ground before him, resting his weary head. Marina was putting her shoe back on. She glanced up and saw Cameron. She stopped what she was doing and looked at him with a vague question in her narrowing gaze.

Cameron turned, giving a wry chuff, and continued walking. All he needed now was to get a goddamn woman stuck in his craw . . .

CHAPTER 9

WHEN CAMERON CAUGHT up to his horse, about a hundred and fifty yards from the scene of the shoot-out, he watered the animal, mounted up, and headed after Perro Loco. The man's trail wasn't hard to follow, marked as it was by bright red splotches of blood on rocks and shrubs—so much of it that Cameron kept thinking he'd soon come across the man himself. There was nothing like a head wound to drain you dry.

But he'd ridden two miles along an arroyo twisting up a shallow canyon lined with boulders, and there was still no sign of the Indian, save for his blood and intermittent moccasin prints.

Suddenly, after another mile, the blood disappeared. Cameron dismounted and looked around, tipping the flat brim of his hat off his forehead and mopping his brow with the sleeve of his buckskin tunic.

He walked several yards up the trail, leading his horse in his hands, peering at the ground. Nothing. Finally he stopped, sighed, and looked up the northern wall of the canyon, which was turning coppery as the sun angled westward, the nooks and crannies between boulders turning a deep ocean-green.

Spying him, a well-fed coyote turned and leapt from a boulder, where it had perched to scan the valley for prey. The beast took stiff-legged strides up the grade and over the peak. Its presence told Cameron the Indian had not gone that way; which left only forward—or up the opposite wall.

Cameron tethered his horse to a piñon, unsheathed his Winchester, and started up the wall, jumping from rock to rock, stopping now and then to crouch and look around. During one such breather he saw a small drop of blood on a boulder to his left. It was about the size of a raindrop, which told Cameron the Indian had stopped long enough to stifle some of the blood flow.

Cameron couldn't believe it. Even if he'd only grazed Perro Loco, the man's feat was amazing. He'd run three miles practically without stopping, bleeding, and now he was climbing a canyon wall. Cameron might have caught old Perro Loco in a bad moment back in Summerville, but the man really was the Mad Dog of the Desert—a true-blue Apache with sand in his blood if ever there was one.

Cameron made a mental note to watch himself. The Apache might not have a gun, but Cameron didn't doubt that the man knew how to fashion weapons from natural objects, and he didn't want to fall into a false sense of security. Hell, he'd seen Apaches kill soldiers with stones thrown from thirty yards away!

Wagging his head, Cameron descended the grade to his horse and unsaddled the animal, then removed the bridle. He hid the tack in a clump of brush under a couple low-growing piñons. He'd leave the animal here while he went after Perro Loco on foot, which was the only way to track him up that steep, rocky grade. In his years scouting for the Army, Cameron had discovered that often afoot was the only way you could effectively track an Apache—Mad Dog of the Desert or otherwise.

He clapped the horse on the rump. The animal trotted a few yards ahead, then stopped and craned its head around to peer curiously at Cameron, who sat on a rock and was replacing his boots with the moccasins he always carried in his saddlebags. "Go on up the trail and find water," he told the horse. "There's bound to be a spring around here somewhere."

The horse just stared at him.

Cameron tucked his boots into his saddlebags, then grabbed his field glasses, and his canteen and rifle, and slung both over his shoulder. "I'll be back tomorrow . . . I hope," he told the horse. "Don't go off with any strangers, now, and stay out of trouble."

He headed back up the wall.

It was hard going for a man who'd gotten used to a saddle. When he was scouting, Cameron had exercised nearly every day in the rocky hills around Fort Hauchuca. That was seven years ago, however, and while Cameron kept in shape working around his ranch, he was not the young, fleet-footed Indian-stalker he once had been.

After several hundred yards, he finally had to stop and catch his breath. He put his head down and sucked air into his lungs. Dark spots formed before his eyes and his vision swam.

"Christ Almighty," he wheezed. "I'm getting old."

When his heartbeat finally started to slow, he lifted his head to glance up the slope, sweat stinging his eyes. Near the sandstone ridge pocked with swallow nests, something moved.

Cameron brought up his field glasses and adjusted the focus, bringing the shaded ridge clearly into view. There against the wall was the shadowy figure of a man; the buckskin breeches told Cameron it was Perro Loco. He was climbing the spur that crested the ridge—a twenty-foot wall of sandstone rock pitted with clefts and small crevices. The Indian's hands and moccasined feet were finding those crevices and using them to pull him up toward the ridge.

Cameron's heart quickened again. He lowered the field glasses and brought up the rifle, levering a shell. He wasn't sure how far away the Indian was—it was hard to judge distances uphill and in this light—but he thought a shot was worth a try. He had no doubt that Perro Loco already knew he was here.

Sighting down the barrel, he didn't like the position he was in, so he slid back on his butt and planted the barrel on his upraised knee. Unable to get the elevation he needed from that angle, he climbed off the rock and used it as a rest for the rifle, crouching low. He took up the slack from the trigger and felt the rifle jump as it barked, spewing smoke and fire, instantly filling the air with the smell of rotten eggs. He lifted his head—the Apache was still there, moving methodically from one hand- and foothold to another.

Cameron dropped his head back down to the rifle and fired. Dust puffed about two feet left of the Indian. The Indian paused for a moment, taking a quick glance over his shoulder, then resumed climbing.

One cool cucumber, Cameron thought, squeezing off another round.

A gout of sandstone blew off the spur six inches above Cameron's last slug. The goddamn rifle was firing to the left. Cameron lowered his head and adjusted his aim. Perro Loco was pulling himself up the last few feet to the top of the spur.

Cameron fired. The bullet spanged below the Indian's right foot as the man was bringing the foot onto the ridgetop.

Angrily Cameron fired three more shots in quick succession, then lifted his head to see the Indian standing on the ridgetop, outlined against the sky.

The man turned, dropped his breeches and bent over, so that for two seconds all Cameron could see was the tan circle of his naked ass.

By the time Cameron had levered another shell and sighted down the barrel again, the ridgetop was deserted.

The Indian was gone.

"Why, you son of a *bitch*!" Cameron hissed.

He replaced the spent lead in the Winchester with shells from his belt, cursed again, and started up the boulder-strewn wall.

He moved as fast as he could over the rocks and boulders and occasional talus slides, pushing through brush to avoid the troublesome cholla, working hard as the grade rose and the sun fell, making it hard to see all the obstacles in his path. His feet grew heavy and his heart pounded like a Comanche war drum.

No, he wasn't as young as he used to be. Thirty-five was old for a man like himself.

Despite the cooling air, sweat dribbled off his brows to sting his eyes. Rivulets streaked the dust on his face and dripped onto his wet shirt. He turned once and saw the valley behind him filling with shadows and the kind of salmon-colored light painters loved. Cameron would have thought it lovely if he were anywhere but here.

When he reached the base of the spur that capped the ridge, he gave himself a two-minute breather, then slung the rifle over his back, made sure the six-shooter was secure in its holster, and resumed the climb, thrusting the toes of his moccasins into narrow crevices in the sandstone rock.

Cameron was halfway to the top when his arms simply played out. His quivering legs felt at once heavy and as insubstantial as air. His bleeding hands were wet and slippery, making it even harder to grab hold of the rock.

He looked down. The base of the spur was a good twenty feet below. If he fell, he'd land on hard, basaltic rock and probably roll a halfmile through cholla cactus and prickly pear and who-knew-what-else? He'd seen men die from infected cholla wounds. At the very least he'd probably end up with a broken leg.

He sucked an angry breath of air through his teeth and cursed. Perro Loco was not going to do him in. He'd worked too hard to die like this—alone on a goddamn sandstone spur in Apache country, his bones stripped and scattered by mountain lions and brush wolves.

No, goddamn it . . . *No!*

From somewhere his anger summoned strength. Suppressing the pain, focusing only on the hand- and footholds he needed to find, he moved, slowly but steadily, until he'd wrapped a hand around the rocky shelf at the top.

There was a fist of rock pushing out of the sandstone to his right. Cameron got his right foot on it and, pushing and pulling, grunting and cursing, hauled himself onto the shelf and over. He rolled onto his back, the breath coming like gusts of sand up and down his windpipe, his heart drumming until he thought it would open his chest.

He stared at the near-dark sky, in which the first stars shone like lanterns, and smiled with relief. Suddenly he grunted in terror and pushed himself onto his knees, bringing the rifle around—the Indian could be waiting for him. The perfect time to attack would have been right after he'd made that energy-sapping climb. A minute ago, Cameron would have been hard put to lift his fist, much less the Winchester.

But there was nothing around but rock and twisted mesquite and some Mormon tea rustling in the night breeze gentling out of the west. Seeing something at his feet, Cameron looked down closely, squinting: a heavy splotch of blood. He'd seen traces of it on the sandstone as he'd climbed, but here was nearly a puddle.

Apparently the climb had been as hard on the wounded Perro Loco as it had been on Cameron. No doubt that's why the Indian had elected to keep moving rather than stay and fight.

"Good," Cameron told himself, nodding. "Damn good." Then he realized, looking into the blackening valleys on both sides, that it was too dark to keep going. There was not enough light to make out the Apache's blood trail or moccasin prints. The new moon wouldn't rise until the end of the week. What's more, high clouds were moving in from the west, and in an hour or two they'd rub out the light from the stars.

He'd stay put until morning, Cameron decided, searching for a place to camp. He found one about twenty feet down the ridge, a hollowed-out place in an escarpment of jagged basalt that lifted out of the hill like lumps of coal glued together by gods amusing themselves.

The hollow was about five and a half feet tall and nearly as wide, with rocks on both flanks, making it easily defensible. To make it even harder for anyone to sneak up on him during the night, Cameron placed rocks and mesquite twigs in a halfcircle around the hollow. An attacker would be betrayed by snapping twigs or the rattle of one of the loose stones.

His chore completed, Cameron relieved himself down the hill, then sat down in the hollow, his back to the wall, and took a long pull from the canteen. He ate two strips of jerked beef, drank more water, and rolled a cigarette, thinking about the others.

He guessed they were probably camping at Mud Wells. That's where he would have camped, and Hotchkiss knew the country as well as he did. If they got an early start in the morning, they should be able to make Contention City by noon—if they didn't run into any damn Apaches along the way . . .

Well, that was Hotchkiss's problem now. Cameron had Perro Loco to worry about.

Cameron sighed, poked out the cigarette in the sand, and kicked his legs out, crossing them at the ankles. He pulled his hat over his eyes and snugged his back into the wall. Sleep came quickly.

———————

In a dream, Ivy Kitchen appeared on that breezy spur. She knelt down before him, adjusting the long white dress she had worn to the barbecue picnic at the Halvorssen ranch, where Cameron had proposed.

"Ivy," he said, half knowing it was only a dream. She was so real he could smell her.

"Oh, Jack," she said. "I went and left you before we were even married."

"You're the only woman I ever loved, Ivy," he said, staring at her, marveling at how young and beautiful she was, how smooth her skin, how blue her eyes.

"We would have had a good life together, Jack. I wanted to have your children—strong boys and pretty girls."

"I wanted that too, Ivy."

"I'm so sorry, Jack. They came so fast, the Apaches. Papa sent us to the cellar but they saw, and opened the doors . . ."

Cameron shook his head, trying not to cry. He'd

never cried in front of a woman. But seeing Ivy again—so real, sweet and pure, just sixteen years old . . . and dead—broke his heart.

"We never even made love," she said.

"You were saving yourself for after the wedding," Cameron said.

"I'm sorry, Jack. I could have given you that, at least."

She leaned toward him and he took her in his arms. He felt the smooth cotton of her dress and wondered if she were really here . . . if she had really come back to him. He gentled her back in his arms, snuggling her head against his shoulder, and lowered his lips to hers.

The kiss was sweet as desert rain, her lips silky and moist.

When he opened his eyes, his breath caught in his throat. It was no longer Ivy Kitchen in his arms, but Marina.

"Oh, Jesus," he said, startled. "I'm sorry."

The Spanish beauty looked at him strangely, as if she had no idea what was happening. She was not wearing a blouse, and her full, naked breasts nestled against his buckskin tunic.

"I thought you were Ivy," Cameron said, pushing her away and looking around for Clark.

Then something touched his outstretched boot. Waking, Cameron looked down and saw a stone by his ankle—one of the stones from the circle he'd made.

Instantly he brought the Winchester to bear. Just as quickly, a moccasined foot kicked it out of his hands.

CHAPTER 10

CAMERON KNEW HE didn't have time to draw his pistol. He threw himself sideways and rolled, trying to separate himself from the Indian.

It didn't work. Just as he was pushing himself up with his hands, the Apache was on him—all sweaty, smelly, grunting two hundred pounds of him—big hands clamped viselike around Cameron's neck, cutting off his wind.

Cameron fell back. The Indian scrambled to kneel on his chest, face twisted into a mask of pure hatred as he pressed both thumbs into Cameron's throat and pounded Cameron's head on the hard rock beneath him.

Cameron wrapped his own hands around Perro Loco's wrists and tried to wrestle free, but the Indian's hard-knotted arms would not budge. Cameron began seeing red, felt himself weakening from lack of oxygen, and knew that in a few seconds he would pass out . . . and then he'd be finished.

His right hand found his pistol and brought it up as he thumbed back the hammer. Perro Loco jerked away, releasing Cameron's throat. Dragging a mouthful of air into his lungs, Cameron pulled the trigger. The gun barked loudly, making his ears ring, but the Indian had shoved Cameron's hand and the bullet spanged off a rock above them.

Then they were fighting for the gun, Perro Loco keeping one hand on Cameron's throat, the other on the gun. They rolled over once . . . twice . . . three times, grunting like embattled grizzlies. Cameron cursed and sucked air down his battered throat, trying to maintain his grip on his gun while keeping the Indian's immensely strong right hand from pinching off his breath again. He wanted to go for his bowie but knew that to do so he'd have to release either the gun or the hand on his throat.

Either way, there wouldn't be enough time to bring up the bowie before he bought it.

Finally he let go of the hand squeezing his throat and placed his left hand on the Indian's big, slippery face, feeling for the eyes. Finding them, he dug in his fingertips, pushing Perro Loco's head back. The Indian released Cameron's gun and yelled in pain.

Cameron smashed the gun against the man's head with as much force as he could muster in such close quarters. It was a good blow. The Indian's other hand dropped away as the man fell sideways. Cameron braced himself on one knee, thumbed back the pistol's hammer, and fired into the dark body of the man only two feet away.

The gun exploded with a sharp flash of orange light, temporarily destroying Cameron's night vision. When he could see again, the Indian was gone.

Cameron heard footsteps, saw a shadow separate from the rock out of the corner of his right eye. Turning that way, he emptied his revolver, but there was nothing before him but a jumble of black rock, ghostly wisps of gunsmoke, and the coppery smell of burnt powder.

Above, the stars shone indifferently, flickering like distant lanterns across a lake.

Cameron cursed, looked around for his carbine, found it, and started running after the Indian. Following a faint trail through the rocks, he stopped to listen. The Indian was dead ahead, only a few yards away. Cameron tracked him by the raspy sounds of his breath and the occasional rattle of rock as he ran.

Cameron hurdled rocks as they took shape in the darkness, racing along the pale ribbon along the edge of the spur, then down the other side, holding the rifle out for balance. He paused twice more, holding his breath, and heard the Indian's labored breathing above the pounding of his own heart.

The third time he stopped—

Silence. Then a cricket sounded somewhere behind him.

He was wondering if the Indian had doubled back when Perro Loco slammed into him from behind, throwing him forward and knocking the rifle out of his hands. Cameron flew face-first into a mesquite shrub.

He turned quickly to the Indian, who was coming at him, holding something over his head. From its size and shape, Cameron could tell it was a good-sized rock. At the last second Cameron sprang to his right.

The rock crashed into the shrub where Cameron's head had been. The Indian was still recovering from the lunge when Cameron hit him with a roundhouse right to the face. The Apache fell backwards and down, beyond the mesquite shrub, and disappeared . . .

Cameron looked for him. Nothing but darkness. It was as though a black cloth were held before him.

He heard a thrashing from somewhere in that blackness, a grunt and several muffled words that could only be Apache curses, then a sudden yell. The yell was loud at first, but it quickly diminished in volume until the man went silent.

The cricket continued to chirp.

Cameron took one cautious step forward, then felt around with his right foot. The ground gave way just beyond the mesquite shrub. It shelved away for several feet, then dropped sharply—how far, Cameron couldn't tell with only the stars for light. But from the sound of Perro Loco's cry, it was a good distance.

Picking up a hefty stone, he dropped it over the edge. It took nearly two seconds to smack rock and clatter away, which told him the drop was enough to kill a man—even an Apache of Perro Loco's caliber.

Cameron gave a sigh and stood there peering over the ledge. He had an uneasy feeling. He wanted to see that the Indian was dead, but there was no way he could know for sure . . . unless he climbed down there in the dark and risked breaking his neck.

It wasn't worth the risk. He'd wait for morning and take another look around. Hopefully, the body would be visible at the bottom of the chasm.

He gave another sigh and, rubbing the sore knuckles he'd nearly cracked when he'd belted Perro Loco, looked around for his rifle. Finding it, he rubbed the sand off it and looked for a good place to settle in for the night, maybe catch a few more hours of sleep. His lungs were raw from the climbing and fighting, and his hand hurt. His eyelids were heavy with weariness, but the adrenaline was still coursing through his veins.

Hoping to calm himself, he dug his tobacco pouch and papers out of the breast pocket of his tunic and rolled a smoke. He smoked and listened to the faint night sounds, trying to empty his mind. Finally he rubbed out the quirley, settled back against the rock wall he'd found in the dark, and slept.

He didn't wake until a gold shaft of sun warmed his eyelids like a hot stove on a chill morning. Birds were chirping and a cicada sang. A breeze stirred. Cameron gave a jump, remembering Perro Loco and what he'd been doing here.

Blinking sleep from his eyes, he got up and looked around, stretching the kinks out of his legs and back. Things certainly looked different in the light of day.

Moving around, he discovered that he had followed Perro Loco southward off the spur, onto a finger of rock that was no more than a hundred yards long and about twenty-five yards wide. It was a jumble of granite, sandstone, sparse grass, and a few shrubs, a piñon or two growing from fissures in the rock. Cameron soon located the mussed mesquite shrub where he'd fallen and Perro Loco had gone over the ledge. Cameron peered over the edge into a wide canyon with serrated walls, filled with boulders, dry water courses, and shrubs.

The Indian lay about thirty feet straight down, his leggings a soft tan in the golden morning sun. The man was lying in a sandslide, head turned to one side, one arm up, elbow crooked. His legs were splayed. There was a red splotch in the sand near his mouth.

He was dead. No one could survive a fall like that. But just to be sure, Cameron jacked a shell and lifted the carbine to his shoulder. Then he thought better of it; a rifle shot would echo around in that canyon forever, alerting who-knew-how-many Apaches to his presence. He regretted leaving his field glasses at his first campsite on the ridge—he could have used them to double-check Perro Loco's condition. He sure wasn't climbing down there—the way was impossibly steep. Then he shook his head. No, he reassured himself; the Apache had fallen nearly straight down—only one broken bush gave sign of his journey down the canyon's wall. The man was dead.

The only problem was, Cameron didn't have any proof. The soldiers at Contention City were going to have to take his word the Indian was dead . . . or ride out here and see for themselves.

Cameron gave a satisfied nod, pursing his lips. "Sleep well, you bastard," he said to the dead Indian, then turned and walked away. "I'll see you in hell."

CHAPTER 11

CONTENTION CITY WAS a sunbaked little wood-and-adobe village nestled in a rock-strewn, saguaro-studded valley. The bald ridges that surrounded it were the same sand color as the town's little church, San Felipe, which abutted the east end of the main thoroughfare, sliding the shadow of its bell tower across the hay and dung-littered earth beyond the stout wooden doors.

The San Pedro River's course through the town was clearly indicated by the cottonwoods and manzanita grass that grew lush along its banks. Miners sauntered there, with sporting women from establishments like the Dew Drop and the Headlight, on warm desert evenings as the sun fell behind the mountains and the night birds cooed. Drifters who could not afford a room in town often slept there in the grass, their campsites marked by cookfires sparking through the trees.

Dogs and chickens ran wild in the streets, as did the children of the whores from the Silver Dollar Gambling Parlor and Pleasure Emporium, one of the few milled-lumber structures in town. Burros ran wild as well—strays and descendants of those once used to haul ore up to the stamping mill before tracks were laid and cars were used.

In addition to its status as a thriving mining town and business center, Contention City was an overnight stop for the bull trains hauling supplies up from Chihuahua, and a watering hole and supply depot for prospectors, cowboys, gamblers, and bandits escaping to or from Mexico.

Adrian Clark had heard the village described as both "deliciously wild" and "hellishly evil," and he wondered why the Arizona, New Mexico, and Sonora Railroad had decided to make the little hellhole its railhead instead of avoiding altogether the "boiling kettle of sin," as many travelers had dubbed it.

Clark rode between the adobe huts, avoiding the dead dogs, dead chickens, dead horses, and dead burros lying bloated in the deep-rutted, manure-packed street. Seeing the mangy lot of ragged, half-shot prospectors and freighters smoking and drinking on galleries, dull eyes taking in the strangers with guarded curiosity, he thought the railroad had made a hasty decision.

Clark only hoped he and Marina would not be here long. Judging by the fetid smells emanating from the restaurants and the seedy look of the hovels that called themselves hotels, he and his young wife would be better off sleeping in the desert, at the mercy of rattlesnakes and Apaches.

Bud Hotchkiss must have been reading his mind. "Not as bad as it looks, Captain," he said, riding next to Clark.

Marina and Jimmy Bronco rode behind them. Bronco was trailing the horse over which Pasqual Varas's body had been tied, attracting only slight attention from the men glancing up from the loafers' benches along the boardwalks.

Hotchkiss said, "I used to spend time here, back when the mine was open, hauling ore. They might look a little rough around the edges, but the people of this little pueblo are some of the nicest you'll ever come across. In fact, I met my first wife here. Lordy, was that a woman! Not the most loyal—I reckon I wasn't, neither—but could she *cook*."

The old graybeard glanced around and rubbed his jaw, his bushy brows furrowing slightly. His voice lowered and acquired a conspiratorial pitch. "Have to admit, though . . . that was a few years back. You know, it does appear this sweet little bend in the St. Pete has attracted a little of the lesser element . . ." Hotchkiss's voice trailed off as he swung his leery gaze from left to right, inching his right hand down to the butt of the shotgun poking up from his saddle boot.

He led the procession around a corner and halted in front of a big wooden barn, the sign above its broad double doors reading, *Establo de Lupido*. The livery barn was weathered gray, like most of the other wooden establishments around town, and several of the shingles missing from its roof had been replaced with flattened tin cans that had turned red with rust. A wooden ramp led into the stable from the street.

Swinging down heavily from his saddle, Hotchkiss said to Clark, "Why don't you and the missus head on down the street there? I believe the hotel where Jack always stays is just around the corner. It's called Ma Jones's Boarding House. You'll see the shingle out front. The boy and me, we'll stable these horses and take old Pas out to boot hill."

Clark looked at the bundle on the horse Jimmy Bronco was trailing. It had considerably less give than it had had when they'd started riding that morning. It was beginning to smell, as well, so that they'd all ridden upwind from it.

"What about his wife? Won't she want him buried at their ranch?" Clark asked.

"Yes, she would," Hotchkiss said with a sigh, and gave his head a grim wag. "But she'll understand. I loved that bean-eater like a brother, I did, but if we don't get him in the ground soon . . . in this heat . . . . No, she'll understand."

"Jesus," Clark said.

"Yep," Hotchkiss agreed.

All four of them sat there for several seconds in respectful, awful silence, casting their sad gazes at the blanketed bundle that, only a few hours ago, had been a living, breathing man. Marina crossed herself and muttered a silent prayer.

"Well," Hotchkiss said, "you two get yourselves a room. Mrs. Jones'll get her daughter to boil you up a couple o' baths." He gave Marina a kindly smile, thoroughly smitten with her.

"Thank you, Mr. Hotchkiss," she said, handing him her reins. "I told Mr. Cameron how sorry I am about the trouble we brought you"—she glanced at the body again—"and I want to apologize to you, as well. I am truly sorry . . ."

Hotchkiss waved the apology off like a fly in his face. "I understand how you're feelin', but you didn't kill our friend, Missus Clark. That was Gaston Bachelard's doin', and I guarantee you that man will pay the piper if me and Jack have to hunt him all the way to Mexico City." He punctuated the statement with a curt nod of his head.

"Me too!" Jimmy Bronco piped up, indignant at being overlooked. Scowling, he led his horse up the ramp.

Clark stepped up and took Marina's arm. "Come along, my dear," he said. "Let's get you to the hotel, shall we?"

"Where will you be, Mr. Hotchkiss?" Marina asked.

Hotchkiss grinned sheepishly. "Jack'll know where to find me, ma'am."

Marina dropped her eyes, smiling timidly, then let her husband usher her down the street, past two gray kittens frolicking in the shade cast by the livery's open doors.

"Anybody run this horse lot?" they heard Hotchkiss bellow behind them.

They found Ma Jones's Boarding House five minutes later. The big two-story structure looked more like a house than a hotel, but the weathered sign hanging on the wire fence encircling the weedy yard verified its identity. A blonde girl of about fifteen or sixteen sat on the glider on the open front porch, reading an illustrated newspaper. She wore a blue gingham housedress with a soiled apron, and she was barefoot. She lifted her toes, then her heels, as she moved the glider slowly back and forth.

As Clark and Marina approached, she tilted her head and squinted her eyes, scrutinizing them boldly.

"If you're here for the hangin', you're a day late," she said.

"We're not here for the hanging," Clark said grimly, indicating his disapproval of the popular spectacle.

"Hey, I didn't hang the guy," the girl said with a chuff. She appraised Marina coolly, then went back to her newspaper.

Clark led Marina through the door, into a dark, cool lobby in which the smells of noon lunch lingered. The floor was bare wood. Faded, threadbare couches and mismatched chairs sat about the room on frayed rugs. An old man as thin as a buggy whip dozed in a chair before the window overlooking the porch.

Clark went to the desk and rang the bell several times, looking around with annoyance. A thin, gray-faced woman appeared in the doorway opening to his right, toting a broom. Breathing heavily, sweat beading on her lip, she cast an angry glance through the window, where the blonde girl could be seen swinging in the glider and reading her newspaper.

The woman scowled. "Ruth Agnes, you lazy—!" She looked at Clark and Marina. "What can I do for you? The hangin' was yesterday, you know."

Clark told her they wanted a room and, if possible, two baths. When he'd signed the register, the woman yelled from behind the scarred counter to the girl in the hammock, "Ruth Agnes, you put that trash away and start the boiler for baths!"

Clark said to the woman, "A friend of ours should be joining us shortly, within the next day or two. I'd appreciate it if you'd let us know when he arrives. His name is Jack Cameron."

Through her bifocals, the woman scrutinized Clark's ornate signature in the register book. "You're friends of Jack's, are ye?"

Clark heard the screen door squeak open and slap shut. "You're friends of Jack's?" the blonde girl echoed.

"Yes," Clark, said, taking a better look at the young woman. She was not beautiful, to be sure, but she had a china-doll's face, with a slightly upturned lip, and she did a rather splendid job of filling out her dress.

"When's he coming?" she asked.

"I hope soon."

"Stop with your questions, Ruth Agnes, and get to work!" the woman told the girl.

"I'm on my break!" Ruth Agnes shot back.

"Not anymore, you're not!"

The girl stuck her tongue out at the woman and stomped down the hall to the rear of the hotel. A screen door opened and shut.

"And get some shoes on!" the woman yelled. She produced a key from one of the cubbyholes behind her and dangled it in front of Clark. "Room five." She glanced over the desk. "Where's your bags?"

"We had some trouble on the stage," Clark muttered by way of explanation. He took Marina's arm and led her to the stairs.

Their room was stale with the smell of old cigarette smoke and sweat, and it was nearly airless. It was furnished with a sagging brass bed, two simple chairs, a wardrobe, and a stand topped with a marble washbasin and pitcher. The towel hanging from the stand looked as though it hadn't been changed since the last person had checked into the room. Flies droned behind the windowshades.

Clark moved to the window facing the street, opened the shade, and heaved and cursed until he'd gotten the window open. Marina sat on the bed, which squeaked with her weight, and looked around. She was so tired she wanted to cry, but she knew she couldn't sleep.

So much had happened in the past twenty-four hours. She was beginning to wonder if she wanted the gold as badly as she'd thought. But then she thought of her daughter at Piro Alta, and she knew she had to endure. She had to get the gold. There was no other way she could get Marlena back and give her a real life.

Clark stood staring out the window, blocking the light. Flies buzzed and bounced behind the shade of the other window. He turned finally, and faced Marina.

"Bachelard and his men ... did they ... harm you?" he asked tightly, as though the thought had been on his mind for a long time and he wasn't sure how to ask it, or whether or not he wanted to hear the answer.

Marina looked at him. A wry smile tugged at the corner of her mouth, but she repressed her anger at his callous disregard for her feelings. She knew that she was little more than a spoilable commodity to him; she'd recognized Clark's superficiality when she'd first met him. It had not mattered then and it should not matter now. He'd gotten her out of a bad situation, and he had the resources necessary to help her find the gold and get her daughter back. Theirs was a marriage of convenience, not of love, though she had hoped that at some point love would grow.

She realized now that there would never be any love, and the thought filled her with anguish.

"Not in the way that you mean," she said, barely able to conceal her disdain.

"They didn't . . . ?"

"They did not rape me," she said abruptly, wanting the conversation to be over.

Clark looked into a corner of the shabby room and sighed with relief. Marina lay back on the bed and turned to face the wall, tears welling in her eyes. After several minutes, Clark lay down beside her and rested his forehead against her arm.

"I'm sorry," he said, his relief plain in his voice.

Inwardly she recoiled from his touch. They'd made love only a handful of times since their sedate private wedding in Prescott, where Adrian kept an office with two other land and mine speculators. She'd tried to please him, because she knew it was her job as his wife—it was an unspoken part of their agreement—but it had been getting harder and harder to feign passion for him, a cold, superficial man forever trapped in his prim Southern past. Holding himself above and apart from others, he gave little of himself, and made love with as much compassion as a dog.

The thought of spending the rest of her days with him made Marina feel as lonely as she'd ever felt in her life, but that's exactly what she would do. She'd dress up his wretched life in return for his liberating her from her uncle and adopting her daughter.

But she couldn't give herself to him now. Maybe later in the evening—but not now. Dios, not now . . .

"I see," he said with a sigh, getting the message. He moved away from her, jerking the bed, and got to his feet. "I'll go out and get us a clean change of clothes. Why don't you bathe and tidy yourself . . . for later."

Then he was gone.

Marina lay there in the gathering shadows of the afternoon, staring unseeing at the faded purple wallpaper, thinking of her life before the Apache attack on her family's rancho . . . the dances and the parties and the long rides across the playa with her dear friend Magdalena, the segundo's daughter . . . the long summer afternoons she'd spent alone with a book in the wind cave behind the stables and across the sandy stream she'd pretended was a moat encircling her own private castle.

She'd never felt more alone than she did now.

She wondered if her heart would ever be light again . . . if she would ever again find pleasure in the simple things of this life.

CHAPTER 12

THAT NIGHT JACK Cameron rode into Contention City under a skyful of stars.

He'd rested only three times since leaving the gorge where he'd left Perro Loco, and he hadn't eaten anything but his two remaining strips of jerked beef. He'd drunk nothing but water. He was craving a stiff drink, food, and sleep, and he intended to pursue them in that order.

But first he wanted to find the officer in charge of the Army detail from Fort Bowie, and tell him what had happened.

He was hoping he'd be able to get the reward money in spite of his not having proof of Loco's demise. It could be a tricky situation, he knew, and it all depended on which of the blueshirts was here. If it was a man he knew personally, Cameron thought he'd get the money. If not . . . well, then he might have some fancy talking to do.

He dismounted his buckskin at the livery barn, slipping out of the saddle with a weary groan. Every muscle in his body ached, and his knuckles were still sore from his fight with the Indian. His skin was burned raw from sun and wind, and his eyes felt like they'd been gone over with sandpaper.

He led the horse into the barn, where he found the

hostler, a short, wiry Mexican whose shaggy black hair was flecked with hay, and negotiated a price for stabling, feed, and a rubdown. He asked the man if he'd seen Hotchkiss and the others. He had, and Cameron felt relieved.

He threw his saddlebags over his shoulder and shucked his rifle from its boot, then asked, "You seen any blueshirts in town, Alvin?"

"Sí," the Mexican said as he loosened the buckskin's latigo, giving Cameron a curious frown. "They hang around here giving the Mexican girls a hard time. Someone's going to get shot if they mess too long with the wrong girl, Jack."

"Where they been doing their drinkin' and . . . and diddlin'?"

"The Dew Drop. They waitin' for you, Jack?"

"I reckon."

"You join up again, fight the Apache?"

"That'll be the day," Cameron said with a grunt.

"Will they go now? Give us Mex boys a chance with the señoritas?" Alvin grinned.

"I reckon. Thanks, Alvin."

"See ya, Jack. Tell the blueshirts good riddance for me, huh?"

Cameron didn't ordinarily frequent the Dew Drop. It was run by a Swede who treated his girls roughly but got away with it because most were orphans who had nowhere else to go. The Army boys liked to frequent the spot whenever they were in town, so they could tell their friends back in Iowa and Illinois what screwing a Mex girl was like.

It was a little adobe building with a second story constructed of rough lumber. The yard was a confusion of ladderback chairs, horse troughs, and chickens. A big saguaro stood sentinel by the low-slung door, its needles silvery with reflected starlight. Pigs grunted in the thatch-roofed barn behind the place. The air smelled of homemade corn liquor and a variety of manures, and Cameron could hear bedsprings getting a workout in the second story.

Inside was dusky with smoky lamplight. There was no music. Four cavalrymen sat playing cards. A fifth sat in the corner with a girl on his knee, brushing his mustache with a small comb. She gave little giggles as the man spoke to her in low tones.

Cameron moved into the room slowly, the saddlebags draped over his left shoulder, rifle in his right hand. The Swede stood behind the bar, his big, raw-boned face ominous in the shunting shadows, his fists on the bar. He stared at Cameron but said nothing. He knew how Cameron felt about him. For that reason, he didn't care for Cameron, either.

The age of the man with the girl on his knee told Cameron this was the soldier he was looking for— that, and the bars on his shoulder. The others in the room didn't look like they were shaving yet. The card game came to a halt. The pounding and singing of the bedsprings above them stopped.

In the silence, Cameron asked the man in the corner, "You in charge of these men?"

The man only now noticed him. He dropped his knee and the girl almost fell, then gained her feet with an angry complaint. She didn't look much older than twelve. Pointy little breasts pushed against her low-cut, lace-edged dress.

"Git," the soldier told her. "You Cameron?"

Frowning, the girl slouched away. The Swede said something to her in a brusque, low voice, and she slipped through a curtained doorway and disappeared.

"That's right," Cameron said.

"Well, well," the soldier said, "you're overdue."

Cameron walked to the man's table, assessing the

officer's blunt face, his broad nose, deep-set eyes, and red hair the texture of corn silk. He wore captain's bars on his shoulders, and something told Cameron they'd been there a long time—and would likely still be there when he died or retired. Probably he had a chip on his shoulder, as well, and wasn't picky about showing it.

Cameron cursed to himself. Of all the lousy luck— why couldn't they have sent Gretchel or McCaig? He wasn't going to get his money, but he sat down anyway.

"There was a problem," Cameron said, a tired sigh rattling up from his chest. He dropped his saddlebags on the floor and slapped his knee, watching the dust billow. "The Indian got away from us. I tracked him and killed him, but I don't have proof. He fell into a canyon."

The soldier watched him for several seconds. Finally he said, "You want a drink?" and indicated the half-full bottle on the table.

"No."

"Well, if you don't have any proof the Injun's dead . . ."

"You could take my word for it."

"That wouldn't be very businesslike, now, would it?"

There was the sound of boots on stairs, and Cameron saw a uniformed young man appear at the bottom of the stairway at the back of the room. The private looked around sheepishly and joined the other soldiers at the table near the bar. One of the men gave a soft whoop and jumped to his feet, making his unsteady way to the stairs.

"You pay first," the Swede said. He hadn't moved from his position behind the bar. The soldier handed over some cash, walked to the bottom of the stairs, then ran up the steps. The other men snickered.

The officer watched with a bemused grin. His eyes were drunk and watery.

"Why don't you take my word for it?" Cameron said. "Ask any officer at Bowie. I always get my man."

"You couldn't have climbed down and cut his head off?"

Cameron shook his head. "Not if I wanted to climb back out again. The walls of that canyon were sheer rock for twenty feet."

"Well, I ain't here to pay for air. If I don't have proof that renegade's dead, you ain't gonna get your money." The man smiled grimly and spread his soft, freckled hands. "Sorry."

Cameron felt a surge of anger. "Why don't you ride out and see for yourself?"

The man wrinkled his nose. "'Cause that ain't my job." He turned to the Swede. "Send her back."

"Corona," the Swede yelled.

"You're a horse's ass, Captain," Cameron said.

What burned him most was that he knew the man was right. It was not the soldier's job to ride out and verify the kill. Either Cameron had proof, and got his money, or he didn't.

He knew it should be enough that the Indian was dead—the Blue Rock Valley would no longer be haunted by Perro Loco—but Cameron had been banking on that money to get him through the winter. His ranch was not yet established, and he was still trying to bring his first herd to market fat. His larder was down to a few pounds of sugar and some wild game, maybe half a bag of Arbuckle's.

The officer crinkled his eyes with a scowl. "And you're nothing but a goddamn saddle tramp."

The girl returned and resumed her seat on the soldier's knee. He gave her a lascivious grin, dismissing Cameron.

Cameron stood up, shoving the chair back with his legs. It went over with a bark. Cameron picked up his saddlebags and rifle and headed for the door, feeling humiliated and angry and just plain shit-upon.

"Stay for a drink?" said the Swede, enjoying the display.

"Kiss my ass," Cameron growled, and stepped out the door.

CHAPTER 13

———✦———

CRESTFALLEN AND MORE tired than he'd ever been, Cameron left the Dew Drop and headed east down the dimly lit main street of Contention City, vaguely in search of food, liquor, Jimmy Bronco, and Bud Hotchkiss.

He wasn't sure which he wanted first. He knew Hotchkiss and Jimmy were wondering about him. Maybe he'd run into them somewhere on his quest for food and drink. He didn't have the energy to make them the sole objects of his search.

Lamplight glowing through its big plate-glass window led Cameron to the Silver Dollar Gambling Parlor and Pleasure Emporium. The place wouldn't have been hard to find if he were blind, for raucous player-piano music and the whoops and laughter spilling from its doors made it the loudest place on the street.

A crowd of Mexican and American cowboys from area ranches spilled out the doors. The smelly, unshaven men in dusty trail clothes stood hipshot or leaning against the horses at the hitch rack, or against the posts holding up the wood awning over the boardwalk, making up for a week or more of solitary silence on the range. They clutched soapy beer mugs in their sun-dried fists; cigarettes drooped from between their lips or smoldered between their fingers.

"Hey, Jack," one said, "where you been keeping yourself?"

"Stuck to a saddle," Cameron grumbled as he weaved his way through the crowd, the saddlebags on his shoulder making it less than easy.

"Hey, Jack," another man yelled above the din, "ol' Hotch said you was after Loco. Ye git heem?"

Cameron stopped and looked around. A tall, long-faced man in a sweat-stained white shirt and suspenders held his gaze. It was Leroy Maxy from the Double T. "Hotchkiss, you say? Where is he?"

The man gave a nod, taking the cigarette from between his teeth, and gestured inside the saloon. "Dirty shame about Pas," he said grimly.

"Sure is," Cameron agreed.

He pushed his way through the batwing doors that had been tied back to let in what little breeze there was, and looked around for Hotchkiss. It took him several minutes, squinting through the smoke and pushing through the crowd, to find him. The old graybeard was sitting at a table near the middle of the room.

Jimmy Bronco sat at the same table. Another man was there, as well—an old Army buddy of Bud's who had lost his mind as well as his left arm in an Indian battle, and who now delivered the Contention City *Weekly Bugle* and did other odd jobs around town when he managed to dredge up a wit or two.

Hotchkiss's attention was on the plump little brunette in his lap, a pleasure girl in a skimpy pink dress hiked high enough on her leg to attract more than a few lusty stares.

Cameron made it to the table and stood there silently for half a minute before Hotchkiss rolled up an inebriated eye and saw him. "Well, look what the cat dragged in!"

"I see you've been worried about me," Cameron said. He turned his gaze on Jimmy Bronco. Two beer mugs sat before the lad. One was three-quarters full, one empty, with webs of froth stuck to the insides. The kid stared into space with a dreamy smile.

To Hotchkiss, Cameron said, "I told you not to give the kid liquor."

"That ain't liquor—it's beer."

"It has the same effect."

The kid's head wobbled, turning, and tipped back. "Hi, Jack," Jimmy said thickly. He grinned.

Cameron looked down and saw that his holsters were empty. Probably Hotchkiss had the kid's pistols tucked inside his own gunbelt. Cameron was thankful for that, at least.

"You get him?" Hotchkiss asked Cameron.

"Yeah, but I lost the body in a canyon. I don't have proof. Already talked to the jackass the Army sent, and he won't take my word for it."

Hotchkiss frowned. "What do you mean?"

"I mean we don't get the reward."

Hotchkiss's face mottled red and his eyes opened wide. He removed his hands from the girl's legs to the arms of his chair, as though to shove himself to his feet. "Well, that's a goddamn *crock!*"

"I know it is, but I don't think there's anything we can do about it. It's my own damn fault."

"Tell 'em to go check it out their own selves!"

"I did. They won't. Sorry about the money, Bud. I know you were counting on it."

Hotchkiss ran his hand down his beard and blinked his eyes as if to clear them. "Well, you were, too. No use cryin' over it. At least you got the bastard."

"Did you bury Pas?"

Hotchkiss nodded sourly. He picked up a full shot-glass and tipped it back, draining it, then slammed it on the table. He smacked his lips. "We might be out a few hundred dollars, but at least we ain't restin' toe-down!"

"Not yet, anyway," Cameron said, his countenance dark as he thought of his Mexican friend and the family Pas had left behind.

"You get the Indian, Jack?" Jimmy said, not having followed the conversation.

Cameron scowled and shook his head. He started away, but before he had taken two steps, Hotchkiss said, "Oh, Lordy . . . Run, Jack, while ye still can."

Cameron looked at him, puzzled. "How's that?"

Hotchkiss was looking at something or someone across the room, behind Cameron. "She's comin' for ya. Been askin' about ya. Said you promised her one thing or another last time you was in town. She's said it before, about other men, and they ain't been seen since. Go, Jack! Go!"

"Who're you talkin' about?"

"Too late," Hotchkiss said. "She's on you like an Apache on a wagon train."

A finger jabbed Cameron's shoulder, and he turned to see the pouting red lips of Dinah Maxwell. She was a redhead, pretty in a hard sort of way, about thirty years old. She wore a dress so low-cut that her full, powdery white breasts appeared about to spring from their lacy nest. She clutched a silk shawl about her slender shoulders and squinted one tea-colored eye like a schoolmarm. She came complete with a distinguishing mole about two inches left of her nose, a full, brightly-painted mouth, and feathers in her hair.

"Well . . . hi, Dinah. How ya doin'?"

"Just fine. Where have you been keeping yourself, Jack Cameron?"

"Well, I been—"

"Been making yourself scarce around here, haven't you?"

"Have I? Well, I been busy, Dinah."

She narrowed her eyes at him. "Don't you give me that horsecrap, Jack Cameron! I know when I been hornswoggled."

Cameron was flushed and feeling faint with hunger, bone weariness, and now this. "I did pay you for your services, Dinah."

Hotchkiss gave an uproarious laugh. Cameron didn't look at him.

Dinah stepped forward and took Cameron by the arm. "Come on. We have some talking to do, mister." Cameron tried pulling his arm away. Dinah hung on.

"Listen, I'm awful sorry if I offended you last time I was in town, Dinah, but I've been on the trail for more days than I have fingers to count, and I just need some food and sleep."

"Food and sleep, eh? Maybe a drink or two?"

"Possibly," Cameron allowed.

"Right this way."

Dinah tugged on his arm. Too weary to fight her, he let himself be led through the jostling crowd, toward the stairs. He glanced back at his friends. Hotchkiss slapped his knee with laughter. Jimmy Bronco just stared into space.

Cameron let Dinah lead him up the stairs, as several cowboys below jeered and whistled. Ignoring them, Cameron concentrated on keeping the saddlebags draped over his shoulder, and on negotiating the steps, which seemed to grow steeper and steeper as he climbed.

"You poor dear, you really are run ragged, aren't you?" Dinah said as she slipped the key in her door and turned the knob.

"Yeah, I really am. If you don't mind, I'd really

just like to put my feet up for a while," Cameron said as she led him into the room.

He let Dinah take his rifle and let the saddlebags fall off his shoulder as he collapsed on a red velvet settee under a gilt-framed painting of Dinah. Dinah liked to tell her visitors that a renowned artist had painted the portrait—which showed her reclining, cloaked in only a slender pink boa, on the very settee on which Cameron was now collapsed—when she was dancing on the best stages in the East. She was a little trimmer back then, and there were fewer lines around her eyes, but Cameron had to admit she was still a fine-looking woman, considering all the years she'd been doing what she did.

He tried to remember what promises he had made last time he was in town, but his mind was too sluggish to offer any clear answers. Besides, he'd probably been drunk on Dinah's liquor—some of the best Spanish brandy you'd find this side of New Orleans.

Now Dinah tugged off his boots, then went over to a big walnut dressing table and poured a glass of brandy. "Now you just relax right there and drink this while I go over to Crow's Kitchen for a big plate of food."

She handed Cameron the brandy and waltzed out of the room.

Cameron sat back, tossed his hat onto a wall peg, and sipped the brandy. As he swallowed, something very close to a smile widened his unshaven cheeks and brightened his eyes. He was beginning to realize how, given enough brandy and the kind of manly comforts Dinah Maxwell was so adept at dishing out, he might have promised her things he wouldn't ordinarily have promised anyone.

He took another sip of the brandy, feeling a warm

glow spread up from the pit of his stomach, feeling as though his stars were realigning themselves.

Go easy now, he told himself. Take it slow with the liquor and don't get yourself into any more compromising situations . . . you goddamn idiot.

But the liquor did taste mighty good. He managed to crawl up from the settee and pad across the room on his creaky legs and in his sweaty socks and pour another glass all the way to the brim. He had just settled down when the door opened and Dinah entered with a plate covered with a napkin in one hand, and a napkin-covered wicker basket in the other. The smell of roast beef and onions mingled with the French perfume Dinah always wore.

She stopped to kick the door closed, then set the plate and basket on the dresser. "Those clods didn't even have a tray—can you imagine!" she exclaimed. "Sometimes I wonder why I stay in this dump."

She removed the brandy and the other glasses from the silver service, set the plate and basket on the tray, and carried it over to Cameron.

"Lordy, something does smell good," he said, dropping his legs to the floor and pushing himself to a sitting position. The smell of the food invigorated him.

"They were about to close up over there, but I told them you were in town, and hungry, and Mrs. Harvey didn't bat an eye." Dinah gave him a sharp look of inquiry. "You haven't been making promises to her too, now, have you, Jack?"

Cameron sighed. "None that I know of, Dinah."

"Well, that's not much of an answer, but there you go. Dig in."

She pulled the napkins away, revealing a plate heaped with several thick slabs of roast beef, slightly charred at the sides and smothered in onions, and a hill-sized pile of fried potatoes overflowing with rich, dark gravy. Next to the potatoes sat a mound of baby carrots boiled in butter.

In the basket nestled three sourdough biscuits, still steaming from the warming rack; their warm fragrance complemented the beef and gravy so well that Cameron's stomach let out a yelp. His hands shook as he seized the knife and fork and plunged them into the beef.

He ate like a ravenous animal. Dinah lay back on the bed and lit a thin cheroot, grinning at him and smoking.

"Get enough?" she said, when he'd mopped the dregs of the gravy from his plate with the last of a biscuit.

Still chewing, Cameron set the plate on the floor and nodded. He washed down the gravy with a slug of brandy, kicked his feet out, and slumped down on the settee.

"That was one fine meal, Miss Maxwell," he said, thoroughly grateful.

"Well, I'd like to say I cooked it, but I only fetched it. It was Mrs. Harvey who did the dirty work."

"Just the same, I'm much obliged." Cameron suppressed a belch, covering his mouth with his hand.

Dinah took a long drag off the cheroot, turning her head sideways, then tipping back her chin as she blew smoke at the canopy over the four-poster bed. "But you know, Jack, I can cook, and I'd be obliged to cook for you regularly if you'd give a girl a chance." She flashed her eyes seductively.

Cameron smiled. "I appreciate the offer, Dinah, but you know me. I'm just a dirty old bachelor from the desert. Ain't fit for civilized company. Throw one of those over here, will you?"

"Don't give me that hogwash," Dinah said, taking a cheroot from her bedside table and tossing it to

Cameron, followed by a box of matches. "I think you're just shy."

Cameron lit the cheroot and waved out the match. "Well, I'm somethin'."

"You can't grieve forever, you know."

"How's that?"

"Over Ivy Kitchen. She's dead these six long years, Jack."

"Six years," he said with a sigh. "It's been that long?"

"Six years she'd been dead, and you're still alive. You gotta start actin' like it."

She paused. They looked at each other soberly.

"Another drink, Jack?"

"Why not?" he said.

She got up and poured them each another drink. She set the decanter on the bedside table and lay back on the bed, cheroot in one hand, glass of brandy in the other. She crossed her legs invitingly.

"My Donovan died back during the war," she said after a while. "Suicide. He had mining interests out here and they all dried up when the fighting began. He couldn't take it."

"I didn't know you were married."

She nodded. "I had to do something so I started dancing again, and eventually . . . well, turned to what I'm doing now. I know it ain't respectable, but I didn't have any other choice. There ain't too many choices for a woman in the West, and I didn't have the money to go back East."

"I never been much of a saint myself," Cameron said, and sipped his brandy, feeling the warmth of the food and liquor in his belly. But he also felt a strange melancholy, talking about such things as Ivy Kitchen and not facing up to life the way he knew he should, but couldn't.

What the hell was he still doing out here, anyway, in this godforsaken country? Why didn't he go up and settle in Nebraska or the Indian Nations where it didn't take so damn much land to graze a single beef, and where it rained once in a while and flowers bloomed and trees greened up the way they should?

It sure would be nice to see a river again—a real river with eddies and rapids, not just a trickle of brackish water in a bed of sun-bleached gravel. He'd like to see geese again, as well—big honkers following the snowmelt rivers back to Canada.

"So what do you say, Jack? Will you make a respectable woman out of me?"

He looked at her and saw her brown eyes on him. They were so vulnerable and tragic that they broke his heart. To cover it, he took a drag from the cheroot and forced a thin smile. He was about to undercut the question with an attempt at humor.

She sensed it coming and said, "Don't turn it into a joke." Her voice was thin.

He watched her for a moment. "I can't," he said finally. "I . . . I don't love you, Dinah."

Her expression remained serious for about five seconds. Then a smile grew. She laughed. "Well . . . hell, Jack, I don't love you, either!" she said. She laughed again and sipped her brandy. "I wasn't talkin' about love. I was talkin' about shackin' up together and keepin' each other's feet warm in our old age."

Her laugh made him feel hopeless and pathetic, and he suddenly wanted to leave. He finished the brandy and stood up. Her eyes followed him.

"Stay with me, Jack. I'll make it worth your while." She smiled. "Free of charge. No strings attached."

Suddenly she looked like a child. Despite how bad he felt and how tired he was, he knew he couldn't leave her alone. She was having one of those dark nights of the soul he was only too familiar with. Such nights brought him to Contention City or Tucson every few months, to lay with women he did not love, and to talk—for the comfort of human company. Not that Jimmy Bronco was not company, but sometimes a man needed a woman.

Dinah Maxwell had fulfilled that need for him in the past. The least he could do was return the favor.

He put his hand on her leg and she pushed herself into a sitting position beside him. He took her in his arms and kissed her.

"I . . . I haven't had a bath," he said. "My horse smells better than me."

"I love the way you smell," she whispered, pushing herself against him, kissing him, running her hands down his back, pressing her fingers into the weary muscles above and below his shoulder blades. Her hands felt so good he almost groaned with pleasure.

Finally she pulled away from him and stood. Giving him a seductive look, she loosened her hair and let the lush, rust-colored mass fall about her shoulders. She stepped out of her shoes with practiced grace and peeled the dress down her shoulders, exposing her pear-shaped breasts.

She was good . . . very good, Cameron thought half-consciously, beneath the passion he felt stirring in his loins. Any woman who could get his temperature up, after what he'd been through, knew what she was doing. Part of him considered marrying her but, tempting as it was now, as he watched her step toward him naked, he knew it wouldn't work.

He simply did not love her and she did not love him. He had not yet become so cynical as to marry a woman he did not love, no matter how much he liked her or how well she satisfied him in bed.

Cameron pulled his sweaty tunic over his head, then fumbled with his holster.

When he'd unfastened the buckles, Dinah tossed the belts aside and helped him with his pants, then unbuttoned his undershirt, pressed her hands deep within the hair at his chest, and ran them down his hard, knotted belly to his groin. Finding his stiffening member, she slipped it out of his undershorts and gave a groan of passion.

Cameron collapsed on the bed with a sigh.

———◆◆◆———

When they'd finished making love, Dinah fell asleep but Cameron could not. She was used to the loud music and the voices booming throughout the building. Cameron was accustomed to quiet nights interrupted by only the occasional yodel of a lonely coyote.

Sleepless, he lay in the bed for a time, hands crossed behind his head, staring out the window. Finally he got up and dressed quietly. He strapped his gun and cartridge belts about his waist, picked up his saddlebags and rifle, and headed for the door.

At the door he stopped, dug in his pockets for some coins, and set them carefully, without a sound, on the marble washbasin. He squeezed the doorknob, turned it, and opened the door.

"Good night, Jack," Dinah said quietly, half-asleep.

"Good night, Dinah." He thought for a minute. "Hey? If I promised you anything last time I was in town—"

"Oh, you didn't promise me anything, Jack Cameron," Dinah said, turning onto her back. "I was just trying to get old Hotchkiss's goat. See ya next time?"

Cameron smiled. "Next time."

He stepped through the door, closed it softly behind him, and walked down the carpeted hall. Laughter and squeaking bedsprings sounded behind nearby doors. Downstairs, men and women were singing an Irish ballad to the tinny pounding of the player piano.

He did not want to walk through the saloon, so he headed for the back steps, which clung to the outside rear of the building. Once in the alley, he looked around to get his bearings, then headed in the general direction of Ma Jones's Boarding House.

CHAPTER 14

GASTON BACHELARD KICKED his gray horse up the rocky ridge and inspected the night-cloaked valley below. A little ranch nestled there in a canyon, starlight glinting off the corral and the thatch-covered adobe barn and cabin.

It was hard to tell in the dark, but there seemed to be three or four horses in the corral. The breeze, from behind Bachelard, must have brought the scent of his horse to the corral, for the animals whinnied and snorted and danced around, shaking their heads.

A dog gave several tentative barks and growled. The butter-colored lamplight in the window of the adobe hut disappeared, replaced by reflected starlight.

Bachelard smiled. He turned to the men next to him. "I'm going to ride around the back of the house, and approach it from there," he said. "You men stay here for about ten minutes. Give me time to disarm our friend Martínez. Then corral your horses and join me in the hut."

Jim Bob McGuffy, whom Bachelard had known since the war, said, "You're gonna ride down there all by your lonesome, Major?"

Bachelard had already started walking his horse out along the ridge. "A man's work is never done," he said with a self-important sigh.

He didn't trust any of his men—not McGuffy, not the two surviving bean-eaters Miguel Montana had sent along with him—to ride down to the house without making a bunch of noise and getting them all shot out of their saddles. As far as he was concerned, they were all dull-witted honyockers, better with a plow and a scythe than a rifle.

But they were all he had. And he knew, from his considerable studies of world history, that revolutions often started with men such as these, led by great men like Napoleon, Caesar, and himself.

Sometimes all it took to change history was one great man leading hordes of cannon fodder into battle. Bachelard was optimistic that it would take only him and perhaps Miguel Montana, coordinating their revolutionary efforts, to take northern Sonora from the Mexican federales and retake his beloved Texas from the Union, forming a separate country . . . with Bachelard himself, of course, as commander general.

He made his way around the ridge, circling the ranchyard, then dismounted and tied his horse to a cottonwood tree that stood in a shallow ravine, about a hundred yards back of the hut. Walking as quietly as he could over the rock-strewn ravine bottom, he came to the ranchyard and took cover behind a chicken coop.

He looked around the coop toward the house, spying no movement there, hearing no sounds. He figured Ramón Martínez and his wife and lovely daughter were wide-awake, however. They'd heard the horses tearing around the corral. That's why the light in the window had gone out, so their shadows couldn't be targeted as they scurried around in the cabin like rats in a cage.

Bachelard smiled. He'd stopped here on several occasions to water his horses and to eat meals he forced Julia Martínez to cook for him and his men. He liked the Martínez family, mostly because he liked the daughter, Juanita, who was beginning to fill out her cotton dresses rather well, and because he liked the look of fear he evoked in the dark eyes of her parents—peons, peasants, low-rent farm stock.

They were a fun lot, the poor. Easily frightened. Easily outwitted. So, so much fun on an otherwise uneventful night. And when Bachelard's fun was through, he'd have a bed to sleep in—a real bed for a change, not the cold, rocky ground. A general deserved to sleep in a bed now and then.

He made the back door of the hut and pressed his cheek against the rough, gray wood. He dimly heard someone mumble something in Spanish. As Bachelard had predicted, the greasers were expecting trouble to come from the front.

He took one step back, then rushed forward, kicking the door open. It splintered as it slammed back against the wall. He remembered where the wall separating the kitchen from the main living area was, and he hunkered quickly behind it just as Martínez's old muzzle-loading rifle boomed. The ball hit the wall with a *thunk*, spraying chunks of adobe that clattered to the floor like hail.

Two screams followed the thunder of the blast, and before their echoes died Bachelard was out from behind the wall and moving toward the ghostly white powder still hanging in the air. He glimpsed a shadow and pursued it, stretching out his hand, grabbing the gun out of someone's grasp and flinging it across the room.

A man yelled in Spanish, "My God! Who goes there?"

"'Tis I, good man—Gaston Bachelard!" the Cajun

yelled theatrically. "You must have mistaken me for common bandits or Apaches."

"Bachelard!" the man yelled in a voice thin with sorrow.

"Light a lamp or I'll start shooting."

"Sí, sí." In Spanish, Martínez told his wife to light the lamp on the wall. "Don't shoot, don't shoot, por favor."

When Julia Martínez had lighted the lamp above the fireplace, Bachelard saw Ramon standing near the window, hands raised high above his head—a short, squat Mexican with an unruly swatch of curly gray hair, dressed for the chilly high-country evening in a striped serape.

Julia—stout, broad-hipped, with a pretty, delicate face, braided hair turning gray—stood before the fireplace, looking with bug-eyed horror at their visitor, whom she'd come to know only too well over the last several months he'd been raiding in the area.

Why, in the name of the saints, did this madman have to stop here? Hadn't she and Ramón always done well by their beloved *Jesus?* They kept up their shrine on the ridge over the valley, even rode to church in the village twice a month—and it was a twenty-mile journey over the mountains!

Bachelard removed his gray Confederate campaign hat and flourished it with as much Southern gentleman's charm as he could muster, bowing elaborately. "Señora," he said, drawing it out, then raising his cold gray eyes to her and grinning. Then he frowned and looked around. "Where . . . where is the señorita? Oh . . . there she is! ¡Hola, Juanita!"

Bachelard had caught a glimpse of the Martínezes' daughter in the open loft above his head. The pale, round face of the girl drew back in the darkness.

"Oh, but Juanita!" Bachelard yelled, as though a

lover spurned, "it is your prince Gaston. Please come down here, ma chérie, and give your prince a kiss!"

Outside a dog barked furiously. "Major Bachelard," someone yelled from the stoop. It was McGuffy. He pounded on the door.

Bachelard threw the bolt and opened the door. "Yes, yes," Bachelard said impatiently. "What is it?"

"Everything secure here, sir?" McGuffy said. A dog stood off a ways, barking at him.

"Yes, everything's secure. Are the horses put up?"

"The greasers are doin' that now."

Bachelard sighed and threw the door back. "Well, then, come in if you must." He stopped, yelled for the dog to shut up, then turned to Julia Martínez.

"I am so sorry we're late for supper, but my men are very hungry, señora." He spread his arms and left the demand at that, little more than the request of a reluctant guest.

Julia Martínez stared at him with her terrified, furious eyes, then shifted her gaze to her husband. Their eyes locked for only a moment.

"Sí" she said, and moved slowly into the kitchen.

"Sit down and rest yourself, Mr. McGuffy," Bachelard said.

"I'm sure Señor Martínez will be happy, as always, to make us feel at home after several long days on the trail. Are you not, Ramón?"

The rancher said nothing. He stood stiffly against the wall, shoulders back, and seemed to be holding his breath. In the guttering lamplight, his dark eyes were shiny as a wounded deer's. There was a gilt-edged crucifix on the wall to his left. It seemed to hold him there.

Bachelard's voice grew tight. "Now kindly ask your daughter to come down and visit me."

A moan sounded in the loft.

Ramón Martínez stared at Bachelard and said nothing.

Bachelard moved toward him, gritting his teeth. "I am not going to rape her, you fool. I am saving her for when she is old enough to bear my children." He gave a thin-lipped smile. "I simply want to say hello."

Still, Martínez said nothing.

"*Call her!* Or I will go up and drag her down myself!"

Martínez's chest fell as he exhaled. He wet his lips and lifted his eyes to the loft. "Juanita," he said softly in Spanish, "come down here. It is all right."

"No, Papa!" the girl cried.

"Do as your father tells you, you little brat!" Bachelard spat, losing his patience.

"Come down here, Juanita. I will protect you," Martínez said.

"Yes, your dear old papa will protect you from the desires of your adoring prince!"

After several seconds, boards creaked and the girl appeared, looking down from the loft. She was fourteen years old and bore all the finer attributes of her mother. Her hair was long and straight and shiny. She wore a white cotton nightgown, and she was barefoot.

"Come, my dear," Bachelard cooed.

Giving her frightened eyes to her father, the girl grasped the ladder, turned, and started down, planting each delicate brown foot in turn. With admiring eyes Bachelard watched the roll of the girl's buttocks as she descended.

"Ah . . . my lovely señorita!" Bachelard cooed as she stepped to the floor and turned away from the ladder. "You grow lovelier with every visit."

Again the girl shuttled her stricken gaze to her father. Her face was as white as her gown.

"Juanita," Ramón demanded. "Come here!"

The girl started toward her father. Bachelard stopped her abruptly, drawing her back with an arm.

"No, no, Ramón. It's okay. Really. Juanita and I need to reacquaint ourselves. Come, my dear. Sit with your prince Gaston." Still holding the girl's arm, Bachelard sat in a creaky chair and drew the girl onto his lap.

Stiffly she complied, keeping her eyes on her father. She straddled one of Bachelard's knees, one bare foot on the floor, the other hanging free.

Bachelard stared up at her lovely face above his, his own features an amalgam of pure insanity and storybook infatuation. "'What light through yonder window breaks?'" he recited from Shakespeare. "'It is the east, and Juliet is the sun. Arise, fair sun, and kill the envious moon, who is already sick and pale with grief that thou, her maid, art far more fair than she.'"

It was obvious by the way the girl shook that she was more afraid of this demon than anything her childish nightmares had ever conjured.

When Bachelard glanced up and saw McGuffy's lusty eyes on the girl, he snapped, "Get your eyes off my bride, sir, or prepare to draw your weapon!"

The tall, lanky man's prominent Adam's apple bobbed in his unshaven throat, and he flushed. "What? Oh . . . I—Sorry, sir." He dropped his gaze to the floor.

Soon the smell of coffee drifted from the kitchen. Julia Martínez brought the big stone pot and set it on the table with cups. McGuffy got up from his chair by the hearth and sat at the table, then poured a cup of coffee. Bachelard remained in his chair, with the white-faced Juanita on his lap. He had just rested his head against the adobe wall and closed his eyes when the dog started barking again and the outside door suddenly opened.

He jerked awake, starting for his gun, nearly throwing the girl to the floor. "Don't you two knock?" he snapped at the Mexicans standing there in their Texas boots and sombreros, worn leather cartridge-belts crisscrossing their chests, half the loops of which were filled with tarnished brass. The men smelled like gunpowder and horses and stale human sweat.

They gave lipless smiles to Bachelard and the lovely little girl on his lap, who did not look at all pleased about being there, then tossed their sombreros onto the floor. Believing he saw something lascivious in their faces, Bachelard drew his gun and aimed it at them.

"If either of you so much as lays a hand on my sweet Juanita, I'll blow your heart out through your spine and chop you up in little pieces!"

Everyone in the room stiffened. In the kitchen, Julia dropped a pan and muttered a prayer.

The two Mexicans looked at each other, turning white, and looked back at the long-barreled Confederate revolver aimed in their direction. The one called Jesus thought at first the man was joking, and he gave a tentative smile. It quickly disappeared when he looked into the crazy man's eyes, and dropped his gaze to the plate Julia now set before him.

"Sí, jefe," he muttered, and leaned forward, grabbing the wooden spoon and digging it into the stew Julia had brought to the table, keeping a watchful eye on her daughter.

Bachelard looked at Martínez, who had taken a seat on the hearth, his stubby hands laced together, staring at the floor. The ex-Confederate gave the girl a less-than-gentle shove as he got to his feet, walked to the table, and sat down. Not hesitating in the least, the girl grabbed the ladder and climbed quickly, short, terrified bursts of air escaping her lungs with every move.

"Ramón," Bachelard said, retrieving a tortilla from a warm plate on the table. "I want you to always remember that your daughter belongs to me. As soon as she's old enough—you know what I mean—I'm going to take her away and make an honest woman out of her. You know what I mean by that, too. So you make sure she stays pure. Make sure none of these little desert rats from one of these ranchos gets their dirty hands on her. I want her clean, understand? Pure. Virgin white. No Cleopatras for me. I'm Romeo and she's my Juliet. Comprende?"

Ramón Martínez looked at him, vaguely astonished, thoroughly confused. He hadn't understood more than five words of what the man had said.

Bachelard turned to him severely.

"Do you understand what I'm saying, Ramón?"

Knowing it was the only answer that would satisfy this demon, Ramón Martínez gave his head several resolute nods. "Sí, señor. Sí . . . sí."

Bachelard filled his tortilla from the stew pot and bit into it, eating hungrily, groaning as he chewed. He told Ramón to run and fetch the wine he'd served them before. Martínez went into the kitchen and came back with a crock jug. He filled each of the cups on the table.

"Well, it's not Napoleon brandy and Tournedos Madeira, but it ain't half bad. No sir, it ain't half bad. Is it, boys?"

Stuffing their mouths as quickly as they could, the men agreed, nodding and grunting, not lifting their faces from their plates.

When the men had finished eating, Bachelard ordered them all to bed down in the barn. They donned their hats and belched as they headed out the door. Bellies full, they were ready to sleep.

When they'd left, Bachelard refilled his cup from the crock jug and sat in the chair he'd shared with Juanita. He crossed his legs with a pleasant sigh, sipped the wine from his cup, and turned his eyes to Ramón.

"I've had a change of heart, Ramón," he said jovially. "At first light tomorrow morning, I'm taking your daughter with me."

Clearing the table, Julia dropped a plate.

CHAPTER 15

CAMERON KNEW THE only place he could get a decent night's rest in Contention City was at Ma Jones's Boarding House. It sat well off the main street, where cowboys whooped and hollered all night, and the din of piano music and occasional gunfire made sleep, at least for Cameron, virtually impossible.

And tonight, of all nights, he needed good, sound sleep.

The only problem was, Ma Jones closed up at nine o'clock every night and went to bed. She believed that anyone out later than nine was up to no good, and she didn't want "nogoods" in her hotel.

When Cameron had ridden into town late in the past, she'd opened up for him and given him a room. His Apache-fighting exploits were known and admired in the area, and she was proud to have him stay at her place. She even had a signed picture of him, wielding a Spencer rifle and decked out in a tan hat, fringed chaps, and red neckerchief—his scouting garb— hanging in the dining room in which she served her guests.

As he climbed the porch steps now, saddlebags draped over his shoulder, rifle in hand, he hoped she'd be as happy to see him tonight as she'd been in the past. He also hoped she wouldn't mistake him for the "rough element" and blow him into eternity with the fabled double-bore with which she always greeted after-hours callers.

He had to pound for five minutes before a light appeared inside. A thin figure clad in white appeared, holding a lantern in one hand, the storied shotgun in the other.

"It's Jack Cameron, Ma," Cameron announced through the glass.

Ma came to the door, raised the lantern and peered out. Her face, drawn with sleep, appeared deathly gray in the lantern light. She threw the bolt and opened the door with more disgust than exuberance. It appeared Cameron was beginning to wear a little thin.

"You're keeping some sorry hours, Jack," she said.

"Sorry to wake you, Ma. Thanks for opening up for me."

The old woman turned and moved toward the desk at the back of the room. Cameron followed her contritely. Hoping to arouse some motherly approval, he added, "I've been tracking an Apache," which was as much of the truth as he wanted Ma to hear.

The woman stood the shotgun against the wall and made her way behind the desk. "When are you gonna get married and settle down, Jack Cameron?"

"When the Apaches give me a chance, I reckon."

She set the lamp on the desk, where it brought out the deep grain of the wood, and produced her spectacles from the pocket of her robe. Cleaning them against her robe, Ma said, "You know, my daughter fancies you—Ruth Agnes."

"Right pretty girl," Cameron allowed, wishing like anything that he could get off his aching legs.

"She's a little lazy now, but I think all Ruth Agnes

needs is a husband to bring her around, show her the way. Get her to cookin' and cleanin' for him, makin' his breakfast of a mornin', his supper of an evenin'. I believe marriage would change her for the good."

"I believe in marriage as an institution," Cameron said woodenly, about to fall asleep on his feet. "Listen, Ma, it's late, and—"

"I think it would do you some good, as well, Jack Cameron. You wouldn't be gettin' bored and lonesome out there, just you and that hammerhead boy, Jimmy What's-His-Name. You wouldn't have to go to Tucson and come here two, three times a year, and practice the evilness that goes on over there . . . You know where I'm talkin' about, and you know who I'm talkin' about, too—that tart."

Cameron just stood there, feeling more than a little like he was standing before Saint Peter at the pearly gates. Finally Ma gave a disparaging sigh and opened the register. Cameron could have kissed her. Placing the glasses on her nose, she ran her finger down a page of the open book.

"Room seven," she said wearily, as if there was no getting through to this sinner. "That's right next to your friends that come in earlier."

Cameron frowned. "Friends?"

Ma Jones ran her finger up the page and tipped back her head to read through her bifocals. "Mr. and Mrs. Adrian Clark. Right fancy couple. What they're doin' here, I have no idea."

She glanced up at Cameron from beneath her thin gray brows, a touch of curiosity flickering in her pious eyes. "I'm sure I don't need to know, either."

Ignoring the implicit question, Cameron nodded thoughtfully, feeling a pang of dread at the prospect of having to parry with Clark and his wife again. They would no doubt still try to convince him to help them find the gold, which he had no intention of doing. He also did not want to see those inky-black eyes of Marina's again, either ... that jet-black hair ...

He accepted the room key Ma held out to him.

"Much obliged," he grumbled, heading toward the stairs.

"Good night," Ma said behind him, closing the register book with a thud. "You give Ruth Agnes some thought. She's a good girl, not a tart like some others."

"I'll do that, Ma," he said, climbing the stairs.

He found his room, stripped off his dusty, smelly clothes, and rolled into bed with a groan.

* * *

He woke up ten hours later, facedown on his pillow.

He wasn't sure what woke him, but he lifted his head from the pillow and turned to his left. The room was filled with orange light as the sun penetrated the shades over the windows.

He looked at the door. Closed. He thought he must have heard something, but whatever it was, was gone. The building was silent, as was the street outside—strangely silent.

Then he remembered it was Sunday.

He reached for his tarnished silver watch on the stand beside the bed and flipped the lid. Ten-fifteen. Sure enough, no doubt everyone respectable was in church. Everyone unrespectable was probably still in bed, as he was. But they were sleeping off drunks and other sundry sins; he was sleeping off half a dozen days of trail and a skirmish with one of the deadliest Apaches Arizona had ever seen. There *was* the little matter of Dinah Maxwell, but that hadn't been his fault.

He deserved to sleep till ten-fifteen, conscience and the voice of his Iowa farmer father, who had never slept later than six A.M., be damned.

He lay back on his pillow and heard the floor squeak outside his door. Someone knocked lightly and whispered, "Jack?"

Cameron frowned and looked at the door with its fly specks and chipped white paint. "Ruth Agnes?"

"You ready for a bath?"

Cameron thought about it. "Yeah . . . I reckon."

"Open the door."

Cameron did not get up, but only reached over, unlocked the door, and twisted the knob. The girl's smiling face appeared, her cherry-blonde hair swept back in a bun.

She wore a light calico dress with lace along the low-cut neckline, and she was barefoot. Thrusting a cup of coffee at Cameron, she said, "Here. This'll tide you until I get the tub brought up and filled with water. It won't take long. I've had the boiler stoked all morning."

"Oh . . . you don't have to wait on my lazy bones—"

"Just never you mind—it ain't no trouble at all, Jack. Why don't you give me your clothes and I'll send them over to Mrs. Donleavy for washin'."

Cameron waved a halfhearted arm at a Windsor chair buried beneath his dusty trail clothes.

Ruth Agnes threw the door wide, strode in, picked up the clothes, and clutched them to her bosom. Striding toward the door, she said, "Be back in a minute."

She pulled the door closed behind her, and the hall's floorboards squeaked under her retreating bare feet.

Fifteen minutes later she'd carted the tin tub into his room and filled it with hot water. Leaving, she asked him if he needed anything else, with a peculiar expectancy etched on her lovely young face, and he told her no, a little perplexed. The girl had always been accommodating, but she seemed especially accommodating today, not to mention cheerful.

Cameron wondered if it could be her birthday, or maybe she'd found a boyfriend and she was practicing for marriage. Then he remembered the conversation he'd had last night with Ruth Agnes's mother, and his stomach took a leap.

Oh, shit. She wasn't thinking . . . ?

Cameron soaked in the cooling water, smoking a cigarette, sipping a second cup of coffee he'd planted on the Windsor chair beside the tub, and stared absently out the window at the sky turning brassy as the sun climbed toward its apex.

He was thinking of Marina and wishing she'd change her mind about heading south when he heard the floorboards in the hall squeak again and the tap on the door.

He knew who it was.

"I ain't decent," he called with the cigarette in his lips.

"That's all right—I won't look at nothin' important," Ruth Agnes said, flinging open the door and striding into the room with a kettle of steaming water. She poured the water into the tub. "Just thought you might be wanting a warmup."

Cameron brought his legs up and cupped his hands over his privates, temples pounding with embarrassment. "Good Lord, girl," he said, "people are gonna start talkin', they see this . . . !"

"There's no one here—they've all gone out," Ruth Agnes said, setting the kettle on the floor. "Momma's at church. She'll be there all day. It's just you and me, Jack. Hand me your sponge—I'll wash your back."

Well, she was here now, and he did need his back washed, so Cameron found the sponge and gave it to the girl, who soaped it up, told him to lean forward, and went to work on his back. The girl's hand was deft, and having his back sponged with hot, soapy water felt so good that Cameron forgot his embarrassment and fairly groaned with pleasure.

Ruth Agnes dipped the sponge in the water and brought it up to the back of Cameron's sunburned neck.

"Momma said you might have a question for me today, Jack," she said demurely.

His frown deepened the already deep-cut chevrons in the saddle-brown skin of his forehead. "Question?" He hoped the girl didn't mean what he thought she meant.

"You know—she thought maybe you might have something important to ask me."

The girl stopped scrubbing. Slowly she dipped the sponge in the water and wrung it out, sliding her now bashful eyes between the sponge and Cameron's face.

He'd turned to look at her.

"You did have a question for me, didn't you, Jack?" Ruth Agnes said, a note of disappointment entering her voice.

Cameron sighed. What was it with the women around here, wanting to marry him? He supposed that any halfway civilized man with a decent job was a prime target in these parts.

He squinted his eyes sympathetically. "I don't know what Ma told you, Ruth, but if she gave you the idea I was going to ask . . . that I was going to propose to you today, she shouldn't have."

A cloud passed over the girl's eyes. "You . . . you weren't going to . . . ?"

"Ruth Agnes, I'm thirty-five years old. I live out in the middle of nowhere with a kid who thinks he's the next William Bonney. I drink too much and, whenever I get the chance, I carouse. You don't want to be married to a man like that."

Ruth Agnes's shoulders slumped as though the sky had fallen on her, and the cheerful light left her eyes without a trace. She stared at him and blinked. "I . . . thought you liked me. You gave me that dress last time you were in town, and that bracelet last year . . ."

"That was because I do like you and wanted to let you know I appreciate how you always clean up after me around here and heat my baths and wash my clothes. I know Ma can't pay you much, and I just wanted to give you something that said I was obliged, which I was . . . am . . ."

She seemed to be only half listening. Her brows were furrowed. Inclining her head, she stared at him as if trying to discern some foreign script. "Don't you think I'm pretty?"

"You're beautiful, Ruth Agnes."

"Then—why . . . ?"

Yes, why? he wondered. She was beautiful and would no doubt get even more lovely with age. Any man in his right mind would marry her, given the chance.

The problem was, as with Dinah Maxwell, he didn't love her. He was a lonely, aging desert rat trying to scrape a living off cattle whenever the Apaches gave him a chance. That was no life for a woman. Ruth Agnes was young and pretty. If she followed him out to his ranch in the middle of nowhere, she'd hate him for it later.

Thinking that, he wondered for the first time if Ivy Kitchen would have hated him for the same reason by now. Maybe the perfect love, he pondered, was the one that wasn't consummated, the one that was never allowed to grow to its fruition.

Maybe he and Ivy had had the perfect relationship.

He looked at Ruth Agnes. Hell, she didn't want to get married and settle down any more than he did. Not yet, anyway. She was young and had her wild oats to sow, though sowing them probably took some imagination with a mother like Ma Jones skulking around with her shotgun. No, Cameron was certain Ruth Agnes was more curious about lovemaking than about marriage, about living out a girlish fantasy than settling down to the grim business of keeping a ranch house for a man old enough to be her father.

He didn't say any of this, however. "Why? Because I'm older than you by a long shot, and I'm even older than my years."

She turned angrily to the window and crossed her arms over her breasts. "There's someone else, isn't there?"

Cameron laughed. "No, there sure as hell isn't, Ruth Agnes." He only vaguely noted the defensiveness in his tone.

She looked at him. "Is it the Mexican woman? The one that came in here with the dandy with the Southern accent?"

"Marina? She's married."

"So? My pa ran off on my ma, an' he was married."

"Well . . . I wouldn't do that," Cameron said. "Foolin' with a married woman is a great way to get yourself back-shot . . . and deserving of it." He frowned, the mention of Marina's name making him feel something he hadn't felt in a long time.

Ruth Agnes turned back to him. "You think I'm just a kid."

"You are a kid."

"I'm fifteen."

Cameron laughed ruefully and shook his head.

"Okay, so you won't marry me," she said huskily, kneeling back down by the tub and dropping her eyes to stare at the soapy water between his legs. "But I don't see any reason why we can't—" She gave a lusty smile that made her brown eyes flash with wickedness. "—you know."

Cameron was flabbergasted. "Good Lord, girl!"

Her hands clutched the tub and her hair brushed her incredibly smooth face. "Come on, Jack. I ain't never done it before, an' I was savin' myself for you."

"Ruth Agnes! If Ma heard you, she'd shoot us both!"

The girl grinned coquettishly. "I'll show you my titties."

He bit his cheek and turned his eyes to the ceiling. "I ain't interested."

"They've gotten big in the past six months!"

Cameron ignored her. "Why don't you go see if my clothes are done?"

"Not that I'm an expert in such matters, but it looks to me like you're interested, Jack."

Cameron looked at her, then followed her gaze to his member lifting its brown head above the water.

"Holy shit!" he yelled, splashing as he covered himself.

Ruth Agnes slapped her hands to her mouth and squealed.

"Now look what you did!" Cameron exclaimed.

"I ain't never seen one that size before!" Ruth Agnes laughed, eyes wide and downcast. "Todie Embers showed me his last summer, but it was just a little wisp of a thing."

"Out!" Cameron ordered, face red with embarrassment.

"Come on, Jack—just one more peek?" Ruth whined.

"Out! I ain't a goddamn circus show!"

Ruth Agnes scrambled to her feet, giggling, and ran out the door. Returning, she poked her head back into the room and asked, "Need more water?"

"No thank you!"

She turned and ran down the hall, squealing.

"I don't know what the hell's so damn funny about it," Cameron groused, taking a troubled gander between his legs. "Women."

CHAPTER 16

WHEN CAMERON HAD recovered from his encounter with Ruth Agnes, he grabbed the towel off the bed and dried himself, then dressed in the clean denims and cotton shirt he'd packed in his saddlebags. As he did so, he considered Gaston Bachelard and how he was going to go about tracking the man down.

The most obvious method occurred to him as he was sitting on the bed pulling on his boots. The idea was so compelling that Cameron froze with one boot only half on.

He'd accompany Clark to Mexico, ostensibly in search of the treasure. Wasn't Bachelard in search of that very same treasure? If their paths didn't cross somewhere along the way, they'd probably intersect at whatever X was drawn on Clark's so-called treasure map.

Cameron got up and stomped his heel into his boot and walked to the window, looking out but only half seeing the half-deserted street below. He was going over the plan in his mind.

It made sense. He would be on the surefire trail of the man who had butchered Pasqual Varas. He'd also verify either the presence or absence of the gold Clark was so certain he would find. The map was probably a fake, and the gold nothing more than a legend, but Cameron would never be sure unless he made the trek to Mexico himself.

As much as he hated admitting it, a small but very real part of Cameron was intrigued by the story of the lost gold. A small but very real part of him had fantasized about what he'd do, how his life would change, if the Treasure of San Bernardo turned out to be real.

Something he did not fully admit to himself was his fascination with the intriguing Marina—and his desire, albeit suppressed, to be near her again . . .

He dug in his pocket for a ten-dollar gold piece and dropped it on the washstand for Ruth Agnes. Then he grabbed his rifle, left his saddlebags on the bed, and walked out the door.

On his way down the hall, Cameron stopped at the Clarks' door and knocked quietly. He wasn't surprised that no one answered. It was nearly twelve-thirty. They'd probably gone out to look for someone else to lead them to Mexico, or to get themselves outfitted for the journey.

Cameron didn't think they would have left town yet. Even if they had, he knew the route they would take to the border, and it would not be hard to catch up to them.

Cameron continued down the stairs, found the still-snickering Ruth Agnes on the porch glider reading an illustrated magazine, and told her he'd return for his clothes in an hour or so. Then he headed over to Crow's Kitchen, where he sat down to a dinner of ham, eggs, fried potatoes, toast with cactus jelly, and tar-black coffee. The only other customer was a retired miner named Jeff Ames.

Ames ran freight twice a week from Tucson, and Cameron enjoyed chatting with him and hearing the news. Cameron was by nature a taciturn man, but living as remotely as he did made him thoroughly appreciate short, intermittent encounters with others, if only to talk about the weather or where Indians had been on the rampage of late.

At last he paid for his breakfast, drained his coffee cup, bid Jeff Ames a hearty farewell, and headed over to the Silver Dollar. There was a quiet game of cards involving five cowboys toward the back. Cigarette smoke lifted from their table and hung suspended in the brown air above them.

A small man with the ravaged face of the all-day regular stood with an arm on the bar and a foot on the brass rail. One hand gripped the half-empty mug of beer before him; the other clutched a cigarette between thumb and index finger.

Cameron tipped his hat to him. The man only nodded and turned shyly away.

"Mornin', Jack—or is it afternoon?" hailed the bartender with a grin. He was a stout man named Ives, roughly Cameron's age, with carefully combed blond hair and a face splashed with freckles. Cameron couldn't remember his first name—Ralph or something. He recalled the man had a deft hand with a foam rake and he only worked on weekends.

"You seen Bud?" Cameron asked the man.

"Not this morning. If he was in last night, he's probably upstairs. You want a beer?"

"Don't mind if I do," Cameron said with an eager sigh.

Only during his trips to town did he ever indulge before dusk. There was nothing quite as enjoyable as the way the bright desert light looked when tempered by a mug of Blatz.

He sipped the beer slowly and talked with the bartender. The cowboys played cards. Evidently they'd sowed most of their weekend oats and merely wanted to enjoy themselves peacefully before riding back to the ranch.

The regular at the other end of the bar smoked and drank his beer, not contributing to Cameron and the barman's conversation. He hacked up phlegm periodically and spat into the brass spittoon beside him.

Outside, the street was nearly silent but for a short-lived dogfight that ended with an abrupt yip. Then the flies could again be heard droning against the dirty windows.

Someone pushed through the batwing doors and Cameron turned to see Adrian Clark walking toward the bar. He smiled thinly.

"Jack." Clark greeted him coolly. "Yes, the pious woman from the hotel told us you'd made it to town. You were successful in running down the Indian, I take it?"

Cameron shrugged. "More or less."

Clark looked at the barman. "I'd like five bottles of your best brandy. Wrap them in burlap, please. They'll be traveling."

"You getting outfitted?" Cameron asked.

"Yes, we're doing quite well. We found a guide who—while not quite as qualified as you, of course— claims he knows the road quite well. He doesn't think we'll have any problem at all."

Clark's tone was smugly confident, and he did not look at Cameron as he spoke. He was watching the bartender fill his order. "How much do I owe you, my good man?"

"This stuff's three-fifty a bottle," Ives said with a disapproving wag of his head.

"Yes, well, we'll be roughing it enough in the next several weeks. I'll at least need a good shot of good brandy now and then. Quells my cough. Picked up a touch of the pleurisy last winter and can't seem to shake it." Now Clark smiled personally at Cameron as he took a small roll of greenbacks from his pocket.

"Who's guiding you?" Cameron asked.

"Man by the name of Hawkins—Jake Hawkins, I believe it is. Big guy. Well armed. Very capable."

"Jake Hawkins, huh?" Cameron said stiffly, rolling a wry look at the bartender, who returned it.

"He's a freighter," Clark said. "He's come up the trail from Chihuahua over twenty-five times. And he's done a good bit of guiding, as well."

"I know who Hawkins is and what he's done," Cameron growled. He drained his beer, wiped the foam from his mouth with the back of his hand, and tossed a coin on the bar.

Clark was hefting the bag of bottles from the bar, careful not to break them.

"You get two beers for a nickel, Jack," Ives said.

"Give the next one to Hotchkiss," Cameron replied, heading for the stairs at the back of the room. "I have a feeling he's going to need a little hair o' the dog."

"Be seein' you, Jack," Clark called after him, a little too heartily.

"Yes, you will," Cameron replied.

As Cameron headed up the stairs, Clark gave a puzzled shrug of his shoulders, tipped his hat to the barman, and headed out the door with his bag of bottles clutched carefully before him.

Upstairs, Cameron passed Dinah Maxwell's door, feeling sheepish about last night. She probably wasn't even in her room, however; she usually went to church on Sundays—which no doubt evoked consternation in Ma Jones and others in the congregation.

Cameron stopped at a door about midway down the hall and tapped. "Anyone seen Hotchkiss?"

He had to ask several times before an angry female voice, drugged with sleep, said, "Last I seen him he was with Franci. Now git—I'm sleepin'."

Cameron thought Franci's room was the last one on the right. He knocked on the door. The only answer was two muffled groans—a man's and a woman's, in unison.

Recognizing Hotchkiss's groan, Cameron turned the knob and opened the door. A naked man and woman sprawled on the bed with the sheets and blankets tangled about their ankles. The man lay on his back, head tilted back on the pillow, guttural snores rising from his open mouth.

Cameron had never seen Hotchkiss nude before. It was a stunning sight—a big hairy belly and thin white legs streaked with blue veins and pocked here and there with old wounds from arrows and musket balls. Cameron reflected that it paid to not let oneself go in one's later years.

"Up an' at 'em, Hoss," he said loudly. "There's a beer waiting for you downstairs."

Hotchkiss grabbed his face as though cold water had been splashed in his eyes. "Oh, Lordy . . . What the hell is happening!"

"It's the dawn of a new day, my man," Cameron said, as obnoxiously as he could. "The sun is shining, the birds are chirping, and the dogs are fighting. Let's go!" He tugged on the man's horny white foot and Hotchkiss pulled it away.

The girl stirred, gave a curse, and glanced over her shoulder and across her naked rump at Cameron. "What are you *doing* in here?"

"Be gone in just a minute, Franci. Excuse the intrusion."

"I done my job for the night . . . now it's time to sleep," she cried, reburying her face in her pillow.

"Where's the kid?" Cameron asked Hotchkiss, who was coughing and complaining as he grudgingly came back to wakefulness.

Coughing, hacking, and grunting, the graybeard scooted up against the headboard and jerked his head at the wall behind Cameron. Cameron turned and saw Jimmy Bronco facedown on the daybed, left arm dangling. There was a half-filled puke bucket on the floor at his side.

The kid's face was turned to the side, mouth open, eyes squeezed shut as though against a storm in his head, and his hair was standing up in sweat-stiffened spikes. His face was the pale green of an approaching storm.

"Good Lord, Bud!" Cameron admonished Hotchkiss.

Hotchkiss turned his head and spat into the spittoon beside the bed, then wiped his mouth and smacked his lips, blinking as though trying to break whatever was holding his eyelids down.

"Well . . . I didn't pour it down him. I lost track of him after Franci started gettin' friendly like she does, and I think the kid here started hittin' up some of the other guys for beer. Fool kid. I told him just one—I really did, Jack."

Cameron kicked the daybed on which the kid snored, spittle stringing from his parted lips into the bucket below. The kid gave a grunt and mumbled something unintelligible.

"Jimmy—haul ass, we're outta here!"

The kid frowned against the thunder in his ears.

The girl stirred, gave a groan.

Hotchkiss said, "What's goin' on? You know I like to sleep on Sundays."

"You too, Bud. Haul ass and get the kid cleaned up. There's a beer waiting for you downstairs, but don't linger. I'll meet you two over at the dry-goods."

"There's a beer waitin' for me, eh?" Hotchkiss said, suddenly coming around. He swung his feet to the floor, then looked at Cameron, who was turning to the door. "What the hell you got goin', anyway?"

"We're goin' to Mexico."

"Mexico? With Clark? What the hell? I thought . . ."

Cameron held the door half-open, and half turned to Hotchkiss. "You wanna get Bachelard, Bud?"

Hotchkiss scowled at Cameron over his shoulder and squinted one blue eye. "For what he did to Pas? You can bet your last pair of calfskin boots, I do."

Cameron smiled cunningly. "Then we're goin' to Mexico."

Clark was standing on the loading dock of the dry-goods store with one other man, a medium-sized hardcase with frizzy red hair puffing out of a leather hat, the band of which was the skin of a diamond-back rattlesnake. In front of the dock stood a pair of mules harnessed to a buckboard.

As Cameron walked up to the loading dock, he recognized the redhead as Jake Hawkins. Hawkins and Clark were sharing one of the bottles of brandy Clark had bought in the saloon. By the sapsucker grins on their faces, it appeared they were having a pretty good time. Clark had finally found himself a guide, and Jake Hawkins had found an easy mark.

"This your guide, Clark?" Cameron asked, smiling.

"That's right," Clark said uneasily.

Cameron shifted his eyes to the frizzy-haired man. Hawkins's nose was blunt and his eyes were dull.

"How you doin', Jake?"

"Just fine, Jack. How 'bout yourself?" Hawkins said. His smile was losing its luster.

"Didn't know you'd taken up guiding for hire."

"Well, I ain't. Not officially, anyways. But when I heard this man and his lovely wife were looking for a guide to take them to Mexico . . . well, I didn't think it'd be right to turn them down." Hawkins's smile widened, flashing a silver eyetooth. "Considerin' my experience and all."

"Oh? What experience is that?"

"Didn't you know, Jack? I been hauling freight up from Chiwowy for pret' near two years now. Know the trail like the back of my hand. All the trouble spots and whatnot." Jake smiled at Clark and reached for the bottle Clark was holding, shifting his gaze uneasily between Clark and Cameron.

The door of the dry-goods shop opened and Marina appeared, carrying a ten-pound sack of flour. She stopped when she saw Cameron. Their eyes met for a second. Then she continued to the buckboard and set the flour in the box.

Cameron saw that Hawkins was watching Marina with more than a passing interest. The owner of the dry-goods came out of the building and set a wooden crate containing miscellaneous trail goods in the buckboard. He was dressed in his Sunday best, and he didn't appear happy about missing church.

Cameron figured the man had been waylaid on his way to morning services by Clark and his "guide." Their shopping list had been too much business to turn down, even on Sunday, but it had still soured the man's demeanor; scowling, he followed Marina back into the store for another load.

Cameron looked at Hawkins. "Get lost, Jake. I'm guiding the Clarks to Mexico."

Clark looked at Cameron curiously. "I thought—"

"Never mind what you thought," Cameron said. "Relieve this no-account of his duties."

Hawkins's eyes blazed with a slow-building fire as he stared down at Cameron, whose head came up to the top of the man's dusty boots.

"Why, this man is a professional guide. He told me so himself," Clark said. "He's guided miners down to Mexico for years. Told me that himself, didn't you, Mr. Hawkins?"

Hawkins didn't answer. His eyes were glued to Cameron—they appeared carved from flint.

"This man is a penny-ante crook," Cameron told Clark. "He and his brother and a small band of other miscreants travel around the territory robbing farmers and stage coaches, and once in a while a bank, when they have the balls. Jake here has spent four years in Yuma Pen for rape, among other things. He has ulterior motives for guiding you and Marina to Mexico."

"Shut your goddamn lyin' mouth, Cameron!" Hawkins exploded.

Cameron said, "The jig is up, Jake. It was a nice try, but it's not going to work. So why don't you and your brother there across the street"—he tipped his head to indicate a man in a shabby derby hat sitting on a loafer's bench before the Traveler's Fancy Saloon—"ride on out of here before you get yourselves shot."

Clark said, "Jack, how do you know these men intend . . . ?"

"To rob you and rape your wife? Because they've done it before."

Hawkins's right hand went to the butt of the .45 he wore tied down on his hip. Just as he reached it, Cameron grabbed Hawkins's feet with both hands and pulled as hard as he could. The man went down just as he got the gun out of its holster.

The gun barked, the slug flying into the roof over the dock. Cursing, Hawkins hit the floor on his back, gunsmoke and dust puffing around him.

Cameron held on to the boot and yanked the man off the loading dock. Hawkins landed in the street with a thud and a sharp grunt, losing his pistol in the process.

The "guide" scrambled to his knees and was climbing to his feet when Cameron kicked him hard in the side and he went over again, cursing, spittle flying from his lips.

Hawkins's brother, Ed, was standing on the boardwalk across the street, watching the fight. Ed's hand had drifted to his sidearm. Cameron was grateful for the reluctance on Ed's face. He didn't want a firefight. There were too many innocent people around.

"That's right, Ed," Cameron called, "you just keep that hogleg in your holster, or you and your brother are gonna need a ride out to boot hill."

Hawkins twisted around on an elbow and looked at his brother, yelling savagely, "Kill him, goddamn it, Ed! Kill this son of a bitch!"

Silence. Hawkins stared at his brother, breathing heavily through gritted teeth.

Cameron watched Ed's gun hand, ready to go for his own Colt the second he saw it move.

Finally the hand came up with a brief wave of surrender. Ed turned, head down, and drifted into the saloon.

"Ed, you're goddamn yellow!" Jake roared.

Cameron picked Hawkins's gun out of the dust and stuck it in his belt. "I'll leave this on the old bridge at the creek south of town," he told the man.

"Fuck you, Cameron!" Hawkins yelled hoarsely, thoroughly defeated and unwilling to accept it.

Cameron looked at him coolly from under the brim of his hat, like a schoolmaster admonishing a belligerent pupil. "But if I catch you trailing us— and believe me, I'll know if you're back there—I'm gonna take it away from you again, shove it up your ass, and pull the trigger."

The man climbed to his feet, still grumbling, and slapped the dust from his jeans. His face was twisted in anger. He picked up his hat, slapped it on his head, and threw another glare at Cameron. "Fuck you!" he repeated.

Then he followed his brother into the saloon.

Cameron turned back to the loading dock. Clark stared at him, speechless. Marina stood before the doors, holding a crate of canned tomatoes.

Cameron moved to the dock and held out his arms for the crate. She lowered it to him.

A smile lifted her cheeks and lighted her eyes, and Cameron returned it.

CHAPTER 17

———◆———

GASTON BACHELARD AND his companions splashed across the foot-deep Rio Rincon and climbed the brushy grade that rose beyond it.

Bachelard halted his horse and surveyed the flat, brushy desert ahead. It rose gradually to the gray-and-blue peaks jutting beyond like enormous thunderheads.

The Sierra Madre, mother of mountain ranges—a hard, rugged-looking range, with deep-blue shadows around its base. But once you got within its foothills and smelled the grass and wildflowers and pines, saw the herds of elk and deer, the briskly flowing rivers, you felt as though you'd died and been generously rewarded for your travails.

"My lovely Juanita," Bachelard said to the girl riding behind his saddle, "I give you the mountains." He gestured broadly with his hand and grinned back at her.

The girl said nothing. She did not lift her eyes. She was exhausted, sunburned, sore, and so dirty that her features were barely distinguishable. So fearful was she of the nightmare her life had become, that she had withdrawn, making her mind as blank as the sky on a cloudy night.

"When we have our power and money, we will

have a stone castle in the mountains," Bachelard said, returning his gaze to the majestic peaks rising above the desert. "We'll fish and swim in the rivers and take long rides through the canyons. You will love it, Juanita. I promise you that."

"I think the cat's got her tongue," Jim Bob Mc-Guffy quipped dryly, and spit a stream of tobacco juice on a flat rock.

"Shut up, Corporal!" Bachelard cowed him. He looked at the two Mexican riders. "You and Rubio ride ahead. We're close to Sonoita, so we'll be seeing Montana's outriders soon. Make sure the fools don't shoot us."

"Sí, jefe," Jesus said. The Mexicans spurred their mounts off across the plain, kicking up dust as they rode.

An hour later Bachelard, the girl, and McGuffy had ridden another five miles toward the mountains, tracing the curving course of a dry creekbed. The two Mexicans Bachelard had sent ahead appeared on their left, galloping back toward them.

In the distance several other riders could be seen looking in Bachelard's direction. Bachelard could barely make out the round brims and pointed peaks of their sombreros and the barrels of their rifles jutting above their heads.

"All is well," Jesus said as he and Rubio approached, then fell in behind McGuffy, riding single file.

Following the dry riverbed, the party soon raised the little village of Sonoita out of the rocky buttes and rimrocks. The squeals of pigs and clucks of chickens could be heard, and the angry Spanish of a farmer complaining to a woman who apparently thought he was asking too much for the watermelon he was trying to sell out of the back of a two-wheeled cart.

When the man saw Bachelard, he immediately ceased arguing and stiffened like a soldier coming to attention. The woman followed the man's gaze and, seeing Bachelard, fell silent as well. A fearful look entered her brown eyes.

Bachelard tipped his gray Confederate hat at the two and smiled mockingly.

He and the others followed the dusty road littered with hay carts, pigs, burros, and children, past adobe-and-thatch huts and up a hill. The hill was wooded with olive trees, dusty tamaracks, and oaks, and lit by hazy sunlight. Men in Mexican peasant garb and armed with rifles, pistols, and machetes strolled along the road, talking and smoking.

The road looped around a dry fountain on which a copper-colored rooster sat preening. Flanking the fountain was a sprawling adobe house with a red-tile roof. An elaborate wrought-iron gate led into the house's patio, where potted orange trees blossomed and filled the air with the smell of citrus.

To the right of the house, beyond whitewashed sheds and barns, was a sprawling hay meadow where small brush huts and tents had been erected, and where milled the men—Mexicans and Texans—Bachelard and Miguel Montana had drafted into their armies.

This was the vast, elaborate rancho Bachelard and Montana had seized from a prominent Mexican rancher. From here they made forays throughout northern Sonora, wreaking havoc on wealthy landowners and their sympathizers.

Their goal was to wrest power from the conservative government and establish their own dictatorship, dividing up the land as they did and "returning" it to the peasants who worked it. They would charge the peasants a nominal fee in the form of a yearly tax for their hard work and the danger they'd endured during the revolution—a reasonable requirement, they were certain. Of course, they'd also expect the peons' utmost loyalty and support. The landless hordes would certainly owe Bachelard and Montana that much!

Once Sonora was secure and their army was legions large, they'd retake Texas from the United States. Then they would declare northern Sonora and Texas a new and independent republic. Which of the two founding fathers would rule this new country— Bachelard or Montana—hadn't yet been discussed. Neither had wanted to broach the subject, knowing it was a touchy one, one that could ignite a small civil war among themselves as well as their troops.

No, it was best to wait and see how things panned out . . .

"Buenos días, Señor Bachelard," said one of the Mexican men guarding the house. He held Bachelard's horse while the former Confederate dismounted and reached up to lift Juanita down.

"Buenos días, Sebastian. Is your fearless leader in?" When speaking of his compañero, Miguel Montana, Bachelard could not restrain from injecting a little sarcasm in his tone. He knew it was not good to parade his and Montana's subtle rivalry before their men, but he couldn't help himself. Bachelard was a self-educated man who read Shakespeare and the Greeks, whereas Miguel Montana was nothing but a bandito, a simple-minded bean-eater with a penchant for killing. But the peasants loved him. Bachelard knew he could not attain what he wanted to without him.

"Sí, el capitán. He is eating," Sebastian said as he led Bachelard's horse away. The other men had already ridden away to the stables.

As Bachelard crossed the flagstone patio—where the late hacendado who owned the place had no doubt taken his morning coffee with his family, and from where they could watch the peasants begin their morning labors in the fields—Bachelard noted a pig hanging from a viga pole jutting from the adobe wall of the house. Blood from the beast's slit throat formed a large, waxy red puddle that had crept past the potted trees and under the wrought-iron fence.

Gently nudging Juanita ahead of him, Bachelard shook his head and grimaced with bemused disgust. Miguel Montana was not a civilized man. Sometimes living here with that slob made Bachelard's blood boil with contempt.

Bachelard went through the heavy, carved door and found his compañero in the dining room, sitting at the end of the sprawling oak table that boasted more than a dozen highbacked chairs. Arched windows let in shafts of golden light, sharply contrasting with the shadows cast by the room's heavy timbers and solid wooden furniture, ornately carved, that appeared several generations old.

"Ah, Gaston!" Montana bellowed when he looked up and saw his American partner enter through the arched doorway, nudging the girl ahead. "Buenos días, mi compañero!"

Montana tossed off the napkin he'd stuck inside his shirt, shoved his chair back, and got up, walking around the table to Bachelard, smiling grandly. His shiny black high-topped boots shone brightly, and his whipcord trousers with their fancy stitching swayed about his ankles. His silk blouse was unbuttoned halfway down his chest, exposing a mat of curly black hair.

"Yes, buenos días, Miguel, buenos días," Bachelard

said, always finding it difficult to muster up much enthusiasm for his partner.

The little man—Montana was only about five feet five inches tall, and slender as a rail—pumped the taller Bachelard's hand with gusto and smiled up into Bachelard's gray eyes.

"How have you been, amigo? Did you find it? Did you find the plat?"

"I certainly did," Bachelard said.

"Have a seat—show me!" Montana intoned, stretching an arm to indicate the table. "I'll have the señoritas bring you a plate of stew.

"Who's this?" he asked Bachelard, gesturing at Juanita.

"Doña Juanita Martínez," Bachelard said grandly, as if introducing the child at her coming-out party.

The girl stared ahead through the arched windows, at the green bushes moving faintly in the faded sunlight. Her filthy black hair hung down both sides of her face. Montana regarded the girl curiously, seeing nothing special about a dirty little peasant girl. He looked at Bachelard befuddled.

Bachelard said, "Have you seen anything so pure and innocent and lovely?"

"Well, I . . ."

"I don't believe I have ever seen a treasure like this one here. When she looks at me I feel like I am twenty years younger, before the war . . ." Bachelard's voice trailed off, and his thoughts drifted back to the bayous of his childhood and the skinny, dark-haired girl who had been the first love of his life. He looked at Montana. "She's a little worse for wear, I admit, but once she's cleaned up, you'll see my future queen shine!"

"Yes . . ." Montana hedged, returning to his place at the table. "Come on, Gaston, have a seat." He half turned to yell through another arched doorway, in Spanish. "Girls—come! Bring another plate. El Capitán Bachelard is back and he is very hungry from his long journey. Isobel, Habra!"

Bachelard helped Juanita into a chair so large she appeared lost in it. Then he took a seat between her and Miguel Montana.

Two girls appeared from the kitchen doorway. One carried a big stew pot; the other carried a basket of tortillas, a glass, and two plates. Bachelard glanced at them, turned to Montana, then quickly back to the girls, shocked to see they were both naked from the waist up.

Bachelard turned back to see Montana staring at him with a wistful smirk. "You like the uniforms I ordered for the girls, compañero?"

Bachelard looked again at the girls setting down the pots, dishing up the food, and pouring the wine. Judging from their faces and the firmness of their breasts, they were about sixteen or seventeen years old.

They did not look at Bachelard. They seemed in a trance, concentrating solely on what they were doing at the moment. Bachelard gave an exclamatory grunt. Then he laughed.

"What have you got going here, Miguel?" he asked, genuinely amused.

Chewing a mouthful of stew, Montana covered his mouth and snickered. "They were acting so damn uppity, these superior rich girls, that I decided to humble them a little, eh? Now, you would think that just being made to serve, when you have been served all your life by the poor peasants from the village, would be enough to cow them. But no! Still I caught them looking at me as though I were a lowly little peon bandit who had invaded their home and killed their parents and brothers just for fun. They do not realize that I—*we*, of course—are the next kings of Sonora."

He shrugged his shoulders and brought his wineglass to his lips. "So I ordered them to disrobe. They've orders not to wear blouses again until I, their king, give them permission to do so."

He took a large drink of wine, swirled it around in his mouth, and swallowed with a loud sucking noise. He smacked his lips and grinned at Bachelard, who had started laughing again as one of the girls refilled Montana's wineglass.

Montana lurched forward and kissed one of her breasts. Ignoring him, she and the other girl drifted silently back to the kitchen.

Bachelard sat back in his chair, facing Montana and shaking his head with admiration. No, he did not care for this little greaser, but apparently he had not given Montana credit for a rather colorful imagination. Bachelard liked men with imagination. Montana had come up a notch or two in his estimation.

He laughed again, picked up his fork, and dug into his stew. After a moment he realized that Juanita was sitting before an empty plate.

Dropping his fork and picking up her plate, he exclaimed, "Ah, Juanita, you must eat! We have another long day ahead of us tomorrow."

He scooped stew onto the girl's plate, set a tortilla on it as well, and set the plate down before her vacant gaze. She gave no indication that she even saw the food before her.

Scowling, Bachelard picked up her right hand, shoved a fork in it, and waited until she slowly began eating, one small morsel at a time. He turned to Miguel, who had been watching the fiasco with cautious reserve, and shook his head as if to say, *Kids.*

"You were going to show me the plat," Montana said, sliding his gaze from the nearly comatose girl to Bachelard.

Bachelard produced the rolled javelina-skin from the inside pocket of his gray coat and set it on the table, then picked up his fork and began shoveling stew into his mouth with hungry grunts. Montana untied the leather thong from the skin and, shoving his plate aside, unrolled it before him.

His brown eyes grew thoughtful as he studied the markings. He nodded, mumbling to himself.

"Does any of that mean anything to you?" Bachelard asked him after a while.

Montana nodded slowly. "Sí, I recognize some of these formations. And this here, this must be a village—San Cristóbal, it appears—and this must be the Rio Bavispe."

He paused. His brows furrowed. He turned the plat toward Bachelard. "What is this?" he asked, pointing to several curlicues within curlicues, forming what looked like a crude turtle, on the bottom left corner of the plat.

"I thought you would know."

Montana lifted his head. "Carlos!" he shouted.

When the guard who had taken Bachelard's horse appeared a moment later, Montana said, "Bring Xavier Llamas to me at once!"

"At once—sí, el capitán!"

When at last a stoop-shouldered old man appeared, holding his hat and looking fearful, Montana beckoned him to his side and showed him the plat. "Tell me, Xavier, do you recognize any of the formations drawn on this map?" He pointed out the turtle. "Do you recognize this?"

The man set his straw hat on the table and shifted his head around to focus his aging eyes on the plat.

Talking to himself, Adam's apple working in his skinny, leathery neck, he ran a dirty, blunt index finger over the drawn lines forming caricatures of mountains, streams, canyons, and villages.

His finger halted at the large X drawn at the base of a butte with an arrow-shaped ridge, then continued on to the turtle.

He looked up at Montana with serious eyes. "Sí," he said with a nod. "I have seen these things, los capitánes. I used to graze my goats not far away."

"What is this?" Montana asked, pointing to the turtle.

The man shrugged as if it were not significant. "The turtle was carved into the rocks by the ancients. I know not what it means."

"Have you seen the turtle anywhere else before?" Bachelard asked the man. "Anywhere but in the region where you grazed your goats?"

"No, el capitán."

Bachelard shrugged at Montana. Montana shrugged back.

Bachelard asked the old man, "Xavier, can you take me to the X on the map?"

"It has been many years, and it is clear across the mountains, but I think I can find the way," the old man said, nodding. He put his finger on the arrow-shaped peak. "I have seen this before. Below, there are ruins left by the ancients. The X is here by the old homes of the ancients."

"How long will it take?"

Xavier shrugged noncommittally. "Two weeks. Maybe three. But . . ." The old man's eyes acquired a haunted cast. "But this is where Apaches are, los capitánes."

"We'll need plenty of men," Bachelard said to Montana.

Montana shrugged. "If you are sure the gold is there, my warrior companion, we will take all the men it takes to get it out. If it is as much gold as you say, we will soon have enough guns and ammunition to take all of Mexico, and all of your country as well!" Montana's eyes were big and his chest heaved as his breaths became irregular.

Bachelard, too, was getting excited. Not only had the map been validated by the legends of the lost church he had heard in cantinas and brothels throughout Sonora, but now this old man concurred, with his recognition of the formations drawn on the map.

Bachelard threw down his napkin and stood slowly. To the old man he said, "Be ready to ride tomorrow at dawn, old one."

"Sí, sí, el capitánes!" the old man intoned, nearly overcome with a newfound sense of his own importance. "Sí, sí. Tomorrow we ride at dawn!"

CHAPTER 18

CAMERON SIPPED HIS coffee and waited for the sun to rise.

A day's ride had put Contention City well behind them. He stood now on a low hill looking east across a flat valley studded with cholla and mesquite, and the occasional barrel cactus, witchgrass, and rocks.

The rising sun touched it with pink. A damn pretty sight. It would have been even prettier if, five minutes ago, Cameron hadn't spied movement out there about two hundred yards away.

It could have been a coyote, but he didn't think so. A coyote wouldn't have slipped from one shrub to another and stopped. It either would have pounced on whatever it was hunting or it would have kept moving. Besides, the shape and size of the form told him whatever was out there was human.

Apache, maybe, or one of the Hawkins brothers. Hell, it could be one of Bachelard's men, sent to keep Clark away from the gold.

That didn't seem likely. Cameron doubted that Bachelard saw Clark as enough of a threat to send men out to kill him. The way Bachelard probably saw it, when he'd gotten the map, the gold—if there was any gold—belonged to him. He must know Clark had a copy of the plat, but he probably also figured he had enough men and guns to fight off anyone who came between him and the cache. And he probably did.

Bachelard probably had enough men to fight off anyone who came gunning for him, as well. Cameron hadn't yet given enough careful consideration to how he was going to get to Bachelard without getting himself and the others killed, but he was confident he'd come up with something.

First he had to locate the man.

Finding the gold was of only secondary importance to him. Still, he had to admit a twinge of gold fever; it came and went, like arthritis pangs or a minor toothache. For the most part, he kept his mind off it and on Bachelard. And on Leonora Varas and her children, whom he would have to tell about Pas's senseless murder. He would have to inform them they no longer had a husband or a father, and he would have to listen to their screams, their begging him to tell them it wasn't true. He'd have to watch them smash their fists against their heads and tear their hair, faces contorted with unbearable grief.

Eventually they'd accept that Pas was gone. But they would always tend the wound. Cameron knew, because it was a wound like the one he tended himself, every day of his life.

Cameron sipped his coffee and turned to look down the other side of the hill, where the breakfast fire glowed orange in the stand of cottonwoods. Before leaving Contention City, Cameron had traded the buckboard for two more mules. Pooling their money, he'd bought three more. He had wanted at least five, to pack a relatively light load of dry food, oats for the horses, extra rifles, and mining equipment in case they needed to dig. It was really more pack animals than they needed on the way in, but you never knew when one of them—or one of the horses, for that matter—would go down. There was no way they'd get a wagon in and out of the country to which they were heading.

The horses and mules grazed in a picket line about thirty yards from the fire.

Beside the dry riverbed where they'd camped, Clark and Marina were taking down their old cavalry tent, which Clark had coaxed the liveryman to throw in with the mules. Hotchkiss and Jimmy Bronco were rigging up their horses, tightening cinches, with the stirrups thrown up on their saddles. They'd already rigged the panniers and wooden pack frames to the mules and were nearly ready to start their second day on the trail to Mexico.

Cameron turned back to look out over the valley where he'd seen something move. He'd left his field glasses in the saddlebags on his horse, so he had only his naked eyes for picking movement out of the ever-pinkening landscape before him.

Whatever it was—if it was indeed anything at all, and not an optical illusion or merely a shadow caused by the rising sun—was keeping out of sight. Whatever or whomever it was had maybe seen him and was staying put behind a mesquite shrub.

Cameron tossed out the cold coffee dregs and walked down the hill to the camp, where Hotchkiss was kicking dirt on the fire. Clark was stowing the tent on a mule. Marina and Jimmy Bronco were mounted and waiting, their horses friskily waving their tails and craning their necks, ready to go.

The tops of the cottonwoods turned gold as the sun rose from the desert and filled the sky with light.

"What's got your tail in a knot?" Hotchkiss asked Cameron, seeing the strange look in his eyes.

Cameron shrugged as he approached, taking long

strides down the grade. "I don't know. Maybe nothin', but I thought I saw something move, just for a second. I think I'll ride out with you, then slip off my horse and hang back for a while. If it's anything except my imagination or poor eyesight, they'll probably want to check out our camp."

"Could just be someone out huntin' deer," Hotchkiss said. "Some farmer or rancher."

"Yeah, that's probably all it is," Cameron said as he fished in his saddlebags for his moccasins, then sat down to put them on. "I just want to make sure, that's all. No sense in not being careful. This is Apache country."

"You got that right," Hotchkiss said darkly, giving one more kick to the fire and heading for his mount.

"Can I not ride drag today, Jack?" Jimmy Bronco asked pleadingly.

"I don't know. You over your hangover?"

"Just about."

"Okay, you got point," Cameron said, shoving his boots into his saddlebags and mounting up. "Keep your eyes open."

Cameron kicked his horse and led up the procession, then halted twenty yards up the trail and turned back to see Clark taking a swig from one of his brandy bottles before corking the bottle and stowing it in his coat. Clark touched his chestnut with his spurs, giving a yank on the lead rope attached to the pack mule, heading out.

Cameron looked at him with mild concern. "How you feelin'?" he asked.

Clark grinned brightly as he passed, the morning breeze playing with the brim of his new black slouch hat. "Never better. I think this dry air is doing wonders for my pleurisy." He gave a raspy cough as he passed Cameron.

Cameron watched the procession jog down the old cattle trail they were following back out to the freight road that would take them across the border and into the foothills of the Sierra Madre. He'd heard enough coughs like Clark's to know the man did not have a simple case of pleurisy; Cameron would have bet his last peg pony it was consumption, and it didn't sound to him like it was getting any better, either. From all the coughing Clark had done on the trail yesterday, Cameron could tell it was getting worse. Trail dust and sleeping on the ground, not to mention the sheer physical drain of travel itself, would take its toll. Cameron just hoped Clark wouldn't succumb before they got back.

Cameron heard hooves clomping and turned to see Marina approach, looking at him with eyes that told him she shared his concern for her husband. Marina looked lovely, her hair bouncing on her shoulders, the horsehair thong of her flatbrimmed hat loose beneath her chin. She wore a white blouse and a pair of boy's butternut slacks tucked into riding boots outfitted with big, Spanish-roweled spurs. A Henry rifle rode in the saddleboot beneath her knee, and around her waist she wore a cartridge-belt and a holster with a light, pearl-gripped pistol—all bought at the dry-goods in Contention City.

"That brandy isn't going to do him any good," Cameron told her.

"I know," she said, reining her horse to a halt beside him. "I've tried to get him to give it up but it seems to give some relief, so he keeps drinking."

Cameron scowled and shook his head. "It's only gonna bring it on all the faster."

"You think it is consumption, don't you?"

"I'm afraid so."

She nodded and turned to look at the Missourian

receding in the distance. "I thought so, too, but I wasn't sure." She turned back to Cameron. "Will he die?"

He was a little taken aback by the baldness of the question. Hers was a mettle definitely forged in fire. "I don't believe there's a cure, but people can live with it quite a while if they take care of it. He's not taking care of it."

"Maybe he will after we have the gold," she said.

Cameron nodded and smiled faintly, vaguely amused at her certainty about the gold. "Yeah, he probably will."

She smiled, her brown eyes suddenly bright with amusement. "It is there," she said, nodding her head and raising her lovely brows. She clucked to her horse and started out ahead of him. "It really is there."

"Show me," he groused to her back.

"I will, Mr. Cameron," she said, half teasing, giving the black her spurs and galloping after the others.

Cameron clucked to his own horse and caught up with Hotchkiss, who was riding up beside Jimmy Bronco, ahead of Clark. "We should make Toke's place tonight," he said to the graybeard.

"Tokente?" Bud asked, looking at him brightly. "He lives out here?"

Cameron nodded. "He ran into a nice-sized vein and bought himself a little spread just west of here, not far off the trail. We can hole up in his barn and fill our canteens and water barrel. In the meantime, I'm gonna drag back and see what, if anything, is followin' us."

He held his reins out to Hotchkiss. "Take my horse. I'll catch up to you later." Holding fast to the horn and cantle, Cameron brought both his moccasined feet onto the saddle, positioning himself to spring onto a passing boulder. Wanting whomever was following them to believe they'd all ridden off together, he didn't want to leave any footprints.

"Be careful," Hotchkiss warned.

"Later," Cameron said.

He shucked his rifle from its boot and jumped smoothly off the saddle onto the boulder, throwing his arms out for balance. Moments later he was on the ground, hunkered down between boulders, watching his back trail.

Seeing no one behind him, he moved out from the boulder and headed back toward the camp, staying wide of the trail, dodging between boulders and trees.

About thirty yards away from the fire ring, he crouched behind a cottonwood deadfall. Hidden by the tangle of roots that had been ripped out of the ground when the tree fell, Cameron peered out from under the tree's rotting trunk.

His field of vision included the campsite, the dry riverbed enveloped in tall grass, and the eroded hill where he'd been standing when he'd spied movement to the east. The sun was climbing fast now, bringing the heat back out of the ground. It was warm on Cameron's face and back, and already he was sweating.

He'd been sitting there for fifteen minutes when something moved on the right slope of the hill. Cameron recognized the faded red headband and black hair of an Apache. A rifle poked up beside the head. Cameron felt his heart quicken. Shit.

All he needed was an Apache attack this early in the trek. The sight of that headband gave him more doubts about how smart it was to head into Mexico and the heart of Apache land. Most of the Indians might have gone to reservations, but there were still enough misfits out here to make travel a living nightmare.

He considered his options. He could engage this Apache now and get him off their trail and be done with it, or he could wait and see if the man intended to follow their caravan. Maybe the man was just curious and wanted to know who was about. Or maybe he wanted to tangle. He was Apache, after all, and there was honor in fighting and killing the white-eyes. The packs probably looked good, too, tantalizingly covered with tarps. Who knew what the white-eyes were hauling? The horses and mules would be some fine plunder to take back to the *rancheria*.

And then, too, there was the woman . . .

Cameron decided to wait a few minutes and see if any other Apaches showed up. If there were only one or two more, as was likely, he could probably handle them if he used the element of surprise to his best advantage. The Apache raised his head a little farther, peered around the hill at the camp.

Apparently deciding all was clear, he got to his feet and walked cautiously around the hill, moving his head slowly from right to left, sniffing the breeze, reading the signs. He held the rifle—an old-model Springfield, it appeared—up under his shoulder, muzzle pointed forward and about chest high.

He was young, maybe in his late teens or early twenties. His face was painted for battle.

At the fire ring, the Indian stared down at the freshly covered coals, then lifted his head and let out what sounded like a cross between a yell and a yelp. A minute later, another Apache appeared, about the same age as the first. He, too, carried a Springfield, and a knife on his belt.

They walked around the camp, picking out the footprints and reading them—no doubt determining exactly how many were in Cameron's party, their ages, and recognizing one set to be that of a woman.

When they were through in the camp, the first brave headed up the trail, following the fresh tracks. The second Indian lingered awhile, taking a drink from the sheepskin hanging from his neck and adjusting the ties on his moccasins.

Then he, too, headed up the trail, following the cavalcade, long hair blowing out behind him.

These two were going to be trouble, Cameron could tell. They'd probably wait for dark and attack the camp or Tokente's rancho, where he'd planned on spending the night. He would have to take care of them here.

To that end, he followed them, staying wide of the trail and taking cover behind rocks and mesquite shrubs. When a hill rose between them and Cameron, Cameron made use of it by running, keeping the hill between him and the two young men and watching the ground carefully so as not to step on anything that could signal his presence.

He climbed the hill and stopped, looking down at the Apaches, who were now walking about ten yards apart, rifles held at their waists. The one in front sensed Cameron's presence and swung around, bringing up the rifle. Cameron's Winchester was already at his shoulder.

He drew a bead on the Apache's chest and pulled the trigger, then immediately planted the bead on the other one, who had turned at the rifle's bark. Before the brave brought his own gun up, Cameron laid him out with a bullet through the forehead.

Cameron walked down to the two bodies lying in the dust, dead eyes gazing at the sky. Some men got inured to killing, but Cameron never had. He'd gotten used to it, so that it didn't bother him as it once had, but he still wasn't hardened to it. There was something simply, clearly wrong in taking the life of another man, and he'd never killed when it hadn't meant being killed himself. He knew that these two renegades, young as they were, with their whole lives ahead of them, would have ruthlessly killed him and the others in his party if he hadn't killed them first.

He dragged the bodies off the trail, leaving them to the scavengers, and headed after his group. He hoped this incident wasn't an omen of more to come.

CHAPTER 19

CAMERON'S GROUP FOLLOWED a faint wagon trail into a canyon where cedars and cotton-woods grew along an arroyo and where a sprawling dead oak was peppered with crows. The crows lifted, cawing raucously, when the party neared the tree.

Cameron was trailing his mule beside Clark. Hotchkiss and Marina were riding drag. Jimmy Bronco rode point, scanning the rims around them where Indians could be hiding. Cameron didn't like the way Jimmy kept his hand on the butt of one of his six-shooters, as if ready to draw at any moment.

He knew the kid was just being vigilant, but he might be a little too vigilant. If one of the others cleared his throat too loudly he was liable to get shot.

"Who is this man whose ranch we're heading for?" Clark asked Cameron.

"Alfred Going. He's about my age, a little older—a Mex from a little village in Chihuahua, but he was raised by Apaches that kidnapped him when he was just a tyke. He and I scouted together one summer, up near Apache Pass, the first time the Army tried to haze the Chiricahuas to San Carlos. We tracked some renegades that separated from the pack and lit out for Mexico."

Cameron shook his head. "That was one bloody summer. We led up a troop from Camp Grant—most of 'em, other than the chief trumpeter and the sergeant-major, greener 'n spring peas. One mornin', me and Alfred scouted up a watershed east of where we'd bivouacked. I told the sergeant-major to stay put till we got back. We were afraid that if the group we were after wasn't east, they'd be north, and he'd run right into 'em in bad country.

"Well, my horse got gutted by a mountain lion, so Alfred and I were late getting back to the bivouac, and guess what? The sergeant-major got itchy feet and went on ahead. Three miles out, he got ambushed at Soogan Creek. The Apaches were waitin' in the rimrocks—had 'em completely surrounded. Alfred and I could hear the guns and the Apache war cries, the horses and men screamin', from a long ways away. By the time we got there, it was all over. Half the detail was lying in the water, and the Apaches had disappeared like they hadn't even been there."

"And the sergeant?"

Cameron shook his head. "Didn't make it. He was a good man. He just got itchy feet. It happens."

"Is that what I have, Cameron? Itchy feet?" Clark asked, with a trace of humor.

"No, you got gold fever. But it amounts to the same thing in Apache country: death."

"I didn't think there were that many Apaches left out here."

"There aren't, but it doesn't take that many. Besides, you have the rurales, the federalistas, and the revolutionaries to worry about. Not to mention the sheer remoteness of the place, and the treacherous trails. If one doesn't kill you, another will."

Clark smiled confidently. "For as much gold as

we're going to find, Jack—you mind if I call you Jack?—it's worth the risk."

Cameron steered his horse off the trail to let Clark and his mule pass through a narrowing between the arroyo and a mound of dry river wash. Then he caught up to him again.

"You see any action?" Cameron asked him.

"No," Clark said, a little defensively.

Cameron had already figured as much. Men like Clark often bought their way out of battle. If he'd fought, he wouldn't have been as eager to tear off with an attractive woman like his wife into Apache- and revolution-ravaged Mexico. He'd have a deeper appreciation for life. He'd know how much even the mother lode was really worth.

But Cameron was glad Clark hadn't fought, because Clark's lack of fear and good horse sense was going to lead Cameron to Bachelard. Hell, it might even lead him to gold he wouldn't otherwise have gone after.

"Stop right there or we blow your heads off!" a man's voice sounded from somewhere ahead.

"Jimmy, keep it holstered!" Cameron yelled at the boy, whose right pistol was half out of its holster. The boy froze and looked at Cameron, his face flushed with alarm.

Cameron had recognized the voice. Apparently Hotchkiss had, as well; he gave a high-pitched laugh as he reined his horse to a halt. Cameron stopped his own horse and waved an arm, looking around for a face in the rimrocks ahead on both sides of the canyon.

"Alfred! It's Jack Cameron."

The man yelled something, in what sounded to Cameron like Apache and Papago mixed with English. Then, as he moved, Cameron spotted him, on the rimrock on the right side of the canyon. The man waved a hand and yelled lazily, "Hey, Jack—what brings you way out here, amigo?"

Cameron cupped his hands around his mouth and replied, "Your cooking, you old heel squatter."

There was movement to his left. Cameron saw someone else in the rocks—a short, round figure with a rifle, on what appeared to be a burro. This had to be the person Alfred had yelled to in the strange mix of languages. Then Alfred and the other were both gone, disappeared behind the butte.

"Let's go," Cameron said to the others. "Jimmy, keep your hands off your guns."

Fifteen minutes later they came around a bend in the trail and saw the headquarters of the rancho. The adobe cabin, with a brush roof, two cactus corrals, and a mud barn, stood before a high limestone rock that loomed like a giant tongue frozen mid-lick, the tip of the tongue hanging about a thousand feet over the cabin.

The wind blew down the canyon, slapping the door of the ramshackle outhouse sitting by a gully that fell away to the right of the headquarters. On a small island of brush in the gully, several goats grazed. They turned their heads when they caught the scent of strangers on the wind, and bleated warily.

Cameron led his group toward the corral, where Alfred Going and an Indian woman were turning loose the horse and burro.

"Dichosos los ojos que te ven una vez mas, Jack," Going said, grinning broadly and moving away from the corral to greet the visitors. "Ah, how happy the eyes that gaze upon you once again."

He was a stocky, barrel-chested man with a double chin, a large round head with kind brown eyes, and a handlebar mustache that had gotten away from him. His hair was still black but his sideburns and mustache were going gray. He wore homespun clothes and a high-topped hat with a narrow crown and feathers in the band.

Smiling, Cameron dismounted and shook the man's hand. "Nice to see you, too, Toke. Been a while." Tokente was the man's Apache name—Toke, for short.

"When's the last time . . . ? Oh, I know, two summers ago you passed through here after you sold some mustangs in Mexico. Remember? You spent a day helping me bury cholla cactus around my chicken coop to keep the coyotes from digging in."

"How's that workin' out, anyway?"

"Pretty good. I ain't lost many chickens, but I seen some coyotes with some pretty sore snoots." Going smiled broadly, hunching up his shoulders, grinning with practically his whole body. His laughter was a soft, steady "heeeee."

"Looks like you got yourself a partner," Cameron told him, nodding at the woman forking hay into the corral. She was round as a barrel, and just over five feet tall, with straight black hair falling in a braid to her buttocks. She wore deerskin leggings and a deerskin poncho painted and decorated with porcupine quills. A necklace of wolf claws hung about her neck.

Going grinned again. "That's my wife, She-Bear. She's really something, Jack."

"She-Bear?"

"That's what I call her because I can't pronounce her Papago name—she's Papago, from over west—but it's fitting if you ask me. If ever a woman looked like a she-bear, it's She-Bear!"

Going smiled broadly and gave a self-satisfied "hee." Turning to the Indian woman, he said something in the strange mix of languages he'd used before. The woman dropped another forkful of hay over the corral, stood the fork against it, and started for the house with a lumbering gait.

Cameron could tell from her profile that whatever Going had rattled off to her had pleased her. A faint smile pulled at her cheeks and Cameron thought he could see some color there, as well. No doubt that was as much emotion as the obviously shy woman ever showed to strangers.

"She has a scar on her nose," Going said. "She was fighting another woman over me—a Puma at the trading post—and she almost got it bitten off!"

"Over *you?*"

"Hee." Going shrugged. "I appeal to women; another man would not understand."

"You can say that again, brother!" Hotchkiss said, coming up trailing his horse and shaking Going's hand. "How you been, Toke?"

"Me? How are you, you old gray-muzzled lobo!" Cameron introduced Jimmy Bronco and the Clarks, Going nodding graciously and smiling and welcoming everyone to his humble casa. Then Going turned to Cameron. "Where you folks going, anyway?"

"Mejico," Cameron said.

Going frowned curiously, as if to ask what all these gringos were doing heading for Mexico.

"It's a long story. We'll tell you over supper—if you don't mind us inviting ourselves, that is."

"I wouldn't have it any other way, brother," Going said. Gesturing to the tank beneath the windmill just beyond the corral, he added, "Help yourselves to a wash, then come inside and light a spell."

"Don't mind if we do," Cameron said.

He let the others go ahead. Going came up beside him and whispered conspiratorially, "That Señor Clark's wife, she is a good-looking woman, but much too skinny. You leave her here a couple days and let She-Bear put some tallow on her bones!"

"Nah, I don't think so," Cameron chuckled. "Hell, those women would get in one scrap after another over you."

"Ah . . ." Going said with a thoughtful nod. "Good thinking."

There was no room for seven people to eat comfortably in the cabin, so Cameron and Alfred Going set up a makeshift table of split logs and food barrels in the yard. She-Bear roasted three plump hens on a spit she built near the table, using mesquite deadfall she gathered in the gully.

While the chickens roasted, juices sizzling as they dribbled into the fire, Going and his visitors sat around the table, drinking wine and talking. When the sun went down, Going lit hung lanterns from the trees. The air freshened and cooled as the sky paled.

As the first stars winked to life in the east, She-Bear served the meat, along with roasted corn. The group dug in with their fingers, as the amenities did not include silverware—She-Bear could barely come up with enough plates and cups. The Indian woman spoke only to Going, when she spoke at all, and while she appeared sullen, Cameron knew it was only because she was shy and awkward among strangers, as were most Indian women he had known. She would not have prepared this kind of meal for unwelcome guests.

Cameron instinctively liked the woman and thought Going had chosen a good wife, but he could not help stealing glances at the poor woman's nose, which bore distinct marks of teeth across the bridge and down the sides of both nostrils. If not for the scar, she would be pretty. Cameron wondered if she had indeed received the bite in a fight over Going, but doubted he'd ever really know. Going was a master jokester, and you never knew when he was serious.

When Cameron was not sneaking looks at She-Bear's nose, or busy listening to another of Going's stories about people he'd known, renegades he'd tracked, horses he'd ridden, women he'd loved, and the money he'd made in the mines, his gaze strayed to Marina. She smiled at Going and Hotchkiss's verbal sparring, throwing her hair back as she ate.

Once, as she tore meat from a bone with her thumb and index finger, looking down and frowning with the effort and against the pain of the hot meat, Cameron indulged in a study of her face. Marina lifted her head to drop a chunk of chicken into her mouth, and as she simultaneously chewed and sucked in air to cool the meat, she caught him staring.

She flushed and smiled. Before she looked away, Cameron felt her penetrating gaze as a sudden flash of fire, all the way to his bones.

When everyone had finished the main meal, She-Bear served queso de tuna, a traditional Mexican sweetmeat made from the fruit of the prickly pear cactus, and rich black coffee with goat's milk. Cameron savored every bite of the dessert, knowing it would probably be his last for several weeks, maybe a couple of months. It was a long way into the Sierra Madre, and a long way out again, with hidden perils all along the trail.

When the meal was finally finished, Going poured another round of wine for his guests while She-Bear cleared the table. Marina started to get up and help but was quickly pushed back into her chair by the grumbling She-Bear.

"Please, you can't do all this work alone," Marina objected in Spanish.

She-Bear turned away with an armload of plates. Going put his hand on Marina's wrist, grinning knowingly and wagging his head. Nothing would have embarrassed the Indian woman more, Cameron knew, than having a young lady of obvious aristocratic breeding help her with such menial chores as supper dishes.

"Clark, why don't you show Alfred your plat?" Cameron said.

Clark flushed in the lantern light playing across his face, and regarded Cameron gravely.

"It's all right," Cameron assured him. "He won't steal it from you."

Cameron had studied the map their first night on the trail, but as he'd expected, he hadn't recognized any of the crudely drawn landmarks. He'd journeyed into the Sierra Madre after Apaches, but he'd been too busy looking for Indian sign to notice much else. His own prospecting, years ago, had taken him farther west, into the Mojave Desert of California. He knew that if Clark had a chance of finding the X marked on the map, he'd have to have help from someone who knew the country and recognized at least one or two of the plat's represented landmarks. Cameron hoped his old friend Going would be that person.

Reluctantly Clark removed the pocket he'd sewn into his coat, undid the thong, and handed the map, copied on a large sheet of parchment, to Going, who accepted it soberly. Going shoved his cup and wine bottle aside and drew a lantern near, then unrolled the wrinkled paper on the table before him, weighting the ends with cups.

"Any of those figures mean anything to you, Toke?" Cameron asked after a while.

Going was studying the turtle in the bottom right corner. Furrows in the bridge of his nose deepened and his jaw loosened as he considered the curious mark.

"This figure here I recognize," he said slowly. "I saw it drawn on some rocks not far from the village of San Cristóbal when I was digging for gold. Just some figures drawn by the ancients," he added with a shrug.

"Have you seen it anywhere else?" Clark asked.

Going pursed his lips, thinking, and shrugged. "No . . . I don't think so."

Cameron sighed and pushed a fork around with his thumb. "There was a miner in the Mojave some years ago. He marked the way to his placer by chiseling little stick figures into the nearby rocks, sort of like Hansel and Gretel dropping crumbs to find their way in the forest. Each one was a little different, depending on how close they were to the mine. They were his secret code, so he could find his way back to the place after shipping out a load of ore."

"You think that's what these are?" Going said, pressing an index finger to the turtle on the map.

"Could be," Cameron said with a shrug. Clark was studying him thoughtfully, eyes bright with hope. "I still don't believe there's gold, you understand," Cameron said to him. "But if there is gold, that mark might lead the way."

Clark nodded slowly. "Of course."

Marina's eyes brightened as she studied the map before Going. "Sí," she whispered. Turning slowly to Cameron, she said, "I have seen the turtle. When I was a child, my father would take me on his hunting trips to the mountains." She shook her head, awestruck. "I had forgotten."

"Were they near this village of San Cristóbal?" Cameron asked her.

She frowned and shook her head. "I remember a village, but I do not remember which one. I was too young."

Clark turned to her sharply. "You must remember, Marina, please!"

"Was it in a valley closed off from the south by three sharp peaks?" Going asked her.

Marina was frowning and studying the table, trying to remember. "I . . . I think so . . . sí," she said, lifting her eyes to Going's. They grew bright with recollection.

"You are looking for the Lost Church of San Bernardo," Going said to Clark, a knowing smile growing on his lips. "Hee."

"You know it?" Clark asked with some urgency.

Going spread his hands. "Who does not know the legend?"

"Have people tried to find it?"

"Of course, señor. But most people believed it was south of San Cristóbal, behind those three peaks. That was what the Jesuit register said in Mexico City. But you know you can never trust the word of a monk. Hee."

"You think there's a possibility it's really there . . . somewhere?" Cameron asked, unable to keep a growing touch of eagerness from his voice.

"You know me, Jack," Going said. "I am just a superstitious old heathen with gold on the brain. I will believe anything until it is proven false."

Marina looked at him urgently. "Please, Señor Going. Lead us to the turtles carved in the rocks. I would not remember the way."

"Hee. That is Apache country. Not to mention that it is also the home of much revolutionary fighting. Hell, there are even scalp-hunters out there, and with a scalp like mine"—Going ran a big hand over his thick black hair—"they might mistake me for an Apache."

"If there's gold out there, we'll find it ourselves," Cameron said to Marina with a thin smile, sneaking a look at Going.

Predictably, the short, stout man jumped to his feet. "Not without me you won't!"

"Wait a minute!" Clark objected, casting an angry look at Cameron.

"You know how big that country is?" Cameron said. "We could spend years scouring one small section of it and coming up with nothing but Apache arrows."

"I don't like the idea of splitting the gold up any more than I have to," Clark said, nonplussed.

Going grinned and said slowly to Clark, in a hushed, reverent tone, "If there is as much gold at San Bernardo as the legend says there is, you could bring the whole Mexican army into the search and still make out a millionaire, señor."

Clark studied the man for a long time, his expression softening. Stifling a deep-throated cough, he poured more wine and threw it back.

Going smiled across the table at Cameron. "Hee," he said.

"It's settled, then," said Marina, relieved, ignoring the look of irritation her husband shot her as he poured more wine.

CHAPTER 20

CAMERON AND THE others were waiting for Alfred Going to finish using the outhouse, around which three goats grazed in the morning sun. The rest of the group was mounted and ready to go.

Going had decided at the last minute—he already had mounted his horse, in fact—to take his constitutional, and the others waited self-consciously. Cameron held the reins of the Mexican's horse; Clark, Marina, Hotchkiss, and Jimmy Bronco sat their tail-whipping mounts by the corral, Clark coughing into his handkerchief every few minutes.

Hotchkiss made small talk with Marina until there was nothing left to say. Finally he asked Cameron, with a touch of anger, "Did he always do this when you were getting ready to go somewhere?"

"Yeah . . . I guess I'd forgot," Cameron said regretfully. "If I'd've remembered, don't think I would have pushed him to come along."

"A damned annoying habit," Hotchkiss allowed.

The outhouse door squawked open and out stepped Going, buckling his gunbelt around his waist and adjusting the soft leather holster on his hip.

"Thought you fell in," Hotchkiss groused.

"Sorry to keep you waiting," said Going. "She-Bear's huevos rancheros sometimes have a bad effect."

"Ain't you gonna tell her good-bye?" Cameron asked him.

Climbing into his saddle, Going shook his head. "She-Bear, like many Indians, does not believe in good-byes. I told her I was going, so she knows that I am going and that, if the Creator wills it, I will return." He accepted his reins from Cameron and touched his steel-dust gelding with his heels.

"I bet she'd like to shoot me for stealing you away from her," Cameron said.

"Of course she would," Going said, chuckling. "What woman would want to see a man like me ride away? But I appeased her by telling her I would come back rich, and that lifted her spirits. She-Bear is a greedy woman—truly an oddity among her people. Once she told me she'd like to live in a city and dress like a white woman. Hee."

A few miles south of his ranch, Going led the group off the freight trail. Cameron was wary. You didn't leave the main trails in this part of the country unless you knew exactly where you were going. The main trails usually led to water and if you left them you had to be sure that your bushwhacking would lead you to springs or creeks, or you would die. It was as simple as that.

Cameron and Going were riding about fifty yards ahead of the others when Cameron said, "You have a trail mapped out in your head?"

Going turned to him with his wide smile. "Don't worry, amigo. I know where I am going. You forget, I grew up in this country."

Cameron shrugged. "Yeah, I know you did. I just hope you remember where to find water."

"I know where to find water. And, just as well, I know where *not* to find Apaches. Apaches have been raiding along the freight roads lately, and I've seen a couple of rancherias along water courses. There has been some rain lately, so the basins should be filled, and that will allow us to stay away from the river-beds and the main springs where the Apaches will go for water."

Cameron nodded, satisfied his old Mexican friend had not lost his touch. He held his hand out to the man. "Toke, your bowel peculiarities aside, I'm glad you're along."

"Me too. She-Bear I love with all my heathen soul, but it is nice to be trailing again," Going said, shaking Cameron's hand and grinning. "But that woman—Señor Clark's wife—she has her eye on me. I know, I can tell these things. You better tell her that, as desirous as I am, I am no man to get entangled with." His voice grew dark as he dragged out the words, shaking his head: "She-Bear is a very jealous woman."

Cameron glanced back at Marina following her husband on her white-footed black. Jimmy Bronco was jawing at her, probably bragging about his lightning-fast draw.

"Yeah, I'll . . . uh . . . tell her," Cameron said.

They rode on, mile by slow mile passing beneath them, taking their time and saving their horses. They all kept a sharp eye on the rolling desert stretching around them, an endless, brassy waste broken by distant mountain ranges, great heaps of rock scattered over the desert floor, and huge spines of red-and-black volcanic dikes poking up from the sand, like the backs of half buried dinosaurs. Occasional playas showed in sinks when they climbed a grade—bleached desert lakebeds in which very little, if anything, grew, and around which the long-defunct waves had deposited ridges of polished rock.

The sand was etched with the tracks of deer,

Gila monsters, coyotes, wolves, and the occasional scratches and blood smears where a raptor had descended on prey.

Cameron was watching for signs of human presence—the prints of moccasins or horses—when he realized they were indeed following a trail, albeit an ancient one, threading around ocotillo and cholla clumps.

Cameron was grateful for the brush but knew that while it concealed him and his group, it could also conceal twenty or thirty Apaches who might have spied them from a ridge. It was true that most of the Apaches had been driven away from the region— some had even been shipped all the way to a reservation in Florida—but renegades and misfits remained. Cameron just hoped none were of Perro Loco's caliber.

In the early afternoon, when the heat became too intense for safe travel, the group descended an arroyo choked with mesquite and papache shrubs, and built a small fire for coffee. They ate beans, tortillas, and dried fruit, and napped in the shade beneath the shrubs. After a quarter hour, Going woke. He rolled a couple of cigarettes from his tobacco, which smelled sweetly of apples, and handed one to Cameron.

"We'll hit the Bavispe in a few days," he said quietly, to keep from waking the others.

"Where it curves south?" Cameron asked, taking a drag off the cigarette.

"*Sí.* We'll follow it into the foothills. I'll feel better in that country."

"How's that?"

"More places to hide."

Cameron nodded.

"It will be nice to bathe in the river," Going said,

sniffing his armpit. "My first day on the trail and already I smell like a horse."

Cameron smiled at him. "That She-Bear's gone and civilized you."

"Sí." Going nodded. "When are you going to get civilized, Jack?"

Cameron shrugged and looked off thoughtfully. "I reckon I ain't the civilizin' type."

"You just need the right woman," Going said. He glanced at Marina, sleeping under her hat. "Too bad that one is married, no?"

"She's not my type anyway," Cameron said. He flushed a little, felt adrenaline spurt in his veins. No, she wasn't his type, he thought. She hadn't been dead for six years.

He waited another half-hour, then woke the others, kicked sand on the fire, and they started down the trail once again.

Four hours later the sun waned behind a red spine of rock in the west, purpling the desert. The heat went with the sun and the horses quickened at the freshening breeze. Quail called and deer came out to graze a grassy flat stretching northward, the sage showing silvery in the blond, sun-gilded forage. There wasn't a cloud in the softening sky.

When the trail Going was following was no longer visible, the party camped in a hollow where boulders and brush hid them from view, and built a small fire over which they brewed coffee and fried bacon.

Cameron unsaddled his horse and picketed the animal in the smattering of grass available. He shucked his rifle from its boot and walked back along their trail for half a mile. Standing on a low rise, he watched and listened for anyone who might be following them.

Satisfied they were alone, at least for now, he

headed back to camp. He set his rifle down and ate one of the biscuits Marina had prepared with bacon, and accepted the coffee she poured.

"Thanks," he said.

They were the first words he'd said to her all day, having wanted to keep his distance from her. Like Going had reminded him, she was married. It might not have been a marriage made in heaven, but it was marriage nonetheless.

"De nada," she said, smiling slightly and meeting his gaze just for a moment.

Was it his imagination or was he falling in love with her? Or was he just aroused by the way she filled out her white blouse and the way her wool skirt pushed against her legs as she moved? Whatever it was, he had to admit that being around her, even when he was trying to ignore her, made him feel more alive than he'd felt in one long, lonely stretch of time.

Grumbling to himself, he turned away and drifted off to drink his coffee and eat his sandwich. He and Hotchkiss were talking several yards beyond the fire when Going approached.

"Nice night, eh, amigos?"

"Right fine," Hotchkiss agreed.

Going sniffed the fresh air that smelled of creosote and the spicy mesquite burning in their campfire. "Ah . . . I have always loved camping in the desert on nights such as these. It brings a man back in touch with his Creator."

"It does, at that," Cameron said. "But I'd just as soon be sitting on my half-finished gallery, sipping tequila and watching the stars over Rockinstraw Mountain." And hearing Jimmy shoot rats down at the trash heap by lantern light, he thought.

"What about the gold?" Going asked him. "In a few weeks, if the map is true, you will be a rich man."

Cameron looked at his Mexican friend. "I'm not out here for the gold, Toke. I should've told you that before, but I'm telling you now."

"I suspected as much," Going said, pursing his lips knowingly. "I know you too well to believe that you would come down here, risking Apaches and rurales, to chase a legend and some figures on a map. Maybe a few years ago, but not now. I can see it in your eyes, Jack. You have lost your—" He looked around, searching for the right word. "—your sense of *romance*. I am sorry for you."

"Yeah, well, just the same, I think you should know I'm going after Gaston Bachelard."

Going frowned. "Bachelard? The Confederate revolutionary? But why?"

Cameron told him about Bachelard following the Clarks and about how Pas Varas was killed.

"He has a copy of the map, so he'll be heading where we're heading. When we run into him, I'm gonna kill him."

Going leaned against a rock, tipped his hat back, and looked off. He sucked air through his teeth, whistling softly. "You're going to kill Gaston Bachelard? That is . . . That is damn near what I would call crazy, Jack. He has many men riding for him."

"I'm betting he'll bring a few, but not all. He won't trust that many men around as much gold as he believes lies behind the X on that map."

Hotchkiss sipped his coffee and cleared his throat. "That might be a mighty risky speculation, but I have a feelin' Jack's right," he told the Mexican.

Going chuckled darkly. "Well, I hope you and Bachelard don't ruin my . . . excuse me, *our* . . . chances at the gold."

Cameron laughed. "Me and Bud and the kid will have Bachelard otherwise occupied, you might say.

If things go as planned, he'll never get to the X. You and the Clarks can go about your excavations without hearing a peep out of him or any of his men. After I kill Bachelard, they'll be after me, and I'll lead them away from you."

"I don't know, Jack. That's Gaston Bachelard you're talking about. And Miguel Montana. Madre de Dios."

Cameron put his hand on Going's shoulder. "Don't worry about it, Toke. You leave them to me and Hotch. You just get us to the X, and if there's any gold out there, you can have my share."

"Well, he can't have mine!" Hotchkiss nearly yelled. "I want to see that murderin' son of a bitch as dead as you do, but hell, I'm lookin' to retire and whore around Flagstaff till my noodle rots off."

Roughly two miles west of Cameron's bivouac, in the lee of a rocky knoll, Jake Hawkins sat around a small fire he'd built in the hole some creature had clawed out for a bed. He was running a rod down the barrel of his big Sharps .56, cleaning the old gun.

The only way you could depend on a gun firing a straight round was by keeping the barrel clean, not gummed up the way his dim brother Ed allowed his guns to get. Then the moron would wonder why the stage driver or freighter he'd shot at didn't so much as blink when Ed tried to pink him from a hill or ridgetop!

Jake took a swig from the bottle by his knee, gave a contented sigh as the liquor plunged down his throat, sending a pleasing chill through his spine. He'd just set the bottle back down by his knee and corked it when he heard twigs snapping and brush rustling somewhere on the other side of the fire.

Instinctively he put his hand on the butt of the Deane-Adams he'd stolen from an Englishman riding the Hatch and Hodges stage line from Contention to Tucson, but didn't bother to draw. Only one man in all the Southwest could possibly make as much noise on a quiet desert night as the one approaching him now.

"Well, I walked a complete circle around the camp and didn't see hide nor hair of a thing," Ed Hawkins said as he appeared through the brush, stepping into the small circle of wavering orange firelight. He plopped himself on a rock, breathing as though he'd run five miles, saying, "Heard a bat flappin' around and a coyote howling for some nooky, but that's about all."

"You know, if I was anybody but me you'd be dead right now," Jake said.

Ed looked at him, puzzled. "What are you talkin' about?"

"The way you just sauntered up to the fire just now, kicking every rock within ten feet, snappin' every branch, and pushin' through the brush like some clumsy ol' Missouri mule."

"Oh, come on, Jake. You knew it was me out there."

"Yeah, I knew it was you because of all the noise you made."

"Well, if I wouldn'ta made so much noise, you mighta gone and shot me!" Ed said, as though he were trying to convey a simple message to an ornery child.

Jake leaned forward and looked angrily into his brother's eyes below the tattered brim of Ed's faded derby hat, which had also come from the Englishman. "Don't make so fucking much noise!" Jake hissed.

"Okay, Jake. Don't get so damn mad." Ed gestured to the bottle. "Pass it over 'fore you hog it all."

When Jake slapped the bottle into Ed's hand, Ed uncorked it and took a long pull. Smacking his lips and recorking the bottle, he said, "You're just mad over what happened in town. But if I told you once, I'll tell ya again, there wasn't no way in heaven or hell I was gonna start anything with Jack Cameron right there on the street. He woulda shot me first and then you!"

"The truth is, Ed, you're a coward," Jake mused.

"You can call me names all you want, but if I was as trigger-happy and hotheaded as you, you and me would both of us be dead, not on Cameron's trail like we are now. We wouldn't know where those two Clark people are headin' for, all bound and determined like they are. You think they woulda hired us after a shoot-out on Main Street with Cameron, even after learnin' who we are?"

Ed wagged his head. "No sir. Brother, the way things stand now, we can trail those people all the way to wherever the hell they're goin', get whatever the hell they're goin' to get after they done got it, and kill Cameron to boot! Back-shoot him, which is just exac'ly what he deserves."

Jake had finished cleaning the barrel and was now rubbing the stock of his Sharps with a rag he'd dipped in linseed oil. He had to admit, his brother had a point.

"Yeah, well," he growled, "things sure woulda been a lot easier if Cameron wouldn't've come along in the first place."

"They sure woulda," Ed agreed. He fished in the pocket of his canvas coat for jerky.

"As soon as I would've found out where they're headed and what they're headed for—it has to be gold or they woulda told me—we coulda killed Mr. Fancy-Pants and had us a party with the girl all the way to old Mexico and back." Jake shook his head hard. "Damn—that's a fine-lookin' woman! Gives me the shakes just thinkin' about what I could be doin' with her right now."

Ed tipped back the tequila and stared into the fire, eyes glazing with thoughts of Clark's lovely young Mexican wife, imagining what a woman like that would look like stripped naked and tied to a tree, maybe, or staked out on the ground. Screamin' and squirmin', pleadin' for her life.

He'd never had any women but whores. His stepsister did him once, back in Kansas, but she'd been big as a heifer and smelled like pig shit.

"I can't wait to catch up with them folks," Ed said, and took another savory pull from the bottle.

Jake grabbed the tequila away from him. "Yeah, well, if you plan on catchin' up to 'em at all, you better learn how to move quiet, you lummox!"

CHAPTER 21

———◆———

MARINA WASN'T SURE what to make of Jack Cameron.

They had been on the trail together now for over a week and he had hardly said two words to her. She could see that he was by nature a taciturn man, but sometimes she sensed that he was attracted to her, only to have her intuition undercut by the way he ignored her.

Maybe he disapproved of how she had married Clark in return for his promise to help her find the gold and get her daughter back. Cameron probably saw her as an opportunistic harlot ready to offer her body to any man who might help her get what she wanted. He must think her no better than the fallen angels swarming around every brothel and cantina on the border, little better than the shapely young blonde at the boarding house in Contention City, whom Marina had seen enter Cameron's room late that Sunday morning.

Every time she thought of Cameron—and she'd found herself thinking of him more and more—she thought of that girl. The memory of her entering Cameron's room was annoying, but she wasn't sure why. She guessed she must be jealous, but that would mean she felt something for Cameron, and that could not be.

She hadn't felt an attraction for any man since she had been fourteen and fallen in love with a handsome, young vaquero who'd worked for her father. He'd been too shy, and too afraid of her father, to approach her. She'd never felt anything more than mild disdain for any man she'd met since the Apaches had attacked her family's rancho. She'd been sixteen then.

Four years later, here she was, riding in search of gold and freedom for her daughter. That was all that mattered to her . . . Wasn't it?

Cameron and Going were scouting ahead. Hotchkiss and Jimmy Bronco rode point while Clark paced Marina at a steady walk, every hour or so taking a pull from one of his brandy bottles.

Clouds were building in the west, and the breeze smelled faintly of wet sage and rain. They would have a damp night, Marina feared. But the water basins upon which they relied would be fresh, making tomorrow's travel easier on the horses and mules.

She was staring thoughtfully at three hawks or vultures—it was hard to tell from this distance—circling off the right side of the trail when she heard horses approaching. Cameron and Going were returning from up the trail, their lathered horses blowing, heads sagging.

Going's horse was favoring its right front hoof. When the Mexican had brought the mount to a halt, he climbed down and lifted the hoof in question.

"Shoe's shot," he said to Cameron. "I'll have to hammer it back on until I can get another one forged."

Cameron nodded. "There's a cave about two miles northeast, up a little canyon," he told the group. "Why don't you rest while I go take a look?"

"Can I ride with you, Mr. Cameron?" Marina asked.

She wanted only to leave the trail for a while, to do a little exploring like she'd done back on her father's rancho. Adrian looked at her and wrinkled his brow disapprovingly, but before her husband could say anything, Cameron replied, "As long as you stay close."

Not casting another glance at her husband, for fear of what he might see in her eyes, Marina spurred the black and followed Cameron up the trail.

They rode single file, not saying anything. Cameron swung his buckskin toward the northeast, following a shallow cut through chalky buttes spiked with several different types of cactus and low-growing juniper. A few gnarled post oaks and willows lined the trail, growing in number as the riders wound through the cut and into a ravine opening between two granite monoliths.

A quarter mile up the ravine, a cave opened on their right—a large crescent worn away by millennia of wind and rain. Large slabs of orange sandstone hooded the entrance.

A freshening wind, heavy with the odor of desert rain, blew down the ravine, giving Marina a chill and a sudden sense of the antiquity of the place. It was the kind of poignant feeling—raw, innocent, and breathtaking in its fleeting power—she hadn't felt since she was a child.

Cameron dismounted, handed her his reins, and told her to wait. She watched him climb the sandy embankment to the cave, where he peered cautiously around—looking for what, Marina wasn't sure. But it was obvious he knew this wild country in all its moods, had identified many of its dangers.

He was a strong, powerful man—half-wild, like his desert-born mustang—and Marina felt unsure of herself around him. At the same time he made her feel safe. Even out here, in this wild no-man's-land, he made her feel safer than she'd felt in years.

He walked beyond the cave, then turned and started back. As he walked toward her, stepping around boulders and avoiding cacti, he caught her staring at him. She did not turn away. Something would not let her turn away.

He came on, glancing at the ground occasionally to consider the trail, but mostly keeping his eyes on hers. His face was expressionless but his eyes were grave.

He approached her and stopped, his sweaty buckskin tunic sticking to his broad, muscled chest which rose and fell as he breathed. Small lines spoked around the greenness of his eyes. Dropping her gaze, she stared at the Colt pistol on his hip and the big, horn-handled bowie in a broad, sun-faded leather sheath.

He poked his hat back, revealing a clean sweep of tan forehead, and reached out to her with his right hand.

She offered him his horse's reins but he took her hand instead, tugging gently. Her heart quickened and her breath grew shallow. Her knees weakened as she threw her right leg over the horn of her saddle and slid slowly down, his hand holding hers for balance.

Standing there before him, smelling the sweat-and-horse-and-leather smell of him, her head coming up to just below his chin, she could not look up. Her ears were ringing and she felt suddenly deathly afraid of this man. But then she realized that the fear was not of him so much as of herself, of the passion she felt stirring deep within her, threatening to bubble to the surface.

Casually, with both sun-darkened, thick-callused

hands, he swept her hair back from her face. With the index finger of his right hand he gently lifted her chin until their eyes met.

He bent down and kissed her, softly at first. Then, as he wrapped his heavy, sweat-damp arms around her, pulling her roughly to him, his mouth opened as it pressed against hers.

She felt as though she'd been struck by lightning. Reacting to the passion she felt, she threw her arms around him and returned his kiss with equal fervor, running her hands over his shoulders and down his back.

Then, breathlessly, she struggled out of his grip and pushed him away. She pressed the back of her hand to her mouth, her mind swirling, her ears still ringing, heart pounding.

Marina turned quickly and mounted her horse. Not waiting for Cameron, she spurred the black down the trail, toward her waiting husband. Tears rolled down her cheeks. Her heart was breaking and she did not know why. All she knew was that she suddenly felt afraid, sad, and very confused.

She needed to be alone.

She turned off the trail, into a slight cleft in the hills, and dismounted. She sat on the talus-scarred hillside, reins in her hands, and put her head down on her knees and cried.

Cameron stood frozen, watching Marina gallop away.

"You goddamn moron," he said to himself.

He kicked a rock and cursed again. What the hell was he doing, anyway, kissing another man's wife? Scared the hell out of her too, it looked like. She probably thought he was going to rape her.

But he hadn't been able to help it. When he'd seen the way she was looking at him—her smoky dark eyes, her black hair hanging across her shoulders—he'd felt possessed, driven to her as though he were a piece of driftwood in a raging rapids.

He hadn't been able to help himself.

Well, now he'd better help himself. When she got back to the group and told her husband what he'd done, Clark would probably try to shoot him, and Cameron could not blame the man.

So here's what your damn life has led to, he thought. Getting shot by an angry husband whose wife you tried to maul.

There wasn't much he could do but face the music, so he cussed again, mounted his horse, and started off down the trail, feeling as guilty as a schoolboy on his way home to his parents with an angry note from his teacher.

But when he rejoined the others, who were resting their horses and mules in some brush, Marina wasn't there.

"Where's your wife?" he asked Clark, a little sheepishly.

"I was about to ask you the same thing," Clark said, rising from where he'd been sitting, half a piece of jerky in his hand.

Cameron jerked his horse around and was about to spur the buckskin back up the trail when Marina appeared, cantering around a butte. Cameron exhaled slowly with relief, squinting at her. She rode up and stopped, looking a little pale but forcing a smile.

"Sorry," she said. "I had to take a side trip . . . to answer a call of nature."

Clark erupted in a fit of coughing. When it subsided he swallowed several times and rasped, "Good

God, I almost had a stroke," he said, grabbing and uncorking his bottle. "I thought Indians had gotten you."

"I am sorry, I didn't mean to frighten anyone," Marina said, sliding her gaze from him to Cameron, then turning sharply away.

"The cave looks good," Cameron said to the group. "Let's head out."

He glanced at Hotchkiss, who grinned knowingly. Cameron turned away from him and headed up the trail.

Marina fell in beside him. "I am sorry," she said softly.

"No, I'm sorry," he said, not looking at her. "I was out of line."

"No, you were not."

Behind them, just out of earshot, Clark watched them closely.

He had suspected that some feeling, a mutual attraction, was growing between his wife and Cameron, but he couldn't explain why. He couldn't pin his hunch on anything conclusive—maybe it was just the way Cameron had been trying so hard to ignore her, or the way Marina turned shy whenever Cameron was in the vicinity. He'd tried to ignore it, because he knew he was prone to irrational jealousy and that Cameron was just the sort of man who brought it out in him.

But when Cameron had ridden up, Clark had seen something wrong in his eyes. Something had happened between them. Something emotional. He could see it now in Marina, as well. It was no call of nature that had waylaid her.

Or was it? Maybe that's really all it was, and Clark was just feeling those old defensive feelings he'd grown up with, the sense that he did not quite measure up to others, the sense that, because his father had always paved his way and made things as easy as he could for his only son, that others saw the weakness in Adrian's eyes and did not respect him.

That's why he had wanted Marina. A woman like that—strong, intelligent, beautiful—might bring him the respect and admiration he so craved. Winning a woman like that—never mind that he'd won her in poker, something no one need ever know—was akin to winning a war.

Now he saw in Marina's eyes what he'd been wanting to see since he'd first laid eyes on her; only, the warmth in her gaze was not for him. It was for Cameron.

And the powerful, passionate feelings he'd sensed in Cameron were the feelings Clark wanted to feel for Marina, but didn't. He'd never been able to give himself, heart and mind, to a woman. He suspected that this, too, had something to do with his father's own relentless wariness of others.

Perversely, Clark didn't want anyone else loving Marina, either. He wished now they'd never met Jack Cameron. Because no matter how much the thought appalled him, Clark was going to have to kill the man.

CHAPTER 22

PERRO LOCO WAS alive and well and riding hell-for-leather toward Contention City.

He knew that's where Cameron was heading, and he wanted—needed—to kill the frontiersman who had shamed him. Killing Cameron was the only way the Apache could get his honor back—and get it back he would, or die.

Vengeful purpose fairly boiled in his blood. He ground his heels into the sides of one of the mules he'd stolen from two miners he'd run into two days after he'd regained consciousness in the gorge where Cameron had left him for dead. The other mule was tied to the tail of the first, following the Apache across the scorching, undulating desert.

The fall into the gorge had fractured Perro Loco's skull, cracked several of his ribs, and broken his front teeth. After a desperate struggle under the baking sun, the Apache had found a cave where the body of an old Indian moldered. The man had broken his leg so that the bones had split the skin and drained his blood. Fortunately for Perro Loco, the old one had died before he'd eaten all the dried mule meat in the elkskin sack around his neck.

Loco slept in the cave for two days and a night. Then he wrapped his ribs in a strip of elkskin he'd cut from the dead one's tunic. The hide collected his own body's moisture and dried, tightening to hold his ribs in place. He relied on his own stubborn will and overpowering sense of purpose to kill the pain in his head and jaw.

Three hours after he'd left the miners' bodies for nature to dispose of, the first mule stumbled onto its knees and rolled to its side, its breath shallow, its eyes rolling up into its head. Its mouth and nose were covered with blood-flecked foam.

The Apache removed the mule's blanket and threw it over the second one, a hammerheaded dun with spindly legs. Then he mounted up and continued the breakneck pace until that animal, too, suddenly halted in spite of Loco's fierce kicks to its ribs.

Its head went up with a sigh as it teetered. Cursing, the Indian dismounted and removed the blanket from the mule's back as the dun slowly toppled like an ancient wickiup in the wind.

"Goddamn white-man's mules," Perro grumbled in Apache.

Fortunately, he'd ridden nearly fifty miles and figured he had only twenty-five more between him and where he was bound—the rancho where the old half-breed tracker Tokente lived.

Perro Loco knew the man had scouted with Cameron, and knew that if Cameron was heading to Sonora with a treasure map—he'd learned this from Bachelard the night the Cajun had freed him—he would no doubt look up his old scouting partner along the way. From the Mexican, Perro Loco would learn exactly where Cameron was headed. At the very least, he would have fresh tracks to follow.

Tokente would have fresh mounts for him to filch, as well.

Loco decided to take the death of the second mule

as an opportunity to rest and to eat. Plucking the miner's bowie knife from its scabbard, the Indian knelt at the mule's sweat-lathered rear and cut several strips of flesh from the still-spasming hip. He sat in the shade of a large, flame-shaped rock and ate the strips of mule meat raw, going back for seconds and thirds and wiping the blood from his hands when he finished.

He drank from the waterskin and set off on foot, making the little village of Wilcox well after dark. He skirted the town's perimeter, stepping quietly, watching the lighted windows around him, until he came to a stable behind a clapboard house with a flagstone walk leading to the outhouse. A white man who could afford such a house could afford good horses.

There were four horses stabled in the dark building, but Perro Loco took only three, as the fourth was so spooked at the Indian's presence that it threatened to tear apart its stall. Perro Loco had the other three bridled and tied nose-to-tail when he heard a door slap shut.

"Harlan, what's going on? Is that you?" a man called.

Perro Loco wasted no time in mounting the first horse and lighting out with a yell his excitement and Apache fury could not contain. He was beyond the town and heading south across the country in seconds.

The first two horses had given out and Loco was riding the third when he topped the ridge overlooking Tokente's cabin and barn, where the pale figures of goats grazed in the misty, lightening darkness.

Loco dismounted, slapped the horse away, and squatted on his haunches. He'd relieved the two miners he'd killed of their shotgun, and the double-bored beast now lay across his knees as he watched the cabin for movement. He could smell bacon in the smoke curling from the chimney. Tokente must be home. Had Cameron already come and gone?

He found a trail and stole down the ridge, keeping a watchful eye on the cabin and outbuildings, and made his way to the cactus corral, where four horses munched fresh hay. Tracks in the powdered dust of the yard told Loco that several more horses and mules had ridden out four or five days ago. The size and shape of the fresh moccasin prints near the corral told him that the person who had pitched hay to the horses that morning had been a woman.

Maybe Tokente had a woman. Maybe that woman was here, alone . . .

The latch on the cabin door clicked and the door scraped open. Loco squatted down behind the feed trough. A stout Indian woman in deerskins swung the door wide and chocked it open with a rock. She stood on the gallery, facing the yard, fists on her hips, sniffing the breeze and looking around. Had she sensed his presence? Loco wondered.

He clenched his jaws and fingered the trigger of his shotgun. Somewhere, a rooster crowed as the sun cleared the eastern ridge and gilded the brush growing from the cabin's sod roof.

The Apache's tension eased when the woman turned to her right, stepped off the gallery, and headed for a chicken coop set back in the shrubs flanking the cabin. She disappeared in the brush, and Loco could hear the excited squawks of chickens.

Loco ran from behind the trough to the shadows of the barn, where he paused to study the cabin once more. Seeing and hearing nothing, he ran to the cabin, stepped softly onto the gallery, and peered in the open door. He turned his head to listen, holding his breath.

Nothing.

He stepped in, holding the shotgun before him, and checked each of the tiny rooms. Finding no one, he went to the window that looked out on the front yard, and waited, holding the shotgun low across his knees.

Finally the woman appeared, slapping dust from her leggings. She drank at the well in the front yard, then started for the cabin. Stopping suddenly, as though realizing she'd forgotten something, she mumbled in Papago and started back to the coop.

Perro Loco stood crouched between the window and the door, waiting . . . Suddenly a floorboard squeaked behind him. A high-pitched, devilish shriek rattled his eardrums. He'd only begun to turn when a rifle exploded. The bullet made a furrow above his lip as he turned.

Behind him the woman stood, jacking another shell into the rifle's chamber.

Dropping his shotgun, Loco heaved the table toward the woman. As it struck her, knocking her back, her rifle went up and barked a round past Loco's head and into the adobe wall. The woman fell, yelling like some she-devil loosed from hell.

Loco scrambled over the table and on top of her. In seconds he had the rifle. He heaved the table away and pointed the rifle at the woman's throat.

The scar on the woman's nose was unsettling. This fat Papago was a warrior squaw, probably more treacherous in a fight than most men. Damn the luck.

Not knowing Papago he said in guttural, halting English, "Cameron—where?"

She scrunched up her eyes and shrieked.

Loco fired a round into the mashed earth beside her face. She blinked, but that was her only reaction. He grabbed one of her legs and dragged her out the door. She grabbed a gallery post. He had to yank several times before jerking her free. Then he dragged her squealing and cursing across the yard.

When he came to the barn, he turned and smashed the screaming woman in the face with the butt of the rifle. That knocked her semiconscious, silencing her.

He went into the barn, returning moments later with a rope, then lassoed one of the four horses in the corral. He saddled the horse with tack he'd found in the barn—an old Mexican saddle worn down to nothing in places—and dallied one end of the rope around the horn. He tied the other end of the rope around the woman's wrists.

Climbing into the saddle while the frightened horse sidestepped and crow-hopped, he gouged his heels into the animal's ribs. The horse bucked frantically and took off at a gallop, dragging the woman, who had regained consciousness, across the yard, then down the trail through the canyon.

The woman bounced over rocks and through brush, moaning and throwing up dust. "Wai-eeeee!" she screamed as she plowed through yucca and prickly pear.

Perro Loco halted the horse and turned to the woman, lying facedown in the dust. "Where go Cameron . . . Tokente?"

She-Bear had decided there was no point in resisting. He was Apache. That meant that no matter how strong she was, he would be stronger, and in the end he would either get the information he wanted, or he would kill her.

If she did not speak, he needed only to follow the tracks. It would take him longer, and rain might obliterate the trail, but chances were that he would still be able to follow Cameron and her man, To-kente, to Mexico.

She knew that the Apache would probably kill her no matter what she said, or did not say, but if she lived, she would have a chance of revenge. She might even be able to track him and kill him before he got to Cameron and her man.

"They go south, to . . . the Sierra Madre," she said thinly, glancing that way.

She lowered her swollen, bruised face and prayed that the savage would spare her.

The rope struck her head; the horse galloped back up the trail. Hope made her heart light. The Apache must have gone back to the corral for more horses. Still, he would have to pass this way on his way south, and he might kill her then.

With all the strength she could muster, She-Bear pushed herself to her feet and stumbled into a cleft in some rocks. She was only about twenty yards off the trail, and her tracks were obvious. If the Apache wanted her dead, she would be easy prey. But maybe he was too preoccupied with Cameron to waste any more time with her.

What was she but a fat, ugly Papago squaw?

Not too much later, the Apache rode down the trail, She-Bear's revolving Colt rifle slung from a rope around his neck, and trailing three of her best horses in a nose-to-tail string. He didn't so much as glance in her direction, and She-Bear bowed her head and thanked the Creator for saving her.

She promised the All-Knowing, All-Seeing One that she would repay him by ridding this world of the evil Apache who was obviously the son of the dark gods from below.

To that end, she struggled to her feet and started back to the cabin. There she would doctor her wounds and prepare for the hunt.

CHAPTER 23

DAY AFTER DAY Cameron's group angled southeast from the Mexican border across Sonora and into Chihuahua, where Alfred Going believed the treasure lay. The little village of San Cristóbal was not named on the map, but Going believed he knew the country the plat described.

Cameron was happy his old friend Tokente had come along. With each mile, each mountain crossing and saddle ford, it became more and more apparent to him that, on his own, Cameron would have gotten them lost. Worse, he might have led them to an Apache hideout.

As it was, they spotted no Apaches, besides the two Cameron had killed back in Arizona. They saw a few old moccasin prints and tracks made by unshod hooves, and, while scouting a side canyon, Hotchkiss stumbled upon human bones; arrows lay among the scattered remains. But no actual Indians were seen, and for that, the group was grateful.

They swam in the Rio Bavispe, a cool, green ribbon of seed- and leaf-flecked water angling through chalky buttes, then led the horses across. In a little village called Dublan, Clark traded his tired mules for fresh ones and Cameron bought two extra, mountain-bred horses for the trail. All the horses were reshod by a one-eyed blacksmith named Ambrosio, who sang Spanish ballads in a pitch-perfect tenor and smoked cigarillos rolled with corn husks.

At Ambrosio's insistence they ate with his family and slept in his stable. Before anyone else in the village had stirred the next morning, the treasure hunters saddled up, rigged the panniers to the mules, and were on their way.

Clark would have little to do with Cameron. Cameron assumed the Southerner suspected there were feelings between himself and Marina. There was little he could do to reassure the man—it was true, after all. Why make it worse by talking about it? When Bachelard was dead and they were all safely back in Arizona, with or without the gold, Cameron would simply take his leave of these people and try to forget that Marina had ever existed.

Meanwhile, Cameron and Marina kept their distance from each other. On the rare occasions when their eyes met, they both flushed a little and looked away, embarrassed about what had happened between them, wanting to forget. But while Cameron lay in his blankets at night, well back from the fire and a good distance from where she lay with her husband, he couldn't help remembering.

If he'd been clairvoyant he would have known that Marina, lying beside Clark, was thinking of him, as well . . . imagining herself wrapped in his arms . . . .

―――――――――

Late the next afternoon they swung deeper into the hills and the terrain grew more and more rough as they followed washed-out canyons and gullies between towering rock monoliths as big as houses. At noon Going led them up a dry creek that traced a zigzagging course through jagged walls of black basaltic rock blown out of the earth's center millions of years ago. They found themselves in a deep canyon.

Like the slash made by a giant knife, it was a forbidding place. The walls were black-speckled granite and sandstone. The caves carved from the terraced rock above were ruins left by the ancients, those the Indians called "those who came before."

No one knew who they were or why they had disappeared, but their stories of deer and bear hunts and battles with other tribes had been etched in the rock on both sides of the canyon. The sight gave Cameron a chill, like a bad premonition.

Going traced a winding course through the maze of rock until the canyon widened and a spring issued from a terraced, flinty wall upon which moss grew. Water prattled onto a bed of polished rock, pooling where the bed widened, and twisted a course down the canyon. They followed the stream through a defile wide enough for only one rider at a time, to a broad, deep pool on the other side.

The pool lay beneath the trail in a basin made from shelving black rock, and was surrounded by green grass, other springs, more ancient carvings.

Clark halted his pack train and dismounted in a hurry, fairly running to the pool and dipping his sunburned and peeling face in the tepid water. He shook his head like a horse and whooped.

"Take it easy," Cameron warned him. "There's plenty. Drink a little at a time or you're gonna get sick."

The man turned to him sharply and gave him a cold-eyed look of pure hatred. "You think I'm stupid?"

"I didn't say that," Cameron said, loosening his saddle cinch.

"I'm not as stupid as you think," Clark said, then

shunted his gaze to Marina. She looked away, and so did Clark, returning his face to the pool.

It was the first time he had openly indicated his jealousy. Cameron felt sick. He could see now that Clark was going to turn what had happened between him and Marina into a royal ugliness.

They picketed the horses in the grass, at a point where the animals could drink from a lower pool. Going gathered wood and broiled the hindquarters of an antelope Cameron had shot the previous day. Night fell quickly, the rock walls above them changing through all the shades of purple as shadows filled the draws and gullies carved by old flash floods and dry slides.

Coyotes yammered at the thumbnail sliver of new moon rising and growing brighter against the darkening sky. The smell of crushed juniper blew down from the heights.

The group sat around the fire and smoked. Cameron, Going, Hotchkiss, and Jimmy Bronco talked quietly. Clark sat against a rock and drank his brandy. Marina wandered off down the canyon. Cameron didn't worry about her. She'd grown up in this kind of country and she needed her privacy. Besides, she had a gun on her hip and was no doubt a fair shot.

When, later, he went down to check the horses, he heard a gentle splash of water and saw her sitting on a rock, thoughtfully kicking her bare feet in the pool. Starlight glinted on her bare, wet legs exposed by her parted riding skirt.

It was too dark to see her face but Cameron knew she was looking at him. He turned away to check the picket ropes. Marina said, "It is a nice evening, isn't it?"

"Yes, it is," he answered reluctantly.

"Do we have far to go?"

"Not far. Three, four more days' travel, Tokente thinks." He knew she was talking just to talk. They had discussed the remaining distance over supper. She was no doubt desperate for conversation—Clark rarely spoke to her, and there were no women around.

Figuring Clark was passed out from the brandy by now, Cameron hunkered down next to her on the rocks. She stopped kicking her feet in the water.

"Nights like these," she said, "remind me of home. I used to ride to a canyon like this, when the Apaches and Comanches were not a threat. I would swim in a big deep pool."

"You miss home?"

"Very much." She paused. "Where is your home?"

"Originally? Illinois. I came West just before the war broke out. Had to run out on my family 'cause my pa wouldn't hear of me doin' anything but stayin' home and takin' over the farm. I never saw any of them again. I heard from a cousin that my parents are both dead. I don't know where my brothers and sisters ended up."

He sighed, and smiled as though the effort pained him, picking absently at a callus on his hand. "I wish now I'd gone back just to see 'em once, before the folks passed on and the kids all left. I regret leavin' the way I did, but I was just a kid. Freedom meant more to me than family."

"Did you marry?"

He told her about Ivy Kitchen without any hesitation at all, which surprised him. He'd always found it difficult to even mention Ivy's name. Something in Marina, though, made him want to talk to her about his most private thoughts.

Suddenly he felt his face heat with embarrassment. "Well, listen to me," he said with an effacing chuckle, coming to the end of the story. "I've never been known to talk a blue streak, but I believe I just have."

Marina ignored the comment. "You have lived an interesting life, Mr. Cameron. A life of adventure."

Cameron shrugged. "Guess it sounds that way."

"What did you hope for, when you left your home?" she said.

He smiled. "Happiness and fulfillment," he said. "A whole houseful of kids, and a wife to talk to when they've all gone to bed." He shook his head. "Not loneliness," he said, surprised at the regret he heard in his voice.

Marina kicked the water and sighed. "I guess we have to make do with what we are given."

"I reckon," he said. He wanted to take her in his arms and kiss her as he'd done before. He wanted to hold her and tell her more about his hopes and dreams, and hear about hers. He forced his mind away from it.

Standing, he said, "I'm gonna turn in." He checked the horses again, then headed back toward the fire.

"Good night . . . Jack," Marina said from the darkness.

"Good night, Marina."

The next morning, before the sun had penetrated the steep canyon, Cameron rolled out of his blankets and took a walk to check on the horses and gather wood for a breakfast fire. He was stooping to retrieve a branch when he saw something in the rock wall before him.

A turtle, the very same turtle etched on Clark's plat.

Cameron dropped his armload of wood and staggered over to take a closer look. In awe he slowly reached out his hand and ran his splayed fingers across the figure that had been carved in the rock. It had weathered some, so that the figure would have been hard to see from far away, but the white lines were still distinct.

"I'll be goddamned," Cameron muttered.

He swung his gaze in a full circle, looking around. This couldn't be the place, the X marked on the map. None of the landmarks matched those on the plat.

Still, he'd found the turtle. He wasted no time in telling the others.

"What do you think it means?" he asked Going when they'd all gathered around the figure etched in the rock.

Going looked around, tipping back his head to study the high canyon walls. After several minutes, Going shrugged. "This can't be the place. It can't be the X. None of the landmarks are the same as on the map."

"Maybe we're close," Clark suggested.

Going nodded. "Sí. Maybe that's all it means. When we see the turtle"—he shrugged—"we're close."

"It may not mean a goddamn thing," Hotchkiss groused. He hadn't put on his shirt yet, so he stood there in long johns and suspenders with his thin gray hair mussed about the crown of his pink, bald head. "It may have been put on the map just to throw us off. I heard they do that sometimes, these old prospectors, to throw a wrench into the search if anyone they didn't want pokin' around for their cache went a-lookin'."

"Could be," Going allowed.

Marina, standing beside her husband, said, "Jack—Mr. Cameron—said before that prospectors used marks to point the way."

"That's right," Cameron agreed, looking expectantly at Going. "I didn't find any more nearby, but they're probably spaced a good distance apart. Maybe we should just ride ahead, the way the turtle's head's pointing."

"I agree, amigo," Going said with a nod.

Too excited for breakfast, they mounted up and headed down the canyon, eating jerked beef as they rode. The trail rose through long-needled pines on a windswept ridge where the sun peered through pink-washed clouds, then descended into another gorge. At a fork in the gorge, they found another turtle, carved in the rock, its head pointing down the left fork.

Two hundred yards farther on, they came to another fork but no turtle. They all dismounted and looked carefully, coming up with nothing. The cool morning breeze murmured in the pines above them and tiny birds chattered in the rocks on the ridgetops. The air was heating up as the sun climbed.

Cameron glanced around and sighed. "Well, I guess we split up."

Hotchkiss nodded. "Jack, why don't me and Jimmy take the fork to the right, and you four continue that way?"

"Meet back here in an hour?" Cameron said.

"Sounds good to me."

Cameron glanced at the kid, whose sun-bleached hair, wispy curls sweeping his peeling cheeks, had gotten shaggy enough to brush against his neck. "No shooting, Jimmy—unless you're sure you're in trouble."

"I ain't no retard," the kid complained, spurring his mount after the graybeard, a packhorse jerking along behind him.

When the pair had disappeared, Going started down the left fork. Cameron paused to drink from his canteen. When he lowered it he saw Clark looking at him, an impudent expression on the Missourian's face.

"Well, Mr. High-and-Mighty—do you believe us now?"

"About the gold? I still have to see it to believe it, but I have to admit, things have gotten a mite interesting." Cameron smiled agreeably.

Clark's eyes grew hard. "What are you gonna do when we find it?"

"What's that?"

"Are you gonna kill me and take my share?" He looked at Marina. "—And my wife?"

"Adrian," Marina objected, "please . . . I am your wife, and I will always be your wife. That was the agreement."

Clark nodded and made a face, as though he'd bitten into something sour. "Yes, that was the agreement, wasn't it? . . . As long as I'm alive."

Cameron leaned forward, resting his forearm on his saddle horn, and pinned Clark with a direct look. He tried to sound as hard and cold as he could, trying to convince not only Clark, but also himself, of the truth in his words. "Get this straight, Clark. I have no intention of taking your gold or your wife. You can't blame a man for lookin' at her. If you were so damn worried about it, you shouldn't have brought her out here. Now just get it out of your head. I have." Then he rode after Going.

Clark fished his brandy bottle from his saddlebags and took a liberal pull. But it only made him angrier—angry at Cameron and Marina, angry at the world, and angry at himself. Would the gold finally bring him happiness? Would it make up for everything he lacked?

Going had just discovered another turtle when the

flat pops of distant gunfire rose from the south, in the direction Hotchkiss and Bronco had ridden.

Cameron reined his horse around, drawing his Colt. "Shit!" he exclaimed, wide-eyed with urgency. "Toke, you three stay here. I'll take a look."

"You want me to go with you, Jack?" Going called as Cameron started off.

"No. They could've ridden into a trap!"

CHAPTER 24

THERE WERE ONLY a few spurts of gunfire before everything went quiet. Cameron felt the blood rush in his ears like waves against a pier.

His tongue tasted coppery. He had long ago learned to take that as a sign that Apaches were close. Some men sweated profusely. For others, old wounds ached. For Cameron it was that coppery, bloodlike taste on his tongue.

He had a bad feeling about Bud and Jimmy. He didn't like the silence that seemed to grow, like an invisible black cloud, as he rode.

The trail twisted through chalky buttes spotted with yucca and catclaw. At the bottom of the gully, along a rocky creekbed, grew gnarled, wind-stunted trees that looked like something in a death dream. Far above these twisted sycamores hung three vultures in a loose orbit. Cameron's breath caught in his throat as he wound around a stunted butte and spied a body about fifty yards beyond the trees.

Keeping his eyes on the terrain around him, Cameron reached down, smoothly shucked his Winchester, and jacked a shell into the chamber. As he rode up to the man on the ground, he talked to himself, trying to remain calm. The hair on the back of his neck was standing upright, his heart was drumming like trains coupling, and his mouth was full of pennies.

It was Hotchkiss. He was moaning and cursing, writhing in pain. The three arrows embedded in his belly, chest, and thigh danced as he moved.

"Stay still, Bud," Cameron said, dismounting, scanning the area as he moved carefully toward the old frontiersman, as though the man were booby-trapped.

"Get . . . Get the hell out of here, Jack" Hotchkiss urged between grunts of pain, breathing heavily. "It's no use . . . it's no goddamn use."

"Sh. Take it easy."

"They had us sittin' down here like ducks on a pond."

"Where's Jimmy?"

"If he ain't dead, they took him. They hit me first. Didn' . . . didn' even know what was happenin' before I was layin' here on the ground and they was screamin' and flingin' arrows from those buttes up yonder. I squeezed off a couple shots but I didn' hit nothin' but air." He lifted his head and smiled with a sharp prod of pain. "Oh Jesus, it hurts!"

"Rest easy, Bud," Cameron instructed. He studied the arrows sticking out of bloodholes in Hotchkiss's body. He knew he couldn't remove the one in the man's belly without pulling out half his stomach.

Cameron touched the other arrow, over Hotchkiss's right lung. Hotchkiss yelled, "Ah, *God* . . . Don't, Jack! It's no use. It's no goddamn use. I'm a goner."

Cameron knew with an overpowering anguish that it was true. He was torn between staying here and trying to do something for Hotchkiss, and going after Jimmy.

Hotchkiss was reading his mind. "Get the hell out of here, Jack. Don't go after Jimmy. There was at least ten of 'em, and they'll get you, too. They're prob'ly heading back to their rancheria. Even if you find 'em, there won't be nothin' you can do. They'll just do to you like they done to me." He arched his back and gave a cry of pain. "Ahhh . . . *goddamn* . . . that smarts!"

Cameron knew Apaches well enough to know they had taken Jimmy alive for one reason and one reason only—to torture him. For Apaches, torture was sport, and they'd honed that sport to an art. He imagined the boy's cries of pain, which the Apaches could prolong for days, and it sickened him.

"Hand me my pistol, will ya?" Hotchkiss said.

The long-barreled Smith & Wesson lay in the gravel about five feet to Hotchkiss's right. Cameron knew why the graybeard wanted the gun; he'd've wanted it for the same reason. Cameron set the weapon in Hotchkiss's outstretched hand. The old man's eyes were rolling back in his head, showing the whites, and he was panting like a woman in labor.

"God, I'm sorry I got you into this, Bud," Cameron said, shoving off his hat and running a rough hand through his curling blond hair.

"It weren't none o' your fault," Hotchkiss said, getting a good grip on the pistol. "It's just that . . . goddamn, we were so close to the gold!"

"If I hadn't wanted to go after Bachelard, none of this ever would have happened. You'd be back in Goldneld—"

"I wanted to go after Bachelard as bad as you did."

"We should've known better."

"Go." Hotchkiss waved him away. "Get out of here. Go back."

"I'm going after Jimmy." Cameron snugged his hat back on his head and lifted his rifle.

"It's no use; he's as good as dead."

"You were one of the very best men I ever knew, Bud," Cameron said. He squeezed Hotchkiss's shoulder for a moment, then stood. The older man grinned briefly, then said, "Just tell me one thing. Do you believe in God?"

Cameron considered this for a moment, dropping his eyes. "Sure," he said woodenly.

Hotchkiss grinned again. "I don't, either. So I guess I'll see ya in hell, then."

"See ya, Bud," Cameron said.

"Later, Jack."

Cameron mounted his buckskin, then looked once more at his friend. His eyes veiled with tears. Brushing the moisture from his cheek with the back of one hand, he rode off, heading down the path the Apaches had left in the sand.

He was fifty yards away when he heard the pistol pop.

He didn't look back.

Coming to a freshet bubbling down from a spring, Cameron stopped and watered his horse. He dismounted to take a good look at the tracks, holding the horse's reins loosely in his hand.

About two twisting, turning miles back, he'd seen from the scuffed tracks of leather heels—a single pair among the prints of unshod hooves—that Jimmy Bronco was being forced to walk, probably with a rope around his neck. The tracks told Cameron the kid had fallen several times and been dragged before he'd regained his feet. In the last mile or so, he'd been falling more and more often and getting dragged farther and farther. It appeared one of the riders pulled him onto a horse now and then, so they could make better time; then he'd throw Jimmy down and make him walk some more.

The kid was wearing out. Cameron hoped he'd get to him before he was dragged to death. At the same time he knew that getting dragged was probably a much more pleasant way to go than what the kid probably had in store if and when the Apaches got him to their rancheria.

Jimmy'd be the main attraction tonight. The women, kids, and even the old folks would come out to enjoy the festivities. To watch him writhe and hear him scream . . .

Cameron winced at the thought, scrubbed the sweat from the back of his neck with his bandanna, then climbed back into the saddle and gave the animal the spurs. He knew the Apaches were gaining ground on him, and it frustrated him no end.

The Apaches could keep up their breakneck pace for hours. Their mountain- and desert-bred mustangs were used to it and even if one or two of the mounts gave out, they could double up on one of the others. On the other hand, if Cameron's gave out, he and Jimmy were dead.

He followed a rugged, twisting trail into the high country. Pines and junipers grew out of the rocks. Grass became less scarce. Deer tracks were plentiful. Once, he saw a mangled juniper where a bull elk had scraped off its velvet, the antler tips laying the trunk open to its mushy red core. Cameron rode with his rifle light in his hands, boots soft in the stirrups, ready to come out of the leather at a split-second's notice.

The sun was angling down in the west, toasting the back of his neck and turning his buckskin tunic into a hot glove. His thought of Jimmy and his old pal Hotchkiss. He'd had no right to bring them along on this foolhardy mission to kill Bachelard.

Bud was too proud to go home, where he belonged. And Cameron had been too focused on Bachelard—and Marina?—to urge the man to retreat to his ranch at the foot of Hackberry Mesa. At least he didn't leave a wife and kids, as Pas Varas had. Bud had been married twice, to Indian women. They'd given him two kids apiece, but had taken them when they'd left Hotchkiss.

The sun was about a half-hour from setting when Cameron's horse came out on the shoulder of a mountain cloaked in pines. The air was fresh and clear. A trickle of snowmelt water sluiced down a trough in the slope to his left.

Cameron stopped his horse to listen. From somewhere in the distance came the sound of low, guttural voices.

His heart quickening, he dismounted quietly, tied his horse to a branch, and donned his moccasins. Then he walked beneath the pines. The air was dark and filled with the heavenly smell of balsam—a sharp contrast to the overall mood of the place.

The needles and spongy, mossy earth were scuffed, making the trail easy to follow. He wound up on a ridge, the slope of boulders, talus, stunted pines, and low-growing junipers falling away in a forty-five-degree angle. Below, a gorge was nestled in more pines and a few deciduous trees, mainly aspens and a few sycamores.

Smoke smelling sweetly of pine rose up from the trees like high-mountain mist. Cookfires sparked through the branches. A dog whimpered and barked.

Cameron crouched low, considering his situation.

It was maybe a couple hundred feet down to the meadow, and the grade was fairly easy, something he could descend without falling if he made use of the handholds. There were plenty of boulders and trees to crouch behind. Also, it was getting darker, though the darkness would work against him as well as for him.

How would he find Jimmy? How could he get him out of there with no light to guide him?

Knowing it wasn't going to get any easier the longer he waited, Cameron stole down the slope. About halfway down, he stopped and scanned the meadow beneath the treetops.

There were two large cookfires tended by old women and girls. The braves were milling around, eating and tending their horses. Cameron could smell the unmistakable aroma of mule. Probably the braves had been out raiding pack trains when they'd discovered Hotchkiss and Jimmy. They must have brought a mule or two back on which to dine. Apaches loved nothing as well as mule—a big, succulent quarter roasted on a spit—washed down with *tiswin*, their near-toxic drink of choice, which turned them into a horde of drunken banshees with the devil's own lust for blood and misery.

Cameron wondered where Jimmy was. He had to get him out of there. He headed for a spot where the trees looked densest, one step at a time, keeping his eyes on the meadow and holding the rifle loosely before him. At last he hunkered down behind a stout pine, removed his hat, and risked a look around the tree.

From what he could tell, there were about twelve warriors, a handful of children, and about five or six old women. An old man with long, stringy gray hair sat before the canyon wall, bare legs folded beneath him. He was singing some chant and looking at the treetops, toward his Apache god, no doubt giving thanks for the safe return of the young warriors with the mules and the skinny young white-eyes.

Cameron did not see Jimmy. He was sure the boy was here, because he'd seen his tracks until the Apaches had half dragged him into the pines. Jimmy had to be here—maybe behind the brush wickiups that sat in a haphazard row before the canyon wall. Setting his jaw and taking a deep, calming breath, Cameron moved out from the tree and made his way carefully around the encampment, stopping behind each tree to scout his position and make sure no Apache was near.

Halfway around the perimeter of the camp, Cameron stopped dead in his tracks as the sound of feet padding through the pine needles and leaves came to his ears—from behind him! He turned quickly and saw a figure moving his way, silhouetted by the light which had nearly faded to total darkness under the pines. Cameron couldn't believe the man hadn't seen him, but apparently he hadn't, for he did not react, but just continued walking, bent a little by the weight of whatever it was that he was carrying over his shoulder.

Slowly Cameron eased his rifle into his left hand and unsheathed his bowie with his right. Suddenly the Apache, who had been on a course that would have taken him only a few feet to Cameron's left, stopped. Obviously he'd seen the white man.

Before the Indian could react, Cameron threw the bowie with an adroit flick of his wrist, a move practiced endlessly when scouting for the Army. He heard the sharp point of the knife crunch through the Apache's breastbone.

The Indian stiffened and made a sound like a single gulp. A raspy exhale followed. Cameron prayed the man would die before he could yell. The load on the man's shoulder fell as he slumped, his legs buckling. The man staggered forward two steps, then collapsed.

He fell to his knees and swayed there for several long seconds, gasping almost inaudibly. Then he fell forward and gave a final sigh.

Cameron sagged with relief, his entire body covered with nervous sweat. He wiped his hands on his tunic, looked around, and walked to the Indian. Crouching, he turned the man over. His bowie was buried to the hilt in the Apache's chest, its wide blade no doubt slicing the man's heart in two.

Cameron had to place one foot on the Indian's chest and pull with both hands to remove the blade. When he'd wiped it clean on the Indian's body, he inspected what the man had been carrying—mule. Cameron wondered how many more men were carving up the meat, and warned himself to watch his backside.

Any more incidents like this one were liable to get him a heart attack, if not get him shot.

CHAPTER 25

CAMERON STOLE ALONG behind the trees, beyond the circle of light cast by the cooking fires. The raw-featured faces of the Apache men and women shone like rough cameos as they milled about, stuffing themselves with food and liquor, no doubt priming themselves for the celebration to come, the celebration for which Jimmy Bronco would be the grand finale.

Behind the wickiups, between the conical brush lodges and the canyon wall, Cameron saw a tree around which the earth was scuffed and flattened. Probably the tree had been used for tying dogs the Apache women were fattening up to butcher. Something—or someone—was tied up there now, too big to be a dog. Cameron hoped, with the blood rushing in his head, that it was Jimmy Bronco.

He was about to leave the shelter of the woods when someone appeared from the velvet darkness behind the wickiups. Cameron squelched a curse and came to ground behind a stump, about twenty yards away. When he glanced around the stump, he realized that the newcomer was a girl. She moved toward the tree, carrying what appeared to be a waterskin. Kneeling, she held out the skin. The man tethered to the tree—Cameron's heart leapt at the sight—accepted the skin awkwardly, fumbled with it, then drank. The girl snatched it away while he was still drinking.

She got to her feet and stood before the prisoner. Suddenly she raised her deerskin blouse, revealing the two brown globes of her young breasts. She said nothing, just stood there for a moment as though awaiting a reaction. Then she dropped the blouse, said something angrily in Apache, and kicked the prisoner savagely with her left leg, knocking him backwards. The man yelped.

The girl laughed, turned, and skipped back to the wickiups and the fires beyond.

Cameron ran, crouching, to the figure before the tree. It was Jimmy, all right. Stripped naked, he was dirty, sweaty, and badly bruised. He lay on his side, wrists crossed over his privates, both knees drawn up in the fetal position. He was shivering in the chill mountain air, teeth clacking together like a pocketful of marbles. Blood streaks plowed through the dirt and grime on his face.

"Jimmy," Cameron rasped, "it's Jack. Are you all right, boy? Can you travel?"

The kid lifted his head a few inches from the ground and squinted painfully. "J-Jack?" His voice, frail as it was, gained a hint of buoyancy.

"It's me, Jimmy. I'm going to get you out of here." Cameron was cutting through the rope tied around the kid's wrists and ankles.

"'P-'Paches, Jack." The kid's voice broke.

"I know, Jimmy. You just stay quiet. I'm going to get you out of here." Cutting through the final knot, he glanced at the kid's feet. They were a bloody mess. There was no way Jimmy could walk, much less run, which they might have to do if the Apaches got savvy to Cameron's presence.

"Here, you hold my rifle," he said, handing the kid the weapon. "Hold on to it tight, now."

He maneuvered his right arm under the boy's neck, the left under his knees, and pushed himself to his feet. Jimmy weighed only about a hundred and thirty-five pounds, and Cameron thought he could carry him a good ways before he'd have to rest. Adrenaline was coursing through Cameron's veins like boiling river rapids, and that made the kid even lighter.

Cameron turned and moved back through the trees, tracing the course by which he had come. Jimmy mumbled, "They come . . . They come down out of the buttes . . ."

"Sh, Jimmy. Be still," Cameron whispered in the kid's ear.

"They shot old Hotch . . ."

"Be quiet, Jimmy. I'm gonna get you of here."

He moved awkwardly with his burden, but he was making good time. To his right, voices grew louder as the revelry increased. Cameron prayed no one would go to the tree where Jimmy had been tied until he was well away from here. He prayed he wouldn't run into anyone out here in the trees. If he did, he knew it would all be over; he'd never have time to drop Jimmy and go for his rifle. The whole band would be on top of him in seconds, and it would be both him and the boy tied to that tree the Apaches used for fattening up their dogs.

When he came to the base of the ridge, the top of which was now capped by a handful of weak stars glittering through the silhouetted pinetops, he set Jimmy down.

"J-Jack."

"It's all right, Jimmy. I'm just resting."

"They come down out of those buttes, slingin' arrows ever' which way." The kid's voice broke.

"It's okay, Jimmy."

The boy was whimpering. His oily skin was clammy to the touch and rough with goose bumps. Cameron was afraid Jimmy was going into shock. No doubt he'd had quite a few good blows to the head. On top of that, he'd covered a long stretch of terrain on his feet, half dragged over about fifteen miles of Sierra Madre.

"You hang on, Jimmy," Cameron cajoled. "I'm gonna get you out of here."

He knew he had to get the kid shelter and warmth—but first he had to gain a good distance from the savages behind them.

With that in mind, Cameron lifted Jimmy once more and started toward the ridgetop. The going was hard and he fell several times, Jimmy rolling forward out of his grasp and falling gently to the grade rising before them. If the Apaches came now, he didn't know what he'd do.

He made the ridge, breathing hard, and set Jimmy down on the lip as if gentling him into bed. Cameron dropped to his knees just before the ridgetop, placed his hands on his thighs, and sucked air into his smarting lungs. His heart pounded and his side ached from the strain of the climb. His thighs and knees throbbed, and he wasn't sure he'd be able to stand again.

But stand he did, and carried Jimmy through the pines. The buckskin was waiting where Cameron had tied him. The horse whinnied with alarm as Cameron pushed through the branches, and skittered sideways. Cameron cooed to the animal, then dropped Jimmy's legs and held the boy against the horse's side.

"Can you stand here, boy?"

The boy gave a grunt and stiffened as Cameron climbed into the saddle. Cameron grabbed the reins in his right hand, slid his rifle into its boot, then reached down and dragged Jimmy onto the saddle before him.

When he'd gotten the boy situated in front of him, Cameron listened for any sign that the Apaches had discovered Jimmy missing. There was no sound but the wind rushing in the pinetops and Jimmy's clattering teeth. Cameron reined the horse around and started down the trail.

Looking east, he saw a thin sickle of moon hanging about halfway up in the sky. Cameron was grateful. A fuller moon would have made the trail easier to follow, but it also would have made him and Jimmy easier to follow. That thin crescent of pearl light was just enough to illuminate the trail before him but not make him or his tracks too conspicuous. If the Apaches discovered Jimmy gone, Cameron hoped they wouldn't search too long in the dark.

They'd come eventually, though. You didn't sneak into an Apache encampment and expropriate one of their captives without ruffling more than a few feathers. They'd let their guard down probably because they hadn't been harassed this deep in the mountains for a long time. Tracking down Cameron and killing him and Jimmy would be a matter of pride.

When they were well off the ridge and had entered the low desert country again, Cameron turned off the trail and headed west through a narrow canyon. If he went back the same way he had come, he would only be leading the Apaches to Clark, Marina, and Tokente. Instead, he'd detour into the western foothills, find a well-used wagon road, and follow it to a village where he would not only find safety from the Apaches, but help for Jimmy, as well.

When he'd ridden what he thought were at least five or six miles by trail, and there was no sign they were being followed, he started to relax. The aches and pains of the long day—the rough ride after Jimmy, carrying the boy up the ridge—became more apparent. Every muscle in his body felt pinched and sore and a sleepy stupor came over him.

Cameron tried to stay alert by taking in deep draughts of cool air. Riding half-asleep, letting his horse pick its own trails in Indian country was dangerous, but the exhaustion of the day simply overcame him. He roused when the trail bottomed out in a valley, magically opalescent in the moonlight, with the toothy silhouettes of mountains jutting against the distant sky.

In the center of the valley was a deep-rutted wagon road. Even in this remote country, wagon roads usually led to villages. Cameron chose to head south, and hoped he would reach the closest village in that direction before the Indians caught up to them or he fell comatose from his saddle.

An hour later, he'd pulled into a cove of rocks to rest his horse when he heard the clatter of a wagon approaching from the northwest. Jimmy was asleep, wrapped in a blanket. Cameron shucked his Winchester from his saddle boot. Stepping onto the road, he jacked a shell into the rifle's chamber and cleared his throat as the wagon approached. You never knew who might be on the road this late, and Cameron was in no mood to take unnecessary chances.

The wagon stopped, the nag blowing in its traces and shaking its head, startled at the smell of a stranger. The driver called out in Spanish. Cameron's Spanish was rusty but he could make out enough of the words to put the sentences together: "Please do not rob me! I am a simple man with not a centavo to my name, and my horse, as you can see, is worthless!"

"Do you speak English?" Cameron said.

"Sí, señor. You're Americano?"

"That's right. Who're you?"

"Porfirio Garza, señor. And you?"

"Jack Cameron. Can you help me, Mr. Garza? I have a sick boy here."

Garza's voice gained a conspiratorial gravity. "Are you a bandit, señor?"

"No, I'm not." Cameron hesitated. What could he tell this man he was doing down here . . . searching for gold, searching for a man he wished to kill? He decided not to say anything unless the man pressed it. Then he'd make up something.

"Can you tell us where the closest village is?" he asked.

"Step nearer so I can see your face, por favor."

Cameron moved toward the wagon, touching the horse's neck to calm him. The wagon was little more than a cart with ocotillo branches woven together to form a cage for shipping chickens and other livestock. The man in the driver's seat was small and round. He wore a colorful serape, dirty white peasant slacks, and sandals. The floppy sombrero on his head was crowned with moonlight. Cameron couldn't see his eyes beneath the brim. However, something about the man—an innocence of manner and voice—told Cameron he could trust him in spite of the alcohol smell on Garza's breath.

"Sí," Garza said after he'd given Cameron a study. "San Cristóbal is just up the road, another three kilometers. I am going there; it is my home."

"Can you give my boy a ride?"

Garza shrugged warily. "What is wrong with him? Does he have the fever?"

"No fever. He was taken by Apaches, forced to run cross-country. He's exhausted mostly, and his feet are swollen."

"Load him up, señor. I will take him to the prefect's wife in San Cristóbal. She is a midwife and cures the sick. Come, come. If the Apaches are not far, we must hasten."

"I appreciate this," Cameron said, turning to retrieve Jimmy. He laid the boy gently in the box. He was happy to see hay there, even if it was littered with chicken dung. He brushed it up around the lad to help keep him warm.

"Can I ride with you?" he asked Garza. "My horse has had it."

"Sí, sí, but hurry. Please. The Apaches . . ."

Cameron quickly tied his mount to the back of the wagon and climbed onto the seat beside Garza. The man rasped a few Spanish words of encouragement to the nag, and they rolled off through the ruts.

"The Apaches—how far are they behind you, señor?"

"At least seven or eight miles. We should be okay. I don't think they'll try to track me at night."

"You took the boy away from the Apaches?"

"Yep," Cameron said with a sigh, not really believing it himself.

"¡Dios mío! You must be a very brave man, señor—and the boy must matter to you very much. Your son?"

"Adopted, I guess you could say. He's a good boy."

"Sí. I wish I had a son, but my Ernestine gave me only daughters—three fat girls too lazy to set the table for their papa. I got rid of two of them today—took them to Bachiniva, to two boys I arranged for them to marry. Their father gave me gold and the promise of four goats in the spring."

Garza chuckled. "A very good deal, considering the fatness and laziness of my daughters. But then, the boys"—he shrugged and shook his head—"they are no great reward, either."

"You're on the road mighty late."

Garza turned to him, grinning coyote-like, and leaned toward him as if to share a secret. The stench of tequila was heavy in Cameron's nose.

"I stopped on the way back to celebrate with a friend. I did not wish to stay so long, but you know how quickly time travels when one is reveling. I could have stayed there rather than risk the bandidos, but then my wife would know I stopped, and she would not be happy. This way I can sneak into the house while she sleeps and she will be none the wiser." He grinned and touched his fingers to his lips.

They'd traveled maybe fifteen minutes when a sound very much like a distant scream lifted over the chaparral. Garza halted the nag as another scream rose from the jagged peaks of the mountains in the northeast. It was a man's scream, filled with monstrous, ghastly pain. Cameron's scalp crawled.

Garza reached up and removed his hat. He placed it over his breast and turned to Cameron soberly, fearfully. "Someone is dying, señor."

"That's what it sounds like," Cameron agreed.

Another scream sounded, even higher in pitch than the others. Cameron guessed the screams originated about three or four miles back. Irrationally he glanced at the wagon box to make sure Jimmy was still there.

"Did you leave other friends in the mountains?" Garza asked.

"Yes, but not there."

Cameron's heart drummed as he tried to think who the Apaches could have run into. Clark? Tokente?

Might one of them have come after Cameron, only to be found by the Apaches?

If that were true, then Marina might have been caught, as well.

They sat there for several minutes, listening. No more screams carried down from the mountains, and at last Garza slapped the reins against the nag's back and continued along the trail.

But Cameron's thoughts remained in the mountains, where someone—possibly someone he knew—had just died . . .

CHAPTER 26

GARZA'S WAGON SQUEAKED and clattered into the village of San Cristóbal. The moon was angling away, casting more shadows than light, but Cameron could still see it was a typical Mexican village, scraggly and dirty, with low adobe huts for houses and business establishments. Corrals were overgrown with chaparral. The smell of burning mesquite hung in the air, and dogs barked from doorways as the wagon rolled up the main street.

They passed a fountain, with its solitary stone obelisk, and turned the corner around a blocklike, sand-colored building whose belfry, too large for the structure, told Cameron it was a church. Garza pulled up at a pitted adobe house. The smell of goat dung was heavy on the night breeze.

"You wait here, señor. I will get the señora for your boy."

It was ten minutes before the door of the shack opened and Cameron heard Garza speaking to someone in a low tone. Then Garza and another man approached the cart. The second man, bald, and as short and round as Garza, was pulling on a shirt.

"Who are you—bandits?" the man said accusingly to Cameron, obviously not happy to have been aroused from a sound sleep. But he did not wait for an answer before peering into the cart.

In Spanish he told Cameron and Garza to bring the kid inside. He held the door open as Cameron slung Jimmy over his shoulder and carried him into the simply furnished room. A mesquite fire burned on the adobe hearth and a single lamp glowed in the hands of an elderly woman who stood silently before the fire in a night wrapper.

"There," the woman said, motioning toward a cot topped by a corn-husk mattress.

As Cameron lay Jimmy on the cot, the kid came awake. "Jack!" he yelled, fiercely clutching Cameron's forearm.

"It's okay, Jimmy, I'm here. Everything's all right. This lady here is going to get you all fixed up good as new."

The kid slowly lay back as Cameron pushed him gently down. When his head came to rest on the flat pillow, he said in an almost normal tone, "Is ol' Hotch . . . Is he dead?"

"I'm afraid so."

Jimmy sighed. "I liked ol' Hotch, even if he teased me more than I liked."

"I did, too," Cameron said, as the woman pushed him aside, moving between him and the boy.

"You go now," she said brusquely to Cameron.

"No, Jack—don't go," Jimmy begged.

"I won't be far, Jimmy. You just relax now. I'll talk to you in the morning."

Cameron stepped aside to let the woman take care of the boy. Garza came up beside Cameron, his sombrero in his hands, and whispered, "I must go now, señor, before Ernestine wakes and finds me gone. It is our secret, no?"

"It's our secret," Cameron said, nodding and smiling at the man. He held out his hand and Garza shook it. "I'm much obliged for your help, Porfirio. Muchas gracias."

Garza clamped Cameron on the shoulder. "De nada, señor. De nada! Your horse is by the barn." Then he turned and was gone.

The second man took him by the arm and led him out a back door. "You can sleep in the barn. There is feed for your horse," he said.

Cameron hesitated at the door, not wanting to leave Jimmy alone with these strangers. He was sure the kid was getting tended just fine, and he had no reason to worry. It was just hard to let his defenses down when they'd been up for so long.

The man disappeared inside and returned with a bottle and a small bowl of tortillas and goat meat. "Go now. Rest. Your boy will be fine."

The man shut the thin wooden door. The clatter of a bolt told Cameron he'd locked it.

In the barn, Cameron sat down with his back to the rough lumber and rolled a cigarette. He needed to unwind. He uncorked the bottle and tipped it back. The raw, metallic taste of mescal flooded his tongue, then burned down his throat. It gave him a pleasing sensation of instant release, and he became very grateful to the man who had offered it.

He took several more drinks and smoked the quirley down to a stub, staring at the sky and the fading moon, the dark backdrop of mountains that surrounded the village, and thought again about the screams he and Garza had heard on the road. He repressed the urge to ride back out and investigate.

Whoever had screamed was long since dead, and Cameron's horse was in no condition for anything but rest. If Jimmy was able, they'd light out of the village tomorrow and try to find the Clarks and To-kente.

Cameron mashed out his quirley on his boot and corked the mescal. He got up with some effort, feeling pangs of fatigue shoot through his body, and led his horse into the barn. He unsaddled the animal and gave it a cursory rubdown and some water and feed.

He found a rickety cot and an old wool blanket in a corner, removed his hat and boots, and sat down. Hungrily he ate the goat meat and tortillas, set the bowl under the cot, and fell nearly instantly asleep. His sleep was deep but fitful, constricted by the sensation of constant movement, of following one trail after another and scanning ridges for Apaches.

At intervals along the trail he'd see Marina, like a ghost behind a thin, dark veil.

In the midst of this he heard, strangely, a door squeaking open. He saw light through his closed eyelids, felt the warmth of sunlight on his face, sensed movement around him.

A metallic rasp and clack jerked him awake. He opened his eyes. Three men in gray uniforms stood before the cot, aiming long-barreled rifles directly at his face.

The previous night, Ed Hawkins had brought his horse to a halt at the base of a sandy knoll, dismounted, and produced a spyglass from a leather sheath tied to his saddle. He tethered his paint pony, stolen from a rancher near Bisbee, to a dwarf pine, and ran, crouching, up the knoll.

The light was fading quickly from the canyon below, but there was still enough to make out the single rider Hawkins was following. Jack Cameron.

Cameron was studying the ground.

"Give it up, fool," Hawkins muttered as he watched Cameron through the spyglass. "Don't you have no sense a'tall? None a'tall? Why, you're gonna get us both skinned and hung and greased for the spit, that's what you're gonna do."

Hawkins considered calling it quits. It was pretty obvious the dumb-ass was following the Apaches who had ambushed the kid and the graybeard several miles back. He was going to try to rescue the kid.

Anyone in their right mind who'd seen the number of Apache tracks would have written the kid off a long time ago and gone back to the Clarks and the Mex, and continued searching for whatever it was they were searching for. It had to be gold. That was the only thing it could be, the only thing that would lure sane people into such a dangerous area.

But now this idiot Cameron was tracking *Apaches!* And right behind Cameron, at the insistence of his brother Jake, was Ed Hawkins.

But by God, enough was enough, Ed told himself, and spat, lowering the spyglass. Cameron was going to get himself killed, and Ed wanted no part of that. He'd seen what Apaches could do to a healthy body, and he'd rather go back and face his brother than even a single Apache.

Hell, he'd just tell Jake that Cameron was dead. By the time he got back to where his brother was keeping an eye on the Clarks, it wouldn't be a lie, either. If Cameron kept heading where he was heading, why, in a half-hour, maybe less, he'd *be* dead—or worse.

Ed nodded to himself and walked back to his mount, where he replaced the spyglass in its sheath. Then he began to think.

What if Cameron wasn't going after the Apaches,

after all? What if he'd found another way to the gold? What if Cameron was following it by himself because he knew Apaches were about and he didn't want to endanger the others?

Jeepers creepers, Ed sighed to himself. He mounted up, and with a heavy air of dark resignation, gave a sigh and continued after Cameron.

Ed followed at a distance. Cameron was a wily guy, with one hell of a reputation. Ed knew he had to give the man a liberal margin of separation not to give himself away, even with Apaches taking up the tracker's attention. Ed was surprised he and his brother had been able to follow Cameron's group as far as they had without getting noticed, but he knew that was due mostly to the distance they'd allowed between themselves and the group. Jake's above-average tracking skills had kept them from losing the trail altogether.

Cameron's tracks suddenly disappeared in an old rockslide. Ed's problem was that the canyon forked at the slide, and by the time he'd picked his way across the bed of talus and flinty shale, it was too dark to pick up the trail again. Ed knew Jake would have been able to do it but, for the life of him, Ed couldn't pick up much more than the cloven print of a deer . . . or was it a mountain goat?

He chose one of the canyon's forks at random and followed the trail into the high country, coming out on a ledge with pines all around him and the smell of juniper and piñon wafting on the breeze. There was still some light left in the sky, but the ground was dark.

He fumbled around in the dark, half expecting to ride right into either Cameron or an Apache encampment. A wolf's howl pierced the gloaming when he was making his way across a meadow, under a ridge built of blocklike chunks of rock. The eerie sound curled the hair on his neck.

Deciding it was time to get the hell out of here—if his brother wanted to track Cameron after Apaches, he could track him his own damn self—Ed brought the horse around and started back in the direction he'd come from. Fuck this. He was ready to go back to the Territories and try his luck again with stagecoaches and small-town banks.

The trail Ed was following down into the semi-arid desert did not look at all like the one he'd taken up, and he was starting to get the willies. He knew how easy it was to get good and lost out here. Hell, he'd heard umpteen dozen stories of men—even good trackers—going into the Sierra Madre and never being heard from again.

Feeling frantic, Ed started riding blind, just letting the horse pick his way, searching for the canyon from which he'd ridden into the high country. If he could get there, he might be able to find his way back to his brother.

Brother. Oh, how good that word sounded all of a sudden! When he saw Jake again, he was going to kiss him right on the mouth.

Ed came to an arroyo that did not look like any of the arroyos he'd seen in the past two hours, much less that day. Heart beating wildly in his breast and legs feeling like lead in his stirrups, Ed brought the horse to a halt and gave his sweating brow a scrub with the back of his gloved hand.

A rock tumbled down from a ridge and clattered against other rocks. A horse whinnied—not his.

Looking up at the low, stony ridge that practically encircled him, Ed saw about a dozen long-haired riders silhouetted against the star-filled sky. They regarded him almost casually.

"Oh . . . Oh, Lord," Ed mumbled to himself, knowing these men in deerskin leggings could be nothing else but Apaches.

Tears welled in his eyes.

"Oh . . . Oh my . . . !"

CHAPTER 27

IT TOOK CAMERON a good ten seconds to remember where he was, and to realize who these three men aiming guns at him were . . .

Rurales.

The dove-gray uniforms and visored military-style hats were all the identification he needed. He assumed the prefect had ratted on him and Jimmy, something Cameron had been too tired to worry about last night. He should have seen it coming, however. The United States and Mexico were not on good terms these days.

Cameron had pushed himself onto his elbows when the man on the far right, wearing sergeant's stripes, grabbed him brusquely by the collar and yanked him to a sitting position. He yelled something in Spanish, too fast for Cameron's comprehension.

Holding up his hands placatingly, Cameron swung his stockinged feet to the floor and reached for his moccasins. While he put them on, the sergeant grabbed Cameron's weapons.

"Come," he said in halting English. "Move, gringo. You are wanted man!"

"Hold on, Charlie, can't you see I'm movin' as fast

as I can?" Cameron carped, yanking on the moccasins, which had shrunk from sweat and sun.

"Move, gringo," one of the other rurales repeated—a reed of a kid with a downy brown mustache barely visible above his mouth. Corporal's stripes adorned his wool sleeve.

"Take your fingers off the triggers, boys, I'm comin'," Cameron said, standing and grabbing his hat.

"Hands up, hands up!" they yelled as they pushed him past his horse to the rear of the barn and out the door into the bright morning sunlight.

Cameron stopped in the yard and said, "I'll go with you in a minute, but let me check on my friend first." He dipped his head toward the rear of the adobe house overgrown with shrubs.

"Move, gringo!" the sergeant yelled again, poking him in the side with his rifle.

Cameron had thought it was worth a try. He'd wanted to know how Jimmy had fared overnight, and he also wanted to make sure the rurales had left him in the house. By the way they hazed Cameron down the street without saying anything about the kid, he assumed they'd left him with the prefect's wife. He was grateful for that, anyway. A Mexican hoosegow was no place for Jimmy in his condition.

The *rurales* ushered Cameron down the street, past jacals and chicken coops and stables made from stones and woven branches. A dog came out from one of the jacals to bark at them fiercely, then turned tail when it saw it was going to be ignored. The woodsmoke hanging in the golden air above the huts smelled of tortillas and spiced meat, causing Cameron's stomach to grumble.

He really could have used a cup of strong coffee and a cigarette, followed by a big plate of eggs and ham and a handful of fresh corn tortillas filled with goat cheese and olives. Instead, he was being hazed down the street like a cantankerous bull, his saddle-sore ass and thighs aching with every shove.

His "morning stroll" ended at a squat, white-washed adobe that stood alone on the eastern side of the street, separated from the other adobes by about twenty yards. Painted above the door was the word Alcalde, or "Mayor." Cameron could see a stable out back, and a corral where a good dozen or so horses milled under a cottonwood tree. Half-dressed soldiers lazed there as well, washing at the well and pitching hay to the horses.

The corporal knocked twice on the hut's plank door and went in, then stepped aside as the sergeant pushed Cameron through the doorway. The third man, a private, stopped outside and came to attention as he took up a sentinel's position to the right of the door.

Cameron blinked as his eyes adjusted to the relative darkness within, then saw a medium-tall man with a soft round paunch, sitting before a small desk on which was a plate of eggs and bacon. Next to the plate sat a covered bowl that Cameron guessed, was keeping tortillas warm. Nearby was a half-empty bottle beside a filmy glass containing one dead fly.

Cameron stood before the desk as the man forked egg into his mouth, followed it with a bite of tortilla, and chewed. Yolk stained the man's salt-and-pepper mustache.

He looked up at Cameron with lazy, colorless eyes. His dove-gray jacket, boasting lieutenant's bars and silver buttons, was open over a washed-out undershirt.

Cameron smelled cigar smoke, and turned to see another man sitting in a wing-backed chair behind him, his fat legs crossed. He wore a straw fedora and a stained suitcoat with tattered cuffs. The alcalde, Cameron thought, whose office had been taken over by the rurales. The unshaven man looked almost comatose, and Cameron assumed he was drunk. Life no doubt had been better before the rurales.

"And who are you?" the lieutenant asked tonelessly as he chewed, as though they were in the middle of a conversation.

"The name's Jack Cameron."

"American?"

"Yes."

"What are you doing here?"

"Hunting Apaches."

The man swabbed his plate with the last of his tortilla and stuck it in his mouth. Cameron's stomach rumbled. "Why?"

Cameron shrugged. "Need the money."

"You a scalp-hunter?"

"That's right."

The lieutenant took a slug from the bottle on his desk and sat back in his chair, which creaked with the strain. He studied Cameron suspiciously.

"What happened to you and the boy?"

"Had a little bad luck," Cameron said. "The Apaches we were following started following us, you might say." He fashioned a smile with only one side of his mouth. "They captured the boy and took him to their rancheria. I snuck in and got him back."

"Who is he?"

"Name's Jimmy Bronco. I found him along the trail and we threw in together."

"He hunts scalps, too, uh?" The lieutenant's eyes narrowed.

Cameron shrugged again. "Why not? We heard you guys down here were paying seven pesos a head. That right?"

The lieutenant did not answer right away. "That's right, señor, but by the look of you, I don't think I have to worry about you breaking my bank, as you say, no?" The man's mustache lifted a little as he smiled, but only with his mouth. His washed-out eyes remained on Cameron's.

Scalp-hunters were about the only Americans welcome in Mexico these days. They were like wolfers, Cameron thought. No one wanted the unsavory breed in their town unless there was a wolf problem.

Cameron knew the man was suspicious of his story, but he also knew the rurale would probably take him at his word. He was a long way from his superiors in Mexico City, and they did not care anyway. Jailing Cameron and Jimmy would only mean paperwork, and Cameron could tell the lieutenant was not a man who enjoyed paperwork. He had obviously grown used to the indolence and lack of supervision out here.

He could haul them out in front of the wall around the square and shoot them, but Cameron did not think the man was a cold-blooded killer. He might be a drunkard, and a lout, but not a killer.

Cameron had an idea.

"Tell ya what else I heard," he said, squinting one eye wistfully. "Gaston Bachelard's out there . . . somewhere."

For the first time, a look of uncertainty came to the lieutenant's fat, florid face. A blush stretched upward into the widow's peak cutting into the curly, gray-flecked hair. He tipped his head a little. "Bachelard?"

"And, no doubt, Miguel Montana."

The lieutenant's voice was furtive, suspicious. "How do you know?"

"One of my men ran into him up north and east of here."

The lieutenant considered this, probing a back tooth with his tongue. "He is heading this way?"

Cameron raised an eyebrow for dramatic emphasis. "Sí."

"What does he want?"

Cameron almost smiled at the man's discomfort. "Well, my man said he had quite a contingent with him. Just guessing, I'd say he's gonna try to take as many villages in this part of Chihuahua as he can. And if what I've heard is true, the peons are no doubt gonna welcome him with open arms." Cameron fashioned a doubtful look and shook his head. "You know how the poor have taken to him and little Miguel."

The lieutenant scowled, his face coloring in earnest. "Yes, the lies he spreads . . ."

"The rurales don't have much support in this neck of the woods?"

Cameron asked it like it was a serious question, but he knew they didn't. The rurales were corrupt, occupying villages and helping themselves to homes, food, livestock, and women. They helped fuel the ubiquitous fires of revolution just as much as the fat politicians in Mexico City did.

Cameron could tell the man wanted nothing to do with Bachelard and Montana, but then again, if he was able to kill or capture the pair, it would be quite a feather in his hat. And it was best to try and track them down before they could ride to the village and attack on their own terms.

Besides, the villagers could and probably would side with the revolutionaries . . .

"You say he is north and east?"

Cameron gestured with a thumb over his shoulder. "Somewhere out that way."

"Could you take me to him?"

"I guess I could if I had to."

"You have to." The lieutenant said something in Spanish to the corporal standing slightly behind Cameron. "Sí, sí, Teniente," the man said, and left in a hurry.

"Go get the boy and your horse," the lieutenant said to Cameron, a kind of fearful resolve in his eyes. "You will take us to Bachelard. If you try to escape, we will hunt you down and shoot you."

Cameron shrugged. "Well, okay, if you say so, *Teniente.*"

He turned and strode casually to the door, making brief eye contact with the mayor. The man turned away glumly and sucked on his cigar. Cameron tugged on his hat brim and grinned. Then he headed up the street, past the fountain, toward the prefect's house, suppressing a smile.

If everything went as planned, he'd avoid a Mexican jail *and* get himself and Jimmy back on the trail toward Adrian Clark, Tokente, and Marina—with a police escort. He doubted the Apaches would attack a fully armed contingent of rurales, even given the *rurales'* reputation for ineptitude and cowardice. But even if they were attacked, Cameron and Jimmy would have a better chance with the rurales than without them.

When they were beyond the Indians, Cameron and Jimmy would find some way to evade the Mexicans, then head for the others. He didn't think it would take much to lose the rurales in the mountains. They weren't known for their tracking abilities, or much else besides drinking and plundering their own villages.

Cameron knocked on the pueblo's door. The door was opened by the prefect's wife. The prefect was sitting at the table eating breakfast. Across from him sat Jimmy Bronco, shoveling in food as fast as he could get it on his fork. Cameron grinned with relief to see the kid looking well on the road to recovery.

"I had to report your presence, señor," the prefect said defensively, standing and turning to Cameron.

"And I thank you mighty kindly, señor," Cameron said.

CHAPTER 28

ALFRED GOING, ADRIAN Clark, and Marina had waited for Cameron the rest of the day he went after Hotchkiss and Jimmy. They had camped on a ledge over a gorge, with a cliff protecting their flank.

Before nightfall Going had considered going after Cameron, then reconsidered. He did not want to leave Clark and the woman alone. If Cameron was in trouble, tracking him would probably only bring trouble for Going and the others, as well. If Cameron, Hotchkiss, and the kid could not handle whatever distress they had run into, chances were that Going wouldn't be able to help much.

No, it was best to wait. And wait he and the Clarks did, watching the sun go down and listening for horses, waking in the morning and listening for horses while they gathered wood, then settling in for the afternoon, peering off across the brassy-yellow waste below, and listening for horses.

Going rolled one cigarette after another, building a supply. Clark paced, got drunk, hacked up blood, passed out, then woke up an hour later and started tipping back the bottle some more.

Marina walked around the grassy ledge, pacing much like her husband did when he wasn't comatose. Every twenty minutes or so, she walked down the trail to where the horses were picketed at a spring-fed pool in the rocks. Going wasn't sure what she did down there, but she stayed there for quite a while—too long for comfort; he didn't want her wandering off and getting nabbed by Indians.

Going knew she was nervous and agitated about Cameron and didn't want her husband to know. She had it bad, that Marina. He guessed she didn't know that Cameron had it just as bad for her. Did the husband know? How could he not? Going just hoped he wasn't around when the sparks flew. When it came to women like that one there, and men like Cameron and Clark, you could always count on sparks, and if not sparks, then lead.

If Cameron returned, that was. By three in the afternoon, nearly twenty-four hours since Cameron had left, things weren't looking good.

"This is ridiculous," Clark said, standing before Going, holding his bottle by the neck.

"You better go easy on that stuff, señor," Going suggested, eyeing the bottle.

"Let's go. We can't wait any longer. Cameron and the others are dead."

Marina appeared behind Clark, coming up from the horses. She stopped, her eyes growing dark as she stared at her husband, wanting to object but unable to find the words.

She couldn't imagine Jack Cameron dead. How could one so capable, so confident—one who made her feel like she had never felt before, who filled her with so much yearning and hope—how could he be dead?

In the last few hours she'd trained herself not to think about it. She'd convinced herself that he would return and all would be well, that they would only have to wait a few minutes more and then they would see his dust trail out in the desert and see his spurs and guns winking in the sun. Then they would hear the clomp of hooves and she would once again be able to look upon his rugged, handsome face, and her heart would grow light and once again all would be right with the world.

If only they could have met in a different life, a different world . . .

"No," she couldn't help saying now.

"'No,' what?" Clark exclaimed, swinging around. Marina hesitated, dropping her eyes. "I think we should wait for him," she said tentatively. "He would do as much for us."

"Ha! That's a joke! Cameron would do whatever he thought was in his goddamned best interest."

"You are wrong, señor," Going said. "He would do the sensible thing." He switched his eyes to Marina. "The sensible thing, señorita, is to continue after the gold. If Cameron returns, he will track us."

"If he's able to track us," Marina said, ignoring the probing stare of her husband.

"Yes, if he is able," Going allowed, pulling deeply on his quirley and tossing the dregs of his coffee in the small fire they had tended. "If he returns and he is not able, he will understand why we left. Cameron knows how the game is played."

Yes, but it is not my game, Marina thought. Staring at her, sneering cruelly, her husband brought the bottle to his lips and drank. His behavior told her he knew very well how she felt about Cameron. He was hurt by it, as any man would be, and wanted to hurt her just as badly.

She did not blame him. Just the same, she could not love him—just as he could not love her. She wanted to be with Cameron. If she ever saw him alive again, she would tell him so, her arrangement with Clark be damned. Clark could have her share of the gold—all, that is, but what she'd need to regain Marlena.

Clark corked the bottle, ran the back of his hand across his mouth, and headed down to the horses.

Going was kicking sand on the fire. "Do not worry, señorita. Cameron will find us." He looked at her and smiled reassuringly.

"Do you really think so, señor?"

"If I told you once, I told you twice—my name is Alfred, or Tokente, if you wish—and yes . . . I am sure."

He touched her gently on the shoulder, winked, and turned and followed her husband to the horses.

———◆———

Gaston Bachelard, little Juanita, Miguel Montana, and ten men—five from Bachelard's faction and five from Montana's—followed their guide, the diminutive Xavier Llamas, through twisting canyons and over pine-studded passes, until the days blended together in a surreal mosaic of disconnected images.

The second day out from the hacienda, they had had a mild skirmish with six Apaches who had apparently been returning from a hunting trip. Packing two mountain goats and several mule deer, the Indians had not been prepared for a hostile encounter, and Bachelard's and Montana's men shot them down like wild dogs and appropriated the meat.

It was good meat, and it saved them time they otherwise would have had to spend hunting.

They did not lose any men in the skirmish with the Apaches, but later they sustained a casualty when one of the men was bit by a rattlesnake while sleeping. He probably would have recovered, given time, but they had no time to spare. Miguel Montana sim-ply stuck his revolver in the sick man's mouth and pulled the trigger. The man sagged backwards, dead.

Holding a protective hand over little Juanita's eyes, Bachelard smiled at the Mexican's cool ef-ficiency, glad that the man Montana had shot was one of his own. It would be one less man Bachelard and his men would have to shoot when they discov-ered the gold. Wealth would be theirs, and so, too, all of Texas and northern Mexico. They would tell the peasants and the rest of Montana's men that Montana had been slain by federalistas or rurales. Miguel Montana would be anointed a martyr and the loyalty of the northern Mexicans would transfer to Gaston Bachelard and his Texas revolutionaries.

Vive le Bachelard!

At the end of the second week, Xavier Llamas brought the procession to a halt on a ridge high up in the Sierra Madre. The breeze blowing through the swaying, creaking pines was tainted with a winter-like chill, so that for several hours all the men had been wearing wool serapes under their bandoliers.

Xavier Llamas sat up straight in the saddle and stared out over the ridge, his small, leathery nose working like a dog's beneath the curled brim of his straw sombrero. The hat was decorated with a pair of crow's feet, snake rattles, and other talismans.

He turned to Bachelard and Montana, riding to his left. There was a twinkle in his cobalt eyes.

"I think we are close, los capitánes."

Bachelard squinted as he studied the patchwork of low-desert watercourses, canyons, valleys, rimrocks, and low, isolated ranges that stretched out beneath them. "I don't see any arrow-shaped ridge," he said.

"No," said Xavier, "but *that* ridge there tells me the other is there"—he pointed to the right, indicating a hill covered with rocks and pines—"beyond that hill."

Bachelard and Montana looked at each other skeptically. Xavier noticed and dismounted his mule. "I show you, los capitánes. Follow me." He handed his reins to one of the other Mexicans and started climbing the hill, his old bowed legs moving with boyish agility.

Bachelard shrugged and dismounted, careful not to unseat the stoic Juanita perched behind the saddle on a blanket. He'd intended to leave her at the hacienda, but when he'd seen how the other girls there were treated, he'd decided it would be safer to take her with him. He would watch over her himself, and when she started to bleed he would marry her.

Bachelard handed his reins to one of his men and started following Xavier up the incline.

"Wait for me," Montana said, following.

The first part of the hill was steepest and hardest, but the old man was negotiating it like a true mountaineer, hardly breaking a sweat. When he reached the summit, he waited for Bachelard and Montana, who came up breathing hoarsely, bent over with their hands on their thighs.

"What is your secret, old one?" Miguel said, gasping for air.

"I limit my tequila to only one liter a day and I fornicate as often as possible," Xavier said with a snaggle-toothed grin, eyes bright with delight.

"Come . . ." he added, jogging off down the other, gentler slope of the hill and stopping on a ledge. Again, Bachelard and Montana followed.

On the ledge, Bachelard sat on a rock to catch his breath and give his aching legs a rest. He gazed out across the desert yawning three or four thousand feet below, a great, water-sculpted, wind-ravaged, sun-baked badlands, home to only the hardiest of creatures. From this vista the centerpiece of it all was a spire of andesite that was capped with an arrow-shaped boulder pointing southeast.

"When we arrive at the spire, we will find the turtles etched in the rock," Xavier said.

"Are you sure, old one?" Montana asked him. He was standing to the old man's right, gazing into the distance.

"I am very sure, el capitán. I would bet my life on it, in fact."

"Oh, no need to do that, Xavier," Bachelard said.

Casually, almost as though he were raising his boot for a shine, Bachelard lifted his foot, planted it firmly against the old man's backside, and shoved. The man dropped over the edge with a sudden, brief yell, and was gone.

Montana, who had turned away briefly, turned back at the sound and saw the old man plummeting down the thousand-foot drop to a sandy slide. Xavier hit the slide without a sound and rolled like a doll, arms flying, tumbling over and over for what seemed forever, finally coming to rest in a brushy crevice.

Montana shouted, "¡Dios mío! What have you done?"

Bachelard shrugged, gazing down at the old man's ant-sized body with dispassion. "He's shown us the way. He is of no more use."

Miguel gestured with his hand. "He was a wise old man, very respected . . ."

"The fewer who know about the treasure, the better, wouldn't you say, Miguel? If there's as much treasure as Xavier claimed, then it will take several trips to bring it all out. In the meantime, we don't want anyone going in ahead of us, and that could be anyone who knows the way."

"That means we will have to kill all the men in our party!" Montana said, red-faced with disbelief.

Bachelard shrugged. "Yes, they will have to be executed upon our return to the hacienda. To appease the others in our armies, we'll say they were conspiring to steal."

Montana's left eye twitched as he pondered this, turning his thoughtful gaze back to the old man, food now for the scavengers. "Yes, I suppose that much gold might lead a few to thoughts of betrayal . . ."

"Exactly," Bachelard said, slapping the smaller Montana on the back. "Shall we?" He gestured to the grade over which they had come.

"No . . . after you," Montana said with a wary smile, not trusting the mad Cajun.

"No, after you," Bachelard insisted.

"Well, together, then," Montana replied.

Each with a nod and a brittle grin, they started back up the grade, hip to hip and shoulder to shoulder, masking their scheming ruminations with smiles.

CHAPTER 29

CAMERON WAS RIDING beside the rurale lieutenant, whose name he had learned was Premierio Gomez. "Maybe we should have left the cannon," he suggested, glancing over his shoulder at the column of gray-clad rurales trailed by a Gatling gun that was mounted on a two-wheeled cart normally used by peasants for hauling hay.

The mule hauling the cart kept wanting to stop to graze along the road, and whenever the cart foundered in sand or alkali dust, the mule wanted to stop rather than push on through. The young soldier who was driving whipped the animal and screamed.

"It's not the gun, it's the mule," Gomez said.

"I think you should have left them both," Cameron said. "And the kid driving the cart."

"If we run into Apaches, we're going to want the Gatling gun. The same is true if we find Montana and Bachelard. If we encounter them, my friend, you are going to thank me for bringing the 'cannon' as you call it."

Cameron peered ahead at the floury white trail twisting over hogbacks as it climbed ever higher into the mountains hovering darkly in the east. "How're you going to get it through the mountains, for chrissakes?"

"You gringos are all alike," Gomez said acidly. "You think you know it all. If you know so damn much, Mr. Cameron, why are you here in this godforsaken place hunting Apache scalps for seven pesos a head?"

Cameron sighed. "You got me there, Lieutenant."

"Unless you were not hunting scalps," Gomez suggested, giving Cameron a sidelong look.

"What else would I be doing?"

"You tell me, amigo."

"Okay, I'm looking for the Lost Treasure of San Bernardo."

Gomez looked at Cameron again and smiled. The smile widened until the lieutenant threw his head back and laughed. "That . . . That's a good one, señor," he said as his laughter settled to a head-shaking chuckle.

"You've heard of it?" Cameron asked.

"Yes, I have heard of it," Gomez said, mopping his forehead with a handkerchief. "Who in northern *Mejico* has not heard of it? Who in northern Mejico has not tried to find it, and died trying? Fools, all."

"I take it you haven't."

"I am not a fool, gringo, and don't you forget it."

That ended the conversation. After about fifteen minutes, Cameron slowed his mount, and Jimmy Bronco, who'd been several places back in the column, caught up to him.

"How ya feelin', kid?"

"Tired, Jack," Jimmy said.

His face was drawn and swollen from the beating he'd taken from the Apaches. The prefect's wife had bandaged most of the cuts, but the bruise over his right eye was a garish purple that covered a good quarter of his face. He was wearing clothes the prefect's wife had rounded up for him—an ill-fitting pair of old denim jeans with holes in the knees, a rope belt, and a cotton poncho with rawhide ties at the neck. Cameron had also bought him a felt poncho and a hat from an old peasant drinking beer in one of the village cantinas. With Jimmy's face badly burned and bruised, he needed as much protection as possible.

"Well, it doesn't look like we're going to be riding very hard," he groused. "Hell, at this pace you can nap in your saddle."

Jimmy turned to Cameron with his jaw set. "They come up on us mighty fast, Jack."

"The Apaches? I bet they did."

"I—I . . ."

Cameron frowned. "What is it, Jim?"

The kid licked his cracked lips and turned his gaze to the rolling, sunbaked hills. "Ol' Hotch, he had his six-shooter out and shot back. But me . . . well, I . . ."

"Froze?"

The kid nodded slightly. His eyes filmed over with tears.

Cameron shrugged. "Same thing happened to me when I was your age."

The kid looked at him, wide-eyed with surprise.

"I was cowpokin' in Nebraska one summer, just after I left home," Cameron continued. "Me and another guy were ridin' drag on a herd when all of a sudden about twelve Arapahos come stormin' down a hogback, a-whoopin' and a-hollerin'.

"Well, me and Joe Luther—that was the older guy I was with—we hightailed it to a buffalo wallow and took cover. Joe Luther, he got his rifle out of his saddle boot and started sendin' some lead after those braves, but me . . . Well, Joe Luther glanced over at me when he was reloadin' and gave me the queerest look. Just then I realized my six-shooter was still in my holster. I hadn't pulled it. I was froze up like a dead cow in a January blizzard."

"You, Jack?"

"Yeah, me. What do you think—I'm not human? I froze up and pret' near got Joe Luther and myself killed. Fortunately, Joe was able to squeeze off enough rounds to hold those braves off until some other drovers arrived to help out."

"Yeah, but ol' Hotch is dead on account of me," Jimmy said.

"Oh, he's not dead on account of you!" Cameron scolded. "He's dead because it was his time to go. Nothin' you or me or anyone else on God's green earth could've changed that. When it's a man's time to go—or a woman's," he added, thinking of Ivy Kitchen, "then they go, in spite of how the rest of us feel about it or what plans we made or how much we want them to stay. That's just the way it is. Even if you'd fired off a few rounds, the Apaches still would have killed Bud, and they probably would have killed you to boot."

"You think so?"

"I know so. Now quit sulkin'. Keep your mind on the moment."

Cameron was about to spur his horse back toward Gomez, when Jimmy said, "Jack, you think I can get another brace of pistols somewhere? Those 'Paches took mine."

Cameron suppressed a smile. "First chance we get, Jim," he said, then heeled his horse up alongside the lieutenant's.

"How is your young partner in crime, amigo?" Gomez asked him with a self-satisfied smirk.

"Better," Cameron said.

An hour later they were off the wagon road and angling into the mountains. It was a rolling, rocky, water-cut country unfavorable for speedy travel, especially when you were pulling a rickety haycart equipped with a Gatling gun.

The main group went ahead of the wagon and two other soldiers, but halted periodically to wait, as the wagon bounced toward them over the eroded, cactus-studded country. The thing looked as though it would lose a wheel or break its axle at any moment. Cameron wished it would; then they would have no choice but to abandon it and really make some time.

Cameron was eager to find his group. The cries he had heard last night still haunted him, and he wanted to confirm that Going, Clark, and Marina were safe.

He still wondered . . . If it had not been one of the men of his party he had heard last night, then who?

The answer came when one of the rurales who had been scouting ahead returned to the column and reported seeing what looked like a human tied to a piñon tree under a distant cliff. Cameron, Gomez, and two other men rode out to take a look.

Fifteen minutes later they ascended a gravelly finger splitting two dry washes, to the base of the granite escarpment. They found the man staked to the tree, facing out from the cliff, head down, long, sandy-blond hair hiding his face.

The man was naked and covered with dried blood, crawling with ants and abuzz with flies. He'd been castrated, partially skinned, and several of his fingers were missing. There were hardly three square inches on him that had not been violated with a sharp knife.

The stench was almost palpable. Even Cameron, who had seen the grisliest of Indian outrages, had to work to keep from gagging.

Lieutenant Gomez said, "Ai-yee," and crossed himself.

One of the men next to him vomited.

Cameron dismounted, walked over to the body and lifted the chin. The man's eyeballs had been burned out with pokers; his nose was smashed and his jaw broken, but Cameron still recognized him.

It was Ed Hawkins—Jake's brother. What the hell was he doing here?

Ed and Jake must have followed him and the others from Contention City. The Apaches must have found him on Cameron's trail last night. Serves you right, Cameron thought, staring into the empty eyesockets. But where was Jake?

The answer came to him like a sudden onset of the flu. No doubt Jake was still trailing Adrian Clark, Marina, and Tokente. Maybe he'd shown himself by now and the others were in trouble. Cameron's urgent need to find the others renewed itself with vigor.

"You know this man?" Gomez asked him.

Before Cameron could answer, the head moved slightly and the lips parted. Cameron's heart thumped.

Ed was alive.

"Jesus God," Cameron breathed.

The man's lips formed the words long before he could give them voice. "Help . . . Help me . . . please . . ." The voice was little more than a labored rasp.

Feeling sick, Cameron pulled his bowie—he did not want to signal his presence with the Colt—and plunged it into Ed's chest just beneath the breastbone. Ed shuddered as if chilled.

When the body was finally still Cameron removed the bowie and cleaned it in the sand. Standing, he turned to Gomez, who was watching him, white-faced, with newfound respect.

"No, I don't know him," Cameron said. He grabbed the saddle horn and climbed back into the leather, then spurred his horse back toward the column.

As they made their way farther into the mountains, Cameron considered ways he could get rid of the rurales and back to Tokente, Marina, and Clark. For the moment, he and Jimmy were safest in the soldiers' company, but tonight he wanted to keep traveling—only him and Jimmy.

There would be a moon by which to navigate, and the Apaches would have a hard time cutting their trail without the sun, so he and Jimmy could travel relatively safely. They'd no doubt catch up to the others sometime tomorrow morning.

It would take these distinguished upholders of Mexican law another week to cover that much ground, especially if they kept packing the cannon.

An hour later Gomez halted the column for the day, in a spot protected by a steep, sandstone ridge on one side, and brushy arroyos on two more. A spring bubbled out of several places in the rocks. The sun turned the sandstone ridge the color of copper; above, a hawk hunted, turning lazy circles in the cerulean sky, where a crystalline moon shone.

There was still at least another hour of good light left, but Cameron was glad the lieutenant had decided to call it a day. Traveling with these men was an exercise in frustration. Nearly all but Gomez looked greener than spring saplings, and had probably spent most of their lives hoeing beans and peppers. Cameron wondered if any of them even knew how to shoot the outdated Springfield rifles poking out of their saddleboots. In addition, could Gomez keep them from bolting or freezing when and if things got sticky?

Something about the man's countenance, no less dubious and defensive for being so overbearing, told him not to count on it.

Cameron slipped the saddles and bridles from his and Jimmy's mounts, then tethered them in a patch of grass near the water. He built a small fire. Gomez left his mount to be tended by one of his men, spread his bedroll in the shade of a boulder and collapsed on it, producing a bottle from his saddlebags, a dreamy cast entering his eyes as he uncorked it.

Cameron and Jimmy shared the dried goat-meat and cheese the prefect's wife had sent with them, Cameron giving Jimmy the brunt of the portion. When Jimmy had finished eating and had a cup of coffee, he went out like a light.

When the sun set, Cameron rolled up in his own blanket and tipped his hat over his face. He wanted to catch a few hours of shut-eye before he and Jimmy tried lighting out on their own.

Sometime later he opened his eyes to a sky full of stars, the crescent moon shimmering and bathing the foothills in ghostly light.

He squeezed Jimmy's shoulder, and touched his index finger to his lips. The boy came awake and instantly began rolling his blanket. When Cameron had done the same, he looked around.

The rurales were dark heaps around the three guttering fires. Their snores rose on the vagrant breeze.

Gomez had posted guards on the perimeter. Cameron knew that he and Jimmy would have to make as little noise as possible so as not to alert them. Cameron figured they'd be seen eventually, but he hoped it wouldn't be until after their horses were saddled.

He and Jimmy saddled the horses in anxious silence, glancing around, then led the animals down one of the arroyos, where the sandy bottom muffled the sounds of their hooves. They'd gone about seventy-five yards down the twisting, turning course when Jimmy's horse started at some night creature scuttling in the shrubs. The animal jerked to a stop and whinnied.

Cameron and Jimmy stopped, listening. Cameron was about to sigh with relief when he heard questioning voices in the distance.

"Let's go!" he said, and he and Jimmy quickly mounted and spurred their horses down the arroyo.

A rifle popped behind them, then another.

With Jimmy following closely behind him, Cameron traced the arroyo for half a mile, then followed a game trail up the bank through a narrow cut in a ridge, then higher into the mountains. Post oaks and piñon pines rose around them, silhouetted by the moon. Last night Cameron had oriented himself using the distant ridges as a guide, and now he rode in what he hoped was the general direction of the rest of his party.

When they were a good three miles away from the rurale bivouac, Cameron halted his horse on a ridge, turned back and cocked his head to listen. He thought he could hear a thin, distant voice or two, but nothing else aside from the labored breathing of his own horse and the mournful howl of a wolf higher up in the mountains.

"I think we're rid of 'em," Cameron said, smiling at Jimmy. "How ya doin', kid?"

"Just fine, Jack," Jimmy said, in a voice that sounded very much like his old self.

"Let's ride, then," Cameron said, giving his horse the spurs.

CHAPTER 30

———————

PERRO LOCO HAD crossed the Rio Bavispe four days behind Cameron and the others, two horses tied behind the mount he was riding. He traveled all day and most of the night, stopping only for catnaps and to eat the birds and rabbits he trapped or killed with a slingshot, not wanting to announce his presence with a gun.

He had reached the place where Cameron had left the others, though Loco could not know exactly what had happened. The Apache knew only that two riders had left the group about a half-mile back and that now another rider was heading back up the trail at a gallop.

Loco traced one of the hoofprints with his index finger, gripping the rifle he had taken from Tokente's woman, pondering the situation.

Three had gone south and three had lingered here for several hours before riding on. Where was Cameron?

Perro Loco slung the rifle over his shoulder and mounted the white-man's saddle, which he had found more comfortable than bareback riding for long distances. Something told him Cameron had ridden south. He reined his horse around in the direction the lone rider's hoofprints pointed, and headed south.

Roughly four miles behind him, She-Bear studied Perro Loco's trail along a dry riverbed. Like Perro Loco, she trailed two horses behind the one she was riding.

One was rigged with packs of food supplies, two extra rifles, a pistol, and ammunition. The other horse she had ridden until an hour ago. She was resting it now. She'd use it later, when the one she was riding had tired.

She-Bear gripped her rifle in her hands, tossed the hair from her eyes, scratched the scar on her nose, and continued on . . .

Alfred Going, Adrian Clark, and Marina came upon another turtle etched in a stone ridge, about three circuitous miles from where they'd waited for Cameron and the others. It was their third turtle that day.

"Well, I'll be goddamned," Clark said, dismounting his horse.

"Not only that, but that," Going said, lifting his chin to indicate something above and behind Clark.

"What?" Clark said, turning.

Marina had already seen it. "Oh my God . . ." she breathed.

Clark lifted a hand to block the sun and squinted at the formation towering above them. It was a stone spire with an arrow-shaped cap. The arrow was pointing due east, straight down the volcanic lava bed they had been following, the ancient path down which the turtles had been leading them.

"We're close, aren't we?" Clark said, feeling as though he were about to hyperventilate. His heart was doing somersaults and his head felt light.

"Hee," Going said by way of reply.

"Well, what are we waiting for?" Clark said, mounting up.

He and Going started off down the lava bed, the shod hooves of their horses clomping loudly on the time-worn black rock of the canyon. Marina watched them go, then turned to look behind her, hoping she'd see Cameron and the others.

But there was no one there, and she was beginning to feel, with a sinking in her stomach, that she was never going to see Cameron again . . . that she would never be able to tell him that she loved him . . . that no matter what became of them, no matter what else she would lose or gain in this life, she loved him . . .

But Marina had a feeling that Adrian Clark was going to remain an obstacle between her and Cameron. Something told her that Adrian would kill either her or Cameron or both rather than let them be together. She turned once more to glance down the trail, seeing nothing but lava rock and the narrow defile shaded by the high rock walls, then rode on.

She caught up to Going and Clark and they came upon yet another turtle, which led them out of the canyon and into the mouth of another. There was a pile of rock between walls of andesite that jutted at least a thousand feet straight up on both sides, sheer walls, with nary a crag or crack, blocking out the sun. It looked as though, relatively recently, boulders had fallen from the clifftops and shattered in the mouth of the canyon.

Clark rode around the wreckage and had started into the canyon when he saw Tokente inspecting the rubble with a puzzled air. Clark paused and asked, "What is it?"

"The church."

"What?"

"Look," Going said, pointing at what remained of the ruined adobe walls and belfry. He saw no bells.

"Of course," Clark whispered, reining his horse back to the pile.

"There must have been an earthquake."

Clark looked at Marina and grinned happily. She returned the look and the smile. It was exciting indeed to find what they had been searching for. She only wished Cameron had found it too.

Clark removed the plat from his boot and opened it before him. He looked around, peered up at the cliffs towering a thousand feet above them, then pointed. "The gold is in there. Back farther in that canyon."

"Hee," Going smiled, staring into the canyon, the opening of which was bathed in golden light.

It was a mythic scene, ominous yet somehow beckoning, welcoming yet chilling. The gold would be in there, hidden in the canyon.

"What are we waiting for?" Clark asked Going.

Going shrugged. "'S awful dark. I think we should wait until tomorrow."

"With walls that steep there won't be adequate light until noon!"

"The morning will bring better light than this. It's dark as night in there now. We won't find a thing." Going dismounted and started unsaddling his horse.

Clark looked irritated. "What are you doing?"

"Set up camp. Build a fire. Make coffee. That gold's been there for two hundred years. It will be there tomorrow."

"I can't wait until tomorrow!"

Going pulled the saddle from his horse and tossed it on the ground, near the rubble. Marina dismounted and began unsaddling her own mount.

Clark watched them, red-faced with anger. Suddenly he coughed. The spasms lasted nearly a minute, irritating his horse.

When they'd subsided and he'd wiped the blood

from his mouth, he said, "Well, I'm going in for a look. The hell with you two!"

When he'd left, Marina said to Going, "Is there water around?"

"There might be water in that little side canyon," the Mexican said, pointing. "If there is, there'll be grass there, too." Going laughed and shook his head as he began gathering rocks for a fire ring.

"What is humorous?" Marina asked him.

"Life is humorous, señora. I grew up near here, in a village—I do not even know if it exists any longer. I hunted and fished in these mountains. Hell, I probably passed within two or three miles of this place. Two or three miles within the mother lode of all mother lodes of Spanish gold!"

"We don't know it's there yet," Marina cautioned.

"No, but if it is there, the joke will be on me."

"If it is not, then I guess the joke will be on us all," Marina said.

Hefting a rock, Going shrugged. "Well, I guess we are just romantics . . ." he said, as if that excused them.

"That's funny—I never used to see myself that way."

Going laughed as he strode over to another rock, wagging his head. "Ho-ho! You are indeed a romantic, my dear. If you were not so fond of Jack Cameron, and I not so fond of She-Bear, we would make a good pair, don't you think?"

Marina laughed. "You know, I think we would make a lovely pair, señor," she said, smiling a smile that wrung Going's heart.

He watched her lead her horse away, shamelessly admiring the way her hips swung as she moved, the way her riding skirt pulled taut across her nicely rounded hips, the way her full black hair shifted along her slender back.

A night with one such as that, he thought, her strong

young legs wrapped around my back, would kill an old goat like me. But . . . ah . . . what a sweet way to go!

Marina had returned from picketing her and Going's horses near water and fresh graze when Clark rode out of the canyon, his dun horse gleaming in the dying light, puffs of golden dust rising about its hooves. Clark's shoulders were slumped, his face drawn with despair.

He said nothing as he drew up next to the fire Going had lit from wood scraps he and Marina had gleaned from the side canyon.

"How does it look?" Going asked Clark good-naturedly.

"Dark," Clark complained, throwing off his saddle.

They were low on food, so Going took his rifle into one of the side canyons and shot a javelina, which he dressed on the spot, then carried over his shoulder back to the camp by the ruined church.

He built a spit from green cottonwood branches, sharpening the skewer with his knife. The sun had gone behind the westward hills as he set one skewered hindquarter of the javelina over the fire, which had burned down nicely and shone with hotly glowing coals. The meat sent up heavenly smells as it cooked. Grease dripped from the cracking skin, snapping and hissing in the coals.

They ate under a sky streaked with the Milky Way, a quarter-moon lifting over the craggy clifftops. They washed down their supper with coffee—in Clark's case, coffee liberally enhanced with brandy. He was no sooner finished eating than he rolled into his blanket and began snoring.

"You better get some sleep, señorita," Going told Marina, who was sitting on a rock, cup of coffee in hand, staring off in the darkness.

"Yes, I suppose . . ." she said vacantly. Going knew she was waiting for Cameron.

"I will take the first watch," he said to her, and got up stiffly, stretching the kinks out of his legs. He picked up his rifle, an old trapdoor Spencer, and moved out from the fire.

He checked on the horses nibbling contentedly on some bunchgrass, then ascended an acclivity on the other side of the spring. It was a steep climb, but mountain goats and probably the ancient ones, as well as the Spanish priests who had once mined this country, had beat a decent switchbacking trail into the craggy, flinty earth. With the moon it was not hard to make out the trail.

When Going came to the top he sat on what appeared to be a barrow, within which some ancient was no doubt buried. He'd seen plenty of such prehistoric graves when he was a kid herding sheep in these mountains and hiking to the alpine lakes to fish for the sweet-tasting trout that spawned there.

Suddenly he stared in astonishment. A pinprick of light flashed below, not far away, maybe a hundred yards nearly straight below him. Going could tell it was a campfire.

Who the hell could that be? Apaches? Bachelard? Hell, it might even be Cameron, looking for them . . .

Crouching and holding his rifle out before him, taking extra care with his steps so as not to loosen any stones that could give him away, Going started down the trail, toward the flickering fire.

Slowly, quietly, he fed a shell into the Spencer's chamber . . . just in case . . .

CHAPTER 31

GOING APPROACHED THE fire quietly, one slow step at a time, zigzagging between boulders. He could see a man sitting before the fire, gazing into the flames. The man held a canvas coat closed at his throat. Wolves howled in the distance, and every time a howl lifted, the man jerked his head around as if expecting to see one of the animals moving in for the kill.

Going made his approach from behind. With the man's back clearly in view, he moved forward, scanning the ground for sticks or stones he might step on and betray himself.

"Easy now, señor," he said at last, holding the barrel of his Spencer about a foot from the back of the man's neck. "No sudden moves now, eh? Slowly lift your hands above your head."

The man straightened, stiffening, and froze. Going saw him shudder.

"Who are you?" the man snapped.

"I'll do the asking, since I have the gun. Lift your hands above your head and tell me who you are."

"I'm . . ." The man hesitated, lifting his hands and jerking his head sideways for a glimpse of the man holding the rifle on him. "I'm Davis, Tom Davis," the man said.

Going had noticed the man's hesitation and wasn't sure what to make of it. Was the man lying about who he was, or was he just too nervous to spit it out without fidgeting?

The man repeated, "I'm Tom Davis, from out Californy way. Who're you?"

"Alfred Going. Some call me Tokente. What are you doing out here all by yourself?"

The man hesitated again, then said, "I'm prospectin'."

"Alone?"

"My partner, he took off on me a ways back. Took all our supplies with him, the bastard." The man chuffed a laugh and shook his head. "Really left me in a fix, he did. I don't s'pose you got any smokin' tobaccy on ye?"

"No," Going muttered, still unsure what to think of this man.

He didn't look like a miner. He looked like an outlaw. But what would an outlaw be doing this far off the beaten path? Hell, there wasn't anyone to steal from in a hundred square miles.

Except Going's own party, that was . . .

———

Jake Hawkins was thinking the same thing. He knew the mining story sounded feeble, considering he didn't look any more like a miner than did Jesse James or Cole Younger, two of his heroes. The problem was, he couldn't concoct a better story on the spur of the moment, especially one this crotchety old Mex would believe.

The man had to be from Cameron's party. What else would he be doing out here?

Hawkins silently chastised himself for getting careless and building a fire out in the open. He was getting as stupid as his brother Ed. And where was Ed? Jake hadn't seen him in a couple of days, since he'd branched off the trail to follow Cameron.

Going slowly walked in front of Hawkins, half shutting one eye and giving him the twice-over. "Maybe you are following me, eh, amigo?"

"Why would I be followin' you?"

Going shrugged. "You are a long way from anywhere. It would be a very long trail out with ore; that is why very few have ever tried to mine this country—except the padres, that is, long ago. But they smelted their own ore."

Hawkins swallowed, growing more and more nervous by the second. He'd known there was something wrong with his story. Sure, this country was too remote for only two men to try hauling out ore. Jake, you dumbshit.

"Well, I guess we just didn't think of that," Hawkins said with a smile, knowing it sounded lame. "Why don't you put the gun down—you be making me nervous—and sit down for a spell? I sure don't mind the company." He gave a brief chuckle.

Behind the grin he used to look benign, Hawkins was concocting a way to get Going to drop his guard. Hawkins only needed a second or two. If the man put the gun down or just looked away for a second, Jake could go for the knife he kept inside his shirt, on his back between his shoulder blades.

"I don't know," Going said, "it seems strange, a man camped alone out here. You know what I think? You got wind of my friend Cameron and the Clarks and their quest for gold, and you decided to follow them to the mother lode."

"What?" Hawkins said. "'Cameron and the Clarks'? I don't know what you're talkin' about, friend."

"You mean to tell me you have never heard of Jack Cameron?"

"Jack Cameron? Who's that?"

"One of the best Indian-trackers in Arizona. You never heard of him?"

Hawkins thought for a moment, then shook his head. "No . . . can't say as I ever have."

"No?" Going said, feigning surprise. "Well, have you ever heard of the name Jake Hawkins?" He smiled and fixed his eyes on Hawkins's plug-ugly face. "A petty thief who steals from the poor and the elderly so he can drink himself comatose every weekend in Nogales or Tombstone or Tucson. A pathetic waste of a man, just like his brother—what is his name . . . Ed? Yes, Eduardo. The Hawkins boys of Tucson. Famous in their own way—their own childish, petty criminal way. Who in the southern Territories does not know them, eh? Certainly not me." Going's voice grew hard. "No, certainly not me, gringo scumbag. I have lived in this country nearly all my life, and I read the Tucson paper. I have read your name in it often." Going smiled.

Hawkins spread his fingers. "Why . . . you're crazy, friend. I don't know what you're talkin' about. I told you, my name's Tom Davis."

"Turn around," Going said.

"Huh?"

"Turn around."

Going had decided to tie the man's wrists behind his back and take him back to the others. He and the Clarks would have to keep an eye on him. Going did not know how the man had found out about the gold, but find out he certainly had.

No doubt the Hawkins boys had planned to wait until his own party had found the cache, then ambush them and take whatever they could carry.

Where was Ed Hawkins, anyway?

Going asked Jake that very question.

"I don't know who you're talkin' about," Hawkins said.

"You don't, huh? Maybe he followed Cameron, eh, gringo? Is that where the charming Eduardo has gone?"

"Go fuck yourself."

Going smiled. "Ah, yes, the charming Hawkins boys."

"Go fuck yourself, you dirty old bean-eater."

Going clubbed the man with the butt of his Spencer. Hawkins yelled and stumbled forward, then hit the ground. Going looked about for something with which to tie him and saw a lariat looped around the horn of Hawkins's saddle, which lay on the ground about fifteen feet away.

Starting for the saddle, Going put his back toward Hawkins. In an instant Jake pulled the knife from the sheath between his shoulder blades and sent the Arkansas toothpick flying end over end through the air.

The weapon entered Going's back point-first, and the man grunted, stiffening and turning at the same time. He swung his rifle around and fired. The Spencer's .45-caliber bullet nearly took off the top of Hawkins's head. Jake Hawkins gave an airy whimper, kicked his feet, and died.

Going staggered sideways and collapsed to his knees, cursing. The rifle slipped from his hands.

What a fool he'd been to turn his back on the man!

The knife had entered just beneath his left shoulder blade. Blood flowed down his back, soaking his shirt. On his knees, he reached around to try and grab the knife, but he couldn't reach it. The pain was hot and intense.

Cursing himself once more, he struggled to his feet. He could not stay here. If he was going to survive, he would have to get back to the Clarks. He wasn't sure he could make it—he was losing blood fast and his legs felt like putty—but he had to try.

The only alternative was to lie down and die, and Alfred Going was not a man who just lay down and died.

At least he'd shot Jake Hawkins. As he moved away from the fire, looking for the trail on which he'd come, that single thought gave him satisfaction.

It took him nearly twenty minutes to cover the hundred or so yards back up the ridge. He had to stop several times as his head reeled. Blood was streaming down his back, into the waistband of his buckskin breeches, then down his butt and left leg.

He wanted to lie down and give up but something pushed him on. Moving as if sleepwalking, he reached the crest of the ridge and started down.

About halfway down the butte, he collapsed. His face hit the ground with a mind-numbing force. He tried to get his arms beneath him, to push himself up, but they would not respond. He felt as limp as an old towel.

Finally, sucking air into his lungs, fighting off the pain that pierced his entire being with every breath, he managed to lift his old Smith & Wesson cap-and-ball revolver from the holster on his side. He thumbed back the hammer, lifting the gun skyward, and fired. The *pop* resounded off the surrounding cliffs, sounding obscene in the heavenly quiet.

He thumbed back the hammer once more, fired again, and then one more time.

Semiconscious, he did not know how long it was before he heard running footsteps and labored breathing. "Here . . . I think he's here," he heard a woman say.

A man coughed, cursed. It sounded as though he was slipping on the gravelly slope. He cursed again. Then Going heard the footsteps approach, smelled Marina's sweet scent just before he saw her kneeling down beside him.

"Oh, señor!" she cried. "What happened?"

It took him a moment to reply, wincing against the pain in his back. "J-Jake Hawkins . . . was dogging our trail."

"Hawkins?"

"Sí. I know not why, but . . . Help me, señora . . . back to the camp."

More footsteps pounded near—dark, breathing raspily. He cleared his throat. "Going . . . what the hell happened?"

"He ran into Jake Hawkins," Marina said. "We have to get him back to the camp. There is a knife in his back."

"Oh, Jesus," Clark complained. "What the hell was Jake Hawkins doing out here?"

"Following us . . . for the gold," Marina said. She was trying to pull Going to his feet. "Help me."

"Don't worry," Going said tightly. "Hawkins is dead." He managed a smile.

Clark cursed again and took Going's other arm. They lifted the man to his knees, then eased him to his feet. He moaned with pain.

"You will be all right, señor," Marina said. "When we get you back to the camp we will remove the knife and get you well again."

"Gracias, señora, but I don't think—" They lifted him to his knees and he gave a yell. Awkwardly they started down the trail.

"I thought we agreed that you would call me Marina," she said, grunting under the injured man's weight.

"Sí," Going managed breathily.

"You sure are getting friendly with the men in our party," Clark groused. Marina ignored him.

They reached the camp fifteen minutes later, and eased the man into a sitting position by the fire. He had passed out, so Clark supported him while Marina removed his tunic and undershirt, cutting the material away from the knife jutting from his back.

"That's nasty," Clark said, wincing at the wound. "This far from a doctor, he'll never make it."

"We have to remove the knife," Marina said.

She clutched the handle and pulled. It came up only a half-inch, pulling the skin up with it, and more blood. Going groaned hoarsely.

"I can't do it," she said. "You'll have to."

Clark scowled, as if to say, *What's the use?* but eased Going into Marina's arms and placed both his hands on the knife. He bit his lip and pulled. He wiped his hands on his trousers, wrapped them tightly around the hilt, and heaved, grunting with effort.

Finally the knife pulled free of the bone. The blood-soaked blade glistened black in the light from the fire. Marina eased Going onto his side, then rolled him onto his stomach so she could inspect the wound.

"It does not look good," she said with a sigh. "We have to get the blood stopped. I need some cloth. In my saddlebags . . . get something, anything . . . please."

Clark grudgingly did as she asked. When he handed Marina a white shawl, she tore it in two and soaked one of the halves with water from a canteen. Then she began, gently to clean the wound.

It took her fifteen minutes, working carefully

around the wound, pouring water into it and delicately removing particles of sand and anything else that might cause infection. Then she stitched the wound with sterilized thread and needle that she had packed in case of such an emergency.

By the time she was finished, there were three piles of blood-soaked cloth and two empty canteens by the fire. She'd tied a makeshift bandage around Going's back, heavily padding the wound. Hoping she'd gotten the blood stopped, she slumped next to the man, dead tired. Her head was almost too heavy to lift.

Clark lay on the other side of the fire, sipping from his last brandy bottle. "A lot of work for nothing," he said with a sneer. It was as though he enjoyed taunting her any way that he could, now that he knew she loved Cameron.

She ignored him. She could give him that small comfort, at least.

She slid back against a rock and closed her eyes. One of them would have to stay awake with Going, in case the wound opened again. She knew she could not count on Adrian, so she would have to be the one.

But for the moment, she needed to shut her eyes, if only for a moment . . . .

CHAPTER 32

ALL NIGHT JACK Cameron and Jimmy Bronco moved steadily and deliberately through the mountains. Even with the moon it was often a treacherous ride.

At one point, when the moon was blocked by a peak and Cameron couldn't see the terrain, Cameron's horse nearly slipped down a ridge into a gorge. If he hadn't felt the cool breeze blowing up, sensed the drop, and reined in the buckskin, he and the horse would have been goners.

Riding through a meadow encircled with pines, they stopped when they heard a hunting mountain lion scream, and Cameron felt a chill in his loins, knowing what such a creature could do to a man and a horse. Other sounds filled the night as well—wolves, night birds, the wind sawing the stony peaks around them, the tinny chatter of water bubbling in a creek or spring, javelinas scuttling in the brush—and Jimmy and Cameron traveled nearly as much by these noises as by sight.

Cameron halted several times to rest the horses as well as Jimmy, who would not complain or ask for a break, but Cameron knew the boy was spent. In the morning they stopped on a grassy ledge overlooking a valley of undulating hummocks of low, juniper-tufted hills. Tying his horse to a picket pin, Cameron produced his field glasses from his saddle-bags, climbed a low, rocky mound, and scanned the terrain behind them.

"Shit," he said after a minute, not quite able to believe what he was seeing.

"What is it?" Jimmy asked him.

"If I'm not loco . . . No, it's them, all right . . . the rurales. Somehow they've managed to follow us."

"With the cart?" Jimmy exclaimed.

Cameron adjusted the focus and surveyed the group, but saw no sign of the cart. What he did see was a bulky object strapped to one of the pack mules. From the size and shape, he figured it was the Gatling gun.

Apparently, after Cameron and Jimmy had slipped away from him, Gomez had gotten serious and decided to get rid of the bulky cart. Cameron had made a fool of him by getting away so easily, and now Gomez was tracking him and Jimmy with fervor.

It looked like he was even using an experienced tracker: A skinny young man in an oversized *rurale* uniform was leading the way, pointing out sign as he rode. As far as Cameron could tell, they were covering the very same ground he and Jimmy had traversed about two hours ago. The kid must have been raised in this country, and knew its every crease and fold.

"Well, I'll be goddamned," Cameron said wonderingly, as he stared at the ragged column moving deliberately through the broken, ridge-relieved, canyon-creased country behind him. "I think we put a burr under ol' Gomez's blanket, kid. We'd better mosey."

An hour later he stopped again.

Scanning the country behind them, he saw that

Gomez was staying hot on their trail. He didn't appear to be gaining ground, but Cameron had a newfound respect for the man. He and Jimmy couldn't dally.

Cameron trained the field glasses eastward and spied a flicker of movement in a narrow defile between two mountain crags. Probably just a cloud shadow, but he stayed with the spot, tightening the focus.

Nothing. Then something moved. It was no shadow.

A horseback rider.

Damn. Apaches.

No . . . wait.

Cameron held the glasses on the split between the promontories. Something passed the opening, and from this distance it was hard to tell even with the glasses, but it looked very much like another rider.

There was another movement, then another and another, and Cameron realized there was a whole column of riders passing behind that rocky upthrust. They didn't ride like Apaches. The only non-Indians out here would have to be Gaston Bachelard and Miguel Montana.

Cameron suddenly felt apprehensive about pursuing the man, yet that's what he'd come here for—to make Bachelard pay for the death of Pas Varas.

Bachelard was a nut, but he was a dangerous nut, and he had a lot of dangerous men behind him. And tracking him down with the intent of killing him, Cameron saw now, wasn't exactly sane.

But whether he liked it or not, he'd gotten what he'd come for. Bachelard was indeed after the gold, and it did look as though their paths were going to cross. Whether he liked it or not, it looked like Cameron was going to get his shot at the man.

Cameron swung the glasses in the direction Bachelard was heading and stopped when a particular formation caught his eye. His heart grew heavy in his chest and he felt a drop of sweat sluice down his spine as he realized he was looking at the tall stone spire, capped with an arrow-shaped boulder, that resided very near the X on Clark's plat.

"Holy Jesus," he muttered.

"What is it?" Jimmy asked. He was taking a breather in the shade of a boulder, holding his horse's reins in his hands.

"I think I just found the X on the map . . . and Gaston Bachelard."

Remounting, they continued on, reckoning now on the arrow-shaped boulder capping the spire, just as Bachelard was doing. Cameron rode with a renewed sense of urgency, his thoughts turning to Marina.

She, Clark, and Tokente had no doubt discovered the spire by now. It wasn't that far from where Cameron had left them. They'd probably found the cache, or at least the place where the cache was supposed to be.

He hoped he could reach them before Bachelard did, and warn them, lead them to safety, if there was such a thing out here. If Bachelard came upon them anywhere near the supposed gold, he'd kill the men with as little concern as he'd have for squashing a bug. There was no telling what he'd do to Marina, but Cameron knew it wouldn't be anything as merciful as killing her.

Mile after twisting, turning mile he and Jimmy rode through one canyon after another, keeping the arrow-shaped spire ahead of them. Several times Cameron stopped to climb a butte and look around. Sometimes he saw the two groups of men following him and sometimes he did not, but he always knew they were there—the rurales slowing in the canyons, Bachelard keeping pace.

In the early afternoon, Cameron was scouting from a low mesa and saw that an ancient, deep river gorge lay in Bachelard's path. Cameron felt a surge of optimism. Bachelard and Montana would lose some time finding a way around the chasm, time Cameron hoped he and Jimmy would be able to use to their best advantage, locating the Clarks and Tokente and getting them the hell out of here.

Cameron would backtrack later and, crazy as it was, find a way to isolate Bachelard from his group and kill him. He owed it to Pasqual Varas and his family.

He knew the reluctance he felt now was due to Marina. Because of her, he wasn't as indifferent as before about putting his life in harm's way. But he told himself that whatever he felt for her was for naught; she was another man's wife. Cameron's sense of honor and decency would not allow him to take the wife of another—no matter how beautiful she was or how much he loved her . . . or how much sense she made of his existence.

It might be better, he mused, if he did not come out of this alive.

Cameron thought it must have been about three in the afternoon when he and Jimmy at last came to the spot where Jimmy and Bud Hotchkiss had been attacked by Apaches.

Cameron recognized the place and saw what looked like half a dozen carrion birds working on an elongated lump on the ground. He'd seen similar things before, but it was still a startling and disturbing sight.

Cameron told Jimmy to wait, and rode on ahead. One of the birds broke away with a raucous cry, beating its wings violently in the unmoving air, then jumped back into the fray. Cameron picked up a stone and threw it, sending up dust near the mass. The birds awkwardly took flight, squawking and flapping their heavy black wings.

Cameron had not had time to bury Hotchkiss before, so now, while the horses and Jimmy rested, he dragged the bloating, stinking, ravaged corpse into an arroyo. With the rurales and Bachelard so close, there was no chance to dig a grave, but Cameron doubted Hotchkiss would know the difference between scavenger birds above ground and worms below.

"You were a good friend," were all the words he could come up with, but somehow they seemed enough. He donned his hat again and walked over to where Jimmy was resting with the horses.

"Forget it, Jim," he said, seeing that the boy was staring with haunted eyes at the boulder-strewn slope down which the Apaches had come. The kid blinked and slowly stood. He wrapped his reins around the saddle horn and poked a ropesoled sandal through a stirrup.

"I can't," he mumbled.

Less than twenty minutes later they came to the point where Cameron had separated from the others, and soon after, they found the campsite on the hillside. Then it was easy, just a matter of basic tracking, then finding the turtles the padres had etched in the rocks and the spire, its arrow-shaped cap looming darkly against the afternoon sky. It was so close that

Cameron could make out the sun-shadowed gouges and splinters in the andesite, the fluted reliefs aimed skyward.

At this altitude the air was thin, the sun intense, and the horses were winded, but Cameron did not want to stop again until he'd found the others. He figured they were two or three hours ahead of Bachelard but he didn't know the country well enough to be sure, and there was no point in taking chances.

Just ahead, in the direct path of the arrow pointing behind them, stood two towering escarpments forming a gateway into a canyon. It was like something out of a kid's storybook, and Cameron's heart tattooed an insistent rhythm as he realized this was the place—this was the X marked on the old Mexican's plat.

Before the entrance to the canyon was a jumble of boulders, strewn and cracked as though fallen from high above. Looking again, Cameron saw what remained of an adobe church, its walls nearly crushed by the boulders so that they were nearly unrecognizable at certain angles.

A woman appeared around one of the boulders—a tall, slender woman with long, black hair. She wore a white blouse and butternut slacks, with a gun and holster on her slender waist. She was holding a hat.

Marina . . .

So great was his relief to have found her still alive and apparently well, that he couldn't help grinning as he rode up to her. Her eyes followed him, looking up beseechingly into his face. There was something wrong.

"What is it?" he said, dismounting.

She turned and he followed her around the boulder to where the fire ring lay surrounded by blankets, canteens, an empty brandy bottle, and cooking utensils. A man lay in the shade of one of the half-pulverized church walls, a blanket over his chest and face. Cameron could tell by the soiled, sweat-stained sombrero lying nearby, and by the boots and buckskin pants, that it was Tokente.

The relief Cameron had felt at seeing Marina again suddenly vanished. His heart sank and a high-pitched hum filled his ears. *No*, he thought, pulling up his dusty jeans at the thighs and squatting down on his haunches. He wiped his hands on his jeans, then removed the blanket from the man's face, drawn yet blissful in death, eyes closed, slightly parted lips revealing a single tooth.

"He died only about ten minutes ago," Marina said quietly.

"What happened?" Cameron asked her.

"Jake Hawkins," Marina said in a voice taut with anger.

Cameron looked at her sharply. "Where is he?"

"Dead. Señor Going killed him with his rifle. He's back there." She jerked her head to indicate the rocky hills behind her.

"Are you sure he's dead?"

"I walked back and saw."

Cameron turned his eyes back to his dead friend and nodded, scowling.

Marina turned to Jimmy. "I'm glad you are well," she said. She frowned, looking around. "Where is . . ."

"He's dead," Jimmy said, turning to her with tears in his eyes, knowing she meant Hotchkiss. He sobbed, and Cameron knew he'd been holding it back.

Marina took the boy into her arms, holding him tightly. He buried his face in her shoulder and cried with abandon.

Cameron disposed of Alfred Going's body the way he'd disposed of Hotchkiss. He felt tired and weak, and he didn't think he had it in him anymore to kill Bachelard. Too much had happened, too many friends had died, and his anger over Pas Varas's death had transformed into a generalized sadness that could not be relieved by vengeance. Killing Bachelard would not bring back Varas. Tracking him, in fact, had only brought more death to Cameron's friends.

He wished now that he'd stayed in Arizona. But how could he have explained to Leonora Varas, with her Hispanic's belief in vengeance, that he had not gone after her husband's killer?

Grimly he walked back to the camp, feeling as hollow as an old cave. Marina had built a fire and made coffee. She'd also heated some javelina meat, and Jimmy Bronco sat on a rock, eating voraciously.

She held out a plate and a cup of coffee as Cameron walked up. "I'm very sorry about your friends," she said, looking boldly into his eyes. "All this"—she held out her arms as though death were some palpable thing around them—"is my fault . . . mine and Adrian's."

"No," Cameron said, shaking his head. "I didn't come down here for you. I came for Bachelard. And I think I found him."

"What?" Marina was clearly startled and a little afraid.

"Him and his army, or whatever you call it . . . they're only about an hour away. I saw them coming from the east. We have to get moving."

Cameron glanced around, remembering Adrian. He'd been taken so unawares by Going's death that he hadn't asked where the Missourian was.

Reading his mind, she said, nodding toward the

black canyon corridor yawning behind them, "Adrian went in there early this morning, looking for the gold. I waited here with Señor Going."

"He find anything?"

Marina shook her head. "I don't know. I haven't seen him since he left."

"Well, we'd better find him and get the hell out of here—with or without the gold, if there is any. Bachelard will be here, and so will about fifteen *rurales* we picked up along the trail."

"I thought you wanted to kill Bachelard."

"I do. But first I want to get you three out of here."

On a bald knob a mile away Perro Loco stood, hunched and watching. The figures in the distance appeared no larger than ants, but the Indian knew that one of them was Jack Cameron. He could tell by the way the man moved and carried himself and by the color of the horse he'd been riding.

A rare wintery smile formed on the Indian's lips as he squatted on his haunches and wrapped both hands around the barrel of the shotgun standing between his knees.

It wouldn't be long now . . .

CHAPTER 33

WHEN CAMERON HAD shoveled down enough food to get through the rest of the day, and slugged back several cups of coffee, he, Marina, and Jimmy broke camp, packing everything onto the mules. He sent the others ahead while he hiked up a butte to check their back trail.

He'd peered across the hazy, broken hills and towering escarpments for nearly a minute before he saw a fine dust veil lifting behind a low ridge about three or four miles away. He recognized the route as the one he and Jimmy had taken, which meant that Bachelard and Montana had made it around the gorge and were making their way in this direction.

It could have been the rurales, but Cameron judged it impossible for them to make that kind of time in the rugged, switchbacking canyons, especially with the Gatling gun.

At the pace the pursuers appeared to be traveling, Cameron figured they'd reach the church before nightfall. But it would be late enough in the day that he didn't think they'd try searching the canyon for gold until tomorrow morning.

Cameron returned to the camp and mounted his buckskin, glancing at the ruins as he made his way past them—the crumbling adobe walls, a smashed window arch, pieces of a broken belfry lying here and there among the boulders. He wondered idly about the bells—could they have been gold, and cached with the rest of the treasure?—and felt an ethereal sense of the place, as though a ghostly presence lingered here.

Riding away, twisting around in the saddle to look behind him, he imagined the people who had designed and built this place so far from civilization, and those who'd worshiped within these long-defunct walls. He knew the descendants of the Pimas and Yaquis were still around, living in villages scattered throughout Sonora and Chihuahua. But what of the Jesuits and Franciscans who had come to convert them?

He caught up to Marina and Jimmy five minutes later, walking their mounts and pack mules up the gradually ascending trail through the boulder-littered, steep-walled canyon, which reminded Cameron of parts of the Grand Canyon in Arizona; the walls were nearly as high in some places.

"Is there anyone behind us?" Marina asked him as he fell in behind them.

"Yep," he said darkly. "But maybe they won't enter the canyon until morning."

It was not easy to make good time on the treacherous trail, and they did not try to get too much speed out of their horses. The trail would slow Bachelard and Montana and the rurales down, as well.

They'd ridden half a mile when Clark appeared, riding around a bend of low-growing shrubs. Cameron could smell fresh manure—probably left by mountain goats that had scattered when they'd heard the horses. The Missourian halted his horse on a rise between two cracked table rocks and waited for Cameron, his wife, and Jimmy to come on.

"Well, well, you made it back," he said contemptuously to Cameron. "My wife was getting worried."

"Stow it," Cameron said. "We have to shake a leg out of here. Bachelard's only about an hour or two away, and a passel of rurales are en route, as well."

"Well, why didn't you bring the whole Mexican army?" Clark snarled.

"It couldn't be helped."

Clark shook his head. "Well, I'm not going anywhere. I found the ruin where they stashed the gold."

"And . . . ?"

"And I've found a pit but I wanted to get help exploring it, in case something happened and I couldn't get out on my own."

"There's no time," Cameron said. "There's probably no gold there anyway." His tone belied his own curiosity. If there really was a cave, like the vaquero friend of Marina's had avouched, then maybe there really was some gold. But with Bachelard and the rurales on their asses, there was no time to get it out.

"Only take a few minutes," Clark said. "I've found the pit. All we have to do is drop a line down and check it out." He reined his horse around and started back up the trail, in the direction he'd just come.

Cameron glanced at Marina. She shrugged as if to say, "Maybe . . ."

Jimmy wore much the same expression under the unraveling brim of his straw hat. If there was gold in the area, how could they leave it behind?

Cameron cursed, clucked to his horse, and followed Clark up the trail. "I take it your friend—Señor Going—didn't make it?" Clark asked with a superior air.

Cameron wanted to say, *You owe him your life, you little fuck*—and he would have if Marina and

Jimmy hadn't been listening. Instead he said, "No, he didn't make it," and rode grimly on.

Shadows stretched out from the canyon walls as the sun angled low in the west. The screech of a hunting eagle bounced off the canyon floor.

As he rode behind Clark, who was pushing his mount faster than was safe on such terrain, Cameron thought about gold. He thought about how little it would take to make him rich. Hell, they might be able to descend that hole and be out in ten or fifteen minutes with enough not only to get Marina's daughter back, but to get them all they'd ever wanted . . . and then some.

He supposed Clark was right. They'd have to try. There was still some time. Hell, Bachelard probably wouldn't even show until morning.

"There it is," Clark said after about ten more minutes of travel. "Right up there."

Cameron lifted his gaze up the cliff face, to where Clark was staring. "Holy shit," he said when he saw the ruins pocking the cliff like giant swallow-nests. He'd seen such places left by the ancient Indians back in Arizona, but none had come anywhere near the size of this place. He'd heard of a virtual city left by the Anasazi in Colorado. Could this dwelling have been left by them, as well? The sun was angling just right to catch the occasional small birds winging in and out of the fifty or so black cave entrances, flashing saffron light off their wings.

"How do you know which one has the gold?"

"There's a turtle carved outside the cave on the third tier—see it?"

Cameron nodded, looking. It was the only opening on the third tier, and it was set farther back in the mountain than the others. The opening was larger than the others, as well, more rectangular than square.

"Must've been the home of a shaman or a chieftain or something, don't you suppose? I looked in several of the others, but none of them has a back door like that one."

"Back door?"

"You'll see." Clark slipped out of the saddle and, half running, led his horse to the base of the cliff, where he tied the gelding to roots sticking out of the bank. He grabbed his saddlebags, draped them over his shoulder, and looked around until he found a stout deadfall mesquite branch, and started up what could only have been the remains of a stone stairway angling up the face of the cliff, to the first tier of caves.

"Bring rope!" he yelled to Cameron.

Somberly Cameron halted his horse next to Clark's, tethered it to the same root, and grabbed the coil of rope from his saddle. Turning to Jimmy, he said, "Kid, you stay here with the horses, keep an eye out for Bachelard and the Mexicans. I doubt they'll be along for some time yet, but we're better safe than sorry."

"I hear you, Jack. Can I have a gun?"

Cameron was surprised at the lack of eagerness in the kid's voice. There was no air of expectant fun in it, no William Bonney grin and flush. It was an innocent, businesslike inquiry.

Had the kid grown up, from all he'd been through out here? It appeared that he had, and Cameron felt a curious, parental ambivalence at the loss.

"There's a spare in my saddlebags," Cameron said, sensing that he didn't need to lecture the kid about its use. "And here, you can have this, too." He tossed Jimmy his Winchester. "I shouldn't be needing it up there."

Jimmy dug in the saddlebags, finding the old

Remington conversion revolver, and Cameron and Marina headed up the steep stairs the ancients had carved out of the cliff face, Cameron throwing the coiled rope over his shoulder.

The steps had been worn down over the centuries by wind and rain so that they were nearly gone in places, and Cameron turned back often to help Marina up the difficult spots. Neither of them said anything—in fact, their expressions were decidedly grim—but secretly they were both enjoying this time together, however brief. Cameron suspected it would be their last.

"Come on—it's up here," Clark called as he climbed.

With a burning branch in his hand—he must have had kerosene and matches in his saddlebags—he disappeared inside a cave on the third tier, and Cameron and Marina followed him into the dusky darkness, Cameron tearing cobwebs with his hand.

The cave went back about twenty yards. Clark's torch illuminated an opening in the back wall, about five by three feet wide.

"Through here," Clark said, passing through the door and starting down a corridor only a little higher than the door, so that Cameron and Clark had to duck as they walked.

They were several yards down the corridor when Cameron suddenly realized he'd taken Marina's hand and was guiding her gently through the darkness, only a few steps behind her husband. Startled, he released her, but she searched out his hand and clasped it again tightly.

The corridor opened onto a circular room, about thirty feet in diameter. Here the ceiling was high enough that the men could stand without ducking. Another door opened in the wall directly opposite the first door. During his first visit, Clark had apparently set out candles on the foot-wide ledge that had been carved about chair-high around the room. Newly lit, they burned steadily.

The limestone walls were nearly covered with petroglyphs—stick people hunting stick deer and bears, and praying to yellow suns and blue moons. The damp air smelled of mushrooms and bat guano. There was a distant, constant rumbling, like an earth tremor oscillating the floor beneath their feet.

In the middle of the room lay what at first appeared to be a circular black rug. Clark's torch revealed it to be a pit, flinty walls of chiseled stone dropping straight down, about five feet in diameter. There were two metal rings in the wall of the room, one on each side of the hole. They were old and rusted but appeared firm.

"Amazing," Cameron said, looking around.

Marina had released his hand and stood behind him. She gave a soft whistle at the pictures on the walls.

"This is the place," Clark said, holding the torch over the pit. "The treasure's got to be down there."

"What do you suppose this was?" Marina asked wonderingly.

Cameron shook his head. "Some kind of church, maybe, or maybe sacrifices were performed here . . . or healings . . . Who the hell knows?"

Marina inspected the floor. "What is making that shaking, that vibration?"

It had grown more intense the deeper they'd plumbed the corridor. A sound like the distant rumble of continuous thunder could also be heard.

"God knows," Clark said.

"Sounds like water, maybe a river," Cameron said.

He nodded to indicate the door across the room. "That tunnel might lead to it."

He studied the pit illuminated by Clark's torch. The sides went straight down for about twenty feet. The torch light revealed a rocky bottom . . . or were those bones?

"Yes, but the gold is here," Clark said, too preoccupied with treasure to be concerned about anything as inconsequential as an underground river.

"How do you know?" Cameron asked him.

"That." Clark pointed out a turtle carved into the wall, nearly camouflaged by the petroglyphs.

"The hole looks empty to me," Cameron said, looking down.

Clark was on his hands and knees, holding the torch over the hole's opening and staring down anxiously.

"No," he said finally. "It opens off that side. There's a tunnel there. You can see it when I hold the torch like this."

Cameron looked again. Sure enough, there did appear to be a small corridor opening off the bottom of the main pit.

Clark grabbed Cameron's rope off his shoulder, ran it through one of the metal rings, and secured it to the other ring across the room. Clark hacked and wheezed as he worked, dripping sweat. He'd turned pale as a sheet. The damp air was nipping his lungs like frost, squeezing out the oxygen. When the knot was fast, he stood and offered Cameron the end of the rope. "Here you go," he said.

Cameron laughed sardonically. "Why me?"

"Can't stand small, dark places."

"I can hold your weight; I doubt you can hold mine."

Before Clark could reply, Marina said, "I'll go," reaching for the rope.

"No you won't," Cameron replied, his dark eyes on Clark, whose thin lips were parted with a supercilious sneer.

Cameron stepped away from the pit, made a double bowline with the end of the rope, thrust his legs through the loops, and took a bight around his waist.

"Hold that torch good and low so I can see what the hell I'm doin'," he groused. "Keep a tight hold on the rope, too. If you drop me I'll shoot you." He was only half joking.

Giving his hat to Marina, he slipped over the edge as the Clarks grabbed the rope in their gloved hands, feeding it slowly through the metal ring, which helped reduce the pull of Cameron's weight. Cameron assisted by finding hand- and footholds in the walls of the pit, in pocks and bores left by the tools used in the excavation. There were more of these than had been apparent from the top. In fact, he was able to climb nearly all the way to the bottom of the pit, and even had to call up for slack.

At the bottom, he stepped out of the double bowline. "Pull the rope up and use it to lower the torch to me."

In a minute, the torch came down horizontally, the rope tied to the middle. He grabbed it, untied the rope from around the base, and held the torch as he looked around the pit. Kneeling and probing the floor with his hands, he saw that the pale dust and chips were indeed bones; there was even half a human skull. A rat scuttled out from under it squealing, and disappeared in the shadows.

"Jesus Christ," Cameron mumbled.

"What is it?" Clark asked from above.

"Human bones down here. This hole must have

been used to keep slaves or sacrifice victims or something. Apparently some died down here and no one bothered to haul them out."

Uninterested in such archaeological observations, Clark said, "Can you see anything in that other hole there?"

Cameron looked around, turning a full circle, the flaming torch burning down toward his hand. Ashes flitted about him and the smoke was getting dense, stinging his eyes.

He squatted down, bringing the torch down with him, peering into the hole opening off the pit. "Looks like another passageway."

"Can you see anything inside?"

Cameron stuck the torch in the hole. It was just large enough for him to crawl into on his hands and knees.

He sighed and tipped his head back to say, "I'll take a look," without enthusiasm. He didn't like small, cramped places any more than the next guy—especially those where people had died and where who-knew-what-else lurked in the dark. But his own reluctant curiosity drove him forward, on hands and knees, bumping his head on the low ceiling.

He moved awkwardly, shoving the torch ahead of him. The air was warm and moist, and the torch increased the heat. He could feel the vibrations from the river or whatever it was each time he pressed a knee or a hand to the rocky, uneven floor.

Finally he came to a room much like the one where the pit started. In the torchlight, Cameron saw the stone walls and the ledges cut into the walls. On the ledges were mounds of heavy canvas bags, rotten with age and rife with mildew, and a large wooden crate like the ones used for shipping muskets.

Two gold bells sat amid it all—big as butter churns

and coated with dust and cobwebs. Cameron didn't know for sure, but he guessed they'd bring about twenty thousand dollars apiece.

Cameron's right cheek twitched and his heart galloped. He sat there on his knees for several seconds, just staring, wondering, hoping . . . not quite believing what he was seeing . . . not quite convinced of the possibility that he'd just found true-blue Spanish treasure.

He parted his lips, taking in heavy lungfuls of air to quell his pulse.

Could it be?

Veins throbbing in his temples, he pushed himself to his feet and walked over to the crate. He took the torch in his left hand, wiped the sweat and dust from his right hand on his jeans, and pulled at the lid, on which there was faded writing. The wood was old and rotten from the high humidity, and it splintered in his fingers as one slat pulled away from the rest with a muffled crack. He threw the slat aside and removed two more.

Then he held the torch over the crate. "Jumping dandelions and hopping hollyhocks," he heard himself say. It was something his mother used to say when she was surprised and he hadn't even known he'd retained the phrase in his memory.

His eyes opened wide, his face expressionless, as he drank in what lay before him—a whole box full of gold and silver trinkets, religious icons, statues, candlesticks, wineglasses, and decanters—the silver shrouded in tarnish but the gold looking as shiny-new as yesterday, as though it had been forged only hours ago.

Multicolored jewels were scattered about like sugar sprinkles on a cake. There were small statues of the saints, about eight inches tall. Slowly lowering his hand to one, as though it would shatter at his touch, Cameron wrapped his fingers around it and lifted it out of the box, surprised by its weight.

He lifted it above his head to peer at the bottom of the base. Scrawled there were the words, *San Bernardo, 1735*. It was typical that the priest-artisan, in keeping with a vow of humility, had not signed it. He hefted it again. It weighed as much as a rock three times its size.

Hearing something that sounded too much like raised voices to be ignored, he stuck his head into the small tunnel leading off the pit. He listened for a moment.

Something popped. It sounded like a gun.

"What is it?" Cameron yelled.

When no answer came, he hurried back through the tiny tunnel to the main pit. The torch had burned down to almost nothing, and he held it carefully to keep it lit.

"What's going on?" he yelled up the hole.

"Jack!" It was Jimmy Bronco. His voice quivered as he yelled down the pit. "We got trouble!"

CHAPTER 34

CAMERON STEPPED INTO the rope and yelled, "Bring me up!"

There was no reply, but the rope yanked taut with surprising force, squeezing the air from his lungs. He was jerked off his feet and slammed against the wall of the pit, smacking his head so hard his vision swam.

Cameron dropped the torch as the rope wrenched him up the wall like a side of beef. Grunting against the sudden, violent jerks, feeling as though the rope was going to pull his shoulders out of joint, he used his feet and hands to push himself away from the stony sides of the pit.

Who the hell was up there, anyway? Cameron already knew it wasn't anyone he wanted to see.

He was at the top of the pit before he knew it, lying facedown beside the hole, his sides sore and burning from the violent chafing of the rope. He'd started to push himself up when a brusque hand took over, grabbing him by his hair and collar, jerking him to his feet. A rancid, sour odor of sweat and human filth filled his nostrils.

No . . . it couldn't be . . .

Marina screamed.

Cameron blinked, then stared.

By the light of the candles Clark had placed around

the room, Perro Loco regarded Cameron with amusement. Cameron would not have been more surprised to see the devil himself standing there.

Maybe Cameron had been knocked out in his ascent, and he was only dreaming. But he'd never dreamed a smell that strong . . .

"H-how the hell . . ." he began. The Indian brought a roundhouse punch into Cameron's jaw. It was a solid, brain-twisting, vision-blurring blow that sent Cameron sprawling across the hole, one leg falling into the pit as he clutched the floor.

Marina screamed again. Instinctively, Cameron reached for his .45. His hand grazed the cool barrel just as the Indian removed the gun from his holster.

He was waiting to hear the hammer click back and feel a bullet tear into his skull when the Indian said in guttural, stilted English, "No. No guns. You, me, Cameron. We fight with knife."

Cameron raised his head to look up into the broken-toothed grin.

"To death," the Indian added happily.

Cameron turned onto his back, got his legs under him, and climbed to his feet, feeling wobbly from the punch that had cracked his lip and sent blood trickling down his jaw. Wiping the blood with the back of his wrist, he glanced around the room, getting a fix on the situation.

Jimmy was lying in the entrance to the room, where he'd apparently been flung, arms and legs spread. He was either dead or out cold. Clark lay nearby, on his chest, blood spreading onto the rocks and dust beneath him.

Marina sat on the ledge above Clark. Her hat was off, her hair was mussed, and her blouse was torn. She stared at Cameron, her brown eyes bright with fear.

Cameron dropped his eyes to the holster on her

waist. Her pistol-gripped revolver wasn't there. Shuttling his gaze to Loco, he saw the gun, as well as two others—probably Clark's and Jimmy's—residing in the Indian's waistband.

The Indian followed Cameron's gaze. He lifted his head and smiled cunningly. He jabbed a finger at Cameron, then thrust it into his own broad chest.

"You, me, Cam-er-on. We fight again. No guns."

He tossed Cameron's Colt into the pit, then removed the three other revolvers from his waistband and tossed them down as well; they clattered as they hit bottom. Grabbing the big bowie from the scabbard on his hip, he held out the wide, razor-sharp blade for Cameron's inspection. It was smeared with fresh blood, probably Clark's.

Perro Loco dropped his eyes to the bowie on Cameron's waist. "Knife . . . we fight like men."

The smile again, drying Cameron's throat and pricking his loins with cold, wet dread.

Cameron grabbed his bowie, trying to convince himself the situation was not without hope. He had a chance. The problem was he hadn't fought with a knife in a long time. He knew that Perro Loco, like most Apache warriors, fought with knives often, and prided himself on his proficiency with the weapon.

Cameron glanced at the Indian's sharp steel blade, buttery with reflected candlelight, and his mouth filled with the coppery taste of fear. Okay, so he'd probably die. He only hoped he could somehow take this big Indian bastard with him . . .

Why the hell he hadn't put a bullet in the back of the man's skull when he'd had the chance, he didn't know, but he didn't have time to kick himself for it now.

Out of the corner of his eye he saw Marina slide

forward. "Stay where you are!" he barked at her. "No matter what happens, just stay where you are! You get too close, he'll kill you."

Another grin formed on the Indian's pocked, broad-boned face. He lunged forward, swinging his bowie in a wide arc. Cameron feinted as the blade sliced his tunic about midway up from his belly button, and jumped to his right, barely avoiding disembowelment. Just one quick, penetrating slash of Perro Loco's well-trained hand, and his guts would be spilling around his ankles.

Loco lunged in again with a grunt. Again Cameron feinted, then reached in with his own knife, opening a shallow gash on the man's wrist. Loco darted away, keeping his eyes glued to Cameron's, trying to read his mind, to anticipate his next move . . . enjoying the fear he smelled in his opponent.

Loco faked a slice from the right, cutting it off midmotion and bringing his weapon toward Cameron's belly. Cameron deflected the arm with his own.

Recovering, the Indian stepped back and kicked him glancingly on the hip. It was a powerful blow, but not enough to knock Cameron off his feet.

"So we're using our feet, eh?" he said. "You should've told me; I'd've taken my boots off."

The Indian responded with a thin smile and came in again with a short jab. Cameron caught the arm with his left hand, swung the Indian to the left, and jabbed his knife at the Indian's belly. Loco deflected the blow with his own knife. The two blades clattered together, the two men locked in a grunting, cursing fighters' embrace.

Ten seconds later, the Apache gave a savage yell and pushed Cameron off with his left arm. Cameron staggered, trying to catch his breath. The Indian drifted right, holding both hands out for balance, the edge of the knife pointing up, the point angling toward the floor—ready in an instant to stab and slice, to plunge straight in and angle up for Cameron's heart.

Cameron was on the defensive, a position he hated. Loco was more adept with a knife than he, and the Indian had him reacting instead of acting . . . for the moment, anyway.

Trying to remedy the situation, Cameron lurched suddenly forward, wheeled, then came around again, this time going in for the kill with two quick slashes that caught the Indian off guard. Loco feinted away at the last second, but Cameron's forward slash had opened a thin red line across his chest.

The Indian looked down, stunned by the accomplishment of his inferior foe. Cameron took advantage of Loco's surprise. Circling, careful to remain at least two steps beyond the pit, he lashed out again, his knifepoint angled up. He thought he had him, but the Indian was suddenly gone, like a ghost. He appeared again to Cameron's left. Screaming, he kicked Cameron in the balls.

Cameron's knees buckled with the pain. He crumpled, groaning.

This is it, he thought behind the agony that seared through his groin and into his stomach, nearly making him retch. Well, I gave it the old college try. If only I could take the bastard with me . . .

Fatefully, Loco hesitated, enjoying the moment. Instead of finishing off Cameron quickly and efficiently, Perro Loco wheeled around in a pirouette of sorts, building steam for a fatal kick to Cameron's head.

The problem was he'd gotten too close to the side of the pit, and nearly fell in. Catching himself, he teetered on the edge of the pit for a full second.

Cameron swallowed the pain engulfing him and

flung himself forward. He rammed his head into the Indian's belly and bulled the man over onto his back.

Loco gave a startled cry as his head hit the rock floor with an audible crack. Still, he managed to bring his knife hand up with a vengeance. Cameron grabbed Loco's wrist just before the knifepoint went into his throat.

The Indian clenched his broken teeth together. His sweat-soaked face wrinkled in outrage. Channeling all his strength into the fist with the knife, he strove to bury the blade in Cameron's neck.

Meanwhile Cameron brought his own knife to bear. The Indian grabbed the hilt with his free hand.

For several seconds they were at an impasse, the Indian's knife only a half-inch from Cameron's throat, Cameron's knife six inches from the Indian's jugular. Each man brought his waning strength to bear. Sweat streamed down their faces—jaws clenched, lips stretched wide, teeth grinding, belabored grunts welling out of their throats.

Slowly Cameron's knife inched toward the Indian's throat. Loco's horrified eyes watched the blade disappear under his chin.

With a final cry and thrust, Cameron shoved the knifepoint into the leathery skin at the Indian's throat. The point went in a half-inch, then an inch.

Loco lifted his chin and yelled what sounded to Cameron like a prayer or a chant, summoning help from the other world.

"Go ahead and pray, you devil," Cameron snarled through clenched teeth, "no god can save you now."

Then he drove the knife into the man's neck up to the hilt. Blood washed over Cameron's hand as though he'd punctured a wine flask. Loco gave a sigh. His head went back and his eyes rolled up in his head.

Resting on Loco's body, Cameron caught his breath

and felt relief wash over him like cool water. He licked his salty lips and swallowed, then heaved himself onto his knees. He stared at the dead Indian, hardly able to believe his luck, then wiped the blood from his knife on the dead man's leggings. Standing, he returned the knife to the sheath on his hip, then headed toward Marina.

She sat on the floor next to Clark, watching Cameron with terrified, expectant eyes, one hand on her chest as if she could not believe he was alive. Cameron wasn't sure he could believe it, either. He sighed and shook his head.

"Are you all right?" he asked her.

She nodded, eyeing Clark. Cameron turned to the man and knelt down.

"What happened?"

"The Indian stabbed him in the chest," Marina said. "He is not conscious but he's alive."

Cameron put his fingers to Clark's throat, feeling for a pulse. The man groaned, coughed, and rolled his head, muttering. He was starting to come around. Cameron inspected the splotch of blood just above his right breast. It looked nasty but not deep. If they could get it bandaged, he'd probably be all right.

Jimmy had sat up with his back against the wall. He was looking around groggily. Cameron knelt before him and looked into his eyes.

"You all right?"

The kid swallowed and nodded, brought a hand up and rubbed the goose egg growing on the back of his head. "The bastard flung me across the room like I was a sack of grain."

"Well, he won't do it again," Cameron said.

"I'm sorry, Jack," Jimmy said. "He caught me by surprise. I would've killed him, I swear I would've, if I woulda seen him. He's just so sneaky."

Cameron nodded. "Oh, I know all about Perro Loco," he said, and gave the kid a grin.

Jimmy's eyes lifted to something behind Cameron, then widened in horror as the kid screamed, "Look out!"

Cameron jerked around and stared, aghast. The Indian stood behind Marina, his big bowie held at his side. Marina turned as well. She screamed and recoiled against the wall.

Blood covered the Indian's chest from the gash in his neck. "Girl . . . dies, Cam-er-on. Too . . . bad."

He lunged toward Marina, bringing the knife back for a fatal thrust. A gun exploded behind Cameron. Cameron saw the bullet smack into Perro Loco's face and knock him back against the wall.

Then the gun roared again. The second bullet smacked Loco's chest. He slid down the wall, smearing blood, and crumpled up on the floor, dead.

Cameron turned to look at the shooter and gaped, befuddled. It was She-Bear.

The squat, round Indian woman lowered her smoking rifle and shuttled her gaze to Cameron, who was still crouched next to Jimmy.

"My man—he not here. He . . . dead?"

Cameron sighed, dropping his eyes, and nodded.

She-Bear accepted the information with her customary stoicism, her expression remaining wooden. She jerked a thumb over her shoulder as she said matter-of-factly, "You got more trouble out there. Many men on horses."

CHAPTER 35

CAMERON TURNED TO Jimmy. "Where's my rifle?"

The kid looked at once somber and frantic. "He . . . The Indian took it away from me, threw it in the rocks down by the horses."

Cameron cursed, standing and walking over to the pit. He couldn't see them in the failing candlelight, but he knew their pistols were down there where the Indian had tossed them. They'd need them now; those were all the weapons they had, except for Cameron's bowie, and he sure as hell didn't want to have to rely on only a knife against twenty or thirty of Bachelard's men; without his rifle he was handicapped enough.

Knowing it was the only way—Jimmy and Marina couldn't hold him on the rope—Cameron got down and dropped his legs over the side of the pit, turning to face the edge and feeling for footholds. Slowly but deliberately he descended, one hand- and foothold at a time, having to move several feet sideways, at times, when the holds in his direct line of descent played out.

It was a hell of a chance he was taking; one misstep and he could end up on the bottom of the pit with a broken leg, a crushed skull, or worse. Any of those injuries would mean certain death, under the circumstances and so far from civilization.

But he had no choice. Worse, he had no time to spare. At any moment Bachelard and his men might take the cave, and that would mean death for them all, except Marina—what it would mean for her, Cameron could only imagine.

Six feet from the bottom, he put his right foot on a protruding rock that wasn't secure. It crumbled, and he slid the remaining distance to the pit floor, with several smarting face and hand abrasions to show for it.

Cursing, he felt around in the dark for the pistols. When he had his own Colt Army in his holster, and the others tucked in his waistband, he wiped his bloody hands on his jeans, reached for a handhold, and started climbing again.

The ascent was relatively easy, and he was at the top in a few minutes, breathing heavily as he clawed his way onto the floor above. He gave Jimmy the old Remington, handed Marina her Colt .38, and kept Clark's Bisley tucked behind his cartridge belt. Clark was sitting against the cave wall, cursing as Marina bandaged the knife wound in his chest.

"What's up, Jack?" Clark asked, his gaunt face pale and sweaty, his dark hair plastered to his skull. His breath was raspy and he coughed every few minutes, bringing up thick gouts of blood which he spat to the side. This humid air wasn't doing him any good at all.

"I don't know," Cameron said. "That's what I'm going to find out."

He shifted his eyes to Marina, who was pressing a handkerchief to the knife wound above Clark's breast. "You two stay here. I'll come and get you if I think we can get out of here."

Clark said, "What . . . What about the treasure?" He turned his expectant gaze to Cameron.

"It's there," Cameron told him. "I just don't know if it's going to do us any good."

Then he was gone, heading up the corridor, Jimmy following close behind.

They found She-Bear kneeling about five feet back from the cave's opening, rifle in her arms, peering down the cliff face. Cameron moved quietly up behind her, careful not to be seen from below.

She-Bear turned her round, lugubrious face to him. She looked even more fatalistic than usual, and Cameron knew that wasn't a good sign.

"What's going on?" he whispered.

His answer came in the form of voices from below, the thud of horses on hard-packed ground. The voices were raised in excited inquiry. Commands were yelled.

Cameron recognized Bachelard's screechy Cajun tenor. "Goddamn it! I thought they were farther behind us. They must have followed some shortcut," Cameron said, to no one in particular. He was trying to make sense out of the situation, which appeared pretty close to hopeless.

Their horses had no doubt been confiscated. Clark was too injured to make a break for it even if they had a place to make a break for—which they didn't. And She-Bear was the only one with a rifle. There was no way in heaven or hell that Cameron, Jimmy, and She-Bear, with or without her rifle, would be able to hold off Bachelard and Montana for more than a few hours.

Jimmy must have seen the doubt in his face. "What are we gonna do, Jack?" he said quietly.

Cameron didn't say anything. He got down on his hands and knees and crawled to the entrance of the cave, lifting his head to peer over the ledge. Several riders were milling on the canyon floor, looking up the cliff, rifles held high in their hands.

Two were Mexicans in fancily-stitched vests and sombreros, bandoliers crisscrossing their chests. Cameron could make out another man taking cover behind a mesquite and two more leading their horses off behind a rise. Those three all looked like gringos dressed in dusty trail garb.

From the voices and sound of boots stumbling up rocky grades and pushing through brush, there were many more men near the cliff base where Cameron couldn't see them.

He gave a sigh. There was no doubt about it— these were Bachelard's and Montana's men. They had seen the horses and pack mules of Cameron's party, and knew they were here. They were positioning themselves for a showdown.

Cameron looked for a possible escape route. There was no way they could get down off the cliff without being seen. They could go up, keep climbing the tiers, but the tiers stopped a good hundred feet from the top of the canyon wall—a sheer wall, at that, impossible to climb, especially with men flinging lead at you from below.

Voices grew louder and men came near, boots thumping on the gravelly stairs in the cliff to Cameron's right. They were beneath his field of vision, but he could hear them approach, whispering and breathing heavily from the strain of the ascent.

"Look—that there's a bootprint," one of them said.

"Sí," another replied.

Boots scuffed, the breathing grew louder. Someone gave a low yell, tripping on one of the steps, no doubt.

"Pick up your goddamn feet, Carmody!" someone hissed.

Cameron crawled farther onto the ledge, dropped his gaze over the side. To his right, three men appeared on the tier beneath him—one Mexican and two Americans.

Cameron grabbed his pistol and brought it up, thumbing back the hammer. Breathing heavily, the approaching men were looking around, open mouths sucking air and showing teeth. The Mexican, lifting his head, saw Cameron lying on the ledge above him.

"There!" he cried, bringing up his rifle.

Cameron aimed the Colt and fired. The man screamed and flew back over the ledge, dropping his rifle. The other two, seeing Cameron and the smoke puffing around his head, brought their own rifles up to their shoulders. With two quick shots, Cameron plugged them both off the ledge, hearing their bodies smack the next tier below, their rifles breaking on the rocks.

A bullet spanged off the side of the ledge a few inches from his face, spraying him with sharp flecks of stinging rock. Looking down at the canyon floor, he saw dust thinning around a rifleman who was smiling and jacking another shell into the chamber. A second bullet buzzed over Cameron's head and barked into the side of the cave behind him.

That slug had come from the left.

Turning that way, Cameron saw another rifleman on the ledge below him, a tall, angular Mexican with a pencil-thin mustache and tattered serape. She-Bear, who had crawled up beside Cameron, brought the butt of her rifle to her cheek and squeezed off a round that chipped the rock wall where the man's head had been a half-second before.

Jimmy sidled up to the cave wall at Cameron's right, planting the barrel of his Remington on his left forearm, aimed, and squeezed off three quick rounds, puffing up dust around two riflemen crouched on the canyon floor.

Seeing a gray-clad figure move practically straight down the cliff, Cameron fired. The man disappeared behind a boulder. Cameron was sure it was Bachelard. He squeezed off another round, out of anger, and heard a bullet buzz past his face and tear through the crown of Jimmy's hat.

"Jesus!" the kid yelled.

"Back! Get back!" Cameron yelled at him and She-Bear, turning and scrambling several yards back into the cave, where they couldn't be seen or fired upon as easily. "We're just sitting ducks out there."

The three of them hunkered down on their knees, weapons held high, staring off across the slowly darkening canyon, listening and watching, trying to get a grasp of the situation.

As many times as he went over it, sweat furrowing the dust on his face and neck, soaked tunic sticking to his back, the smell of gunpowder hanging heavy in the air and the sound of conspiratorial voices reaching his ears from only about fifty or sixty yards away, Cameron could not figure a way out of the pickle they were in.

At least, one that wouldn't get them all killed.

Behind a boulder at the bottom of the canyon, Gaston Bachelard crouched beside Miguel Montana, removed his hat, and lifted a cautious gaze up to the cave opening on the third tier of the ruins.

"Well, compadre—any suggestions?"

Montana looked carefully over the boulder, squinting his eyes and biting down hard on the thin cheroot in his front teeth. He shrugged.

"How many do you think there are?"

Bachelard turned to call to one of his men hunkered down by a boulder about fifteen yards behind and to his right. "How many are in the cave, Jumbo?"

"I've seen three. Looks like only one has a rifle, though."

Bachelard turned to Montana, who frowned. "Only three?"

"That's what the man said."

"Where are the others?"

"Maybe there are no others."

"This gringo—Clark—he came down here with only two other people?"

Montana was incredulous. He sucked the cheroot, puffing fragrant smoke, and blinked his mud-brown eyes. His face had been sunburned nearly black; he never wore a hat. He feared a hat would make him go bald, and he was vainly attached to his impeccable thatch of tight, curly black hair; the touch of gray in his sideburns lent what he considered an air of distinguished maturity.

"There might have been more when he started," Bachelard said, raising his eyes and bobbing his shoulders. "I only saw three separate shooters myself, but even if there are four, or even five, they are badly outnumbered."

"Sí. And in a very dangerous spot."

Bachelard smiled. "There's no way up, and there's no way down but through us."

"So what do we do—wait?"

"'Fortune favors the brave,' says Virgil."

"Who?"

"Never mind."

"You will lead the charge?" Montana's face broke into a grin.

Bachelard looked at him coolly. "Yes ... I will lead the charge, my friend. And so will you. We're sharing the spoils, are we not?"

The grin faded from the little Mexican's face. He turned back to the cave and swallowed. "Sí."

Bachelard turned back to one of the men hunched behind the nearby boulder, awaiting orders. "Jumbo, go back and make sure Juanita is secure. Keep her out of the line of fire."

Crouching, the man ran back to where Bachelard had cached the girl in a protected hollow across the canyon.

"And keep your hands off of her!" Bachelard called to his back. Jumbo scowled. Imagine bringing a girl along on such a journey and then not even taking your pleasure!

Bachelard turned back to the cave. He cupped his hands around his mouth.

"Hello!" he shouted. "Clark ... in the cave!" He listened to the echo.

Silence followed. Then: "What?"

"Do you want to live or die?" Bachelard shouted, drawing out the words to distinguish them among the echoes.

"What about yourself?"

Bachelard chuffed. "A real funny man up there," he said to Montana. "That can't be Clark." Turning back to the cave he cupped his hands around his mouth. "Who are you?"

"Jack Cameron." The sepulchral voice echoed off the rocks.

The man beside Bachelard turned to him expectantly. Montana looked at him as well, seeing the peculiar expression on the ex-Confederate soldier's skeletal features. "Who?" Montana said.

Bachelard waved him off. "Ah . . . we meet again, Mr. Cameron! The lure of gold too much for you, eh?"

"The lure of killing the dirty rebel dog who killed my friend was too much for me . . . you fuckin' shit-for-brains asshole!"

Bachelard's face colored. He fought to regain his composure. "Listen, Cameron," he said congenially, "I am going to make you an offer. You and your friends can leave the cave, and the gold, now, and we won't kill you. How does that sound to you?"

"There isn't any gold."

"Oh?" Bachelard said. "Why don't you let us look for ourselves?"

"'Cause you'll shoot us in the back."

"I give you my word as an officer and a gentleman. We will give you unimpeded passage if you leave the cave now—empty-handed."

On the heels of the last echo Cameron returned, dry with irreverence: "Kiss my ass."

Bachelard bit his lip. One of his men stifled a laugh. Bachelard turned around sharply to see who it was. He saw four or five faces regarding him cautiously. He turned back to Cameron, said icily, "Don't be so hasty, my friend. I have twenty men. What do you have—three, four, five at the most?"

"I've got a whole fuckin' army up here."

Bachelard chuckled loudly enough for Cameron to hear. "No . . . I don't think so." He paused. "I tell you what: We will give you until dawn to reconsider your answer to my offer."

There was no reply.

Bachelard turned to his men, in various positions around the base of the canyon.

"Hark, you soldiers of a free and independent Texas and Sonora! Do you want more gold than you have ever seen in your life and ever will again—even in heaven?" His voice echoed loudly, resounding around the canyon like a bullet in a lead-lined room.

A murmur arose.

"Well, *do* you?" Bachelard shouted at the top of his lungs.

Responses of "Sí," and "Sure," and "Hell yes," rose a little louder.

"Then, at dawn we will charge the cave," Bachelard intoned. "Any man who cowers from his duty will be drawn, quartered, and gutted like a pig."

Bachelard licked his lips and smiled at Miguel Montana, who had turned to him with an unguarded look of misgiving.

Bachelard cleared his throat and cupped his hands around his mouth, raising his voice for Cameron's benefit: "And the first one to kill Cameron gets to fuck the lovely Marina de la Guerra!"

A soft din rose from the rocks around the base of the cliff. Someone said incredulously, "De la *Guerra?*"

As Bachelard had suspected, the name was well known to these Mexican honyockers. Some may have even worked for the de la Guerra family. More than a couple obviously knew of the lovely Marina, whose beauty was no doubt legendary.

Bachelard let the din settle. Then he added, with a smile, "At the crack of dawn, then: *Let fly the gods of war!*"

CHAPTER 36

———————————

BACHELARD'S PATHOLOGICAL laughter sailed skyward on the cooling evening air, dying out gradually, finally replaced by the breeze shunting down the canyon and by the chirps of the small birds that had found homes in the walls of the empty ruins.

Cameron's face was purposefully expressionless. He did not want Jimmy or She-Bear to know what kind of an effect Bachelard's last statement had had on him. The thought of that devilish horde storming up here in the morning, guns blazing, and . . .

Marina.

The light was nearly gone from the canyon, though the sky remained bright. Cameron holstered his pistol and stared off across the chasm to the sheer wall of fluted, crenelated rock turning gradually from pink to purple to black, and strained to come up with a means of escape.

Cameron turned to Jimmy and She-Bear, who had drifted to separate places against the cave walls. She-Bear was eating from a small pouch of jerky, her rifle lying across her large thighs, that same emotionless, self-contained look on her round face with its hideously scarred nose.

Cameron knew she must have loved Tokente very

much to have tracked him this far—or to have tracked the man tracking him, anyway. She'd displayed no emotion over his death, but Cameron wasn't fooled. There was plenty of pain behind those mud-black eyes and her phlegmatic demeanor, probably all the more intense for being so squelched.

"You two stay here and keep a sharp eye peeled, will you?" he said. "I'm going to go back and check on Clark."

Back in the pit room, several of the candles had gone out, but Marina had lit more and set them on the rock ledge around her and Adrian. Clark was sitting against the rock wall, his shirt off and his arm in a makeshift sling. Marina had padded the wound with strips of Clark's shirt, and secured the pad with a band tied around his chest.

"How you doing?" Cameron asked him.

"Not so good," the Missourian said wistfully. "I could sure use a drink."

"You're out?"

Clark nodded.

"Well, I'd offer you a snort of mine, but it's in my saddlebags, which are now the property of Gaston Bachelard."

Clark cursed as a frightened light entered his eyes. "So it's him . . . Damn." He pondered this for several seconds. "What are we going to do?"

Cameron had squatted on his haunches beside Clark. Marina sat on the ledge on the other side of her husband, regarding Cameron fearfully, expectantly.

"Well . . . I'm not sure," Cameron said with a sigh. "He's giving us till dawn to think it over . . . Wants us to give ourselves up—says he'll let us go."

"That's a crock!" Clark laughed ruefully.

Cameron nodded. "We can't go up or down. There are no trails across the cliff, so I guess the only thing to do is to leave this cave when it gets dark, and hide in another one. They maybe wouldn't find us. Hell, maybe once they've gotten the treasure, they won't bother lookin'."

He hated the idea of running and hiding from Bachelard. If it were only himself in this dilemma, he probably would have stayed and fought. But he had others to think about—namely, Jimmy and Marina. He didn't want to see them hurt.

"They can't have that treasure, Jack! It's mine!" Clark's eyes turned fierce and his back stiffened against the wall.

"Easy, easy. I think we've already lost it. We *may* be able to get out of this alive—and that's a *big* maybe—but there's no way we'd get out with the treasure. I'm sorry, but there just isn't any way. There are at least twenty men down there."

Clark pondered this, the fervor in his eyes becoming tempered with frustration and disappointment. "Goddamn him . . . Why the hell did he have to come along? We were so close . . ."

Cameron nodded. He felt the same way. When he'd held that statuette in his hand, he'd felt the gold fever leak into him like a fast-working drug, making his heart beat fast and his knees quake. How gold could change one's life!

Maybe he could go back down and get just a little. Hell, Bachelard didn't know how much was there. If Cameron took a few of those statuettes, the Cajun would be none the wiser. One of those statuettes would probably go for at least four thousand dollars . . .

Cameron said to Clark, "I'll see what I can do."

He glanced at Marina and their eyes locked. He couldn't help feeling jealous of Clark, being under her ministrations. She must have sensed it, for she smiled curiously and turned away.

Cameron stood and walked back down the corridor to Jimmy and She-Bear, who sat with their backs to opposite walls. Jimmy was holding his Remington in his lap and chewing jerky that She-Bear must have given him. She-Bear sat stonily with her rifle across her thighs, head tilted back against the wall as though asleep, but her eyes were open. Cameron knew she was listening as only an Indian could listen.

Outside, the canyon was nearly dark. The sky had paled. No sounds lifted from below. Bachelard's crew must be settling in for the night.

"Here . . . eat," She-Bear said, offering Cameron some jerky.

He shook his head. "No, thanks."

He remembered Adrian saying that this cave was the only one with a back door. Maybe . . .

He turned, ducked through the opening in the back wall, and walked to the room with the pit. Clark was asleep and Marina was leaning against the wall with her arms around her legs, resting her head on her knees.

"I'm going to check something out," Cameron said to her, picking up one of the candles planted in a puddle of dry wax.

He ducked through the door and stepped into another corridor similar to the first, the guttering candle shunting shadows of protruding rocks around the walls, his own shadow crawling down the ceiling.

Ducking uncomfortably, he walked for several minutes. The walls and ceiling remained the same height and width. The only thing that changed even slightly was the rumbling. It seemed to grow louder the farther he moved down the corridor.

Suddenly the floor began to drop at a slight angle. The ceiling rose a little, for which he was grateful; his neck was getting sore. Fifty yards farther on, the candle went out. Blackness like he'd never known before engulfed him. He reached into his tunic pocket for matches, relit the candle, and continued walking. He'd moved only about six more feet when the candle went out again.

"What the hell?" he said, his voice sounding eerie in the tight confines of the stone corridor.

He lit the candle one more time, and again it went out. Giving up, he continued without it, feeling his way along the wall. The candle had to have been blown out by air funneling down the corridor. He thought he could smell it, however faintly. If there indeed was air, it had to come from somewhere outside.

Maybe the corridor traversed the mountain, opening on the other side! If that was true, Adrian had been speaking more literally than he'd realized when he'd described this as a back door.

Suddenly Cameron stumbled on a shin-high rock. There had been no other such rocks in the corridor.

Curious, he bent down and touched the stone, feeling it on all sides. On the other side of the rock was nothing but air—even below the level of the floor. A chill ran down his spine.

He struck a match and cupped it in his palm, bending low to reveal a pit, much like the one in the room where he'd left Adrian and Marina. His heart thumped. If he'd simply stepped around the rock, he would have now been lying at the bottom of the pit!

Who knew how many more pits lay in the corridor? He didn't have enough matches to keep lighting one after another, either, and since the candle wouldn't stay lit, he'd have to go back. If there was air coming from outside—he could feel it now, a

slight freshening against his sweat-soaked tunic—
then there would have to be light coming from outside, as well.

The sky was probably nearly completely dark
now, however. He'd wait until dawn, then he and
the others would return this way, hopefully literally
see the light at the end of the tunnel, and get the hell
out of here.

It was a better chance than merely hiding in another cave. Chances were Bachelard would detail at
least a few men to find them. Back where he'd started,
he told Clark and Marina his plan. Clark was awake
and blinking with interest.

"What about the treasure?" he said fervently, then
turned as a coughing fit gripped him. Marina handed
him an already bloody handkerchief.

"I've got an idea about that, too," Cameron said.

Getting up from where he'd been sitting on the
ledge beside Marina, he slipped into the passageway leading to the cave entrance. Finding that all
was quiet—relieved that Bachelard at least appeared
to be keeping his word to wait for dawn—he told
Jimmy and She-Bear his plan. She-Bear listened stonily. Jimmy's eyes were bright with hope.

Cameron turned to She-Bear, vaguely wondering what her real name was. Going had told them
only "She-Bear," but Cameron knew she had a Pima
name. If she'd been a little more talkative he would
have asked her.

"Can you handle it alone out here for a few minutes? I have a job for Jimmy."

The woman only nodded.

Back in the pit room, Cameron looped the rope
around Jimmy's waist. "I'd go back down myself,
kid, but you're younger than I am. Besides, I can
hold your weight; you can't hold mine."

"I don't mind, Jack," the kid said eagerly. "So the treasure's down there, huh? It really is?"

"That's right."

Clark and Marina were watching from the gargantuan shadows the candles cast on the wall.

"We're gonna be rich, ain't we!" Jimmy exclaimed.

Cameron pulled the rope taut and turned the boy around by the shoulders. "What have I told you about sayin' 'ain't'? These people are gonna think I haven't taught you anything at all." He grinned. "Be careful now. Go slow. I'll have the rope in case you fall."

Gently he lowered the boy into the pit, kneeling on one knee beside the hole and running the rope through the second ring and over his shoulders. When Jimmy had made the bottom, Cameron brought the rope back up, and used it to lower a long candle into Jimmy's waiting hands.

"Jeepers creepers, it's dark down here—even with the candle." Jimmy's voice rose hollowly from the pit.

"Wait now," Cameron said. "I'm lowering the saddlebags."

When Jimmy had the bags, Cameron said, "Right through the side hole there, about twenty yards. You'll find another room, like a root cellar. There are some burlap bags and a crate. Take five of the small gold statues from the crate. Put them in the saddlebags and hightail it out of there."

"Gotcha," the kid said, bending to peer into the hole.

"Why only five?" Clark asked Cameron.

"They're heavy; it's all we'll want to carry without horses."

"Shit."

"Yeah . . . well, it's better than nothing at all. Each of those statues is worth all the money I'll ever need."

"Yeah, but what about me?" Clark growled. "My tastes are a little more refined and cultivated than yours, I would suspect."

"I'd suspect that, too," Cameron said, trying not to let the Missourian rile him.

It wasn't long before Jimmy reappeared at the bottom of the hole, toting the saddlebags, which had grown considerably bulkier and heavier, his face lit specterlike by his candle. He tied the rope around the bags, and Cameron raised them. Jimmy himself crawled out three minutes later.

"Jiminy! A real treasure cave! I can't believe it!" he exclaimed, dusting himself off.

Marina smiled at him, thoroughly affected by the boy's enthusiasm.

"There was really a lot, huh?" she said, leaning forward with her elbows on her knees, hair falling from a shoulder.

While Jimmy described the treasure to Marina, Clark inspected the statuettes in the saddlebags, candlelight gleaming off the smooth-polished gold. Cameron disappeared down the corridor, to the cave opening where She-Bear sat alone, rifle held across her knees.

He sat down across from her, stretched out his legs and crossed them at the ankles, took a long pull from his canteen lying there, and dug in his tunic pocket for his makings.

"Smoke?" he asked She-Bear.

She said nothing, only held out a hand. Cameron tossed her the pouch. When she had what she needed, she tossed it back to him. Slowly, ponderously, he rolled a smoke, stuffed the makings back in his pocket, and lit the quirley on his boot sole.

She-Bear had already lit hers. She sat across from Cameron, hiding the glowing coal in her palm—no use giving Bachelard's men a tempting target—and smoked silently.

Cameron drew deeply on the quirley, enjoying the taste of the tobacco, the slightly heady feeling the smoke gave him. It was all he enjoyed, however. His thoughts were not pleasant.

It was almost over. They had the treasure. Cameron needed only to get the others safely out of here. When and if that was accomplished, he would return for Bachelard.

The Cajun was not what filled him with dread, however. What did, was his knowing that soon he would be saying good-bye to Marina. He could not take her from Clark, despite the fact Clark was who he was and that their marriage was a loveless one. It just wouldn't be right, and it would always be between her and Cameron.

She was not a woman who could break a vow and be content with the decision, no matter how empty the vow may have been. No, it just wasn't in the cards. Besides, Cameron fully expected to die when he went back to kill Bachelard. It was just as well. He didn't want to live with another woman haunting his past.

After a while, Jimmy returned. Cameron got up, stretched, looked around.

All was quiet. The canyon was velvet-black with a milky wash of stars hovering low over the jagged peaks. Below, a horse whinnied and fires flickered—a half dozen or so spread a good distance away from each other. Bachelard wasn't taking any chances. No doubt he had men posted around the cliff, not far from the cave, to make sure no one in Cameron's group slipped away.

It appeared he was indeed going to give them until dawn to decide, apparently hoping that the tension would drive them to a desperate, foolhardy decision. That way he wouldn't lose any men, and the gold would be his without a fight.

Cameron, Jimmy, and She-Bear took turns staying awake and keeping watch. Cameron's vigil was first. He woke She-Bear at one o'clock, then lay down, snugging his back against the wall, crossed his legs at the ankles, folded his arms across his chest, and fell fast into a sleep troubled with dreams of tunnels—one dark corridor after another, curling deep into the earth with no light, no end in sight.

"Hello the cave . . . Cameron, what's your decision?"

The words came to him as if from deep underground. He stirred but couldn't wake.

Someone had grabbed his shoulder and was jostling him. "Jack! Wake up! It's Bachelard!"

Cameron suddenly opened his eyes. Jimmy was kneeling over him, silhouetted by a sky filled with golden light. It was morning.

Holy shit!

CHAPTER 37

———◆———

HE JUMPED TO his knees, drawing his revolver.

"What happened?" he demanded. From the light in the sky, he could tell he should have been awakened at least an hour ago.

Jimmy slid his gaze guiltily to She-Bear, kneeling just inside the cave with her rifle butt snugged up against her shoulder. "I—I fell asleep," Jimmy said repentantly.

Cameron couldn't blame him—he hadn't had much sleep in the past few days, and had been through holy hell to boot—but it was a perilous blunder. He'd hoped to sneak back into the corridor as soon as the first rays of dawn pinkened the sky, well ahead of Bachelard's stirring.

"I'm going to count to three," Bachelard yelled. "You'd better tell me your decision by then, or we're going to start shooting."

Gun in hand, Cameron got down and crawled to the lip of the ledge. He was about to drop his gaze over the side when he saw a half-dozen unshaven faces staring up at him from the tier just below. They were only about twenty yards away, spread about six feet apart, and they all had their rifles trained on him.

Bachelard was counting: ". . . three!"

Cameron pulled his head back and scrambled inside the cave as a volley of shot pinked the ledge and outside walls of the cave, spanging and throwing up dust and rock chips.

"Charge!" Bachelard yelled below.

She-Bear squeezed off a round, slipped another shell into the chamber of her single-shot, fired again. Cameron heard the growing sound of footfalls. A face appeared on the left side of the cave's opening. The gun in the man's hand barked. She-Bear flew backwards, dropping her rifle.

Cameron lifted his Colt, fired, and watched the man grab his throat and stagger backwards off the ledge. Another man appeared on the right; before he could fire, Cameron shot him in the belly, and Jimmy blew a hole through his knee. The man yelled, crumpling and crawling out of sight.

"Jimmy, go!" Cameron yelled. "Tell the others to run for it down the back corridor! Go!"

"Here!" The boy tossed Cameron his gun and disappeared through the low door at the back of the cave.

Firing another round at the canyon floor and keeping his eyes on the opening, hearing yelling and the sound of boots pounding rock, Cameron knelt on one knee beside She-Bear. He was about to check for a pulse when he saw the bullet hole in her forehead, dripping dark red blood.

"Goddamn it!" he said tightly.

A blindly fired bullet struck the cave ceiling, ricocheting dangerously before it died. Cameron fired a round at the opening to hold the hordes at bay, turned, and ducked through the door.

He was halfway down the corridor when he stopped suddenly. He'd heard something. It sounded like the *rat-tat-tat* of a woodpecker.

It was a rapidly firing gun.

The Gatling gun.

Cameron smiled. The rurales had caught up to him—or to Bachelard, he should say. It couldn't have happened to a better guy at a better time.

The yelling picked up, and so did the rifle and pistol fire, only this time it sounded as though the shooting was directed away from the cave; Cameron could no longer hear the muffled *pings* of slugs hitting the walls and ceiling.

Curious, wanting a grasp of the situation, while knowing he should go on after the others, he made his way to the door and stepped back into the cave. He could hear the Gatling gun clearly now above the din of rifle and pistol shots.

The *rurales* had indeed ridden into the canyon and joined the fray. Apparently Bachelard and his men were well occupied, for no more men or bullets appeared in the cave.

Smiling with satisfaction, Cameron turned and jogged down the corridor, feeling the way with his hands. When he came to the room with the pit, the candles burned down to nubs told him the others had gone down the corridor.

Suddenly his stomach filled with bile. The pit in the floor of the corridor. He hadn't mentioned it to Jimmy!

"Wait! Stop!" he shouted, tearing off through the dark chasm, feeling his way with his hands, knocking his head on low-bulging stones. "Jimmy! Wait, goddamn it . . . Hold up!"

Dead ahead a light appeared. Someone yelled.

"Wait!" Cameron returned. *"Don't take one more step."*

He approached the group breathlessly, relieved to see them all together. Marina and Jimmy were standing sideways, facing each other, holding candles. Jimmy had the bulky saddlebags draped over his shoulder. He and Marina looked at Cameron fearfully, wondering what had happened now. Clark sat against the wall with his knees up, looking tired and weak.

"I forgot—the way is blocked by a pit," Cameron said. "I'll have to find it." He took Jimmy's candle and turned to Clark. "How you doing?"

"I'm not going to make it. I've lost too much blood; I'm too weak."

"You'll make it, come on." Cameron reached down and gentled the man to his feet, throwing one arm over his shoulder. Starting out, he held the candle out with his right hand.

"Why don't you just leave me?" Clark said. "You know you want to."

Cameron made no reply to this. He didn't want to think about it.

"She'd like you to, too," Clark said dryly. "You two would be as snug as two bugs in a rug."

"Shut up so I can hear myself think," Cameron said, holding the candle down at waist level as he searched for the pit. He should have counted his footsteps last night.

His candle went out. So did Marina's. He took a deep breath and smelled fresh air.

"There!" Marina said excitedly. "Do you see it?"

Peering ahead, he saw what appeared to be a dim pinprick of light. There was an opening about one hundred yards ahead!

"I see it," Cameron said. "But I don't see the pit. You two stay behind us a good four or five feet. I'm going to walk slow until I run into the same stone I ran into last night."

He'd walked maybe thirty feet when he found the

rock. Gently setting Clark down against the wall, he lit his candle and held it over the pit, cupping the flame with his free hand.

The flickering flame revealed a pit about five feet in diameter. It also revealed a fairly shallow bottom, only about six feet deep—an apparent sinkhole sucked under by a water table that had lowered at some point in the last two or three hundred years. The stones around it must have been heaved up from the floor much later, when the ground had contracted.

Cameron took a giant sideways step across the narrowest end of the hole, then held out his hand for Clark. "You're going to have to stretch," he said.

"I don't have the energy," Clark groused.

"Hold out your hand, goddamn it!" Cameron ordered.

Clark did as he was told. Cameron pulled him across and Clark cried out in pain as he fell into Cameron's arms. Cameron eased him down against the wall, then turned to help Marina and Jimmy across the pit.

Giving Clark a moment to rest, Cameron squatted on his haunches. Marina did the same, mopping the sweat from her husband's brow with a handkerchief.

"I don't know why you're doing this," Clark said, his voice pinched with pain. "You know you two would like nothing more than to have me out of the picture."

"Please be quiet, Adrian," Marina said, her voice not so much admonishing as sad.

He looked at her keenly. "Can you tell me it's not true?"

Marina said nothing. Clark scoffed, and squeezed his eyes shut against the fatigue and pain racking his body. He crumpled, coughing.

"I'd give my share of the gold for one slug of brandy," he moaned.

Frowning with puzzlement, Marina looked at Cameron. "The woman . . . ?"

"Dead."

Marina softly closed her eyes.

"The rurales arrived just as we were pulling out," Cameron said. "That might be why Bachelard isn't behind us. We have to keep moving, though, because sooner or later one of them will be on our tail— either Bachelard or the rurales . . . Whoever wins, I s'pose."

He turned to Clark. "You ready? We're almost there."

"No," Clark groaned.

Cameron pulled him to his feet and led him down the passage. After several yards there was enough light from the opening to see any other possible sinkholes.

The rumbling grew louder and louder, vibrating the floor and walls of the chasm. The humidity was rising. The air funneling down the passageway smelled freshwater-clean and refreshing.

Sure enough, Cameron thought, it's a river. And this must be where it spills out of the mountain.

As they approached the end of the tunnel yawning wide before them, the ceiling lifting and the walls fanning gradually out around them, he realized he was wrong. The tunnel gave out on a slope terraced by the river. In a bed about twenty feet below, the river boiled loudly between limestone banks about thirty feet apart.

The three of them stood looking hopelessly around the room, about fifty yards wide and a hundred yards long. Fluted columns of pink limestone rose up along the walls, like sacred reliefs straining toward the heavens. Several swordlike stalactites hung from the domed roof as well, now lit an iridescent salmon by the rising sun, sliding shadows across the red, rocky floor.

Looking around, Cameron saw that they were not outside, but deep in the mountain, in a high-domed chamber. The light was coming from a high, open dome about a thousand feet above the river.

The chamber appeared to be the inside of a volcano. Years after the volcano blew its top, the river had apparently carved a passage through the heart of the mountain. It entered through one tunnel it had carved through the ages, and left by another.

The ancients must have seen the place as sacred, and carved a passage to it. They maybe worshiped here or—who knew?—sent sacrificial victims plummeting to their deaths.

Clark sank down against the wall and started to laugh. The laugh grew until it resonated off the walls and the high-domed ceiling, rising even above the thunder of the river gushing through the chasm below. It was a laugh of desperation, expressing the horrible futility of their situation. It was a mocking laugh, as well, mocking Cameron for even trying. There was no humor in it at all.

Cameron stared down at the river and sighed.

Bachelard lifted his head up from the cave where he'd been pinned down when the *rurales* had opened up with the Gatling gun, thumbed back the hammer on his old Gunnison revolver, and loosed a ball at the gray-clad horsemen swarming down the canyon and yelling in Spanish.

He couldn't tell if he hit any of them. Just then the Gatling gun was trained on him, and about five quick rounds chipped rock from the ceiling above him, raining shards down around and on him.

Of all the lousy luck, he moaned. Rurales!

They'd caught him and his men by surprise as they'd charged up the old stone staircases toward the cave where Cameron and Clark had bastioned themselves, laying out nearly half of Bachelard's and Montana's force in one fell swoop. The others were pinned down on the various tiers, returning fire with their rifles and revolvers, a feeble reply to the metallic barks of the Gatling gun backed up by the riflemen nestled in the rubble at the bottom of the canyon.

Those sons-of-bitches bean-eaters really wanted them dead, and they didn't give a damn if they back-shot them all!

"Cowards . . . Oh, you greaser cowards!" Bachelard roared.

What troubled him more than anything, however, was the gold. He had to get to the cave where Cameron and Clark were pinned down. He'd deal with the *rurales* once he had the gold.

He thought briefly of Juanita, hidden in the rocks. She'd be safe there until he could rally his forces with the gold. Then he'd fight his way through the *rurales*, and rescue his damsel in distress.

Above the raucous clatter of gunfire, Bachelard heard boots thumping near, saw shadows move on the ledge outside the cave. Then four men stumbled into the cave, one falling and grabbing his leg, the others turning and slamming their backs up against the cave walls, panting, their eyes filled with terror.

They were all Montana's men. Bachelard wondered if any of his own Texans were still kicking.

"Reload your weapons and get ready to storm the cave with the gold," Bachelard ordered. "It's just above and to the left."

The men looked at him with dumb cows' eyes, as if they hadn't comprehended his orders. He knew they'd understood. They were just scared.

"Do you hear?" Bachelard intoned. "Do you want the gold or don't you?"

One of them opened the cylinder of his revolver and started filling it from the bandoliers crisscrossing his chest. The others looked at each other in silent, conspiratorial council. Fortunately for Bachelard, they were only half-reluctant. They were nothing if not loyal, even to this crazy gringo, and if he'd wanted them to try for the gold at the very gates of heaven, they probably would have done it. He was the one with the brains, after all. Who were they but ignorant peon banditos? If it hadn't been for him and Montana, they'd probably all be dead or moldering in prisons.

One by one they shrugged and began reloading their revolvers. Bachelard smiled to himself and peered out over the ledge, where the gunfire was growing more and more sporadic. The Gatling gun had gone silent.

"I think it's time, my good men," Bachelard said through a smile.

Groans rose nearby. Shuttling his gaze, Bachelard saw Miguel Montana crawling on his hands and knees around the entrance to the cave. He clutched his stomach with a blood-soaked hand.

"Gaston!" he cried. "I'm injured."

"Oh, Miguel," Bachelard said with theatrical lament, feeling a thrill.

Even in such a situation he was not unhappy to see Montana taken down, something he had been secretly yearning for, for some time. He hadn't wanted to be the one to do it, for Montana's men might have turned against him and joined forces with some other revolutionary faction. Now it appeared the vain little greaser was indeed on his last legs—gunned down by rurales, no less!

Vive le Bachelard!

His face the very picture of concern, he ran crouching to the man, helped him sit back against the wall. The other men, murmuring despondently, gathered around. One of them offered his canteen.

"Let me see, Miguel," Bachelard said, gently lifting one of the hands crossed over the gushing belly wound.

"Does . . . Does it look bad?" Montana asked in a pinched, grunting stammer.

Bachelard sighed and shook his head, thoroughly enjoying himself. "It doesn't look good, Miguel. I tell you what—these men and I are going to go after the gold and try to secure our position. When we've done that, we'll return for you."

"Don't leave me, Gaston—I'm *dying*," the little Mexican cried, rolling his head to his chest.

Looking embarrassed, Bachelard glanced at the men, then lowered his head to Montana's ear. He whispered something. Montana nodded sorrowfully. Bachelard stood and turned to the men.

"He told me he wants us to go get the gold in his honor. What do you say?"

All four men heartily agreed, even the one with the bullet in his leg.

"Let's go, then," Bachelard said, stepping back to let the others lead the way.

When they'd run out of the cave for the steps angling up to the next tier, firing their guns into the canyon, Bachelard hesitated, turned back into the cave, and squatted next to Montana. He lifted his revolver, thumbed back the hammer, pressed the barrel to the Mexican's forehead, and said, "Here, this will make you feel better, Miguel."

The dark eyes widened with horror as the pistol fired, drilling a slug through Montana's brain.

Bachelard turned and followed the others up the stairs, firing into the canyon to cover himself. The Gatling gun had not opened up until he and the other four men were inside the cave where Cameron and Clark had bastioned themselves.

They hit the floor, cowering under the heavy slugs pocking the ceilings and walls, looking around.

As Bachelard had suspected, no one was here except a dead Indian woman. Also as he had suspected, there was a back exit to the cave, possibly leading to a room where the gold was stashed. He'd have to be careful now, for it could be a trap.

"This way," he ordered, leading the way through the door.

Lighting a match and cupping it in his hand, he led the way through the low-ceilinged corridor. When they came to where it opened into another room, he dropped the match, sidled up against the wall, thumbed back the hammer on his revolver, and called, "Cameron?"

No reply.

"Clark?"

Silence.

He heard no breathing, sensed no presence in the heavy darkness. The only sound was the distant rumble he'd heard as soon as he'd stepped through the door at the back of the cave.

"Where the hell are they?" he mumbled to no one in particular.

He stepped softly into the room, lit a match and cupped it away from his body in case someone would train a bullet on the flame. No gunfire sounded, however.

Perspiration streaming down his face and into

his scraggly goatee, Bachelard lifted the match and walked around the room as the four Mexicans shuffled around the entrance, their backs to the wall, breathing fearfully.

Bachelard found the candles, lighting several. No one was here. But there was a pit, and a rope dangling into it.

"Damn! They got the gold!" he cried. Swinging his gaze around, he saw the back entrance. "And they've taken it out!"

He bolted through the door, and the four Mexicans followed.

"I've got you now, Cameron!" Bachelard screamed. "I've got you now!"

CHAPTER 38

CAMERON HAD NOT heard Bachelard's yell, but he heard the shooting—seemingly random shots echoing within the chamber.

"Everybody back against the wall!" he said, drawing his Colt, aiming it into the tunnel, and squeezing off two quick rounds.

The ground trembled. Several chunks of rock broke away from the dome and plunged into the river and onto the banks, dangerously close to Cameron and the others.

Inside the mountain, Bachelard felt the trembling as well. Rocks fell from the ceiling, and cracks appeared in the walls.

What the hell was happening—an earthquake?

He stretched out his arms to steady himself against the walls as he made his way awkwardly down the corridor, toward the circle of light growing before him.

"Onward, men! Onward!" he ordered the Mexicans, whom he'd shoved out in front of him to absorb any more bullets Cameron's group decided to fling his way.

Cameron, too, was thinking it was an earthquake. Then he remembered the Gatling gun. The loud reports and heavy, thunking rounds of the big weapon, in addition to all the other shooting, had probably opened some fissure inside the mountain. It probably wouldn't take much of a crack to start a chain reaction and to get the whole mountain coming apart at the seams.

Marina, Jimmy, and Clark pressed their backs against the chamber wall and darted wide, frightened eyes this way and that as several stalactites loosed from the ceiling like spears from an angry god and shattered on the rocky floor of the chamber. One fell only a few feet to Jimmy's right. Marina jerked the boy away from it.

She turned to Cameron. "We have to get out of here!"

Cameron nodded fatefully. "The river's the only way."

She seemed to have drawn the same conclusion herself, and looked at Clark.

"No way," he said. "I'll never make it."

"You have to," Marina pleaded.

Clark laughed. The bandage on his breast was bright with fresh blood. The wound had opened. "Now you're trying to drown me! Forget it. I'll stay here." He turned to Cameron. "Give me my gun."

Another stalactite plunged to the floor only ten feet away, spraying them with pink-and-white sandstone.

Cameron grabbed Marina and Jimmy by their arms and led them to the lip of the bank, staring at the dark water boiling below. He grabbed the saddlebags off Jimmy's shoulder and draped them over his own.

"The river'll take you through that tunnel and out

of the mountain," he said, with more certainty than he actually felt. "It's the only way. Don't fight it. Just try to keep your head above water and let the current do the work."

"I can't swim!" Jimmy exclaimed, terrified.

"You won't need to, Jim. Go!"

Marina looked at him desperately, then shuttled the look to her husband, crouched against the wall with his Bisley in his hand.

"I'll take care of him," Cameron told her.

She brought her eyes back to him. "I'll see you on the other side?"

"It's a date," Cameron said, conjuring a feeble smile.

"Let's go, Jim," Marina said to the kid. Grabbing his hand, she said, "When I count to three, we'll both jump."

Jimmy stared at the water and shook his head. He was saying something but Cameron couldn't hear it above the rumble of the mountain and the boiling of the water.

"... three!" Marina said. Hand in hand, she and Jimmy plunged into the river, disappearing at once. Their heads reappeared several feet downstream, barely discernible in the foam-ravaged tumult. They bobbed for a few seconds before passing into the tunnel on the right side of the chamber.

"Come on," Cameron said, turning to Clark.

"I told you, I'll never make it. I'll die here—dry, at least. Maybe I can even take one of the bastards with me."

Clark coughed several times, peered into the tunnel, jerked away as several shots chipped stone from the side of the entrance, then fired two quick rounds into the darkness.

Cameron stood on the lip of the bank, staring

at Clark, not sure what to do. He knew Clark was right—he'd never make it in the river.

Clark laughed angrily. "You stupid bastard. This is the best thing that could happen to you. Now she'll be all yours—if you make it, that is—and I'll be out of the way." He laughed again, but it was mostly a cough.

"I don't deny that I love your wife, Clark. But it was a marriage of convenience, for chrissakes!"

Clark could not argue with that. He hauled himself to his feet and stepped to the edge of the bank. "All right, I'll jump—on three." He shot Cameron a dark look.

Cameron counted to three and stepped off the bank, plunging into the icy water, surprised to find it wasn't as deep as he'd suspected. His feet hit the bottom, and he shoved himself back to the surface even as the enormous weight of the saddlebags urged him back down.

Looking around as the current pulled him toward the tunnel, he saw Clark standing on the bank, smiling and giving a broad wave. Hearing something behind him, the man turned. That was all Cameron saw. Suddenly he was in the tunnel and careening downstream, bouncing off rocks, fighting against the deadly weight of the saddlebags.

He knew that if the river were any deeper he would have to let the bags go. As it was, however, whenever they pulled him to the bottom, he got his legs beneath him and propelled himself back to the surface, keeping one arm hooked around the leather band between the two bulky bags.

———•—•———

Back in the chamber, Clark had turned to face the two Mexicans aiming revolvers at him. He lifted the

Bisley but before he could fire, both Mexicans triggered their own weapons. One slug went through Clark's chest, just beneath the knife wound; the other entered his belly and lodged against his spine. He flew off his feet with a shriek.

It wasn't the bullets that killed him, however. What killed him—and the two Mexicans who had shot him—was the collapse of virtually the entire domed ceiling of the chamber. In seconds the men were buried under a mountain of sandstone and limestone.

But as the roof disintegrated, Gaston Bachelard flung himself off the riverbank. With rocks falling all about him, he shot into the tunnel.

The rushing water spun Cameron like a top, slamming him against submerged rocks—first a knee, then his jaw, then a shoulder—until his whole body was numb with scrapes and bruises.

His biggest enemies, however, were the saddlebags containing the statuettes. A collision with a boulder stunned him. The weight of the gold pulled him down. Before he realized what he was doing, he'd inhaled half a lungful of water.

He kicked, trying to get back to the surface, but the current swept his legs out from under him and he sank even farther. He was about to release the bags—five statuettes, even if they were worth four thousand dollars apiece, were not worth his life—but from somewhere he mustered the strength to get his legs beneath him again. Finding a shallow boulder, he fought for the surface.

When his head broke through, he sucked air into his lungs while coughing and vomiting up water. Opening his eyes he saw the eerie, twilight world of the tunnel, with its low-arching, vermilion ceiling. Two boulders grew larger and larger before him, until he smacked into them, hard, with his face and chest.

Losing consciousness, Cameron released the bags, which immediately sank. He clawed at the smooth-polished stone, pain searing his skull. The current quickly swept him away from the rocks and dragged him under.

Suddenly the current weakened noticeably. He was vaguely aware that he'd passed from the darkness of the tunnel into bright sunlight, and was swirling between low, red banks. Weak from exhaustion and nearly drowned, he tried once more to find a purchase on the bottom.

His boots dug into the sand. He tried to stand, fell, tried again, fell again. He reached instinctively for a rock on the bank. Surprised to find himself clutching it, he ground his fingers into a cleft.

He hung on for a long time, coughing up water and sucking in air, his body racked with pain. When he finally felt as though he'd purged himself of the river and his head had cleared, he glanced around.

The water was churning around him with less vigor, and the level seemed to be dropping, judging by the old waterline.

Frowning, puzzled, Cameron looked back at the mountain. Dust was billowing skyward in great mushroom clouds that were slowly dispersing.

The whole chamber must have collapsed and dammed the river. He thought of Clark with a surprising sadness.

Cameron began to search for Jimmy and Marina. No doubt they'd been propelled farther down the canyon; they'd had no gold weighing them down, and the river had not yet dammed when they'd gone through the tunnel.

The bank was too steep to climb here, so Cameron waded downstream, steadying himself on the rocks, watching the river sink lower and lower, its eddies straightening, the riffles around snags disappearing. Submerged rocks rose, shining wet in the bright, midmorning sun. It was good to feel the heat through his wet tunic, to see birds twittering and bouncing in the shrubs up high on the bank.

Tempering his own relief at having been spit from the river alive was his distress over Marina and Jimmy. Had they made it or had they been slammed against the rocks and drowned? He didn't want to think about it, but he kept an eye out for corpses just the same.

He'd walked maybe twenty yards, the water down around his knees, when he stopped suddenly and peered ahead, feeling his heart skip a beat. Lying close to shore, in a cove of the stone embankment, was a body.

Cameron ran clumsily, splashing through the water, nearly tripping. Relief buoyed him as he approached the corpse. The body lying facedown, long silver hair floating about its head, was not Marina or Jimmy.

Gaston Bachelard.

The crazy old Cajun Confederate floated there in the dying current, legs angling beneath him. His gray hair wafted out around his skull like the tendrils of a sea creature. His open eyes, a washed-out, reptilian blue, dully reflected the sun. Already the hollow cheeks were darkening. The river must have propelled him past Cameron as Cameron struggled with the saddlebags.

"Do you feel cheated?"

Cameron turned sharply to his right. Marina stood

on the stone embankment across the river. She was soaked, long hair plastered to her head and shoulders, blouse pasted to her breasts. She looked fine. She looked wonderful.

Cameron smiled at her. He'd never felt so relieved.

He shook his head. "No," he replied to her question.

It was enough that Bachelard was dead. He was even grateful he hadn't had to kill him. There'd been enough killing.

"Are you all right?"

She nodded. "A few bruises here and there, but I am fine. Jimmy is resting back in the bushes. I think he is more terrified than anything."

"I guess that's to be expected."

"Adrian?"

Cameron shook his head. "He wouldn't come."

"I didn't think that he would," Marina said with a fatalistic sigh, looking upstream with a melancholy expression on her face. "The gold?"

"I lost it upstream a ways, but with the river going down like it is, I bet it won't be hard to find." He held out his hand to her. "Join me?"

She looked at him, tears glistening in her eyes. She climbed down off the rocks and moved quickly toward him. She flung out her arms and wrapped them around his neck, burying her face in his chest.

"I was so worried," she cried.

He engulfed her in his arms, rubbing his hands down her slender back, pressing her close, never wanting to release her again.

"I was, too."

She looked at him with tears of relief and joy in her large brown eyes. "I love you, Jack Cameron," she said huskily. "I wanted to tell you when you returned with Jimmy, but Adrian was there, and—"

"I know," Cameron said, looking down at her, smiling a knowing smile. "I felt the same way."

"I thought we would never be together. I thought I would never again know such happiness."

He pressed her close to him again. "Me too, Marina," he cooed in her ear. "Oh God . . . me too."

They stood there in the river as the water gradually dropped from their knees to their shins to their ankles, holding each other close, never wanting to separate.

But separate they did, finally. Cameron bent down and kissed her mouth. Then they turned and, holding hands, walked upstream.

They said nothing as they walked. Words were not enough to express the relief and joy they felt at being together at last. It was enough to hear the tinny chatter of the water and the birds, to feel the warm sun radiate through their wet clothes.

"Here we go," Cameron said, seeing the saddlebags wrapped around the base of a boulder, all but exposed by the disappearing river, which was only a freshet now, curling down the middle of the sandy bed.

"Oh my God," Marina whispered.

"Yep, it's ours," Cameron said, stooping to pick up the saddlebags. He turned them upside down, dumping the water, and draped them over his shoulder.

"No," Marina said. "I mean . . . what an awful thing we did—Adrian and I—getting all those people killed for such a pittance. Even if we had gotten the whole treasure, it would still be a pittance."

Cameron took her hand and led her back downstream. "It's happened before," Cameron said. "It'll happen again. Many times. Gold is one hell of a temptation, and a harsh mistress to boot."

He stopped and stiffened as a gun barked once, twice, three times. The reports came from dead ahead.

"You wait here," Cameron told Marina, dropping the saddlebags. He drew his Colt and ran ahead, heart beating wildly, wondering what the hell could be happening now. Hadn't they been through enough?

When he'd run back to where he'd found Marina, he stopped and lifted the Colt to his shoulder. Just ahead were two men on mules. They were both dressed like Mexican peasants, with sombreros and patched boots. They wore serapes and gunbelts, and they were holding old-model rifles in their hands.

At first Cameron thought they were men from Bachelard's group, but then he saw the girl riding behind the stout man with the thin black handlebar mustache. Each man trailed a pack mule on a lead rope.

"Hold it right there!" Cameron yelled. "Throw those guns down."

Both men and the girl—a girl of about twelve, Cameron speculated—turned to look at him with fear in their eyes. They stiffened, hesitating in their saddles.

"Amigo, we . . ." the man with the handlebar mustache started to say.

"Throw 'em down!"

The man with the mustache turned to the other, shorter man. He turned back to Cameron, took his rifle by the barrel, leaned down and set the butt on the sandy riverbed, and let it drop. The man beside him did likewise.

"Your pistols—those, too."

When the men had tossed their pistols on the ground, Cameron stepped toward them. "What were you shooting at?"

Both men turned their wary eyes to something on the ground before them. Cameron walked around the front of the mules and saw Bachelard lying where he had left him. With the water gone, the dead Cajun lay on the wet bed of the river, arms and legs spread.

There were three nickel-sized holes in his head.

Cameron turned a questioning look at the men.

The one with the handlebar mustache shrugged and gestured to the girl riding behind him. She had snugged her head up tight to the man's back, burying her face in his serape.

"He took my dear Juanita," the man said, his hate-filled gaze on Bachelard. "Said he wanted to marry her." He gestured to the other man—an old, cadaverous-looking gent with one blind eye and hollow cheeks, his head nearly swallowed up by the big sombrero—and said, "Old Juan and me, we tracked them all the way from Arizona to here, waiting for an opportunity to sneak her out of his clutches. It came this morning, during the firefight below the ruins. We snuck down and grabbed her while he and his men were shooting at the rurales."

Cameron nodded, stealing another look at the girl, her face still buried in her father's back. What hell she must have been through at the hands of that mad old Confederate. Her father must have been through hell as well.

Cameron holstered his pistol, bent down, picked up the rifles, and handed them back to the men. Then he returned the pistols, as well.

"Sorry," he said. "I'm afraid I'm a little gun-shy these days." He held out his hand to the man riding with the girl. "I'm Jack Cameron."

The man nodded knowingly. "I have heard of you, the Indian fighter. I am Ramón Martínez. This is old Juan. He fought the Apaches in Mejico. They took his eye." He gestured at the girl with his thumb. "This is Juanita. I am taking her home to her mother."

"I bet her mother will be very happy to see her."

"Sí," Martínez said. "It was good to meet you, Mr. Cameron." He started to rein his mule around.

"Wait," Cameron said.

He turned to see Marina coming up behind him, dragging the saddlebags. He went to her and opened one of the pouches. Removing a statuette, which shone radiantly in the bright sun, he took it to Ramón Martínez and held it up to the man.

"Here, take this," he said. "For your trouble."

"Dios mío, look at that!" Martínez shuttled his astonished eyes to old Juan, who grinned toothlessly.

"Señor, I could never . . . !"

"Yes, you could," Cameron said. "You must."

"I . . . I must give you something in return."

"How about one of your mules and some matches?"

"Sí, sí," Martínez sang, still in awe over the statuette in his hand. He tossed Cameron the pack mule's lead rope. "You can have the mule, the packs, and all. There is food, coffee, and even some tobacco."

"Señor," Cameron said, "That's the best exchange I've ever made in my life. We're even."

Martínez shook his head. "Oh, we are far from even, señor, but I am happy to make the gesture."

"Farewell," Cameron said.

"Farewell, Mr. Cameron," Martínez said as he and old Juan reined their mules away, toward a cleft in the rock through which a trail threaded. Martínez removed his sombrero and swept it to his chest with a flourish. "And you as well, señora."

"Buenos días," Marina said, smiling brightly at the man.

When the trio had left, Cameron turned to Marina.

He took her in his arms and kissed her. He held her away from him and stared deeply into her smiling eyes.

"Let's go get Jimmy and your daughter and go home," he said.

Marina's smile brightened even more. "Home? Where is home, Mr. Cameron?"

"Home?" he said, turning a thoughtful gaze northward.

"Home is up north, in the high desert country. I've got some good grass, a sound spring, and one hell of a view of Rockinstraw Mountain off my gallery."

"And it's not so hot? I'm tired of the heat," Marina said.

"Cool breezes blow through the cottonwoods, even in summer."

"I think we would have a good life there, the four of us," Marina said.

"I think so, too." He smiled and kissed her again.

She draped her arms over his shoulders and looked into his face lovingly. "You know what I think, Jack? I think you are a romantic."

Cameron leaned down, picked up the saddlebags, and heaved them onto the mule. He took the mule by the rope and Marina by the hand, and they set off to find Jimmy.

"You know what I think, Marina? I think you're right."